Daisy Wood has lived in London for most of her life. She started writing this book when she was 20, but then life took a different path and it was left. Many years later when she had retired, she found her work hidden at the back of a cupboard where it had lain for nearly 50 years. Having time on her hands now, she decided to finish the story, which has taken two years to complete, never dreaming it would be published.

For my mum and dad, because they always believed in me.
Thank you.

Daisy Wood

FULL CIRCLE

AUSTIN MACAULEY PUBLISHERS™
LONDON • CAMBRIDGE • NEW YORK • SHARJAH

A CIP catalogue record for this title is available from the British Library.

ISBN 9781528911351 (Paperback)
ISBN 9781528959773 (ePub e-book)

www.austinmacauley.com

First Published (2020)
Austin Macauley Publishers Ltd
25 Canada Square
Canary Wharf
London
E14 5LQ

Table of Contents

'Yea, all which it inherit, shall dissolve,
And, like this insubstantial pageant faded,
Leave not a rack behind. We are such stuff
as dreams are made on; and our little life
is rounded with a sleep.'

The Tempest Act 4, scene 1
William Shakespeare

Prologue

The year is 1786 and the small Willows Estate nestles deep in the quiet countryside of Wiltshire, not far from Mere. The roaming country manor "The Willows" in the heart of the estate has been in the family for some generations. It was an estate once owned by the late Earl of Fenwick, and was inherited by his great nephew George MacMartin from Lochiel who left Scotland and took up residence there in 1716, later marrying the Lady Abigail Pembroke from Wilton in 1717. They had had two children, George and Jane, but tragedy struck the family just four years after the birth of their daughter, Jane, when in 1724, Lady Abigail died of a fever that took only two days to consume her, leaving her grieving husband to care for his two small children. They lived their lives in relative peace till the son, it was said, met with an untimely death while serving with the army abroad. It was after his death that George MacMartin changed his name to Martin, devoting his life to his daughter Jane, wanting above all else to keep her shielded from the world around him. She was, after all, his sole heir.

While visiting a friend's home in London, Lady Jane, at the impressionable age of nineteen, met her mild-mannered Scotsman Charles Hamilton who hailed from Edinburgh. Lady Jane's heart was his from the beginning, but when Charles Hamilton offered a proposal of marriage to her father, he met stern opposition. It was only after much pleading and many tears that her father consented to the marriage with the proviso that they made their home in The Willows in the West Country; he would not have his daughter taken from him to live in some wild remote area of Scotland—he loved his country but he knew only too well the dangers there.

Charles Hamilton was the third-born and youngest son of a family of five; his father was a Scottish Lord of the house of Hamilton from Edinburgh. Being the youngest son, he had no claim to title or lands, just money left to him by his grandfather. So when they married in 1739, Lady Jane's father made the estate over to his daughter and Charles Hamilton, to be held in custody for their first born son. If there be no son, then the first born daughter. In the event of no children and Charles Hamilton survived his wife, he would inherit. Their happiness though was to be short-lived; for just over a year into the marriage in 1740, Lady Jane died in childbirth. Four years later, her father George Martin was also dead, some said of a broken heart; he had already lost his son, and when he looked at his granddaughter Elizabeth, he could see only his beloved daughter Jane—their deaths were too great for him to endure. Charles Hamilton bereft

16

with grief himself, having been married only a year, never re-married, but lived his life through his only daughter, Elizabeth.

Elizabeth Hamilton (like her mother Jane) also married for love. She met Andrew Duncan when his family visited the willows in 1759. He was the second-born son from the Duncan's of Dundee, and likewise had no claim to lands, just monies endowed to him by his mother. For Andrew Duncan it was a good match. He had no inclination to go into the clergy, which was expected at that time of the second-born male child of any noble family, for he would then become the owner of a substantial estate, albeit in the south west of England. Things were fine within the family until Elizabeth's father died of the lung sickness which consumed him within six months, just three years after the marriage of his daughter Elizabeth in 1763, but not before he had seen his only grandchild Stewart come safely into the world in 1762.

It was only then that Andrew Duncan changed in character. During the next few years, and after having sold off many acres of land from the estate to pay debtors, he left Elizabeth to go back to Scotland, under circumstances Elizabeth knew only too well. Over the years since then, these dark secrets within The Willows have been bubbling like a cauldron, keeping its occupants in constant reminder of what had happened all those years past. Circumstance and fate will determine the outcome now; and it is very close to surfacing...

Chapter One
Stewart

The hot July sun came streaming through the latticed windows onto the large four-poster bed where Stewart Hamilton lay languidly on his stomach. The hour was just before eleven—or so the clock said as it ticked away in its soothing fashion on the mantle shelf above the fireplace. He had spent two years in Italy, studying, amongst other things, astrology with an old family friend Rodolfo Visconti, the relationship with the families going back two generations to his Grandfather Charles Hamilton. As a child, Stewart had been fascinated by the subject, so later when life had become intolerable at home—because of the animosity Stewart held for his father Andrew Duncan—his mother Elizabeth had urged him to go; she did not want this, but the alternative was not an option. The problems had been masked while Stewart was boarding at Winchester College, but when he returned home at the age of eighteen, he realised at once the extent of the damage done by his father. At times the fights between father and son had become so intense—though never physically coming to blows—there was a festering resentment between them, and Elizabeth came to fear for her son that in his rage Stewart would strike out at his father. Both had a temper that once lit could not easily be doused. So in 1782, Stewart left England to find refuge with his mother's friend Rodolfo in "Rapallo", Italy. Stewart found an inner peace while he was there; Rodolfo listened without passing judgment, letting Stewart pour out his anger and bitterness as they sailed the waters of the Mediterranean. But as with all things, this peace was short-lived. Stewart became restless for home and his mother—she was an all-consuming part of his life—he needed to return, he had been away too long. So in the late summer of 1784, he set sail for England.

Stewart stirred slightly, pushing his hands up under the pillow. The sun felt warm and luxurious as its rays beat down on his back. Stewart Hamilton was twenty-four years of age and handsome, a fact he knew only too well, inheriting his mother's thick black hair and deep blue eyes. His slim agile frame stood over six feet in height, with broad shoulders and a lean strong body, excelling in most sports, like riding and fencing. His face was rather lean in appearance, almost rugged, with a finely chiselled chin which had a slight cleft, and while his nose was straight and aquiline, it was inclined to turn up at the tip. A small black moustache-fringed full lips, and when he smiled, they exposed two rows of perfectly even white teeth. Most women were attracted to him like bees are to the honey pot, and men despised him for the same reason—a fact that Stewart was very much aware of and played it many times to his advantage. In such company, he had an enigmatic smile, but one which never touched his eyes—these always remained sharp and alert to his surroundings. His true smile, which set alight his deep blue eyes and opened a window into his soul, was used only for those that he loved. His manner towards his fellow men made enemies of them, and while women worshiped him, he was closed to many as they only reached the surface, never penetrating to the sweetness within.

There was only one woman who could understand his dark temperament: his mother. Just by looking at him, it seemed, she could read his inner-most thoughts. They had a bond which transcended that of mother and son, and Stewart revered her. To him, her smile was like the kiss of a warm summer breeze, and her touch a comforting angel in times of trouble and darkness. After the desertion of his father when Stewart was just three years old, they became so inseparable that people whispered it was un-natural and unhealthy for a child to be that close, but both mother and son had witnessed things that Elizabeth would be haunted by, and Stewart would trap into the far most corners of his mind. People would often talk of his sanity, yet he was to prove them wrong in the years to come.

Stewart moaned and turned over, stretching his left arm as he did so across the bed. He lay there in a half sleeping daze with his eyes trying to focus onto the canopy above him, letting his mind wander back over the events of the previous evening. Oh God, he had got so drunk! Looking about him now he could see the detritus of clothes decorating the floor; he certainly didn't remember getting home *or* into bed. Stewart raised his head but immediately let it fall back onto the pillow again as a striking pain stabbed at the back of his eyes. Somewhere in the distance birds chirped merrily, and he thought how was it they could be so cheerful when his head felt like it had drums inside it.

'Damn drink,' he muttered. 'God, why do you have to drink so much?' But he knew the answer without having to voice it.

Little things were coming back in waves now, especially Maggie with that soft comforting voice and her long, sweet smelling auburn hair which was always so silky. Stewart breathed in and smiled in remembrance; she was a good woman—Maggie—like Mother in some ways—all heart. He felt a pang of guilt thinking how he had intended to visit her that previous evening, but the stop in Mere at the Angel Inn had prevented that. The pull of the ale and friends' company had been too strong to resist, particularly after the hot and dusty coach journey from Exeter. Pulling the pillow from under his head, he pushed it down over his face, trying to block out the sun and the unwanted memories that were now returning.

'You use her and she does not deserve it,' he murmured into the pillow, as if by saying it, it would render legitimacy to how he behaved. He had met the Lady Margaret Stanhope not long after returning from Italy, having gone to her home with his cousin Alexander Hamilton—a relative on his grandfather's side of the family. Alexander knew her from London, where she had been married from an early age to a man many years her senior. It had by no means been a love marriage, but a "*grand match*" which would secure her for life (as her father so delicately put it). Her husband, Lord Stanhope, had died two years previous in 1784, leaving Margaret a home in London, as well as a fine house not far from the town of Mere. It was in this house at a dinner party she had held that Stewart was introduced to her by Alexander.

Lady Margaret was a strikingly beautiful young woman, slim in stature, just a little over medium in height and very elegant. Her hair was one of her most redeeming features; thick, curly and deep auburn in colour it had a distinct lustre to it, which only enhanced the translucent creaminess of her skin—skin that most auburn haired people are blessed with—and eyes the colour of emeralds. Her facial features were soft with high cheek bones, a small nose, a full pink mouth and long elegant neck, but her qualities went far beyond her appearance, and Stewart knew this well.

Stewart closed his eyes and sighed. 'Ah, Maggie, you never question me, pursue me, or want anything from me except my company… You comfort me and expect nothing in return except… kindness…'

Stewart's thoughts were suddenly interrupted and drawn to other sounds coming from the garden beneath his window. He sat up slowly, leaning on his elbow, straining his ears, then grinned with pleasure on hearing his mother's voice ring out in clear syllables from below.

Elizabeth Hamilton was almost the antithesis to her son. She was small and slim in stature, but moved with a grace of those much taller than herself. Though pale in complexion, her facial features were soft and gentle to the eye, and when she smiled, she had a way of radiating kindness. In her appearance she was neatly dressed in style, though not always in the first mode of fashion. Elizabeth Hamilton was a well-respected person within the society she walked in.

'Oh, there you are, Spike,' Elizabeth called breathlessly, seeing her gardener weeding amidst the flower beds. She watched him for some moments as his fingers deftly separated them from the flowers, turning over the earth around the plant where it had become compacted.

Spike turned and looked up at his mistress as she stood there smiling at him; he had known her since he was a young lad when he had first been taken onto the estate to work with his father—who had been head gardener to Lady Elizabeth's father before him. He had lived in a small cottage on the estate since he was born, and then with his wife who had worked as housekeeper for Elizabeth. Sadly, Spike's wife had been dead some four years now, taken with the sweating sickness that had claimed many in that area then, and as they had never been blessed with children, he lived alone.

Elizabeth had grown up with him and there was more than just a bond of servant and master—he was almost regarded as one of her family. Even his name was a "nickname" given to him by Elizabeth, as when he was young, he had an uncontrollable piece of hair that stood up on the crown of his head (hair that had long since gone). Elizabeth would tease him, and the name had stuck. Spike's real name was John Wood, a man of 49 years of age, thick set, muscular even, and medium in height, though from years of working in the gardens his shoulders had taken on the stoop of his manual labours.

'Thank goodness I have found you,' she continued. 'We have some guests coming for dinner this evening and I need some flowers for the table.'

Spike stopped his weeding and stood up, taking off his hat and nodding to Elizabeth. It was hot in the garden and Spike had the sleeves of his shirt pushed up, pulling them down quickly he spoke.

'Mistress.'

Looking at her he noticed the frown that always appeared across her small forehead when she was confronted with the unexpected; it wrinkled the place just between her eyebrows.

'Could you pick some for me please, and I will see that they are arranged?' Elizabeth asked, turning her eyes searching the numerous flower beds, whilst drumming her fingers lightly over her cheek.

Spike watched her; this was another trait she had when she was perplexed or thrown off guard as she was now.

'Oh, Spike, which ones?' she turned to face him. 'It is Milady Morris, you know—' Elizabeth broke off in mid-sentence thinking why Eleanor Morris had put it upon herself to call on her at such short notice—another prospective daughter-in-law no doubt.

Spike smiled. 'If I may be suggesting, Mistress, roses?' he replied in his soft Wiltshire lilt. 'They be at their best this time of year'—Spike inhaled deeply—'smell their fragrances,' he added as he closed his eyes. It was true the air around them was pungent with it, and the heat of the day only seemed to add to the heady bouquet. A smile of relief came across Elizabeth's face as he said this.

'Milady Morris always admires your roses,' she replied as she nodded slowly and smiled; this pleased him, as he knew he had made the right choice.

'Spike, thank you,' she added, resting her hand on his arm, looking warmly into the weather-beaten face. 'You always have such impeccable taste, Spike.'

A slow smile came across Spike's face in response. 'I will be picking them directly, Mistress,' he added, giving a small nod, and placing his hat back on his head he turned to go. 'Impeccable taste, aye,' he mumbled happily to himself, turning back once more to look at his mistress. Spike knew her secret from that night twenty-one years past; he had done what he could for her then, and would do it all again if asked. He would defend her to the death if needs be, and if any man so much as laid a finger on her, well he would kill them with his own bare hands. He could feel them now clenching to fists at his sides as he remembered. Spike took a deep, slow breath, letting the memories and the anger slip away from him until he relaxed, and then picking up his step, he continued on his way to cut the roses.

Just as Elizabeth turned to go to the kitchen, Stewart's voice called to her, stopping her.

'Good morning, Mother!' Elizabeth's head swung round in surprise, her eyes immediately resting on Stewart's tanned form as he leaned from his bedroom window above.

'Oh, good morning, Stewart.' She paused to shelter her eyes with her hand from the sun's glare. 'Did you sleep well?' she added in jest.

Stewart smiled; he could sense the intonation of those words. 'As sound as the dead,' came the reply.

'I left word with Pip not to wake you; was the journey bad?' she added with concern.

Stewart grinned, as his eyes took in the sereneness of his Mother, there could be a raging storm in her head, but one would never know from her seemingly calm appearance.

'Mother dear,' he paused shaking his head a little, 'sometimes I think you know my mind better than I,' answered Stewart thoughtfully. As he sat there now looking down at her, he could feel that powerful bond that bound them, like an invisible umbilical cord that could never be severed. Was this something that every mother and son experienced? After all, he had only had his mother beside him for guidance; his father? Well, that was another life. Elizabeth frowned as she watched him, and he noticed a look of apprehension come over her face,

'Never mind,' he continued, dismissing the subject hastily, before questions were asked.

'So we are to have Milady Eleanor Morris to dinner?' he asked. *Who else has she to parade before me?* he added under his breath. There had been a long procession of future wives of late and he was in no mood to be polite this day.

At the mention of food, Elizabeth's mouth opened.

'Stewart, you must be hungry,' she paused. 'I am on my way to the kitchen now to discuss tonight's food, shall I ask Mrs Cottle to prepare you something to eat?'

'NO,' came Stewart's quick reply. 'No,' he repeated softening his tone. 'No, thank you.' His stomach churned at the thought of it.

'I could not eat a morsel,' he added, putting his hand up and rubbing his brow. Mrs Cottle's food at any time of day was mouth-watering but at this moment, his head or the foul taste in his mouth would not let him swallow a mouthful. Besides, Mrs Cottle would find a way of making him pay for having to find him breakfast at midday. Stewart chuckled to himself then took a lungful of clean air to clear his head. 'I will saddle my horse and go for a ride, Mother; this day is too glorious to waste by lying in bed.' Waving to her, he stepped back into his room.

***

As Pip entered the kitchen, Mrs Cottle turned to look at him.

'He be awake then, Mr Pip.'

Pip smiled slightly and nodded.

'And you be wanting a bowl of hot water, no?' she added.

22

'If you would be so kind, Mrs Cottle,' Pip replied.

'Hmmm… If it were me, I would be throwing *cold* water over him. Such a commotion last night, you cannot be telling me that my Mistress be hearing none of it.' She stood there with her fists on her hips shaking her head.

'That young man needs a wife, only that will curb his exuberance.'

Pip chuckled to himself and shook his head. 'I be doubting that very much, Mrs Cottle.'

Mrs Cottle was a lady of ample proportions, with light brown hair and eyes to match. Although of the same age as her mistress, she looked much older. Outwardly, she gave the impression of a very stern matriarch, but under her brusqueness was a warm, gentle loving character, who when worried or upset gave the appearance of someone very angry.

Violet Cottle clucked her tongue as she lifted a bowl from the wall and filled it with hot water. 'He be a trial to my Mistress ever since he was but a small lad. Master Pip, I do not be knowing how you be keeping your temper with him.'

Pip took the bowl from her, smiled and inclined his head. 'I thank you kindly, Mrs Cottle,' saying this, he left.

***

As Stewart stepped back into the room, Pip entered, carrying towels over his arm and the large bowl of steaming water, pausing slightly as he entered to survey the room. Pip, whose real name was Peter Wickens, was a man in his late 40s, slightly thickset, and shorter than average, with plain features; a nose a little larger than his face should have, but with sharp eyes that missed nothing.

'Good morning, master Stewart,' he greeted bowing. 'I trust we be feeling a little better this morning.' Pip added, putting his head to one side and raising his eyebrows. Stewart's eyes narrowed, immediately filling with mischief.

'Why, you old rogue, so it *was* you who put me to bed, though you might have taken my breeches off,' Stewart exclaimed.

Pip stopped where he was, closed his eyes and took a breath. He had been Stewart's valet since he was 13 years old, but had known him since he was as a young boy, and a very difficult boy he had been, but he hoped by now that he had earned Stewart's respect, as on many an occasion Stewart had turned to him for guidance, counted on him, knew that he would never lie to him, and could always rely on his discretion.

'If you be permitting me to say so, sir,' Pip continued. 'When trying to…' he paused, thinking carefully before he spoke. 'After I be undressing the rest of you,' Pip cleared his throat and eyed his master, 'with some difficulty may I add, I did be receiving an unkindly boot in my stomach. You then be proceeding to be telling me—if I may be using your very words, sir—'*get your bloody hands off me, I WANT MAGGIE.*' Pip paused for effect. The last three words were drawn out with distinction. 'Whoever Maggie may be?' he questioned; raising his brows once more he walked to the dresser, placing the bowl and towels down.

Stewart's eyes widened then narrowed. 'Good God, was I that bad?' he questioned.

Pip smiled as he looked out onto the gardens. *If only you knew,* he thought to himself. There had been one mighty struggle just trying to keep him in the room, then he had passed out on the bed. 'Not really, sir, you do not be throwing the candle stick at me on this occasion,' he replied, turning to look at him.

Stewart looked hard and long at the man; he knew that Pip disapproved of his behaviour, which had become increasingly worse since his return from Italy. The man did not deserve to be treated like that. Stewart nodded, then walked across the room and placed his arm about the small man's shoulders.

'Pip, you are the epitome of diplomacy,' offered Stewart with the hint of teasing in his voice, a smile playing at the corners of his mouth, then adding rather sheepishly, 'My mother does not know any of this, does she?'

Pip smiled again for a moment then straightened his face before he replied.

'No, sir,' Pip assured him, as he stared up into Stewart's face. He too, like others, had seen and heard too much, but out of loyalty not only for Stewart but all the family, had said nothing.

Stewart moved away and paused before he asked the next question. 'Tell me, Pip, did I say anything else I should not have?' Stewart eyed Pip with a sideward glance.

'No, sir, you then be passing out cradling the pillow,' Pip replied.

Stewart laughed in relief; he knew his tongue got the better of him when he drank, and as he did not remember what had happened. Well, he slapped Pip on the back, thinking how blessed he was with such loyalty.

'Do you wish me to be shaving you now, Master Stewart?' Pip asked, as he walked towards the closet for a fresh linen shirt and breeches.

There was a moment's pause as Stewart seated himself in front of his mirror; rubbing his hand over the black grown of beard which was beginning to show.

'Pip, I think I will grow a beard,' he replied musingly. Stewart looked at his reflection as he said it, but Pip just closed his eyes, shook his head, sighed deeply and laid the clean things onto the bed.

'As you wish,' he said in resignation—he had been through this scenario before.

Stewart sat looking at his face. 'I know that you do not approve, but I thought it would look rather different,' he offered.

'Hairy be the word that comes to mind, sir,' Pip responded, a feint trace of a smile playing at the corners of his mouth.

'I used to have one, you remember, during the time I spent in Italy,' replied Stewart, turning in his chair to look at him.

Pip paused before replying, 'Master Stewart, that be when you spent most of your time aboard ship, sir, there were not much need for such toiletries then. But, if I may be so bold, you be home, and while a moustache is quite acceptable, a full beard could be seen as…' Pip held up his hands and the rest of the sentence was left in the air.

'And we do not want my reputation to be enhanced any more than it is,' finished Stewart. For a moment there was silence while Stewart re-examined his chin, thinking all the while was it worth the argument, and having decided it was not, he tucked the white towel around his neck.

'You know that I can never argue with you, Pip, then let us be truthful, I would never win anyway,' Stewart exclaimed, chuckling. 'Come on, shave me *and* my moustache, you old rogue!'

***

The wind blew warm into Stewart's face, ruffling his hair, and billowing out the wide sleeves of his shirt as he raced through the countryside. Everywhere the sun came through the trees like streaks of gold, casting its glow to whatever it touched, while the grass all around lay like a thick green undulating carpet, the breeze tipping its blades showing a multitude of greens and yellows as the sunlight refracted at different angles. Stewart breathed in deeply; the air smelt sweet and warm, for it was days such as this that it felt so good to be alive. Reining his horse down to a trot, he came to a halt by the lake, where he sat for a while taking in the beauty of the countryside, breathing deeply once again, letting his senses take over, filing his mind and head with the beauty of the moment. If there was heaven, then surely this was it. Patting his horse on the neck, he dismounted and walked slowly to the lake's edge, stooping to pick up a stone on the way.

'Is this not the most beautiful, the most peaceful and relaxing place we know, old friend?' he said, turning to his horse that was busy pawing the ground with his front hooves, nibbling now and then contentedly at the leaves of a low-hanging branch of a tree nearby. Stewart allowed his eyes to roam slowly around the lake, taking in every detail. He knew the countryside hereabouts like his own lands—beautiful, virgin country. Before he went to Italy, there were times in the summer months when he would steal out of the house and come here to sleep by the lake under the stars. Nobody, not even Pip (he thought), knew about this. It was his secret, about the only one he had, as everything else he did was known the second after it had happened. He chuckled to himself like a small schoolboy, pleased that he had managed to keep it for so long.

'*La mia baia di pace,*' he whispered.

No sooner had the words left his lips than he became suddenly aware that he was *not* alone. He felt a presence just behind him to the right, and although they were very still, he could still feel them watching him. Frowning, he reached up and scratched the side of his face. Stewart gradually lowered himself to the ground and sat there for some minutes, his knees pulled up in front of him, while his fingers picked at the blades of grass beneath his hands, aware of the pair of eyes that watched his every move.

'Damn them,' he whispered, 'is nothing sacred.' His face clouded over at the thought he had been followed there. Slowly he shifted himself sideways and, in one quick movement, swung round. His eyes opened wide with surprise as they immediately rested on the statue of a small young girl, slender in build, no more than seventeen years of age.

'Well,' he breathed in amazement. 'I had not expected to find someone like you here,' he added, at last beginning to regain his composure. Stewart lowered his head while his fingers made circles in the grass, then looking up once more he watched as a water fowl glided over the lake; leaving that strange wake behind it, like a ship in the ocean. It was some moments before he spoke again.

'How do you known of this place?' he enquired, turning his head a fraction, trying to get a glimpse of her out of the corner of his eye. When no answer came, he moved his head further so that he could see her better, letting his mind take in every detail as she stood there, motionless; he thought she looked like a water nymph—yes, that was it, like *Volvi* the Limnade nymph that had just risen from the depths of the lake. Her eyes met his for a brief moment, large, grey eyes, sad in expression. Quickly, she looked away.

'I do not bite,' he said quietly, smiling at her. 'Will you not even tell me your name?'

Still there was silence. A gust of breeze caught her corn-coloured hair, whipping it up into soft whirls, framing her heart shaped face, which was at this moment was devoid of colour, with the exception of a full cherry red mouth whose upper lip rose up to a cupid's bow. She was beautiful, the very essence of innocence and purity, and Stewart felt a strong compelling desire to reach out and touch her, if only to confirm to himself that he was not hallucinating. He was perplexed; maybe he was having a vision of some kind, or maybe he was just dreaming and would wake suddenly to find himself at home.

'You should not be out here alone, you know, it is not safe. Your family must be looking for you.' He paused, still looking at her.

'You are extremely beautiful,' he whispered, then bit his lip as he realised he had voiced his thoughts so openly, turning away as he noticed the blood rush to her cheeks in embarrassment. He watched a bird as it skimmed across the lake calling to its mate, the sound echoing around them. Stewart had no conceivable idea why he had just said that, except that it was true. There followed a silence with just the intermittent chirping of birds, and the sound of the breeze soughing through the trees.

'I wish to beg your pardon, Mistress, for my behaviour,' he added quietly, as he rose walking slowly towards her.

'It was impertinent of me, embarrassing you, please forgive me.' His voice was so gentle and warm that a smile crept into a corner of her mouth.

'But you are, you know,' he added in a whisper to himself. Stewart stood, staring down into her face. Her skin was very fair and had that softness of youth, with her hair hanging heavy now in large, loose coils about her shoulders. She meekly lowered her head in reply.

Feeling the sense of anxiety slip away from him, he spoke again, 'May I be so bold as to tell you something else? You should always use your smile.' Stewart cleared his throat uneasily and gestured with his hand at the countryside before him. 'Pray tell me, do you come from here?' Still no reply came from the young girl, who just stood motionless watching him.

The air seemed charged suddenly; there was a tension that made him feel uncomfortable and out of control which was something that was alien to him. To cover this, Stewart swung backwards in a sweeping gesture.

'Allow me to introduce myself,' he continued, moving his left arm back while crossing his right arm over his body and bowing lowly as he spoke. 'I am Stewart Charles Hamilton, at your service, Mistress.'

The girl started to shake her head from side to side and became agitated, entwining and untwining her hands. Stewart thought that she might scream, but instead she lowered her head then spoke for the first time. 'I cannot, sir, for it would not be right to speak, as you be of noble birth, do you not, sir?'

Stewart frowned and was amusingly astonished at her reply. Her voice was sweet with the soft Wiltshire lilt behind it. Taken aback by her answer, he righted himself before replying, unsure at that moment of what he was about to say.

'What? I am no nobleman, and what does it matter, as we meet on neutral ground.' It was the first thing that came into his head before he swung his arm about him as to encompass the lake and fields. 'Surely, convention does not apply here?' he questioned amusingly. 'Please do not call me sir,' he added softly.

Stewart turned on his heel to face the lake once more, throwing the stone that he had been fondling into its depths. He stood there for some moments, watching the ripples flow out from where the stone had landed as a strange sense of detachment came over him—it was as though for once in his life he had been taken unawares, not in control of the situation, and this troubled him.

'What is your name, Mistress?' he enquired finally, glancing back over his shoulder. She stood there for what seemed like an eternity, twisting a piece of grass between her fingers before she spoke.

'Jenny. Jennifer Martin, sir,' she answered quickly.

Stewart was again unprepared, as he had not expected her to answer him, so he picked up another stone and tossed it into to the lake while he gained his composure.

'Do you know what I call this place, Jennie?' he questioned, turning once again to look at her as he spoke.

Stewart raised his hand and beckoned to her to come closer, speaking in a calm tone so as not to alarm her any more than she was. 'Come here, Jennie.' But she made no effort to move towards him.

'Please,' he asked with gentle encouragement, lifting his brows, but there was still no movement on her part. Stewart shrugged his shoulders then walked back to her once more, hesitating now and then till cautiously he reached her side. He could see that she did not know what to make of this strange large man that stood beside her, and that all of her instincts told her to run. Her arms were interlocked tightly before her, while her whole body was putting up an invisible barrier between herself and him. He knew in all propriety that he should leave, but... Stewart swallowed hard, emotions were running though his body as the wind blows through a field of ripe corn, pushing, moving, swaying, while the corn struggles to stay upright. Stewart felt his chest contract as he struggled to push air into his lungs.

'*Baia della pace,*' the words came from his mouth in a whisper, like they travelled on the breath of air that had been trapped within him and was suddenly expelled, freeing the obstruction making Stewart breathe deeply through his nose.

'It is Italian,' he explained, at last gaining his equilibrium. 'It means *bay of peace.*'

Suddenly, she turned and lifted her head to gaze innocently up into his face, her eyes seeming to hold his own in a trance that he could not turn away from; yet again he felt that overwhelming desire he had before to touch her.

'I have a name for it also,' her words broke the spell, and Stewart smiled nervously, but he was shaken, out of his depth, and he didn't like the feeling.

'Really?' he spoke at last, clearing his throat which had suddenly taken upon itself to close again. 'Pray tell me,' he added.

Her body turned from him then and her arms came defensively up and across her chest once more as she looked down to the ground and shook her head.

Stewart turned and walked a few paces towards the lake before sitting down again and drawing his knees up against his chest. He was perplexed, and as he looked out onto the lake, other images came into his mind and he began to think of Maggie. There was no logical explanation for this, except that his thoughts were always drifting towards her lately, and what had happened by the lake here just amplified the situation. 'I wish I loved her as she should be loved,' he confessed to himself. Oh, he loved her, but not with that passion that tears at your insides when you cannot be close to one another. That all-consuming love which gnaws at the heart till you think it will burst. The love he had for her was a slow, warm love, one that comes from mutual respect, trust and admiration. The screech of a water fowl brought him back from his thoughts, remembering Jennie, but when he turned, he found to his surprise that she had gone. He rose to his feet, slapping his thighs as he did so to dust himself. What had happened to him here had shaken him and he did not like the feeling.

'Old friend,' he said, patting the horse on the neck. 'I think it is time that you and I returned home.' Mounting his horse, Stewart sighed, a note of sadness in his voice. 'Oh well, perhaps we will see her again someday.' Pulling gently at the horse's reins, he started on the ride back to the house.

Chapter Two
Andrew and Elizabeth

Stewart sensed there was something wrong the moment he entered the hall. There was a tense atmosphere all about him, one he was unfortunately familiar with, and one he did not like. Lilly closed the large front door behind him, and began to make her way back to the kitchens.

'Lilly,' he called softly. Lilly stopped and turned.

'Yes, sir?' she replied curtseying. Stewart could see by her body language that she did not want to be there; she was as scared as a rabbit wanting to run.

'Where is Thompson? And what is going on here?' he asked, motioning to the drawing room where raised voices were coming, but Stewart knew before the words had passed her lips.

'Begging your pardon, Master Stewart, 'tis your father. He be coming down from Scotland.'

Stewart's face had frozen, and his eyes had taken on a glassy stare which made Lilly back away.

'When did he arrive?' he asked tonelessly.

'Ab-bout 2 o'c-clock,' she stammered back the reply.

Stewart's eyes never left the drawing room door. 'And my mother?' But he knew that also, without Lilly having to say.

'She be in there... with him, sir.'

'Thank you, Lilly,' he said in a low, cold voice as he made his way across the hall, his footsteps echoing on the stone flags.

'I should not be going in there, sir,' Lilly called to him, her voice tight with fear. 'He do say that on no account was anyone to be disturbing them.'

'Oh did he indeed,' replied Stewart, even more determined to enter. 'We will see.'

Lilly raised her arm in vain, but she knew it was futile to try and stop him. She could do nothing at all. Looking up she saw Pip standing at the top of the stairs. He raised his arm to indicate he was there, and to go back to the kitchen.

As Stewart threw open the doors to the drawing room, the two occupants swung round in astonishment. He waited, looking from one to the other, his mother he could tell had not expected him home so soon, and his father... well, he could tell his thoughts by the look on his face. Taking a step into the room, he slowly pushed the doors close behind him, leaning against them as he did so. It was Elizabeth's voice that broke the silence.

'Stewart,' her breath caught in her throat as her hands pressed into her stomach.

Stewart stood with his feet astride while his two hands rested on the doorknobs behind him; better there, he thought, than round his father's neck. The urge to attack was strong, but he refrained; his mouth was dry with anger now, as his eyes darted from his mother to his father, swallowing several times before he spoke.

'I gather that Lady Morris will NOT be coming,' he said dryly to Elizabeth. 'And what is he doing here?' he added, motioning to his father. By now Stewart was having great difficulty in restraining himself. He knew that if he let go of the doorknobs, he would fly at his father, and there would be no one to stop him. A cold sweat had broken out on his forehead, which in turn was trickling down the sides of his face. The remark made Andrew Duncan stiffen and tighten his jaw.

'What is the matter, Father?' he asked with sarcasm, 'feeling guilty? Or could it be that your latest mistress has grown tired of you, or no… wait, you have run out of money and your debtors are at your heels. Is that it, Father?' Stewart asked, saying the last word with disdain. He was now shaking from head to foot, and his hands were wet with sweat, but he kept his voice level and calm.

Andrew Duncan had gone a very deep shade of red, and Stewart noticed the right side of his father's face twitch, but neither man took their eyes from one another. Elizabeth all the while sat motionless, as though she had seen the Medusa, and had suddenly been set to stone.

'How dare you speak to me like that!' Andrew Duncan, who at last found his voice, got to his feet. 'Who do you think you are?' he continued, but the rest of the words seemed to be trapped, as he stood there open mouthed.

Stewart swallowed once more to control himself. 'And who are YOU to give ME orders?' he retaliated. 'A man who left his wife and a child of three these twenty-one years past, to go off with some… some—Do not question or moralise to me what I can and what I cannot do.' It was an effort to keep his voice steady now but he knew he had to; knowing just one spark would ignite a full scale brawl, as the two men stood looking at one another. They were equal in height, maybe Andrew Duncan an inch taller, but their tempers were identical.

Out in the hall Lilly had been standing in the shadows by the stairs. She was terrified at the sound of Stewart's voice; never before had she heard him raise it as he had now. Things were racing through her mind, and at this moment it was in turmoil, for what could she or anyone do, and what if they fought, what if someone was hurt, or even worse—the mere idea of it sent a cold slither of ice down her spine; her only thought was she had to get help. Thompson the butler and Carter the footman had gone to Mere, maybe Pip would come, had she not seen him on the landing. It was as she turned to make her way to the kitchen that Pip came up beside her. He placed his finger to his lips for silence, and then pulled her into the darkness to wait.

Stewart finally let go of the doors and walked towards his father; there was anger and contempt in his eyes for the man he saw before him. '*Oh God,*' he thought, '*I could hit him and think nothing of it.*' It was only seeing his mother's petrified face out of the corner of his eye that stopped him. He stood still some feet away, his mouth set.

'Oh, if only I were just one year older.' His voice seemed to come from outside of him, calm and flat, as though someone else had spoken the words. 'And do you know why?' he continued, 'because then I would have the pleasure of personally being able to remove you from this house.' Stewart raised his hand to stop Andrew Duncan from answering. 'But, until that day'—he swallowed hard, and shook his head slightly—'I will suffer you here for her sake,' he gestured to his mother, who he saw was about to drop to the floor.

Andrew Duncan flew at Stewart then, his face contorted with resentment. 'You know nothing of me... how I feel... what I am...'

'NO!' Elizabeth's piercing scream resonated around the room. 'For God's sake, NO!' she cried as she threw herself between them, looking up into her husband's face. 'This hate between you,' her words fell away to silence as her eyes looked into her husbands, pleading.

At hearing her voice, Stewart's body relaxed a little, and his eyes looked down at her. 'Mother,' he said softly, 'how can you defend this.' He paused to look at his father. 'This...' he shook his head in disbelief.

Elizabeth saw the hurt and pain in her son's eyes, but he did not understand how could he—he was but three years old when it happened.

'It is quite simple, Stewart,' she answered softly in reply, a deep sadness in her voice. She turned her head from him then and wept.

Stewart watched his mother, her shoulders trembling slightly, but he could not comfort her. Turning to face his father, he stared long and hard into his eyes.

'Well, she may defend you, she does not know how to hate, but by God I will get my revenge on you for what you have done to her.'

Saying this, Stewart turned and walked towards the doors, pausing before opening them, but not looking back, he spoke. 'I will not be here for dinner, Mother, I will be out.' His voice was void of any emotion.

'But when will you be back?' Elizabeth's voice was pleading now.

'God knows,' he replied as the doors closed behind him, the only sound that could be heard in the room was the gentle tick, tick, tick of the mantle clock.

Andrew Duncan walked to the fireplace, resting his hand to the mantle, standing there for some moments to collect his thoughts before turning to face Elizabeth, clasping his hands behind him. Though he was a man of average build, he stood over six feet in height. He had strong features with a very straight aquiline nose. His eyes were a pale blue, while his hair was brown, interspersed with grey at the sides, and surprisingly, still thick, in spite of his 55 years. Pushing his shoulders back, he walked forward to where Elizabeth was sitting.

'Andrew,' she breathed, raising her hand up, palm facing him in a gesture to stop him. 'Before you start, I have no more money.'

There was a pause as she raised her head up to look into his eyes.

'Oh come now, Lizzie,' he laughed, 'you have no more money, yet you are able to maintain the running of this estate.' His hand made a circular movement around him as he stood. 'Which is hardly a cottage,' he added, seating himself once more in the chair by the fireplace, crossing his legs. 'So do not tell me you have none.' He raised his brows in a mocking gesture, while Elizabeth watched his foot as it rocked back and forth in time to the clock.

'Andrew, truly I have not, not the sort of money you desire.' There was a resigned pleading in her voice. She knew he could take what he wanted, and there was no way to stop him. Elizabeth's eyes turned to the window, as the first rumblings of thunder rolled over the landscape outside, and a cold shiver went through her.

'If it were not for me, you would have been…' he paused, biting the inside of his mouth as Elizabeth looked up at him in horror, colour draining from her face.

'Yes, Lizzie,' he nodded at her. 'Our little dark secret.' He knew he had her now, but he was desperate; there was nowhere else to turn. As he looked at her, he lifted his mouth into a smile.

Elizabeth placed her hand to her throat, staring at him, her eyes searching his face, and swallowed deeply before answering. 'I did NOT kill him, and you know that,' she replied in a low frightened voice. Her mouth was suddenly dry.

'I know it, but what would anyone else think, eh?' His tone was thick with innuendo, and then a cynical grin appeared on his lips.

'Ohhhh, dear God,' she breathed. 'I killed him accidently, to save you, you know that. You were drunk, Andrew, filthy drunk when you started arguing and he pulled that knife on you.' Elizabeth shook her head slowly in disbelief. 'You are the one who would have been dead now.' She stood up, pacing slowly. 'If I had not come down to see what the disturbance was about…' she paused in mid-sentence, her eyes staring into some distant memory.

'But you stabbed him, Lizzie,' he said, hitting back at her.

At this Elizabeth swung round to look him in the eye. 'I did it to save your *life*!' she screamed.

'Why?' Andrew questioned, his voice was calm in reply to her hysteria. 'You did not love me.' There was a question in the words that hung in the air, and then a silence ensued where a pin could have been heard if dropped.

Elizabeth dropped her head down in resignation. 'I did, once, a very long time ago…' her words trailed off into a whisper, as though time had taken them and put them into the past.

Andrew stood there, regaining composure once more. 'Well, that is all past and gone, is it not?' Andrew Duncan shrugged his shoulders as at that moment his clothes felt too tight; he had not intended this to happen as it had. '…That is, if you furnish me with the money. I need five hundred pounds.' His last words were spoken as though he were bartering for some sheep at a market, while Elizabeth just stared at him in disbelief.

She looked at her husband now and remembered how it had been; wondering how could a person change so much? How could a man hide so much of himself that she had believed that he loved her? Her feelings for him then were so profound, she would have given up her life freely for him had it been asked of her. Now, he would give up her life for the sake of five hundred pounds. Andrew's voice broke into her thoughts.

'After all, you would not want your precious son to know that his devoted mother was a murderess, would you now?'

Elizabeth looked up at him; his passive face looking back at her gave her no inclination to his feelings, as outwardly he looked very calm.

'You would not dare?' she answered.

Andrew stared back at her. 'Would I not?' Andrew raised his brows and nodded at her. He was *more* than desperate now.

After a short silence, Andrew shifted his shoulders once more and cleared his throat... *Dear God, was he actually doing this?*

'Your father was clever, was he not, Lizzie? He put that codicil, very slyly might I add, into the Marriage Contract that gave this house over to you on your marriage... as custodian...' He paused for effect, looking up at the ceiling and tapped his finger on his chin sardonically. 'Let me see, it went something like: *"If there be children from the marriage, then the house and surrounding property will revert to the first born son on his 25th birthday. If no son, then to the eldest daughter."'* Andrew sniffed hard with derision here, remembering the humiliation he had felt then. 'Oh, your father was a canny Scotsman, all right, he never disclosed this when we married.'

Elizabeth watched him closely and could see now that he was trying hard to contain the anger and something more—anguish, which was rising within him.

'I have my jewellery.' She paused to swallow before adding. 'You are welcome to that.'

The moment had passed. 'Oh yes,' he replied, now remembering, 'that emerald necklace your father gave you as a wedding gift... that should be worth something.' He was mentally counting now.

Elizabeth saw that his face was a myriad of emotions, and amongst these was still anger; she shook herself, trying to come out of the fear that was little by little enveloping her.

'I will fetch it at once,' she replied, walking to the door and disappearing quickly before he could answer.

As the door closed, Andrew Duncan closed his eyes and let out the breath he had been holding. He was shaking from head to foot and it seemed his whole body was perspiring. He could not comprehend where some of the words he had spoken had come from, how could he have said such things, but desperation leads a man down a path that he would never imagine treading.

***

As Elizabeth mounted the stairs to her room, her legs felt as though they were about to give way beneath her, and the ground kept coming up to her in waves of nervous sickness. Things were colliding around in her mind, terrible things. If Stewart found out, what would he think of her? If he knew all that had happened that bleak winters evening, would he ever be able to understand?

As she reached the landing, Elizabeth distractedly wiped the beads of sweat that had formed on her forehead with her handkerchief. Turmoil was the least of the emotions she was feeling at the moment. She was brought back to her senses as somewhere along the corridor a door banged shut, and heavy footsteps could be heard coming towards her. Elizabeth ducked quickly into the dark shadows of a recess, just in time to see Stewart fly past her, bag in hand, as he tore down the stairs. She watched him cross the hallway, jumping nervously when the front door slammed hard behind him as he left the house.

Elizabeth, now in a state of despair, continued to her room, lighting a candle from one of the sconces along the corridor before entering. She closed the door quietly, then stood for some moments to still her nerves, before she made her way across the room to the small table where her jewellery box stood. Steadily, she placed the candle down beside it and picked up the box. She stared at it, her finger tracing the thistle pattern on the lid; it had belonged to her mother. She looked around herself carefully, as if to find someone there watching her and sighing with relief at seeing no one, she seated herself on a stool. Opening the box, she emptied the contents into her lap, watching the stones sparkle as they caught the candle's flicker; then she separated the emerald necklace from the rest and held it to the light. It was beautiful—the most beautiful piece of jewellery she owned. It consisted of a large emerald drop set in gold, with smaller ones at intervals set into the gold chain. Its clasp was an equally large emerald drop with a row of smaller ones set in gold that hung beneath it. The stones at that moment cast large green spots on Elisabeth's face as she held it aloft, watching it glisten in the candle's flame. She shook it gently, gazing at the colours as they danced before her eyes. It was then a large tear escaped and trickled down her face, leaving a wet line in its wake.

How could she part with it, and yet she had to; either way was meant for Stewart's sake. She had intended to keep it and give it to him when he married, for his bride to wear it on her wedding day, just as she had done. But now she had to give it up, so that he would never know the truth about her. Elizabeth buried her head in her hands and sobbed, her tears wetting the stones, as though the emeralds shared in her sorrow.

In the drawing room Andrew had helped himself to a glass of whisky to steady his nerves while waiting, and was unconsciously leafing through the pages of a poetry book that he had found on a window seat.

'Paradise Lost by John Milton, how very appropriate,' Andrew whispered ironically. 'We could have been so happy, Lizzie, but circumstance and fate stopped that.' There was a noise behind him and he quickly dropped the book back to the seat just as Elizabeth re-entered the room. Turning on his heel, he saw her standing by the door clutching the necklace in her hand.

'Here, take it!' she called, holding her hand out to him. 'Go on, take it. Take it and get out!' Her voice had been slowly rising in pitch; Elizabeth was near to hysteria now.

Andrew closed his eyes for a moment, and then slowly and deliberately he placed his glass on the small table by the sofa. He paused, carefully choosing his words.

'Thank you, Lizzie,' he nodded. 'Now Stewart can go on thinking what a martyr his mother is, to put up with such a man as I, for a little while longer that is.' With that, Andrew took the necklace, carefully wrapped it in a large handkerchief, and placed it in the pocket of his coat.

'I will take my leave of you now, Lizzie,' he bowed his head slightly. Elizabeth made a move to open the door when Andrew put up his hand and said calmly, 'No, please do not bother to see me out. I know my way,' he added, walking towards the door. Within seconds she heard the large front door close behind him.

When he had gone, Elizabeth sat on the sofa, put her head in her hands and gave in to her tears once more.

All this while, Lilly and Pip had been standing in the shadows of the hall. They had heard Stewart leave and had been very fearful to leave their mistress alone with this man; they were powerless but had witnessed everything.

***

As Andrew Duncan left the house, he breathed in deeply. Dear God, was this sufficient to keep his debtors at bay? He doubted it, but if he paid some of what he owed, it might suffice to keep him out of prison. He swallowed hard, how had he come to this demise? But he knew the answer: jealousy. He looked around him at the estate and shook his head; time was a harsh reality, if he could turn it back. He felt for the ring in his pocket and turned it gently with his fingers. Placing his hat on his head, he went out into the rain to the stables to retrieve his horse.

35

Chapter Three
Lady Margaret

As Stewart left the house, he looked towards the heavens to find that the heat of the day had now culminated into ominous rain clouds. The air all around was thick and heavy and you could feel the power held within it; a storm was brewing, he knew, but not only in the heavens. Stewart shrugged and concluded that the storm matched his temper at this present moment, like primed gunpowder ready to explode. Looking once more heavenward, he shook his head. Would he reach Lady Margaret's home before it broke? He doubted that very much. Pulling himself into his coat, he smacked his hat on his head and headed for the stables, while unconsciously crossing himself, asking for forgiveness for what he was about to do. He saddled his own horse and left the stables just as the first drops of the summer storm were hitting the earth.

By the time Stewart had reached Lady Margaret's house on the other side of Mere, he was soaked to the skin. He dismounted, retrieved his bag from the back of the saddle then looked once more heavenward. 'God, forgive me,' he whispered.

Leading his horse to the stables, he returned and mounted the front steps, ringing the bell; he had to wait some moments before it was answered. The door opened slowly, letting out a warm glow from the candle stick that was held aloft. Stewart looked at the small frail man that stood before him and thought absently that he had not been expecting callers, his coat had been hastily buttoned using the wrong buttons, leaving the bottom one with nothing to hold on to, and his wig was also slightly askew. Stewart's first thoughts were, *Poor man, and what the hell am I doing?*

'Why, Mr Hamilton sir,' said Giles, startled, 'what on earth brings you here so unexpectedly, and on such a night as this?' Giles looked at him puzzled, and as he spoke his eyes were looking over Stewart's dripping form, as though he was in two minds whether to admit him or not.

'My father,' answered Stewart, walking past him into the hall and placing his wet things on a table there. Giles looked at him in amazement; the poor man's mouth was gaping as his mind tried to get in sync with his voice.

'Your father?' he began,

'Is Lady Margaret in?' Stewart interrupted before Giles could finish. Giles had regained enough composure to turn and shut the door, noticing that the rain had made a rather large puddle on the floor just inside it. Then looking towards

Stewart, he saw that an even bigger one was now forming around Stewart's feet, as he stood by the table placing his wet hat and coat there. Stewart's impatient voice snapped him back.

'Is Lady Margaret in?' Stewart repeated firmly.

Giles pulled himself upright before replying, 'Yes, sir, yes she is in her personal drawing room, writing.'

Without waiting, Stewart turned on his heel and mounted the stairs two at a time, calling back, 'Thank you, Giles, no need to announce me, I'll announce myself.'

'Very well, sir,' Giles said to himself as he watched Stewart reach the landing and disappear into the darkness of the passage above.

Stewart steadied himself and breathed deeply as he reached the landing and for the third time that night asked God for forgiveness. He saw the glow from under her drawing room door before he reached it, pausing to compose himself once more; he placed his hand on the handle and opened it. He saw Margaret at once, her back towards him, sitting at her bureau writing. Closing the door quietly behind him, he walked across to her. All of his senses seemed heightened now; he could feel his feet squelch in his boots as he walked, the fire to the right of him cracked suddenly, making him flinch, but most of all he could smell Margaret's roses and jasmine perfume—she had bathed then.

'Hello, Maggie,' he whispered as he bent and kissed the back of her neck. *God*, he thought, *she tasted sweet.*

Margaret froze for an instant, then stood up and in one fluid movement, turned, her eyes betraying all of her emotions at once.

'Stewart!' she cried as she threw her arms around his neck and kissed him; he had taken her unawares, he knew that, as she disentangled herself from his embrace, pushing him gently away.

'Why did you not tell me you were coming?' she questioned. 'I was expecting you yesterday.' Margaret looked down at herself, smoothing out the folds of her robe with her hands, embarrassed. 'Look at me.'

Stewart clasped her hands and held them out, running his eyes over her. 'You look breath-taking to me,' he breathed as he pulled her into his arms and kissed her again. Margaret once more pulled herself away, feeling the wetness in his clothes seep into her own.

'You are soaking wet!' she exclaimed, eyeing him critically, 'and you have shaved your moustache,' she added as her finger ran softly over his upper lip. 'Come now, what are you doing here at this late hour and in this storm?' nodding her head towards the window as she spoke. Stewart made a move to pull her into his arms once more.

'Oh no!' she stopped him by placing her hands between them and pushing gently onto his chest. 'I am sure that you have not come out in this storm just to see me.' Her eyes were sparkling with laughter, but her voice betrayed a slight edge. Margaret eased out of his embrace and moved to seat herself on a small sofa, patting the place beside her for him to join.

'Come,' she encouraged, 'sit down here next to me and tell me all, you are not in trouble, are you?' Her brows rose and her head slightly inclined as she spoke. Stewart shook his head, breathed deeply through his nose, and came to sit next to her.

'No,' he sighed, 'I am not.'

Margaret took one of his hands into both of hers as she looked up into his face. 'Well, that is a relief at least,' she paused for an instant before carrying on. 'Well, what is it then?' she coaxed squeezing his hand. 'Tell me.'

Stewart looked down at their clasped hands, trying to collect his thoughts before answering.

'It is my father, Maggie, he has come down from Scotland again, we thought...' Stewart paused and took a breath, 'we exchanged the usual pleasantries with one another, you know.'

Margaret put up her hand and stoked his cheek. 'I see,' was all she said, and that was enough for Stewart, for only Maggie did see. Her hand felt cool as she held it cupped against his face that he closed his eyes, covered it with his own and tried to let all of the anger drain away from him.

'Maggie, I hate his very being,' he said with harshness in his voice, and Margaret noticed a cold expression come into his eyes as he spoke of him. 'One day he will push me too far, and I swear I will...' The tone and the flatness of his voice unnerved her.

'You must not say such things, Stewart, you frighten me,' she said, as her eyes searched his face. Releasing his hand, she stood up. 'But where are my manners, you are soaking wet, and I wager you have not eaten?' she added. Stewart looked hard at her; he had unnerved her, he knew that, and he had not meant that to happen. He stood up now to face her.

'Maggie, I...' The words trailed away as they looked at one another with an unspoken acknowledgment. 'No, I do not want anything to eat, Maggie,' he added softly in resignation.

'Well then, let us get you some dry clothes.' Margaret's smile broke the tension, but as she went to move past him to summon her maid, Steward grabbed her arm, pulling her round with a jolt. Margaret's look was that of bewilderment as she tuned round to face him. The look he returned as he stared down into her eyes was serious.

'Whatever is the matter?' she questioned. Margaret looked down at his hand which was gripping her arm like a vice, the grip was not vicious, but of need with and underlying element of fear. 'Stewart, you are hurting my arm,' she exclaimed. Stewart made no move to loosen his grip, and his voice was low as he spoke.

'Maggie,' there was a slight pause, 'Will you be my wife?'

Margaret's mouth fell open; of all the things she had been expecting, this was NOT one of them. 'Wha... what did you say?' she faltered, finding it hard to speak.

'I said, will you be my wife?!' he repeated, this time his voice was stern, this was not the response he had been expecting. 'What is the matter with you? Have

I said something *so* strange? I have asked you to be my wife, is that bad?' he was gently shaking her as he spoke.

Margaret's face showed total confusion. 'No, Stewart, but…'

'But what!' he interrupted. 'Good God, Margaret, I have shared your bed, I do not know how many times, and now, because I have asked you to be my wife, you think I have gone mad!'

Margaret finally released herself from his grip and walked to the window, her hands twisting nervously; turning her eyes, she searched his face for some kind of answer. 'Stewart,' she coughed, trying to clear the tightness in her throat. 'It… it is not the same,' she answered. Shaking her head, she paused to see if he would speak, but no answer came so she continued. 'Lying with someone is one thing, marrying him is another, especially when the love is one-sided.' Her look said it all as she continued. 'You have never once said that you loved me, have you, Stewart?' Before he could reply she continued. 'Oh yes, you have said it, when'—she put up her palm to stop his retort that she could see coming—'when you have been so full of drink that I am sure you did not know if it were I or some other woman you were caressing.'

'MARGARET!' Stewart's voice broke in like a clap of thunder, making Margaret flinch badly; her mouth remaining open in mid-sentence. Finding her voice once more, she continued.

'I have accepted this, Stewart, taken you for what you are with all your faults.'

'Stop it!' Stewart shouted. 'Stop it! Enough. What is the matter with you, how do you know what I feel?' He was moving slowly towards her now. 'Would I ask you to be my wife if I did not love you?'

Margaret stared at him wistfully. 'In truth, Stewart, I do not know, would you?' Margaret's anguished answer came out on the exhalation of a breath she had been holding.

Stewart straightened himself and looked at her with gentleness.

'Maggie, I have always, always shown you the greatest respect, this you cannot deny. There has been nothing that I would not have done for you, nor would I yet do. You talk as though I treat you badly.' His eyes were searching her face all the time he was speaking.

'Stewart,' Margaret broke in gently. 'You still have not answered my question.'

He said nothing for a few seconds, his eyes staring fixedly at her.

'Would I ask you to be my wife if I did not love you?' he questioned

Margaret inclined her head, smiling slowly. Stewart swallowed hard before replying, and she saw the muscles in his face contract, but Stewart's eyes never left hers.

'No,' came his firm reply. Once it was out, it was easy to say the rest. In fact, it was true, he did love her. It was a love borne of need, mutual respect and companionship. Lots of marriages did not even have that. 'No, Maggie, I would not.'

Stewart saw the relief on Margaret's face as she smiled at him. 'That is all I wanted to hear,' she said gently. 'I trust...' Margaret paused to swallow and compose herself. 'I trust you,' she continued, her voice steadier now. 'And I know that you would never lie to me, thank you.' She came to him slowly and cupped his face in her hands. Kissing him lightly, she whispered, 'Yes, Stewart, I will be your wife.' As the last words caught in her throat, tears clouded her eyes. 'Yes, yes, yes,' she answered softly as the tears brimmed over her lashes and ran down her cheeks.

Stewart drew her towards him then, cradling her in his arms tenderly.

'Oh, I love you so much,' she whispered as she allowed herself to be taken up into his arms. She did not care how he loved her, so long as he did.

Outside, the rain fell heavily, the heat of yesterday having been extinguished by the fierceness of the storm. In Margaret's bedroom a fire had been lit and the flickering flames from it threw shadows dancing on the walls and ceiling like spirits keeping watch. Stewart lay there deep in thought—sleep would not come to him yet. He turned to look at Margaret, her mouth slightly parted and her breasts rising and falling in the even rhythm of slumber, while her hand rested gently on his chest. Stewart reflected that when asleep, her face resembled that of a small child, peaceful and serene, but, when awake, and showing those deep green almond shaped eyes, they reflected the wholly beautiful young woman that she was. They had made love with such a slow tenderness and with such depth of feeling, the like he had never before experienced; it had left him not sated, but with every nerve in his body heightened.

Stewart turned away. Slipping gently out of the bed, he rested her head on a pillow, then pulling a cover about his shoulders, he walked to the window. He ran his fingers through his hair to clear his thoughts, turning once to look at Margaret as she lay at peace. Shaking his head, he rubbed his eyes with the heels of his palms.

'Love is unconditional,' he said under his breath as he gazed out onto the gloomy wetness of the night. He turned and, for several moments, paced in silence up and down the room, seating himself finally in the winged chair facing the fire. What Maggie had given him was just that; she was kind, warm, loving and, above all else, truthful and trusting. Stewart leaned forward and buried his face in his hands.

'I do love her,' he said in answer to his own thoughts. 'She is so like you, Mother, she has your strength and courage, and may I be damned to hell if I ever hurt her.'

'Stewart?' Margaret's voice split the silence.

'I am here,' he answered, turning to look round the chair as he roused himself from his thoughts.

Margaret slipped from the bed, pulling her robe around her before she came to kneel by his feet, and then Stewart lifted her gently up onto his lap and cradled her in his arms.

'Stewart?'

'Mmmm?' came the reply as his lips pressed into the hair on the top of her head.

'Is there something the matter?' she asked

'No, nothing,' he replied, laughing softly, moving her slightly to take her hands in his and bringing them up to his lips to kiss.

Margaret looked up at him, her green eyes searching his face. 'Stewart, you will never hurt me, will you?'

'Never,' he said. 'I will *never* hurt you, Maggie, I swear it.' Picking her up as he said the last words, he made his way to the bed and laid her gently down. Suddenly, his mouth came down onto hers with such ferocity that Margaret recoiled, but in a split second her mouth answered his with the same fierceness. Stewart's arms came round her, crushing her to him, as Margaret pulled him closer, wrapping her legs around his thighs. They rolled and pulled at one another, crashing to the floor in a tangled mass of bedclothes and limbs. The act of possession was so intense that when their final release came, it was as though their souls had fused together. They lay there for some time till Stewart lifted his head and looked down into Margaret's face; it was then a great wave of peace came over him.

'I will never hurt you, I swear,' he breathed again. Margaret gave the slightest of nods and pulled his head down to kiss him gently on the lips.

'I know,' she whispered as she released him.

They remained there, just listening to the rain outside and the fire crackle and burn within, before Stewart picked her up and placed her back into bed. Easing himself gently down beside her, he pulled up the bedcover and held her to him tucking her head under his chin, stroking her back, cradling her as you would a baby. She fell asleep instantly, and, in the next breath, so did Stewart.

***

It was late afternoon before Stewart arrived home with Margaret. They had come in Margaret's coach as the weather had made the roads like mud, and though the rain had stopped, there was still a chill dampness left in the air. Stewart shivered slightly as he handed Margaret down from the coach.

'Are you nervous?' he asked, squeezing her hand.

'A little,' she replied, rubbing her hands up and down her arms as the coldness seeped through the material chilling her skin. If she were truthful, it wasn't only the weather that sent chills up her spine. All of her organs seemed to be moving in some form or another, as she placed her hand across her stomach to stop it churning. She had never been to the Willows before, she did not even know if his mother knew of her existence. On reflection though, she must, as the rumours would no doubt have reached even his mother's ears.

'Do you think your mother will approve of me? What I mean is...' Margret paused. 'Does she know about us?'

Stewart smiled. 'About us? What about us?' Stewart shrugged his shoulders. 'My mother does not believe in idle gossip,' he leaned towards her smiling,

41

'especially not about me, come on, Maggie.' He held his arm out to her and Maggie gratefully took it. 'Everything will be fine,' he assured her, holding her arm tight to his body. 'Let us get you inside, you look chilled. One would never believe it was July,' he commented, looking up at the darkening sky.

'Where is my Mother?' Stewart enquired as Thompson the butler opened the door. Thompson was the epitome of his profession as he stood there straight as an arrow and dressed to perfection, his eyes betraying nothing.

'She is in the drawing room, Master Stewart,' he replied, stepping aside as they came into the hall. 'Milady,' he greeted, bowing sharply to Margaret. 'Shall I announce you...' but before he could finish, Stewart had pulled Margaret towards him and reached the drawing room door.

'I live here, Thompson,' Stewart said with a smile on his face. 'I need no announcing.'

Thompson looked from Stewart to Margaret and mused to himself that he rather thought he did, but he bowed in his dignified manner as though there was nothing amiss and went back to his duties.

Elizabeth had been sitting on the window seat with the view to the garden at the back of the house, so was unaware of Stewart's arrival. The previous evening had left her drained and empty. Although she had retired early, sleep had been her enemy; her mind was so full that she could feel the memories colliding with one another, so much so that when Stewart's voice called from the door, she stood up so abruptly she knocked a small table and its contents to the floor.

'Mother,' his voice was gentle. 'I am sorry I startled you.'

Elizabeth's face lit up. 'Stewart,' she called as she advanced across the room towards him, 'where have you been?'

Stewart stepped to the side then, and drew Margaret out from behind him.

'To Lady Margaret's,' he replied, placing an arm around Margaret's waist; then releasing Margaret, he drew to the side. 'Margaret, my Mother, Milady Elizabeth,' he swept his left arm out towards his Mother before continuing.

He then turned towards Margaret, looking into her eyes giving encouragement. 'Mother, this is Lady Margaret Stanhope.'

A little of the happiness faded from Elizabeth's eyes as she saw Margaret, though only those who knew her well would have noticed the change. She had heard rumours about the two, only rumours, but it worried her. Regaining her composure, Elizabeth held out her hand, and made a kind gesture of letting Margaret kiss her cheek.

'Hello, Margaret, I am pleased to meet you, will you not sit down?' Elizabeth motioned to the sofa.

Margaret looked at Stewart for support, his eyes meeting hers, then smiling he made the merest of nods and led her to the sofa.

Elizabeth regaining her self-control once more came across and tugged the bell pull by the mantle. 'Where are my manners, you must be hungry, I will ring for some tea, and I am sure that cook has some cold meats, bread and pickles...' Elizabeth broke off her agitated speech as Stewart caught her hand.

'Mother,' he smiled at her, then held his stomach, 'yes, I am hungry,' he answered, looking towards Margaret who smiled up at him. Leading his mother to the sofa, he continued. 'Come, sit down with me. I have something to tell you, then we can ring for the food.'

Elizabeth allowed herself to be led back where Stewart seated her next to Margaret.

'I... well, we have something to tell you,' said Stewart. Elizabeth's face was blank as she looked from her son to Margaret, then back again.

'What do you mean?' but Elizabeth's words were stopped by Stewart.

'Mother, there is nothing wrong,' he assured her, 'for once I have good news,' he added.

Elizabeth was becoming more anxious by the second, as her hand pleated the material of her gown.

'What do you mean?' she repeated, then shook her head puzzled.

'Mother, I have asked Lady Margaret for her hand in marriage and she has accepted.' There was a silence in the room, where it seemed like nothing moved, not even the air till Elizabeth spoke.

'Oh, Stewart!' she exclaimed which could have been interpreted in any one of two ways.

A light tap on the door caused all eyes to turn as Lilly the maid entered and curtsied; she looked at her mistress and asked, 'You rang, Milady?'

'Oh, Lilly,' Elizabeth replied, trying to gain control. 'Yes, could you ask cook if we may have some food, tea and cakes if any, please?'

'And a large glass of Port for my mother,' Stewart added. 'I think she is in need of it.' He turned to Lilly and grinned.

'Yes, sir.' Lilly tried hard not to giggle, as she too had seen the startled look on her mistress's face. 'Right away, sir.' Curtsying once more, she turned to go.

As the door closed, Stewart turned to his mother, grinning. 'Well?' he asked, as Elizabeth looked at him hard and long.

'Really, Stewart,' she exclaimed, 'you know that I do not—' but Stewart broke into her sentence.

'If you had seen the expression on your face a moment before, Mother, you looked as if you could drink the whole bottle.' Stewart eyed his mother keenly, waiting for her retort.

'Really?' she said, laughing somewhat nervously, her mind trying to take in the shock that she had just been given. Her son had left the house the previous evening in a temper fit to murder, and now he had come home, not only smiling, but with a woman he had betrothed himself to. As her brain clicked into motion though, she registered what this carefully managed pretence was all about. Surely, he would not do this, not to the woman she had sitting next to her, who was at this moment looking lovingly up into her son's face. The Stewart she knew was not so callous, nor would he marry someone where no love was involved, she was sure of that. Elizabeth turned to look at Margaret, and then to her son. It was at this point Stewart understood what his mother was registering in that logical brain of hers.

With a smile still on his face, Stewart came across and raised Margaret to her feet, pulling her to him by placing an arm around her waist. He looked askance at his mother, then down into Margaret's eyes.

'Well, are you not going to congratulate us?' he questioned, raising his eyebrows.

Elizabeth drew in a silent breath, directing her gaze to Margaret. 'If my son has chosen you, then I know you will both be very happy. God bless you both.'

Elizabeth saw her son's face and shoulders visibly relax. Stewart knew that his interrogation regarding this surprising revelation was not over. As soon as she could speak with him alone, he would have a *lot* of explaining to do. Coming back to her senses, Elizabeth stood up.

'Margaret, I am sure that you would like to freshen yourself before the food arrives,' in saying this, Elizabeth had already reached the mantle and pulled the bell, 'and of course you must stay here tonight, as it seems we are headed for more rain,' added Elizabeth as she looked out the window into the garden where the trees seemed to be swaying in an alarming fashion, while dark grey clouds were chasing one another across a very angry sky. It seemed to Elizabeth that the nightmare events of yesterday evening were still not over, both outside and within the house.

'If it rains again like yesterday, the roads will be impassable for your carriage.' Elizabeth paused as Lilly entered the room. 'Ah, Lilly, please show Lady Stanhope to one of the guest rooms so that she may refresh herself, and then ask Martin to arrange for her horses to be fed and stabled, and her carriage put away. I think we are in for another storm.'

Lilly curtsied low. 'Yes, Milady.' She then turned to Margaret, curtsying once more.

'And if you will be coming with me, Milady Stanhope, I will take you to your room.'

Stewart squeezed Margaret's hand. 'Go on Maggie,' he said as he kissed the top of her forehead, 'go make yourself beautiful.'

Margaret smiled and nodded. She understood that his mother wished to speak with her son. Margaret reflected that maybe she should take her time, as she understood there were many questions to be answered, not least those about herself. What mother would not have questions when her only son comes home with a woman who has been widowed just two years and announces his desire to marry her; had her own mother been alive, she would never have taken this news as majestically as Lady Elizabeth had. Margaret respected Elizabeth's stoicism in this. She could tell that his mother was no stranger to sudden unexpected developments in her life. She had nothing but admiration for the woman.

As soon as the doors closed, Elizabeth turned to her son and met him eye to eye. Stewart did not move—he could feel the tension within the room—and as he looked at his mother, he knew that most of it was emanating from her, till finally she spoke.

'Stewart, you have never lied to me—not that I know of, that is—and I do not want you to lie to me now, so tell me, are you in love with her?'

The words hit at him like a landslide, causing a sudden silence in the room, as though he had suddenly lost his hearing.

'Well, are you going to answer or explain all of this for me?' her tone of voice bore no nonsense.

Stewart rubbed his hand over his face; regaining his composure before he spoke. He raised his hands up before him palms out, as though to stop any onslaught that his mother might have ready to aim at him again.

'Before you say anything, Mother, I just want you to know that I do love her.'

Before Elizabeth could retaliate, Stewart stopped her. 'Let me finish, please?' he added, and Elizabeth nodded, turned and seated herself once again on the sofa.

'Carry on,' she offered.

'I have known Maggie—Lady Margaret Stanhope,' he corrected.

Elizabeth folded her arms and looked up at him slightly sardonically.

'Please, Mother, let me finish,' he reiterated.

Elizabeth breathed deeply and waved a hand at her son, 'Please continue, but—'

Stewart stopped her words again. 'Please, Mother! Hear me out.' Elizabeth nodded.

'I have known Lady Margaret Stanhope for over a year now. Alexander took me to a dinner party she was hosting for a distant cousin of hers,' he stopped beginning to pace the room, 'oh the details have no consequence here,' he continued.

'I met her at the dinner party,' he said emphatically. 'Mother, she is just like you, she asks nothing of anyone, would do anything for anyone, but most of all she has a heart so...' his words trailed away. 'She is a truly beautiful person, believe me.'

Elizabeth eyed her son but did not move to say anything in response.

Stewart continued to pace the room, then clapping his hands together he turned to face Elizabeth. 'I have not done this to get control of The Willows!'

Elizabeth raised her eyebrows and put her head to one side her face unyielding in its look.

'Mmmm,' she offered.

'No, no, no!' he shouted

'Who are you trying to convince, Stewart, me or *you?*' Elizabeth's voice had also risen; she meant to get to the bottom of this.

'Oh God, I am not explaining myself well,' replied Stewart exasperatedly. He stopped pacing and came to sit beside his mother, taking her hands in his.

Elizabeth's expression did not change. 'Tell me this, Stewart, if your father had not come here yesterday, would you have asked Lady Margaret to marry you?' Her question hung between them in the air. 'Answer me truthfully, Stewart, or not at all,' she added. Elizabeth silently thought that he had never

45

openly lied to her, only glossed the truth a little to save her embarrassment over some of his indiscretions.

'No,' Stewart paused, 'not at this time, but, I do love her.' His eyes looked pleadingly into his mother's. 'Given a little more time, we would have married…' Stewart paused once more. 'The love she gives me is unconditional.'

'So that means it is acceptable for you to marry her?' retaliated Elizabeth. 'Stewart, I have been in a marriage such as this, where I worshipped the very ground your father walked on, to later have my heart broken and my spirit crushed, left to feel unwanted, rejected…' She paused to get hold of her emotions. 'This woman has been through one traumatic marriage, married to a man who could have been her grandfather!'

Stewart stood up suddenly. 'Mother, I know all this.' His voice was level but his hands were shaking, thinking well before he spoke his next words.

'Mother, do you put me in the same category as my father?' He did not look at her as he said the words, but his body was as rigid as a piece of wood.

Elizabeth slowly stood up next to him, placing a hand into one of his.

'No, Stewart, I do not.' It was the finality with which she said the words which made him turn his head to look at her.

'I am very glad for that.' Stewart's voice had a tremor to it which could have been anger or deep emotion, as he gripped his mother's hand and swallowed hard.

'Mother, she is my goodness, my gentleness, my pathos, all these things that I am not. I will never hurt her, I swear to you.'

Elizabeth looked at her son and said her next words very gently. 'I hope not, Stewart, for if you did, I will never forgive you.'

As that moment, the door to the drawing room opened, revealing the butler and two servants bearing trays of food and a steaming pot of tea.

'Just leave them on the side dresser please, Thompson, we will help ourselves later,' Elizabeth ordered.

Thompson looked at his mistress and nodded. 'Very well, Mistress, as you wish.' With that he bowed and ushered the two other servants out and closed the doors quietly behind him.

Stewart eyed his mother; he knew that his interrogation had not ended.

'I will be honest with you, Stewart; I have heard rumours about the two of you…' Elizabeth broke off for a moment. 'This woman has known no love for the first part of her adult life. She was married off by her father, for a king's ransom some would say—I cannot imagine what her life must have been like with that man—this was his third marriage, and some would say he was not of a very calm temperament. Two years must have seemed a lifetime, and it was a blessing that there were no children.'

Stewart for once did not interrupt her.

'Stewart, to marry for love is the greatest gift that God can bestow upon a person. To have that love returned is a double blessing.' As Elizabeth spoke, she was looking out to the garden to that far distant place of her youth where love was new and all that mattered. Without a sound two large tears spilled down her face. 'It has been my prayer that you would find that.' As Elizabeth finished, Stewart went to his mother and pulled her gently into his arms.

'I can promise you, Mother, that her love for me is returned,' saying this he leaned down and kissed the top of his mother's head. He knew what she meant; had she not been alone these past twenty-one years—without a husband—even if he tried, he could not imagine what that would be like. Elizabeth took his hand and pressed it to her cheek, and then two pairs of identical blue eyes met, conveying their message without words.

'Be very careful, Stewart, please, please be careful.'

Stewart closed his eyes slowly in acknowledgement of what his mother had just said when a small tap came from the door, making them both turn as Margret slowly entered the room. Wiping her hands over her cheeks, Elizabeth composed herself before speaking.

'Margaret,' she called, holding out her hand to her perspective daughter-in-law. 'I think you and I are going to be great friends.' She paused looking from Margaret to Stewart. 'Very, very great friends.'

As Margaret looked at Elizabeth, she felt that from that moment a bond was formed between the two women, though as yet neither knew the strength of it.

Chapter Four
Alexander

Stewart rose early the next morning, leaving Margaret and his mother sleeping. He needed to see his cousin Alexander about many things, not least to go over the accounts. He had been very lax of late, leaving the running of the business to him; he knew that Alexander did not mind but it was inexcusable on his part to have left things this long.

The main industry on the estate was the growing of flax, and Mere was the local centre of this industry at this time. It was Alexander who kept up the running of this as Estate Steward, which involved the overseeing of planting, harvesting, then the laborious washing and cleaning of the flax so that it could then be combed and separated, ready to be spun by the tenants in their cottages; then in turn to be woven and made into any number of uses, like bed ticking, aprons, shirts, cheesecloth for wrapping foods to the very finest bed linen (if the flax was of the best quality). Some of the land was given over to crops, sheep, and a small herd of dairy cows, which kept the whole estate fed, and what was surplus to need was sold off at market. Even the sheep's wool was sold, as the estate did not have the means or manpower to wash, card, spin and weave this as well as the flax. Though through necessity, land had been sold off, there still remained a substantial amount to work and provide income.

As Stewart approached the building which Alexander had as his office, the weather seemed to be brightening, and the breeze had lost most of its chill of yesterday. He re-adjusted his coat and took a deep breath; this was not going to be easy and he knew that. Stewart was acutely aware of Alexander's feelings for Margaret, and that Alexander rued the day that he introduced his cousin to her. They had had many a disagreement on this subject, and Stewart recalled that one time it had nearly come to blows. There was a small stable next to the building where Alexander kept his horse so that he could ride out and oversee the daily running of the estate. It was here that Stewart found him taking great pains and pride in brushing his horse's main.

Alexander was a year older than Stewart, around the same height but smaller and slimmer in build. His hair was fine and fair, and although his face was lean, it gave the appearance of a person much younger than his years. He had the blue eyes of the Hamilton's, but Alexander's eyes were a penetrating ice blue circled at the edges with a deep blue limbal ring.

'Good morning, Alex,' called Stewart. 'I'll wager you do not take as much trouble to brush the local wench's hair,' he added, pointing to the horse's main with the tip of his riding whip.

Alexander spun around. 'Why you…?' he began while taking aim. Stewart ducked just in time to see the brush fly over his head.

Stewart eyed his cousin, as he picked the brush up off the floor and dusted down his breeches and jacket. 'Temper, temper, dear cousin. I come in peace, or at least I think I do.' Stewart mumbled the last words to himself, as he threw the brush back at him.

'Where in hell's name have you been these last weeks?' questioned Alexander, as his horse whinnied, gently nudging his master's arm for him to resume the brushing.

Stewart stroked his chin with his left hand while tapping the whip gently against his boot with the other. 'Well, for one I had to go to London on some business for my mother, and then to Exeter.' Stewart paused, eyeing his cousin.

'How is the town? God, I bet it smells like hell in this weather.' Alexander suddenly stopped, turned and eyed his cousin.

'You have been at Margaret's?' exclaimed Alexander as he walked slowly to where Stewart stood, realisation showing on his face

Stewart sighed. 'There is no easy way to tell you this, Alexander. I asked Margaret for her hand in marriage and she accepted. We are betrothed.' Even as the words left his mouth, Alexander was upon him, grabbing Stewart's arms in a firm grip.

'To Maggie?' Alexander answered disbelievingly. 'You are going to wed Margaret?' Slowly, Alexander's arms dropped to his sides as he turned and walked to the door, and just as the silence was becoming more than uncomfortable, Alexander spoke in a very cold and controlled tone. 'I never knew you were in love with her.'

Stewart coughed gently, to break the atmosphere if nothing more. 'Alex…' he paused. 'I do, I love her dearly.'

Alexander swung round and in an instant was facing Stewart. 'You never once led me to believe that you were in love with her, let alone any intentions you had of marriage with her.' His tone was flat.

Stewart noticed that his cousin's nose was pinched and his lips had taken on that white hue of anger. He knew he had to tread very carefully here, as Alexander was at the point of losing his self-control, and if he did, it would wedge a rift between them that ultimately would be irreconcilable. Stewart moved past him and walked through the door out into the day. Standing there, he closed his eyes and breathed deeply, and as the sun hit his face, he could feel some of its warmth slowly make its way into his body, which at the moment felt frozen to the marrow. Turning, he saw that Alexander was standing next to him.

'Alex, I do love her, truly, she is everything I am not, and so like Mother, you would not believe.' Alexander rounded on him at once.

'We do not marry our mothers.' He stopped, searching Stewart's face. 'You realise that she has never given herself to anyone else but you.' He paused. 'Apart from that bastard husband of hers.' He shook his head. 'If you do not love her like she deserves to be loved, then you will answer to me.' He finished. Alexander smiled. 'I will tell you something, dear cousin, if you break her heart, I will break your neck.' He nodded to Stewart as though to seal the threat that had just been made.

Stewart breathed deeply. 'Between you and my mother, I will be cattle feed next week if I am not honourable and worthy of her.' Stewart's teeth bit into his bottom lip before he smiled.

'Oh you can believe that, cousin,' Alexander answered sardonically as he turned and slapped Stewart on the back, a little harder than a friendly slap Stewart thought. 'Now shall we go in and go over the books, and maybe have a mug of ale to toast your betrothal.'

Alexander gestured with his arm for Stewart to accompany him, and Stewart took the peace offering that was being given to him if somewhat reluctantly.

'After you, cousin.' Stewart smiled, reciprocating the gesture.

***

They spent most of the morning going over the ledgers, pausing around midday to ride into Mere to the Angel for some well-earned repast of bread, cheese, pasties and a jug of ale.

As they sat comfortably in the inn, Alexander turned to Stewart.

'Where will you marry?' he paused to take a sip of ale, raising his eyebrows over his mug in question. 'London?'

Stewart rolled his ale mug in his hands and thought before answering. 'I think we will wed here in Mere, at St Michael's. Just family and a few friends.' He nodded in agreement with himself. 'A quiet affair, in a peaceful setting.' He stopped and looked up at his cousin.

Alexander smiled in return, nodding. 'I agree with you, St Michael's is beautiful at this time of year, Mag...' he stopped correcting himself, 'Margaret would like that.'

'She is very special to me, Alex,' offered Stewart.

'Yes, and to *me* also,' answered Alexander

The tavern was abuzz with the lunchtime trade, along with those who were awaiting their transfer to the coach bound for London; Mere was on the main Exeter to London road. and the return; in fact, all of the inns in the town did a good trade, even in the winter months, as there was always someone wanting to travel, and most of the inns had rooms for passing trade.

Stewart rose from his seat. 'Shall we get back to the ledgers then?'

Alexander downed the last drop of ale and stood up. 'I think we must, come on, Cousin, let us be done with it, else we will still be there when the sun sets.'

Stewart smiled and pushed his hat on his head, leaving a coin on the table for the serving girl. 'Yes, let us get it over with cousin, but I have a favour to ask of you before we do.' Stewart paused looking around. 'We will talk outside,' he gestured.

It was late afternoon when Stewart slowly made his way back to the Willows. After he left Alexander, he had had time to reflect on all of the repercussions that had come about from the events that happened just two days previous. He pulled his horse down to a trot and removed his hat, feeling the coolness of the breeze brush through his hair. He was at peace, he reflected, even though he had nearly alienated the two other people in his life that he held dear. He hoped that they would understand him, and that he meant no harm against Margaret—he DID love her. She was the best of him. Without her, he reminded himself, he would not be the man he now was.

When he had first met her, he had been very wild, out of control, everything and anyone irritated him. He had drank to excess, womanised (he wiped his hand over his face at the thought of this); that dinner at her house was the first time he had not drunk himself under the table and into oblivion. She had seated him next to herself and engaged him in intelligent conversation, and was truly interested in him as a person. By the end of the evening, he had known nothing about her, but she had known everything about him.

He dismounted, took the reins and began to walk slowly alongside his horse. All of those things that Alexander had said about Margaret, he knew them to be true. She had known no other man except her husband, and of him Margaret never spoke. Stewart paused to take off his coat—the day had warmed and at this quiet time of the evening the air was sweet, and the breeze a welcoming balm as it blew gently through his shirt.

That first time he recalled she had been as nervous as a bride but had neither refused his advances nor pushed him away. Maggie had wanted him, he knew that, as much as he had her, but she was hesitant, afraid, as though she did not know what to expect. Stewart remembered holding her close to him, stroking her back and feeling the tenseness leave her. Afterwards she had said, 'I never knew it could feel like that.' It had been addressed to the air rather than to him.

Stewart stopped walking and sat down pulling his knees up under his chin. 'Dear God, Maggie, what did that man do to you?' In truth, he had never thought about it till now, but now was different, the scales had tipped. His mother's words rang in his ears. 'He was not of a very calm temperament.'

He stood up, shook himself, laid his coat over the saddle and mounted. Clicking his tongue and gently tapping the horse with his heels, he set off for home.

***

Stewart could hear their voices in pleasant conversation before he opened the drawing room doors. As he entered, Elizabeth turned to face him and smiled.

'So, you have at last decided to honour us with your presence,' she raised her eyebrows in mockery, but her eyes were laughing. Stewart looked towards Margaret, and her smile gave him a warm feeling inside.

'Mother, I am sorry for my lateness,' he apologised, 'but I have been very neglectful of my duties of late, and Alexander has been running the estate singlehandedly, very well indeed, but nonetheless without help. We had a lot to discuss and time just ran away with itself.' Stewart bent and kissed his mother's cheek.

'It is not my cheek, or forgiveness, you should be seeking, my young man, but Margaret's,' she nodded in Margaret's direction. Stewart looked at Margaret and could see from her eyes that she was trying hard to contain herself from laughing. He bent down as though to kiss her cheek but whispered in her ear.

'Laugh and I will never be able to live it down.' She felt the laughter in his lips as he kissed her and squeezed her hand.

'Mother, I am full of the dust of the road, so I must wash and change, but afterwards do I have time to take Margaret for a walk around the gardens before we sit to dinner.' Stewart looked at his mother.

'As long as you are seated at the table by 7:30 then yes,' his mother's eyes were sparkling as she said it, 'otherwise you will incur the wrath of cook, and we do not want to do that, do we?' Elizabeth smiled and turned towards Margaret. 'Mrs Cottle times her meals to the second.'

At this, Margaret, not being able to contain herself any longer, burst out laughing, covering her mouth with her hand as she did so.

***

As soon as Stewart entered his room, he stripped down to his breeches, then stopped and looked at the bowl of hot steaming water that had miraculously appeared on his table along with clothes for washing and drying. It never ceased to amaze him how the servants of the house would conjure things up as though out of thin air the moment they had been asked for; or even if they had not as was the case now. As he washed, he thought of Alexander winging his way to Ellicott's in London. He had asked a lot of him he knew that, but both knew that it was for Maggie's sake, not their own. He hoped that he had not left it too late, and that the article in question would still be there. It was the only place it could be; knowing the value of it no one else in London would handle such a thing.

Stewart washed the heat and dirt away from his body, and then dressed into the fresh clothes that had already been laid out onto his bed, smiling to himself. Yes, Pip was another miracle of nature where things materialised out of thin air without being asked for. In spite of everything else he knew, he was blessed with love, kindness, faith and loyalty—what more could any man ask? He looked around him, adjusted his coat and left the room.

***

The air was heady with the perfume from the flowers and the birds were singing their final chorus before nesting for the night, as Stewart and Margaret walked the gardens companionably together. They ducked as they passed under a jasmine and honeysuckle arch—their smell was at its most powerful at this time of evening, especially if the day had been warm and calm like this one. Stewart looked down at Margaret and stroked her hand that was tucked safely into his arm. They stopped and Margaret turned to face him.

'Penny for them,' she said softly.

Stewart smiled and laughed, raising a hand to push back a piece of her hair that had come loose. 'I was thinking a little while ago, just how fortunate I am.' He gazed at her tenderly. 'I...' he paused. 'I had never really thought about it until today. The small everyday things that people do for you, not because they have to, but because they want to out of love and loyalty, maybe friendship.' He paused again to stroke her face. 'These things we take for granted, that are given so freely by others, yet we never stop to think. Oh we hope that we repay their kindness, and that they know this...' His voice trailed away as the birds continued their evening song.

'What made you think of this now?' she questioned.

Stewart raised his eyes to the evening sky; it was clear with just small puffs of cloud, and somewhere towards the east it was darkening to a pale purple hue, heralding the beginning of dusk.

'When I went upstairs just now,' he began, 'there was a bowl of steaming hot water ready and waiting for me, with fresh towels, and Pip had laid out fresh clothes for me, I did not have to ask.'

'But that is only natural,' began Margaret, when Stewart interrupted her. He took both her hands and looked down into her eyes.

'In my mother's house, these people are like family; they have known me since I was born; like my extended family if you understand.' Stewart shook his head. 'I am not explaining myself very well.'

Margaret placed a finger to his lips to stop him. 'Oh, I understand very well, Stewart. They love you, they are loyal and kind, I can see that and I have only just met them.' She pulled him to her, resting her head near his shoulder.

'My family were never like this,' she continued, 'our household were not loyal, most of them did not want to be there, but out of necessity they had to, otherwise they starved.' Stewart pulled her away from him to look at her.

'No, please let me finish.' Stewart nodded and pulled her against him once more.

'There was not much love to be found within the walls of my home. My mother died when I was 13, and my father had no use for a girl, just my two brothers. I was, shall we say, surplus to their needs.' Stewart tightened his arm about her, and held her head to his chest as Margaret continued. 'So, when I was of marriageable age, I was sold to the highest bidder... like a prized heifer auctioned at a cattle market...' her voice trailed away.

'Maggie, stop, you do not need to say this.' Stewart's voice was soft and tender in her ear.

'Oh but I do, Stewart, please let me finish.' Maggie felt him rather than saw him nod.

'I had no knowledge of men; my father had kept me hidden away on our estate in Devonshire. The first that I saw of my husband was the night before my wedding. I was dressed up and presented like a game bird at a banquet.' Her voice had got lower now and tremulous with emotion. 'When I saw him, I almost collapsed with fear, but I knew if I did, then I would pay the price.' Margaret swallowed hard, trying to calm herself. She knew she had to tell him; he was to be her husband and he had a right to know.

'Stewart, he… he used me like… I thought that this was normal, and that all women were subjected to this when they married, I know that this is not the case now,' she said, her speech had quickened as though she was racing to get it out of her mind. 'He made me do things… Oh God, I have to tell you because I am not the person you think I am.' At this, Stewart pulled her away from him staring hard down into her face.

'Margaret, I do not care.' His voice was stern but not angry, and Margaret saw the compassion in his eyes. 'Listen to me please, it was not your fault, do you hear me?' Stewart shook her gently and pulled her against him again. He could feel Margaret shaking again, but this time she was sobbing. 'You are safe now, and no one will ever hurt you again, I promise.'

They continued to walk a little way till they found a seat hidden under a huge old oak tree that had spread its branches nearly to the ground. For a while they sat in silence. He had his arm about her shoulders and was stroking her head like a father does to a child to comfort them. Her revelations to him had shaken him to his core. Had he been so wrapped up in his own world that he did not see the suffering of others? He knew Stanhope had been a mean angry man, he also knew that there were men who revelled in such practices, but for him to have done that to the woman sitting next to him was unpardonable. He also now knew what it had cost her to give herself to him as she had done, thinking that he would be the same, expected the same. It was unbearable to even think it.

Margaret's voice broke into the silence.

'When I first met you at that dinner party, Stewart, you aroused feelings in me that were so alien, I did not know how to handle them. Then each time I saw you, they became stronger, my stomach would turn in on itself when you looked at me, when you smiled, when you held my hand…' She paused to swallow. 'As I told you I had never known love from a man, only the tender love of my mother, and when she died, so did the love. I only knew that when I was with you, I felt similar feelings, but on a far greater scale than I could deal with at that time.' Margaret sat up to face him now. 'You had awoken something in me, something so powerful it terrified me. I would long for those days, moments that I could be with you, and when you were not there, it was as though I was only half alive.'

Stewart cupped her face in his hands and placed his forehead against hers.

'I am so sorry, Maggie.' His voice held all the emotions he was feeling. They had sat in silence for some moments, when Stewart laughed softy. 'Mrs Cottle is going to be furious with me when we get back, we are late for dinner.'

The mood was broken. Margaret smoothed her hands across her face and laughed gently. 'I will tell her it was all my fault,' she answered smiling.

Chapter Five
St Michael's

St Michael's Church in Mere was old, dating back as far as 1090. It also held a Royal coat of arms of the deposed King James I, and some said it was the first to be erected in the Monarch's short reign. It had moreover been the church that the family had worshiped in for over seventy years now.

Alexander looked around St Michael's and nodded to himself. The preparations for the wedding had been undertaken so quickly, but what had been achieved was beautiful. It seemed that every conceivable flower from the gardens of the Willows estate had been used in some form or another, and when you entered the doors of the church, the perfume hit your senses with a wave of heady fragrances. Alexander had arranged for someone to come and prepare the church, but as soon as Spike had heard, he and the tenants had emphatically insisted it was their job to prepare for their master, and they would brook no interference. So they had decorated the church, they had strung the Jacobean carved pews with garlands of jasmine and honeysuckle, roses and flock stood in huge pots of clay down the nave the centre aisle, as well as at the altar. The finest linen had been laid on the table at the top on the dais, and the floor from door to chancery was strewn with rose petals. The total effect was stunning. Alexander swallowed hard, then turned and made his way out through the porch. As he walked through, he stopped and turned, there it was; set into a niche the carved statue of St Michael the Archangel, dating back to the mid-1100s. Alexander crossed himself and gave up a silent prayer. He felt in his pocket for re-assurance, it was there; his aunt Elizabeth's mother's silver wedding ring nestling gently in a piece of velvet. In his other pocket lay something very precious, something that had nearly cost him his life Alexander reflected. He turned sharply at the thought and made his way out into the late August sunshine.

The congregation was arriving; all of the tenants were gathered there in their best. If not new clothes, they had been washed and pressed to a high degree, with every child's face scrubbed to perfection. Stewart will feel both proud and humbled by this show of affection for him he thought.

The church bells had just begun to peel when his Aunt Elizabeth's carriage came into view. Alexander watched as it came down the path and turned around to stop in front of the church. Her footman, Carter, stepped down and placed a small box of steps in front of the carriage door before opening it to help Elizabeth down. Alexander smiled with sheer joy as he saw her adjust her gown. It was of soft silk, midnight blue in colour, a demurely low cut bodice which was edged in the most delicate of lace with three-quarter sleeves edged also in the same lace. The dress had a panel of paler blue inserted from bodice to the bottom of the skirt and this too was edged at both sides with the lace. Her hair had been swept up in curls and studded with small jasmine flowers, and atop her head was a small hat made from the same midnight blue silk of her dress adorned also with the lace. The overall effect was beautiful.

Alexander walked forward and bowed lowly kissing her hand.

'Aunt, you look wonderful,' he complimented.

Elizabeth smiled, pulling him down to speak in his ear. 'Dear Alex, if you think I look wonderful, then wait until you see Margaret.' Elizabeth nodded her head in the direction of the second carriage that was coming down the path. It was then that Elizabeth looked into her nephew's eyes and saw not sorrow, but of what might have been.

'You were very fond of her, Alex, were you not?' It was not a question; she was merely stating what she saw so clearly etched into his face. Her heart went out to him.

'I was, Aunt,' Alexander said wistfully, 'but she was never mine, she was always his from the first moment they met.'

Elizabeth placed her hand on his arm, then looking round Alexander to the church she questioned.

'Where is Stewart?'

Alexander roused himself from his thoughts. 'Oh he is in the church, Aunt. I do not think I have ever seen him nervous, but he is today,' he replied, eyeing the church door. 'I had best go in and keep him company.' With that he turned on his heel and disappeared through the door.

Elizabeth watched him go, then looked round to see Margaret's coach pull up. The tenants had decorated her coach also. The horses had white plumes on their heads and the sides of the coach were festooned with garlands of cream roses. As Elizabeth turned to look at them, she could see that every tenant was beaming with pride at what they had accomplished. She sighed deeply, marvelling at the depth of feeling they had for her family; turning, she led the congregation into the church to take their seats.

Margaret was helped down from the coach by her footman. There was no one to take her in, her father had died two years past, and as for her brothers, she did not exist for them. She pulled herself upright and started to walk towards the door when suddenly from the left-hand side an arm was produced, hooked at the elbow for her to take. Margaret turned slowly, and there in all his glory was Spike, Elizabeth's head gardener. He had on a new brown coat for the occasion, light brown breeches, beige waist coat complete with new buttons, new shirt and stock, stockings and highly polished shoes with a pewter buckle. A new tricorn hat completed his dress.

'Milady,' he offered, 'I be no relative I know that, just a humble gardener by trade, but I will not be seeing you enter that church alone.' He paused to push himself upright. 'Will you be taking my arm, Milady?'

Margaret could neither speak nor move. Her mouth quivered and her eyes filled; she knew if she so much as blinked the tears would tumble down her cheeks. Spike nodded, then took her hand and placed it in the crook of his arm, tapping her hand lightly.

'Shall we be going in?' he smiled warmly, and all that Margaret could do was nod. As they reached the inner door, she tuned to him.

'Why could I not have had a father like you?' She paused, reached up and kissed his cheek. 'Thank you,' she said.

***

The air inside the church was warm and fragrant; the sun at that moment was filtering through a stained glass window, which acted like a prism refracting its light into a spectrum of colours over both people and floor.

'Are you ready to be married then, cousin?' questioned Alexander as he came up to sit beside him.

Stewart eyed him out of the corner of his eye. 'Any more remarks like that, cousin, and we will be having a funeral instead of a marriage.'

Alexander laughed softly. 'We look like a couple of bookends, do we not?'

Stewart looked at him, thinking that he was not in the mood for jokes or riddles at present. Then suddenly he realised what Alexander meant, they were dressed identically. Dark blue coats, white linen shirts, lace frilled stocks, cream waist coats, breeches, stockings, and rounding off the ensemble new black shoes with silver buckles. Stewart chuckled to himself. 'One dark, one fair,' he offered. Both their hair had been sleeked back and neatly clubbed with a deep blue satin ribbon.

'This is my mother's doing,' he smiled.

Suddenly, Stewart turned to Alexander. 'Do you have everything?' he asked urgently.

'Calm yourself, cousin,' replied Alexander, tapping first one coat pocket and then the other. 'Though this part cost me dearly,' he added, tapping the right hand side again.

Stewart shook his head. 'I am indebted to you, cousin for, that,' Stewart pursed his lips, 'though no doubt you will find a way to make me pay…' The rest of the sentence trailed away as the congregation all arose and faced the door.

Margaret stood at the top of the aisle with her hand tucked into Spike's arm. Slowly, Spike released her and stepped back into one of the pews.

Margaret literally glowed, as the light from the side windows hit her. Her dress was very simple, made from a deep cream silk with ribbons of emerald green satin threaded throughout the bodice. The skirt was ruched up at intervals by a small emerald satin bow showing a lighter cream lace underskirt. The neckline was edged with a frill of the same material, as were the edges of the three-quarter length sleeves. Her hair had been pulled up onto the top of her head, with the exception of one large coil which ran from the back, then round and down her left shoulder. Small tendrils of hair had been pulled from the sides so

57

as to frame her face. She wore no hat, just small pieces of lace which had been intricately wound into her curls. The effect was stunning.

Stewart never took his eyes from her as she slowly walked the length of the aisle to stand beside him. He took her hand in his and kissed it. Alexander coughed softly to get Stewart's attention.

'You will need this first I think,' he said as he placed the article in question into Stewart's right hand.

Stewart pulled himself together and lifted the emerald necklace, then placed it gently around Margaret's neck, securing the clasp at the back. As he leaned back, a pair of eyes matching the emeralds brilliance looked up at him.

'You look beautiful, Maggie,' was all he said

There was a slow murmuring around the congregation, and Elizabeth who had been watching this grabbed the pew in front of her to stop herself from falling. Her legs had gone to jelly, the buzzing in her ears was painful and her head was swimming. A million things were fighting themselves in her brain, but first and foremost was, 'Dear God, what has he done!'

Alexander, who had been watching his aunt, left Stewart's side and came to stand next to her, placing his arm around her waist to hold her up, as he whispered into her ear. The relief on her face was instantaneous. She looked up into his face then mimed the words, 'Thank you.'

Alexander's reply was, 'You are most welcome, Aunt.'

The rest of the ceremony concluded without incident, and when the silver wedding ring was placed onto Margaret's finger, a small applause went up from the back of the church. The vicar frowned, but both Stewart and Margaret smiled broadly, the tension was lifted.

Elizabeth had insisted that the tenants would celebrate the wedding breakfast on the lawn at the back of the house just below the terrace. They had given so much of themselves in preparation of this wedding, they deserved to celebrate it with the family.

It was late-afternoon as Elizabeth stepped down from the terrace; her eyes were searching for one man. She found him on the end table on the right at the back, sitting deep in thought, supping his ale. Coming up to him from behind, she placed a hand on his shoulder.

'Spike,' her voice was gentle, 'will you walk with me a while?'

Spike raised his head, then stood and nodded.

They walked for some moments in the flower gardens; the early evening air was tranquil and warm, and the only sound that could be heard was the chirping of birds till Elizabeth spoke.

'Spike, what you did today was…' She broke off, unable to finish the sentence, walking all the while further into the gardens, till Spike stopped suddenly. Elizabeth turned and could see that his mouth was working, as though he were searching for the right words to say.

'Mistress…' he paused slightly then continued, 'When I saw Milady step down from that carriage today, she reminded me so much of how my Merryn was on our wedding day.' He looked away now his eyes searching for some far

58

distant memory only he could share. 'She was as scared as a rabbit, and her face be deathly pale'—Spike smiled here as he remembered—'that is until her father be giving her his arm to hold onto. There be such a change in her, like dark to light. What he had offered her was security, that she be doing the right thing...' He paused again to clear his throat. 'No bride should be going into the church alone on her wedding day.'

Elizabeth looked at him in amazement. 'You truly are the most generous, kind, thoughtful and wonderful man.' She then linked arms with him and walked on. She knew the ale had mellowed him, or he would never have let her take his arm as she did, this was just the right time to ask.

'If I ask you something, will you please consider it?'

'For you, Mistress, anything,' came the heartfelt reply.

'Oh, Spike, please, just for this one night, can you not call me Elizabeth like you used to when we were children?' He saw the pleading in her eyes and nodded acquiescence.

'Will you come up to the house to live?' Elizabeth broke in before Spike could utter a word, '...to live in with the servants, be part of the household...' Her words were coming quickly. '... Oh, Spike, it would be warm, you would be dry...' She paused before saying the last words, 'you would not be alone.' She turned to face him and rested her hand on his arm. When there was no reply, Elizabeth continued. 'You can spend all of the daylight hours in the gardens, we need not see you from dawn till dusk.' She was pleading now. 'Please, for me, will you consider it?' Elizabeth finished and waited.

Mis... Elizabeth,' Spike corrected, 'I will consider this... but when I have made my decision, it will be final.' Elizabeth nodded

***

Back at the Willows, most of the house guests had departed, and it was only a handful of tenants still left who were clearing and taking down the tables with the servants as Elizabeth returned. She came up onto the terrace just as Stewart came out through the door.

'I was coming to find you,' he questioned. 'Where have you been? Or need I ask?' His eyebrows went up and he smiled.

'I have been walking in the gardens with Spike,' she replied. 'Stewart...' she continued, 'I know that this is your house now, but I have asked Spike to come and live here with the servants... to be one of the household...' Before she could finish, Stewart took her hand.

'This is my house in name only, you are the mistress here, and will continue to be until...' the words hung in the warm air. 'Margaret has no intention of taking your place here,' he continued, 'she has her own household to administer to; we will live between the two, but *you* will always be mistress of The Willows.' Elizabeth just stared at him.

'Have I made myself clear, Mother?' he questioned.

Elizabeth nodded; this was not what she had expected. Somewhere in the distance she could hear chattering; it could have been the birds or the servants, but for that split second Elizabeth could not comprehend. It took a few moments for her to gather her thoughts before she spoke.

'Stewart, the necklace, how did you...' but her speech was stopped by Stewart placing a finger against his mother's lips

'That is of no consequence, Mother, did you honestly believe that I would let him take that from you?' Stewart placed his arm around his mother's shoulders and turned her towards the house. 'Come inside, it has been a long day.'

The warm still air was like a calming balm on her senses; breathing deeply, she allowed him to lead her into the house.

***

Margaret was sitting on the window seat that faced the garden, looking down at the wedding ring that Stewart had placed on her finger this day; she twirled it around. It was quite wide, silver and consisted of two interlocking vines that had no beginning or end. Set into some of the spaces of these were Scottish thistles. It was so beautifully intricate, and yet so simple. She wrapped her other hand over it and held it tight, remembering the last time a ring was placed there causing a shiver to run down her spine.

Her thoughts were drawn back when the door opened and Elizabeth entered followed by Stewart.

'I found her,' he smiled, 'she had been walking in the gardens.'

As Margaret began to speak, Stewart stopped her.

'I have told Mother that she is still the mistress here at The Willows, and will remain so for the rest of her life.' Stewart looked down at his mother.

'It is all legal; I have been to Exeter to see Mr Mortimore and all the documents have been drawn up and duly signed.' Elizabeth went to reply but Stewart placed his hand upon her shoulder to stop her.

'There are no loopholes; every avenue has been sealed, you have my word.' He inclined his head in affirmation.

There was a pause where all that could be heard was the gentle talking of the servants. They were happily merry and their voices reflected this as they collected up the last of the dishes that had been piled onto the terrace.

'Elizabeth,' Margaret began. 'This ring is beautiful, how could you bear to part with it?' Before Margaret could finish, Elizabeth had crossed the room to sit next to her and took her hand.

'It was my mother's wedding ring; my father Charles Hamilton had it made for her in Scotland. It represents two souls intertwining forever in an eternal circle.' Elizabeth's eyes glistened as she slowly placed her fingers on the ring and pushed it around Margaret's finger as she spoke. 'They should have been together for years, but the fates did not allow it.' She had never known her mother, only what her father had told her; that she resembled her, had her gentleness and compassion. Elizabeth was back in that faraway place now, where only she could go, remembering all the things her father had said.

The voices from the garden were slowly quietening, as the last of the servants came past the window, their arms full of tablecloths bound for the laundry.

'But surely you should wear it?' Margaret broke in, looking at Stewart for support.

'My mother was never married with that ring,' he began. 'My father wanted to use his own ring.' Stewart's voice was cold as he spoke.

Elizabeth pulled herself upright and coughed lightly; touching the ring that she still had on her finger, she covered it with her hand.

'I always intended it for Stewart's bride.' She smiled. 'So, Margaret, wear it with love and good health, and may your souls forever be entwined.' As she said the last words, she kissed Margaret lightly on the cheek, then stood up and slowly made her way to the door.

'Now, I will bid you both good night.'

Stewart followed her and kissed the top of her head.

'Good night, Mother. I love you dearly.'

***

Stewart closed the door to their bedroom, walking towards Margaret taking off his coat, shoes, breeches, and stockings as he did so, coming to a halt in front of her in only his shirt. He pulled Margaret towards him while his hands moved up and down her spine. As he looked down at Margaret, he frowned, and one side of his mouth went up into a half smile.

'Margaret Hamilton,' he paused, 'you have kept me out of your bed for three weeks?' He raised his brows in question. 'And now you give me buttons!?' Saying this he ran his hands over them, trying to count. Slowly he shook his head.

'I do not think so,' he said as he took her into his arms and kissed her deeply. Placing his hands either side of the bodice he pulled.

Margaret's lips parted in a smile under his, as she heard the popping then the pinging of the seed pearls hitting the floor.

Chapter Six
Revelations

Over the next few days, life settled to its usual rhythm on the estate. It was Friday when Alexander revealed he had secured Stewart and Margaret a short trip to his friend Edward Trowbridge's home near Freshwater on the Isle of Wight. His friend having left to go on a voyage to Spain to settle a business arrangement he had made. The whole house and servants were at their complete disposal.

'What more can you ask?' stated Alexander. 'Peace and quiet, a whole house to yourselves.' Alexander lay back in his chair, watching the August sun as it came through the open window of the office, leaving streaks of muted colour on the wooden floor, while the dust motes swam in its light. The air in the room was still and very warm and both he and Stewart sat in their shirt sleeves.

'I should not be leaving you on your own at this time of year,' he answered

'Why not?' replied Alexander. 'The harvest is in, the washing and combing are almost complete. The only thing left is the spinning and weaving, and you cannot help with that, Stewart.' Alexander raised his brows in jest. 'We should have good quality this year, as it was harvested just after the flowers bloomed, meaning we should get a good price for the cloth we weave,' he added.

Stewart nodded. 'Alex, I need to ask you what happened in London.' He leaned forward, placing his elbows on his knees looking up at his cousin.

Alexander stood up, coming round to sit back on the edge of the desk. 'All I can say is, it was a blessing that it was I and not you that went to Ellicott in Sweetings Alley.'

He pushed himself up and for some moments Alexander paced, the air in the room was becoming more humid, as though there was no oxygen to breathe; stopping to turn, he looked at Stewart.

'There were two other interested parties; one a foreign dealer and the other...' he paused looking at his cousin. 'The other was Northcott.' At that Alexander walked out the door and into the sun.

Stewart stood up and followed his cousin out, grabbing Alexander's arm and turning him towards him.

'How to hell did he know; how did either of them know?' The question hung in the air. 'It had only been taken two days previous,' Stewart added in astonishment as he paced back and forth, the sun burning through the material of his shirt now. Unconsciously, Stewart pulled the material away and waved it to let in some air.

Alexander thought for a moment before replying. 'The jeweller had notified them, as they were looking for stones of that quality,' he paused. 'It is common practice, Stewart, people often put in requests for such quality jewellery, and any goldsmith worth his trade will keep his clients informed if they come onto the market, especially those he knows will pay a high price.'

Stewart nodded; he knew such practices went on, 'But Northcott?'

Alexander shrugged his shoulders. 'Cousin, you and he are not the best of friends, are you not?'

Stewart eyed his cousin warily. 'The man's a scoundrel and a rake; he would sell his own mother given the chance.' Stewart rubbed his chin with his hand. 'I... I have had a few encounters with him, where I have not particularly liked his treatment of others.' He paused. 'I threatened to run him through the last time I saw him.'

Alexander breathed deeply. 'That accounts for it then.'

Stewart rounded on him, grabbing his arm again. 'Accounts for what?'

'Why he tried to have me killed,' answered Alexander. The silence that followed was emotionally charged; Alexander could see his cousin trying to process the words that he had just heard.

'He did what?' The anger was showing in Stewart's face now, as his hand tightened on his cousin's arm.

Alexander looked back sternly at his cousin, then prized his fingers away.

'Stewart, when I visited Ellicott and enlightened him of the fact that the necklace in question had been stolen from its owner, he withdrew all other interested parties offers.' Alexander thought for a moment before continuing. 'Northcott, shall we say, was in no mind to accept this.'

'The hell he was!' rounded Stewart.

'Will you let me finish please?' Alexander said in exasperation. 'The man as you rightly said is a rake and a scoundrel. He has no moral code; come to that he has no morality at all.' Alexander looked towards his cousin. 'He wanted it at any cost, especially when he knew it was yours.' Alexander breathed deeply. 'God, Stewart, did you have to make an enemy of the man? Could you not have left the moralising to someone else?' The moment the words had left his mouth, he shook his head. Looking into his cousin's eyes, he added, 'No, you would not would you.'

Stewart shrugged his shoulders in reply.

Alexander resumed. 'After I had obtained the necklace, at a much greater cost than it was sold for might I add, I left the building just before mid-day. As I came up the alley to Cornhill, someone grabbed my arm from behind. I swung round and hit him full in the face with my elbow, to which he slid backwards and down the wall, revealing a small dagger in his right hand. This, I gathered in an instant, was to cut my throat with. I can tell you, cousin, I did not stay around there to find out why or who he was.' Alexander paused here. 'I then proceeded down Cornhill into Cheapside, mingling with the crowd, keeping my head down, till I reached the coaching house "The Swan with Two Heads", you know the one in Lad Lane, and booked onto the next available stagecoach to Exeter. This happened to be at mid-day, thank God.' Alexander paused again to look at his cousin. 'I travelled under the name of James Cameron—my middle name and my mother's name—the coach consisted entirely of gentlemen passengers and would stop only for the changing of horses and...' his voice trailed off. 'They were all bound for the assizes at Exeter, and I made no move to tell them that I was not. I had booked my passage to Exeter, so that I would not be traced.'

Stewart stood there in silence, and then ran his hands down over his face. 'Alex... if I had known that anything like this was going to happen, I would never have sent you.' With that he went and sat himself on the grass under the nearest tree.

Stewart's mind was working as he shook his head. 'I did not even think that in such a small space of time, people would get to know about the necklace.' He paused to look up at his cousin. 'Why did you not tell me, Alex, when you returned from London?' he questioned

'Well, Stewart, you were about to be married in three weeks, and I did not want you racing to London to confront Northcott.' Alexander's mouth quirked up into a sardonic smile. 'A wedding can only take place when both participants are there, no?' he questioned. Alexander walked slowly across to sit next to Stewart under the tree.

'Hmmm,' was the only reply Stewart gave.

It was midday and the air was oppressive. There was no movement in the trees at all now, even the birds had stopped chirping, giving in to the heat of the day.

Stewart stood up, dusted himself then walked into the office to retrieve both his and his cousin's coats and hats.

'I need a drink,' was all he said before mounting his horse.

***

As they approached Mere, they could see that the noon coach to Exeter had just disgorged its cargo onto the road outside the Angel. A cacophony of sounds abounded where its passengers who were ending their journey in Mere fought to find their baggage amongst the many boxes and bags piled in a heap. They were hot, tired and thoroughly disgruntled. One young woman had given up completely and was sitting by the road with her head in her hands. Stewart dismounted and walked towards her.

'Can I be of assistance to you, mistress, can I get you some water maybe?' he asked.

The woman, who must have been in her late 30s, just nodded her head and waved her hand at him. As she looked up, Stewart observed she was a comely sort of young woman with large grey eyes set in a round face with a small nose and a pointed chin; she wore a snow white cap on her head, but her fine fair hair could be seen at the sides and was pulled into a neat bun at the back of her neck. Her dress was blue grey in colour, not of the finest quality, but good cloth nonetheless.

'Thank ye kindly, Sir, I be alright in a moment; when my head stops a spinnun.' She breathed deeply. The sound of her Wiltshire accent was prevalent, but the lilt was soft and musical.

Alexander, who had been watching the events, made his way into the tavern and procured from the owner a pitcher of water and goblet. Bringing this out, he poured some and offered it to the woman. She looked up at him and nodded. 'Bless ye, sir.' She took the goblet, poured some onto her handkerchief and dabbed at her forehead and neck, then drank slowly. 'We be set upon by highwaymen some hours back. Coach for Andover were coming toward us, and when they see it, they left us and took off the other way they did.' The woman took another long drink and closed her eyes. 'I be feeling much better now. Thank ye, sir,' she added, trying to stand up.

Both Stewart and Alexander took and arm each and pulled the woman gently to her feet.

'Where is your luggage, mistress?' Alexander asked, eyeing the mound that still seemed to be abandoned on the roadside.

'Mine be a red carpet bag, sir,' she replied, squinting at the pile. Stewart nodded to Alexander to see if he could find it, while he helped the woman to a bench that was outside the tavern, which was shielded somewhat from the suns glare.

'Where have you to go to, mistress?' queried Stewart.

'Oh no worries to you, sir, thank ye. My husband will be a meet'n me with the buggy soon.' Just then she looked over and saw that Alexander had managed to retrieve her bag. 'Oh God, bless ye, sir!' She looked from one to the other. 'Your mother must be proud of you, to help a woman such as myself.'

Stewart smiled at her and bowed respectfully.

'We were happy to be of assistant to you, mistress,' he offered, 'can we get you anything else—some bread and cheese maybe, or a drop of ale?'

The woman looked up, smiled and placed her hands together.

'Lordy no, sir, I be fine now, and you have done too much for me a ready, you be going about your business; you have done me a great service this day and I truly thank ye,' she replied. 'Who be ye?' she asked, fanning herself with her handkerchief once more. 'I wish to tell my husband how kind ye both were.'

'It was our pleasure, mistress,' Stewart smiled as he took off his hat. 'I am Stewart, and this is my cousin Alexander, Hamilton is the name. And your name, mistress?'

'Merryn Martin, sir,' she replied. 'My husband be Stephen Martin, the blacksmith at the end of the town.'

Stewart and Alexander bowed in farewell. 'Good day to you, Mistress Martin,' said Stewart, as they made their way into the tavern out of the sun.

By luck they found a seat by the window and Stewart ordered two tankers of ale and some bread and cheese from the serving girl.

Alexander eyed him. 'I can hear your brain working from here, cousin. What troubles you?'

Stewart looked out the window to where the woman was now being helped up into a small buggy by her husband.

'I have heard that name before, but I cannot quite place where or when,' he paused here, still thinking. 'No matter, it will come to me maybe later, or maybe not.' He shrugged then eyed his cousin. 'A month past you would have been on that coach, or one like it, would you not?'

Alexander shrugged his shoulders. 'Mine reached here in the early morning, but yes, thinking about what had happened in the alley, God must have been with me at that time.'

Stewart rounded on him. 'God, Alex? If anyone had known what you had about your person, then you would be dead!' Stewart rubbed his hands over his face and breathed deeply.

The air inside the Angel suddenly became suffocating. It smelt of ale, bodies and tobacco, and Stewart felt decidedly unwell at that particular moment. When their ale and food came, he motioned to his cousin to follow him outside leaving payment on the table.

They sat down on the bench that the woman had just vacated and quietly ate their lunch and drank their ale. Stewart chewed and swallowed his last mouthful, before washing it down with the rest of his ale.

'Alex, when I sent you to London, I really did not think about the danger that I was putting you in, and for that I apologise to you profusely.'

Alexander eyed him out of the corner of his eye. 'Cousin, do you think that I did not know what the dangers were when I accepted?' He paused. 'I knew what the consequences were, and even if I had sat down and thought about it, I would still have gone.'

'And you say I am reckless,' Stewart countered

'Would you not have done the same for me?' questioned Alexander. 'You know you would, without question, and more had I had asked.'

Stewart put his hand on his cousin's shoulder and pressed his fingers in silent thanks.

Alexander turned smiling to look at his cousin; the smile had reached his eyes in mischief. 'Well, cousin, how does it feel to be married?'

Stewart grinned; the tension was broken. 'Alex, I know what you are implying with this question,' he grinned, 'you are incorrigible, so I will not even grace it with an answer.'

Alexander slapped him on the back. 'I will say one thing, cousin, you look happy and contented with it.'

Stewart thought for a moment before answering, 'Do you know Alex, I am. I never believed I would say this, but I feel at peace with myself. She is truly the best of me.'

Alexander gave him a rueful smile, and then slapped his hat on his thigh to rid it of dust. 'Well, cousin, let us get back and finish what we started; you have a trip to ready yourself for.'

As they stood to go, Stewart noticed that the pile of baggage had disappeared as if by magic, and all was quiet on the street once more. Mounting their horses in unison, they rode back to the Willows.

Chapter Seven
Isle of Wight and More Revelations

They travelled by coach to Lymington and from there boarded a ferry boat which would take them across the Solent to Yarmouth, a small port on the north western part of the Island. Trowbridge's house was situated some six miles inland on high ground near Freshwater; from there on a clear day you could just see the Needles, the group of three chalk stacks on the western most tip of the island.

The Solent was calm, as the boat left its moorings in Lymington, and Maggie was standing by the rail as Stewart came behind her and placed his arms around her waist.

'They assure me it will only take an hour or so to reach Yarmouth,' he spoke into her ear as the noise from the boat and the gulls that were following them drowned out all other sounds.

Margaret turned her head to look up at him. 'I have never before been on a boat,' she called. Her hair was escaping her bonnet as the boat's sails caught the breeze. 'Stewart, look how the wind opens the sails,' she paused to look up, then back at Lymington Harbour as it slowly receded into the distance. 'I feel like a child that has just been given a sweet for the first time. When the sugar melts on the tongue, and that rush of pure joy that follows, Stewart this is heaven.' Her eyes said it all.

Stewart turned her towards him and smiled down at her. 'Margaret, this is a ferry, just wait till I take you to Rapallo in Italy aboard a ship!' he grinned widely. Her child like joy left him humbled. 'Maggie, Maggie, Maggie, you never cease to amaze me,' he added as he pulled her to him holding her tight. 'Life with you is like a present that has been wrapped into several packages. As you unfold each one, you never know what you will find within.' He felt Margaret laugh against his chest, and then slowly she pulled away from him, placing her arms about his neck.

'As I have told you, I led a sheltered life, Stewart Hamilton, you are showing me things I could only dream of.' Stewart kissed her forehead, then turned her to face the rail once more.

'Then feast your eyes, Maggie, this is only the beginning.'

***

As they docked in Yarmouth Harbour, Trowbridge's coachmen were there waiting to take possession of the luggage that they had brought with them. In twenty minutes all things were loaded aboard the carriage, including Stewart and Margaret. Thankfully, the drive to the house was uneventful and by the time they arrived, it was close to 5pm. As Stewart stepped down from the carriage, he looked up at the house; it was a very prepossessing building made of what looked like stone, standing in its own grounds with a sweeping drive. Holding his hand out to Margaret, he helped her down.

'This will be our home for the next week, maybe two?' he questioned. 'However long you want to stay, Maggie, it is your choice,' he added, squeezing her hand.

The butler who had been waiting at the front door to greet them bowed as they entered, then escorted them into the dining room where a tea had been prepared, complete with cold meats and cakes, laid out on the large table.

'Before eating, would Sir and Milady like to freshen yourselves?' the Butler asked.

Stewart looked at Margaret. 'Yes, thank you,' he replied

'If you would care to follow me, Sir, I will show you to your rooms then,' he answered. With that, he bowed and went out of the door before them.

Stewart walked quickly behind him and called. 'We will need just the one room, thank you.'

The butler's face betrayed nothing, he just nodded. 'As you wish, Sir, I will have the servants bring Milady's baggage to your room at once.' With that he called down the corridor and issued his orders in a brisk and final fashion.

Stewart quirked his eyebrows up at Margaret. 'After you,' he offered, smiling with his eyes.

Once inside their room, Stewart dismissed the servants, saying they would not be needed at this present time and closed the door, pulling Maggie to him he kissed her for some moments.

'I have been wanting to do that since we were on board that boat.' He kissed her eyes, and then his lips travelled down to her ear and neck.

'We are supposed to be washing.' Margaret's eyes smiled up at him, as Stewart's hands felt for the laces at the front of her bodice and pulled.

'But…' as he paused to untie the fastenings to the skirt, 'to wash, we have to undress first, do we not?' His eyes were dancing over her, as he shed his coat and shoes.

From there it was like a well-choreographed ballet as he walked her back to the bed. Skirt, bodice, breeches, stockings and finally corset went to the floor. By this time Maggie was left in nothing but her shift when her legs hit the bed causing them both to fall onto it.

'Are you not going to remove your shirt?' Her voice was soft in his ear as his lips and tongue stroked and caressed the small dip between her neck and shoulder. Margaret arched her back in pleasure as she felt the shudder run through her, entwining her hands in his hair.

'I have not got the time,' he breathed; pushing her shift down, his arms came around her, pulling her against him. 'Oh God, I love you, Maggie,' were the last words he uttered.

Margaret lay there for some moments afterwards, eyes closed, waiting for her senses and all her organs to fall quietly into their correct places. Stewart lay on his side beside her, head propped on his hand watching her, his finger tracing the rise of her breast. As she rolled towards him, she looked up into his face.

'I love you too,' she whispered.

***

As time passed peacefully, it afforded them the luxury of familiarising themselves with one another. They had known each other before, but this was different, their lives were separate then, now their lives had become inexplicably joined. Stewart had not known just how naive Margaret was; he had only known her as a beautiful young woman who was kind, caring, unquestioning, and, above all else, loyal. She had given nothing away of her hidden self, which included having no self-worth. It had taken a lot for her to open up to him that night at the Willows, he knew that, to reveal also her anxiety, and lack of self-esteem which lurked within her, hidden under a mask of a young woman who looked totally in control, when all the time she was nursing insurmountable fears. He believed that now she was finally letting him through that invisible barrier which would allow him to build her confidence.

She had never refused his advances from the very first time she had taken him to her bed. Now though, he could feel the difference in her responses to him, which also made him realise how much she trusted him now, and just how much she had held back before.

They had taken a picnic out onto the headland overlooking Freshwater bay; the coach had left them there on the understanding that they would return at 4pm or if the weather changed to rain. Margaret was strolling along the top, looking down to the beach just below them, watching the waves come in onto the shore. She had taken her hat off and her hair was being gently blown by the sea's breeze while her face was serene and relaxed. Stewart studied her for some moments, watching her joy in the freedom they had here, just to be themselves. Slowly, he stood up and came towards her.

'Margaret Hamilton,' he called, 'have you abandoned your husband.' His eyes were alive with mischief. 'Will you not come and eat with him?' he added, grinning widely.

'Stewart, you always call me by my full name when you are about to tease me, or,' she drew her brows together mockingly, 'you are about to tell me something of grave importance.' She came up to him laughing, placing her arms around him in a tight hug. 'I think you are teasing now.'

'Maggie, I do not know you at all these days; you are like a chrysalis that has opened up to reveal a beautiful butterfly.' He hugged her back. 'A beautiful butterfly with sparkling green eyes.' He could feel her laugh in response against his chest, breathing in deeply, he smelt the salty air and it was exhilarating, standing there with nothing but the seagulls squawking above them and the sound of the waves hitting the beach below, just for that split second it felt like they were the only two people in the world.

Reality brought him back at the sound of horses' hooves and coach wheels approaching.

On the ride back, Margaret sat next to Stewart, holding his hand in both of hers, stroking it, then holding it up against her own linking her fingers in his. Stewart could tell that there was something on her mind that she wanted to unburden herself with. He would not ask her though; when the moment was right, she would reveal it to him herself, just as she had the other times. Stewart looked out of the coach window; the evenings were drawing in now, and the sky was dusky as the sun dipped westward. He always enjoyed this time, giving closure to whatever had happened during the day, good or bad. It was peaceful.

'Stewart,' Margaret broke into the silence. 'When I was a girl,' she began as she turned to look at him, 'I spent most of the daytime in the nursery at lessons with my governess. The evenings were spent with my mother who taught me, amongst other things, to sew and embroider.' Stewart turned and faced her.

'Go on,' he encouraged

'When my mother died, I spent nearly all my days in the nursery and my bedroom, which was adjoined to it.' She swallowed here. 'I had my meals there, and maybe three times in the afternoons, after lessons, my governess would take me down to the garden, where I was allowed to play and wander for no more than an hour.'

Stewart nodded. 'Go on,' he said for the second time taking her hands in his.

'I never saw another child, nor had the opportunity to see one either. I was never taken anywhere, just left there out of the way. My governess informed me that I was to be married two days before it happened, just two days after my eighteenth birthday.' She paused and swallowed. 'I need you to understand why I am like I am.' Her eyes filled with tears, and Stewart went to pull her against him but Margaret stopped him shaking her head.

'I cannot tell you everything now, but you must know that there are some things I will never be able to say. They are locked away, and I never want to re-open them.' Stewart nodded in acknowledgement.

Margaret continued. 'You have unlocked so many emotions, so many wonderful things for me, it is like I am re-living the childhood I never had. Did you know I had never seen the sea till will we came to Lymington?' With that she threw her arms about him and hugged him tightly. 'You are my husband, my lover and my guardian angel that has come and rescued me from hell, and I love you so much it hurts.'

Stewart's mouth was dry. He could not speak lest the emotion he was feeling would show, but just held her very close. This explained her unbridled joy at all the things she was now seeing and feeling for the first time. When he had first met her, she had held tight to all these emotions. How she had done this he did not know, and more, he could not imagine. The Maggie he knew then bore no resemblance at all to the Maggie he held tightly in his arms now. If he was her saviour, then she definitely was his.

***

It was three weeks before they finally left the Isle of Wight. Stewart had sent word to Alexander to have the coach waiting for them when the ferry docked in Lymington, as he had no intention of remaining in the town with his wife. The place was thriving because of its salt flats, supplying most of the southern part of England with salt, and exported by the ton, even to the Americas. It had close connections with Portsmouth where the navy moored ships and housed a quantity of naval personnel, the barracks not being far away. It was also notorious for its smugglers; daytime was fine, but by nightfall it had another life. Stewart did not want to risk staying the night there, not with Margaret. Instead, they made their way to Salisbury, and there spent the night at a place called "The Sun and Lamb" coaching inn on High Street. Rising early next day, they ate a light breakfast and were on the road again by 10 o'clock.

They sat in gentle conversation for most of the way, when Margaret brought up the subject of "The Willows".

'How long has the estate been in your family, Stewart?' she questioned—there was no underlying agenda to her question, just interest.

'To be truthful, I do not really know the story, but I believe my great grandfather inherited it,' he paused here. 'My mother will know the history though, when we get back you must ask her.' He thought for a moment. 'I do know that all of the males were of Scottish decent, they married the daughters of the previous owners.' Stewart grinned here. 'I am not making much sense, am I?' He pulled her to him and sat with his arm about her shoulders.

'Are you happy, Maggie?' This was not a question, more an affirmation of the fact.

Margaret turned to look up at him.

'You know, for the first time in my life I can truly say that I am. I am very happy, Stewart Hamilton.'

Stewart looked at her and smiled softly. 'You know something, Margaret Hamilton, so am I,' he answered.

***

Elizabeth watched the carriage as it came up the drive to stop outside the house. When Stewart and Margaret stepped down, Elizabeth looked from one to the other and breathed a sigh of relief. One look at their faces told her all that she needed to know; and as Margaret came and hugged her, Elizabeth pulled back and looked at her.

'I do not need to ask if you are happy.' She smiled. 'It is written on your face for all to see.' Then Elizabeth turned to Stewart to kiss him welcome, but instead

72

found herself pulled into his arms in a warm hug, as he placed a kiss on the top of her hair.

'Hello, Mother, I am afraid we stayed longer than we intended,' he glanced at Margaret. 'I believe tomorrow I have some explaining to do to my cousin.' He raised his eyebrows.

'Alexander is fine,' she offered, 'he told you to stay as long as you wished, and he meant it. Now let us all go in and when you have refreshed yourselves, we can sit to dinner.' Elizabeth held out her arm for them to go first.

Elizabeth breathed deeply as she watched them walk up the steps, and thought. '*If your father was your retribution, Stewart, then most certainly Margaret is your deliverance.*'

***

The morning had that chill of autumn which mid-September brings; there was sun but it held little warmth now, as the earth was sleeping at this time to replenish itself for the next planting season. Those fields that were given over to late potatoes, cabbage, turnips and parsnips were yet to be picked and stored for the winter. All of the vegetables for the estate were grown in one small corner, more than enough to feed the house and its tenants.

Stewart noticed that the leaves on some trees were just beginning to turn brown, but the hedgerows were still thick and abundant as he and Alexander rode around the estate taking stock of the fields. The tenants' houses were grouped together at the far side near the River Nadder, which flowed at the edge of the estate, down and round to the back of "The Willows". Nearly all of their water came from this.

'Some of the houses we are about to see need some repair before the winter sets in on us,' stated Alexander. 'It is the rooves that need it mostly, the thatch has rotted. I anticipated that maybe we could repair them before the end of October,' he added.

'It will have to be undertaken now then,' Stewart answered. 'Do we know of a craftsman locally that can carry out this work?' he added

'There is a thatcher in Mere, a gentleman by the name of Freeman, I will ride in this afternoon and ask if he can come and assess the work,' he paused. 'There is not much damage, but I believe that you have to remove some of the surrounding thatch as well, to assure that it will stay watertight.'

Stewart nodded. 'Most of these cottages consist of two rooms down and two rooms above, am I right?' he questioned.

'That is correct,' Alexander replied, knowing what his cousin was about to say next.

'So while the repairs are undertaken, they can cover or remove any pieces of furniture to the lower floor, and live there for the duration of the works?' Stewart queried.

Alexander smiled. 'The tenants of the two cottages that need repair are already in agreement with that.' Alexander looked sideways at his cousin; he could tell by the way he sat his horse that he was relaxed and contented.

'Married life seems to suit you, cousin.' Alexander grinned.

Stewart quirked his mouth up at one side and grinned back. 'I feel like I have been through a reformation,' he paused, 'a reformation of the soul, which is not a bad thing, as my soul was getting decidedly black of late,' he added grimacing slightly.

'Oh I do not think so, cousin,' laughed Alexander, 'maybe a little grey around the edges, but definitely not black.'

Stewart laughed heartily. 'You are too kind, Alex, but what I have learned from Margaret these past weeks has made me re-think my life. Can you understand that?' he asked.

Alexander thought before answering. 'Oh, I can understand that of Margaret. She is definitely the best of you.'

'On that we are in full agreement, cousin,' came Stewart's reply, as he buttoned his coat up to the top. A very keen wind was blowing in from the east. 'Now, let us go see these cottages, and estimate the cost of the repairs, plus anything else that needs to be completed before winter.'

***

Stewart made his way back to the house around mid-day, leaving Alexander to ride into Mere to find the thatcher. He knew that Margaret would not be there; she had gone to her own house in Mere to open the mail that had accumulated there for over three weeks, as well as dealing with other issues that had arisen in her absence. If they were to live between the two houses, she needed to put various things in place to ensure that the house ran smoothly while she was not in attendance there.

As he entered the drawing room, he found his mother in the far corner of the room, sitting at her bureau writing. He knew she had heard him come in, as anyone else would have knocked.

'Good afternoon, Stewart,' as she said the words in greeting, she turned her head and smiled at him.

'Mother, why are you in here attending to your letters and not in the study?' he questioned as he came to kiss her cheek.

Elizabeth looked up at him, a smile still playing on her lips. 'That is your room now, Stewart.' With that, she stood up, took his hand, and guided him to the window seat.

Stewart said nothing but seated himself next to her with an amused, puzzled expression on his face.

'When my last Estate Steward died two years ago, Alexander took his place.' She waved her hand here. 'You were in Italy at that time, and I knew I could trust him, he was family. He also has a very level head on his shoulders and a keen business eye.' Elizabeth looked at him sideways to see if Stewart would respond.

'Please continue,' Stewart offered.

'Stewart, I have run this house since your father left, as when he left so did the housekeeper.' She paused again here to see his reaction, but Stewart's face was closed, he just nodded for her to continue.

'Above all things,' she began, 'when I was old enough to understand, my father involved me in everything connected with the running of this estate. He treated me like he would have treated a son.' She paused once more to consider what to say next.

'He wanted me to be strong and to be able to manage if the time ever arose. He was a very forward thinking man, your grandfather, he raised me alone with a nanny, governess and a tutor, but wanted me to be able to stand alone if need be.' Here, she stopped to clear her throat.

'I thank him and God every day, as if he had not...' her words trailed away.

'What I am trying to say is, I will continue to deal with the running of the household, but you will handle the running of the estate with Alexander.' She took his hand in hers; when he said nothing, she continued.

'You told me that Margaret was so like me in many ways.' She paused again. 'She is strong and resilient, she has had to be out of necessity, as when her husband died, all she had for help were lawyers and the executors of his will. He left her with a house in London. He had three there, did you know, hers being the smallest; his two sons from previous marriages occupied the other two in Kensington and had joint ownership to the estates in Devon, which are vast. She also inherited the small house in Mere.'

Stewart looked at her. 'I understand what you are trying to tell me, Mother, go on.'

'You must take over the running of the estate along with Alexander.' She breathed deeply then continued. 'You work well together, like brothers, and the people here respect and love you both.' She paused again to reach up to stroke his face.

'Oh, Stewart, you have found a woman of great worth. I know that she built a barrier around herself and was distant at times, because of all that happened to her, but I can see that she is slowly letting that go. Margaret has changed so much in the three weeks that you were away, I hardly recognise her.' Elizabeth became slightly agitated. 'Oh I am not explaining things very well, am I?' Her voice trailed away.

Stewart placed his hands on his mother's shoulders and smiled warmly. 'Like you, through necessity, she has had to take command, but like you know she can relinquish some of that responsibility to me. Am I right?' Stewart nodded to her.

Elizabeth relaxed, shook her head slightly and smiled. 'Oh, Stewart, if I can see into your thoughts, then you most certainly can also see into mine.' She leaned forward and kissed him on the cheek.

Stewart stood. 'Now, Mother, can we possibly have some lunch? I have been out of the house since 6 o'clock this morning and I am ravenous!'

***

Alexander had returned to the house just before dinner to notify Stewart of what he had resolved regarding the repairs of the tenants' rooves. It was late evening, and as night came early now, rather than let Alexander return to his own house, Elizabeth had asked him to stay the night and eat with the family. It had been a quiet, relaxing dinner, but Stewart could see that his cousin had something other than work on his mind.

The women had retired and the two men now sat with their whiskies in the winged chairs either side of the fire place; the hour was late, the curtains had been drawn and a fire had been lit in the hearth while several candles burned around the room.

'Are you going to tell me about it, Alex, or are you just going to sit there thinking?' asked Stewart.

'God, how do you do that?' queried Alexander. Stewart hunched his shoulders and smiled.

'I digress,' continued Alexander. 'I found the man Freeman who said he would come and inspect the thatches tomorrow. He said he hoped they did not need a re-thatch. To which I replied to all intents and purposes, so did I,' stated Alexander.

Stewart chuckled to himself. 'And so do I, cousin, it would cost a fortune, no?' Stewart lifted his eyebrows in question. 'Please continue.'

'After that, I went to The Angel to avail myself of some well-earned food and a mug of ale. It was while sitting by the window that I saw George Wheatley approach the inn and enter.' Stewart's ears pricked up at the mention of this name.

'He saw me as he came through the door and came to sit opposite me. After much questioning, and threatening might I add, he unburdened himself with his story.'

Stewart eyed him cautiously. 'And what story might that be?' he questioned as he sat up and rested his elbows on his knees, holding his glass between his palms.

Alexander thought well before answering. 'You, I, Wheatley and Northcott were all at Winchester together, were we not?' Stewart inclined his head in acquiescence.

'Also,' continued Alexander, 'you may remember that Wheatley acquired a great wealth after the death of his father.' Stewart nodded his head again.

'Do you recall Northcott's sister, Alison? Well, Northcott inherited his father's estate near Crediten in Somerset; she will just get a dowry from her mother when she dies. So, she set her designs on Wheatley, or rather the Wheatley estate near Frome in Somerset.'

Stewart frowned, then gulped back the last of the whiskey in his glass. 'Go on.' His voice was flat.

Alexander stood up and placed a hand on top of the mantle. 'Once she had enticed him into her bed, she thought that she had gained the prize she sought.

Wheatley, on the other hand, had other thoughts: he does not want her.' Alexander paused. 'She had threatened to go to her brother and tell him that he has ruined her, and was now refusing to marry her.' Alexander turned to face Stewart. 'If Alison was a virgin when she took him to her bed, then I am the son of the King!'

'Oh, I wholly agree with you there, cousin.' Stewart stood up and went to pour himself another whisky. Holding the decanter up to his cousin, to which Alexander held out his glass to be filled.

'It does not end there though. The day before yesterday she came and told him that she was with child.' Stewart's eyes narrowed, and his shoulders stiffened. 'Wheatley looks ill. He said that there is nothing he can do short of shooting himself, or fleeing the country. To which I told him neither of these ideas would help his situation.' Alexander returned to his seat.

'Where is the fool now?' questioned Stewart.

'He has taken rooms in the Angel Inn, and he stated that he is not returning home any time soon.'

Stewart rubbed his hand over his face. 'There is nothing we can do tonight, Alex, so let us both go to our beds, let the servants go to theirs and we will go see him tomorrow, and try and talk some sense into him.'

'No, no, no, Stewart, not *we*. I will go and see him,' stated Alexander.

Stewart said nothing but just looked at his cousin. 'Goodnight, Alexander. I will see you in the morning at breakfast.' With that he put his glass onto the tray and left.

As he entered his dressing room, he could see by the light of the candle that Pip was still there waiting for him.

'For God's sake, man, go to your bed. I am fine,' he whispered as he patted the man on the shoulder, lit another candle for him and sent him on his way.

Entering the bedroom he could hear Maggie's gentle breathing; the curtains were still open he noticed, as she had this aversion about sleeping in the dark, he would get to the bottom of this another day. He quietly undressed then slid in beside her, gently spooning her next to him. She was warm and her hair smelled of jasmine as he stroked her shoulder and kissed her neck gently. Maggie roused and placed her hand back onto his thigh, pulling his leg over hers. 'Stewart.' Her voice was husky with sleep, then she turned, pressing her whole body into his, as his fingers raised her head and his mouth covered hers. His last thoughts were a prayer of "thanks" for how lucky he was.

Chapter Eight
Wheatley

Stewart and Alexander left the house very early the following day. There had been a slight frost and the air was chill and fresh as they rode out into the morning, the heat of the summer had turned into the crispness of the first days of autumn. The fields lay around them carpeted in a mist that seemed to float inches from the ground, and all sound was muted with the exception of the occasional call of a bird. The land was resting. The two cousins rode on in mutual silence just enjoying the freedom of the moment.

They met with Freeman the thatcher, who assured them that the rooves, although they had some damage, it was contained to just the one place. A price was negotiated, and as Alexander stated, 'it would not cripple their finances.' From there they made their way to the estate office to organise the payment of bills that had come in over the three weeks of Stewart's absence. Customarily, Alexander would have gone to the house for Elizabeth to arrange, but now it was in Stewart's hands.

Alexander lit the fire that had been laid in the small hearth. When the weather turned cold like now, it was always laid fresh for him when he left in the evenings by one of the workers, but he generally only lit it if he was to stay there some time. It was still cold in the office at present, and both men had their capes wrapped around them for warmth until the fire took hold.

'Alexander, why do you not organise all this work up at the house in the study?' Stewart questioned.

Alexander thought for a moment before replying. 'Before, I would complete the payment slips so that all your mother had to do was put her signature to them.'

'So,' interrupted Stewart, 'you can come to the house write the payments in the study, and I could put my signature to them there.'

'To do that, Stewart, the study would have to house all of these ledgers, folders and chests.' Alexander held out his arm to show the wall that housed these things. 'Besides all that, I like to sit here in the peace, quiet and solitude of my office. It helps me think better,' replied Alexander.

Stewart shook his head. 'My mother knew something when she employed you as Estate Steward. You have a good business head, Alex, she was right about that.'

Alexander smiled. 'Have your fingers thawed enough, cousin, for you to place your signature on the ones I have prepared.' There was mockery in his voice.

Stewart grinned at his cousin. 'Let us get it over with, or we will never get to see Wheatley today.'

***

Arriving at the Angel, Stewart enquired of the inn keeper which rooms Wheatley had taken, being told that they were on the first floor overlooking the back yard. The inn was a one of the better ones in the town, but it was still an inn. Customarily, people only stayed one night, or maybe two, its amenities were sparse but functional.

As they both entered the room, they could see Wheatley lying on the bed in the corner. Wheatley, having seen the two cloaked figures, jumped up, hitting his head hard on the table next to the bed and then proceeded in trying to hide himself beneath it.

George Wheatley was tall, slim and gangly in appearance, like a young man that had gone to sleep, then awoken to find that his arms and legs had suddenly grown, so that he did not know how to use them. He had a comely face with mid-brown hair and large soft brown eyes resembling a young buck deer which were shielded by long dark lashes, the envy of many a female. His smile was refreshing and warm, which gave him the appearance of a young boy. After Winchester, he had gone to Cambridge to study Law, but having completed only one year had returned home as he had no interest in the subject; he was of the disposition where he would take *the path of the least resistance*. He would never make a lawyer, and as his family owned a vast estate in Somerset as well as houses in London, he would not need this.

'Wheatley, what are you doing?' called Stewart from the doorway. Advancing towards him, he went down on one knee and tried to pull him out.

'For God's sake, George, it's me Stewart!' he shouted.

Wheatley poked his head out and looked around him, seeing startled expressions on the faces of both Stewart and Alexander, and having established that they were not there to harm him, he slowly eased his way out and sat on the bed.

'I thought you were Northcott's men come to take me,' came his nervous reply. 'I cannot marry Alison. I am pledged to my second cousin from Cornwall. My mother will kill me, her parents will kill me, and now Northcott will kill me!' By the end of the sentence, he was screaming.

Stewart looked at Alexander. 'Get us some drink from below will you, something strong.' Alexander nodded.

The air in the room was stale and rancid. Stewart wrinkled his nose in distaste; walking to the window he threw it open, and took a gulp of air. Looking out of the window he could see a hive of activity below him in the stables, where

79

the noon stage to Exeter was about to change horses before continuing on its journey.

'Just how long have you been locked up here?' Stewart eyed him sternly. 'You have one of the riches estates in Somerset, and here you are living in…' his voice trailed off.

With that he turned on Wheatley. 'Right, George, stop babbling like a fool and tell me exactly what you have done.' Stewart quirked his mouth up in an ironic smile, as he rubbed the place between his brows and shook his head.

'Only you could get into such a disastrous mess,' he continued. 'Do you never stop to think before you…?' Stewart's voice trailed off as Wheatley looked at him.

'All right, all right,' offered Stewart, raising his hand up. 'I have been known to be rash and short tempered on occasion myself, but…' his voice trailed away again. 'Where was your head, George? What were you thinking? Northcott's sister?!' Stewart raised him arms up and shook his head in disbelief, then turned and seated himself on a stool.

'Your stupidity knows no bounds.' He raised his arms once more for effect. 'The woman has had more…' Stewart stopped himself from going on. Getting up he paced the room trying hard to calm his temper.

'Can you not read people, George, can you not see the reason behind their actions, are you that blind, Wheatley?' Stewart's voice was slowly rising in tone again.

At that moment Alexander entered carrying a tray with mugs, and what looked like whisky.

'In the name of God, can you not keep your voices down,' he whispered, 'They can hear you down in the tap room,' he added. 'If any of Northcott's men are in this establishment, by now they will know exactly where to find you.'

Stewart nodded. 'One thing is for certain; you cannot remain here.'

Alexander looked at Stewart, then at Wheatley. 'You can stay at my house,' offered Alexander. 'If we leave by the back door under the cover of darkness, no one will know you are there,' he added. Wheatley nodded. 'Do you have a horse, George?' questioned Alexander.

'It is stabled at the back,' answered Wheatley.

Stewart shook his head. 'No, no, that will not do, it would be too easy for Northcott to take him from there, ride away, and force the marriage.' He paused, rubbing his chin. 'We will take him to the Willows.'

'Have you lost your mind, Stewart?' Alexander rounded on him. 'You would be deliberately incurring Northcott's wrath, as well as endangering your family, you have too much to lose.'

'Northcott would never invade my home!' retorted Stewart,

'Stand up, George.' ordered Stewart. Wheatley stood, eyeing him with suspicion. 'You are almost of our height, maybe slightly slimmer in build, but with the cape around you and hat on, there would not be a man who could tell the difference,' he added, removing his cloak and hat. 'Put these on, George, you and my cousin will be leaving together. I will follow on your horse.'

Alexander was about to protest when Stewart stopped him.

'Do you have a better proposal, Alexander?' Stewart raised his brows.

'I will go to Margaret's house, where I will stay the night. No one will be watching the comings and goings of her household.' Stewart's voice was final.

'And what am I to tell my aunt, *your* mother, Stewart, *and* your wife?'

'Tell them I was detained on business, in connection with the repairs to the cottages and that it was easier to remain in town, as I had an early appointment in Mere,' he stated emphatically.

'Stewart, do you think that your mother for one moment will believe that?' It was not a question, more a fact.

'My mother knows nothing of Wheatley's dilemma, she will believe it.'

Stewart threw his cape around Wheatley's shoulders and pushed the hat onto his head.

'Go now, and ask the stable lad to saddle your horse. I do not intend to remain any longer than I have to.' Stewart opened the door. 'Go now while the noon coach for Exeter is still unloading, you will be less noticeable amid the noise of the passengers.' He nodded in dismissal.

***

Stewart rang the bell to Margaret's house and was confronted by a very startled butler.

'We did not expect you, her ladyship sent no word,' he apologised.

Stewart looked at the man, who must be in his sixties, and raised his hands in apology. 'Please, do not worry yourself, I had business in Mere today, and tomorrow early I have to see a craftsman regarding some repairs. Her ladyship does not know I am here, but my cousin Alexander is taking word to her now. Tell the cook I will need only a cold supper, some meats, cheese, bread, whatever she has to hand.' By this time Stewart had reached the stairs.

'Please, just light a fire in the small guest room for me, I will eat there so as to cause as little disruption to the household as possible,' he added

'But, sir, her ladyship will be—' Giles was stopped by Stewart placing a hand on his arm.

'Her ladyship will be fine,' he assured him.

'Very good, sir,' came the reply, but by the look on the Butler's face he thought that everything was not fine, and there would be repercussions.

Stewart was lying full stretch by the fire, with the remnants of his dinner lying on the tray beside him. He stretched comfortably placing his hands behind his head, then leaning up he took a sip of his whisky—it was peaceful with just the crackling of the fire and the creaking of the house settling for the night. He should not be here alone, he thought, Maggie should be here; strange how he sought her company now, where before he only sought solitude. His brain was whirring like the cogs of a perfectly oiled clock, his father, he considered, had done him a great justice when he came down, for without that he would never have had what he had now. So engrossed in his thoughts, he did not hear the door open till Margaret called his name.

She was standing there with her hand on the door knob, head to one side, smiling at him. Stewart shook his head slightly and breathed deeply, then within two strides he had her in his arms, closing the door behind her.

'What?' was his surprised exclamation as Margaret pushed him away slightly to look up at him, her face a mixture of emotions, but most of all it was questioning. Behind them the fire crackled warmly in the hearth, but everything else in the room was quiet. As Stewart stood there holding her, he realised there definitely was not much warmth emanating from Margaret's greeting at that moment.

'Well?' she paused, still smiling. 'Are you going to explain things? Did you really think that your mother and I would believe Alexander and George's story?' Her words were coming fast and Stewart had to think hard what to say.

'I am waiting, Stewart Hamilton,' she added, her eyes were sparkling but not all of it was from joy.

Stewart sighed. 'George has got himself into a bit of bother.' It was better to tell the truth he thought as he searched her face.

'I did not mean to involve Mother and yourself at all.' He pulled her across the room and seated her on the bed. 'Please believe me, there was no other solution, will you forgive me?' he added

'You seem to have me at a disadvantage,' she replied, looking around her and then at the bed. Stewart's eyes twinkled.

'I have always thought that if you are to impart something of a delicate nature to your wife, then here is the best place.' He smiled teasingly and raised an eyebrow.

Margaret slapped him on the chest and pursed her lips. 'It is a good thing that you are honest, Stewart Hamilton, as your cousin, after much interrogation from your mother might I add, told us everything.'

Stewart wiped a hand over his face. 'Alexander is a worse liar than I am.'

'Are you a one man crusade, Stewart?' Margaret countered. 'Must you take on everybody's troubles? Your mother said...' her voice died away; he was stoking her face with his finger, which continued down her neck to the back of her head, where his fingers massaged the top of her spine.

'Stop that!' Margaret held his hand and swallowed visibly, then she grasped the other hand as it came up to do the same.

'You are incorrigible! Stop, and get your clothes on, we are going back.' But her words were cut off as Stewart placed his mouth over hers.

'We… are going nowhere, except…' His eyes looked behind her, as he took off her bonnet and started to undo her laces.

'You came to be with me, did you not, Maggie? His voice was soft in her ear, as he started to take out the pins from her hair and run his finger through it.

'You know I did,' was all she said.

***

As they lay peacefully entwined in one another's arms, Margaret pushed her fingers into the hairs of his chest thinking, then brushing her lips on his shoulder she turned to him.

'I could not bear to lose you now,' she began, 'I have only just found you, and to be alone again…' Her voice had lowered to a whisper.

Stewart pulled her on top of him, folding his arms around her in a tight hug, their noses and foreheads touching.

'I have no intentions of going anywhere,' he said, 'and neither will I do anything to put myself in harm's way, I swear, Maggie, you are, as my mother says, "*The best of me.*"' He rolled her over onto her side and pulled her tightly next to him. 'And I love you very much.'

She squeezed him hard before replying.

'You have shown me love, how to be loved and to love in return. I could not go back to that solitary existence I had before… when you are not with me… that is why I came tonight.' She paused. 'I wanted you…' she breathed as she looked up at him. Gently he smoothed the hair from her eyes, kissing her deeply.

'Come and show me how much, Maggie.'

Chapter Nine
The Unexpected and First Child

It was a week now since they had taken George Wheatley back to his estate in Frome, Somerset, with strict instructions for him to remain there until such a time as things could be settled with Alison Northcott. As far as could be established, Northcott knew nothing of his sister's affairs, but if Alison saw that her plans were to be thwarted, then she might take more drastic action.

The day was peaceful. Margaret and his mother had gone into Mere to purchase some lace, and Stewart had ridden out to the Estate office to see Alexander. It had turned pleasantly balmy for the end of September; though the sun held no real heat, it still warmed the face where it touched it. An Indian summer, his mother had called it, usually occurring after a bout of frost. Stewart thought more aptly it was likely the calm before the storm, in more ways than one. He dismounted, tied his horse in the stable to feed, then came into the office where Alexander was seated at his desk engrossed in a ledger.

At the sound of his footstep on the boards, Alexander looked up.

'Good morning, cousin, what brings you here?' Alexander's tone was pleasant and welcoming.

'The women have taken themselves off to Mere, so I have come to discuss Wheatley,' answered Stewart.

Alexander twisted his quill between his fingers, then placed it down and sat back.

Alexander sighed. 'Cousin, do you not think that we should leave things be? George is safely at home, and no one is likely to storm his estate to kidnap him in the near future.'

Stewart frowned and seated himself. 'Alex, this thing will not go away, it has merely shelved itself for this present time. As soon as Alison informs her brother, there will be hell to pay.' He sat there, unconsciously chewing the inside of his mouth.

'If she tells him this, and she will, mark my words, he will spread the word far and wide regarding the treatment of his sister by one George Wheatley. Northcott will reap his vengeance on George, and he will be shamed, no matter what. The man will never be able to hold his head up in society again.' Here he paused. 'Plus, he will have to marry her.'

Alexander stroked his chin and closed his eyes.

'Then we must find others who have availed themselves of the fair Alison's embraces.' Alexander steepled his fingers and waited for Stewart's reply.

'Alex, you know as well as I that no one will come forward and admit to such. Northcott's reach weaves a wide web. They would be terrified of the consequences. He is a very vindictive man,' answered Stewart.

'Then what is left?' responded Alexander.

'We have to find someone to distract her.' Stewart raised his brows. 'In the amorous sense, do you follow?' Alexander nodded, but he did not like the direction this was taking.

'At the same time we have to contrive for Northcott to come across the passionate pair, finding them *In Flagrante Delico*, so no matter what she says after that, Northcott will never believe her.

Alexander looked totally astounded. 'And who in hell's name are we going to find to perform such act. Northcott will call him out!'

'Not necessarily,' countered Stewart, 'we have to bid our time till after she has disclosed to Northcott about Wheatley.' He paused here, mentally going over the scenario. 'Then, if the new man is reasonably attractive'—he paused once more—'he could fool her by omission. Let her think he has capitol and land but up in the northern part of England.'

Alexander was shaking his head as he watched his cousin mentally map out his plan.

Stewart stood up and paced. 'Do you not see, if he gives the appearance of great wealth...' he paused once more. 'She is fickle, and only sees what she wants to see. Let him shower her with gifts and jewellery.'

'Stop there Stewart,' Alexander broke in. 'Just where are we going to find such a man?' he pushed the chair back and started to pace the room. 'Northcott will still call him out – rich or poor, if only to save his sister's reputation!!'

'Cousin, you are missing the point here. If she has already disclosed the affair with Wheatley, then is found *In Flagrante Delico* with another, whatever she says from thence will hold no weight. He cannot call them both out.' Stewart paused for Alexander to take this in. 'She has compromised herself in the eyes of her brother. He can then never believe a word she says.'

Alexander nodded. 'But again I ask, who are we going to find to take on this part?'

Stewart looked at his cousin then looked away. 'I know of such a man who will do it... for a price.'

Alexander shook his head. 'Sometimes I feel I do not know you at all, Stewart. I need some air.' With that he walked out of the door.

Alexander raised his head up to the sky and breathed deeply. He let his mind take in the tranquillity of countryside around him, calming his thoughts like a soothing balm. He did not hear Stewart come out, so when he spoke, he jumped.

'Alex, I have been an observer to all this many times, *not* the participant. I have seen men beguiled and thought how stupid they are, being led by their noses to a doomed fate.' He paused and walked around.

85

'Cousin, I have seen first-hand what this can do to a person, to be taken in, led to believe that they are loved and wanted. Only to find out later that it was not them they wanted but their status, money, land.' He paused again to get control of his feelings. 'Not only men get trapped and taken into this web of deceit and lies. Women do too.'

The realisation on Alexander's face was so transparent that Stewart turned on his heel and walked back into the office.

Alexander followed him, not knowing what to say, but say something he must.

'You are talking about my aunt, your mother.' He stopped, picking up things absently on the desk and putting them back again—all the while his brain was whirring.

'All this aggression you had, all this hate built up inside you, why did you never tell me, Stewart, why?'

Stewart shrugged his shoulders in reply, and sat down again breathing deeply.

'I love my mother more than anything else in this world. Apart from Maggie.' He raised his hand to indicate this and stop the words that Alexander was about to say. 'It was not until I came down from Winchester that I could see exactly what had been happening in my absence.'

Alexander said nothing, but let him continue.

'He has slowly been taking money from her for years.' Stewart held his temples tight; his head was throbbing. 'But that is not the only hold he has over my mother. There is something else, dark and sinister which I have yet to discover.' He closed his eyes here and breathed deeply again.

'Do you not see now why we must do something for Wheatley?' Stewart bent to retrieve his hat from the stool.

'I will arrange something, and then set it in motion when the time is right.' He looked at Alexander and nodded. 'I must get back now before the ladies return, we will expect you tonight for dinner, that is not a question, cousin, that is a fact.' He nodded again, smiled and left.

Alexander stood there stunned as he watched his cousin depart.

***

The dinner had been a quiet one, it held nothing of the revelations that had taken place that afternoon. Stewart and Alexander now sat in the chairs by the fire, talking about estate business, while the ladies sat on the sofa and talked of the lace they had bought that day.

'It is a beautiful piece, and so intricately woven,' stated Margaret. 'Where will you use it?'

'Ah, I have a very plain green dress, nothing to speak of, but if I add this to the neck and the sleeves, it will bring out the colour and turn something ordinary into something a little special.' Elizabeth smiled, but as she looked at Margaret, she could tell that all was not well. Her face was pale, and her eyes had lost their sparkle. This had been evident for a few days now, but tonight she had hardly touched her food, and now looked as though she would drop where she sat.

'Are you well, Margaret?' she questioned.

'I am fine, really, Elizabeth, just a little tired that is all. I did not sleep well last night.' She looked towards Stewart and smiled. 'He was very restless, and took most of the bedcovers when he moved.'

Elizabeth nodded and smiled back. There was something else though, she could tell; Margaret was not her cheerful self at all. It was like the Margaret she had been when she had first come to the Willows, and this troubled Elizabeth.

'Stewart!' she called. 'You must take your wife and bid us good night, else she will fall asleep where she sits.'

Stewart turned in his chair and saw in Margaret's face what his mother had seen. Getting up, he came towards her, holding out his hand.

'Margaret Hamilton, we shall bid good night and retire I think.' Saying this, he smiled warmly and pulled her to her feet.

'Alex, I may or may not see you in the morning, depending on how early you rise. So if not here, I will see you at the Estate office.'

Alexander stood up smiling and bowed. 'Good night, Margaret, sleep well.'

***

Stewart looked at Maggie; she was seated at the table looking into the mirror as she brushed her hair. There was something troubling her, he could tell that; she had been distracted at dinner, where normally she would have joined in the conversation. His mother had looked at him twice, and then when they said good night, she had caught his arm.

'There is something troubling her, Stewart, you must find out what it is.' Elizabeth nodded to him.

Margaret placed the brush very precisely on the table then turned, stood up, and came towards him. Lifting her shift, she took his hand and rested it very lightly on her stomach, looking up at him. Stewart did not move or take his eyes from hers.

'Stewart,' she whispered. 'I am with child.'

Stewart's face went through a myriad of expressions, till finally his brain registered what she had just imparted to him. He licked his lips and swallowed hard, as his mouth had suddenly gone dry. There was a slight buzzing in his head, as though for a split second everything seemed to stand still. He saw Margaret frown and shake her head slightly. It was then that he pulled her into his arms, almost crushing the breath from her. He coughed, trying to clear his throat before he spoke.

'Maggie!' His voice was husky with emotion. 'Oh God, Maggie!' was all he said as he pulled her to him once more. The room was warm and so was Maggie, as he stood there, savouring the information that she had just bestowed upon him.

'I never thought I would be able to have children,' came her muffled reply as she buried herself into his shirt.

'I…' Margaret began. 'When my…' she paused again. 'When he first took me, it was so violent.' She paused again. 'I bled for days.' She was breathing hard now, and Stewart knew just how hard it was for her to tell him this.

'He said…' She breathed in deeply again through her nose to steady her voice. 'He said, "*Your father was correct there then. I received what I paid for.*" I was in so much pain but he did not care, he just took me again and again. I knew that I was screaming as I could hear myself calling as though it came from outside my head. From that moment I thought I would never be able to bear children.' Her voice trailed away into the silence.

She knew Stewart was crying as she could feel the vibrations through his chest. When the tremors subsided, he picked her up and went to sit in the winged chair by the fire, cradling her on his lap. They must have sat there in silence for some time; she realised this because when he finally moved, the fire had burned down to a red ember.

Stewart stirred as though waking from a deep trance. He picked Margaret up and took her to bed. Placing her gently down, he slid in beside her, pulled the covers up and held her very close to him, wrapping his legs around her, till finally they slept in peace in one another's arms.

Not a word had been spoken.

***

As Stewart entered the dining room, he could see that his mother had nearly finished her breakfast. She raised her head and they stared at one another for a few seconds before Stewart came towards her.

'Good morning, Mother,' he said as he kissed her cheek.

Elizabeth was still staring up at him, and Stewart knew that she was waiting for some explanation regarding Margaret.

'You have a letter that came this morning,' Elizabeth began, but Stewart interrupted her.

'I have it, and that is why I must leave now to see Alexander.' He eyed his mother to see if she would question him. 'It is to do with the renovations to the cottages,' he continued. 'I have left Margaret in bed as she is feeling slightly unwell this morning.'

His mother eyed him suspiciously.

'Mother, she is fine, could you get Lilly to take her a tray this morning, just an egg and some bread with a pot of mint tea?' He smiled at her. 'When I return, we can all have lunch together,' he concluded

Elizabeth nodded. Stewart knew his mother did not believe a word of it, but it would have to wait till lunchtime; then they would impart the good news. He reached across, took a slice of bread spread liberally with butter and waved good bye.

Stewart felt euphoric as he rode towards the estate office; his thoughts were colliding against one another, two pieces of news in just twelve hours, one phenomenal, and one bad. The best was that he was going to be a father; in the space of two months he had wed and then found out that Margaret was with child—his child. Just thinking about it made him want to call out to the countryside, he had never felt so elated and so much love for one person before. All of his senses had become heightened, as though he could smell, taste and hear for the very first time. There were sheep bleating in the next field, birds chirping their chorus in the hedgerows, and rooks in the high trees calling one another. The world at this moment for him had turned on its axis.

The downside was that the letter had been from Wheatley, stating Northcott had written to him declaring that if he did not marry his sister Alison, he was a dead man. He had requested his lawyer to draw up a wedding contract, and by the end of the month, they were to be wed.

The hell they will, thought Stewart. He had to get to Exeter and quick to set his plan in motion, but first he had to see Alexander on both counts.

As he rode up, he could tell that Alexander was out. He could be in any number of places, mused Stewart; in the fields, the tenants' cottages, Mere—the best thing to do was to wait, so he stabled his horse and walked back to the office. As he opened the door, he saw that a fire had been lit, which indicated that wherever he was, he did not intend to stay out for long. He took his hat off and seated himself in the chair by the fire to wait. As he sat there watching the flames flicker, he thought how much his life had changed, how he had changed. At this very moment, he could not imagine a life without Maggie. What she had told him last night had invoked anger and happiness, but happiness had won through. Before Maggie, it would have been the anger.

Fifteen minutes later, Stewart heard Alexander return and stable his horse.

'Good morning, cousin,' were Alexander's first words. 'We are keeping aristocratic hours now we are wed, no?'

Stewart chuckled and got up to greet him.

'Firstly, you are expected up at the house for lunch.' Stewart put up his hand when he saw that Alexander was about to protest. 'No, we will go together when we have concluded our business, we are expected.'

'Secondly, I received this in the mail this morning.' Giving his cousin the letter, Stewart waited for him to read the contents.

Alexander whistled though his teeth loudly. 'Now what are we to do?'

'We set into motion my plan, which means that I have to go to Exeter tomorrow at the very latest. Fairweather is there at this moment and I need to talk with him.' He watched Alexander to see what the reaction would be.

Alexander thought about his words very carefully before imparting them.

'Stewart, last evening… Margaret is not well, even I could see that. How can you go off to Exeter?'

'Maggie is fine,' interrupted Stewart, 'and even if she were not, my mother is there with her, as well as the servants and a physician on hand. So there is no worry for that.'

'Why would Margaret need a physician?' Alexander's brain had picked up on that one word: physician.

89

'She does *not* need a physician, I said this metaphorically. Look, let us go back to the house now, wash, and have some lunch, as I have had no breakfast this morning!'

'Well, if you will keep patrician hours, what do you expect?' Alexander replied mockingly.

'Let us just go, Alex, please, can we?' answered Stewart

Alexander smiled, took his cloak off the peg, and put his hat on his head.

'I will not argue, as I breakfasted at six this morning, and my stomach is complaining too right now.'

****

Elizabeth was sewing and Margaret reading as they sat companionably in the window seat looking out to the garden. The sun rays were welcoming as it came through the glass windows, heating the two women. It was peaceful, but Elizabeth could not help but steal the occasional glace in Margaret's direction. Though serene she looked very pale in complexion, and she hoped with all her heart that she was not sickening for something. She had finally come down around 10 o'clock, looking decidedly fragile. If Elizabeth was honest, she had looked wan for a couple of days now. Her thoughts were cut off as the door opened and Stewart and Alexander came into the room.

Stewart came straight to Margaret, lifting her to her feet and kissed her.

'Am I missing something here, Stewart?' was Elizabeth's response.

'No, Mother,' he replied. His face was alight with pleasure.

'Now that you are both here, we have something to tell you.' He smiled down at Margaret and pulled her in to him, looking at her all the while he spoke.

'Mother, you are going to be a grandmother and you, Alex, an uncle.'

There was a moment's silence as it registered in their minds what Stewart had said. Then Elizabeth's eyes filled with tears as she pulled Margaret into her arms and held her.

Alexander's face went from shock to disbelief to joy. Smiling broadly, he came and slapped his cousin so hard on the back that Stewart nearly lost his balance.

'You are supposed to shake my hand, cousin, not slap me so hard as to knock me through the window.' Stewart laughed.

'This is wonderful news,' exclaimed Alexander. 'I cannot believe it!!'

Stewart sat next to Margaret on the window seat and kissed her forehead.

'If you cannot believe it, imagine how I feel. It is as though my life has been reborn.' He was answering Alexander, but his words were addressed to Margaret.

Elizabeth wiped her eyes, and came to take Margaret's hand.

'Right, Stewart, I shall now take Margaret upstairs, where I will tuck her safely up in bed, with a book and a pot of mint tea, it does wonders to calm a stomach ache. Now I know the reason, I can apply the remedy. What she needs at the moment is rest, till these symptoms pass—and they will I know—so you

90

two,' she waved her hand at them to dismiss them, 'can go about your business and leave us to peace and quiet.' She looked at Stewart who was about to protest. 'She will be perfectly safe; I will sit by her till your return.' Stewart nodded, then kissed Margaret very softly.

'I will be back early,' he whispered as he squeezed her hand.

Turning, he looked at his cousin.

'You and I will take ourselves off to invade Mrs Cottle's kitchen. If she berates us and tries to evict us, we will play our ace card and tell her of our good news. On hearing that, she will probably get out her freshly cured ham from the pantry, and a flagon of ale with which to wash it down, and if she is completely ecstatic, we will probably get dessert!'

Alexander was about to say, 'You always could charm the women,' but thought it totally inappropriate under the circumstances.

'If you cause my cook any grief, you will both find your own food for the next two weeks!' Elizabeth called after them as they left.

Chapter Ten
Exeter and Lady Catherine

Sitting by the window in the coach bound for Exeter, Stewart's mind was a jumble of thoughts, but foremost of these was Maggie. She had been so ill the last few days, unable to retain anything, even water, that he had not wanted to leave her. His mother had assured him that this was normal, and that things would right themselves within a few weeks, but Stewart was uncertain of everything at present.

When he had been alone, he had thought about no one, not even himself—most definitely not himself. Danger did not concern him; if he saw an injustice, he would be the first to denounce it, regardless of the cost. However, now suddenly everything had changed, and soon he would have not one but two people to protect and put before himself. How could one's life alter so much in the space of two months, from someone who cared nothing for his position in society or reputation, and who had disdain for those who flouted the moral codes of justice, to what he had become now.

He was roused from his thoughts by the voice of the young woman who was sitting opposite him.

'Sir, if you will pardon my asking, would you perhaps know if the inn where the coach stops is a reputable hostelry one that a young woman may stay for a night? My family, who are coming to collect me, will not arrive until tomorrow.'

Stewart removed his hat and inclined his head. 'Mistress, the place where this stagecoach stops, The Mermaid Inn, is one of high repute I can assure you it boasts of comfortable rooms and is renowned for its food. You should be quite safe there,' he replied.

'Thank you kindly, sir, you have been of great help to me.' She inclined her head and went back to her small book that she had been reading.

Stewart looked at her, and then her clothes, and thought that her speech had the ring of the aristocracy. He wondered what such a woman of breeding was doing on a stagecoach without a chaperone. This seemed to Stewart very odd, and set off signals of alarm in his brain. Either she is eloping with someone, or, is fleeing someone; there could be no other logical explanation. All the signs told him that he should not implicate himself in this, but his sense of justice once again won through. He would not be leaving the inn for it was there that he was due to meet with James Fairweather, so he would bid his time and keep watch—he was good at that.

On arrival at the Mermaid Inn, he waited for his bag to be unloaded, then watched as the young woman's bag was handed down—she too had only a small carpet bag. A woman of her breeding would normally be carrying a portmanteau.

'Mistress, may I be of some assistance?' questioned Stewart.

'Thank you kindly, sir, but no, the bag handler will take in my luggage,' she replied respectfully.

Stewart doffed his hat, bowed and went into the inn. There was something amiss and he knew it, but that was secondary at present to the task he had come for. If he had time later, then maybe he would amuse himself with this conundrum.

He found his friend in the dining area partaking of his evening meal. Coming up behind him, he tapped him lightly on the shoulder.

'Fairweather, how are you?' greeted Stewart.

The man coughed loudly and turned around. 'God, Hamilton!' he exclaimed. 'You nearly made me choke on a piece of beef!!'

Stewart grinned and seated himself opposite.

James Fairweather was shorter than Stewart by at least three inches, but had a well-proportioned athletic figure. He had mid-brown hair that was inclined to wave, and hazel colour eyes which seemed to shine out from his face even when he was angry. His complexion was ruddy, giving the appearance of having been out in the sun too long, but his demeanour was of a very pleasant, amiable young man.

Stewart knew that his family ranked just under that of an aristocrat and were very wealthy owning land in many counties, and on leaving Winchester, James Fairweather had gone up to Oxford to study philosophy and politics.

'Sorry, James, could not resist it,' replied Stewart mischievously. 'Have you been here long? What is the food like?' He nodded to the half-eaten plate that Fairweather had before him.

'It was perfectly fine, till some rouge nearly choked me,' he retaliated, but with good humour.

At that point, the serving girl came and Stewart ordered himself some of the same. When they had finished their meal, they sat at leisure talking about their lives.

'You are married?' came Fairweather's shocked response. 'You, of all people!' He shook his head in disbelief. Stewart smiled and leaned back in his seat.

'You should try it someday, Fairweather, it will change your life. It changed mine.'

Fairweather's response was to shake his head. It was at this point that the young woman from the coach came into the dining space and seated herself by the window. Fairweather looked from the woman to Stewart and back again.

'You did say you were married, Hamilton, happily married?' he queried.

'No, no, it is not what it seems,' replied Stewart.

'Then pray do tell me otherwise,' countered Fairweather.

'She is an aristocratic young woman, travelling alone, on a stagecoach to Exeter, with no luggage, and nowhere to stay. The only answer she gave was that her family were coming to collect her tomorrow.' Stewart raised his eyebrows in question.

'Ahhhh,' was all the reply he received.

'Quite,' said Stewart, but as he watched him, he saw his friend's face pale.

'Do not move, Stewart, or our game is up.' Fairweather's voice had lowered considerably in pitch. Seeing that his friend was about to turn his head, he kicked Stewart firmly in the shins.

'It is Northcott, he is here,' he hissed through closed teeth.

Stewart's face froze. 'We have to get out of here and quickly, where is he now? Is he facing us or with his back?'

Fairweather seemed to be stuck dumb.

'Fairweather, pull yourself together man,' exclaimed Stewart.

'He is going to sit next to the young woman from the coach,' he replied incredulously.

Stewart's face went from dark to light. 'James Fairweather, our plans have been altered for us.' He motioned for James to follow. 'Let us get out of here, now!'

***

They had seated themselves in the tap room in full view of the door which led up to the rooms above. It was only a matter of waiting, Stewart knew this.

All about them was the contented mumble of voices as people enjoyed their ale, recounting stories of their travels. Stewart looked around the room; the air was thick and muggy from smoke, tobacco and bodies, as some of these people had been on the stagecoach since London, and still had further to travel. They were tired but jovial.

Fairweather's elbow in his side brought him back.

The young woman came out first. Going through the door, she mounted the stairs. A silent message went from Stewart to his friend.

'Right,' Stewart whispered, 'go up and avail yourself of the room that she is occupying. Then watch for Northcott to follow her.' He added.

James Fairweather nodded in agreement.

No more than a few minutes passed before Northcott followed her. Stewart waited till he had disappeared, then went up the stairs himself, trying carefully not to make much noise, as the stairs creaked from age and use. Having reached the top, he found his friend hiding in a recess in the passageway.

'They entered that door at the end,' pointed Fairweather.

The light in the corridor was not good, only a few candles burned in the sconces along the wall. Then Stewart saw the soft glow that emanated from under their door.

'We will give them some time, then Northcott will get all that he deserves.' His voice was low and menacing.

Fairweather looked at Stewart, puzzled.

'Did I not tell you that Northcott tried to have my cousin Alexander killed in London, while he was on a mission for me?'

James Fairweather's only reply was to shake his head.

'This way I will *kill two birds with one stone*",' smiled Stewart.

Seeing his friends face turn complete blank, he added.

'James, I will tell you all once we have accomplished what we came for.' Both friends nodded at one another in agreement.

After waiting some minutes, they advanced cautiously towards the door; placing his hand to the door knob and his shoulder to the panel, Stewart pushed hard. The door gave way to reveal the young woman in question and Northcott in an amorous pose. Stewart's eyes surveyed the room quickly; there was a fire, two candles were lit, one in the sconce above the bed and one on the table beside it. The young woman was dressed only in her shift, while Northcott was in his stocking feet, breeches and shirt. Northcott was tall and dark haired, with grey deep set eyes that held no warmth. His face was hard and bony, with high pronounced cheekbones and square jaw, but at that moment as his face caught all of the shadows from the candles' flicker, it gave the appearance of a skull.

Stewart advanced upon the pair, causing them to part, then reached between them. Pulling at one of the bedcovers, he held it out to the young woman, keeping his eyes all the while on Northcott.

'James, please take the lady into my room, number five at the end on the right. She can remain there till the morning, when we will put her on the next available stage to wherever she wishes to go. I will stay here.'

By this time, Northcott had regained his senses; he waited till the door closed then slowly backed away to where his coat lay across a chair. Reaching down, he drew out his sword and lunged at Stewart.

But Stewart had anticipated this, and just as the sword was about to enter his shoulder, he threw himself sideways, drew the dagger out of his coat and slammed it hard against the swords blade, sending the object flying across the room.

As Northcott backed away towards the wall, Stewart advanced rapidly, grabbing him by his stock and pushing the blade of the dagger up under Northcott's chin. The point pierced the skin there and a small trickle of blood ran down his neck.

Stewart was ridged, his face blank but so full of anger that his eyes sparked like steel.

'You will tear up the marriage contract between your sister and Wheatley, am I making myself clear?'

There was so much menace in his voice a weaker man would have crumbled, but Northcott stood eye to eye with him, and matched glance for glance.

'I will run you through for this, Hamilton, I want satisfaction.'

Before he could continue, Stewart threw his head back and laughed loudly.

'As I recall Northcott, you have NEVER beaten me at fencing.' He sneered and quirked his eyebrows to make a point.

'But that is not the way you carry out your threats, is it, Northcott?' He held the man so close to him now Stewart could feel and smell his stale breath on his face.

'You prefer to come from behind and slit their throats, no?'

Northcott paled significantly, even by the candles' light, Steward could see that his skin had gone grey.

'Did you think I would not find out? Do you take me for a fool?' Stewart's voice was slowly rising.

'If you EVER harm, or go to harm any member of my family again...' He pressed his nose against Northcott's, eye to eye. 'I will split you like a suckling pig and roast you on a spit!' He paused to swallow. Pushing Northcott at arm's length and tightening the hold on his stock while putting more pressure on the dagger.

'Do I make myself clear?'

Northcott did not respond, but spat to one side. His face was contorted with rage and malice.

'If you think you have got the better of me, Hamilton, then you are very much mistaken, my vengeance runs deep, and with you it is fathomless, you have my word.' His voice was steady and hard.

Stewart threw him to the floor. 'Your word is worth about as much as your honour. Just try, then we will see who bleeds the most.'

***

He left Fairweather in Exeter. From there James Fairweather would travel to Wheatley's home in Frome Somerset, and relate to him that he was now freed from the marriage contract with Alison Northcott. No doubt he would elaborate the conditions under which this occurred, thought Stewart, but he did not think that this piece of information would travel far under the circumstances. It was best for all parties concerned that this remained secret.

As the coach made its way out of Exeter, Stewart turned to the Young woman who was seated opposite him.

'So, are you going to tell me who you are, or do I have to find out by other means?' His tone brooked no nonsense.

Sitting in a dignified manner, she raised her head up high before answering.

'I am the third great niece twice removed of The Earl Cornwallis.'

Stewart breathed out, whistling through his lips.

'Good God, My Lady, do you not realise that your... your uncle twice removed, will turn the country on its head to look for you!!!'

He pinched the top of his nose very hard.

'My Lady, where did you board the coach?' he questioned.

'From Salisbury,' came her curt reply.

And were you staying there with family? Or was this just a stop along the way?'

She looked at Stewart with distaste. 'I came from Bath, my family have a home there and were taking the waters at the Spa,' she paused, 'why are you asking me all of these questions?' she added.

Stewart shook his head in disbelief as he did not like what he was hearing.

'Do you...' he paused to gain his composure. 'Your uncle must have half the country out by now!' He looked around the coach as people were becoming aware of the conversation between them. Stewart put his fist over his mouth to stop him from saying more.

'You will alight with me at Mere; from there I will send word for my coachman to bring my mother's coach to take you to Bath.' Stewart saw that she was about to protest and stopped her.

'I will brook no argument on this, My Lady. I am putting myself and my family at great risk to restore you to your family.' He shook his head. 'How in the name of all that is holy did you get involved with this man?'

The minute the words left his mouth, he knew. Was the man that obtuse, to think he could do this, was he so vain? No, he could see it clearly now how he had lured this young woman into eloping with him; it was money that he sought. He had said it many times that Northcott would sell his own mother for gain. Once he had taken her, it was either marriage or shame. But the aristocracy had a long arm as well as memory, and one day they would have found Northcott skewered or strung up. This was not such a bad thing, Stewart considered, but then berated himself for such thoughts.

It was around midday when the coach stopped outside the Angel; there was a fine rain which gave the appearance of mist, as Stewart helped the young woman down and took her into the inn. He saw Alexander immediately sitting in the inglenook. Stewart put his arm out for the young woman to proceed to the fire, as he could see by the expression on her face that she found her surroundings most abhorrent.

Stewart looked down at his cousin, who seemed about to explode and spoke.

'Alexander, may I present you to the...' he paused here... 'I must get this right, the third great niece twice removed of The Earl Cornwallis.' With that, he took off his hat and bowed.

'If we do not get this young woman to her family in Bath very quickly, we will all be resting in the tower by nightfall.'

Alexander's mouth had remained open throughout. Finding his voice again, he stood up, sharply bowed and spoke.

'Your servant, My Lady.'

Stewart seated her near the fire, then pulled Alexander to one side.

'Either you or I, cousin, must ride out to the Willows, get my mother's coach and bring it here with all haste. Then we must get her to Bath without further delay.' Stewart nodded.

'I will go,' replied Alexander. 'My horse will run faster with me in the saddle.' He looked towards the young woman. 'Can you not hide her somewhere?' It was not a question, more a statement.

'Were would you have me put her, Alex?' he lifted his brows.

'Cover her up, people are becoming curios,' Alexander replied looking around the tap room.

'Alex, they have seen me get down from the coach with her, come into the tap room with her, and now you wish me to cover her up with a cloak. Would that not draw even more suspicion?'

Alexander nodded in agreement, pulling his own cloak around him, he left.

***

It had been agreed when Alexander came back with the carriage that he would escort the Lady back to her family in Bath. He had no other obligations than to himself, and if he were delayed for some days, it would not affect anyone other than himself.

Stewart reached the Willows about 6pm, and as he entered the hall, Elizabeth was waiting for him. Calling him into the drawing room, she closed the door behind him. Elizabeth turned and paced the room for some moments, trying to get her thoughts together. Stewart eyed his mother, but did not offer anything in explanation, waiting for her to speak.

'Stewart, you have done many stupid, desperate things in your life, but nothing even approaches what you have done this day.' She rang her hands in despair.

'You have not only implicated yourself but by what you have done today, you have implicated our name and the estate.' She paused again. 'If Alexander cannot explain satisfactorily to her family what has taken place over the last twenty four hours, you will be accused of false imprisonment.' Elizabeth held her head in her hands.

'Do you not know who these people are, and what they are capable of?' Shaking her head, she walked away and sat on the sofa.

Looking up at him, she shook her head. 'Have you nothing to say for yourself?'

Stewart swallowed hard. 'Mother, I... Mother, to say I am sorry is futile and cowardly. I have tried to right a great wrong before it was made, for that I am guilty. For implicating this family, I cannot express my sincerest apologies and regret enough.' He offered as he walked to the window.

'That young woman is about eighteen years old. She had been seduced by a man who wanted her for the status and the wealth she has. He would never have obtained this by legal means so he did this by subterfuge and cunning. I know this man, and when I saw what was about to happen...' he paused again, 'Do you think that I could have sat idly by and watched this happen?' Stewart started to pace the room again.

'I went there in the first place to prevent such an injustice happening, only to find an even bigger one was playing out before my very eyes. Would you have had me do nothing in defence of this?' He paused once more then continued.

'Right now the young woman in question is still "*virgo intacta*".' He eyed his mother but her face was impassive. 'She is being restored to her family exactly as she left them. Even though at this time she believes that the world is against her, and her family have thwarted her one true chance of happiness. In time she will see the error of her ways, and this man for what he really is.'

Seating himself next to Elizabeth, he took her hands in his. 'I thank God every day for these bounties I have been given, and feel rich beyond my expectations for the love that I have bestowed on me every day.' Stewart looked deep into her eyes.

'Mother, I am truly sorry if I have let you down.'

Elizabeth stoked his hands, and looked at him. Placing her hand upon his cheek, she spoke.

'Go see your wife, Stewart, she needs you.'

***

Margaret was seated at her looking glass when Stewart came in. She watched him approach through the mirror; coming up behind her, he placed a hand on her shoulder. Margaret, still holding her eyes on his through the glass, picked up his hand and placed it gently on her cheek, then turning it round, she kissed it gently in the palm, holding it there stroking his fingers.

Stewart turned her gently, pulled her up and held her to him, then Margaret turned her face up and spoke.

'I know why you did it, Stewart, it is alright.'

There was no accusation in her words, just an affirmation that what he did was noble, and done with a good heart.

Chapter Eleven
James Fairweather, Bearcroft and Exeter

It was the middle of November. Stewart looked out of his study window, marvelling at the changes in the countryside; the leaves were turning from green to a multitude of browns, yellows and reds. Each season had its beauty, and this one was magnificent at the moment. He could see in the distance that the roses had been cut back to allow for new growth in the spring, when the land would begin its rebirth. He thought of Maggie and their child which was due to be born in May, God willing. The trees would be in full blossom by then, and the land would have awoken from its hibernation, just as their child would. But when he thought of the child and what she would go through to bring it to life, it terrified him. His grandmother had died to give life to his mother, and he could not imagine his life without Maggie now. She was the constant in his world; when everything else was in turmoil around him, she was the base to come home to, knowing that the universe would right itself again. He shook himself. Putting his quill down, he got up and came to stand by the window.

Standing there, Stewart recalled the events that had taken place a month ago. It had taken some explanation on Alexander's part when he had delivered Lady Catherine back to Bath. Alex had told him that her mother had nearly collapsed and been helped to her room. The Father was angry but outwardly calm, and after seeing his daughter to her room, he had summoned their physician, then taken Alexander into his study. It was a good hour later, and after much interrogation, when the physician entered the room and nodded to her father. Alexander had breathed easier then and relaxed, she had been unharmed. There followed more questions; her father wanted names, but Alex had told him that they did not know the name of the man responsible. It was just by chance that his cousin Stewart had been travelling to Exeter to meet a friend when he had encounter Lady Catherine on the stage coach, and thought it rather odd for a lady of her standing in society to be un-chaperoned, on a public coach, heading to Exeter with no place to stay when she arrived there. This was duly noted by her father, and after a few more enquiries, Alexander had been offered accommodation for the night, he then returned home late the following afternoon.

Stewart closed his eyes as he stood there; he had had no word from anyone since then, and he assumed that his story had been believed. But the family would not stop there; they wanted Northcott's name at any cost.

'Penny for them,' Margaret's voice split the silence.

Stewart blinked. Coming back to the present, he turned to see Margaret standing just behind him. She placed her hands inside his jacket and around his back, pulling him close.

Stewart held her tightly, feeling her warmth.

'Daydreaming?' she questioned, talking into his shirt. 'You should be working. Alexander will want all of those papers signed by tomorrow.'

Stewart smiled into her hair, then pulled her away to look at her.

'Are you well now?' he asked.

Margaret nodded her head and smiled. 'Yes, I am fine now. Everything seems to have settled, and I ate a small breakfast this morning *and* managed to keep everything.' She eyed him curiously.

'Your mother tells me this is perfectly normal, that she was the same when she carried you, so there really is nothing to worry about.' Margaret poked him gently in the stomach.

'You look much worse that I do,' she added with humour in her voice.

'I know,' he replied, 'but it is not only you that I have to worry about.' He pulled her to a chair and sat her on his knees. 'I have been expecting some sort of repercussion from the events that took place in Exeter. I have not fooled myself by this peace that has pervaded since Alexander returned. They want a name, and they will not rest till they get one.' He paused here to move Margaret into a more comfortable position, then sat back into the chair.

'Surely, it is for the girl to disclose the name of the man that beguiled her to elope with him,' answered Margaret.

'That young lady would not give up his name even if they held her over hot coals. She is stubborn, high handed and very disagreeable.' Saying this, he made a noise in his throat close to contempt.

'What do you think they will do then?' questioned Margaret.

Stewart eyed her, then pulled her back to rest on his chest. Stroking her hair he continued.

'I have been expecting to be called before a magistrate to give account of the happenings on that evening.' Stewart picked up her hands and stroked them, as he sat there listening to the fire's crackle behind them, when a small gust of wind found its way down the chimney into the room, causing the flames to leap.

Margaret sat upright. 'But why would they do that, you saved their daughter from this man.'

'Maggie,' Stewart interrupted, 'they want justice, they are not going to sit back and accept this violation of their family. God, if anyone did that to our daughter, he would not live to see the sun rise again.'

Maggie turned to look at him smiling. 'Oh, so you have decided that it is a daughter?' She took his hand and placed it over her stomach.

Stewart looked at her and laughed softly. 'Daughter, son, I really do not care, just as long as you and the child are safe. Now, Margaret Hamilton, I must get back to my work, go and busy yourself, and I will come find you again for lunch.' He lifted her to her feet and kissed her gently. 'Go find my mother if you want, you two are as thick as two thieves these days.'

101

Margaret kissed him back, smiled and left.

***

It was a week later when the summons came. Stewart was to report to the Assizes in Exeter on 5th December to give evidence at the inquest regarding the abduction of one said Lady Catherine. That was two weeks away. Stewart read the letter three times before he laid it on his desk. His first thoughts were to send word to his friend James Fairweather, and then to go and seek out his cousin Alexander, but his primary task was to speak with Mortimore, his lawyer, and that meant a trip to Exeter.

He sat down and looked around the room. If things went wrong, he was cruelly aware that he could lose all of this, all that he held dear and all he had fought so hard to keep. Why? He knew the answer: because of one man and his greed.

Stewart picked up his quill and wrote a small note to Fairweather to arrange a meeting with himself and Alexander in Exeter. The letter gave nothing away of the reason, just three friends meeting; he would time it so that it would be on the same day that he would arrange to meet with his lawyer Mortimore. That way suspicion would not arise, he hoped. If he put one foot wrong, he knew also that he too would be held to account. He closed the letter, addressed it, then sealed it with wax. Stewart then wrote another letter to his lawyer, requesting a meeting with him regarding family business. Sealing this also, he stood up. He must find his mother and Margaret, then go and see his cousin, but first he placed the summons into the draw of his desk; he would show them both when he returned.

As he passed the hall table, he placed the letters into the dish. Stewart paused to breathe deeply; it would be taken to Mere today along with his mother's, then turning he made his way to the drawing room.

When he entered, he saw that his mother was sitting at her bureau writing, while Margaret was on the window seat, embroidering what looked like a small cot sheet. He swallowed deeply and thought, *Oh God I have so much to lose.* Kissing his mother on the cheek, he then went to sit next to Margaret.

Margaret looked up and smiled warmly at him. Her hand with the needle poised in mid-air, ready to make another intricate stitch into the cot sheet, where she was embroidering a vine with small yellow flowers along the edge.

Stewart stroked his fingers along the stitches so tiny and yet so beautifully done. If anyone had told him six months past that his heart would fill with joy to see his wife embroidering their unborn child's cot sheet, he would have laughed openly in their face. He roused himself, then bent and kissed her gently on the lips.

'I must go and find Alexander; there are some bills that need attention. Do not wait for me for lunch, I will lunch with him.' Looking deeply into her eyes, he squeezed her fingers with one hand and stroked her cheek with the other.

'Did I ever tell you, Margaret Hamilton, you are one very beautiful woman?'

His mother coughed from behind him.

'Stewart, there are three of us in this room, and one of them is your mother. I should not be hearing this.'

There was laughter in her voice, and Stewart knew she was jesting. He smiled, stood up and went to stand by her. Kissing her cheek, he added. 'And so are you.'

He could hear Maggie's laughter as he left the room.

***

He found Alexander on the road half way between the estate office and the house. It was cold; in fact, the air was freezing and white plumes of condensation could be seen coming from both horses and men alike. An eerie mist seemed to be swirling about them, causing everything it touched to become damp and stiff. Stewart pulled up the collar of his cloak and pushed his hat further onto his head.

'I was on my way to see you,' called Alexander as he pulled up his horse. 'I have received a summons to give evidence at an inquest for the Lady Catherine on the 5th of December,' he added

'So have I,' replied Stewart. 'I was on my way to you for the same reason, but I think it is best we go back to the estate office to discuss this, where we will not be interrupted.' Stewart nodded his head. 'I have not told Margaret or my mother as yet. I wanted to wait till we had agreed a plan of action first.'

Alexander nodded back. 'Let us go back there then. I left the fire burning, so it will be warm at least.'

'You are most considerate, Alex,' Stewart replied eyeing his cousin. 'It is a trifle cold out here.'

Neither man said another word until they were inside the office.

'I did not realise that they would call you too,' said Stewart distractedly as he watch Alexander put more wood to the fire. Then Stewart nodded his head in affirmation. 'But naturally they would, it was you who delivered her back to her family, it was you who told her father exactly what had taken place in Exeter.' He paused. 'They need my side of the story, if only to check what you had told them was the truth.'

Stewart removed his gloves and put his hands out to the fire for warmth.

'Alex, you must tell me exactly what transpired when you took her back, my testimony must not veer from your statement at all.' He sat back rubbing his hand over his chin thinking.

'You know,' he paused slightly, 'I would not doubt for one moment that she would use all her feminine guile and say it was I who led her to Exeter. That I was her assignation.' Stewart stood up and paced the room. 'I have to speak with Fairweather; he is my only defence here.'

Alexander's face was completely blank. 'Dear God, Stewart, I had not even given a thought about that, but she would not, she could not...' His voice trailed away.

Stewart looked at him and raised his eye brows. 'Oh could she not? I believe that she is capable of anything, after what she tried to do.'

'Where does Fairweather live?' questioned Alexander. 'We should go straight to his home, not wait for the letter to reach him.'

Stewart was nodding, his brain was ticking over now like cogs on a wheel.

'He lives in Salisbury; his mother owned a house there which he inherited. It is where he stays when not in London,' Stewart responded, all the while his mind was taking stock of the situation, and how best to tackle the circumstances in which he now found himself, then rapidly everything fell into place.

'What a fool I have been, Alex,' he walked to the fire then turned round to face his cousin. 'I have been trying to think of a way not to reveal a name, when in retrospect, and in the eyes of her family, it *could* have been I who was the perpetrator in this travesty.' Stewart ran his hands through his hair, and down his face.

'By my letting you take her home to her family, it could be seen…' His voice trailed away.

'Dear God, Alex, do you not see what has happened!' The realisation was plain to see on Stewart's face as he paced the room now; fine beads of sweat had appeared on his brow, as he turned to face his cousin.

'It was I in that coach with her that day; she questioned me regarding the hostel, the food. This could all have been perceived as a code by those that occupied that coach then. If they locate those occupants, which I am sure that they have, I will then be served up as a lamb to the slaughter.'

All this while, Alexander had been staring at his cousin in disbelief.

'God, how could I have been so stupid, Alex?' Stewart threw up his hands.

'Look at me. I am tall, dark, as for those people that dined there that evening, who just caught a glimpse of a man; who is to say that it was not I that sat with her then?'

'Fairweather…' came Alexander's stunned reply.

Stewart seated himself and put his head in his hands.

'Northcott has had a hand in this. I will wager he has reached the Lady Catherine through his sister, who might I add, has had her designs on Wheatley destroyed, again by my own hand. So not only does the brother want vengeance, so does the sister, one alone is enough but combined they are a formidable force.'

By this time, Alexander had paled and become decidedly agitated.

'Just how are you going to prove your innocence in all this, with so many people plotting against you?' He stopped and stared hard at his cousin.

'Stewart, you have to leave the country, take Margaret with you.'

'Are you mad, Alex!' Steward rounded on him. 'And let the wrath of God come down on my mother and her home? By running away I just proclaim my guilt to everyone. No, I have to find both Fairweather and Wheatley, then see my lawyer.'

Stewart rubbed his forehead, pinching his nose hard to clear his mind. Then his eyes opened wide as he turned to Alexander, shaking his head in disbelief.

'She even slept in my room that night, did she not?' With that, Stewart walked out into the cold.

***

It was not until the following evening that they reached Salisbury. Both Stewart and Alexander had returned to the Willows the previous day to inform Stewart's mother and Margaret of their intention to travel to Salisbury, on the pretext of business. His mother had taken one look at Stewart to know that something was amiss. She said nothing until after dinner in the evening when she found him in the study and confronted him. As he retold the story, he saw his mother notably pale. She waited till he had finished, then kissed him on the cheek, held his hands in hers and whispered the words, 'God go with you.'

He had told Margaret that there had been a problem with one of the bills which had not been paid; they had to go into Salisbury to see the gentleman in question and get some answers, as to write would be a waste of time. Margaret had nodded to him; she knew that he was anxious about something, but was content with the answer he gave her.

They rode out in the cold light of daybreak the following morning for Salisbury.

***

As they came into the town, they were tired and horse sore. They had made only one stop at The Green Dragon in Barford St Martin, where they ate, and fed and rested the horses for a while.

'Where shall we room?' questioned Alexander.

Stewart coughed and shook his head to clear his thoughts. His voice rasped as he spoke.

'There is a coaching inn on the corner of New Street and High Street called "The Sun and Lamb". Margaret and I stayed there on our return from Lymington. It is a safe place to rest for the night.'

Alexander nodded.

'We must rise early and hope that we find Fairweather at home.' He paused. 'If he is in London… Well, we will resolve that problem when we come to it,' Stewart finished.

***

James Fairweather's house was situated at the eastern end of Salisbury. It was a large red brick building consisting of two upper floors and what looked like a semi-basement, presumably where the kitchens were, thought Alexander as he surveyed the building.

Stewart hit the knocker against the door with a sharp rap that resounded in the air around them. It was opened by a tall man in complete livery, who looked down his nose at them and informed them that tradesmen should use the back door.

Stewart drew himself up to his full height and took off his hat. Holding it across his chest, he nodded slightly.

'Pray forgive me, but my name is Stewart Charles Hamilton of the Willows in Mere. I seek your master James Fairweather on urgent business.' The look he gave was enough to make the man submit and bow deferentially back.

'Sir, my master will be back around 10 o'clock, having stayed the night with some friends in the town,' he replied.

'Would sirs like to wait in the drawing room?' He opened the door wide and waved his hand for them to pass, leading them to the left-hand side of the hallway into a large room very comfortably furnished, with a wall at the far end covered in books from ceiling to floor.

'Would sirs like some refreshment?' he asked before leaving them.

'That would be most kind of you, and very welcome.' Stewart smiled and inclined his head.

Alexander looked around him and whistled. 'Dear God, how much is this man's estate worth?'

'A great deal more than mine,' he replied eyeing his cousin. 'Sit down, Alex, and let me do the talking.'

Alexander was about to reply when Stewart added, 'Yes?' in a tone that brooked no argument.

Some minutes later, two servants brought in trays of cold meat's bread and pastries, together with a decanter of Port and two glasses.

When they left, Stewart poured two glasses, handing one to his cousin and drinking the other down in one swallow. Alexander looked at Stewart as he poured a second one.

'Should you not remain sober for when he returns?' It was said in jest but there was an element of reprimand in his tone.

'Alexander, it is not you that will be transported or your neck that will end up in the noose.'

Alexander watched his cousin consume another glass. 'No, cousin, but as your accomplice, I will be sentenced to the same fate, no?' he replied.

Stewart sank down heavily into a chair.

'My apologies, Alex, I am not thinking logically at the present time. It is not only I that will suffer. Both my mother and Maggie will feel their wrath.'

'Do they know?' questioned Alexander.

But before Stewart could answer, James Fairweather entered the room.

'Good day to you, gentlemen! What is amiss?' Fairweather called as he shut the door and came to stand in front of them, looking from one to the other.

'Good God!' he added. 'You look as though you have just been sentenced—' his speech was cut short by Stewart.

'You do not know just how true those words could be,' Stewart replied.

James Fairweather took himself a glass from the side, filled it with whisky and poured equal amounts into both Stewart and Alexander's glasses. Then raised his own glass in acknowledgement.

'Go on, tell me about it.' With that he seated himself and waited for Stewart to impart his story.

It was some half an hour later before Stewart finally finished his account. No one spoke for some moments, then Fairweather stood up and pulled the bell pull. Stewart and Alexander looked sideways at one another.

When the servant entered, Fairweather gave his orders in a brisk military manner. They were to prepare the coach immediately for travel to Frome in Somerset. A person was also to be despatched to his lawyer Edward Bearcroft in the Inner Temple London. He was to return with him post haste.

'But, James,' Stewart offered, 'I have a lawyer in Exeter.'

'Not like mine,' was his response.

Stewart's head was spinning, apart from the fact that he had had very little sleep or food for the past twenty-four hours, and having consumed two glasses of Port and one of whisky in the last half an hour, he wondered did James Fairweather know something he did not.

Fairweather looked at him. 'Stewart, you are dealing with people far beyond the reach or capability of your lawyer in Exeter, who at best deals with family law and disputes over land and money. Mine on the other hand has appeared at the high court for several major trials. You are dealing with the aristocracy, Stewart. Their lawyers will deride yours before he can even utter a sentence.'

Stewart nodded and rubbed his eyes with the heels of his hands. They felt at that moment as though all the dirt from the road were swimming in them.

'James, I do not know how to thank you,' replied Stewart humbly.

'Hamilton, how many times at Winchester did you defend me, take a beating for me? Now I can repay you and right an injustice at the same time,' Fairweather answered.

Alexander, all this while, had been listening intently to this debate. He had been at Winchester with these young men, albeit a year above, but could he have been so blind as not to see what was happening around him each day. He shook his head, and thought, evidently, he had. He viewed his cousin with different eyes from that moment.

Chapter Twelve
To Speak the Truth

Stewart sat in the quiet of Wheatley's Study, and as he looked out onto the dark grey landscape, he wondered just how it had come to this? In truth he knew, without asking himself. He had not been thinking straight; if he had, then he would have escorted the Lady Catherine back to her parents in Bath and not his cousin Alexander. His mind had been on other things at that time, as he had just learned that he was to be a father for the first time, and that Margaret had been extremely unwell as a result of her condition. The inquest was scheduled for the day after tomorrow, but right now all he could think about was his wife and mother back in Wiltshire. His mother knew all the circumstances, but Maggie had been told only that he had been called to give his account of what had happened.

He got up and walked to the window. The countryside looked devoid of all colour, as though it had taken up the grey hue from the clouds that raced across the sky. Stewart thought that it resembled how he was feeling at the moment. It was bitterly cold, and he hoped that it would not snow before he could get back to the Willows.

Contemplating all the events that had taken place in the last two weeks, he realised that he had given Northcott all the information he had needed to set in motion his plan. Stewart clenched his fists in anger at his own stupidity. If he had taken her back and explained, he would not have found himself in the nightmare that he now did. All the while he had waited for the summons to the inquest, Northcott had carefully put his plans into motion. It never once occurred to him that he was now the suspect.

Fairweather had taken over everything. His Lawyer Edward Bearcroft had come directly to Wheatley's home, and it had been there that he had taken control of the situation. Edward Bearcroft was a slight man of average build, but his face looked to hold a wealth of knowledge, though quietly spoken, he was a man that exuded intelligence. As he stood bewigged before them now, Stewart thought him more than good he was remarkable. He had set his people at once to gather every piece of information that was available. With great diligence he had sought out and found all of the occupants of the coach that night, trying to ascertain exactly what their impression had been when they overheard the conversation between the Lady Catherine and Stewart. There had been two journeys, and he had also managed to contact those that had occupied the return coach to Mere.

Even to those people that were in the Angel when they arrived. Fairweather had given his own account of the proceedings also, stating that he had gone there to find Stewart to discuss their friend Wheatley's predicament, and if anything could be done to prevent a tragedy similar to the one, they now found themselves in. Stewart had imparted to Fairweather his tale of the woman on the stagecoach, who was by then sitting by a window in the eating area, and things had developed from there.

The information that Bearcroft had acquired regarding Northcott was astonishing. For the past two years, Northcott had gambled a small fortune away in the clubs of London. There were many IOUs out bearing his name, and it was reported that he had sold one London house to help pay for his debts. He was still a wealthy man, but if he carried on in this vain, in a few years he would soon lose everything. Northcott's sister he now understood had been a party to this whole charade; if she had secured Wheatley, then between them they would have amassed a huge fortune.

No names were to be mentioned at the inquest though. It could not be proven without a doubt that it was Northcott in the room with Lady Catherine that evening. The owner of The Mermaid Inn in Exeter did not remember seeing any person matching Northcott's description that night. They could not use his sister Alison either as this would implicate Wheatley. The argument would be totally on disproving the evidence given by Lady Catherine, and other testimonies, but mostly it would come from Fairweather's proof that Stewart was with him, and that they had seen this travesty play out before their eyes. The only honourable thing they could have done was to try and stop it, before lives were ruined.

Stewart sighed and placed his head in his hands. He felt like he had aged overnight. He was so deep in thought he did not hear Fairweather come up behind him and place a hand on his shoulder. Stewart jumped and turned quickly.

'God, Fairweather, do you want to stop my heart!' Stewart eyed his friend and shook his head, then turned and walked away from the window to sit in one of the chairs by the fire. James Fairweather said nothing but came and sat in the chair opposite him.

'Stewart, I have never seen you like this,' He began. 'You never gave up on anything or anybody. You would fight others battles with impunity; you cannot give in now.'

Stewart looked up and eyed his friend. 'Oh I am not giving up, it is just I have so much to lose now, not just materially, but personally.' He paused. 'I could be tried, and if I am found guilty, I could be transported, no?' Stewart raised his hand to stop his friends reply. 'At the very worse, I could be hanged. People have been for a much lesser crime than this, stealing a loaf of bread comes to mind.' Stewart breathed deeply. 'If he cannot induce The Lady Catherine to tell the truth, then it rests solely on mine and your testimony. Am I right?'

Fairweather nodded.

'There are many out there, who would revel in my disgrace.' He paused again to look at his friend, raising his brows and nodding. Fairweather nodded back and Stewart continued.

'Those whom I have thwarted in their attempts to ruin, disgrace and bully others. I have made many enemies in my life in the defence of others less capable than myself to fight back. They will see this as their reckoning, will they not?' Stewart smiled. 'Your lawyer Bearcroft has one of the sharpest analytical minds that I have ever seen, and I understand that I would not stand a chance in hell without him. As you say, he can turn an argument on its head and reverse it. I have seen what he is capable of by what he has found out about Northcott's demise.' He paused again to get up and walk about the room, picking up objects distractedly and putting them down again as he passed.

'But the law should be the truth,' exclaimed Fairweather

Stewart shook his head. 'James, the truth is as the person who sees it.'

The room went quiet, each man was within his own thoughts till Stewart spoke again.

'What I am trying to say, James, is that I do not hold you responsible at all if the outcome is not the one we intended.'

James Fairweather said nothing. He rose out of the chair, coming to stand before Stewart and raised his hand out to him, which Stewart took. Both friends looked into each another's eyes then Fairweather pulled him into to him and slapped his back in friendship and recognition of what Stewart had done for him in the past.

'You will be vindicated, Stewart, I know that.'

***

As Alexander stood looking at his aunt in the drawing room of the Willows, he noticed for the first time the streaks of grey in her hair that had appeared just around her temples. She looked tired and her eyes had a blue tinge all around them. Walking towards her, he pulled her into his arms and held her there.

'Aunt, I know all will be well, you have to believe me.' He pulled her away and held her by the shoulders. 'I have to go back to Exeter today as the inquest is tomorrow, and, I must leave now if I am to make Wheatley's house by nightfall.'

Elizabeth cupped her hands around his face and looked intently up into his eyes.

'We will take my coach, and I will hear no argument on that.' Elizabeth saw that he was about to protest. 'When this ordeal is over, we can bring him home.'

Alexander eyed his aunt cautiously. 'We?' he questioned.

'I am coming with you, and I will hear not another word on the subject. I intend to bring my son back with me, do you understand, Alex?' Alexander nodded.

'I have told Margaret that I intend to see my lawyer Mortimore in Exeter on personal business, and when the inquest is finished, I can then travel back with both of you,' she finished, with the accent on *both*. 'I will stay overnight at The Mermaid Inn, as I do not want my presence known to Stewart at this time. My coachmen Carter and Fulton will accompany us.' Her words held such finality, Alexander did not try and dissuade her.

'Is Margaret well?' he asked.

'She is resting at present. Since Stewart left, she has been a trifle unwell, complaining of pain in the lower part of her back. So I have made her stay in her room, and lay on her bed for as much as she can. I will not allow her to use the stairs, so she takes her meals there. At all costs my grandchild will not be a casualty in this.'

'She is worried, Aunt, and I believe she knows more than we think. Before she married Stewart, she had to live by her wits and awareness of the people around her. Whatever Stewart has told her, she will have deduced for herself exactly what is about to happen at that inquest,' replied Alexander

Elizabeth nodded in agreement.

'But by not voicing this, she can hold some kind of agreement with herself that all will be well,' Elizabeth replied as she raised her brows at her nephew and nodded.

'May I see her, Aunt?' enquired Alexander.

'Of course you can, Alex, you do not need my permission to speak with her.' Elizabeth waved her hand in dismissal.

As he left, she sat down on her seat, as though her legs had suddenly disappeared. She looked around her, listening to voices and memories, hearing Stewart's laughter as he would run from one end of the room to the other, while his governess chased him. All the echoes of the past were compounded by the silence that now pervaded the room. She sent up a silent prayer for her son's safe return.

As he mounted the stairs, he thought he had never seen his aunt so totally in control. However, on reflection, his aunt was a strong woman, had had to be for many years, he suspected, that of the circumstances she found herself in now, she had coped with either equal or worse in her lifetime.

Alexander knocked at Margaret's door before he entered, and as he came into the room, he saw Margaret sitting with her feet on a stool by the window, her embroidery abandoned on her lap as she looked out onto the garden. There was a fire burning heartily in the hearth and everything was at hand, her book, some savouries and mint tea. There was even a bell so that she would not need to use the pull by the mantle.

'It seems that my aunt has thought of everything,' Alexander nodded to the table beside her. 'I hear you are banned from using the stairs.' His voice held laughter but his eyes were serious.

Margaret turned, smiled and held out her hand in greeting.

'I am to be coddled like an egg in the nest,' she laughed. 'How are you, Alex, and how is Stewart?' Although her words were light hearted, there was an underlying urgency within them.

'We are fine, and we are totally prepared for tomorrow, and I am to be conveyed back in my aunt's coach, as she has some business in Exeter with her lawyer Mortimore. Of which I am truly grateful, may I add, those stagecoaches are fine, but they do not have the comfort of hers.' He sat down beside her, smiling.

Margaret smiled back. Then leaning forward, she placed something into the palm of his hand. Alexander stared at it, and then at Margaret.

'Tell him that this symbolises our eternity, and I will expect him to bring it back with him when he comes. Our lives are not over yet.'

Alexander could not speak, as he turned the ring over and over in the palm of his hand.

'He will return, you know,' he said in earnest. 'Of that I am in no doubt at all.'

'Oh I know, just tell him I am taking care of the other half of our bond.' She rested her hand lightly on her stomach and stroked gently. 'Tell him I love him very much, please.'

***

He had left his aunt, her maid, and coachmen at the Mermaid Inn, after dining with them and seeing his aunt and her maid safely to their rooms. He then took one of the horses and made his way out to Wheatley's estate.

By the time he reached there, it was late evening, and found everyone in deep conversation in the library. As he entered, all heads swung round in unison to look at him.

'Good evening, gentleman, sorry I am slightly late, but I had some other business to attend to, my apologies to you.' He bowed slightly coming into the room and seating himself next to Stewart.

Bearcroft was the first to speak again.

'I have found out today that the Lady Catherine will have to give evidence at the inquest tomorrow. If she refuses to attend, then there will be no case to answer to.' He paused here to look around at his audience. 'They need her to state first hand exactly what transpired that night, as well as those that were witness to part of some of it.' He coughed here. 'It is the testimony of those others that I mean to disprove. Someone had seen you, Hamilton, when you entered the dining area, seating yourself next to Fairweather; this piece of information came to light yesterday. I have spoken to the person and he is willing to attest under oath that it was not you, Hamilton, that sat with the Lady Catherine. He states that he saw you and Fairweather leave and sit in the taproom. From there it is both yours and Fairweather's statements that the other council will have to disprove.' He shuffled his papers before he continued.

'I have called all those who were in the coach, both on the inward and outward journeys, also those who were present at the Angel Inn where you alighted with the Lady Catherine. From what they have told me, you made no means to conceal any of your movements at that time. You did it in open view of all present.'

It was at this juncture in the speech that Stewart looked at his cousin Alexander and gave a knowing nod.

Bearcroft then rose, nodding to all present. 'I will take my leave of you now, gentlemen, and go to my bed, which I hope you will all do likewise. We have a long day tomorrow.' He looked towards Stewart. 'You and I will go over the procedures tomorrow at breakfast.' With that he left the room.

Stewart breathed deeply and closed his eyes. 'Dear Lord, do not let evil prevail tomorrow.' Saying this, he raised his eyes upwards.

'Amen to that,' responded Fairweather. Standing up, he shook Stewart's hand. 'Till tomorrow, my friend.'

Wheatley did the same and left with him.

The two cousins sat quietly together, each deep in his own thoughts. Then Alexander reached into his pocket and placed the ring into Stewart's hand.

Stewart looked from his hand to his cousin with total confusion showing on his face.

'I have a message from your wife,' said Alexander.

Stewart nodded.

'She said,' began Alexander, 'Tell him that this symbolises our eternity, and I will expect him to bring it back with him when he comes. Our lives are not over yet, and I am taking care of the other half of our bond. Tell him I love him very much.'

The expression on Stewart's face was unreadable. He took the ring, kissed it, and then placing it onto his little finger, he stood up, nodded to Alexander and left the room.

Chapter Thirteen
The Inquest

The courthouse was packed from wall to wall, but as Stewart looked around, he saw many of the men that were lining the walls at the back were his tenants from the Willows. Stewart swallowed hard.

'Did you think they would not come and support you, Stewart,' answered Alexander.

Stewart turned and inclined his head to them; in turn they took off their hats and nodded back. He knew he was to give evidence first, then to be called back again if further questions were to be answered. His eyes searched the room looking for anyone that could be associated in some way with Northcott, but there was none. The Lady Catherine was seated just to his left on a raised platform with her father. She was very pale, and sat as rigid as a piece of wood.

The Magistrate beat his gavel three times to bring order to the proceedings, then as everything quietened, he went on to state the reason for the calling of the inquest, naming all parties to be summoned.

Stewart took his place to give evidence, which was directly facing The Lady Catherine and her father. Then as he relayed all that had happened that night, he looked directly at the magistrate and her, with a voice that was unwavering and precise in all detail. When he had finished, Sir Richard Sutton lawyer for The Lady Catherine stood up and paced before him. Though portly in appearance, the man held himself as though he were Royalty. He paced the room now, surveying his audience for some moments, then turned his eyes to Stewart and spoke.

'Can you tell us just why you were in Exeter that evening, sir?'

'I went to meet with James Fairweather a friend I have known since Winchester, sir. On the following day, we were to go to the estate of George Wheatley of Frome—also a friend from Winchester.'

'And you just happened to meet with The Lady Catherine on the coach that you travelled to Exeter on?' he questioned.

'Sir, I did not meet with the Lady Catherine at all. Whilst on our journey, she questioned me regarding the inn that we were to stop at, as to whether it was a suitable establishment for a young lady as herself to be staying the night,' replied Stewart.

'So, she spoke to you first?' his question held a note of sarcasm.

'Sir, as I told you, she posed a question to me. Until that time my thoughts had been elsewhere; in truth, I had not even noticed The Lady Catherine.' Stewart was interrupted here.

'Oh come now, Mr Hamilton, you would have us believe that a lady of her standing, travelling on a public coach would not have drawn your interest!' he countered.

'Sir, not until she spoke to me, no. As I said, my thoughts were elsewhere at that time. It was only after she spoke that I took notice of her appearance, and my first thoughts were, why a lady of her standing and rank should be travelling alone on a public stagecoach without a chaperone,' responded Stewart.

'Did you not think that the others on the coach that evening would have thought the same?' he questioned again.

'In truth, sir, I do not know as I neither knew them nor spoke with them,' came Stewart's curt reply.

'Let us move further along, sir, what happened when you reached the Mermaid Inn? You spoke to her again I believe.' The intonation in his words made Stewart sit up straight. He knew too well what he was implying here.

'I did, sir, we were awaiting our bags to be unloaded from the coach. I was under the impression that a lady like herself would have more than just a carpet bag with her. To my astonishment, she had no more than that. It was that piece of information that set bells ringing in my head, that all was not right.'

Stewart's voice had risen, biting the insides of his mouth to try and get his saliva flowing he continued.

'Why would any young lady of breeding be alone on a coach, going to an inn they knew nothing about, or, may I say, had no knowledge of at all, without a chaperone,' retorted Stewart.

Sir Richard Sutton paced the room turning to Stewart, then the magistrate.

'Quite, my point exactly,' he offered.

It was at this point his own lawyer Bearcroft stood up, and bowed to the magistrate.

'If I may, sir?' he gestured as he looked at the magistrate.

The magistrate closed his eyes and nodded, resting his arms on the desk.

'Please continue.'

Bearcroft turned and looked Stewart in the eyes.

'Did you carry Lady Catherine's baggage into the inn? He paused for Stewart to reply.

'No, sir, she informed me that the baggage boy would carry out this service,' he answered

'And did you see the Lady Catherine when you received the key to your own room?' He paused once more.

'No, sir,' came Stewart's short reply.

'And did you proceed straight to your room from there?' Bearcroft nodded to his associate Sutton, as he saw that he was about to protest.

'I have this one more question, if you please.' Sutton inclined his head begrudgingly.

Bearcroft looked at Stewart. 'If you can answer please, sir.'

Stewart swallowed, composed himself and then answered.

'I headed straight to the dining area where I found my friend Fairweather seated enjoying his meal, so I joined him.'

'Thank you,' replied Bearcroft, bowing slightly both to the magistrate and Sutton.

Sutton stood up, pacing a little, rubbing his chin with the fingers of his right hand.

'Let us proceed, what happened then?' he queried.

'I ordered myself a meal, and while I waited for this, Fairweather and I chatted amiably, till I saw The Lady Catherine enter the dining area, taking a seat by the window. My friend looked at her and asked me who she was, it was then that I informed him what had taken place on the coach to Exeter,' finished Stewart.

'Ah, so by this time your friend was also aware of the Lady Catherine,' he replied cynically.

'As he had just asked about the Lady, yes, that is correct,' replied Stewart curtly.

'So he too was aware of the Lady's demise?' Sutton questioned again.

'Yes, I have just told this to you,' responded Stewart impatiently.

'Let us continue.'

Stewart looked at the magistrate as though to ask why, as he had already disclosed his account of the evening in the beginning.

The magistrate who was looking slightly annoyed just closed his eyes and nodded in Stewart's direction for things to continue.

'As I had my back to the door, my friend Fairweather saw the man come into the room. He made his way to sit opposite the Lady Catherine,' continued Stewart.

'Oh, so you observed this man and his general appearance?' queried Sutton

'No, sir, I did not. The lighting in the dining area was dim, I could only see the gentleman's profile,' responded Stewart

'But your friend was facing him when he entered the room, no?' he argued.

'My friend saw only a tall dark-haired man,' snapped Stewart.

At this point, Bearcroft stood up.

'I really must protest, sir, you are treating these proceedings as though my client were on trial!' His voice was rising as he spoke. 'I understood that this was an inquest, to establish what transpired that night.'

The magistrate nodded in acquiescence. 'Maybe we should hear The Lady Catherine's account of what happened before we proceed.'

Stewart saw the young woman pale significantly, and her eyes fluttered as though she were about to drop to the floor. He eyed his council, and then the Lady Catherine.

'If I may suggest, sir,' Bearcroft addressed the magistrate, 'should not that part of the proceedings be held in private?'

The magistrate nodded slowly. 'We will go to my chambers, but after lunch.'

Stewart's head was buzzing, he saw no one as he left the court, and his mind was a jumble of words and thoughts, which was maybe a good thing, as then he did not see his mother seated at the very back, swathed in a dark cloak.

***

Stewart ate very little as they sat in the dining room of the Mermaid Inn. Bearcroft was examining his papers and reshuffling them into the order that the proceedings would now take, as Stewart looked around him, but without seeing. The smell from the food was making him nauseous, to say the least. Though the weather outside was very cold, icy even, the air within was suffocating, and he found he was having trouble breathing. He had to get out of here quick. As he rose, Bearcroft held his arm.

'Hamilton, you will say nothing during this part of the proceedings. Do I make myself clear?' His words were stern and would counter no intervention while The Lady Catherine gave evidence.

Stewart nodded in agreement.

'When I counter question, I will ask her to think very carefully before she answers me. If she can read me, which I am sure she can, she will know that I have something that will put her testimony into disrepute.'

Stewart nodded again.

'If you will excuse me, sir, I think I am about to vomit.' With that he ran towards the door, making it out of the back door just in time.

Stewart breathed deeply through his nose, and then sank onto a barrel nearby. The world was spinning and his hands and forehead were clammy with sweat. He lowered his head to his knees and waited for the sensation to pass. At that moment, a dark skirt came into view and he felt a cool hand at the back of his neck. He lifted his head to the side just a fraction, then sat up quickly as he recognised the form that was standing beside him was his mother.

She held out a mug of water, then placed her other hand on his brow.

'Did you think I would leave you here to face this on your own, Stewart? You are my child, all I have left, and I love you with a passion that knows no words.' Elizabeth pulled his head towards her and stoked his back.

Stewart stood up, held his mother, then kissed her on the cheek.

'I must go back,' he nodded to her. 'Let us hope that she will see reason and tell the truth, so that we can end this farce.' He tucked his mother's arm through his and went back into the inn.

***

The magistrate's room was panelled in heavy oak, with numerous shelves sinking under the weight of law tomes. It smelt of dust and wood, and his desk was covered in an assortment of books and letters, all of which had been either dog-eared or marked in some way. The magistrate pulled out two chairs for both the Lady Catherine and her father, and then went to sit in his own. Eyeing everyone, he shook his head and tapped his quill lightly onto the ink well before he spoke.

'I am hoping that this can be resolved without a trial.' His eyes moved round the room looking at all present.

'Proceedings of this nature are always very distressing and very unpleasant for all parties concerned.' Here, he sucked his teeth, drew a deep breath, then sat back in his chair, folding his hands across his stomach, watching.

Sitting up sharply, he addressed The Lady Catherine.

'Right, My Lady, you will state your name, and the reason you have been called to this inquest.'

By this time, eyes were darting in all directions. Both lawyers looked at one another, then at the magistrate.

The magistrate sat there, watching their reaction.

'I have dealt with many inquests in my time of office here, but none so farcical as this one,' he paused for effect. 'This ends now, do I make myself clear?'

Stewart looked towards the Lady Catherine and knew that if she had not been seated, she would have dropped like a stone.

'Maybe we can get you some water, Lady Catherine,' offered the magistrate as he nodded to his clerk to fetch some.

Stewart stood with his hands clasped behind his back, feeling detached like a spectator that was hovering above rather than a participant. He carefully looked at each one present, trying hard to establish exactly what had transpired while he was at lunch. It occurred to him that either the magistrate had heard something or knew something that the rest of the assembled group did not.

The clerk appeared with a jug and a glass which he offered to the Lady Catherine. She sipped it gently, then passing it to her father, she spoke for the first time.

'It is true, I encountered this gentleman on the coach bound for Exeter,' here she paused to look at her father and then at Stewart, 'but, he is not the gentleman that I had agreed to meet there.' There were sharp intakes of breath from everyone, including her father.

'This man is innocent, the only thing he is guilty of is helping me at a time when I did not want to be helped.' She paused again, trying to gain composure.

'I met the other gentleman at a soirée whilst I was staying with my aunt in London in the summer.' She paused again, picking violently at the lace of her dress, then looked at her father.

'I am so very sorry, Papa, that I have brought our family to this demise, I am a foolish young girl who had her head turned by someone who had cunning and guile enough to persuade her to elope with him.'

'I will have his name!!!' shouted her father. His voice was so powerful it reverberated around the room, moving the air quickly, pushing it with pressure into the ears, giving one the feeling that they were submerged in water. Everything went quiet.

'He gave the name as Robert Northbury, which I now know to be untrue,' she replied meekly.

'Just how did you know this, young lady?' boomed her father once more.

She held her head down and passed him a note.

Stewart noticed the man turn from white to red to puce in as many seconds. Stewart was stunned, as his brain had still not had time to register the last shock. How did she get this note? Was it given her today? But more important, by whom?'

Then it seemed that everyone was speaking at once. Questions were being thrown about the room like an echo, when the magistrate's gavel hit the desk hard.

'I will have order here!' he called authoritatively.

A silence ensued so intense that Stewart thought someone had shut off that part of his brain that allowed him to hear.

The magistrate turned to the Lady Catherine.

'I have kept your family name out of these proceedings so far, but if you incur my displeasure or waste anymore of my time, I will disclose it. Who gave you the note?'

'In all truth, sir, I do not know. As I left the dining area, someone pressed it to my hand. When I turned to see, they had vanished.'

With that the magistrate stood up and turned to Stewart.

'You are now free to go, Mr Hamilton, the remainder of this inquest can be undertaken without your presence, and within this office. I will send word to dismiss the crowd gathered in the courtroom. I bid you good day, sir.' He then inclined his head and waved his arm for Stewart and Bearcroft to leave.

***

As Stewart and Bearcroft walked slowly back to the inn, Stewart turned to him.

'What just happened in there? Did I miss something?'

Bearcroft smiled. 'I have a small network of people that I rely on, Hamilton. Some are like you and I, others shall we say are of a lower, more debased nature. You may recall that I informed you I had a key witness to all this, one who could destroy everything she said. Well, it was that person who handed her the missive that she received in the dining area of the inn.' Bearcroft raised his brows before continuing.

'He is small, inconspicuous and very fast.' Bearcroft nodded his head at Stewart.

It took some moments for Stewart to process this information, till he realised what he meant.

'You mean a child!?' Stewart's face was blank.

'If you will excuse me for one moment, sir?' With that Stewart ducked into the nearest alley and emptied the contents of his stomach for the second time that day.

119

Bearcroft eyed him curiously. 'Might I ask, do you make a habit of this?'

Stewart wiped his mouth on his handkerchief and breathed through his nose.

'Only when I face transportation or the noose,' was his reply. 'Now I must go find my mother who will be waiting in the inn for my return. By the way, she was the first person to see me do this in the inn yard.'

'Your mother is here!' exclaimed Bearcroft. 'I admire her tenacity and courage,' he added. 'You must take me to meet with her.'

***

Stewart sat back in the coach with his eyes closed. He was seated next to his mother while Alexander and James Fairweather sat opposite.

James Fairweather nodded to himself. 'I never knew just how good that man was until today. His web of spies and informants radiates from the aristocracy down to the smallest pickpocket.'

Alexander nodded, then looked over to his cousin.

'Can you believe he has stopped this coach three times since we left Exeter?'

Elizabeth looked at her son, and took his hand in hers.

'Ah,' said Fairweather, 'the touch of a mother's hand, I cannot remember what that feels like,' he added smiling.

Stewart opened one eye and looked across the coach at them both.

'I may have lost the contents of my stomach along the way, but I have not lost my hearing.'

Alexander and James laughed softly.

'Would you like me to come and sit between you both and hold your hands?' Elizabeth's voice had humour in it as she spoke. 'Well?'

Alexander smiled. 'Forgive us, Aunt, we mean no disrespect at all, it is just a way to release the stress of the day.'

'I know, Alex, I was just teasing you,' she replied

As they spoke, the coach slowed, turned and began its way up to the house. The front door opened just as they were alighting, and Thompson beamed and bowed low as Elizabeth came up the stairs.

'All is well, My Lady,' he smiled

Elizabeth placed her hand on his arm. 'Yes, thank God.'

She then turned to face the three men behind her.

'Stewart, go to your wife. You two, come with me.' It was said with such authority they obeyed her without a word.

Stewart undressed in his dressing room, then rinsed his mouth out with water from the pitcher there. He threw some to his face to take the dust from him and washed his hands and arms.

As he came up to the bed, he knew that she was awake. Sitting on the edge, he reached out to stoke her hair.

'Just hold me, Maggie, please,' was all he managed to say before Margaret threw herself into his arms, squeezing so tightly he heard his ribs creak. They stayed like that for some time, until Margaret pulled him gently into bed beside

120

her, folding her arms and legs around him, lest he should disappear. Stewart felt for her hand, then separating her fingers, he placed her ring back, curling her fingers around it with his own hand. In less than the time it takes for a breath, they were asleep.

Chapter Fourteen
The Thank You and Spike

It took a few days for things to settle back into some essence of normality. The everyday flow of the house was undisrupted, but the occupants within felt as though they had been through a tempest. Stewart sat quietly now in his study, writing letters to both James Fairweather and George Wheatley. He had slept on and off for the past two days, and at this present moment to say he felt disorientated was an understatement. He had eaten very little in the days he had been back. Everything seemed to sit like a stone within his stomach; he knew that it was just a consequence of all that had happened, but Mrs Cottle the cook seemed to be of the impression that his stomach was in sympathy with his wife's.

When he allowed himself to think about what might have been or what he could have lost—and all for nothing—it sent a cold shiver through him. He had seen the look on Lady Catherine's father's face. The man had been out for blood, there was no doubt of that, but then who could blame him? No one. The Lady Catherine could have been no older than eighteen, very wilful, but also very gullible. He did not put blame on her family for his dilemma. Would he not have done the same, or worse?

He rose and looked out of the window; it had snowed the previous evening, and now all the countryside was a luminous white for as far as the eye could see. There was little difference between the sky and the horizon of trees; each had iridescence to it, so bright that it hurt the eyes to look at. It was as though all anguish, pain and fear had been cleansed away, leaving a new canvas for life to begin again.

Stewart shook his head and pinched the top of his nose. He did not delude himself that what had transpired between he and Northcott would go away; it was when, and in what form, his retaliation would materialise itself that worried him.

A knock from the door brought him back, as he turned, he saw it was Alexander.

'How did you get here in this?' questioned Stewart.

'Ah… it is not that thick. The ground beneath is frozen, but the snow is only two to three inches at the most. I do not think it will last, Stewart, as the trees are already beginning to thaw.'

Stewart stood up and motioned Alexander to the fire. As Alexander stood with his back to it, warming his buttocks, Stewart smiled in amusement as he came to sit in one of the chairs.

'Cousin, it is very cold on that horse, believe me.' Alexander rubbed his thighs and shivered.

'Some of us have been working.' Alexander paused here to look hard at his cousin.

'Whilst some of us have been sleeping.' Alexander continued mockingly.

'No, in all honesty, Stewart, your face looks skeletal, have you not eaten anything?'

Stewart closed his eyes and leaned back into the chair.

'It was the mere thought of what might have happened to my family...' Stewart's voice trailed away. 'I still ask myself just how I could have been so blind...' he paused again, 'when I think about it, Alex, it terrifies me.' He opened his eyes and looked up at his cousin. 'Can you understand that?'

Alexander just nodded, and seated himself.

They sat for some moments just listening to the silence around them, each to his own thoughts, when the door opened again and Elizabeth entered. Looking at them both, she shook her head.

'Have I interrupted something?' She questioned. 'The silence in here is as a church at night when it is empty.'

Alexander laughed gently. 'No, Aunt, we were just... contemplating.'

Their conversation was stopped abruptly by a cacophony of sounds which appeared to be emanating from the front of the house. The occupants looked from one to another in complete bewilderment, then made their way out into the hall.

Thompson the Butler was standing by the door, his face showing one of complete confusion, and as Elizabeth went past him out onto the porch, she too abruptly stopped as though she had met with an invisible force, and her hands came up to her face. Stewart and Alexander stood where they were and just looked from one to the other.

'What in the name of all that is holy...?' Alexander's words trailed away.

Coming out to stand by Elizabeth, the site that greeted them was astounding to behold. There was a large coach with a crest emblazoned on the side and four liverymen unloading what seemed to Stewart to be crates of some description. These in turn were being carefully carried up and placed into the hall.

Behind the coach was the cause of the noise that seemed to resound around the countryside, the source of which was plainly to be seen, as at least twenty-five caged geese on three large wagons were giving full vent to their lungs, in resentment at having been bounced and knocked on their journey to the Willows.

It was at that moment a liveryman came up the steps, bowed formally and handed Stewart a missive which bore a coat of arms within the wax seal that Stewart could not quite identify. The liveryman then bowed again, took three steps backwards and went back to the coach to finish the unloading.

'Stewart!' called Alexander as he came out of the hall. 'Do you know what is in there?' Stewart answered by shaking his head, as Alexander pulled him into the house.

Stacked neatly on the stone flags of the hall were:

4 crates of Port from Portugal

6 crates of the finest French Wines

2 crates of French Champagne

1 crate of Whisky and

6 hogsheads of what looked to be Ale

Stewart heard one of the liverymen enquire of Thompson where he should put the Geese. It was at this point that Elizabeth, who had been in a state of complete disorientation, came to her senses.

'There is a barn over there a way to the West which houses the dairy cows, could you possibly take them there?' she questioned.

No sooner had her words been spoken, the wagons were turned and with directions from Carter the footman were on their way within minutes, with further instructions from Elizabeth to put down straw and release the animals into the barn at the other end away from the cow stalls.

As the last of the wagons were unloaded with what seemed to be cheeses, Stewart slowly opened the letter. It read:

Stewart Charles Hamilton,
I did you a grave injustice.
My humblest apologies and heartfelt thanks.
Sir Henry Portman

Beneath this was the same Coat of Arms as was on the door to the coach and the seal.

Stewart looked around him in astonishment, then handed the letter to Alexander adding, 'It is from her father.' Looking up, he saw Margaret at the top of the stairs, then turning, he mounted them two at a time.

'Stewart, what is all this?' Margaret's face was a mixture of laughter and puzzlement.

Stewart reached her, pulling her into him. 'Her father is saying thank you for rescuing his daughter,' he replied, shaking his head and holding her close. Picking Margaret up, he carried her down to the hall.

Elizabeth looked at her son and smiled.

'Your thoughts are the same as mine, are they not?'

Stewart smiled back and nodded. 'We are in agreement then.'

Alexander looked between Thomson and Margaret. 'They appear to be communicating in some sort of code, that neither I nor you have the privilege to understand.'

Stewart laughed. 'We will share this bounty between ourselves and all of the tenants, Alex, each house will have a goose and a cheese.' Stewart nodded, calculating as he spoke. 'We will keep back one of the hogsheads of ale for the house, but the rest will go to the tenants, plus a bottle of wine, a bottle of port, and a bottle of whisky to each house if there be enough to go around.'

Margaret looked at Elizabeth smiling. 'I could not agree more,' she offered.

Elizabeth took Margaret by the arm. 'Margaret, let us get you into the drawing room, you should not be standing and it is cold enough in here to freeze us all to statues.' As she turned with Margaret to go, she called back over her shoulder.

'Thompson, close that door!'

Thompson, who seemed to have been mesmerised by the comings and goings, pulled himself together, and with a brisk shrug closed the door with a resounding thud.

Margaret felt the warmth as they came into the drawing room; it was filled with brightness, as the reflection of the snow from outside seemed to illuminate the room through the windows. Having seated Margaret by the fire with her feet elevated on a stool, Elizabeth sat down opposite.

'Margaret, I have a small favour to ask of you.'

Margaret looked at her and smiled. 'Anything, what is it that you want?'

Elizabeth bit her lip and thought some moments before answering.

'Do you remember, after your wedding I went to see my gardener Spike?'

Margaret inclined her head. 'Yes, I believe that you had asked him to come and live with the servants here.'

Elizabeth nodded. 'He told me he would consider it, make a decision, and that his decision would be final. I agreed to that and did not push the subject anymore.' She paused here looking down at her hands.

'He has never replied to me, Margaret, that man is like a brother to me. He has served me well for all of these years. I just want to do something for him now, can you understand that?'

Margaret reached over and took her hand. 'You would like me to talk to him.'

Elizabeth just nodded.

'I have never been able to repay him for what he did for me on that day, this may be my opportunity,' Margaret finished.

Elizabeth stood up. 'I have furnished two rooms for him behind the kitchen. The windows there look out over the garden, and they have their own door. He need never come into the house if he does not choose to, but he can come and eat with the other members of the household in the kitchen.' Elizabeth's voice was pleading now. 'Margaret, he holds you with great affection, I know this.'

'As I do him,' came Margaret's soft reply.

Elizabeth smiled down at her. 'I will go tell Stewart to bring him up to the house now. I will say I need to speak with him urgently on a private matter. He will come for that.' Elizabeth turned to go then looked back once more.

'Thank you,' she answered gratefully.

***

125

Spike's cottage was not far from the main building. It was within a walled garden where most of the herbs, onions, leeks and the like were grown at hand for the kitchen. Stewart knocked on the door; he knew that Spike was in, as there was smoke emitting from the chimney. Spike's face was that of complete surprise as he beheld Stewart standing at his door.

'Master Stewart sir, what brings you here now?' he questioned.

Stewart saw the confusion mingled with apprehension on the poor man's face. Placing his hand on his shoulder, he smiled.

'There is nothing amiss, Spike, please believe me. I come at the request of my mother who wishes to speak with you on some private matter, which I am not privy to, may I add.' Stewart took off his hat as he spoke. 'So I am here to escort you to the house,' he added with a grin.

'Please do come in, sir, I will fetch my coat and hat,' replied Spike.

Stewart looked around. It was clean, furnished sparely but well. A welcome aroma was emitting from a pot hanging over the fire. It smelt good to Stewart, rabbit more like he thought. Stewart licked his lips, as his stomach made protesting noises of hunger.

'I be ready, Master Stewart sir,' called Spike.

Stewart turned and smiled. 'Your supper smells good, Spike.' He offered, nodding at the pot.

Spike smiled back, then went and pulled the pot a little away from the flames. 'Do not want it to be burning while I am gone, sir,' he nodded.

As they walked back, Stewart's face was thoughtful.

'How long have you lived here, Spike?' he asked.

'All my life, sir,' was the contented reply. 'I be born in that cottage, as were my younger brother and sister.'

Stewart stopped and turned to look at Spike. 'You have a brother and sister?' he asked in astonishment.

'Only a sister now, sir, she be married and lives in Cornwall as housekeeper to an elderly lady there. My brother died very young of the septic throat. I caught it too, but I was much older and stronger than he was. All of my family are buried in St Michael's, all paid for by the grace of your family, sir.'

As they continued walking, Stewart's mind was working hard.

'Has my mother ever visited your home?' Stewart enquired.

'Only the once, sir, when my Merryn died…' Spike's voice trailed off.

Stewart looked at the man. He was content; he could see that just by his demeanour. It crossed his mind that maybe his mother was wrong by forcing him to abandon his home to come and live at the house. She was doing it to be kind, and with Spike's welfare at heart, but maybe the way forward was not this. He thought of Spike's cottage that he had just left; there was a peace there, warmth, not a home that a man would live in dread to go back to. Most of all, there were memories, and Stewart felt these above all else. He stopped walking again and faced Spike.

'What is your real name, Spike? I never have known,' he asked.

Spike smiled and nodded. 'Your mother be giving me that name when we were children together,' he paused and looked at Stewart, seeing a puzzled smile on his face. 'It had to do with my hair, sir,' he continued, tapping the top of his hat. Spike saw that Stewart looked even more puzzled.

'When I be young, sir, my hair was a trifle unruly shall we say. There be a piece at the crown that would not lay down.' Here, Spike chuckled. 'Just like a spike, sir.' He saw the realisation come into Stewart's face.

'Ahhh,' replied Stewart.

They continued to walk in silence,

'So what is your real name then?' Stewart enquired.

'John Wood, sir,' answered Spike.

They continued again in silence.

'Pip my valet, what is his real name?' Stewart was intrigued now.

'It be Peter, Peter Wickens, and you gave him that, sir; as when you were young, you could not be saying Peter, you would call him Pi which ended up as Pip.' Spike shrugged his shoulders and smiled.

By this time they had reached the door.

Stewart took him into the drawing room where Margaret was seated. Eyeing her behind Spike, he shook his head in the negative, and hoped that Margaret had read his signals correctly.

On seeing Margaret, Spike held his hat to his chest and bowed.

'Milady,' he offered.

'Wait here, Spike, while I fetch my mother.' He looked at Margaret again. 'My wife will entertain you.'

At the last remark, Spike turned a confused face at Stewart.

Stewart placed his hand on Spike's shoulder and smiled. 'I mean that she is very good at putting people at ease,' he added, grinning.

Spike nodded but did not see the relevance of it at all and his mind began to tick. Could it be that they now thought him to be too old to carry out his duties? Did they mean to replace him? Oh he was a lot slower than he used to be, he knew that, but he could still do the work.

Margaret saw the agitation in his face and stood up.

'Spike, are you well?' she asked.

Her words brought Spike out of his thoughts.

'Oh yes, Milady, please do not get up.' By this time he was even more disconcerted and began to move his hat around in his hands. It was at this point Stewart entered with Elizabeth.

Elizabeth looked at her gardener, and knew at once what he must be thinking; how could she have been so stupid. Coming towards him, she smiled broadly and placed a hand on his arm.

'Spike, Stewart tells me that I have disturbed your supper, and for that I truly apologise.'

Spike looked at his mistress and blinked.

'Think nothing of it, Milady, it will keep,' came his reply.

'You must be wondering why I have brought you out of the warmth of your home to see me, well…' she paused here and looked at her son. 'We are going to repair your cottage as Cook noticed when she was in the garden that some of the thatch was in need of attention. So…' she paused once more to swallow. 'While this is being carried out, amongst some other small things that also require some repair, you will stay in two rooms that I have made for you at the back of the kitchen.' Elizabeth moved to the dresser and poured out two glasses of port. Coming back, she held one out to Spike.

'It will take maybe more than a week, but when it is finished, it will be much improved.' She raised her glass to him and sipped her own.

'You will receive an increase in your yearly income also, to £20.'

Spike looked astounded; his mouth moved but no words were emitted.

'Now,' continued Elizabeth, 'I will take you to see what I have prepared for you temporarily. I know you will like it as it has its own door out into the garden, so you need not enter the house at all.'

She nodded to him, and Spike nodded back. She knew that he understood what she was telling him.

'Thank you, Milady,' was all he managed to say before they left the room.

Margaret looked at Stewart. 'What just happened here?' she questioned, looking towards him for answers.

'Maggie, when I went into his cottage just now, I could feel the warmth within; not just from the fire but it was filled with love, and most of all memories. Maggie, that small cottage holds his whole life within it walls, and I was not about to take that from him.' Stewart stopped here and looked at her.

Coming towards him, Margaret looked up into his face; her eyes were glistening with tears.

'You truly know the meaning of the word home, Stewart.' Placing her arms about him, she held him tight.

***

Elizabeth looked at Spike as they stood in the living area of the two rooms.

'Well, Spike, will this be comfortable for you? Naturally you can bring all of your things with you…' Elizabeth broke off as Spike looked at her and smiled.

'It will do me fine, Mistress. Thank you,' he nodded his head in respect. He could tell a great deal of thought had gone into the furnishing of the rooms.

'I have but one small favour to ask you,' began Spike. 'If I may be so bold, Mistress.'

'Of course, Spike, what is it, tell me.'

Spike chewed the inside of his mouth for a few seconds before responding.

'There be a lad…' he began, eyeing her to see if she would interrupt, but Elizabeth just nodded.

'Go on.'

'Well, Milady, he is the eldest son of Doryty and Cadan Bligh, your tenants. His name is Kenver and he be a good lad, fourteen years of age and has a great love of the plants.' Spike paused again to look at Elizabeth, but she just nodded for him to continue.

'He has been coming down and helping me sometimes, with a little of the heavy work. Oh I know that we be employing people from the town, but he is special.'

Elizabeth smiled. 'Go on.' She knew what Spike was saying; he was giving her a solution to their problem that would serve both of them without hurting anyone.

'I was wondering like, if we could be taking him on as my apprentice—no payment mind—till he learns the trade well…' Elizabeth stopped him here.

'Would he come and live with you, Spike, as it is very far to walk each day from where the tenants live?' By saying this Elizabeth was giving him back what he had given her.

'If Milady be in agreement, I do not use the upper floor of the cottage, so he can be sleeping there. He be a good lad and I would like to do something for him.'

Elizabeth looked at the man before smiling warmly. He was one of the kindest people that she knew, and loyal to the point of sacrifice; he would do anything for her, and had done many times. As they looked at one another, there was no need for words. Spike knew he was loved as a brother, but both knew there were boundaries between mistress and staff that were never passed. Elizabeth took a silent breath then spoke.

'That is a wonderful idea, Spike, but he will be paid.' Elizabeth put up her hand here when she saw he was about to protest. 'He will get two Crowns a year, and once he has proven himself, listened to you and passed your expectations, he will receive one Pound.'

Spike nodded and smiled back.

'So we have an agreement then, Spike?' Elizabeth raised her brows at him.

'We do, Mistress.' Spike closed his eyes and nodded.

'Good,' she replied, holding out her hand for him to shake. Spike looked down at her hand, then up at her face before nodding and taking her hand in his. The bargain was sealed.

'Just one more thing before you go, Spike, you will be expected at Mrs Cottles table for luncheon on Christmas Day, that is not a request, Spike, that is an order.'

Spike smiled and nodded once more.

Chapter Fifteen
Christmas 1786 and the Threat

Christmas 1786 was a quiet one at the Willows. Stewart had sent invitations to both Fairweather and Wheatley, but only Fairweather came. Wheatley was to spend Christmas with his betrothed and both their families at her home in Cornwall. He wrote of his betrothed that she was a sweet young thing, with large brown eyes and brown wavy hair that seemed to frame her heart shaped face. Wheatley said that she reminded him of a very beautiful china doll. On reading this description, Stewart had laughed to himself, and thought that George Wheatley was totally smitten.

The servants dined at the large table in Mrs Cottles kitchen, and Spike had taken pride of place beside her. It was noted by all that she fussed over him like a mother hen. Two geese were cooked for the occasion; one for the family, one for the servants, and Mrs Cottle stated emphatically that every feather was to be saved, the larger ones for quills, and the soft down for a pillow she was making, though she would not disclose for whom.

Margaret was seated on the sofa propped up by many pillows, with her feet on a small stool. As Elizabeth watched her, she could see that she was much better now; her face had colour, and her eyes sparkled, especially now as she watched every move Stewart made as he sat playing cards with Alexander and James. She could not have wished for a better daughter-in-law had she picked her herself.

'Are you tired, Margaret?' Elizabeth asked.

Margaret turned to Elizabeth and smiled. 'No, Mother, I am fine. It has been a peaceful day, after all the turmoil of two weeks ago, it was badly needed. At the time I never believed we would see a Christmas like this.'

Elizabeth sent up a silent prayer of thanks for that, as she herself at the time had thought the worst of the situation. Watching Margaret, she smiled; it was the first time that Margaret had addressed her as mother, and it gave Elizabeth a warm feeling within her. If only life could always be this simple.

As the mantle clock struck ten, Stewart rose.

'I will leave you two gentlemen now to fight over your winnings of buttons, as I shall take my wife up to bed, else she will fall sleep where she is on the sofa.'

Alexander turned in his chair to look at her. 'I bid you good night, Margaret. Sleep well.'

James Fairweather stood unsteadily and bowed low, 'Good night, Mrs Hamilton.'

Stewart eyed him then grinned. 'Sit down, you fool, you have drunk too much champagne, I fear. Cousin, I leave him in your capable hands, and do not leave a candle in his room.'

Alexander laughed. 'Please do not worry yourself, cousin, I will see that all is safe. We will go to our beds soon, and then the whole house can sleep.'

'I shall also bid you good night,' added Elizabeth standing up, which caused Alexander and Fairweather to do the same again.

Stewart then dismissed all the servants saying they were no longer needed, and that he would see them all at St Michael's in the morning.

***

He gently stood Margaret by their bed and kissed her softly. Reaching up to her hair, he carefully removed all of the pins, and as her hair fell about her shoulders, he pulled his hands through it, fanning it out with his fingers. Slowly, he undid the laces to her bodice, and then turning her, untied her skirt which sank to the floor. Her corset was the next to fall, till finally he pulled her shift above her head. Stewart stood back a little and for some moments to let his eyes take in the beauty of Margaret's body. The only light in the room came from the moon as it fell through the window silhouetting them against the darkness within.

His fingers traced over the small mound that had appeared in Margaret's stomach; all this while, she stood still watching him.

'Our child,' he breathed.

Her answer was to place her hand over his and hold it there.

He undressed himself, keeping his eyes on hers all the while, till at length both stood naked as the day they were born. Stewart kissed her eyes, then, very slowly, his tongue made its way down to her ear, while his fingers massaged the back of her neck. His mouth came down her body now till it covered her breast, and he felt the shiver go through Margaret. Placing his hands round her waist, he lifted Margaret and gradually lowered her onto him. Margaret's body arched and her arms and legs came up round him, her hands entwining in his hair pulling his face into her neck. Stewart gradually placed her gently onto the bed, laying full stretch upon her. Raising himself onto his arms, he looked lovingly into her eyes.

'I love you, Margaret, with all of my heart, soul, and body.'

'And I love you, Stewart, more than you will ever realise.' Margaret's reply came out as a whisper just before his mouth came down to hers.

He made love to her so tenderly, it was as though his body floated above hers, their skin just barely touching, and when their release came, their eyes locked onto one another's, conveying its message like nothing else could.

They fell peacefully asleep wrapped in each other's arms.

***

It was customary on St Stephen's Day for those with money to give alms to the poor, so the family went to St Michael's Church in the morning armed with two bags of pennies to give to all of the children of the congregation.

As they came into the hall on their return, Stewart noticed a letter which stood on the hall table. Picking it up he looked at it and turned it over in his hand. The only writing it bore was his name on the front.

'Thompson, when did this arrive?' he questioned.

'What would that be, sir?' he replied, his arms laden with coats and hats.

'The one on the table here,' answered Stewart, holding out the letter to show his butler.

'But no one has called this morning, Master Stewart,' he answered puzzled.

Stewart's face paled considerably and his hand shook as he read the message inside. Alexander, seeing this, came to him. Stewart said not a word but passed the letter for him to read.

I can reach your family anytime I wish, Hamilton.

Alexander looked up at Stewart.

'How in God's name did they enter this house without anyone knowing?'

The question hung in the air.

'I do not think that God had anything to do with this,' replied Stewart.

It had been agreed that all members of the household and tenants should be aware of the threat made against the family. Only that way could everyone remain diligent and alert to any strange occurrence, or person, that had been seen in the surrounding area. The peace of Christmas had abruptly ended on St Stephen's Day, but of course that had been Northcott's plan; why should they be allowed to relax in their contentment, while he wallowed in his own self-pity?

***

It was January 6th, and Twelfth Night had come around quickly. As tradition dictated, Mrs Cottle had baked two cakes; one for the household and one for the family. A dried bean had been secreted in the half to be cut by the men, and a dried pea in the half for the women. Down in the kitchen the dried bean had fallen to Thompson the butler, and the dried pea to Lilly the maid. They would be King and Queen for the night.

Whereas upstairs, the bean had fallen to Fairweather and the pea Elizabeth. It was a welcome relief to all the inhabitants just to relax and enjoy the moment of one night of amity. Tomorrow the search would start in earnest for whoever had placed that note, as finding him would then lead them to the web of others that worked hand in hand with Northcott.

Fairweather left the following day, giving profuse thanks to all, especially those in the kitchen who had fed him so well his breeches were now too tight. Mrs Cottle had blushed deeply, and stated a perfect gentleman as himself was welcome at any time. Elizabeth commented to Stewart that the young lad could charm the birds out of the trees. To which Stewart replied, 'He has a big heart, Mother, and would do anything for anyone.'

In point of fact, that was exactly Fairweather's trouble; he would help anyone, even if it meant danger to himself. Stewart thought wryly that it was usually himself that got him out of such scrapes, but he didn't mind as James Fairweather was a good person. Without his help at the inquest, he would not be here right now.

The morning was cold and crisp, as James' coach came round to the front of the house. Looking out, Stewart thought that the trees in the distance stood out like stark fingers reaching up to the sky, trying to find the sun which had hidden itself above the cloud. Though all of the snow had gone the wind was as chill as that from the Arctic.

Fairweather took Stewart's hand and slapped him on the shoulder as he spoke.

'I thank you for all of your hospitality, Stewart. I have enjoyed one of the best Christmas' I have had for a long time. My best compliments to your mother, your wife and the entire household for making me so very welcome,' he finished.

Stewart slapped him back and smiled. 'You are most welcome, believe me. What you did for me at that inquest exceeded more than just friendship.'

James nodded in acknowledgement. 'I will contact Bearcroft as soon as I reach London, so he can set his minions to finding out the plans—if any—that Northcott has put in place to reap his revenge on you. Do not worry, Stewart, we will thwart him.' Just as Stewart was about to answer his friend, he was stopped.

'And I will hear no more of money; the man is under my retainer, and this is a debt well overdue to be paid.' With that Fairweather got up into his coach.

'Goodbye, Alexander and Stewart, I expect to be Godfather to your child.'

'After me, you are second,' exclaimed Alexander from behind Stewart.

James smiled, and then doffed his hat in acceptance, as the coach moved on.

Chapter Sixteen
Inquest of Lord Stanhope, Laudanum and the Inner Temple

It was now mid-April, and not a word had been heard after the letter on St Stephen's Day, and everyone in the house was alert to the slightest change or movement within the town; all comings and goings were watched closely, as were any new comers to the area. But Stewart knew that any attack would not be visible to anyone; it would come without warning and with such ferocity that the family would not have a chance to avert it. Bearcroft's search had revealed nothing—after that one occurrence, they had gone underground.

He stood by the window, watching Margaret as she walked on the lawn at the back of the house. She was heavy with child now; he prayed that whatever Northcott had set in place—and he was sure he had—it would not fall upon the house till after she was safely delivered of their child. A knock on the door brought him back from his thoughts.

'Master Stewart,' called Lilly, 'Mr Fairweather is here to see you.'

At the mention of his name, Stewart swung round.

'James,' he said in surprise, 'what brings you here?'

James Fairweather waited till Lilly had closed the door.

'Stewart, my lawyer Bearcroft has sent me word,' he paused here to look out at Margaret, 'there is to be an inquest regarding her late husband's death.'

James Fairweather was pale and nervous as he conveyed the last words.

Stewart looked at him in total confusion. 'What are you saying, James?' he shook his head as though he had not heard correctly. 'An inquest, but the man has been dead these past two years or more,' he answered incredulously.

James placed his hand on Stewart's arm. 'I came in all haste to tell you this, as new evidence has come to light regarding how he died,' he paused again. 'Someone has come forward to say that just before he died a request was sent to the Apothecary in St Thomas' for Laudanum.'

Stewart shook his head again. 'I do not understand what you are saying, James, how can...' Stewart cut off his speech and looked at Fairweather astounded.

'My wife?' he whispered. 'They are saying the request came from Margaret?'

Fairweather saw Stewart's face turn ashen.

'When?' he asked flatly.

'Bearcroft has heard that she will be summoned to an inquest in June.' He paused. 'He has already put in motion his links to ascertain who has alleged this, and why had it not come to light before. Believe me he will leave no stone unturned, he will get to the bottom of these lies, for lies they are.' Fairweather paused again. 'Northcott would not stoop this low, would he, Stewart?'

Stewart's eyes were on his wife who appeared to be coming back to the house. Grabbing Fairweather by the arm, he pulled him to the door.

'Into my study now!' his voice was low and angry.

As Margaret came through the hall, the study door closed quietly.

'I was just coming to collect you, Maggie,' Stewart smiled. 'I think you should rest now you look very tired, so I will take you up and get Lilly to brink you some tea,' said Stewart hastily.

Margaret looked at him and her brows knit together. 'Is there something wrong, Stewart? You look worried,' she asked.

'No, no, just that I have to complete a lot of paperwork by this evening, and I want to know you are safe. Mother is in Mere, and I do not want to leave you alone at this time that is all,' he smiled again and kissed her forehead.

Margaret nodded and smiled, but she could see that there was something amiss. Stewart was tense, his eyes betrayed his thoughts.

'You would tell me if you have worries, Stewart?' she asked.

He laughed softly. 'I would, I am fine, and there is nothing for you to worry about. Now let us get you upstairs.' He held her round the waist and guided her up to their room, where he promised faithfully that in half and hour he would come and make sure everything was well.

As Stewart came into the study, he closed the door, then leaning back against it, he breathed deeply.

'Good God, Stewart, is that man capable of such an atrocity? That he would cause harm, even murder, to avenge what happened to him?' Fairweather sat on a chair and held his head in his hands.

Stewart moved towards him, sitting in the chair by the desk. 'I have said before that he would sell his own mother for gain, and I believe that to be true.' He swallowed audibly.

'Margaret is about to be confined in just one month. If I tell her this, it could cause the child to come before time, which would endanger not only her but the child as well. James, the shock could kill her.' Stewart's voice trembled and his hands were shaking.

'We were waiting for a physical assault on our persons; instead, he has circumvented this by bringing hell down on the weakest of us in such a way that he is not implicated, again,' he added.

'But, Stewart, even Bearcroft knows that he has instigated this…'

Stewart stopped him. 'We all know it was by his hand, but proving this—or any other trap that he has now set into motion—will need something of military precision. Do you not think that he would have set up every provision for this?' his voice trailed away.

'Dear Lord, I am not thinking straight!' Stewart exclaimed, getting up and pacing the room.

Fairweather eyed his friend before he spoke the next words.

'Stewart, Bearcroft needs to know before he puts further wheels in motion…' he paused to sand up. 'Stewart, he asks, has Margaret ever procured or asked someone within the household then to procure Laudanum for her?' He saw Stewart's face change as he turned towards him.

'Please, Stewart, do not get angry, he just needs to know, like your mother may have used it in very small doses in times of stress to help her sleep. Oh I am not explaining myself well at all. I mean you and your family no harm, my friend. I just want to help you.'

There was pleading in his voice, and Stewart in the logical part of his brain that still worked could see why this was needed.

'I understand you, James, I am sorry,' he offered. 'But how am I supposed to find this out without first explaining to her why I need such information, tell me that?'

It was at this point in the conversation that Alexander came through the door, stopping abruptly when he saw the expressions on both their faces.

'What has happened?' was all he said.

As Stewart filled three glasses of whisky, Fairweather relayed to Alexander what had taken place in London. The silence in the room that followed was eerie, as though someone had sucked out all noise, and all that remained was a little air to breath. Stewart's hands shook, in fear as well as rage. He placed his hands on the table to steady himself, then picking up two glasses, he turned and handed them to Alexander and James.

Stewart was the first to speak. 'I must tell my mother, James, as I believe I can see a way of giving you that information.'

The look he received from both men was as though he had lost his mind completely.

'Please, you have to trust me here. My mother is made of much sterner substance than we give her credit for.' He was pacing the room now. 'James, you will stay here tonight and hopefully by tomorrow, I will be able to give you all the information that you need.' He looked at them both but neither offered a word.

'I must go to see Margaret now, to make sure she is comfortable,' he nodded and turned, but before he left the room, he turned once again to face them.

'I will see you both at dinner tonight, and you will be at your most cheerful when you present yourselves, is that clear?'

Both Alexander and Fairweather nodded in reply.

As Stewart left, he saw his mother making her way to the kitchens. Following her, he entered just behind.

Elizabeth turned. 'Stewart, are you following me?' she queried.

'No, Mother, I just wanted to tell Mrs Cottle that there would be two more for dinner tonight. My friend James has come down from London, and as Alexander has just graced us with his presence, he can stay too.'

As they entered the kitchen, Mrs Cottle looked up; her face was flushed as she had been making a pie, and the small wisps of hair that had escaped her cap were peppered with flour. Over the fire steamed four great pots which were being stirred frequently by Lilly.

'Lilly,' she called, 'do not let any of that burn or you will get no supper this evening.'

Stewart looked towards Mrs Cottle beaming.

'Mrs Cottle, I beg your forgiveness, and hope that it is not too late…' he paused looking at his mother. 'My friend James and Alexander have just arrived… Would it be a bother to you to accommodate two more for dinner this evening?' he finished.

Mrs Cottle lifted her hand once more to brush her forehead, eyed him sympathetically, then nodded her head while her other hand came up to shoo him away. 'Out of my kitchen this instant,' she ordered

Lilly stood open mouthed; she had never before seen both her mistress and master in the kitchen.

'Keep stirring, Lilly!' shouted Mrs Cottle.

Stewart bowed graciously and then made his way back down the passage. Elizabeth caught up with him just before he reached the hall, turning him to face her, before she spoke.

'Right, my son, are you going to tell me what is going on here?'

Stewart nodded and led her into the drawing room.

It took some time to unravel the events of the afternoon, to put them all into a sequence that Elizabeth could understand.

Elizabeth was stunned; she had paled considerable and at one point, Stewart thought she might collapse, but she drew herself up and nodded. When she looked at the pain so clearly reflected on her son's face, it broke her heart.

'Leave it to me,' was all she said before she left the room.

***

It was a quiet dinner, and Elizabeth had sent word to thank Cook for a splendid meal, having to cater for two extra guests at such short notice, then standing up she turned to Margret.

'Margaret and I will bid you all good night, for there is something that I wish to show her, something I have found which has been hidden in the attic for many years now.' She looked to Stewart as she said these words.

Margaret stood carefully, and took Elizabeth's arm.

'Good night, gentleman.' She nodded and smiled.

When they reached Elizabeth's room, she dismissed her maid Molly and said she would call for her when she needed her, then lighting another candle, she led Margaret to sit on the chair by her table, placing the candle down beside her. On the table, Margaret observed, was her looking glass, her brushes neatly laid out and a neat pile of what looked like very small night clothes. Looking around once more, she also noted a small scent spray and next to this a bottle of Laudanum.

'Do you take Laudanum, Mother?' she enquired.

'No, no, just sometimes at night if I have had a very arduous day or I am troubled with something, I put just the merest drop into my tea. It helps me relax and sleep.' She looked at Margaret who was staring at the bottle.

'I used it when I was with my first husband.' Her words seemed to be addressed to no one in particular—she was remembering something, Elizabeth thought.

'When I wanted to forget or... to help me through the night.' She touched the bottle lightly with her finger. 'They were bad times.' She breathed.

'Margaret, are you well, child?'

Elizabeth's words broke Margaret's thoughts. 'I am fine, Mother, what is it you wished to show me?'

Elizabeth picked up Margaret's hand and held it.

'I found these in the attic, perfectly preserved in cloth. They were Stewart's when he was born; I embroidered them myself. There are six in all and I wondered if you would like them,' she finished.

Margaret's eyes glistened by the candles glow.

'Oh, Mother, they are beautiful.' She looked at Elizabeth and smiled. 'I will take great pleasure in teasing Stewart with these.' She giggled as her fingers touched the embroidery around the neck and hem. 'Can you even imagine that he once fitted into these small garments?'

Elizabeth moved closer and held Margaret to her.

'Margaret, you are so precious to me. You must know this,' Elizabeth whispered.

Margaret tilted her head to look up. 'As you are to me, Mother.'

***

When Stewart came into the dining room for breakfast the following morning, Elizabeth inclined her head to him. Stewart knew that this was a greeting, but it also gave him the answer to the question he posed yesterday.

'Will you stay another day with us, James?' questioned Elizabeth.

'No, thank you for your kind offer, Milady Elizabeth, but I have to go to London on family business, so I will make my way home and go from there by my coach,' he replied as light hearted as he could manage.

'I had thought to take Stewart with me for some company, but I can see that he will be needed here.' Fairweather smiled and looked at Margaret.

Margaret smiled and looked up from her egg. 'I am very well, James, and Stewart can go with you if he wishes. I do not think it will take a whole month to conclude your business matters, am I right?' she asked.

'It will do him good to get away from the house for a few days, he is becoming morose.' Saying this she looked at Stewart with mischief in her eyes.

Stewart grinned back. 'My wife is trying to rid herself of me, Fairweather, and only after nine months.'

Elizabeth smiled at him, but he could see that it was hard for her to contain her fears. 'We do not need men around at this time,' she offered, reaching over to take Margaret's hand. 'What Margaret will go through does not require her husband here to upset the whole household.' She turned to James Fairweather. 'Please take him with you, James, he is surplus to our needs at the moment.'

Alexander sat there, watching this carefully orchestrated speech, and to say he was astounded at what had taken place around the table was an understatement. He thought it was definitely a form of code they used, but now Fairweather seemed to have gained the art also.

***

Stewart and James Fairweather had sat in mutual silence for most of the way to London. They had stopped twice to change horses and eat, but it had been an uneventful journey, thank God.

'How long is it since you last visited London, Stewart?' asked Fairweather.

'About nine months, if I remember correctly.' Stewart's eyes never left the landscape outside as he answered. He remembered well he had taken some documents to Coutts, his mother's bank, in London for signature; then the day after his return, his father had visited, which led him then to ask Margaret for her hand in marriage. Stewart wiped a hand over his face.

'They could hang her for this, James, could they not?' It was not a question, he was merely voicing a truth.

'Stewart, it will **never** come to that. You have my word,' countered Fairweather

Stewart shifted in his seat and lay back closing his eyes. 'Just so that you know, James, I will go to the gallows with her if it should come to that.'

James Fairweather sat speechless. There was no answer he could give.

***

So this was the Inner Temple that Fairweather had told him of. Stewart looked around him in awe; to him it resembled more of a monastery than a place of law. Amid the buildings lay tree-lined walkways and grass, where people clothed in black robes walked in silence, carrying their mounds of papers tied up with coloured ribbons. Each ribbon, he imagined, denoted what type of law case it held. They entered a small building then proceeded up to the first floor, where a small frail gentleman bowed them into a room which seemed to hold hundreds of the same mounds of paperwork also bound in ribbon. In the middle of all this, and just in front of a wall of legal tomes that outweighed those of the magistrate's office in Exeter tenfold, was a large, highly polished wooden desk. Seated behind this was Bearcroft engrossed in one of the tomes, writing notes on a paper that seemed to be covered in scribble. Stewart turned to James and raised his eyebrows.

Bearcroft nodded to himself, then tapping his quill lightly on the tome in agreement, he took off his glasses and raised his eyes to them in greeting.

'Good day to you both, and welcome to my chambers. I trust you had no difficulty finding me?' said Bearcroft.

Stewart doffed his hat, held it to his chest and bowed. 'Your servant, sir.'

'None at all, sir,' answered James Fairweather, removing his hat, bowing also.

Stewart noted that there was no fire in the room, but thought that that was very wise considering the amount of paper stacked from floor to ceiling. One spark could set the whole building ablaze. One could be heard though in the room adjacent, where from the corner of his eye Stewart observed a very large leather sofa.

'I have made some progress in finding the source of these accusations. There was a housemaid in the employ of your wife, a girl by the name of...' here he broke off to read from the notes, 'a one Rosie White, who was approached—by persons unknown to us at the present time—and given money. It is stated that she had previously obtained a vial of Laudanum for the Lady's maid of the then Lady Margret, two weeks before the Lord Stanhope died. The Butler to his Lordship, who is also in the employ of these—persons unknown—has given testament to this fact,' he paused again here to look up at the two men.

'One would assume that they were paid handsomely for their troubles.'

Bearcroft shuffled his paperwork, retrieving three sheets which he placed before him.

'Do sit down, gentleman, please. Remove the papers from the chairs and just place them on the floor beside them,' he motioned with his hands.

Stewart and James looked at one another, then did as they were instructed.

'The house that your wife occupied while married to Lord Stanhope was the larger of the two in Knightsbridge, now the residence of his eldest son.' He paused again to see if there were any questions. On receiving none, he resumed.

'The house as I stated is large. Stanhope's bedroom was in the left wing, while Lady Margaret's was in the right. Meaning, gentleman, there was a considerable distance between the two. So you follow me?' he questioned.

Stewart nodded. 'Yes, sir, I follow. Meaning, if my wife had poisoned him, to do this she would have needed an accomplice from the rooms of her husband.'

'Ah, so you are following my thoughts, good,' came Bearcroft's reply. With that he stood up and called to his clerk to fetch three glasses and a decanter of Port. 'You will take a glass, gentlemen?' he asked.

'Thank you, sir,' Stewart and James answered in unison. Having received their glasses of Port, the clerk bowed and left, leaving Bearcroft to resume.

'It is my belief, what is happening here is an attempt to inflict as much pain and suffering to the person concerned—your wife—as can possibly be achieved,' he nodded towards Stewart.

'Are you saying that my wife will not go to trial?' questioned Stewart.

Bearcroft put up his hand and closed his eyes. 'Master Hamilton, let us not race before ourselves here. Most of what we have is supposition, we need proof that money changed hands to bring about these lies. Do I make myself clear?' he questioned.

Stewart nodded solemnly.

'The maid is our first undertaking. She is the most vulnerable. No longer in the employ of the Stanhope house, she is with another family called Spencer. Not gentry, but they own a small estate in Suffolk and also have a house in London,' he paused again to take a sip of port. 'I should know by tomorrow, or the next day at the very latest, if my mission has been successful. If, however, the family have retired to Suffolk, it will take a while longer,' he concluded.

Stewart bit his lips. 'Is there the remotest chance that my wife will not be summoned to an inquest? The reason I ask, sir, is that she is due to be confined in one month from now, our first child will be born, and she knows nothing of this at the present time,' he added.

Bearcroft nodded. 'I fully understand your predicament, Master Hamilton, I will do everything within my power to prevent this, but,' he stopped to breathe deeply. 'There could be other contingencies set in place that we know nothing of at present, do you follow me?'

Stewart closed his eyes and nodded.

Bearcroft stood up. 'I will expect you both for dinner tonight at my club "Brooks", St James St. We can then go over various other aspects which might enable us to stop the proceedings, but I can give you no certainty of this.'

Stewart and James Fairweather both stood, bowed and shook his hand in farewell.

***

As they descended from James Fairweather's carriage in St James Street, Stewart looked up at the famous Brooks Club Building.

'Very impressive, James,' exclaimed Stewart. Rebuilt just eleven years before by a wealthy wine Merchant, the building now bore his name.

'How are we to get into this place?' he queried.

'No problem, Stewart, he would have left word at the signing room that we are expected.' Fairweather eyed him sideways. 'If not, then we can always call my father...' he paused here and blushed slightly.

Stewart turned on him. 'Your father is a member?!'

Fairweather looked very awkward and inclined his head.

Stewart looked at the building again. It was made of yellow brick and Portland stone, and each window emitted enough light so as to cast golden shadows onto the pavement outside. He wondered to himself if this is what the famous Versailles had looked like.

'After you, James,' he offered, taking his hat off.

As they mounted the stairs, Fairweather looked back.

'Stewart, I do not frequent these establishments, although I was born to this, I would much rather have what you have,' he paused slightly. 'A Wife, a child and, most of all, to be loved.'

'Well, if Wheatley can find that, then I am sure you can, James,' he answered smiling at him. 'Let us go inside.'

They were shown to a private room where a table had been laid ready for supper. A young male servant took their capes and hats, saying that Edward Bearcroft KC would be with them shortly. Stewart was walking around the room admiring the paintings when Bearcroft came through the door.

'I trust we are hungry, gentleman, we have pea Soup, venison with potatoes followed by cheese. Would that suit everyone?' he asked.

Stewart looked at James then inclined his head. 'That is most gracious of you sir, thank you,' he replied.

Chapter Seventeen
The Telling and the Birth

Sitting in James Fairweather's coach on their way back to Mere, Stewart reflected on what had taken place in London. He looked at his friend who was comfortably asleep in the opposite corner of the coach, and thought he wished his brain were that relaxed so that he might do the same. He went over everything that Bearcroft had said the previous evening. Bearcroft's clerk had spoken to the eldest of the two sons of Lord Stanhope. He was aware of the rumours, but did not give much credence to them. He knew that his father had taken laudanum on a regular basis, which accounted for his violent mood swings. His father, as far as he was concerned, had died of an apoplexy as he had seen it happen. When asked would he give evidence to this effect, he had smiled deviously. The words *Quid pro quo* had been mentioned, in that he wanted the London house back. To do this, Stewart knew that he would have to tell Margaret everything. There was still a fifty percent chance, nonetheless, that she would be called to the hearing. This alone, Stewart knew, would strike terror in Margaret, but what was the alternative? Either way he would have to tell her.

Then it suddenly came to him that this was ultimately what Northcott wanted. Realising also that Bearcroft thought the same in that calculating brain of his, that was why he had approached the son. Northcott wanted to inflict as much damage and pain on his life as he possibly could. If Margaret lost the child and maybe her own life in the process, what did it matter? Stewart's hands were shaking and he felt the bile rise up in his throat. Thumping hard on the side of the coach, the driver stopped just in time for Stewart to jump down and wretch by the roadside. Looking up, he saw James Fairweather looking at him in bewilderment.

'Stewart?' he questioned.

As the coach resumed its journey, Stewart sat back in the seat and tried to calm his stomach. Fairweather watched him intently; then when he felt that Stewart had composed himself enough, he spoke.

'Want to tell me about it, Stewart?' he asked.

Stewart spoke for some fifteen minutes, explaining to James exactly what had brought him to this conclusion, and how he believed that Bearcroft thought the same. As he watched his friend, he saw his colour change.

'Dear God, the man is the devil incarnate,' he breathed. 'So no matter what happens,' he continued, 'you must tell Margaret.' He put his head in his hands then, and rubbed hard at his temples.

They did not continue on to Mere, but broke the journey by staying the night at James Fairweather's house in Salisbury. In the morning, after breakfast, Stewart came down to the hall with his bag, seeing his friend waiting there.

'James, words cannot express my thanks to you for what you have done for me these past months. I will go the rest of the way by Stagecoach now, as I fear I have taken too much of your time already.' Stewart offered his hand to Fairweather.

James Fairweather picked up his own bag and with quick instructions to the servants, made his way to the front door. Stewart watched him puzzled.

'Come on, Hamilton, if we do not leave now, we will not get to the Willows in time for one of Mrs Cottle's fine dinners,' he called. With that he descended the stairs and jumped into the carriage. Stewart shook himself and followed.

***

It was 5pm by the time they reached The Willows, having stopped at the estate office to collect Alexander and inform him of everything that had taken place in London. As Stewart stepped down from the coach, he could see his mother at the window of the drawing room. When he entered the hall, she was there to greet him; then looking round him, he turned to his mother, kissing her lightly on the cheek.

'Where is Margaret, Mother?' His look was anxious, and his mother could see the fear in his eyes.

'She did not sleep well these last two nights. The baby has grown big now, and every time it moved, it caused pain and discomfort to her. The only relief that she gets is to lie on her side with a cushion beneath her stomach.' She looked at her son, then held him tight.

There seemed to be a lot of voices all talking at the same time behind him; looking to his mother, he pulled her into the study. As he informed her what had happened in London, he saw his mother visibly pale—at one point he thought she might fall and reached out to stop her, but she held him at bay with her hand upon his chest.

'Do you have to tell her, Stewart? Can it not wait till after the baby is born?' Elizabeth's eyes were pleading. 'Stewart, if you tell her now,' she swallowed, 'you run the risk of bringing on an early birth, endangering Margaret in the process.'

'Mother, would you have me wait till the summons comes to her, which could be any day?' he paused to pace the room. 'Do you not believe I have not thought about all this after I learned what was to happen,' he shook his head. 'I will be the minister of all that is evil to her!' his voice had risen. 'Dear God, I hold hers and the child's life in my hands,' he shook his head again. 'This is his vengeance on me!'

Elizabeth came to him and, placing her hands on his arms, she shook him.

'Stewart! You are her strength, her courage, remember that.' Releasing him, she stood back. 'Go to her, Stewart. If you need me, I will be right here.'

Stewart pulled himself upright and breathed deeply; nodding to his mother, he left the room to make his way up stairs. As he mounted them, he felt as though he had become detached from his body, as if he was watching himself go through the motions, like a ghost hovering above. The activity in the hall below seemed like a dream that he was not part of, a fantasy, and if he blinked, then everything would restore itself to how it was before, and the world would go on as it had been. He entered their room without knowing how he had got there, till Margaret called his name from the bed.

'Stewart! You are back.' She smiled warmly at him, trying to sit up.

Walking towards her, he took off his coat and shoes, then climbing onto the bed he pulled her towards him, her back resting on his chest. Finding her hands, he clasped them in his own and put them around her. They sat this way for some moments before Stewart spoke.

'Maggie, you should know that I love you more than my own life, I would do anything to protect you, keep you from harm,' he paused here to kiss the top of her head. 'Do you believe that?' he questioned.

Margaret nodded, but made no move to talk. Stewart knew that she was anxious, as he could feel her heart quicken under his hands.

'I have to tell you something, but I need you to know that no harm will *ever* come to you. Do you understand me?'

Margaret nodded her head once more but he could feel the panic rise within her. Slowly, he turned her sideways to look into her face.

'I have been to London to visit with the lawyer Bearcroft.' Stewart paused again swallowing hard. 'Maggie, you used Laudanum when you were with your first husband, I know that, out of necessity, to help you overcome pain and fear,' he paused again. 'Northcott, to get revenge on me, has paid two people from your household then to say that you acquired this to poison your husband.' Before he could continue, Margaret had started to shake badly, her eyes staring at him in disbelief. Stewart grabbed her by the arms and shook her lightly.

'Margaret Hamilton, we have proof that this is *not* true. Do you hear me, do you understand me?!' his voice was stern.

Margret shook her head agitatedly as the tears came down her face. Stewart pulled her to him forcefully, holding her so tight he could feel the child within her.

'Margaret, the eldest son knows this is a lie, he informed the lawyer that he will testify to this effect, but he wants the house in London put back into his name.' Stewart paused, hearing her breathing ease.

'Bearcroft will draw up a legal document, where you will return back the house to the family as a gift. No money will change hands.' Again Stewart paused to lift her face up to his.

'Northcott has instigated this to inflict pain and suffering on my family, to harm the most vulnerable person. I will not let him do this,' he nodded to her. 'Do you believe me?'

Margaret inclined her head slowly. She was still shaking visibly, her hands were as cold as ice, and her face devoid of all colour. Stewart pulled at the bedcovers to wrap them around her.

'Maggie, there was no other way,' he paused again to get control of his emotions. 'I had to tell you; I could not avoid this as this document needs your signature.' He held her close to him to try and quell her mounting terror.

'Dear God, Maggie, if there was some other way, I would have taken it, but there was not.' His voice held a sense of inevitability in it that she would understand, he knew that.

'I am going to get up now to ring the bell for some hot tea,' said Stewart cautiously.

Margaret gripped his arm and shook her head.

'Maggie, I am not going to go anywhere, just to the mantle, do you hear me?' Stewart's voice was calming, all the while he was stroking her face. Slowly, he eased himself up and went to the mantle and pulled the cord. Coming back, he lay down once more and held her tight.

As they lay there, Stewart detected a strange stillness within the room, as happens before a storm. All he could perceive was a high pitch whistle noise which seemed to emanate from within his ears, as though air was gusting through his head at an alarming rate. Neither heard the door open, nor saw Elizabeth come into the room bearing a tray. It took some moments for Stewart to become conscious of his mother standing at the foot of the bed.

'I have brought you both some tea,' was all she said as she looked at her son and then Margaret, who seemed to have buried herself within his chest. Stewart nodded and closed his eyes. Elizabeth made her way to the door, turning as she got there. 'Lilly will bring your dinner when it is ready,' she added, and then left so quietly it was as though she had never been there.

***

It was some time after midnight when Margaret awoke suddenly shouting in pain. As she looked up, she could see that Stewart was holding her in his arms, calling her name. The bed and her clothes were wet, but she could not imagine where it had come from. Then another pain gripped her which seemed to commence from the bottom of her back, round and through her stomach till she thought that it would burst.

'Maggie, Maggie, listen to me, I have to ring for my mother.' His voice was urgent and full of fear. Leaping from the bed, he pulled hard several times on the bell pull, then opened the door and shouted loudly for help. Looking around him, he saw the water pitcher by the window; pouring some into a glass, he came and lifted Margaret's head up and tried to make her drink.

'Talk to me, Maggie, please talk to me. What can I do?' As he sat there watching her, it appeared to him as though her whole body was racked with pain.

'Maggie, listen to me, what can I do?' At that moment her hand grasped his so hard, making him flinch as her nails dug deep into his skin.

'Stewart!' Elizabeth's voice shouted from the doorway. 'Get some clothes on now, and get out of here!'

Stewart stood and looked at his mother, startled by her orders, then realised too late that he was standing naked next to the bed. Grabbling Margaret's robe, he pulled it around him, then hugging Margaret to him and kissing her, he reluctantly left the room.

Elizabeth came round to Margaret and smoothed her hair back from her face. She looked deathly pale, and was shaking so hard her teeth were chattering.

'Margaret, I am going to get you to stand, can you hear me?' she questioned.

Margaret nodded, just as another pain gripped her.

'Lilly!' ordered Elizabeth. 'Get as many old sheets as you can find, as well as candles, then put water on to boil, but first tell Master Alexander to run with all haste and bring Mistress Beryan Penhale our tenant. 'Tell him to take the coach if need be,' she called after her as Lilly left the room.

Elizabeth lifted Margaret slowly, pulling her legs around over the bed.

'Place your arm about my shoulders, Margaret, I have to get you walking.' Elizabeth could see that Margaret was still shaking.

'Margaret, listen to me, you will be fine, it is just that the child is arriving early. All will be well, I assure you,' offered Elizabeth as they began to pace the room.

'My midwife did this for me, it will work, believe me, as it helps to bring the child down,' she added.

Many times they stopped when the birthing spasm came over Margaret, so that she could work through the pain.

'Breathe, Margaret, take short breaths, it will help, you must not hold your breath.' Elizabeth's head was throbbing, not just from exertion but from fear. Would Alexander never arrive with Beryan Penhale?

It was some half hour later that she came, then everyone, but those who were needed, were banned from the room.

***

Stewart sat in the study with his head in his hands. He was oblivious to everything around him, so much so that when Pip came in, he looked at the man as though he did not know him.

'Master Stewart?' he questioned. 'I have brought your clothes for you.'

Stewart looked at the man, then down at Margaret's robe that he still had wrapped around his body. Looking once more at Pip, he shook his head.

'Master Stewart, you must get dressed,' he implored. 'You may be needed, sir.'

This seemed to pull Stewart out of his stupor. 'My wife?' he questioned. 'How is she?' he entreated.

'She is fine, sir, now you must dress.' There was urgency in Pip's voice that Stewart understood. Slowly he stood up and nodded his head.

'Can I see her?' Stewart pleaded as he began to pull his shirt over his head.

Pip eyed his master seeing the pain imprinted upon his face. 'Not at this present time, Master Stewart sir, the midwife is with her.' Pip stopped here to hand the breeches to his master. 'She will be fine, sir, I know she will,' he paused again. 'Beryan Penhale has helped more than fifty children into this world, sir, Milady is in safe hands,' he added.

Stewart nodded as he pulled them on. 'How long have I been in here Pip?' he questioned.

'For some hours, sir, but now you must get ready.' Pip said, nodding his head.

'Have you ever been married, Pip?' asked Stewart.

Pip smiled and nodded. 'Yes, a long time ago, sir, you were up at Winchester at the time.' He stopped here to think.

'Alice was her name, and she was a spritely young thing then, full of life.' Pip smiled as he remembered.

'Did you not have children, Pip?' questioned Stewart, buckling his breeches over his stockings.

'No, Master Stewart, they did not come for us, much as we wanted them.' Pip thought for a while, his mouth moving trying to get the words together.

'Neither Spike nor I were blessed with that, but you, Master Stewart, you are truly blessed,' he added as he passed Stewart his coat.

'My wife be your mother's maid,' Pip chuckled to himself here. 'Myself your valet, and her your mother's maid, we thought we be very privileged.

Stewart looked at the man and thought well before he voiced the next words.

'What happened, Pip?' he asked gently.

'She caught a fever, sir, and was gone within two days. Oh, your mother did everything, even be calling her own physician, but it was to no avail.' His voice trailed away.

Stewart got up and placed his arm around the small man's shoulders.

'All of these years that I have known you, Pip, and I have never bothered to ask, I am truly sorry,' answered Stewart sadly.

Pip turned to look at his master smiling. 'That is no worry to you, sir. She passed on when you were but sixteen and still at Winchester.'

Stewart shook his head again. 'God, Pip, I have been very selfish in my life. I never asked or questioned anything, that is until I married Margaret.'

Pip looked hard at his master. 'You have been no different than any other young lad. You had to be finding your own way in this world with all of its trials, and pitfalls. I do not think, if I may be so bold as to say so, Master Stewart, that you be turning out so bad.' Pip winked at Stewart and nodded his head. Picking up Margaret's robe, he moved to open the window drapes, letting in the dawn light. The sky was a pale, pale blue and it held the promise of a fine day.

148

As the door opened behind him, Stewart swung round to see his mother standing there.

Elizabeth smiled at him. 'You are the father of a very beautiful son, Stewart,' was all she said.

Stewart was out of the door and mounting the stairs before another word could be spoken.

Pip looked at his mistress smiling broadly. 'He will make a fine father, Milady.'

Elizabeth looked after her son. 'Oh I know he will, Pip, I know,' she answered.

Pip nodded his head in a bow and left the room.

***

Elizabeth found Alexander and James Fairweather in the drawing room, sitting on the sofa. As she entered, two pairs of eyes looked up, then both men stood to attention.

'Aunt?'—'Milady Hamilton?' they questioned in unison.

'They have a son,' was all she said, but that was enough, as they then proceeded to act like two schoolboys who had been told they had won first prize. Elizabeth laughed and waited for them to finish.

'If you would like to come with me, Cook has prepared breakfast for us in the kitchen.' With that she turned on her heels and left with Alexander and James in her wake.

***

Stewart entered the bedroom just as the midwife was laying their son into his wife's arms. Seeing him, she turned and curtsied.

'Master Stewart sir, you have a very fine son, who be having very good lungs, may I add.' Looking at Margaret, she curtsied once more. 'I will leave you now, Milady; if you should be needing anything, just be sending for me.' She picked up her bag and made her way to door. 'I bid you both good day, and a fine one it will be too,' she added as she looked towards the window.

Margaret looked up at Stewart and smiled. 'Do you want to hold your son?' she asked softly.

Stewart stood motionless; he was mesmerised by the small bundle that Margaret held in her arms. He saw a small round face, with lips that were moving slowly as if the child was eating. He could see he had no hair, and that his eyes were shut.

'Stewart?' she called softly. 'Come, sit beside me,' she coaxed, patting the bed.

Stewart sat gently on the bed beside Margaret, not taking his eyes off his son.

'Here, hold his head in one hand and cup your other hand and arm under his body.'

As she laid his son in his arms, she could tell from his face the emotions he was going through.

He swallowed several times before he spoke. 'He is so small,' he breathed. Getting up and moving to the window, he held his son up higher and marvelled at him. 'This is ours, Maggie, our son.' It was then that the tears came down his face. Sitting down in a chair, he shook his head and smiled widely. 'Dear God, he is so small,' he repeated.

Elizabeth had entered the room quietly, and coming up behind her son, she placed her hand on his shoulder. 'Did you ever feel such a love before, Stewart?'

He looked up at Margaret and smiled. 'Oh yes, but different,' was his answer.

Margaret smiled back. 'Mother, say hello to Charles, Stewart, Alexander, James, Hamilton.'

Elizabeth looked at Margaret startled. 'You are naming him Charles?'

'Yes, Mother, he was his great grandfather, was he not.' Margaret's words stated that she would brook no argument on the subject.

Elizabeth put out a hand to stroke the child's cheek, 'Charles Hamilton,' she said softly. Turning towards the door, she brushed her cheeks with her hands.

'Stewart, Mrs Cottle has prepared a special breakfast for us all in the kitchen, you can bring Margaret's to her in a while, as I am sure she will want some rest after the night she has been through.' She looked at her son. 'Put your son in his crib, then when you are ready, you can come and join us. Lilly will be in the next room if Margaret needs her.'

Before she left, she turned to Margaret. 'I will send you some tea, you will need plenty of liquids now you are feeding.' Smiling, she left the room.

The air in the room was so still, Stewart could feel the small heart that beat in his hand, like a bird's. It felt as though the child had no weight at all; he was as light as holding a feather in his hands. Suddenly, a small fist came out of the coverlet, with fingers so transparent you could see the veins beneath. Resting his son on his knees, Stewart placed his small finger within its reach. The fingers closed around it so tightly that Stewart was startled. Then his son's hand brought his finger up to its lips and sucked tightly, its tongue pressing against it. Stewart raised his head to look at Margaret in question.

'Your son is hungry, Stewart,' she laughed. 'Bring him here and I will feed him.'

Placing their son back into Margaret's arms, he sat on the side of the bed and watched as she put the small mouth to her nipple. It latched on so tight that Stewart gasped.

'He is so strong, when he gripped my hand just now...' The words died away on Stewart's lips.

'Your mother tells me that they are very strong. Do not be deceived, Stewart.' She laughed as she watched the child drink. 'There will be no wet nurse, I will feed my children, put them to bed, and love them. They will **never** feel alone and unwanted **ever**, only loved.'

Stewart nodded, he knew what she meant, as he sat there gazing in awe at what they had created.

150

'He is wearing a gown that was yours, Stewart, imagine that you were once that small.' Margaret laughed gently.

Stewart raised his head in query, his mind was far away, and it was as though she had spoken to him in some foreign tongue.

'His gown?' he questioned smiling.

'Your mother made them, they were your own, remember?' Laughing, she put a hand up to stoke his face.

'Go eat some food, Stewart, you will feel better then.' Margaret held his hand. 'We are quite safe here, I promise,' she added, squeezing his fingers.

Stewart looked up into her eyes, leaned forward and kissed her lightly. Margaret held his head there and kissed him back.

'Go.' She laughed.

***

As Stewart entered the kitchen, all eyes were on him.

'My wife is NEVER going through that again!' he stated emphatically.

Alexander and James looked at one another then laughed loudly.

'What have I said that is so funny, pray tell me?' Stewart looked irritated.

Alexander tried to straighten his face before replying. 'Think about what you have just said, cousin, and then think of the consequences.'

Mrs Cottle chuckled to herself as she coddled her eggs.

'What do they mean, Mrs Cottle?' asked Lilly innocently.

'Never you mind, my girl,' Mrs Cottle replied sternly. 'Get on with your work!'

Chapter Eighteen
Daisy, the Journey to London and Vindication

It had been two weeks since the birth. After Margaret had signed the documents that Bearcroft had sent by one of his special messengers, they had heard nothing. He watched now as she walked on the lawn with the baby tucked safely away in its Perambulator. James Fairweather had sent it from London, saying it was the latest thing. You could walk anywhere with it and the baby was safe and warm within its body. It consisted of a wicker crib which was supported on a structure similar to that of the stagecoach, but with two large wheels and two smaller ones. It had a hood which could be raised or lowered and a handle with which to push the object, situated at the foot of the crib. Looking at it, Stewart thought it was a marvellous invention.

Coming out of the house, Stewart made his way across the lawn calling, 'Mrs Hamilton, you have abandoned me.'

Margaret looked up and laughed. 'I believe that he will have your eyes, Stewart,' she said as she took Stewart's arm.

'He has no hair as yet, but that will come in time.' She smiled at him. 'I hope it is just like yours,' she added as she reached up and kissed him. 'When we have a daughter, then she can look just like me,' she teased.

Stewart shook his head, smiling, and then leaned in and kissed her. 'I have to go to the estate office; I must get back to my duties.'

'Go to your work.' She smiled. 'I will see you at dinner,' she added pulling him down to her by his coat and kissing him for some moments.

'Margaret Hamilton, you never cease to amaze me,' he answered as she released him.

As she watched him go, a shiver ran through her. She knew the summons was coming, it was just a matter of when. Margaret looked at her son and then at her husband as he made his way back across the lawn, then sent up a prayer.

'Dear God, please do not let me be taken from them.'

Elizabeth had hired a nanny for her grandson, who came very well spoken of by a friend. Elizabeth was aware that Margaret—because of her own childhood—wanted to be with her child as much as she could, but there were times when this would not be possible. Elizabeth also knew that when, and if, the time came for her to go to London, she would never leave the child at the Willows; she would need somebody with her in London, a person she could trust.

Both Elizabeth and Margaret had interviewed the numerous ladies that came for the position, but one stood out amongst the rest. She was not a young woman, in her early forties, but she had a kind and placid disposition, as well as a firm hand. Her name was Daisy Harrington, a vicar's daughter, and she hailed from London.

Daisy was tall and slim, with dark brown hair and eyes. She had soft features and a gentle smile, which seemed to put people at ease, but most of all her voice was so calming that even Elizabeth and Margaret had been taken by her. She had been the nanny of a wealthy merchant's family in London, but the master's business had taken him, and his family, to the Americas, and Daisy Harrington had not wanted to go. Like others of her profession, she had never married, and when asked if she would mind leaving London to reside in Mere, she had smiled and said that her duty was to be where the child was, as long as it was in England.

Margaret watched her now as she came towards her, dressed in a deep blue gown buttoned to the neck with a crisp while lace collar. The sleeves were narrow and to the wrists, and she wore a long white apron to cover the front. Her hair was parted in the middle and pulled softly back into a bun at the back of her neck; over this she wore a snow-white cap.

Margaret thought that were she given the chance, Daisy Harrington could be a beautiful woman.

Daisy curtsied, 'Good day, Milady, I have come to tell you that lunch is ready.' She smiled. 'I will take Master Charles to the nursery and change him, then call you when he is ready to feed.' She smiled warmly to Margaret.

Margaret placed her hand on Daisy's arm and smiled back. 'Thank you, Daisy.' Bending down to her son, she kissed him gently on the forehead, stroked his hand and then walked away back to the house. Looking back, Margaret saw Daisy bending over the perambulator laughing and talking to her son, tucking the sheet around him as she did so. Margaret breathed deeply and thanked God for all his small mercies.

***

As Stewart rode up to the estate office, he could see Alexander coming towards him from Mere.

'Good day to you, cousin,' shouted Alexander.

Stewart bowed and took his hat off in jest. 'And a good day to you too, Alex,' he sent back.

Both men dismounted and led their horses to the stable, where they removed the saddles and left them to drink and eat their fill. Coming into the office, Alexander opened the window, and then wedged the door ajar. Removing his coat, he placed the mail onto the desk.

'It is very warm for the middle of May, do you not think so, cousin?' he offered as he removed his waistcoat as well.

Stewart looked closely at his cousin and raised his brows. 'It has come, has it not?' he said, nodding his head.

'It is in the post, Stewart. There are also two for you; one from James and one from Bearcroft,' Alexander answered as he picked up the mail from his desk, handing the three letters to Stewart. 'The rest are bills and such like.'

Opening Bearcroft's letter first, he stood and read in silence. Alexander knew there was something amiss from the expression on Stewart's face.

'Dear God, Alex, the London property has not been transferred as the court is disputing the reason for the transaction. Alex, they think it is a bribe to the eldest Stanhope, on the part of Margaret.'

Stewart's face showed disbelief and terror at the same time. Grabbing the letter from his hands, Alexander read for himself.

'Stewart, how did they know about this?' came Alexander's fierce reply. 'Where did they acquire this information? They have to have informants within the courts, this is a private matter, it will not even be listed, it is a gift!' Alexander's voice had risen slowly.

'Bearcroft has set his clerk and people to discover the source of this, but is not sure that he will obtain it before the inquest starts.' Stewart paused here to sit in a chair. 'She has to be present by next Thursday to give evidence to this fact.'

Stewart rubbed his face with his hands several times, then standing, he smashed his fist onto the desk with such power the ink stand and its contents went crashing to the floor.

'I will kill him for this!' his voice was cold and very calm.

Alexander could see Stewart's anger being held carefully at bay, but his face and lips were the colour of ash. Thoughts were colliding in Alexander's brain, as he knew if Stewart found Northcott now, he *would* kill him—he had no doubt of that. But if he did, then both he and Margaret would hang. Turning, he walked out of the office into the May sunshine.

'Alex,' came Stewart's voice from beside him. 'Calm your fears, I will do nothing to prejudice Margaret's chances, I swear.' Alexander looked sideways at his cousin then nodded in reply.

'Have you read James's letter?' Alexander questioned just as Stewart was breaking the seal.

'He offers his house in London, it is at my complete disposal, he also states he is coming here this Saturday to take us to London in his coach,' finished Stewart.

Alexander placed his hand on Stewart's arm. 'Stewart, I cannot come with you, the planting of the new crop will start next week. I have no one to leave in charge of this. The growing is easy; it is all that has to be done to get the seeds into the ground that takes the time.'

Stewart covered his cousin's hand with his. 'I know, Alex,' he answered. 'Before two weeks have passed, we will all be back here again, and life will resume as before, please God.' Pausing, Stewart looked at Alexander. 'Come now, cousin, let us go finish what we have to do so that I can return to the house. You will come to dinner, no?'

Alexander nodded. 'Thank you,' he answered.

***

As Stewart entered their room, he saw Margaret sitting in the chair by the window feeding their son. Coming across to her, he kissed her, then smoothing his palm over the small head as it fed, he kissed his son lightly on the cheek. Margaret looked up into his eyes and knew that the letter had arrived. She reached out her hand and held his tightly. Stewart lowered himself onto his knees, then pulling her to him, he rested his head against hers.

When the small Charles Hamilton had finished his dinner, she stood up holding him to her shoulder. Stewart held out his arms and took the infant from her, patting his back as he walked to the window, when a loud belch emitted from his small mouth, letting a trickle of milk run down Stewart's shirt.

As Margaret went to take him back, Stewart shook his head. 'He is fine, Maggie, let him be.' Seating himself, he held his son to his shoulder, wrapping a sheet around his small legs. Reaching into the pocket of his jacket on the floor, he pulled the three letters out, handing them to Margaret.

'Maggie, sit down and read Bearcroft's one first.' He knew she understood his meaning, so with shaking hands she opened the letter.

'Dear God,' was all she said as her hand come up to cover her mouth.

'Maggie, this will be disproven, you have to believe me.' Standing up, he walked over and pulled the bell pull. When Daisy entered, she curtsied as Stewart handed his child over to her. Looking at the wet patch on his shirt, he smiled.

'I fear he needs changing, Daisy,' he said, smiling.

She nodded, wrapped him in a blanket and left.

Coming towards Margaret, he could see she was shaking badly. Sitting beside her, he took her hands into one of his then lifted her onto his knees and held her tightly.

'Someone disclosed this information, and Bearcroft is at this present moment engaged in pursuing the offender.'

There was nothing that he could say to her to quell her fears, only time would do that. It was also foolhardy to tell her that she must not worry herself; that would be to tell her not to breathe. All he could do was to be there for her when she needed him. These lies would be refuted, he was sure of this, but if they could not be, then there were ways and means where a person could be spirited away and out of the country—there was always someone who could be purchased for the right money. What was happening now proved that to be so. But what he wanted foremost was to clear her name. She was innocent in all this; he was the one that should bear the wrath of Andrew Northcott. Damn the man to hell for all eternity for what he had done to his family. Lifting her face to his, he kissed her deeply.

'Did I not tell you, Margaret Hamilton, that I would *NEVER* let any harm come to you? Look me in the eyes, Margaret, did I not?'

Margaret nodded. Stewart stood her on her feet, then brushing his thumbs over her cheeks to wipe her tears, he kissed her once more.

'Get dressed, we are going down to dinner.'

155

She nodded, but before she could move, he had pulled her to him, kissing her again as he pushed her shift over her shoulders. Pulling at his own clothes in a frenzy to remove then, he threw her back onto the bed, crushing her with his body. It was so quick neither had the chance to say another word. Afterwards, they lay that way for some moments till their breathing eased and their bodies returned to them. Lifting himself up onto his elbows, he rested his forehead against hers.

'God I am sorry, Maggie, I did not mean to…' his words trailed off.

Margaret pulled him back down to her, stroking his back with one hand while the other entwined itself into his hair.

'I needed you, Stewart, as much as you needed me. We should not be sorry for that,' she whispered.

***

The drive to London would be a long and arduous one. James Fairweather, as promised, arrived with his coach early on the Saturday evening, but as Margaret would take both her nanny and her maid, it was decided that two coaches would go, Fairweather's to take Stewart and himself, and Margaret's to take herself, nanny Daisy and her maid Millie. Millicent Weaver had been Margaret's maid from the day she left her home and married Lord Stanhope. Millie was twenty-eight years of age, with mouse brown hair and eyes to match. She was small in stature, but like her face, she was softly rounded. She too had a gentle disposition, and loved her mistress dearly, as she had known all that had happened to her with her first husband, and many times had bathed Margaret and tried to ease the pain. If anyone knew what she suffered now, it was Millie.

The weather was warm and sunny, and as the party set out on the Sunday morning, Elizabeth sent up a silent prayer that this was a good omen. They proceeded slowly, stopping first in Salisbury to Fairweather's for lunch, then on to Andover where they dined and stayed the night at the George. From there they continued their journey to Basingstoke to stop once more for food at the Feathers Inn. Their last stop was at the White Hart in Maidenhead, to dine and rest for the last night before continuing into London the following day.

Stewart noted for the entire journey Margaret had seemed very quiet and detached. He had wanted to ride with her, but this was not possible, as she needed to feed their son, and to have both her maid and nanny with her at all times. It was as though she had reverted to the Margaret he knew before they married; she was keeping him at bay.

When they finally arrived at James Fairweather's house, it was late into Tuesday afternoon. The journey had taken its toll on all of the occupants with the exception of the young Charles, who had been totally oblivious to the trip. Stewart had insisted that they take the perambulator with them, so it had been disassembled and the wicker body placed within Margaret's coach, while the carriage wheels were strapped to the back of one of the coaches. This enabled the child to lie in his crib while he was not being fed or changed, and thereby sleeping for most of the journey. Margaret's maid here had been invaluable in the cleaning and washing of the clouts, pilchers and clothing of the young Charles. It was not for her to do, but she would allow no one else.

Amid the general bustle and chatter of the servants taking down the bags, Stewart helped Margaret from the coach. She was ashen and disorientated, Stewart could see this, as he held her firmly by the waist, looking into her eyes. She smiled weakly at him and shook her head. Leading her inside, he turned to James Fairweather who was opening a letter and handing out another to himself.

'Stewart, this is from Bearcroft, he states that he will be here tomorrow by 10 o'clock in the morning. He is presently residing at his chambers; he obviously did not know when to expect us here, so I will send a carriage for him early tomorrow,' he finished.

Stewart seated Margaret on a chair then read his own letter, handing it to James to read afterwards.

'Northcott's sister!' he exclaimed. 'Just how did she get this information?' he questioned alarmingly.

Stewart shook his head. 'We will know more in the morning. The whole family are as beasts of the underworld; "*Arachne*" comes to mind when I think of Alison. They can enter and exit people's lives when and how they wish, causing pain, anguish and damage.' He shook his head and looked at Fairweather.

'I must take Margaret to her room. When she is settled, we can talk this through.' He looked at Margaret who he thought was about to fall from the chair.

'I fear for her sanity, James. You have no notion at all what that woman has endured through her short life, and for that man to have done this to her…' his words trailed off.

James Fairweather watched his friend as he turned to look at him. There was a cold hate in his eyes; he knew that if Stewart encountered that man now, he would run him through without compunction. The destruction that Northcott was bringing down on Stewart's family was unfathomable.

'Go, take your wife to rest. I will have a maid bring food and tea. What she needs at this present time is to be with you, Stewart, we can talk tomorrow after breakfast before Bearcroft arrives.' Fairweather nodded.

Margaret allowed herself to be taken up the stairs; she knew that Stewart held her firmly around her waist, but her legs appeared not to be attached to her body. Her head was swimming and her vision blurred, and somewhere a voice was talking, very calmly, she knew that by the tone. Looking around she saw Stewart beside her, his mouth moving, but no words were registering within her brain. She wondered, could this be how it felt when you were about to die, whereby one by one your senses ceased to function—first taste, smell, feeling, then hearing, till finally the sight goes and one is at peace with one's body where no pain or harm can ever hurt you again? The last thing she remembered was a sense of weightlessness, then oblivion.

Slowly her senses were returning, people were talking, and a cool cloth was being wiped across her brow. Margaret felt the bile rise in her throat; sitting up quickly a chamber pot was thrust under her head just as she wretched uncontrollably into it. She was leaning back now onto someone's chest and feeling the hands which clasped hers tightly, she knew it was Stewart. Leaning back into him, she closed her eyes till the sickness passed.

Stewart reached up and smoothed the hair from Margaret's face, then loosened the bodice lacings to allow her to breathe easier. Looking up at her maid at the foot of the bed, who he could see was loath to leave her mistress, he spoke quietly.

'Millie, go get some tea, please. Mistress Hamilton will be fine now, she just needs to rest,' he nodded towards her.

'Yes, sir,' came her short reply, but Millie was hesitant, looking at her mistress who was looking anything but well.

'She will be fine, Mille,' Stewart assured her. 'Go get the tea, I am here,' he added softly.

As Millie left, Margaret turned to him her eyes searching his face. Stewart returned her gaze puzzled. At that moment Margaret suddenly grabbed at his shirt and started to kiss him ardently; pulling back, he clasped her hands.

'Maggie, Maggie, please talk to me, what is it?' he questioned as he felt her hands tremble in his.

Her reply came back urgent and laced with fear. 'Stewart, please, make me feel something, anything than that which I feel now.' She paused looking at him.

'I want you, Stewart, please.' She was on her knees beside him now.

Stewart placed his hands around her face and kissed her softly.

'It is alright, Maggie, please, just let me lock the door.' Nodding to her, he released her. Getting off the bed, he looked back at her as he made his way to the door. His mind was working hard, as he knew exactly how she felt, had he not felt the same way when he had come back from the inquest at Exeter. He undressed without haste, and then slowly took Margaret's clothes from her. His hands unpicked her hair and then stoked her neck, shoulders and back as he knelt before her; pulling her legs around him, he kissed her deeply. He could not take away her pain, but he could ease it, if only for a short while.

Margaret lay on top of him, her head resting on his chest while her finger traced the muscle of his upper arm as it rose and fell. She felt his fingers as they mapped out the bones of her spine, and breathed deeply. If she had nothing else in this life, she had had two years with this man who was her redeemer in every sense of the word. Her life had begun when she met him, so let it end now with the touch of his caress and the feel of his lips upon her.

***

Bearcroft arrived promptly at 10 o'clock. Having refused any refreshments, the three men proceeded to the library, where the household were told that on no account were they to be interrupted.

As Stewart looked around him, he could see various paintings of ancestors high on the walls. One over the fireplace was a painting of a man, and from the likeness was almost certainly James' grandfather. His own family, the ones he knew about went back just three generations. Further back from that, one line came from Scotland, while the other from Wiltshire. Bearcroft's voice brought him back from his thoughts.

'I will tell you one thing, Hamilton, the man is devious and cunning. His web of lies and deceit was so embedded that to another lawyer without my resources to hand would have taken at least six months to unravel.' Bearcroft was eyeing them both over his spectacles.

'But unravel it I have; now we have but to convince the magistrate that this whole debacle is a pack of lies.' He thought for some moments before continuing.

'It would appear that Alison Northcott had managed to avail herself of the now Lord Stanhope at a party. She then used all of her feminine guile to acquaint herself of the history of his father's marriage to Lady Hamilton.' He paused again. 'Lord Stanhope the younger was, shall we say, having consumed the best part of two bottles of champagne, very free with his voice.' Stewart and James looked at one another in astonishment.

'To continue, the Lord told her of the plot that some scoundrel had concocted regarding his ex-stepmother, who he could not even imagine had the capability to think up such a plan.' Bearcroft looked directly at Stewart.

'No disrespect to your good Lady, sir, these were his words, not my own,' he then resumed.

'He continued saying that he knew his father had died of an apoplexy, as he and the physician had been present at the time. The rest regarding the property you know,' he paused again.

'Let me make this quite clear to you both; the woman then proceeded to make her charms available to the magistrate, informing him that there was bribery afoot.' As he finished, Stewart stood up and poured himself a large whiskey, holding the bottle out to the other two men in the room, he poured them one also.

Bearcroft raised his glass to both Stewart and James. 'How is your good wife, Mr Hamilton? Will she stand up to the rigours of questioning at the inquest?'

Stewart pressed the place between his brows with his fingers and thought well before answering.

'My wife has not long been confined, and we have a three-week-old son, which due to reasons of feeding, we have had to bring with us. How she will react when questioned, I can truthfully say I have no way of knowing.' Stewart drank the remaining whisky in his glass.

'She gave birth a full two weeks early, brought on, may I add, when I informed her of these accusations.' Stewart started to pace the room.

'To say that she is not in a rational frame of mind at this present moment is an understatement.'

Bearcroft pursed his lips and breathed deeply through his nose. 'With your permission, sir, may I talk with her?' he asked, adding, 'With yourself present, naturally.'

Stewart looked at the man. Had he not just told him that his wife was not quite balanced in her thoughts?

'I will go and enquire, sir, but if she refuses…' his voice trailed away.

'Just inform her that I require a few facts that only she would be privy to.' Bearcroft saw Stewart eye him suspiciously.

'I will cease speaking the moment you raise your hand, sir. You have my word,' he added.

Stewart walked to the door, turning back. 'I will go and speak with her now, sir, if you will excuse me.' Inclining his head, he left the library.

***

All three women were seated by the window, sewing. He had told both Daisy and Millie that on no account were they to leave their mistress alone. His son, he could see, was laying peacefully in his crib, his hands and legs moving, as his nanny talked to him in quiet tones. As he entered, the nurse and maid stood up and curtsied.

'Please, ladies, remain seated, I have just come to borrow my wife for a moment.' He smiled at Margaret and held out his hand to her.

As they left the room, Millie looked after her mistress nodding.

'He be a good man to her, this second husband, and he loves her something fierce I be knowing that.'

Daisy smiled in agreement. 'A rare thing in these times too.'

***

As Stewart and Margaret entered the library, Bearcroft stood up and bowed deeply. 'Your servant, Milady Hamilton.'

James Fairweather smiled and bowed also. 'Your servant, Milady.'

Stewart looked at his friend and shook his head. Coming over to him, he whispered in his ear, 'Sit down, you fool.'

Bearcroft pulled a chair from the side and turned to Margaret. 'Please be seated, Milady. I will try to make this as short as possible, and if at any instance you wish me to discontinue, you have only to raise your hand. I wish not to cause you the slightest discomfort.'

Margaret inclined her head.

'As I have informed your husband, I have untangled this web of lies and deceit, but because certain processes have been set into motion, I cannot at this stage prevent the inquest,' he looked at Margaret and smiled. 'Do you understand me, Milady?' he questioned.

Margaret inclined her head once more.

'The perpetrator who forged these events missed one vital piece of information, being that both Lord Stanhope's elder son *and* his physician were present at his death.'

Margaret's eyes opened wide. 'I never knew this,' she breathed.

160

Bearcroft looked askance at Stewart, who was as baffled as Bearcroft.

'Let me be specific here, Milady, you were aware only that he died of an apoplexy?'

Margaret shook her head. 'I was aware that he had died, but I thought it was from his heart.' She glanced round at Stewart looking agitated.

'Did no one tell you of the circumstances of his death, Milady?' Bearcroft questioned soothingly. He also had seen the agitation in her face.

Margaret shook her head in the negative. 'My rooms were at the other end of the house. It was only that his valet came to inform my maid that I heard of his death.'

'I see,' replied Bearcroft, his face changing with his thoughts.

James Fairweather thought he could hear Bearcroft's brain working from where he sat. It was as though a light had been turned on somewhere in his mind. He turned to Stewart who seemed to be thinking the same thing.

'Thank you, Milady Hamilton, that is all I needed to know. Pray return to your infant, I am truly sorry that I had to raise such delicate questions with you,' he bowed deeply again, as Stewart led her from the room.

Bearcroft looked towards James Fairweather. 'If jurisprudence prevails, we will end this travesty tomorrow.

***

Leaving James Fairweather's house, Bearcroft proceeded to the magistrate Robert Marshall's home. He now had sufficient evidence he believed to stop this inquest taking place.

The inquest, if held, was to be in Brooks Club's small drawing room, which had been obtained at great cost. It would be presided by the magistrate and not a coroner as there was no inquest held relating to suspicious circumstances at the time of Lord Stanhope's death. Bearcroft had, as a precaution, called the Lord Stanhope's physician and surgeon James Hunter to give evidence, when and if it should be needed.

On entering the house, both Bearcroft and Marshall observed the social graces of the time then proceeded to Marshall's study, where Bearcroft seated himself and watched his adversary keenly before he spoke.

'We have an inquest tomorrow, Marshall, which both you and I know is a travesty of justice.' He paused to see if Marshall would comment. Having received none he continued.

'If this happens, then certain details will come to light which for all involved should be kept unspoken.' Seeing the magistrate's face change, Bearcroft resumed. 'Am I making myself clear, Marshall?'

Marshall was flustered, he could see that.

'Bearcroft, what are you suggesting?' he queried irritatedly.

'Sir, it has come to my knowledge that certain information which has been acquired has been done so by nefarious means.' Here Bearcroft raised his brows for effect.

'I have sworn testimonies from both Lord Stanhope's eldest son—the now Lord Robert Stanhope—and his father's physician James Hunter stating they were both present at the death,' he paused again. 'The woman who acquired this information missed one vital part in her gathering of such evidence: that of the physician.' Bearcroft could see that by this time Robert Marshall had become decidedly agitated.

'The physician stated that there had been evidence of "hard pulse disease" and several times he had let blood, and applied leeches to Lord Stanhope.' He was interrupted here by Marshall raising his hand.

'Bearcroft, let us dispense with the rest of the formalities. I have been very cleverly duped, and this will not go unpunished. I want names, and now!' His voice has risen as he spoke.

Bearcroft watched the man carefully before he answered.

'You hold a certain document, do you not? One which gifts back a small house in Kensington to the Stanhope family? I want this released today. This was never my client's to keep; insofar that she held it only until the event of her death, when it would once again become the property of the Stanhope estate.'

'Agreed,' came Marshall's short reply.

'As to names, I have none, none that is, which would reflect the true names of the offenders, each preferring to adopt a pseudonym.' Bearcroft paused.

'I will have my clerk present to you all of my searches and findings that I have acquired over the past months. Each one is carefully documented and cross referenced.' Bearcroft was stopped abruptly by Marshall rising suddenly, knocking his chair to the floor, then coming round and opening the window.

'Do you know what enrages me most, Bearcroft? Is the fact that I cannot pursue these people for false evidence, and perverting the course of justice. They have circumvented my authority for their own debased enjoyment of watching another person suffer.'

Bearcroft watched the man closely; he had some notion what had pre-empted his seeing the greater picture. Men were gullible where the female prowess was concerned. This man had had his head turned by a conniving 'Femme Fatale', he nodded to himself in agreement; for this fact alone, he had chosen to remain single, as he would never have retained his sharpness of mind had he married. Of that he was sure.

'I can now go back to my client and inform them that there will be no further action taken regarding this matter. We seek no form of compensation, as in hindsight the damage done to my client can never be rectified, only time may blur its edges a little.' Bearcroft collected his papers and tied them neatly within their ribbon. Standing up, he bowed. 'Your servant, sir. Good day.'

Chapter Nineteen
Return, Confessions and Threats

After Bearcroft's news, they spent a full week in London before departing for Mere. They needed the time to quieten their nerves and replenish their energy before the arduous journey back home. Stewart had sent word immediately to his mother of the news that all charges had been dropped against Margaret; he knew she would be waiting for any letter, good or bad. They left the following Tuesday, taking the same route they had chosen last time, stopping at the same inns to rest and eat, but this time it was with light hearts and without the "*Sword of Damocles*" poised above them.

They reached Mere around mid-day on the Friday. Here the coaches stopped as Stewart wished to see if his cousin Alexander was at the Angle Inn; being told that he had just left, they made their way to the estate office.

Alexander was deep in thought writing the last entries into his ledger when he heard the sounds of wheels and horses approaching. Laying down his quill, he emerged from the office to see Stewart jumping down from the coach. Stewart watched his cousin as he came towards him, knowing that his mother would have told him the good news. The two cousins clasped one another so tightly that Millie who had been watching gasped.

'Oh my!' she exclaimed.

Margaret leaned round to see what Millie had found so alarming. Smiling, she looked at her maid, then reached and patted her knee.

'In truth they are cousins, Millie, but in kinship they are more like brothers.' Margaret smiled deeply, as she knew that Alexander would have given anything to have been with them on that journey.

Margaret watched as Alexander closed the office and saddled his horse; then talking to Stewart, he raced off to inform the house of their return. Looking at the countryside around her, she breathed deeply, seeing the plush green meadows, and trees, the scent of grass and hedgerows filling her senses once more. She lay back and closed her eyes—she was home. Turning, she looked at her son who was sleeping peacefully, then gave up another silent prayer of thanks for their deliverance.

As the coaches came up to the house, Stewart saw his mother standing there waiting; at a second glance he noticed that the whole household was present. Stewart looked at James Fairweather and grinned.

'We have a welcoming party, James,' he called as he opened the carriage door.

As Margaret stepped down, Elizabeth threw her arms about her and clasped her tightly. Margaret responded with tears streaming down her face. Cupping Margaret's face, Elizabeth kissed her on the forehead and released her. As she turned, Stewart pulled his mother into him, kissing the top of her head.

'Hello, Mother,' was all he managed before she kissed him also.

Fairweather by this time had become a little nervous as he could see that he was next in line, but before he could react, Elizabeth had cupped her hands to his face and kissed him too saying, 'James Fairweather, I owe you my life for what you have done for this family.' As she released him, Stewart noticed that his friend had gone crimson to the roots of his hair.

Elizabeth then turned her attentions to her grandson, scooping him from his nanny's arms into hers; she mounted the stairs and entered the house.

Stewart looked at his friend whose colour seemed to have reduced slightly to a lighter shade of pink and grinned.

'Welcome home, James.' Slapping him on the back, all three men walked into the house.

***

It was Sunday evening, dinner was over, and the women had long since retired to their beds.

The three men sat on the steps of the terrace at the back of the house, looking out onto the lawn. The light was beginning to fade, and the sky having lost its blueness was turning into varying shades of pink and purple. The air was warm, and a light breeze tickled at the shrubs and trees, while birds could be heard tweeting softly—their last song before nightfall. Each man sat deep in thought, neither wanting to speak first to intrude on the others' private reflections. It was James Fairweather who broke the silence.

'You are a very lucky man, Stewart. I would give up my wealth to have what you have here. Within this house there is love, respect, kindness and, above all, a feeling of warmth that I could only dream of.' He stopped to sip his drink.

Stewart looked at him and said nothing, letting his friend unburden himself of all his thoughts.

'My mother died when I was small, giving birth to my younger brother. There was no doubt that my father loved her, as he never remarried, and always carries a small miniature of her in his pocket.' He looked at Stewart and Alexander. 'How do I know? I found it some years ago. It must have fallen onto the floor. I knew who it was immediately, so I just placed it on the table for him to find.' James paused to take more of his drink.

'My father is a good man, Stewart, but he is born of an age where one does not show one's feelings, no matter how bad they are hurting. He lives for his work, and I know that he loves me, just by the small things that he does.' James stopped to run his hands over his head.

'If I could find but one quarter of what you have, I would be…' he stopped to swallow the last of his drink. Standing up rather unsteadily he smiled.

'I think I have said too much, gentleman, so I will bid you both goodnight and go to my bed.' As he walked away, he turned once more.

''Your mother is a wonderful warm human being, Stewart, I wish that she were mine also.' With that he walked into the house.

Alexander raised his glass as he looked out onto the lawn. 'I will second that,' he added, draining his own drink he stood up. 'Good night, Stewart, I will see you tomorrow at the office.'

***

As Stewart reached the landing, Pip came out of his dressing room. Stewart smiled, and handed him the candle that he held.

'Go to your bed, Pip, I am fine.' Patting the small man on the shoulder, he nodded.

Margaret watched him as he came into their room. He removed his clothes slowly, placing them on the chair, and as the dim light from the window shone onto his face, she could see it was wet. She lay there quietly, waiting to see what he would do. Turning, he walked towards the window, resting his hands on the wood at the side. As she heard him sigh, she slipped out of bed and coming up behind him, she placed her hands round his waist, while resting her head on his back.

'What is troubling you, Stewart?' she whispered.

Pulling her round to face him, he looked down into her eyes. 'I am not troubled, Maggie, just humbled,' he traced his thumb over her brow, down her nose and over her mouth.

'Maggie, I am nothing without you.' His thumb moved down to her chin then down the front of her neck.

Margaret shivered and pushed her body close to his.

'If I ever lost you…' his words stopped as he placed his mouth over hers. Raising his head, he moved her backwards to push her shift over her shoulders. Bringing his hands up again, he let his thumbs trace the whirls of her ears, barely touching her, then he moved his hands slowly down round her neck to stroke her spine. Stewart felt Margaret's hair rise on her body from his caress. Softly, his hands slid over her shoulders, lightly touching the skin of her arms before moving inwards till his thumbs stroked her breasts and cupped them. Margaret moaned in pleasure, not taking her eyes from his. Placing his hands about her waist, he lifted her up and let Margaret rest her legs around him, then gently he lowered her to the ground, and with the dying light from the window playing on her skin, he held himself above her, watching her face go through all the emotions till their release came.

'I love you, Maggie,' his words came out as a whisper.

***

It was mid-July as both Alexander and Stewart rode out over the estate. The flax fields were lush, green and tall—it would be a good harvest this year. In a few weeks the flowers would bloom, and then would begin the laborious task of pulling the flax from the ground. Alexander had already arranged for help with this from the town and surrounding area. Each year since he had been there, they had come and pulled the flax. This was necessary as it had to be taken out of the ground with the root intact, then it was tied in bundles and stooked, which made it easier for the sun to dry the stems. When it had become the colour of corm, the arduous task of rippling started; to pull the flax through nails which had been hammered into a board. This separated the seeds which would be used for next year's planting.

Alexander sat on his horse, explaining the process to Stewart.

'I truly did not know just how much work was entailed in the production of the flax,' Stewart answered.

'Oh it does not stop there, Stewart, we then have to soak the flax in water. By soaking, the inner stalk rots which frees the fibres outside.' Alexander looked at his cousin. 'This is called retting.'

Stewart nodded. 'You are going to tell me there is more?'

Alexander grinned. 'Yes, we then break the stalk within so that it falls away leaving just the fibre. Then, cousin, the gruelling task of hackling takes place, running once again through beds of tightly-spaced nails. This smooths the fibre till it is glossy and supple; that is the finest flax for spinning used for bed sheets, shirts and shifts to name but a few. Anything that falls away is used to make bed ticking and more.'

Stewart looked at him astounded at his knowledge.

'The shirt that you are wearing and mine came from this.' Alexander pulled at his shirt.

Stewart shook his head in amazement. 'I am the owner of all this, yet I know nothing of the process, you my, cousin,' he broke off shaking his head once more.

'When did you acquire all this knowledge, Alex?' he questioned.

'When your mother first employed me as her Estate Steward.' Alexander looked at his cousin.

'I knew a little of the process before, then the tenant farmers guided me. This farm could run very well without me,' he added.

Stewart shook his head. 'No, Alex, without you to oversee this process, nothing would happen.'

'How is my godson?' asked Alexander to change the subject

Stewart smiled. 'He is the apple of everyone's eye, and will be spoilt beyond belief.'

Alexander laughed. 'Like father, like son then.'

Stewart gave him a darting look. 'I was never that spoilt.'

'When is he to be baptised?' queried Alexander.

'With luck, the first week in August, cousin, and no, we do not have a godmother, as Margaret knows but one female relative, a distant cousin, who resides in Norfolk,' Stewart replied emphatically, watching his cousin for his response.

Alexander smiled and inclined his head. 'Noted, cousin.'

As they rode on, the sun was steadily getting warmer, causing both men to remove their coats and waistcoats.

'Will you come to the house for dinner when we are done Alex?' Stewart asked.

'That is most generous of you, cousin,' Alexander replied with mischief in his eyes. 'I would come just for the company alone, but I have to admit that Mrs Cottle's meals are a great enticement.'

'You are welcome, Alex,' Stewart said with warmth.

'Did you know that Mrs Cottle takes Charles into the kitchen? I do not know what she feeds him, but when he is returned, he sleeps very soundly,' remarked Stewart.

Alexander laughed loudly. 'Come, Stewart, let us finish here for the day, so that I may go home wash the heat and dust from me, change my clothes, then come to your home and enjoy my meal.'

***

As Stewart came into the hall, he saw the letter waiting on the table. Picking it up, he looked at the seal and knew it was from James Fairweather. Walking through the house and out onto the terrace, he found Margaret sitting in the shade, the perambulator beside her. He bent to look for his son but saw that it was empty. Raising his brows to Margaret in question, she smiled.

'He has gone to be changed, Stewart.' Saying this she rose out of the chair and came to kiss him.

'Mmmm… you smell of the fields, Stewart Hamilton.'

Stewart pulled her to him, then remembering the letter he sat down with her on the seat.

'James has written me a letter,' he said, breaking the seal.

Margaret saw his face change as he read the contents. 'What is it, Stewart? Is something amiss? Is James well?'

'Where is my mother, Maggie?' he spoke distractedly.

Margaret looked at Stewart warily. 'Why? She went to Mere as one of the ladies there had received some fine embroidery silks from France.' Margaret was getting agitated.

Stewart turned to her and pulled her to him. 'It is fine, Maggie, you have no need to worry. It is just some news regarding my father that my mother needs to be acquainted with. Do you believe me?' Stewart nodded to her.

'I believe you, Stewart,' she replied, holding tight to his hand.

Looking up, Stewart noticed their son's nanny Daisy coming towards them, holding young Charles aloft in her arms and laughing. On seeing Stewart watching her, she quickly lowered the baby down onto her shoulder.

167

Daisy curtsied as she came near. 'Sir, Milady, baby Charles loves to be held like that,' she said nervously, 'he laughs so much… but I will not do it again, if you think it inappropriate.'

Stewart took his son and held him up just as Daisy had done, seeing him smile, as his arms and legs moved agitatedly. 'You are right, Daisy, he loves it.'

Daisy smiled. 'If I may be so bold, sir, there are not many fathers who would do that to their infant—hold them even.'

Margaret watched Stewart as he placed his son to his shoulder.

'I have a rare husband.' Margaret smiled up at him.

'Leave him with us,' Stewart smiled. 'I will call you if he soaks my shirt as he did the last time.' Stewart gave his son his small finger to hold, as he held him in his arms.

Daisy curtsied once more. 'Thank you, sir, Milady.' Turning, she walked back to the house.

Maggie held her small son's foot. 'She knows not what to make of you, Stewart, and, if I may be so bold, neither do I.' Margaret laughed teasingly.

'May I join you?' called Alexander as he came towards them.

Stewart looked up. 'Here, come hold your godson!' he called.

Alexander raised both his hands and shook his head. 'I have only now put on a clean shirt and breeches for dinner, and as I recall, the last time I held young Charles, he soaked them both.'

Margaret laughed. 'I will take him in and feed him, so that I may have my own dinner in peace also.' Taking her son into her arms, she went into the house.

Stewart and Alexander sat in peace, the evening was tranquil and not a leaf moved around the garden. Alexander could see that Stewart was deep in thought; he was looking to the distance maybe seeing some distant memory, or what was to come. He was loath to break into his reflections, as everyone succumbed to moments like these where you re-visited an event that had passed, seeing the images as clearly then as you had done the first time. It was Stewart that broke the silence.

'It was on this same day a year past that I asked Margaret for her hand in marriage,' he stopped for a moment to gather his thoughts.

'There was such a storm raging that night, Alex, in this house, as well as across the countryside,' he turned to look at Alexander. 'My father had come to the house. He needed money.' Alexander nodded his head in understanding.

'The necklace?' offered Alexander.

'Exactly,' came Stewart's reply, then he handed Alexander the letter from James.

Alexander read the letter through three times before answering.

'Stewart, correct me if I am wrong. Northcott has contacted your father?' There was total bewilderment on Alexander's face.

'I believe that it was my father who contacted him,' Stewart replied flatly.

'Yes but, Stewart,' he paused, ''the other information? Is your father insane?' Alexander read the letter again. 'Where does all this come from? My aunt, what does she say?' Alexander got up and walked.

'Alex, I am awaiting my mother's return from Mere. I must speak with her first, but I will leave it till after dinner.'

Stewart stood up and came to stand by Alexander, looking sideways at him.

'Could any of this be true? Knowing my father, I do not doubt it. I believe he is capable of anything. It is the fact that Northcott is now privy to this information and with the blessing of my father...' Stewart shook his head.

'There is something we are missing here, Alex, something vital, and I am very afraid that it involves my mother.' As he spoke the last words, Elizabeth came out onto the terrace. Stewart watched her come towards them, smiling and at ease. He thought to himself that he had not seen her this happy for a long time. Her face was flushed and small tendrils of hair had escaped which gently floated around her ears and neck as a light breeze suddenly lifted them. He also noticed for the first time small smudges of grey that had appeared around her temples, as though they had been brushed there with ash. Stewart smiled warmly as he bent and kissed her cheek.

'Good evening, Mother,' he greeted.

Elizabeth turned towards Alexander, the smile still on her face.

'Good evening, Alex,' she rose up on her toes and kissed him on the cheek. 'You will be staying for dinner, yes?'

Alexander smiled back and nodded. 'I will, Aunt, thank you. It seems that I am never in my own home of late. My cook thinks that I am not over fond of her food, so to convince her otherwise, I ate two helpings of her pudding yesterday.' Alexander patted his stomach. 'She may not have the culinary skills of Mrs Cottle, but if she left me, I would be most saddened. She is a fine woman and has been with me since I acquired the house.'

Elizabeth smiled. 'Would it interest you to know Alex that Mrs Cottle knows her? On the odd occasion that she goes to Mere, she has tea with her at your home.'

Alexander shook his head and laughed. 'You must think me very arrogant, Aunt, not to know things about the people that care for me.' Alexander looked at his aunt. 'I will wager that you know everything about your household.' He raised his eyebrows and inclined his head.

'Alexander, most of my household have known me since I was small. I grew up with them, it is not the same thing at all.' She placed a hand on his arm. 'You are a good, kind person, Alex, never think otherwise.'

Stewart coughed breaking the conversation.

'Mother, did you manage to purchase any of the French embroidery silks?' he questioned.

Elizabeth came out of her thoughts. 'Oh yes, I bought one of deep blue, that is for Margaret, and one of gold and one of a rich scarlet. She does not know that I have it, so do not say anything till after dinner.' The look that she gave her son and nephew was enough.

'Now I must go and see my grandson before he sleeps, then freshen for dinner.' As she went to walk away, she turned to them once more.

'And do not be late!' she added.

The two cousins sat once more companionably together, but the thoughts that raced through both their minds were not peaceful.

'What will you say to her, Stewart? How will you ask her these things?' Alexander queried.

It was some moments before Stewart answered.

'Alex, before I say anything to my mother, I think that I will go and speak with Spike.'

Alexander looked at him questioningly.

'If any of these things are true, then he will know about them, of that I am very sure.' Standing up, he turned to Alexander.

'I must go in now, as I too want to see my son before he sleeps, and wash for dinner. Help yourself to a drink, cousin.'

***

Stewart sat back from the table and looked around at the other three people seated there. His mother looked very happy; he could tell by the way she spoke, and her whole appearance bore this out to be true. Margaret, his wife, looked radiant; she had a glow to her face, and was truly vibrant when she spoke. He wondered if there was something that he was missing; it couldn't be the silk as his mother had not yet given it to her. Alexander was worried, but he had concealed it so well no one would ever have known. Standing up he spoke.

'Mother, Margaret,' he inclined his head politely. 'Alexander and I beg your apologies but we must go over some bills that he brought with him this evening. So we will retire to the study and as it should take no longer than half an hour, we will come find you both in the drawing room.'

Elizabeth looked at Alexander. 'There is a discrepancy regarding a payment, Aunt. They say it is more, but we are not entirely sure that is correct.' Saying this, he got up and bowed his head.

'Let us get this over with, cousin, so that I can savour some of that fine whisky you were given last Christmas.' Alexander smiled.

'*We* were given, cousin, not just I,' corrected Stewart

Alexander's eyes glinted in amusement. 'I stand corrected. Shall we go?'

As they left the room, Elizabeth turned to Margaret. 'Is there something they are not telling us, do you think?' she said with an air of scepticism in her voice. Standing up, she came and took Margaret's arm.

'Mother, I think it is just as they said, but I can understand your misgivings after all that has happened in the last few months. Let us not worry unnecessarily,' she offered as she took Elizabeth's arm and laid it gently through hers as they made their way into the drawing room.

It was warm in the room and although there was still enough light, the brightness of the afternoon was slowly creeping towards dusk. Lilly was just lighting the last of the candles above the mantle when they entered.

Curtsying, Lilly asked, 'Will there be anything else, Milady?'

'No thank you, Lilly,' answered Elizabeth, 'go have your supper now.'

'Thank you, Milady,' replied Lilly as she turned and curtsied once more before leaving.

Elizabeth walked to her work basket and picked up the blue silk embroidery skein.

'I have a little surprise for you, Margaret. I know that you were searching for a deep blue silk to embroider Charles' monogram on his bed sheets. Well when I went into Mere today, I found this.' Elizabeth held out the skein to Margaret.

'Oh, Mother, that is beautiful,' she answered with joy as she felt the softness of the silk between her fingers. 'It must have cost you a great deal,' she added, looking up at Elizabeth. 'Charles does not know how lucky he is to have you as his grandmother. I fear he is spoilt,' Margaret said, laughing.

'I have but one grandchild, Margaret,' smiled Elizabeth, 'that is my privilege.' Elizabeth replied, seating herself beside her daughter in law. Taking their work in their hands, they sat companionably in silence with just the ticking of the clock on the mantle.

***

As Alexander closed the study door, he turned to Stewart.

'You cannot go out to speak with Spike now; it will arouse suspicion from everyone, including the household. You must leave it till tomorrow, and then create an opportunity whereby you can speak with him about this letter.'

Stewart nodded. 'You are right, cousin, did you not see the way my mother looked at me? No, it is best left until tomorrow. I will seek out Spike in the gardens before I come to the office.' Stewart sighed deeply. 'I truly thought that all of this ended in London, but to now turn his assault on my mother!' Stewart rubbed his hands over his face. 'Alex, this is unthinkable. Let us go back to the drawing room, as I am in need of that drink.'

As they entered the room, two heads came up from their needlework to look, then Elizabeth's eyes met her sons. He knew that no matter what he said she would be questioning it, it was best to leave the explanations to Alexander. Stewart looked towards his cousin.

'Whisky, Alex?'

'Thank you, cousin, it would be most welcome,' he replied smiling. Turning to Elizabeth he continued. 'It was an error on my part, Aunt, and very remiss of me as I had forgotten one order. I will issue a new payment tomorrow and take it to the weaver personally.'

Elizabeth looked at her nephew and then at her son. 'That is so unlike you, Alex, but we are all fallible at times, even I.' She shook her head slightly, 'I had promised Spike new rakes for the garden, and have still yet to write the order.'

Stewart glanced quickly at his cousin. 'Mother, I will go to him tomorrow and ask him to make an inventory of what is needed. If it needs to be crafted, I will ride to Mere and talk to the blacksmith there, so that it can be made at his earliest possible convenience.' Stewart picked up the glasses. 'Besides, I wish to see how his new apprentice is shaping; it will be amusing to see how Spike is tutoring this young lad. I know from personal experience he is a very patient man, having had to deal with myself, when I pulled flowers instead of weeds.' Stewart chuckled to himself, and then looked at Margaret. 'He put me to another task of watering the seedlings.'

Handing Alexander his drink, he sat in the opposite chair and raised his glass.

***

Chapter Twenty
Spike, Secrets, Cousin Charlotte and Re-Interment

It was very early morning when Stewart made his way to Spike's cottage. There was a stillness at this time of day, similar to that before nightfall, but nightfall was closure, morning was the pleasure of what was to come. He hoped that this one brought with it good news, thinking this he tapped the letter in his pocket. As he approached the cottage, he saw the lad Kenver come out and quietly close the door. Kenver was tall and spindly in appearance, his body not having yet matured into a young man. He had thick blond hair, which at the moment was fighting to be loose from the tie that held them back, and light blue eyes that made his face shine. There would be many a young lass vying for his affections soon thought Stewart.

On seeing Stewart, the lad clasped his hat to his chest and bowed his head.

'Good morning, Master Hamilton sir,' he spoke in greeting, keeping his head bowed.

'Good morning, Kenver,' returned Stewart, looking at him, thinking to himself that the lad had not been expecting to find his master walking towards him at this hour of the morning.

'Is your master in?'

'Oh yes, sir, he be finishing his breakfast, sir.'

Stewart could tell that he was anxious to leave, as he hopped from one foot to the next, moving his hat from one hand to the other in turn.

'Thank you, Kenver,' Stewart replied. 'I will not detain you a moment longer as I know you have your work to go to, as do I. Good day to you, Kenver.'

'Good day to you, Master Hamilton sir.' With that, he bowed again and was gone before Stewart could turn around and see him go.

Stewart tapped lightly on the door and waited. From within he could hear Spike mumbling.

'Young Kenver, what have you forgotten this time, lad...' his voice trailed away as he opened the door and found Stewart not Kenver.

'Master Stewart sir,' the surprise in his voice was evident, 'what brings you here to my cottage at such an hour?'

Stewart saw the look of alarm on the man's face and put out his hand to rest on Spike's shoulder.

'Be at peace, Spike, I come on a mission from my mother. I am here to take an inventory of the tools that you need, and she apologises greatly for she said that you requested these things a month or more past.'

Having regained his thoughts, Spike stepped back. 'Please, Master Stewart sir, come in.'

Stewart took his hat from his head and, ducking under the lintel, entered. It was just as he remembered it from the last time he had come. Still the same sense of warmth pervaded the atmosphere, but now there was a stronger presence which must come, he thought, from Kenver. Strange how one person can make a difference to a home; there were small things of the lad's—an extra cup, his coat hanging behind the door, a different smell even, but above all of this there still remained that sense of peace and love.

'Please, Master Stewart, take a seat.' Spike offered the good chair that stood by the fire, but Stewart sat himself on the stool.

'Can I offer you some tea, Master Stewart?'

Stewart inclined his head. 'Thank you, Spike.' Stewart watched as Spike took down a fine china cup and saucer from his small dresser and poured some tea into it.

'Your mother gives me this tea. Always has since I can remember.' Spike smiled with pleasure. 'I savour it and have but one cup in the morning and one at night after my supper.' He handed the tea to Stewart. 'When you be finished, sir we can go to the tool shed and I will show you what is needed. Mayhap we can be mending some of the tools, Master Stewart.'

'Thank you, Spike, we shall see.' As he watched the man ready himself to go out, he realised what his mother saw in him, and also why she felt the deep regard she had for the man. If anyone knew anything about the contents of that letter, he would.

As they made their way slowly to the tool shed, Stewart turned to Spike.

'Spike,' he paused, 'I do not mean to sound impertinent in any way, but do you read?'

Spike smiled. 'Oh yes, Master Stewart, your mother be teaching me when I were a lad, and how to write too; though not that beautiful fancy writing, the one that your mother be doing. What makes you ask?'

Stewart swallowed and then took the letter from his pocket. 'I was in receipt of this yesterday.' He stopped to gather his thoughts. 'My mother has always told me that her regard for you is akin to a brother and because of this...' his words trailed away.

'Spike, if anyone is privy to the contents of this letter, it will be you,' he finished.

Spike searched Stewart's face. 'Is it something bad, sir?'

'It could well be, Spike, it could well be.' Stewart handed him the letter.

Spike opened the thick paper sheet with its crest emblazoned at the top and slowly read the contents. Stewart saw his face harden and then lose all of its colour.

'Are you well, Spike? Would you like to sit?' Stewart did not like the shade of the man at all, and thought he would drop like a stone at any moment.

'Are you well, Spike?' he asked again.

Spike folded the letter and handed it back, and then looking at Stewart, he inclined his head.

'I think we best go back to my cottage, Master Stewart sir, take a strong drink, and then I will tell you everything.'

Stewart followed him back in silence. His stomach at that moment felt heavy and hollow, as though a stone had been dropped into it. On entering the cottage, Spike drew down two mugs from the dresser and filled them with strong ale.

Handing one to Stewart, he raised his. 'I am thinking we may need this, Master Stewart sir.' He then seated himself on the stool, gesturing for Stewart to take the chair.

'It be twenty-three years past on a cold November evening,' he began. 'Your father be having five gentlemen to dinner that night, and after they had eaten your mother retired to her bed and they proceeded to play cards' He looked up at Stewart. 'Your father was never a good loser, and he had, shall we say, a very quick temper, which could be lost in a moment,' he paused.

'Please continue, Spike, I understand,' replied Stewart.

'They had been playing for some hours, it were well into the night, and your father had lost heavily,' he stopped again.

'I must tell you, Master Stewart, that when your father be bringing such guests here to the house,' Spike took a deep breath, 'I would be staying in the kitchen watching.' He eyed Stewart warily, waiting for him to comment.

'Please, Spike, I know what my father is, I realised this all too late when I came down from Winchester.' Stewart took a long swig at his ale. 'Please continue, Spike, I comprehend what you are telling me. You wanted to keep my mother safe.'

Spike nodded.

'All had been drinking heavily, and when the brawl do start, it could be heard all over the house. Chairs were sent a banging in the dining room, and I heard the sound of breaking glass. It were then they came out into the hall. Your father and one of the gentlemen—I know not his name—they started to fight something fierce. There be shouts of cheating, striking blows at one another wherever they landed, they both be unsteady on their feet. Then your father tripped and fell. By now your mother and some of the servants had appeared on the landing above. As your father fell, the other gentleman he be seeing his advantage and came down on him hard. He struck your father several times...' Spike stopped to take a mouthful of his ale. 'The other gentleman then retrieved a small dagger from inside his coat, but your father, canny as he was, had seen this and hit his arm, knocking the dagger from his hand and across the room, where it stopped at the foot of the stairs.' Spike breathed deeply and closed his eyes his face showed that he was reliving every second. 'The gentleman then placed his hands upon your father's throat, meaning to be choking the life from him.' Spike looked up at Stewart his eyes pleading. 'It all be happening so fast, Master Stewart, your mother had descended the stairs, picked up the dagger and plunged it into the gentleman's back.' Spike stood up and walked the room; when he turned to Stewart, his face was wet with tears.

'Dear God, I should have stopped her, but I were too late, sir.' The finality with which he said the last words made Stewart's blood run cold.

Spike drank the rest of his ale and tried to compose himself.

'Those other men had fled out of the door the instant the fighting started; they be wanting no part of what was taking place. Pip—he was first Footman then—came running down and ordered your mother's maid to take her to her room.' Spike looked at Stewart with pity in his eyes.

'Oh, Master Stewart, she just stood there as though she be set to stone, staring into nothing with the dagger held tight in her hand.' Spike paced the room once more, wringing his hands. Then swallowing hard he composed himself to continue.

'Pip and I knew he were dead. Your father had removed himself from under him, still staggering, and made his way up to his rooms.' Spike shook his head once more. 'There be so much blood. She must have hit his heart or lungs, dying directly.' Spike slumped onto the stool and placed his head into his hands.

Stewart all this while had been sitting there, trying to comprehend what Spike was revealing to him. He was sick to his stomach and he knew that if he did not move quickly, he would wretch in the cottage. He stood up, knocking his mug into the fire place and raced for the door.

When Stewart returned, his face was ashen. He wiped his mouth on his handkerchief and looked at Spike.

'I seem to have made a mess in your garden, Spike, my apologies to you.'

Spike looked at his master stunned. 'Master Stewart, please…' the words would not come.

'Can you tell me what transpired next, Spike, please,' he asked calmly. Coming into the room and retrieving the mug, he held it out to be filled again.

Spike filled it, then refilling his own mug, drank deeply and sat once more.

'The servants; they be bringing out all the old linen they could find, and we wrapped the body in it. There were a carpet in the hall, and we made use of this as well, tying it with rope.'

The words came easier now—it was like retelling a tale that one had heard years past. Spike felt detached from the story, as though it were not himself that was speaking.

'Pip; he brought the cart around and together we be loading the body onto it, and then with the aid of a torch we drove into the night down to the River Nadder.' He nodded to himself here in remembrance.

'There be five willow trees there once—that be where the house gets its name from, but there be only three now—we buried him under one of those.'

The silence that followed was heavy, as though a great pressure were being put on the cottage, pushing the ceiling down.

Stewart stood up in a daze.

'Did anyone see you? Follow you? Did my father follow you?' Stewart's questions came quickly.

'In truth, sir, I do not know.' Spike replied.

'Did I see any of this? Spike, I have to know.' Stewart was anxious for any information now.

Spike inclined his head. 'Yes, sir, you must have followed your nanny, for when I be looking up, you were standing on the landing.' Spike sat with his head bowed, holding his mug between his hands.

'The nightmares I had when young, it all makes sense now. Why I clung to my mother as I did, the affinity between us.'

Spike could see plainly the realisation on Stewart's face, as the answers to the many problems throughout his life came clear.

Stewart stood up, placed his cup onto the table and turned to Spike.

'We must remove those remains as soon as possible. If my father—and I do not doubt for one moment that he did not—saw where you buried him, he will have proof!'

Spike stood also. 'Master Stewart sir, do you realise what you be asking? Pip and I are not young men now, we would need some help to dig...'

Without hesitation, Stewart answered. 'Alexander and I will carry out the digging, Spike. My mother's life is in danger here. That man Northcott, for all that I know, could have requested someone to do just that: dig!'

Stewart ran his hands over his face. 'Is there no end to this madness?'

There followed a silence where each man was alone with his thoughts. The room was getting warmer, and the sun was slowly rising higher in the sky as could be seen by the stream of light that came gently through the window now.

'Master Stewart,' Spike's voice broke into the silence. 'We must do it in the early morning, sir. Before the sun has risen.' He picked up his hat and placed it upon his head, walking to the door. 'But first we must go see the tools.' He was nodding to Stewart as he spoke. 'That be the reason your mother sent you to me is it not?'

Stewart knew what the man was telling him, and placing his own hat on his head, he rose and followed Spike out of the door.

Just as they got outside, Spike turned to Stewart. 'Some men have black souls, Master Stewart, some can be redeemed, but others, like your father's, are black from the core. There can be no redemption for them.'

Stewart laid his hand on Spike's arm. 'I know, Spike, and I know of only one other man like that,' Stewart swallowed. 'God help me...'

As the two men walked in silence, Stewart's mind was racing. Just as with Margaret, there was no way to resolve this, other than showing his mother the letter.

Stewart and Spike went unconsciously through the motions of inspecting the tools, as each man was acutely aware of the other's thoughts. When the inventory was concluded, Stewart placed a hand on Spike's shoulder and pressed warmly.

'I will go into town and ask the blacksmith to come and take stock of what can be repaired and what needs to be replaced. I will talk to my cousin regarding the other matter.' Stewart gave the merest of nods in affirmation to Spike.

'Now I will return to my mother and tell her what has been decided.' As Stewart turned to go, he stopped and looked back.

'I owe you and Pip a debt that I fear I will *never* be able to repay.' Without waiting for an answer, he turned and left.

***

Stewart stood still as he came through the passage from the garden. He blinked several times as he looked at the small young girl who was standing next to his wife. She was a mirror image of Margaret, down to the deep auburn hair and the almond shape green eyes. Looking at Margaret, he shook his head. He was not in the mood for more surprises, good or bad, as he felt as though his body had just been disassembled and put back together again but in the wrong places.

Margaret looked at him warily. 'Stewart, do you remember my telling you of my distant cousin from Norfolk? Well, she has come to pay us a visit.'

There was a tautness in her voice that Stewart instantly picked up on.

'Stewart, may I introduce you to my cousin, Mistress Charlotte Masters.'

Stewart bowed. 'Your servant, Mistress Charlotte.'

Charlotte curtsied and lowered her head, but Stewart thought that the young girl looked rooted to the spot with panic. He pulled himself together and smiled deeply.

'You are most welcome, Mistress Charlotte, have you both breakfasted yet? I myself have not as my business took me out very early in the day. May I ask you to join me?' Raising his arm, he inclined his head towards the door.

Margaret watched Stewart closely, keeping her eyes on his for any sign that he may give her, but none came.

'Come, Charlotte, let us go and eat, then I can introduce you to my mother, Milady Elizabeth Hamilton, mistress of this house.'

***

Stewart rode slowly out to the estate office. Breakfast had been a strange affair; his mother's reaction to the Mistress Charlotte had been the same as his own. After formal introductions, the young Charlotte had said no more than yes, please and thank you, in response to any question. He had no idea why the child had come, for child she was, her age could be no more than eighteen. Stewart reflected here that his own wife had been of such an age when she had been married to Stanhope, a man old enough to be her grandfather, and he shuddered at the thought. Putting his hand up to his brow, he tried to calm his agitation. He felt as though the world was spinning out of control at this present moment, and his brain was having trouble comprehending all the things that were whirling into it like a rainstorm. He needed time to think.

As he approached the office, he saw Alexander seated on a stool outside. Alexander waited for Stewart to dismount and take his horse into the stable where he removed the saddle and set the horse to eat and drink. Watching Stewart come out, he stood up.

'Stewart, you look as though you have not slept for a week. In God's name, what has happened?'

Stewart walked towards him, taking off his coat, then going into the office he brought out another stool, placed it beside his cousin's and sat down heavily. It took some time for Stewart to unravel the story enough, so he could relay to his cousin as near as he could, an exact account of what had taken place. Alexander sat without saying a word for some minutes. Several times he went to speak but stopped himself. Turning to look at Stewart, he found that he was at a loss for what to say.

'Alex, I know what you are thinking, have I not been over and over this in my mind so many times this morning till my head hurts.' Stewart closed his eyes then held his head.

'There is no doubt in my mind, Alex, that my mother did this to save my father—or there be any doubt that she did not mean to kill the man—just to stop him from choking the life from her husband. God knows why, I would have let him.' Stewart's voice was rasping.

'Cousin, we must remove the remains and take them to another place far away.' Stewart was nodding to himself as he said the words. 'I know of one, where I used to go when I was younger, no one with find him there.'

The silence was intense when Alexander stood up abruptly and went into the office, returning with two mugs of ale.

'Do not tell me you do not want this, Stewart, because if you do not, then I will drink both.' With that he drank his down without pausing for air.

'When will we do this? It is my belief that it should be done with all haste, as we do not know when they will come to search,' Alexander questioned.

'Tomorrow morning at dawn,' came Stewart's reply, as he drank from his own ale.

'Alex, this is the third mug I have had today!' he exclaimed.

'You need it and so do I., he countered as he took Stewart's mug from him and drained the remaining contents.

'The revelations of the day do not stop there, Alex. When you come to dinner tonight, you will see for yourself. But now I must go into Mere to see the blacksmith and ask him to come and assess the gardening tools. They are in sore need of repair.' Standing up, he went into the office to retrieve his coat and hat.

'I am coming with you, cousin, I fear I have no appetite for paperwork right now.'

Stewart nodded and went to saddle the horses.

***

179

Margaret sat peacefully on the terrace with baby Charles. She held him now into a sitting position with the crook of her arm supporting his head and neck. He now had a fine down of very dark hair all over his head, and eyes of the deepest blue. She gently let her fingers play with the soft fluff, feeling its silkiness.

'You are truly your father's son, Charles,' Margaret said to herself, letting him hold her finger in his fist.

Charlotte was amazed at the infant as she sat next to Margaret watching his every movement.

'How old is baby Charles, cousin?' she asked, holding out her own finger to his fist.

'He will be three months in one week,' answered Margaret proudly.

They sat companionably, looking out over the lawn, watching the breeze lift the leaves of the flowers that were in pots along the stairs leading down.

'It is very beautiful here, Cousin Margaret. The gardens are so big I cannot see the end of them; they seem to stretch to the horizon.'

Margaret looked at her young cousin and smiled.

'Do you not have a garden in Norfolk?' she asked.

'Oh yes, but nothing to resemble this,' was her reply.

Margaret watched her cousin—this was the most that she had spoken since she had arrived that morning. As Margaret looked at her face, she could see the reflection of her own image there, albeit younger.

'Was your mother, my mother's sister, perchance?' she questioned.

'In truth I do not know, Cousin Margaret, my mother had dark hair and dark eyes, my father is fair and has blue eyes. Why do you ask?'

Margaret thought well before she replied.

'Surely, you can see the likeness between us, we have the same colour hair, well, yours is a lighter shade than mine, but the eyes are the same.' Margaret was curious now.

'My father told me that it came from my grandmother,' came her reply, as she tickled Charles' feet and made him gurgle in joy.

Margaret was beginning to feel a little uncomfortable, though for what reason she could not say.

'Charlotte, I must go in and feed my son now, will you stay here? Or come into the drawing room and read?' she questioned as she rose up off the bench.

'Oh I will stay here please, it is so beautiful.' Her eyes roamed around the garden as she spoke.

Margaret watched her; there were certain mannerisms that were akin to her own as well, and this puzzled her.

'I will call you for lunch, Charlotte, enjoy the garden.' As Margaret reached the door, she looked back at the young girl and smiled to herself. Two years ago, she had sat with her and her father around the dinner table in her house. No suspicion had arisen then, but remembering, she thought it would not, as she had eyes only for the man that was seated next to her. Alexander's cousin, Stewart Hamilton.

Stewart was seated at his desk in the study when his mother came in.

'Good evening, Stewart.' She placed her hand in greeting on his shoulder and leaned down to kiss his cheek.

Stewart raised his eyes to her and smiled. 'What do you make of our new guest, Mother?' His eyes were smiling but questioning. 'A striking resemblance, would you not say?'

Elizabeth seated herself next to him. 'She says they are related through her grandmother,' Elizabeth stopped. 'There is something amiss here, that we are not seeing, Stewart. The likeness is too great to dismiss.'

Stewart smiled at her and covered her hand with his. 'We will discover all in good time, Mother, for now let us just enjoy her presence here. It is a welcome change from men, do you not think so?' Stewart smiled as he raised his eyebrows at his mother in jest.

'Oh, I cannot get any sense from you today, Stewart Hamilton, just tell me that you managed to arrange for the blacksmith to come here.'

'I did, Mother, and he will be here early tomorrow morning, I am just about to leave and inform Spike of this. So, if you will excuse me, I will go now, or else I will be late for dinner.'

'You are incorrigible, Stewart.' She waved her hand at him in dismissal. 'Go and inform Spike, I will see you at dinner.' With that she left the room.

Stewart approached Spike's cottage with trepidation. How long could he keep up this pretence with his mother? Long enough to remove the remains of the man to a secret location, he answered. Stewart raised his arm to knock on the door when it opened suddenly, revealing both Spike and Pip. Removing his hat, he went inside.

They spoke in detail for over half an hour, till it was agreed that the remains should be removed the following morning just before sunrise. Stewart would arrange for Alexander to stay the night and they would walk to the edge of the gardens, where Spike and Pip would meet them with the wagon.

As he came back to the house, he crossed himself, sending up a prayer that all would go well. He thought silently that he had been doing that a lot of late. On entering the hall, he could see Alexander in conversation with Margaret and Charlotte; from the expression on his face, he looked totally astounded.

'Quite a remarkable likeness, is it not, cousin?' Stewart's look dared his cousin to deny it.

'Astonishing!' was the only reply Alexander could give.

'Do you both not remember her when you came to my dinner party two years ago?' Margaret questioned.

The look that Stewart gave her was enough to stop further talk on the subject.

Elizabeth had seated Charlotte between herself and Stewart, while Margaret and Alexander sat opposite them. It was a pleasant meal with more questions than answers, and when they rose to go into the drawing room, Alexander grabbed Stewart by the arm pulling him backwards.

'Where did she come from, cousin?' queried Alexander.

'From a coach, early this morning, Alex,' Stewart replied, grinning. Alexander looked at him indignantly.

'Well, what would you have me say, Alex? I am as astounded and mystified as yourself. We know her to be a relative, as it is plain for even a simpleton to see, the likeness is…' Stewart shook his head.

'She says we met her father? I cannot for the life of me remember what he looks like,' offered Alexander

'Neither can I, cousin, she is a complete conundrum. Though I fear she was rather taken with you, as every time you asked a question of her, she coloured to her roots,' Stewart teased.

Alexander raised his hands up and breathed deeply though his nose. 'Enough, cousin, I am in no mood for jokes at this present moment. What I need is to clear my head for what we have to do tomorrow.'

Stewart could see that his cousin was anxious—how had he felt this morning when Spike had related everything to him. He had emptied the contents of his stomach into the poor man's garden. It was something he had done since childhood, whenever he was confronted with something terrifying.

'Point taken, Alex, but till tomorrow there is nothing we can do, so come and enjoy a glass of whisky and try to relax. We have to try and act as normal as is humanly possible, cousin, as my mother will be aware of any sign from us that there is something amiss.'

***

As Stewart and Alexander approached the end of the gardens, they saw the cart waiting. No one spoke, but Stewart gave a nod to Spike to continue. There was light, but as yet the sun had not shown itself above the horizon of trees in the distance, and the only noise came from the cart as it rumbled on out to the river and the sound of the horse's hooves hitting the earth.

Stewart saw the three willows ahead long before Pip turned and motioned to them. Stately trees with their feathered branches bent low to the ground; some were touching the river as it slowly flowed pulling the leaves with it. *How could a place so peaceful hold such horror in its earth?* he thought.

Stewart dismounted and came round to the back of the wagon, taking two shovels from the back he handed one to Alexander.

Spike looked at his master and shook his head. 'I never thought to be doing this a second time, sir,' was all he said as he went before them to the place of burial. He and Pip stopped at the willow on the end to the right, talking quietly together before Spike spoke again.

'This be the one, Master Stewart sir, it should not be that deep a grave, as the earth has a way of pushing things to the top after a while.'

The air around them was warm as they dug into the earth. Both men were down to their shirts and breeches, working methodically and in rhythm, and from the exertion, sweat ran down their faces and soaked their shirts till finally Stewart saw what looked to be a dark piece of cloth. They paused in their efforts and Stewart called to Spike.

'Is this what we are looking for?' his voice was breathless.

Spike swallowed visibly, his face had lost most of its colour, and his hands trembled as he took the shovel from Stewart to move the earth from either side, looking up at Pip, who nodded to him slowly in confirmation.

'We must be going carefully from here, Master Stewart, so as not to disturb it too much. That way it will be easy to take it from the ground and transport it. I think it best if we be using small shovels from here, as it will be but bones that are left.' Spike was on his knees now, carefully removing the earth from each side till the roll of what once was carpet was uncovered.

Spike looked up at his friend. 'Pip, be bringing the sheet close now, so that we may try and lift it out whole.'

Pip nodded and spread the sheet as near to the hole as was possible. Stewart was watching intently then gestured to Alexander to kneel beside him, so as to lift the roll from the middle, while Pip and Spike took both ends.

'When I give my signal, we will all lift together,' said Stewart, looking at all three men in turn.

Stewart and Alexander pushed their hands beneath the object, spreading their fingers in an effort to cover as much of the area to be lifted as they could. He thought that the earth felt cool and soft under his hands, not like earth at all, but as some strange fibre that had the ability to move and shift at will. Stewart raised his eyes to the heavens, asking God to bless the man's soul, that he may rest in peace in the place where they were to inter him.

'One, two three: lift!' Stewart's voice was low but firm.

The bundle was so light, it took little effort to remove it from its grave and place it into the shroud that awaited it. Then all four men crossed themselves as they lay the shroud into the wagon.

'Quickly, we must fill in the hole now,' Stewart ordered in a muted voice.

When he and Alexander had finished, they placed the turfs of grass that they had been carefully removed before digging upon the mound, stamping them down with their feet, so as to make it look as though the ground had never been disturbed.

Then just as the sun came over the tree tops, they rode out to the lake.

***

The four men sat inside Spike's cottage, looking at their feet, each had a mug of ale in their hands and sipped at it from time to time. Not one word had been spoken throughout the whole occurrence; each man had been deep within his own thoughts, and even now they sat in silence.

Pip was the first to speak. 'I have brought clean clothes for you, Master Stewart, Master Alexander. The water is hot in the cauldron over the fire, so while I be taking your shoes to clean them, you can wash yourselves.' It was said so calmly and so matter of factly, as though nothing at all had occurred that morning.

Spike rose also, taking his hat and bowing. 'I be off now as well, Master Stewart, Master Alexander, I be expecting the blacksmith any time now, and also to keep an eye on young Kenver, make sure he be doing things correctly. I bid you both a good day.' He bowed, put his hat on his head and left the cottage.

Stewart looked at his cousin, and saw the same bewildered expression on his face.

'It is my guess, cousin, that this is the way they deal with matters as traumatic as the one we have experienced today. Let us not forget that they have been through this once already, albeit twenty-three years ago. We should wash, change and go up to the house and act as normal as is possible.' Stewart nodded as he spoke.

Alexander watched his cousin as he poured water into a bowl and stripped himself to wash the earth away from his skin. At this present moment, Alexander thought he did not know where he was, it was as though he had stepped into some other life quite alien to the one he knew. He could not comprehend at all what he had done this morning, and if anyone questioned him at this time, he would think them mad to suggest such a thing, but he had done all of those things. He was searching hard to find a word to describe his feelings and the only one that came to mind was that he felt *detached* from everything, nodding to himself in agreement, that was exactly what it felt like.

'Alex?' Stewart's voice called him back. 'Alex, are you quite well?'

Alexander looked up at Stewart watching him dry his body before putting on his clothes.

'Alexander, you have to wash now.' Stewart's voice was stern. 'Alexander, are you listening to me?'

'I am sorry, cousin, I am feeling slightly…' he paused, '*detached*… yes that is the word, detached.'

Stewart advanced towards him. Taking his cousin by the arm, he pulled him to his feet. 'Alex, snap out of it please. We have to wash and go back to the house, are you listening to me?'

Alexander looked at his cousin, and the look he saw returned was of worry and confusion. Pulling himself together, he started to take off his clothing.

'I will be fine, Stewart, I am sorry it is just that… well it is not every day a man gets to dig a corpse up and re-bury it.' Splashing water over his head and body, he turned. 'I promise you I am fine.' Stewart took the bowl from the table, opened the door, throwing the contents onto the garden. Coming back, he refilled the bowl and nodded to his cousin. Alexander continued washing automatically, then turned again to his cousin, water dripping from his hair and face.

'You will still have to tell my aunt, will you not?'

Stewart breathed deeply. 'Yes, Alex, I will, God help me, but at least she will know that he no longer rests where he was—if she ever knew where he was—and she will not know his new resting place.' He shook himself. 'We need a drink, Alex, more than one.'

It was then that Pip entered with their shoes. 'Master Stewart, no one has risen yet in the house, so you will be the first down to breakfast.' Pip collected the clothes, bowed and left.

Stewart knew what he was telling them, that the house was quiet and no one would know they had left, least of all where they had been.

***

Chapter Twenty-One
Cousin Charlotte's Letter, Second Child and Alexander's Story

The day had been a customary one. After breakfast Alexander had gone directly to the Estate office, while Stewart had followed Spike to the tool shed to see the blacksmith. It was decided that most of the tools could be repaired and just a few would need to be replaced. The blacksmith had taken those for repair, promising that they would be delivered back either the next day, or within two at the latest. The new tools could take a week, but as Spike pointed out, they had sufficient for their needs, and they could wait.

His mother had had the ladies from the Church for lunch, and as she said they had not come for her but to see baby Charles. The said baby Charles was enthralled at being cuddled then bounced about and generally made a fuss of that Stewart thought Daisy would have extreme trouble in getting the child to sleep that night after such excitement. But when he returned from his regular visit to Mrs Cottle late in the afternoon, the young Charles Hamilton was so sound asleep in his mother's arms that his whole body was as limp as a rag doll. Passing her infant over to his Nanny, Margaret and Stewart went up to their room.

Margaret closed the door behind her and looked at Stewart smiling. 'Your child will sleep till noon tomorrow.' Coming towards him she held his coat and pulled him down and kissed him. 'Penny for them?' she said as she released him.

Stewart wrapped his arms around her, holding her tight against him. 'Oh, Maggie, I never thought they would leave... the noise resembled that of the geese we had delivered at Christmas.'

Margaret giggled loudly and looked up him. 'What will happen when we have more children Stewart Hamilton, will you run and hide yourself away?' As she said this, her finger was gently prodding him in the chest in amusement.

Stewart bent and kissed her for some time. 'And just how many children are we likely to have, Mrs Hamilton?' he said as he smiled down at her, stoking her face.

Margaret placed her arms around his neck and kissed him back. 'As many as they come, Mr Hamilton.' Her eyes were alight and sparkling as she deftly removed his coat. 'We have a few hours before dinner, do we not?'

Stewart was already undoing her laces, as her hands unbuttoned his shirt. 'There is no need to rush; we have two hours before dinner,' she spoke softly into his ear.

Stewart turned her round loosening her corset and skirt, dropping them to the floor, and then quickly removing the rest of his clothing, he pushed her shift over her shoulders, and watched as that too fell. Pulling her into him and kissing her deeply, his hands ran down her spine and cupped her buttocks, pulling her even closer.

'Dear God, Maggie, you expect me to wait…' his words trailed away as he buried his face in her breasts. Slowly he walked her to the bed and sat, then lifting her onto him he held her away and watched her as he moved her gently on him. Every hair on Margaret's body was standing by now as she put her arms around his neck and held her legs tight around him; sensations were moving through her in waves, feeling as though all of the nerves in her body were laid bare and tingling even to her toes, as if small eruptions were going off all over her body, till finally she cried out. Stewart turned her quickly onto the bed and lifted her hands above her head, pushing himself into her.

'Now, Maggie,' he breathed as he fell onto her crushing her with his weight.

It was some moments later when he pulled himself up onto his elbows and smoothed the hair from her face with his hands, neither could speak, as they waited till their breathing slowed. Margaret noticed small beads of sweat on his forehead and chest, touching his forehead with her finger she brought it up to her mouth and licked it.

'You taste of salt, Stewart,' she whispered, smiling she brought his head back down again to kiss him. They lay there for some time motionless, his forehead resting on hers, till Stewart spoke.

'Maggie, I want you so much sometimes it hurts, can you understand that?'

Margaret just nodded and stoked his back.

***

Dinner was peaceful, with just the chattering of Charlotte as she spoke of her home and asked questions of both Margaret and Elizabeth. She was a pleasant young girl Stewart reflected, not yet hardened to life's traumas. He wished that she could stay that way, seeing only the good in people, and not the evil that existed in some souls. Watching her he could tell that she liked Alexander, the way her eyes wandered, watching his face and the movement of his hands, listening to his every word. Had he not seen that before in her cousin? He turned now to look at Margaret, smiling with his eyes. She knew what he was thinking without having to voice the words. Studying Alexander now, he could see that he did not know what to make of the young girl. He must feel her attraction for him, he knew that also. No man is oblivious to that kind of feeling. When he had questioned him before dinner, Alexander had been shocked, answering flatly the he was nearly ten years her senior. Smiling to himself now he thought that ten years was nothing, as long as he was loved, and there was clearly a very strong emotion emanating from Charlotte to Alexander at the moment. He would talk to Margaret later.

Turning to Charlotte he spoke. 'Charlotte, when is your father returning from his business travels, did he tell you?'

'No, Cousin Stewart, but I have a letter he gave me for Cousin Margaret.' She stopped and blushed deeply here. 'I am so sorry, I had forgotten about it till now; I was so excited to come here…' her voice trailed away. 'Please forgive me, cousin; I will go fetch it directly.'

Margaret placed a hand on her arm. 'Charlotte, be still, it is of no consequence, you can bring it when we have finished dinner.'

Stewart saw the young girl relax. Another letter he thought, what would this one reveal, he had had his fill of revelations of late. Better that Margaret opened it tomorrow, when if there were things that needed to be done it could be looked at with a clear head, and *after* a good night's sleep.

'I say we leave the letter till tomorrow, Charlotte, it cannot hold anything so urgent that we need to see it now. What do you say? Let us just enjoy the evening.' Stewart nodded his head to her in affirmation.

'You are right, Cousin Stewart; I will find it and bring it down in the morning,' she replied relieved.

Stewart stood. 'Now, let us all retire to the drawing room, so that the household can clear away the dishes and sit in peace to their own supper.'

Elizabeth had sat silent throughout, watching this play out around the table. Her heart went out to Alexander, as he looked out of his depth with the whole situation, but then knowing the depth of feeling that he had had for Margaret, she wondered what he felt when he looked at her mirror image in her cousin. This was not a good situation for him to be in.

***

The following morning Charlotte found Margaret sitting out on the terrace chatting amiably with her Nanny, while Charles gurgled softly in his perambulator.

'Good morning, Cousin Margaret,' Charlotte called as she came out of the door.

Daisy immediately rose to her feet and curtsied. 'Good morning, Mistress Charlotte, I trust you slept well?'

'Very well, thank you, Daisy,' came Charlotte's reply as she stooped to tickle her cousin Charles' foot.

It was warm in the garden, and an equally warm breeze was blowing through the shrubs around them, rustling their leaves like music.

'It will be a hot day today I fear,' commented Daisy. 'I will take Master Charles in to change him and put him for a nap before his next feed Milady.'

Margaret rose as Daisy lifted him from the crib, running a hand over his head she kissed him gently on the cheek.

'Thank you, Daisy,' she replied, placing a hand on the Nanny's arm.

Watching them walk back to the house she turned to Charlotte.

'Come, cousin, let us sit together in peace, and then I can read your father's letter.'

Elizabeth stood by the window and watched the two cousins as they sat on the terrace. There was something about them that she could not quite place her finger on, something did not sit right in her mind, and this troubled her. She had spoken to Alexander the previous evening regarding the young Charlotte. Was he aware of the attraction that she felt for him?

'What can I say, Aunt, I defy any man not to see and feel such a thing, but she is a child, Aunt,' he had stopped to run his hand over his face. 'How can I dissuade her without hurting her feelings?'

She had not disagreed with him, she was a child, but a child of marriageable age, and one with a woman's heart. He had been troubled, she could see that, but he was human after all. He had been alone too long, and he needed a wife, but it was for him to find her, not to have these affections thrown at him. Oh why could life not be simple just for once.

She watched now as Charlotte gave the letter to Margaret. It was more than one page, Elizabeth could see that from the thickness of the packet. As Margaret sat back and proceeded to read, she saw a change come over her face. It was not fear, more a look of enlightenment, as she read occasionally she would look sideways at Charlotte, and then continue reading. When she had finished Elizabeth saw Margaret carefully fold the letter again, and lean towards Charlotte taking her into a warm embrace.

Moving from the window, Elizabeth made her way outside.

'Good morning, ladies,' she called affectionately.

Margaret's head looked up, and Elizabeth could see that there were tears in her eyes.

'Margaret, your son is awaiting his feed; you must go to him before he brings the whole house down with his crying.' Elizabeth could see that Margaret needed to compose herself.

'Oh, thank you, Mother, I will go to him directly.' She looked at Charlotte and smiled. 'My cousin will be staying a while with us till her father returns; he has entrusted her into our care, as he did not want to leave her alone in Norfolk.' Getting up she walked towards Elizabeth, placing the letter into the pocket of her gown.

'I will be back very soon, and then maybe we can all have lunch on the terrace.' She kissed Elizabeth and went into the house.

Margaret's first thoughts were to find her husband. If he were not in the study then it would have to wait till lunch, or dinner. Her mind was racing, so many thoughts were coming and going that it was hard to put them into order. Charles' cry broke into them, resulting in her going straight to the nursery.

It was as she was coming out of the nursery she heard Stewart and Alexander's voices echoing from the hall.

'You have come for lunch? Oh good.' Stewart could hear the merriment in her voice and turned to look at Alexander grinning.

'At least she is still pleased to see me, Alex.' Alexander shook his head laughing.

'Go to your wife, and feel very lucky,' he said, pushing him towards Margaret.

Margaret pulled him down to her by his stock and kissed him warmly.

'Maggie, we are in the hall,' whispered Stewart, his colour changing to a rose pink as he looked back at Thompson the Butler.

Margaret was oblivious to anything as she took his hand and pulled him to the back of the house. 'We are going to have lunch on the terrace, and then...' she paused to look up into his eyes, 'I have something very special to tell you.' Kissing him once more they went outside.

Alexander looked at Thompson, but not a muscle moved on his face. He just took Alexander's hat and left.

***

As Stewart closed the door to their room, he looked at Margaret very carefully.

'Right, Margaret Hamilton, are you now going to tell me what has you so animated that you cannot contain yourself to sit still for longer than one second.' His voice held laughter but his face was puzzled.

She came to him and pushed the coat from his shoulders, then pulling his shirt out from his breeches she pushed her hands up inside to stoke his back.

'Margaret, what are you doing...' his words were stopped by her placing a finger onto his lips.

'Shhh,' was her reply.

Taking his hand she pulled him to sit on the bed beside her, and then very carefully she took out the letter, opening it and smoothing out the pages she handed it to him. Stewart looked at her and shook his head.

'Read it, Stewart,' she whispered.

The air in the room was suffocating, so while he read Margaret rose and opened the windows wide, letting in a very welcome breeze. She stood leaning against the table by the windows watching Stewart's face go through many changes. Had not hers done the same when she had read the contents?

Reading the last page, Stewart carefully folded the letter again, letting his hand drop to his lap.

'She is your sister?' he said incredulously. Margaret's head was nodding vigorously.

Suddenly, she was upon him, holding him so tight. 'Oh, Stewart, is it not wonderful, she is my sister.' It was then the tears came.

Stewart sat up, pulling her onto his lap, holding her tight, he breathed deeply. 'What was the other piece of news you had for me?' he questioned. 'Please do not let it stop my heart, Maggie. One shock today is enough.' He laughed gently.

Margaret sat up, took his face into her hands and looked deep into his eyes.

'I am with child again.' Her voice was so quiet it took some time for Stewart to register what she had said.

'You are,' he breathed just as Margaret nodded her head and kissed him deeply once more.

Sometime later as they lay entangled in one another's arms Stewart leaned away from her and placed his hand over her stomach. He was looking into her face but the words would not come. Margaret placed her hand upon his and pulled him close resting her head on his chest.

'I love you, Stewart Hamilton,' was all she said as she drifted peacefully off to sleep.

***

Alexander raised his brows as Stewart ducked into the office.

'To my estimation, cousin, it is around noon now?' he queried light-heartedly. 'You look as you did after drinking all night in The Angel, though I know that not to be true.' Alexander's eyes were full of mischief, as he beckoned his cousin to sit down. 'Have you slept at all?' he teased.

Stewart put up his hands and breathed deeply.

'I feel totally disembodied, Alex. I will leave it to you to understand why when you read this letter from Cousin Charlotte's father. I will then tell you the second part, when you have digested the first.'

Stewart took off his coat and waistcoat, and then poured himself a mug of water from the stone pitcher on the floor, before walking outside to sit in the shade. His mind was so cluttered he could not think straight, and he had a raging headache which seemed to commence in his shoulders and rise to his temples ending at the place between his brows. Margaret had been elated; she was no longer alone without kith and kin: she had a sister.

At the other end of this dimension was his mother. She knew nothing of the other letter, the involvement of his father with Northcott. Stewart shuddered at the thought of it. This would never go away, it was reality, and no matter how hard one tried to forget, one could not. This happened. It could not be disproven, it was the truth. All they had done was to remove it from its resting place, to another underground location.

He had written to James to invite him to the Baptism of his son on 5th August, of which he had accepted. There would be time then to talk in depth.

What would he make of Cousin Charlotte? No, Sister Charlotte, Stewart corrected himself. He would probably be as perplexed as Alex.

Then the last revelation, that Margaret was with child again, well he had been jubilant, what man would not. Rubbing his hands over his face, he stood up and walked back into the office.

As Stewart entered Alexander raised his head up, the letter still in his hand.

'She is her sister?' he said in disbelief.

191

Stewart just inclined his head. 'Alex, we will know no more till her father arrives, which will not be till the end of August. Meanwhile the child knows nothing of this only that she is to stay here till her father comes for her.'

Stewart refilled his mug with water and sat on the edge of the desk.

'Maggie could have been no more than five years old when Charlotte was born.' He swallowed hard here. 'What possesses a man, Alex, to give up his daughter—his own blood—simply because she is a daughter and not a son? Can you comprehend that, Alex? Because I for one cannot,' he paused. 'Which brings me to the last surprise, are you ready for this?' saying this Stewart smiled broadly. 'You are to be an uncle again.'

Alexander's face matched that of Stewart's, coming round the desk he clasped his cousin tight and thumped his back.

'Out of everything that has occurred, God in all his mercy has given us one piece of joy, cousin, congratulations,' smiled Alexander. 'Does your mother know yet?' he questioned.

'Margaret is giving her the news now, along with Cousin Charlotte,' Stewart answered.

'Alex, it is my mother that troubles me greatly.' Stewart sighed heavily. 'I have written to James and he says he will be present at young Charles' baptism. I will talk to him then.' Stewart paused. 'This is not something that will go away, Alex, and that is what scares me most.' Stewart looked down at his hands. 'Amidst all this joy, there is this pain, and my heart is breaking for my mother, who has never done anything but good in her life.'

Alexander looked at him and saw the anguish in his eyes.

'Sit down, Stewart, I wish to tell *you* something.'

Alexander poured out two mugs of ale from the earthenware bottle on his desk, handing one to Stewart he beckoned him to follow him outside taking a stool with him he motioned to Stewart to bring the other. Seating themselves under the cool shade of a tree they drank quietly for some moments.

'When I was eleven,' began Alexander. 'I lived in a small village a little outside of Edinburgh. My father was a Minister, as was his father—my grandfather—before him.' Stewart looked at him and inclined his head.

My grandfather, your grandfather and my great uncle were brothers from the House of Hamilton in Edinburgh. My... our great uncle,' he corrected himself, 'was the first born and so inherited the house and land, your father was the third born and inherited monies left to him by his grandfather, my grandfather was a Minister—most second sons went into business or the clergy. When he died my father took the position.' Alexander paused to sip his ale.

'I am following you, Alex, please continue,' replied Stewart softly.

'It was during that year my father and mother died of a lung sickness which rots the lungs, causing the person to spit blood – consumption was the name they gave for it. My father would visit the sick and infirm of the parish regularly, and they say it was from there that he brought it home to my mother. They had both died before I reached the age of twelve—it never harmed me.' Alexander swallowed hard and drank more ale.

'They were very harsh times in Scotland then, and our great uncle was the only survivor—your grandfather had died just after you were born. He knew that your mother was still living, so he wrote her asking her to take me. She did with open arms.' Stewart sighed and raised his mug to Alexander drinking deeply.

'Our great uncle settled some money on me, which he sent to a bank in Exeter. It was for my schooling in Winchester, and to be used for my needs till I was eighteen years of age and able to go out into the world to seek a living for myself.' Alexander paused again to look at Stewart.

'Your mother used none of that money. She paid for my schooling, and all of the expenditure that was necessary for my stay at Winchester. When I left, she presented me with a small fortune, and to say that I was amazed Stewart—well, she found the house in Mere, which I purchased, and then the cook—who I now also believe is a relative of your Mrs Cottle—a butler and maid.' Alexander saw Stewart begin to speak and stopped him.

'My Butler acts as my valet, my needs are simple, Stewart.'

Stewart by this time had stood up and was pacing slowly up and down.

'Your valet Pip took care of me as well as yourself at Winchester, and every break from studies I would come and spend it here with you and your mother.'

Stewart turned and walked into the office, returning with the bottle of ale he refilled their mugs, held his up to his cousin and sat down once more.

'I worked closely with her then Estate Steward, and so when he died, she asked if I would be prepared to take on the task—with payment. I told my aunt that I would not accept payment; I had enough for my needs and required none.' He paused to turn and look at Stewart. 'I have since discovered that money goes regularly into my name at the bank in Exeter—that will be for my godson.' Alexander drank down his ale and stood up.

'Your mother has been a mother to me for all these years, she knew nothing of me when I came, if I was a bad person or not. I was family she said, and families should always give help to one another.'

Stewart stood, then coughed to clear his throat, swallowing several times to compose himself. Looking at Alexander he placed a hand round his shoulders.

'Alex, you have always been a brother to me. You should know that.' His voice was so tight with emotion he could not utter another word.

***

Chapter Twenty-Two
Affection and Baptism

James Fairweather smiled broadly as he stepped down from his coach.

'Good day to you, Stewart!' he exclaimed. 'And a very hot one it is, too, not one you would want to spend travelling in a coach.'

Stewart came down the steps, inclining his head. 'Good day to you, James,' he greeted his friend.

'How is Master Charles?' asked James.

'Noisy,' replied Stewart with a grin on his face.

As they ascended the steps, Elizabeth greeted him warmly. 'Hello, James,' she called as she reached up and kissed him on both cheeks. 'It is good to see you once more. Come in and take some refreshment, you look hot and very travel weary.'

James Fairweather took off his hat and bowed to Elizabeth. 'Good day to you, Milady.' Not having time to right himself, Margaret came out and clasped his hand.

'Oh, James, we are all so pleased you could come,' she said with laughter in her voice.

James clutched his hat to his breast and bowed once more. 'It is my pleasure, Milady, and I thank you for the invitation.'

'Oh, James, you need not stand on ceremony with me,' she said as she placed her hand through his arm pulling him into the house. 'Come see how Charles has grown!'

As James came into the living room, he stopped dead, looking at the young girl he saw before him and then turning to Margaret.

Margaret giggled. 'No, James, you are not seeing visions, this is my cousin Charlotte, and she is staying with us while her father is away on business. He has entrusted her into our care and will come for her at the end of August.'

James bowed for the third time in as many minutes. 'Good day to you, Mistress Charlotte.'

Stewart looked sideways at his friend. 'James, go up and refresh yourself, then come and take some tea, or another beverage if you so wish, with us on the terrace, while we await Alexander who will be with us shortly.'

'Thank you, I will, as I fear that my clothes have jointed with my flesh, the sun is relentless, and not a cloud to be seen or a breeze to be felt.'

'Pip has everything ready for you,' said Stewart, nodding to his friend.

194

James Fairweather smiled. 'I give you a heartfelt *thanks*.' With that he left the room.

Stewart looked from his mother to Margaret to Charlotte. 'Go out to the terrace, there is shade now, and I will join you presently. I just have some paperwork to attend to in the study first.' Taking Margaret's hand, he squeezed it. 'Go bring Charles down if he is not asleep, let James see how much he has grown.

His mother gave him one of her surreptitious looks, smiled and left.

Stewart made his way to the study, removing his coat as he went and unbuttoning his waistcoat. The house inside was cool in comparison but the heat was oppressive, seeming to suck the air out from one's lungs. He threw open both windows, and breathed deep. He did not hear Alexander enter till he was standing by him.

'James is here,' Stewart offered.

'I know, I saw his carriage being led away as I came up to the house.' Looking out, he nodded. 'How is Margaret?'

'She is much better this time, Alex, she has had just a few days where she has not been able to contain anything, but this time she is radiant, she seems to have some inner glow…' his voice trailed off

Alexander watched the ladies. 'Maybe it has something to do with the Mistress Charlotte.'

'You could be right, cousin, she has changed since the young girl came. There is a warmth within her now, I cannot truly explain.'

'What of the, cousin, Charlotte?' Alexander lifted his eyebrows.

'Oh she is still yours, cousin, of that I am in no doubt.' Stewart grinned.

'I do not find anything to jest about, Stewart, the girl is a child—' before Alexander could finish, Stewart broke in.

'A child perhaps, but as my mother pointed out to me, a child of marriageable age, and one with the heart of a woman,' he paused to look hard at his cousin. 'Alex, do you not get lonely? Do you not feel the need to have someone other than yourself to care for, and likewise someone to care for you?' Stewart shook his head. 'She is beautiful, Alex, she is kind and is of a very loving disposition, and as my mother in all her wisdom said, she puts you next to God.'

Alexander sat heavily. 'What of my feelings, Stewart? Is it me here who is to be sold so that I will not be lonely?' he breathed through his. 'She is warm and loving, I can tell that, after having known her just these two weeks, and I find her very agreeable to speak with, but I do not love her, Stewart. You alone should know what that feels like.'

'I have but one thing to say to that, cousin. Love can grow.' The words hung in the air.

There was a light tap on the door, and then James Fairweather walked into the silence.

'My humblest apologies, have I interrupted anything?'

'No, James, come in, come in,' Stewart said as he walked towards him. 'We were just speaking of Cousin Charlotte.'

195

'Ah!' came James's reply. 'There is a remarkable likeness between them. There are some subtle differences, but nonetheless remarkable.'

Alexander looked hard at his cousin, daring him to say a word.

'Let us join the ladies out on the terrace, and for God's sake, James, take off your jacket, you will melt. We hold no social graces here, just the common respectful ones.'

Alexander stayed back, trying to collect his thoughts together. Of course he was lonely. He had needs like any man, though he could find that elsewhere, but it was not the same as having a wife. When he saw his cousin happy and content, with a beautiful child and another to be born next year in March, he wanted that, but not at any cost. Taking off his jacket and laying it over the chair, he went out onto the terrace.

'Good day to you, ladies, Mistress.' Alexander inclined his head.

Elizabeth rose from her seat between Margaret and Charlotte. 'Come, take my seat, I have to go to the kitchen to see cook regarding the dinner tonight.' She beckoned Alexander.

Stewart looked at him. 'You should be very honoured, Alex, to be sitting in the midst of two very beautiful ladies.' His eyes rested on Margaret, sparkling with mischief.

'Pay him no heed, Alex, he teases me frequently.'

They sat pleasantly, talking for some while, then Margaret was the first to leave to feed her infant, followed by Stewart and James. Alexander knew that his cousin needed to speak with him quite pressingly, regarding his aunt, but this then left him alone with the cousin Charlotte. He also knew that she had been watching him, so when he turned to speak, she blushed pink to the roots of her hair.

'I understand, Cousin Charlotte, you are to be Charles' godmother tomorrow?' Alexander spoke softly.

'She lowered her head and nodded. 'Yes, Cousin Alexander, but I fear I have no gift for baby Charles. I knew nothing of him till I came. I have written to my father requesting that he find something suitable, a shawl maybe, or a silver rattle.'

'Do not trouble yourself, Charlotte, I have bought him a silver plate, mug and spoon with his name engraved onto them. It will suffice for both of us tomorrow,' he paused before he said the next words. 'I believe that you should say his names when asked by the vicar, it is only right as you are her cousin by birth, I am just by marriage.'

'Oh, cousin, you do me a great honour, but it should not be I,' she answered as she turned her head up to look at him, which caused her colour to change once again to a pink hue.

'It will be fine, Cousin Charlotte.' Alexander smiled softly. 'Let us go in for lunch.' He rose, bowed slightly, and offered her his arm.

Elizabeth, who had been secretly watching this play out from the drawing room window, smiled knowingly to herself.

***

Dinner had been a pleasant, happy one, with stories from Elizabeth of Stewart's baptism, and how he too had baptised the vicar. Margaret would use her husband's baptismal gown, which had been carefully washed and pressed, the small bonnet and shoes did not fit though, as Stewart had been just one month old, and Charles was now three months and growing fast.

The days were long now; even though the hour was nine o'clock, there was still daylight, as the three men walked the lawn together, deep in thought. James had informed Stewart that no word had been heard since that first time when Northcott had contacted his father. Stewart had spoken in depth to James of what had taken place as a consequence of that, but neither had commented further. James now looked towards Stewart and thought his words over carefully before he spoke.

'Stewart, it is his word against your mother's that all of this occurred. Nobody knew the man except your father, and for all we know he could have been a rouge, a seaman, a friend from Scotland… the list is endless. None of your household knew his identity, and if he were someone of consequence, you would have heard of a disappearance.' He stopped walking and turned towards Stewart.

'There is no longer any trace of this man on your land, and only yourself, Alexander, Spike and Pip know of his final resting place. As you said, the other men fled wanting no part of what was taking place, they were not present when this happened, only your father and the deceased.' He ran his hand over his face. 'I will go to London after the baptism and speak with Bearcroft, to get his thoughts from a legal aspect, but I am sure he will be of the same mind as I. I would advise not telling your mother at this present time. Let us wait and see what transpires. If other circumstances come to light, then, and only then, will she need to be told.'

Stewart inclined his head in agreement. 'A clear head can always see things differently, thank you, James. Now I shall take my wife and go to my bed as we have to be at the church by twelve noon tomorrow. Goodnight, gentleman.' Turning back, he looked at Alexander.

'Why do you not take Cousin Charlotte to see the gardens, they smell beautiful at this time of evening.' There was no teasing in his voice, just a polite gesture.

'I will also take my leave of you, Alexander, it has been a long day for me. I will see you early in the morning.' With that James walked back with Stewart to the house.

Alexander came up onto the terrace and approached his aunt.

'Aunt, Cousin Charlotte, will you walk with me in the gardens for a while, I fear it is too hot to sleep.'

Elizabeth looked at the tall fair man that stood in front of her and her heart went out to him.

197

'I will be very happy to walk with you, Alex. Come Charlotte, I will show you the roses.' Taking Alexander's arm and that of Charlotte's, they walked down slowly together. Elizabeth looked up at him, smiling warmly and squeezed his arm.

'Thank you,' she mimed with her lips.

***

The tower to St Michael's in Mere was very imposing. Dating from the 14th century, it stood around one-hundred-and-twenty-five-feet tall with four tall pinnacles atop pointing up to the sky. The tall double doors were open, awaiting the congregation to enter for the baptism of young Charles Hamilton. The octagonal font could be seen clearly directly in the centre of the tower, as the tenants entered spreading themselves around the back of the interior, then came the Ladies of the Parish with their families, and finally Stewart's family, with young Charles laying peacefully in his mother's arms, contented having been fed before the party left the house.

The weather was hot, and many of those gathered were fanning themselves vigorously to cool down. Margaret handed her son over to Charlotte while the family positioned themselves around the font, the vicar then progressed through his speech of questions and answers till the moment came where Charlotte placed her godson into his hands. Holding him over the font, he then poured water over Charles' head three times to represent the father, son and holy spirit, while Charlotte's clear voice read out the names he was to be given, and the vicar repeated them. Alexander watched Cousin Charlotte from the corner of his eyes and noticed her hands were trembling. Taking the hand next to him, he placed it gently into the crook of his arm. Charles Hamilton looked up into the vicar's eyes and never uttered a sound.

As with the wedding of Stewart and Margaret, the tenants and staff celebrated on tables set out on the lawn at the back of the house. It was a cold luncheon, as much of the food had been prepared either that morning or the day before, as well as pickles and cured ham. Two kegs of ale stood on the terrace where jugs were filled frequently.

The family had joined them and sat to theirs on the terrace, while Master Charles slept peacefully in his perambulator under the watchful gaze of his nanny.

Stewart stood up, raising his glass. 'To my son, my wife, and my mother, and to friends and two very treasured godparents.'

James Fairweather stood, raising his glass also. 'I second that!'

Stewart bowed slightly. 'Now if you will all excuse me, my wife and I must go and thank my tenants.' Looking at Margaret, he inclined his head and offered her his arm.

Margaret turned to Charlotte. 'You did splendidly, Cousin Charlotte, your father would have been proud of you, and so would your mother,' she added, squeezing her hand.

Alexander looked at her as she sat next to his aunt. 'My cousin is correct, Cousin Charlotte, young Charles should regard himself very lucky and be proud to have such a godmother as yourself.' The words were warmly spoken and Charlotte's colour heightened as he spoke them.

Elizabeth who had been watching this exchange spoke. 'Young men, why do you not take yourselves off for a stroll into the gardens, while Charlotte and I go freshen ourselves?'

James stood up at once and bowed. 'Thank you, Milady, and thank you also for a wonderful ceremony and food,' he patted his stomach. 'I tell everyone regarding your cook, her meals are ambrosia.' He kissed his fingers to confirm this.

'James Fairweather, Alexander, go for your walk. I fear you have both had too much to drink.' Elizabeth smiled as she waved her hand for them to leave.

'Come, Charlotte, let us go and see some of the presents that Charles has received.' Standing up, Elizabeth took Charlotte's arm and walked into the house.

'Oh, upon my word it is cool in here,' Elizabeth exclaimed as she walked into the darkness of the passage. Coming into the hall, she saw Stewart by the table holding some letters.

'Stewart? I thought you were talking to the tenants.' queried Elizabeth.

'Oh, I was, Mother, but Thompson said there had been some mail brought here today, and then Alexander asked me if I had put the letters out for posting that he brought here yesterday, so here I am,' he answered.

Elizabeth's face was puzzled. 'Strange, I did not think that mail came here on a Sunday?'

'Oh it does not, Mother, one of your ladies from the church brought them with her and gave them to Thompson. Otherwise they would have come tomorrow as normal.' Placing the letters back onto the tray, he nodded. 'Nothing that cannot wait till then. I shall now resume my duties, Mother,' he grinned playfully.

'I fear you also have had too much to drink, as well as those two lads that I have just sent into the gardens to walk off their over indulgence. Be off with you, go and join your wife.' Elizabeth waved her hands to shoo him away.

Charlotte giggled to herself. 'Oh, Aunt Elizabeth...' she bubbled.

Elizabeth turned. 'Believe me, Charlotte, men are still children, no matter how old they are, and need a firm hand.' With that, both ladies laughed and made their way to the drawing room.

Many gifts were piled onto the small table there, amongst them a beautiful shawl.

'Aunt Elizabeth, look at this, is it not beautiful?' exclaimed Charlotte.

Elizabeth looked at it and read from the card. 'That is from my friend Josephine, the one that I bought those silks from. I believe she has some relatives in France.'

Together they looked through the gifts, reading the cards. 'Aunt Elizabeth, mine will come when my father arrives at the end of August. I wrote to him regarding baby Charles, and asked him if he could choose something for me, a silver rattle maybe or goblet with his name on or a shawl.' He eyes were drawn to the gift that Alexander had given.

'But Alexander said that his gift was from both of you.' Elizabeth took Charlotte's hands in hers, looking into her face. 'You have a fondness for him, do you not?' Charlotte blushed, pulled her hands free and walked to the window. All three men were just coming up the steps, their laughter could be heard clearly.

'He is a very fine gentleman, Aunt.' It was the wistfulness in her voice that made Elizabeth pull her into her arms.

'Oh, Charlotte, my dear child.' Holding her away, they sat down. 'Alexander is a very kind man indeed. He is loyal, generous to a fault and very loving.' Elizabeth stroked her hands.

Charlotte swallowed. 'Aunt, when he is near or speaks to me, my heart leaps. In secret I find I watch his every move. I know he is much older than I, oh, Aunt, I should not feel this way I know, but I do. I feel disloyal to my father by having these emotions. It will be better when he comes to take me back, in time I will forget.' There was such anguish in her voice.

Elizabeth raised her head up and saw the tears in her eyes. 'You are young, Charlotte, this is the first time that a man has roused such emotions within you.' Elizabeth pulled her against her, holding her till her tears were spent.

'Come,' Elizabeth said firmly, handing Charlotte her handkerchief, 'wipe your face. I will introduce you to the tenants, I am sure that their curiosity is fit to burst with the need to find out who you are.' Laughing, she pulled her to her feet.

***

The three men sat in silence.

'Is there something troubling you, cousin?' asked Alexander. He had seen that look before and it did not bode well.

'Later, when the women have retired, we can speak. I have a letter on my person which is from my father to my mother. I intend opening the said letter to find out its contents.'

Before anyone could speak, Daisy appeared with a thoroughly disgruntled Charles. Curtsying, she said, 'Begging your pardon, Master Hamilton, but would you know where Milady can be found as I fear Master Charles is hungry.'

'Go back to the nursery, Daisy, I will find her immediately,' he said as he took his son into his arms. Curtseying once more, she left.

'James, go find my wife for me please, I dare not take him out into that sun. Tell her Charles her son is hungry,' he grinned, as he walked back into the house.

Watching Alexander as he returned, James seated himself once more and breathed deeply. 'There is a breeze now, Alex, can you feel it? Maybe we will get some rain to cool us, but for now the breeze will do.'

He saw that Alexander as deep in thought, then following his gaze realised he was looking at Charlotte.

'You do not know what to make of her, do you, my friend?' asked James. Alexander shook his head.

'She has a fondness for you, I can see that, and it is a little more than an infatuation I believe.' James shifted in his chair. 'Pray tell me if you want, that it is none of my business, but did you know my father was twelve years older than my mother?' Alexander looked round at him.

'She was seventeen when she met him at a party in London. When her father proposed a marriage between them, my father would have none of it. In fact, he was astonished that her father could even think of such a thing. But, marry they did, and she doted on him, so much so that when she died, a part of my father died with her. You could do worse, Alex. I wish someone would show me such affection, but alas I think am bound for bachelorhood.'

Alexander smiled softly. 'I take the gift of what you are telling me and thank you for it. In truth I do not find her repulsive, on the contrary I find her very beautiful, and I also feel affection for her, but I do not love her, James.'

'Neither did my father when he married.' James nodded, stood up and went into the house.

Chapter Twenty-Three
The Letter, Sorrow and the Mending

It was early morning, and the house was still asleep as Stewart sat alone in his study. Turning the letter over and over, watching it go from writing on one side to seal on the other repeatedly. He looked out of the open window to the garden for guidance, but there was nothing to be heard, only the chirping of the birds and the wind rustling the trees and shrubs. Placing the letter into the pocket of his coat, he stood up and went to saddle his horse.

As he rode through the countryside, he knew where he was going without thinking. His horse knew the way without guidance, slowing down unconsciously as he saw the lake stretch out before him. '*Baia della pace,*' breathed Stewart, but now it was anything but a "Haven of Peace", and he shuddered when he thought what was now buried there.

Getting down from his saddle, his hand picked up a stone as it was custom to do, throwing it into the depths, watching the circles emanate from where the stone had entered. He tethered his horse to a tree, then sat with his knees drown up to his chest. Slowly, he pulled the letter out from his pocket and carefully released the seal without breaking it, so that it could be sealed once more.

His father's handwriting stood out stark and black against the creaminess of the paper. There were very few words on the page, but what was there was spelt out in very clear syllables what he wanted. For his silence, his mother was to sell the estate and give him half of the proceeds.

'The hell she will, I will kill you first.'

As he said the words, it was a though they were taken and pushed into the depths of the lake for safe keeping. Breathing deeply, he let his head fall onto his arms. Stewart sat there for some time, clearing his mind, thinking only of his mother. Slowly he rose up, throwing one more stone into the lake as if to seal the bargain that had just been made, then mounted his horse and rode for home.

Margaret, wrapped in her robe, was descending the stairs as Stewart came into the hall.

'Stewart, where have you been so early?' her voice was questioning, but worried.

Coming towards her, he pulled her into his arms and kissed her.

I woke too early, and rather than wake you, I went for a ride to clear my head; we drank too much yesterday. In fact, I do not remember getting into bed at all.'

Margaret stepped back and looked at him. 'You remember nothing, Stewart Hamilton?' Her eyebrows rose up as she stared at him.

Kissing her once more, he whispered in her ear. 'Well, some things are quite clear.'

Trying to pull away from him, she laughed. 'As your mother rightly says, you are incorrigible!'

Stewart squeezed her once more. 'Of course, we could always go back to bed?'

Pushing him away from her, she laughed. 'Stewart Hamilton, your son will be making a rather large noise very soon if he is not fed, out of my way.'

He grabbed her arm as she passed. 'Take him to Mrs Cottle,' he grinned. 'He will sleep till noon.'

A loud cry then went up from above and Stewart groaned. 'My wife prefers her son to me…'

As Margaret moved past him, she whispered. 'Go wash yourself for breakfast, Stewart, I will see you after lunch.' Tapping his cheek lightly, she went back up the stairs.

Breakfast passed pleasantly, with easy banter as they sat around the table. Margaret watched her sister as she sat next to James. He was an easy man to talk to, thought Margaret, funny, respectful, but as she watched Charlotte, she was acutely aware that her eyes strayed constantly towards the blond man sitting across from her. It was more than infatuation, she knew that; had she not felt the same about Stewart? Turning to watch her husband now, she sighed, and a quiver went through her. He was a handsome man, and, she thought thankfully, he was all hers. Stewart turned, suddenly catching her gaze with his; Margaret replied with a hint of a smile, but it was enough. There was another language without speech.

The moment ended quickly as Elizabeth spoke to her.

'Margaret, would you and Charlotte care to come into Mere with me today? I am just visiting a friend and we should be no more than two hours.'

'Please forgive me, Mother, but I am a little tired today. I think I will just rest for a while. I was up very early this morning with Charles, but I am sure that Charlotte would love to go.' Looking towards her sister, she saw her eyes light up.

'Oh, I would love to, Aunt, thank you,' she replied

'Then it is settled, we will leave here in half an hour. I will just go and tell Carter to bring round the carriage.'

Elizabeth saw that her daughter-in-law had hardly touched her food, and there were dark shadows under her eyes.

'Stewart, take your wife up to rest. I will send Lilly up with some tea and maybe a few biscuits.' Reaching across, she squeezed Margaret's hand and nodded.

'You know it will pass,' she whispered.

***

The three men sat in their shirts outside the estate office, leaning back against the wall. The air was hot and dry, and seemed to suck the life out of everything, even the light breeze of the morning had ceased and now not a leaf moved, and the sun was relentless as its rays beat down on the parched earth, turning the grass from green to varying shades of yellow and brown.

James Fairweather fanned himself with his hat. 'God, it has to rain soon. I feel as though I have been placed into an oven and slowly cooked hard like a biscuit.'

Stewart learned forward and looked sideways at his friend.

'We could always go down to the lake and swim.' No sooner had he spoken the words, he realised what he had said.

'You would have us go to that place, knowing what lies there?' questioned Alexander.

'Alex, he is not IN the lake, but somewhere in the thicket on the west side,' was his reply. 'Besides, we can no longer swim in the River Nadder, we are grown men now, what would the tenants who live there make of us,' he added.

Stewart got up, went into the office and brought out the letter.

'Read this,' handing it to Alexander, he sat back down.

Alexander read the lines quickly, passing it on to James.

'When did the letter arrive, Stewart?' queried James.

'I found it amongst the mail that was brought back from Mere after the baptism. I only read it this morning.'

James looked at his friend and thought that he seemed too calm, too detached, as he passed the letter back to Alexander.

'What will you do, cousin? What can we do?' Alexander questioned.

'This letter should have been addressed to me,' he answered as he took the letter from Alexander's hand. 'There is a method in what my father is doing, but as yet I do not quite know what it is. What I do know…' he paused to look at his cousin and friend. '… I will never sell this estate, even if I have to kill him to keep it.' He rose from the stool, turning. 'Now, I am going for a swim, even if you are not,' he added, turning towards the stables to saddle his horse.

James looked at Alexander, lifted his shoulders and the two men followed him.

***

As Stewart surfaced from the water, he pushed back his hair and breathed deeply. Laying back, he let the water take him as he floated, looking upwards to the sky. Pip had taught him to swim in the River Nadder when he was small—he smiled remembering. He had thrown him in and told him to kick with his legs and strike out with his arms or he would drown, and he had done just that, as he did not think dying at the age of six very appropriate at that time, least of all what his mother would have said. Looking over at Alexander and James as they splashed and pulled one another under, he swam to the shore, sitting in the sun to dry. Alexander, he thought, must have learnt in the rivers of Scotland, and

James from his own estate in Cornwall. Maggie could not swim, he knew that, girls did not enjoy the same freedom as boys, but then she had also not been allowed out of the confines of her garden till she was eighteen. He would love to bring her here, take her into the depths and hold her, letting her float in his arms. The unbridled freedom she would feel, letting go all of her inhibitions. His son would swim as soon as he was old enough, and his daughter—if he had one. Why should the mere fact of being a girl stop you having the same freedoms, even if it meant defying convention damn it; had he not done the same all of his life? Yes, he answered himself, and look where it had got him.

He was aroused from his thoughts by a shower of cold water being splashed on him, courtesy of James and Alexander.

James seated himself on the grass beside him.

'Excellent idea of yours, Stewart, I feel totally invigorated.'

Stewart looked at him and smiled. 'James Fairweather, you are fool but a very nice one. Why have you not found yourself a wife yet? Someone to take care of you? Someone to love you?'

'Ahh, Hamilton, if it were as easy. I am afraid no one will have me.' With that, he stood up and spread his arms out. 'Am I not a fine figure of a man?'

Stewart shook his head. 'Get dressed, you fool!' he laughed.

***

As they rode up to the house, Stewart knew that there was something wrong when he saw his mother walking up and down.

Jumping from the saddle, he was by her in just a few strides, and he could see she was crying.

'Mother, what is wrong?' he shouted.

Elizabeth clung to him and sobbed. 'Oh Stewart…' She held his face in her hands. 'It is Margaret, she has lost the child,' she sobbed.

Stewart was in the house and up the stairs before anyone could stop him. Bursting into the room, he saw Margaret laying as though dead on the bed, and so much blood around her—his stomach churned and he held onto the door for support.

'Maggie!!!' he screamed before Alexander and James pulled him from the room. He fought them all the way down the stairs screaming her name, till they got him into the study and shut the door.

'Let me out of here or I will kill you both!!!' he yelled.

Elizabeth came into the room then and slapped him hard on the side of his face.

'Stewart!!' she screamed. 'Sit down now!!!' her voice shook with emotion.

It was then that he fell to the floor, head in his hands and sobbed. Elizabeth waved Alexander and James away with her hand and sat down with him, cradling his head in her lap.

'We will be just outside, Aunt,' said Alexander quietly before closing the door.

She waited for him to quieten, and then lifted his head up to look into his eyes.

'Stewart, can you hear me?' He nodded in reply, tears streaming down his face.

'After you left, Maggie went to your room for a while. She told Lilly when she came to take the tea things that she felt much better and she would go down to sit on the terrace in the cool. She left the room to come down, then just six stairs from the bottom Lilly saw her fall like a stone hitting her head on the post at the bottom.' She breathed deeply here and took his hands in hers.

'It was then that the bleeding started. I sent Carter to Mere to bring my physician, while Pip carried her upstairs.' She kissed his hands and sobbed.

'There was nothing he could do, Stewart. I came out onto the porch to look for you and…'

He gripped her hands tightly. 'Mother, I want to see her, please!!' he pleaded.

'I will send Lilly up to see if the physician has finished, then we will go.' She was nodding all the while she was speaking.

***

As they entered the room, he could see her laying high upon the pillows looking deathly pale even unto her lips.

The physician bowed. 'Mr Hamilton sir, I have administered some laudanum for the pain, and to calm her. The bleeding has stopped, all that was meant to come has, and she will sleep now for some hours.'

Stewart moved to the bed and gently sat next to her; smoothing her hair back from her brow and taking her hand in his, he turned to the physician.

'I will stay with her till she wakes,' he replied softly.

Elizabeth turned then to her physician. 'Mr Hardiman, words cannot express my gratitude for what you have done.'

'It is of no consequence, Milady Hamilton, I will stay here till she wakes to make sure that she is well, as I fear she may be troubled in her sleep with hallucinations from the laudanum. It can take a person that way some times.'

Elizabeth looked once more towards Stewart, and then turned for the door. 'Come, Mr Hardiman, I will get cook to prepare you something to eat.'

***

Alexander and James were seated in the drawing room.

'Do you not find it ironic, Alex, all that she endured before the birth of her son…' James Fairweather's voice stopped.

'What I do know, James…' Alexander paused to find the words, 'is that we were swimming when this happened, and he will never forgive himself for that.'

As he was speaking, Elizabeth entered.

'Alexander, no one was to blame. As she descended the stairs, Margaret became unsteady and collapsed. The blow to her head rendered her unconscious, but the fall caused her to lose the child,' Elizabeth spoke the words softly.

'Stewart is with her; he will not leave her side. My physician will remain here until she regains consciousness, as I fear that the laudanum he administered could cause her to hallucinate.'

'Aunt, what can we do?' came Alexander's anguished reply.

Elizabeth placed her hand on his arm. 'Dear Alex, I fear there is nothing that any of us can do. Charlotte was whiteness to all of this and is most traumatised, my maid is with her now on the terrace.'

'Would it help, Milady Hamilton, if Alexander and I went and sat with them?' asked James Fairweather.

'James, it cannot do any harm, but maybe take her thoughts from what she witnessed. We came back from Mere just as this occurred, and Charlotte believed her cousin to be dead, and so did I...' Elizabeth sat heavily onto the sofa as she said the last words.

Alexander walked to the side cupboard and poured his aunt a glass of port.

'Drink, Aunt,' was all he said as he held it out to her.

'James, I am going up to see Stewart, please stay with my aunt.' Nodding, Alexander turned and left.

Alexander tapped lightly on the door before entering. The room was in semi darkness, as the drapes were pulled. Walking towards the bed, he placed his hand on his cousin's shoulder and squeezed.

Stewart's voice came out as a rasp. 'Alex, for God's sake open those drapes. Maggie cannot bear them to be drawn.'

Walking straight to the windows, he pulled them apart, allowing a stream of bright sunlight to flood the room, and then pushing the windows open to let in some air, he turned to his cousin.

'Stewart, this is nobody's fault. Margaret became unwell as she descended the stairs...'

'I know, Alex, but I should have been there...' There was so much remorse in his voice that Alexander's heart went out to him.

Standing behind Stewart, Alexander looked down at Margaret's inert body as it lay in the bed.

'The physician said that the laudanum may cause her to have visions, nightmares...'

Stewart put up his hand. 'I know, Alex, I will be here for her.'

Opening the door, Alexander turned. 'If you want anything, cousin, I will be down stairs.'

***

When he came down, he found James on the terrace with Charlotte and Elizabeth's maid Molly. Daisy was there also with baby Charles but before he could speak, Elizabeth came out of the house.

'I have arranged for my grandson to go to my friend's wet nurse in Mere.' Turning to look at James, she continued. 'James, may I be very presumptuous in asking, would you escort them there please? They will remain for a few days, as my physician states Margaret cannot nurse him while the laudanum is in her blood.'

James Fairweather stood up and bowed. 'I am at your service, Milady Hamilton, I will stay at Alexander's house if I may till their return, in case they should be in need of any assistance,' he nodded to Alexander for approval.

'Of course, James, I will write a missive for you to take to my butler and cook to inform them of your requirements.'

'I will need very little requirements, Alex, just a bed and food.'

'My butler is my valet also, James,' began Alexander

'I have no problem with that in the slightest, pray tell him I will not be of a bother to him.'

Alexander shook his head. 'To hear you speak, James, no one would believe you are from the family that you are,' he smiled warmly.

'I was brought up to be respectful, Alex, and I hope that I will always remain so.' Turning to Daisy, he bowed. 'Shall we go, Mistress?'

As Elizabeth led them back into the house to prepare themselves, Lilly came down the corridor from the Kitchen.

'Begging your pardon, Milady, but Jenifer Penhale is wanting to speak with you in the kitchen.'

Elizabeth turned to James and Daisy. 'Please excuse me, but I must see what she wants, she is the midwife's daughter, my tenant.'

As she entered the kitchen, Elizabeth saw her seated at the large table. She was a small girl, no more that seventeen, thought Elizabeth, but looking older than her years. Jenifer, seeing her mistress, rose and curtsied.

'Begging your pardon, Milady, I have a message from my mother. She be sending you a tea for Young Milady Hamilton, and I am to be telling you that a small amount is to be brewed in boiling water, then when it be cooled, Milady Hamilton is to drink it. It helps with the pain and stops the bleeding. I know this to be true, Mistress, as did she not give it to me when I lost my child. I have to tell you not to be giving Milady Hamilton anymore laudanum as this is bad.'

Elizabeth was speechless. 'You lost a child, Jenifer?'

'Oh no worries to you, Milady, I have my bonny Beryan, she be named after my mother, and another will come in time.' She curtsied again, handing over the small cloth bag to Elizabeth.

'I best be going now, Milady, I bid you good day.' She curtsied for a third time and turned to go.

'Jenifer, be still, child.' Elizabeth turned to Millie.

'Please find Pip and ask him to take Jenifer Penhale home in the cart. Beg his pardon, and tell him that I need Carter to take nanny Daisy, my grandson and master James to Mere.'

Mrs Cottle took the small cloth bag from her mistress. 'This will be fine, Milady, Beryan Penhale be knowing what she is doing. I will brew it immediately and get it sent up to Young Mistress Hamilton.'

Coming out to the cool of the terrace once more, Elizabeth saw Alexander talking softly to Charlotte.

'Oh, Alex, she would be so good for you,' she said softly to herself.

***

Stewart sat in the chair by the bed watching Margaret. He could tell that she was waking as her head kept moving and her eyelids fluttered. When the scream came, he was unprepared.

Stewart jumped onto the bed and held her tight in his arms.

'Maggie, Maggie, Maggie listen to me,' he spoke softly.

Maggie was moaning and fighting to be free of his hold.

'Maggie, listen to me!' His tone was harsher now, as he pulled her face round to look into her eyes. He could see that her eyes were trying to focus on him but there was terror in them. Again, she pounded him with her fists, shouting incoherent words.

'Maggie, it is I, Stewart!!!' he shouted, holding her arms firmly by her sides.

'Listen to me, please, you are safe, you are safe...'

Slowly, Margaret's eyes seemed to focus, darting from his face to around the room and back. Gripping his shirt in her hands, the tears spilled over her lashes.

'What has happened?' she pleaded, holding her stomach.

Stewart pulled her into him rocking her in his arms, there was nothing he could say.

***

It was a week before Margaret left her room, and even now as she sat in the drawing room by the window, she was very frail. The blow to her head just above her left eye had caused bruising to her eye and face, while her cheeks were drawn and devoid of colour. She had been told by Elizabeth that the physician had stated emphatically that she must not get with child for at least six months, to give time for her body to heal. Even now she could not walk on her own; wherever she wanted to go, Stewart carried her. Today was the first time that he had left her side since the accident happened, to go work in his study.

Margaret looked out of the window now—her head so full of words, but none could be spoken. Her heart broke when she looked at Stewart, knowing that he put blame upon himself for not being there. Even if he had she told herself, it would still have happened. She watched her sister now sitting in the window seat beside her, pretending to read a book. Margaret knew that she had been distraught, for had she and Elizabeth not witnessed the aftermath of the fall. So many lives affected, not just her own.

'What book are you reading, Charlotte?' asked Margaret.

Margaret looked up in surprise. 'It is *Cecilia* by Fanny Burney, cousin. But in truth, sitting here with you, none of the words have entered my head.' Closing it, she smoothed the book cover.

'Then we shall hear the story together, will you read to me? My eye hurts so when I try to focus on things.'

Charlotte beamed at her. 'Oh, Cousin Margaret, that would give me great pleasure!'

Margaret smiled and thought that maybe it was she that had to do the mending of the other lives affected by this tragedy.

As Charlotte read, Elizabeth came quietly into the room and sat near them, listening, but as she watched them both, something lifted from her heart, and she knew that all the hurt would mend now.

No one heard Stewart come in, until baby Charles gave out a squeal of delight. Margaret watched as her husband brought their child to her, then two large tears fell over her lashes as she held out her arms to take him.

'Mr Hardiman the physician said you may have him back,' he smiled lovingly at Margaret, placing Charles in her arms; then kissing her warmly, he too sat down to hear Charlotte read.

***

Elizabeth looked around the table at lunch and she thought to herself that life was at last settling down to how it had been before the accident. She knew that many things could never be forgotten, but at least the pain had eased, and Margaret was coming out of the black hole that she had placed herself within, to shut out all feeling and pain. James Fairweather was talking spiritedly as was his character. He was a good young man, observed Elizabeth, never morose, always full of life, and very funny with his constant anecdotes. Here was another young man who needed a wife. She smiled at the thought; life with him would never be dull. James turned to Elizabeth and spoke, bringing her out of her thoughts.

'Milady Hamilton, I must thank you profusely for your unbridled hospitality. I feel as one of the family when I stay here.' He placed his hand on his heart and bowed across the table at her.

Elizabeth shook her head and smiled. 'James, you are like one of our family, and a *very* welcome one.'

'I am afraid I must leave you though as I have business in London,' he looked towards Stewart as he said this. 'Then I will be back once more for the wedding of our friend George Wheatley in two weeks' time in Frome. It will be a grand affair, I feel, with hundreds of guests, and I am hoping that all here will be present.' He looked towards Margaret as he spoke.

'Mother, Margaret,' Stewart broke in, 'my sincere apologies, the invitation came the day of Charles' baptism, and then… well'

Margaret placed her hand over James'. 'Of course, we will go, James, and we will take Charlotte with us.' She turned to smile at her sister, who she saw could hardly contain herself with joy.

'Oh my, you are going to take me with you!?'

Elizabeth turned to look at her smiling. 'Did you think we would leave you behind, Charlotte?'

James then turned to Alexander who was seated next to him. 'You will come too, will you not?'

'I will, James,' nodded Alexander. 'If only to see Wheatley safely married,' he smiled musingly.

'Right, that settles the matter. We can all depart from here, and my coach is at your disposal for anyone that wishes to travel with me.'

'Thank you, James,' replied Elizabeth rising from the table. 'Now let us all sit on the terrace and enjoy this weather while we may, as I fear autumn will be upon us before we know it.'

***

James Fairweather left a little after 3 o'clock, and then the house went to rest to replenish their minds as well as their bodies. It had been a long week.

As Stewart sat Margaret on the chair in their room, he knelt down and removed her shoes and stockings. Looking into her eyes he smiled.

'You have come back to me, Margaret Hamilton, and I am very glad for that.' He stroked her hair behind her ear, and then his fingers pressed into her neck, massaging her spine. He swallowed deeply, kissing her brow.

'Let us get you to bed, you need your sleep to make you stronger.'

Maggie placed her hand behind his head and pulled him to her, her eyes searching his face. She kissed him deeply, undoing his stock and pushing his jacket from his shoulders.

'Let *us* go to bed now, there are other ways to love, Stewart, no?'

Chapter Twenty-Four
Wheatley's Wedding

James Fairweather had agreed to meet with his lawyer at his Chambers in the Inner Temple. Walking towards the building now, he was confident that he would hear some good news.

'Your servant, sir,' bowed James.

'And yours, sir,' responded Bearcroft. 'Please take a seat.'

James removed the paper contents from a chair and sat.

'Your friend Northcott, sir, is a very conniving man, and so is Duncan. They are conspiring together to take the Hamilton Estate, by the process of blackmail.' He paused here, steepling his fingers thinking.

'You have brought all the documentation with you?' he asked.

James Fairweather placed the file before him, and watched as Bearcroft opened it and searched the papers, reading quickly, going backwards and forwards as he muttered to himself.

'This is all in order, so I fail to see what possible hold the man has over Milady Hamilton.' He rubbed his hand over his chin and looked up into James Fairweather's eyes. 'I think there is something that I am not privy to here, am I right?'

James reached into his pocket and handed over the letter from Stewart.

'Perhaps, sir, all will be clear when you read this,' offered James.

Bearcroft read it through three times before taking off his glasses and pinching the top of his nose and replacing them again.

'My friend Hamilton requests that you burn this after having read the contents, sir,' said James

Bearcroft looked over the top of his glasses at James Fairweather and nodded gravely.

'We know not who the gentleman was, no clue as to his identity, where he came from... he could have been a seaman, sir, or from another part of the country, even Scotland as that is where Duncan is from, a place called Dundee, as I recall,' offered James.

'This was twenty-three years ago, a lifetime for some,' replied Bearcroft. 'I can see from what is written that it was in defence of her husband, no malice aforethought.' Bearcroft's brain was thinking hard.

'I will send someone post haste to Scotland to delve into Duncan's past and contacts there. If the man came from there, we could maybe retrieve a name.'

His mind was going over every scenario now, James could tell, he had seen the man work before.

'He cannot have been of any consequence, or his whereabouts would have been traced at the time of his disappearance. You must leave this with me, sir, as this will take much thought and investigation on my part. Pray tell Mr Hamilton I will do my utmost to put this to an end, and...' he paused. 'I will destroy this paper now.' Saying this, he went into the next room to where a small fire was kept and tossed the letter into the flames.

Coming back out, he looked squarely at James Fairweather and said, 'I have never received or read any such document, do I make myself clear, sir?'

James nodded in reply.

***

Margaret sat looking at her sister, watching her embroider tiny flowers of yellow onto Charles' cot pillowcase. She reminded her of herself at such an age, sitting with her governess in her rooms overlooking the garden. But Charlotte had freedom, a peace about her that she could only have hoped for then. She was beautiful, with her hair flowing down her back in ringlets. As Margaret thought of Alexander, she hoped that Charlotte would not get her heart broken, as it was plain to see that she had a deep affection for him.

'Your work is beautiful, Charlotte,' Margaret spoke as she leaned over to look at the work. 'Who taught you?' she asked.

Charlotte looked up and smiled. 'Oh my mother, cousin, her work was exquisite, I have many handkerchiefs that she made for me with my monogram on. I will show you some when we go inside.'

Margaret leaned over to the perambulator that was beside her seeing Charles peacefully asleep, blowing bubbles with his lips.

'He is a very good child, Cousin Margaret, not bad tempered in the least, I think that he favours you.' She smiled. Then correcting herself, she continued.

'Oh I am not saying Cousin Stewart is an angry man; on the contrary he is one of the most congenial men I have met, and Cousin Alexander.'

Margaret placed her hand on her sister's arm. 'You have feelings for Alexander do you not?'

'Oh no, no, no, I mean he is a good man, and very easy to talk to.' Her face had gone the colour of the Pelargonium flowers in the pots beside her.

'It is acceptable to have feelings, Charlotte, we all do, no matter who we are. I also know that your feelings are more than just a young girl's fancy?' Margaret saw she was about to deny this. 'No, please let me finish. Alexander is a good man, he is also eight years older than you are. His feelings are... different, they are more mature than your own. Give him time, and I am sure that he will see you for what you really are, a very beautiful young woman.' Margaret nodded to her.

'Oh, I shall be leaving here soon, cousin, and I will become just another memory for him,' she replied, keeping her eyes on her work.

Margaret closed her eyes and sent up a prayer.

Charles' cry brought them both back from their thoughts.

'I fear he needs changing again, Charlotte.' As she bent to pick him up, she saw Daisy's tall figure come out of the house.

'I will take him and change him, Milady, and then perhaps he will be ready for his feed,' she said, taking Charles from her arms.

'Thank you, Daisy, I will follow you in.' Standing up, she looked to her sister. 'Please stay and enjoy the afternoon, Charlotte, I am sure my mother will be out soon to keep you company.'

As Charlotte sat there deep in thought, she did not hear Alexander come out.

'Good afternoon, Cousin Charlotte and a very warm one it is to,' he exclaimed.

'Oh my, you startled me, Cousin Alexander.' Her face was flushed

'My humblest apologies, I never meant to frighten you.' Looking down at her hands, he asked, 'Is that for our godson? He should feel very privileged to have a godmother such as you.' Seating himself opposite, he smiled.

'We have a wedding to go to this weekend do we not. I hope that the weather holds, so that Wheatley can enjoy the same as Margaret and Stewart. It was glorious that day.'

Elizabeth's voice cut in, 'Oh there you are, Charlotte, my dressmaker will come for you soon, so that she can make the necessary alterations to the gown that you are to wear on Sunday. I have given her the lace, it needs only you to tell her where it should go.'

'And good afternoon to you, Alexander,' Elizabeth greeted as she turned around to face him. 'Are you prepared for the wedding?'

'Yes, Aunt, I will wear the same clothes I wore to Stewart and Margaret's. They are new, I wore them only the once.'

Elizabeth inclined her head and seated herself between them.

'We will be staying overnight at George Wheatley's estate, so we must take clothing with us.' Looking at Alexander, she added, 'If you provide Pip with your clothes, then he will pack them with Stewart's. There will be three coaches departing. My own, Margaret's and James'. Charlotte, you will ride with myself and my maid, Margaret, Daisy, Millie and Charles will go in Margaret's coach and you two gentlemen will ride with James Fairweather, and I want you all on your best behaviour, understood?' She looked at her nephew and smiled.

'Of course, Aunt, would we be anything else?' he grinned.

'I know what you three are capable of when you are together, and not a drop of drink will pass your lips until after the wedding. Do I make myself clear?' She aimed this at her son as he came towards her.

Stewart bowed teasingly to her. 'Understood, Mother.'

Charlotte was pressing her lips tight together so as not to laugh.

'Right, come now, Charlotte, let us get your dress finished so that we can sit down to eat our dinner in peace.'

Stewart watched his mother go in and turned to Alexander.

'I have had no word yet from James, so maybe he will inform us of anything that has happened when he comes on Saturday. It is my guess that he does not wish to put pen to paper.' Stewart seated himself next to Alexander.

'How is Margaret?' asked Alexander. 'When I saw her as I came in, she looked a lot brighter, but still a trifle unsteady on her feet. Will she be able to stand throughout the ceremony?'

'We will sit at the back, Alex, that way if she wants to sit, she can and nobody will notice. Do you know the church he is to marry in? It is quite large, and seats over two hundred people, which in its self is a good thing, as I believe there will still be those that will have to stand at the back and round the sides.'

'It is the Church of St John the Baptist, is it not in the centre of Frome? I believe that St Michael's would fit inside it twice over.' Alexander smiled

'Do not forget, Alex, that his father's cousin was a Lord, there will be quite a few of the aristocracy present.'

Alexander sat there smiling to himself. 'We will be the poor relations, will we not? James can hold his head with the rest, his estate is vast, though you would never think it would you. He is so unpretentious.'

'That is James, he was never brought up to be anything else. Good breeding they call it,' Stewart replied.

Alexander watched his cousin as he got up and walked back and forth along the terrace. He was still troubled, and who could blame him after what had happened. There was a heavy gilt that sat upon him, in that he had been swimming when Margaret had lost their child. Nothing could erase that, and then there was his mother. The horrors of the past four weeks weighed heavy on everyone, even himself.

Stewart sat next to his cousin and looked sideways at him.

'Cousin Charlotte will be gone the weekend after the wedding. Her father has written to say he will be here on the Saturday. Norfolk is a very long way away, and I think that Margaret will miss her greatly. Do not forget, Alex, that she is her sister. I do not mind telling you that it troubles me also a great deal.'

'I would agree with you, Stewart, this whole sequence of events has very bad timing. In truth I believe I will miss her too. She is very easy to talk to did you know that, and very intelligent.'

Stewart smiled to himself and said nothing.

***

On arriving at George Wheatley's estate, he had greeted them warmly. Stewart thought George had not changed a bit. He was still the amiable foolish boy he had been at Winchester. The house was vast, like a palace, with footmen running in all directions taking guests to their rooms. How much would it cost for the upkeep of such a place? More per month than the Willows produced in a year was his answer.

'Come in, come in, welcome to my humble abode.' George Wheatley threw his arms out and hugged Stewart, Alexander and James in turn.

215

Then he bowed very deferentially to Elizabeth, Margaret and Charlotte.

'Stewart, and who is this beautiful vision of a young lady you have brought with you?'

'Have you no eyes Wheatley? Has your wife to be completely addled your brain? Look at her closely.' There was a silence where Stewart looked at Wheatley and shook his head.

'She is Margaret's cousin, George,' added Stewart.

'Oh my word, what a striking resemblance,' replied George.

'And he is not even married yet,' commented James.

Which was followed by hails of laughter.

'Elizabeth looked towards Margaret and Charlotte and whispered.

'And they have not touched a drink yet.' She raised her eyes upwards. 'Please let them remain sober tonight.'

Margaret laughed, then took both Elizabeth's and Charlotte's arms and followed the maid up to their rooms.

When they reached the top of the stairs, they were shown three rooms, but Elizabeth shook her head.

'Thank you kindly, young lady, but Charlotte and I will share a room. This young lady is under my care and will not be sleeping alone. If you could bring her baggage into my room, I would be most grateful.'

Elizabeth looked down into the hall, the noise from there was deafening. People were arriving consecutively. She put her hand up to her brow and sighed. She would go and lie before dinner, and with a little hope, the walls of the rooms would be sufficiently thick so as to block out the din, else they were in for a wakeful night, as once the dinner started... Well, one night was all they had to endure, then they could return home.

Maggie was lying on the bed when Stewart entered.

'Are you well, Maggie?' he asked, coming to sit on the bed by her.

'Yes I am fine, just tired,' she answered, turning towards him. 'Your mother has taken Charlotte into her room with her.'

'Yes, I know, and rightly so. I know George and James, they would not hurt anyone, but the other people that are here I know nothing about. If anything were to happen to your sister, my mother would never forgive herself.'

She stroked his face. 'If they were all like you, she would have no need to worry.'

'Ah, well, I was a trifle wild in my youth,' he answered warily.

'Stewart Hamilton, I refuse to believe that you were anything but chivalrous,' Margaret replied teasingly.

He held her hand and stoked her fingers lightly. 'We should go down to dinner, but I think that I will tell George that the drive here has made you tired, and could we have some food sent up for us. I will do the same for my mother and Charlotte also.' Kissing her hand, he walked to the door. 'I will be back directly.'

Knocking on his mother's door, he waited. It was opened by her maid Molly.

216

'Molly, please tell my mother that I will ask for our food to be sent up to us, as I fear Margaret is very tired, and I know that my mother will not be open to the sort of conversation that will be bantered around the table. Thank you, Molly.'

Molly curtsied. 'Thank you, Mr Hamilton, that is most thoughtful of you, my mistress is very tired.' Stewart nodded and left.

Moving through the throng in the huge hall, he found James, Alexander and George laughing heartily by the entrance.

'Gentleman, you must excuse us, but Margaret is exhausted after the journey, and my mother is not young anymore, so if you would be so good as to ask for a tray of dinner to be sent up to our rooms, I would be most grateful, George.'

'Not at all, not at all. They are well though, are they not, Stewart? My physician is amongst the guests here I will ask him to come up.'

Stewart raised his hand to stop him. 'They are well, George, just tired, and Mistress Charlotte is staying with my mother to keep her company,' he looked at Alexander. 'She will be sharing a room with her too.'

Alexander smiled and inclined his head slightly to say that he understood.

'Now if you will forgive me, I will go back to my wife.' Bowing to them in mockery, he left.

Alexander watched him go, and wished he could go with him.

'His wife is well, is she not, Alex?' questioned George a second time.

'She lost a child two weeks past now, by having a fall,' he watched Stewart go up the stairs. 'She will be fine, she just needs to be cared for that is all.'

***

The Church of St John the Baptist was quite a grand building. The central western door stood open, and on either side of the entrance were two statues of Evangelists. As Stewart looked in down the naive, central aisle, he could see rows of pews either side, and intermittently at the outer ends to these pews were huge stone columns reaching up, arborescent in structure to hold the roof. Looking around him, the congregation was slowly moving into their seats, and from what he could tell by their speech and dress, most were from titled families. An organ was playing in the far back of the church, to the left of the altar, and he had the notion that he could hear choristers singing somewhere, but it could well be the reverberation of the organ.

Leaning towards his mother, he asked, 'Shall we go in now? We can sit in the last pew on the right, which is George Wheatley's side.'

James and Alexander went in first, followed by Charlotte, then Elizabeth and Margaret with Stewart in the aisle seat. The church filled rapidly, till all those that were allotted a seat had them, and then the rest of the guests filed in around the sides. The organ stopped suddenly, and the congregation rose up. Turning their heads, they saw Edwina Beaumont his bride, a small vision in what looked to Elizabeth to be the finest Irish lace; holding tight to her father's arm, she progressed down the aisle.

Charlotte was standing on tip toe to try and see when Stewart beckoned her to stand in front of him so that she could watch the ceremony. Elizabeth smiled to herself, as she saw Alexander watch her. She looked beautiful in a very pale green dress that could be mistaken for cream. The lace had been placed around the high neckline and sleeve edges, and her hair had been pulled back from her face and caught up with ribbon allowing the ringlets to fall around her shoulders. Elizabeth thought she looked quite enchanting, and so did Alexander by the look on his face. Smiling once again she thought that her plan seemed to be working.

It was extremely hot inside the church, and even though they sat by the entrance, very little air was circulating within. Margret sat halfway through the service, and Elizabeth gave her the fan she carried.

'Margaret child, do you want to go outside?' she asked.

'No, Mother, I am quite well just tired, I will be glad when today is over and we can all go home,' she answered.

The wedding concluded when George came back up the aisle with his young bride on his arm, and Stewart thought that George had been right; she did resemble a small china doll. Nodding to his cousin and James, they departed quickly before the rest of the congregation began their exit from the church.

'We will go back to the house, as I know that young Charles will be bringing the house down if he does not get fed within the next half hour,' exclaimed Stewart as they came out into the sunlight.

Alexander laughed. 'Ah, Stewart, the joys of parenthood.'

Stewart eyed him warily. 'When you have children, Alex, I will remind you of that.'

'Why did they not have the wedding at Wells Cathedral, or Salisbury for that matter, particularly since there were to be so many guests?' asked James.

'I believe they were too far away from the estate, James, and as many came from London, having the wedding here enabled Wheatley to put many of the guests in his home,' replied Stewart. 'Not ideal, but convenient,' he added.

'They could have had it within the grounds of the estate,' answered James.

'Wheatley's mother would have none of it—it was inside a church or nothing,' was Stewart's response.

'Let us leave now so that we can be ready to depart as soon as the wedding breakfast is over,' added Stewart as he handed Margaret into her carriage.

***

It was mid-afternoon by the time the wedding breakfast finished, and they left the house soon after, to slowly make their way home.

Sitting in the coach, Alexander turned to James.

'James, will your wedding be like that?'

'Not if I have any say in the matter, it will not. You have forgotten one very important thing though, Alex, I have yet to find a wife…'

Laughing, Stewart answered. 'You will my friend, you will, just give it time. You will be smitten by some beautiful young girl, as though you were hit by a gale.'

All three laughed loudly, then sat back and fell asleep.

Chapter Twenty-Five
William Master, a Sister and a Betrothal

The Coaches came up the drive close to 8 o'clock in the evening, the occupants tired, weary and hot. They were greeted by Thompson who informed Elizabeth that a Mr William Masters—Charlotte's father—had arrived by mid-day and was now waiting in the drawing room having been fed by Mrs Cottle. On hearing this, Charlotte raced up the stairs into the hall and into her father's arms.

'Papa, Papa, you have come early!' she cried, hugging her father tightly. 'Come meet my cousin, her husband, his mother, and their cousin Alexander, also friend James,' she called, the words tumbling out of her as she pulled him towards the door just as they were entering.

'Your servant, Milady,' he said, bowing respectfully to Elizabeth.

'You are most welcome to my home, Mr Masters,' Elizabeth replied. 'May I introduce you to my son Stewart Hamilton, his cousin Alexander Hamilton and of course your daughter's cousin Margaret, my son's wife, who I believe you have met before, and my son's friend James Fairweather.' She paused here while greetings were exchanged. 'You must forgive us, sir, but we have just journeyed from Frome in Somerset, and are very travel weary. My daughter Margaret has not been well of late, so you must please pardon her as she must go up to rest. I will join you in the drawing room with Charlotte as soon as I have refreshed myself.' Smiling at him, she lowered her head slightly, and then went up the stairs followed by her maid Molly.

On the landing she found Stewart, Alexander and James talking.

'If you three wish to sit for a while, please go into the study, I shall settle Mr Masters, then inform him that I will speak with him tomorrow. I am too fatigued to hold intelligent conversation this night,' she said as she put her hand to her brow.

'Be off with you now, tell Thompson to bring drinks into the study if you so require. I bid you all good night.' Saying this, she went into her room.

Alex turned to James and Stewart. 'Would you like a nightcap? Or shall we just retire to our beds?'

'Alex, I think we have had enough to drink this lunchtime. Myself I will go to my bed,' replied James.

'I am definitely for my bed,' replied Stewart.

'Then I will go also, it has been a long day, and it looks to be another one tomorrow, with many revelations I believe... better on a clear head... yes?' Alexander inclined his.

***

Millie helped Margaret out of her clothes and then, seating her on a stool, she brushed her hair. Margaret turned on the stool and placed her hand on her maid's arm.

'Thank you, Mille, please go to your bed, I will not require you anymore.'

'Very well, Milady, I bid you goodnight,' she replied.

Margaret breathed deeply as she sat there; she had made her decision, and tomorrow before Elizabeth spoke with Charlotte's father, she would tell her mother what she had chosen. There would be no more lives destroyed, not least her sister's. She was innocent of all this, and Margaret was not about to shatter her faith in humanity. She was so deep in thought she did not hear Stewart come into the room till he was behind her. Taking his hand, she placed it to her cheek and held it there.

'What troubles you, Maggie?' he asked softly.

Margaret turned and stood up, placing her arms around him and resting her head on his chest.

'I have decided that she will never know her true parentage.' She looked up into his face.

'She has known nothing but love and kindness all of her small life, Stewart, and I will not take that away. She will always be my sister, but he will always be her loving father. I would not have her know that her real father gave her away for a price, simply because she was a girl—just like me—but she got the better bargain, and I thank God for that.'

Stewart lifted Margaret in his arms and laid her in bed, then undressing himself, lay next to her, spooning her into him.

'I agree,' he whispered in her ear. 'Now sleep, Maggie, I will see my mother in the morning.'

Pulling her tightly into him, he whispered, 'I love you, Maggie,' as they drifted off to sleep.

***

Breakfast was a joyous occasion. Charlotte's eyes shone and her face glowed with pleasure as she related to her father all that had happened at the wedding. It was the most that she had spoken since she had come thought Stewart.

Margaret looked at her father's eyes as he watched his daughter; seeing so much love there broke her heart. Elizabeth, observing all of this, saw the sorrow and the joy in Margaret's face. Placing her hand over Margaret's, she squeezed.

'Charlotte, before the sun reaches its heat, you must take your father and show him the gardens,' suggested Elizabeth.

'I will, Aunt, thank you.' Turning to her father, she continued, 'You must come and see the rose gardens, Papa, they are so beautiful, and the fragrances are so heady…' She closed her eyes, as though smelling them now.

William Masters looked at his daughter and laughed. Then looking around the table, he spoke.

'If all present company will excuse us, we will go.'

'Go, sir, your daughter loves the gardens, it is the place we look for her when we cannot find her here.' Stewart looked at them both and smiled broadly.

Margaret watched as Charlotte took her father's hand and led him out of the room.

Seeing this, James Fairweather rose.

'If you will pardon me, Milady Hamilton, Alexander has offered to show me around the estate, then we will go quench our thirst in the Angel in Mere,' he said, bowing respectfully.

Alexander also rose. 'We will see you all for lunch. Will you come with us, cousin?' he asked as he turned to Stewart. 'I will call in at the estate office as well to see if there are any bills.'

Stewart looked at Margaret and raised his brows smiling.

Margaret shook her head and returned his smile. 'Take him with you, Alex, he will only brood if he remains here,' she said, waving her hand for them both to go.

Waiting for the door to close, she turned to Elizabeth.

'Mother, Stewart has told you what I have decided, has he not?'

'Yes, Margaret, her secret is safe with me. I have also informed her father, and he is in total agreement with you. Knowing now all that you have suffered through your young life, he does not want his daughter to feel such horror and pain, or be subjected to such unbridled hate.'

Elizabeth saw Margaret's shoulders slump in relief. How could one man inflict so much pain on a family, but Elizabeth knew that was possible, had she not been the subject of such pain?

'Go, be with your son, Margaret, sit in the rocking chair in the nursery and rest, and then when the sun leaves the terrace, you can come sit in the cool of the shade before lunch.' Coming round beside her, Elizabeth held her daughter-in-law to her and stoked her head. 'You must rest, child, to regain your strength. I will ring for Millie.' Saying this she walked to the mantle and pulled the bell pull.

***

Charlotte and her father sat on a bench in the shade of a huge oak tree. Sitting there listening to her, he remembered when he had been approached by her father. He had told him that her mother had died—he knew that to be untrue now—and that as he Masters could not have children, would he be in a position to take his daughter, and he would pay handsomely. Which he had done, setting him up in Norwich, as a merchant of the finest Worsted Cloth. Her father had bought him a house in King Street, a warehouse along the river, and two single-masted craft called Keels for use to ferry the cloth up the River Wensom to Yarmouth. There it was shipped on seagoing vessels to Europe to be traded for wine and spices.

He and his wife could not believe such luck could come to them, and to have a beautiful child of their own to love and cherish.

He had been a miller by trade, but learned the art of a merchant very quickly. He knew how to barter, sell and buy goods; they had prospered greatly over the years. But now to find that all this had been paid for by the sorrow of others, cut him deeply, as he now knew that her mother had lived for another seven years before dying.

'Charlotte child, you are speaking so quickly your poor father cannot follow what you are saying, and moreover, he is a little deaf,' he smiled deeply at his daughter as he heard her laugh loudly.

'Oh, Papa, you say such funny things, but I love you deeply.' With that she threw her arms around his neck and hugged him tight.

'I think that we should go back to the house now, Papa, then I can show you young cousin Charles, he is the most beautiful baby you ever did see, and so good tempered, he hardly ever cries, only when he is hungry.' Charlotte pulled her father to his feet and tucked her arm in his tightly.

'You like it here, do you not, Charlotte?' he asked as they slowly walked back.

'Yes I do, Papa, but that is not to say that I do not like our home in Norfolk,' she replied anxiously.

'I know, child, do not worry yourself. I was thinking though when I was away, that it is time I sold my business, and become a gentleman of leisure.' He looked sideways at her.

'We could come to live here? Buy a house, and then you could come see your cousin whenever you wished, Charlotte. What say you? Would you like that?' The look in her eyes was enough to tell him what he wanted to know.

'It is settled then. I will enquire of Milady Hamilton if you might be allowed to stay here with her, until such time that I have sold my business and properties to be able to purchase a house hereabouts.'

'Oh, Papa, I love you dearly,' was all she said, kissing him on the cheek and squeezing his arm.

***

Stewart and James were sitting in the Angel in Mere, each to his own thoughts, in quiet reflection. Till James' voice cut into the silence.

'Correct me if I am wrong, Stewart, but I have observed that cousin Charlotte has some affection for Alexander...' he paused to see Stewart's reaction.

'I am afraid you are right, James, and I think it a little more than fascination.' Stewart studied his mug before continuing.

223

'She is a very beautiful young lady, albeit that she is still only eighteen, and to my understanding, much wiser than her years and well educated.'

'But Alexander does not share this affection, no?' queried James.

Stewart leaned back in his chair and closed his eyes.

'She would be good for him, I know that, but… he is of the opinion that he is too old for her.'

'Oh, he told me that as well, but I pointed out that my father was twelve years older than my mother when they married, and he had affection for her but did not love her then. It was after the marriage he fell in love with her.'

'Ah, James, if only Alex was as wise as your father, it would make life much simpler, would it not. He is lonely, as I have told him many times. He needs someone to love him, take care of him, and I know that cousin Charlotte would do all of these things and more, even though I have only known her just this one month.'

'Perchance if she could stay here a while longer, would he change his opinion?' he questioned.

Stewart sat up abruptly, 'Hush, James, Alex is coming,' he said quietly.

'The post coach has not come in, it is well overdue, and so I can only hope that it has not been detained by certain persons of the criminal variety,' Alexander said as he sat and picked up his mug to finish his ale.

'I had heard that they were stopping these coaches, as some have been found to carry large amounts of money, though I would not entrust any of mine to such delivery merchants,' voiced James.

Stewart stood and stretched. 'Let us get back to the house then, we will have to wait till tomorrow for any mail, as I fear I will not be making the journey into Mere again today.'

'Neither will I,' replied Alexander. 'I must stop at the estate office though to finish the payments. I will join you for dinner later, if I am expected?' he teased as he turned to go

'Some day your cook will refuse to make you dinner, you are never there,' called Stewart.

'You need a wife, Alex,' shouted James as Alexander went through the door.

'Love comes later, my friend, when you really know one another,' he turned to Stewart. 'Do you not agree my friend?'

'Oh yes, James, I agree.' He raised his mug and hit it to James' in salutation.

***

Stephen Masters sat on the terrace next to Elizabeth deep in thought. It was peaceful here, giving his mind leave to think deeply. He closed his eyes, letting the coolness of the breeze blow over him, soothing him, heightening all the sounds of the countryside around him. A man could rest in peace here given the chance.

'Something troubles you, does it not, Mr Masters?' asked Elizabeth.

William Masters opened his eyes, returning to reality. Looking to Elizabeth, he nodded. 'You are a very perceptive woman, Milady Hamilton, yes it does. I would ask a great favour of you, and I do not know how to voice it.'

'Just tell me, that will suffice,' responded Elizabeth. 'I gather it concerns your daughter Charlotte?'

'Mmmmm,' came his reply as he nodded his head.

'You would like her to stay a while longer here, am I right?'

'My word, Madam, how do you do that,' replied William Masters amazed.

'Years of practice, sir.' She smiled.

William Masters shifted in his seat slightly. 'If I may be so bold, I have a proposition to put to you, Milady, you can stop me at any time if you think I overstep my bounds.'

Elizabeth nodded and smiled. 'Go on.'

He then recounted what had been discussed with his daughter in the gardens that morning, watching Elizabeth very carefully for signs of disapproval. He knew what an imposition this would be to the family, and that he somewhat felt he held them to ransom after the revelations of that day.

Elizabeth listened to him till the end, and then breathed deeply.

'Mr Masters, you do not know how that gladdens my heart. She has been a great help to her sister throughout this crisis we have all been through, and to take her away now I feel it would be detrimental to my daughter's well-being. So yes, Mr Masters, I would be more than happy for your daughter to stay with us.'

Elizabeth saw the instant relief on his face as he got up and bowed deeply to her.

'You do not know what a weight you have lifted from my heart, Milady, I send you a thousand thanks.'

'You are most welcome, Mr Masters, now I have a proposition to put to you.'

***

Alexander was seated in the drawing room, reading a book when Charlotte's father came in.

'Good evening to you, Alexander.'

Rising sharply, Alexander bowed. 'Your servant, sir,' he offered.

'Alexander, you are good, kind man, I see this and I have only met you these past two days. I also see that my daughter holds you with a great high regard.' He paused, rubbing his chin.

'I have a proposal to make to you, sir, in that would you think me impertinent if I asked you to consider a proposal of marriage with my daughter? You must bear in mind, sir that my daughter is very green when it comes to the ways of men,' he paused once more, looking at Alexander hesitantly. 'I am a merchant by trade, and being so have many such men come to my house, I have kept my daughter away from such men as I would not want an alliance with any of them. Do you follow me?'

Alexander nodded.

'Would you be in a mind to accept such a proposal?'

There was a silence where both men looked at one another, trying to read their thoughts.

Alexander swallowed hard before he answered, 'I would, sir.'

Alexander saw her father's shoulders visibly relax. 'I cannot tell you, sir how happy you have just made me. My daughter at this present time knows nothing of this proposal, and will not till things are settled and finalised. Am I making myself clear?'

Alexander nodded once more.

'I intend to settle an amount on her, and buy her a house wherever she chooses to live, be it here or in Norfolk...'

Alexander stopped him here. 'Sir, if I may speak out of turn, she needs no dowry, I have sufficient money to keep her safe and well cared for. I also have a house which is mine, in Mere not far from here. I am Estate Steward for my aunt of which I get a salary of £50 per year. Your daughter's hand in marriage would be all that I ask. She is very dear to me.'

'Your aunt told me that you were a kind and generous man, and I believe her. Nevertheless, she will have her dowry by her own right. What she chooses to do with it—'

Alexander stopped him again. 'Will be entirely in Charlotte's hands, it will be hers to use as she sees fit, sir.'

William Masters came across now and took Alexander's hand in such a tight shake he thought that every bone would be broken.

'I will leave my daughter to her peace this night, then tell her what we have discussed tomorrow, but if she is not in agreement...'

'I truly understand, sir, you want her to be happy, and to desire the man she marries,' replied Alexander.

Her father nodded. I will say good night to you, sir, you have made me a very happy father this evening.'

Alexander drew in a deep breath as he watched him leave the room, and then let it out again slowly. 'I hope that I can live up to your expectations, sir,' he whispered after him.

He found Stewart in the study. Coming in, he seated himself in the chair next to the desk. The windows were still open and a warm breeze was blowing the drapes either side; it was peaceful, closing his eyes he inhaled the fragrances from the garden, roses, honeysuckle and jasmine were the most prevalent.

Stewart looked at him and smiled teasingly.

'Well, have you accepted the man's proposal?'

This made Alexander sit up suddenly. 'Dear God, it only just happened, how did you know so soon?' replied Alexander astonished.

'Did you think my mother could keep anything like that a secret, Alex? No, she will be good for you, Alex, and I fear she loves you deeply, so remember Margaret's wrath will come down on you if you do not treat her well,' said Stewart.

'God, cousin, pray what do you think I am going to do to her, she is a very warm loving person, and as I have come to know Charlotte, I have formed a deep affection for her.'

'I am very glad to hear that, cousin,' replied Stewart teasingly. 'Shall we go and tell James the good news?'

'I do not think that advisable as Charlotte is not privy to this information at the present time. Her father will tell her after breakfast tomorrow, and if she is in agreement, only then will the proposal be finalised,' answered Alexander.

'Done! We can toast to the good health of you both tomorrow. Now let us eat.'

***

Alexander was seated on the window seat when William Masters and his daughter came into the room the following morning after breakfast.

Standing up, he bowed. 'Good morning, sir, Mistress Charlotte.'

'I have spoken to Charlotte this morning in great depth, on what we discussed yesterday, and she is willing to be betrothed to you, Alexander. There will be many things to be settled and thought through, but may I suggest an October wedding? That will give us two months.'

Alexander smiled and nodded as he came to where they stood. Taking Charlotte's hands, he found them to be as cold as ice and trembling so much that his own hands shook as he brought them up to his lips to kiss. 'I am greatly honoured, Charlotte, that you have consented to accept my proposal of marriage.'

William Masters coughed. 'I will leave you for a few moments to go find your aunt, sir.'

Alexander placed a finger under her chin and lifted her head up to look into her eyes. She was shaking from head to foot.

'I do hope, Charlotte, that this is in happiness, and not fear that you shake so,' he smiled warmly.

'Come, sit with me.' Saying this he took her hand in his and led her to the window seat. Holding her hands once more, he continued.

'You need never be afraid of me, Charlotte, I would NEVER do anything to hurt you or cause you pain or sorrow. You have saved me from loneliness and solitude. I thought that I was destined to become a bachelor, the godfather to many children, never a father to my own.' He saw her blush deeply and stroked her face with his finger. 'I am sorry I did not mean to do that, please forgive me.'

Charlotte nodded and kept her eyes on his.

'May I kiss you, Charlotte?' Her reply was just to nod very quickly.

Many things were racing through Alexander's mind as he looked at the young woman before him. She was beautiful, and yet so innocent that his heart went out to her. Raising her head up to him, she closed her eyes as he pressed his lips to hers very gently. Leaning back, he saw that her eyes were still closed, so he kissed her again, pressing his lips more firmly to hers, causing hers to part. He felt the shudder run through her, as it went through his own body too.

Leaning back, he found that his lungs had suddenly stopped.

'That seals our betrothal, does it not,' he said huskily as he still found it hard to breathe, but he steadied himself and placed his cupped hand to her cheek.

It was then the door opened and Elizabeth entered. They parted so abruptly that Elizabeth smiled.

'Would you like me to go out and come in again?' she teased.

Alexander shook his head and smiled. 'No, Aunt, you are welcome.'

'May I ask the others to come in now?' Elizabeth smiled again and thought it must be hard for them, but in retrospect at least they had had time to become acquainted with one another, and love would grow, she was sure of that. Something her sister never had with her first husband.

Walking to the door, she called to Stewart, then told Thompson to bring glasses as there was to be a celebration.

***

Later that evening, Alexander asked her father for permission to walk with Charlotte on the lawn. Her father had looked at his aunt, who had inclined her head very slightly, saying all would be safe.

As they walked, Alexander turned to her; he knew that the house would be watching them, but he would do it anyway.

'May I kiss you again, Charlotte?' he asked gently.

'Yes, I think I would like that very much,' she replied.

Alexander breathed easy then, she was not repulsed by his advances.

He held her shoulders and placed his lips on hers. This time her lips parted, accepting him, kissing him back. Placing his arms around her, he pulled her to him, feeling her body yield to his embrace.

'We will be fine, Charlotte, I know we will,' sighed Alexander.

'Yes I know we will, Alexander,' she replied, enfolding her arms around him.

Chapter Twenty-Six
Margaret and Charlotte

Stewart stopped writing and looked up at his cousin as he came into the study and knew from his face that all was not well.

'There are three letters, two for James… and one for your mother,' he said as he handed it over to Stewart.

The hand writing told him who it was from. Placing it into his pocket, he stood up.

'Not here, Alex, we will go to the office.'

As they came along the corridor, Stewart could hear the cries of his son.

'What ails Charles?' asked Alexander. 'Is he unwell? I have never heard him cry so, even when hungry.'

'My mother tells me that he is cutting teeth and that this is perfectly normal, and nanny Daisy agrees. Even so his gums and cheeks are red, and he is so fretful,' he replied. They entered the hall just as his mother was descending the stairs.

'I am just on my way to the kitchen, will you be dining with us this evening, Alex?' she enquired.

'That is very kind of you, Aunt, thank you. I hope my godson will find peace soon, he sounds in great pain,' he replied.

'Mrs Cottle is at the moment preparing an infusion, which she claims will sooth his gums and ease the pain,' she answered, but her face was full of scepticism.

'What would that be, Aunt?' queried Alexander.

'Her remedy is cloves steeped in oil. Apparently, it has a soothing effect when the oil is applied to the gum, so I am told. I only pray that it works, for until that tooth—or teeth—makes its appearance, we are all in for a fractious period.'

'I am off to the estate office, Mother, please tell Margaret I shall return as soon as possible.'

His mother waved her hand in dismissal, then turned and headed for the kitchen.

They rode slowly in silence, when Stewart pulled up his horse and stopped.

'Alex, I need to talk to you about Charlotte…' he began.

Alexander raised his brow up and smiled. 'I know what you are about to impart, Stewart, and I am aware of that very fact. I am a man of the world you might say, and she is just a young girl,' he breathed in through his nose. 'I would never do anything unless Charlotte invited me to do so... does that solve your problem?' he offered.

'On the contrary, cousin, no, that is just what I was afraid of,' he responded.

'What would you have me do, Stewart, ravage her? I have to show tolerance and know that she will come to me in time. I know that I do not disgust her, and that when I kiss her, she yields to my touch. She is warm and loving, I will not destroy that to satisfy my own needs. I will wait.' Alexander shifted himself in his saddle and looked intently at his cousin.

'You are a very generous man, Alex, there are others that would not be so giving. I will tell Margaret to speak with her though, she has no mother to turn to, better her sister than no one. Come let us find out the contents of this letter.'

As they came up to the office, they saw James Fairweather waiting for them.

'I saw you two depart and guessed that you would be headed here. I too have received letters today,' he held the letters aloft.

Stabling their horses, they went inside. The air in the office was heavy, it had been closed for some days, and with the sun beating relentlessly on its roof, it resembled an oven, where everything inside seemed to have been baked solid. Alexander opened the window and propped the door back with a small wedge of wood. The effect was slightly better, but as there was neither much breeze to be found outside, the air inside was loath to circulate itself.

Seating himself at Alexander's desk, Stewart took the paper knife and carefully loosened the seal. James and Alexander knew immediately by the changes on his face that it was not good news.

'The effrontery of the man, and he dares to call himself my father!' He banged his fist hard onto the desk, and then handed the letter to Alexander.

My Dear Lizzie
I see that you have chosen to ignore the last letter that I sent, so you leave me no alternative but to set my other plans into motion.
It could have ended differently, but you chose this route.
Yours
Andrew Duncan

Alexander paled and passed the letter on to James.

Stewart stood up and paced the room, then hitting the door hard with his fist he turned.

'How dare the man have the impudence to call my mother Lizzie!!!' he bellowed. Grabbing his hat, he attempted to leave the office but was stopped by Alexander and James.

'Get out of my way if you value your lives!' he was ashen to the lips.

'I will kill him, and then there will be an end. Only that way will we be able to live in peace.' He was struggling hard now to free himself.

Alexander grabbed his face and made him look at him.

'Stewart, what then of your mother, your wife, your son.' Alexander saw the hate in his eyes lessen, as he shook his head in despair.

'What would you have me do, Alex, stand by and watch her hang? I would kill her myself first.'

'Maybe when you read the other missive from my lawyer, it will show you a way forward,' offered James. He nodded as he held out the letter. Taking it from his hand, Stewart walked out the door.

Standing there he looked out around the countryside; everything was as it always had been, there was peace. Looking up to the heavens, he closed his eyes and prayed. His life had been one long succession of battles, and he was tired. He wanted nothing more than to live in amity with his family, was that such a hard thing to ask for in this life. He swallowed hard and rubbed his eyes with the heels of his hands. Just two men brought chaos and destruction to his world, and for what reason? Greed, avarice, cupidity, they all meant the same, and any other name that held so much weight. He looked down at the letter that James had handed him and started to read.

Stewart came back into the office and handed Alexander the letter.

'My other letter is a request from my father,' began James. 'He asks that I go to London to attend some business there for him as he has to depart for Cheshire where we have some property.' He paused and scratched his head here looking from Stewart to James. 'My father owns many such properties throughout England, and they have to be maintained,' he broke off.

'James, you do not have to apologise to me for your wealth,' said Stewart, 'but I fear that I have to come with you though, and speak with your lawyer,' he added.

'Then you will stay with me at my father's house.' He could see that his friend was about to decline. 'Do not refuse, Stewart, for how many times have you made me welcome here? Besides, maybe I can be of some assistance to you there. Two heads are better than one, no?'

'I thank you, James, yet again for your hospitality and friendship. One day I may be able to repay you…'

'Friendship courts no payment, Stewart. It is given freely for what it is,' countered James.

Stewart bowed his head. 'Then I take it in the manner that it is given, James, and give you my heartfelt thanks.'

***

As they entered the hall, there was silence. Stewart looked towards Thompson the butler and shook his head.

'It appears, sir, that the infusion Mrs Cottle made has soothed the young Master Charles' gums to the extent that he is now sleeping.' He bowed, took their coats and hats and left the hall.

'Your Cook, Mrs Cottle, is a marvel of nature. Has she had children of her own?' enquired James.

'No, James, but she nurtured her sister's three children from a very early age, when her sister and her husband died of the sweating sickness. As I understand it, Mrs Cottle has not herself been married,' replied Stewart.

'Now I must go to my wife in the nursery and see how my son fares,' he added, making his way up the stairs. Reaching the top, he called out.

'Please go sit on the terrace, and, Alex, go see your betrothed. I expect you will find her in the gardens.' He smiled and disappeared along the corridor.

As he entered the nursery, Margaret came towards him and pushed him out of the door.

'If you disturb our son, Stewart Hamilton, now that he has found a little peace, you will stay with him all through the night as punishment,' she whispered.

'Maggie, I need to speak with you, let us go to our room.' Pulling her by the hand, he walked her down the corridor.

As they entered their room, he pushed the door shut and pulled her to him.

'Oh, Maggie, you feel so good,' he groaned.

Margaret looked up at him and touched his face, then pulling him to the bed, she unbuttoned his waistcoat and pushed it off his shoulders and then proceeded to untie his stock.

Stewart held her hands tight in his. 'No, Maggie we cannot...'

'Hush! As I said before, Stewart...' He placed his finger to her lips and finished her words.

'There are other ways, no?' Pulling her into him, he kissed her deeply.

***

A warm gentle breeze came through the open windows, wafting over them, cooling their skin, making the small hairs on Margaret's body stand up.

Stewart stroked her hair, and as they lay together, he let his hand softly caress her upper arm, going down to her waist and over her hip.

'You are a very beautiful woman, Maggie,' he breathed.

Margaret smiled and looked into his eyes. 'What was it you wanted to tell me?'

'Oh,' said Stewart, shifting slightly. 'Well yes... Firstly, I wish you to speak to your sister about Alex.'

Margaret frowned at him perplexed. 'What do you mean?' Stewart hunched his shoulders, then Margaret smiled and nodded, realising what he was trying to convey to her. 'Ahhh...'

'Yes... precisely. Does Charlotte have any knowledge of what occurs between a man and a woman and the consummation of marriage?' he paused slightly. 'Oh I fear I am not making myself clear... what I mean is...' Stewart paused again to look at Maggie and pursed his lips, trying to find the right words.

'Alexander was never as gregarious as I,' he began.

Maggie laughed, softly stopping him. 'Go on...'

'He always held back, would let people and things come to him. What I am trying to state is that he will not make the slightest advances towards her less she gives him permission to do so,' he paused once more glancing at Margaret for help. 'Maggie, you understand what I wish to say, do not make it more difficult for me.'

'I know,' she replied, pushing his hair back from his face.

'Maggie, she has no mother to go to for guidance, you are her sister, and she trusts in you. Please?' He kissed her nose.

'What was the second piece of news you had?' asked Margaret.

Stewart sat up pulling on his stockings. 'I must go to London with James tomorrow. I have to visit the bank and will stay but a few days, then I will return by Stage Coach, as James has business of his father's to attend to.' Stewart reached over for his breeches and lightly slapped her thigh smiling.

'Now, Margaret Hamilton, we must get dressed and go down to lunch.'

'Not before I have been to see our son, Stewart Hamilton.' She pulled her shift over her head and leaned in to kiss him. 'Come tie my corset, and then I will see you downstairs.'

***

Daisy had brought young Charles down to lie in his perambulator in the cool shade of the terrace. Leaning over him she smiled.

'Milady, come see.'

As Margaret leaned in to her son, she saw what Daisy had, a small white jagged piece protruding from the bottom of his top gum. Placing her small finger there she felt its edge.

'Oh, my darling, no wonder you were in such pain.' Margaret smoothed her palm over his small forehead.

Daisy stood there beside him, smiling. 'Sadly, Milady, the poor lamb has many more to come yet.' Margaret smiled in reply.

'I will walk him up and down a while, Milady. Mayhap he will sleep some more.'

'Thank you, Daisy, you are truly a treasure,' Margaret answered.

She watched as Daisy wheeled him along, singing all the while to her child. She had not wanted a nanny, but Elizabeth in all her wisdom had insisted, and had been quite right, she thought. Daisy was an amazing person, patient and loving—she could not have wished for better. Then seeing Charlotte come through the door, she reflected it was just the right time to speak with her. The men had returned to the estate, and her mother was resting.

'Charlotte,' she called. 'Come sit with me a while.'

Margaret watched as she came towards her studying her face. There was something different about her, the way she walked, her appearance and radiance. Yes that was it. Charlotte's face glowed.

Charlotte kissed her sister and sat next to her, as Margaret took her hand and looked into her face.

'Tell me, Charlotte, are you happy?'

'Oh yes, cousin, very, very happy,' was her reply, but then really it was plain for all to see without asking.

'Charlotte, what do you feel when Alexander kisses you?' asked Margaret. She could see her sister trying hard to pull together the words to describe her feelings, till finally she spoke.

'Oh, Cousin Margaret, when he kisses me, it feels as though all of the parts of my body have dissolved to liquid.' Her face was alive with joy at the thought. 'Sensations rise up from my toes going around my body, like a thousand butterflies are passing through it.'

Margaret smiled and closed her eyes. She was not repelled by his touch then. Margaret coughed slightly and took both of Charlotte's hands in hers looking into her eyes.

'Charlotte, did your mother ever tell you what happens between a man and a woman in order for a marriage to be consummated?'

Charlotte blushed deeply, trying to pull her hands away, but Margaret held on and nodded to her to answer.

'A little, in that he has to enter me to take by maidenhead, and that is the way a child is conceived.' Her voice was very low, and her eyes were on their clasped hands in her lap.

Margaret squeezed her hands, then releasing one, she raised Charlotte's head.

'Charlotte, it is not something to be afraid of, it is something very beautiful between two people. The sensations that you feel when he kisses you will be magnified a hundred-fold when this happens. It is only the first time that you will feel a little pain.'

Charlotte's hands were shaking.

'Charlotte, you know that Alexander is a kind patient man, he would never do anything that would cause you harm, he will be gentle I know.'

Margaret closed her eyes and a cold slither of ice went down her spine when she thought of the time her first husband had taken her. Her sister would not have to suffer that. She pulled her sister in and enfolded her into her arms, smoothing her hair.

'You will come to me after your marriage and tell me how happy you are, and how wonderful it is to be loved by your husband,' Margaret assured her.

'I know, Cousin Margaret, I feel such waves of emotion go through me when he is near, and when he touches me, it takes my breath away. I know that I will be afraid, but in truth I will not stop him,' Charlotte replied.

Margaret pushed her away to look at her.

'Charlotte, we are all afraid the first time, but if you love and trust him and your love is returned, as I know yours is. You will be fine.'

Chapter Twenty-Seven
The Loan and Compassion of a Debt Paid

As Stewart sat in the office of Bearcroft's Chambers in the Inner Temple, London, he recalled the last time he had been there, Maggie was facing an inquest to her late husband's death curtsey of Northcott; now it was his mother who faced a similar fate, but this time there were two adversaries to fight—Northcott and his father.

He felt as he did last time, strangely detached by the quiet somnolence of the atmosphere which surrounded him. It was peaceful, yet unnatural. It was as though he were looking down at himself from a great height, watching himself go through the motions, without actually being there. Stewart looked to the back of the room to the shelves of Law tomes and thought how many years had they sat there, silent and steadfast, giving out their edicts and judgements, to how many people.

Bearcroft sat before him behind his desk, browsing through one such tome at this present moment. While he, Stewart, sat hat in hand, awaiting his decision. James had had business to attend to and said that he would meet him here later, but he was yet to arrive. Bearcroft coughed suddenly, removed his glasses and looked up.

'Your father, Hamilton, is wanted both in Scotland and here for debts amounting to thousands of pounds. He faces the debtor's prison, even worse, deportation to the colonies, if he cannot produce these amounts by the end of October.'

Stewart swallowed hard, and his palms were suddenly wet with sweat. Here was his chance to rid himself of his father for good. He looked the lawyer firmly in the eyes.

'Exactly how much are we talking of, sir?'

Bearcroft watched Stewart intently, then replaced his glasses and shuffled the papers before him, retrieving one which Stewart observed to have many figures on.

'It is in the region of around £15,000 sterling, sir.' Bearcroft paused still staring at Stewart.

'Mr Hamilton, are you perchance thinking of *paying* this money?' The emphasis was on the "paying".

'Sir, that is probably more that the whole income of my estate in a year, from those monies bills, wages, and one hundred other items will need to be paid or bought. My final profit would be no more than four thousand, maybe five. This will also depend on how good or bad a year has been.' Stewart rubbed his hand over his face before continuing.

'I know what you are thinking, sir, and there have been many times you must believe me, when I wished to choke the life from him. I have moved a man's bones from his resting place to inter him elsewhere to protect my mother, but for all that, he is still my father. I am not a vindictive man, sir, but I believe in justice.'

Bearcroft nodded slowly. 'You are a remarkable man, sir, in that you see your enemy for what he is, but still have compassion.'

Their conversation was interrupted by footsteps running up the stairs. James Fairweather entered the room breathless, and bowed to both.

'Your servant, gentlemen, I graciously beg your pardons but I was delayed at my father's bank for longer than I intended to be.' James Fairweather looked from one to the other breathing quickly from the exertion of running. 'Dare I ask what has happened?'

Stewart stood up bowing to the lawyer. 'I will return tomorrow, sir, when I have had time to clear my head. If it be at your convenience, sir that is, we can discuss other matters then?'

Bearcroft stood and bowed. 'I will see you tomorrow at the same hour, Mr Hamilton. I wish you well in your deliberations, sir, but I do not envy the decisions you have to make.'

'Good day to you, sir,' said James, as he left the room with Stewart.

As they made their way out of the building, Stewart turned.

'Is there a church nearby, James?' he asked.

James Fairweather looked at his friend and thought that he had maybe lost his mind but offered his knowledge of one anyway.

'The Temple Church, Stewart, not far down.'

Turning to look at his friend, he spoke, 'James, I am perfectly sane, I need to talk with someone who will just listen to me and not question me. Then, when I am done, mayhap he will make me see the way forward as in a form of enlightenment.'

James looked at him perplexed, but understood the logic of his thinking.

As they entered through the west doorway, all that could be heard was the sound of their shoes on the stone flagged floor. It was cool, and the silence instigated a high pitch whistle which emanated from within the ears. Stewart sat in a pew then placed his head in his hands and prayed.

Some half an hour later, Stewart nodded to his friend that they would go. Walking though the gardens, he stopped to look at James.

'You have decided, Stewart?' he asked.

'James, I will go to my mother's bank and request a loan for £15,000 to be paid back with what interest? I do not know, over a period of 1 year; more than that I doubt they will give me. If I fail, then they will claim from the estate, there is nothing else I can do, as I do not have that money at this present time in my hands to give to him.'

236

James opened his mouth to reply but was stopped instantly by Stewart.

'Please, think very carefully before you speak, James, do not say anything that will make me hit you, as I do not wish to do that. Do I make myself clear, James?'

James Fairweather looked at his friend with empathy and inclined his head. They continued to walk in silence till they reached James' coach.

'I would be most grateful if you could take me to The Strand, James, which is where my mother's bank Coutts is situated,' asked Stewart.

James turned and looked at his friend.

'No, Stewart, we are going to my bank Hoare's, in Fleet Street, where you will acquire a loan with no interest, and for a longer period as I shall be your guarantor. Now if you wish to hit me'—here he offered Stewart his chin—'you may do so.'

Stewart raised his eyes up to the heavens and gave up a prayer of thanks.

***

Leaning back in the coach, Stewart closed his eyes; he was hot, tired and sore, and to add to these ills the growth of beard on his chin itched madly. He was on the last stage from Andover now, and he hoped to be in Mere early evening, giving him time to go to Margaret's house, saddle a horse and ride home.

The meetings with the lawyer Bearcroft and the bank had drained him, and he had not slept more than six hours since he set out two days ago. He had obtained the loan at no interest, which he would never have thought possible, thanks to James. The letter of credit had been drawn out in Bearcroft's name, as he would contact the courts and settle the debt, with the proviso that if so much as one penny was owed after settlement, there would be no *quarter* next time. He would go to prison or be transported. It was not to be disclosed where the money had been obtained from or from whom. To secure all paths, Bearcroft had drawn up a document to this effect, which Andrew Duncan had to sign, or the payment was rescinded, and Duncan would go straight to prison.

Stewart reflected that in the space of two years, his life had been reduced to a living hell. The only good thing to come out of it all was that he had a beautiful wife and child, but they too had been threatened. Stewart raised his eyes to the heavens again, saying quietly to himself, *'Sufficient unto the day is the evil thereof,'* as he mentally crossed himself and said, *'Amen.'*

As the coach pulled up outside the Angel Inn, Stewart alighted, then stood and strained the muscles in his back, neck, arms and legs, with an effort to bring some life into them. Lifting his bag from the pile, he made his way slowly to Margaret's house just at the edge of the town.

Margaret's butler opened the door with a mixture of surprise, shock and trepidation on his face, as he looked at his master standing there in a state of dishevelment.

'Giles, you have my humblest apologies,' he said, taking hold of the man's arm.

'I have this hour stepped down from the stage coach from London. I ask nothing but that you saddle me a horse so that I may ride home please.'

'Mr Hamilton sir, I will go and ready one this instant.'

Before Stewart could utter a word, he had gone. Looking round, he made his way to the drawing room; taking a glass from the salver, he poured himself a rather large whisky, and then seated himself by the window. His shirt stuck to him, and he could smell the dust from the road on his coat. He would give anything just to dive into the lake right now, and wash away the memories of London. Just to cleanse himself of the malevolent feelings, both towards himself and against others.

'Begging your pardon, sir, your horse is ready.'

Stewart started, being so deep in his own thoughts he had not heard the man come in. Standing up he came towards the door.

'Giles, I have some clean breeches, stockings and a shirt here, do I not?' asked Stewart.

'You do, sir, would you like me to bring them, or lay them out for you upstairs?' Giles queried.

'Just bring them, Giles, I will take them with me.'

Giles looked at his master but said nothing.

'As you wish, sir,' he replied rather tentatively, and left the room.

***

Stewart stood in the hall his hair wet and loose about his shoulders, his shirt was open minus his stock, and his breeches seemed to be wet. Holding out his roll of dirty clothes to Thompson, he spoke.

'Sorry, Thompson, but these will need washing and cleaning.'

Then turning to his mother who seemed to have lost the ability to speak but was standing there open mouthed, he bowed. Behind her were Alexander who was trying to contain himself from laughing, his shoulders visibly shaking, and Charlotte who seemed to be in the same predicament as his mother. Margaret, conversely, seeming to have no inhibitions was standing at the top of the stairs holding her son, her hand over her mouth, with tears streaming down her face both in laughter and thanks that he was home safe. Lilly the maid, who had just been handed the dirty clothing, had eyes as big as saucers.

Stewart came across to his mother and holding her in his arms, he kissed her forehead gently, and then stepping back he bowed to all present.

'I bid you all a good evening,' he said, mounting the stairs he took his son in his arms and made his way to the nursery.

Elizabeth looked after him, and finally finding her voice, she said, 'I do believe my son has lost his mind.'

***

The moon's glow fell into the room illuminating, and casting its silvery glow, adding to the warm light emitting from the candle. Stewart had been talking for some time as he lay there with Margaret held tightly in his arms. He told her everything that had transpired that night twenty-three years ago, and all that had occurred since because of it. The words came pouring out of him like a flood, while Margaret lay there listening, knowing now what pain he had been going through, not just hers, and his mother's, but his own also. When he had finished, she looked up into his eyes, then kissed him softly.

'Go to sleep, Stewart, you are safe now,' she whispered, tightening her hold around his chest.

Stewart breathed deeply, then whispering as he always did. 'I love you, Maggie,' he fell to sleep in an instant.

***

Neither man had any appetite for work as they sat outside the office. With Stewart's horse tethered to a tree nearby, they leaned back against the wall in companionable silence.

'How many labourers do you employ at this time of year, Alex?' Stewart's voice broke into the silence.

'I would estimate 40, though some will bring their sons with them if they are of age and capable. Why do you ask?' replied Alexander.

'Oh no reason cousin, just idle curiosity.' spoke Stewart

'You are thinking about the loan, are you not?' asked Alexander quietly.

Stewart looked hard at his cousin. 'I am thinking, cousin, that if the next five years, harvest be not as good as the last two, our expenditure will be more than our gain. That being so, through necessity I may have to sell off some of my land.'

Stewart sat there, deep in thought. It was peaceful here, no interruptions, and he now saw what Alexander did, in that the mind worked better under these circumstances. The loan he had secured was over five years with no interest, which meant that in five years, he would have to pay back the same amount £15,000 sterling. James had told him that Hoarse Bank charged no interest, in that it encouraged people to invest, as by investing it would in some strange way help the bank. Though for the life of him, Stewart could not fathom the logic in that. His loan was small in comparison to what other men borrowed, but then they had the means to repay, for them it was more a question of being able to draw that much money at that time. The capital was there but not in money.

Stewart pressed his fingers into his eyes.

'How much do you think that this estate is worth, Alex?'

Stewart was thinking out loud and Alexander knew this, and thought some time before he answered.

'In all honesty, cousin, I would estimate between £30 to £35 thousand pounds sterling. The acre is worth in the order of £40 pounds, and we have how many? To my knowledge, 450 acres, not all of which we farm, which would amount to

239

£18 thousand pounds sterling, the rest of the money would be taken up by the house, and farm buildings and rights to use the River Nadder.' Alexander watched his cousin intently.

Stewart rubbed his face several times. 'If I could not pay back the loan, Alex, I would be forced to sell off some... 375 acres... No?' he raised his brows for effect. 'That is, of course, if the price of land holds steady.'

Alexander stood up and paced, several times he stopped to talk but the words would not come, till finally he rounded on his cousin.

'Stewart, I have money, together we can pay this debt within the year... No, please do not say anything... I owe your mother a debt that I could never think to repay for all that she has done for me since I was twelve years old,' he paused here to swallow and calm himself.

'I owe her my life, because without her help, I believe that I would not be here today.' Alexander paused again to stand in front of Stewart. Holding out his hand he continued.

'So, we are in agreement, cousin, we will pay this debt together.'

Alexander could see that his cousin was thinking hard; the muscles in his jaw were moving as he reflected on what he had said to him. Finally, Stewart stood up and faced him, and then nodding slightly Stewart took Alexander's hand in his.

'We have an agreement, brother, because that is what you are to me.'

Stewart turned quickly before Alexander could answer, mounted his horse and rode off.

Alexander watched Stewart disappear into the distance, then sat down heavily on the stool.

***

It was late afternoon when Margaret found Stewart deep in thought in the study. He was standing in front of the window, hands clasped at his back, looking out to the garden. He knew she was there, for as she came up behind him, he opened his hands and took hers, bringing them round in front of him. Margaret rested her head on his back and sighed.

'Maggie,' he began, turning to face her and pulling her into him, 'In the last two years I feel I have aged beyond my years... my life has always been in some turmoil or other... but these two years have exceeded what I thought was physically possible.' He paused to look down at her, searching her face as though to take it to memory.

'I need you to know that I could bear to lose many things from my life, but if I ever lost you, my life would be worthless. You are the only reason for me to exist, the only thing that makes my life tolerable, you *are* my constant, where no matter what befalls, I can always come back to you, and I will be safe. I could not go on if you were no longer there.'

Margaret looked intently up into his face, cupping her hand to his cheek as she stroked his lips lightly with her thumb.

'Stewart, you rescued me at a time when I was in a very dark formidable place. You pulled me from that darkness and showed me light, warmth and love. I would never leave you, but if I should get taken, you would go on for our son's sake. He would need you to guide him, give him your wisdom and, more preciously, your love'

He held her so close she could hear the thud of his heartbeat in her ear. He was melancholy, she knew that, ever since his return from London. What his father had done to them, then the loan, it was insurmountable at this time. Margaret knew that she had that money, some of it came from her mother, the other left to her by her first husband, no doubt for services rendered. Margaret shivered at the thought. Nevertheless, she could not at this time offer that money to him, as he would presume in that stubborn head of his that he could not provide for her and their son. She would bide a while, and when the time was right…

Stewart pulled her away from him and smiled mischievously, lightening the mood.

'And if it were I that was taken first?'

Margaret thumped his chest with the flat of her hand.

'As for you, Stewart Charles Hamilton, I would be free of your teasing.' Margaret swallowed audibly.

There was a rap on the door, causing them to part suddenly. As the door opened, Charlotte's head appeared.

'May I come in?' she asked shyly.

Margaret smiled broadly at her, and then went to take her hand to pull her into the room.

'Come in, Charlotte, has Alexander arrived yet?'

Charlotte lowered her eyes. 'Not yet, cousin, he will come at seven o'clock when he has finished his work.'

'Then you and I shall walk the gardens for a while,' stated Margaret as she turned her to leave the room.

Charlotte stopped suddenly and turned back. 'Oh, Cousin Stewart, there is a letter for you,' she said as she handed it to him.

Stewart looked at the seal and smiled. 'Thank you, Cousin Charlotte, it is from my friend James. I will read it and come join you both.' Looking out of the window, he observed that Daisy had brought his son out and was sitting there with him on her lap.

'Margaret, our son awaits you on the terrace,' he grinned amiably.

Charlotte clapped her hands together in delight, 'Oh good, I shall take him for a walk with me.'

Margaret just lifted her shoulders to Stewart in reply and blew him a kiss.

***

Stewart sat on the steps of the terrace and looked up to the sky. It was that strange time of evening where it was neither day not night—twilight they called

241

it; a half light where the colours were still visible before night fell and all was grey or black.

Alexander was sitting quietly beside him and sipping his drink, loath to break his thoughts, Stewart was the first to break the silence.

'Alex, you remember what you did for Margaret and I, finding us a place to go to, just to be away from everyone and be alone? Well James has done just that for you.'

Alexander turned to face him frowning. 'What do you mean, Stewart? We are to go to London?'

Stewart rested his arm about his cousin's shoulders and shook his head. 'No, my cousin, you are to go to Torquay in Devon. He owns a small house there which overlooks the bay, it will not be warm, but he tells of spectacular views of the sea from all windows that face that way. He needs me to tell him when you will depart so that he may tell the people of the village to go and prepare the house for you. It stands empty, so either he will send his own people to look after you, or you may take your own household staff.'

Alexander looked at him. 'James has done this for me? That is truly an amazing gesture, Charlotte will be thrilled. I know she will.'

Stewart slapped his back and laughed. 'Alex, I do believe that you have a very deep affection, or are in love with Charlotte?'

'She is a very warm-hearted gently person... and—'

Stewart stopped him before he could continue. 'If she is anything like her sister, cousin, you will be one very happy man.' Stewart's grin said everything.

Chapter Twenty-Eight
An Unexpected Proposal

Elizabeth looked out to the lawn from the drawing room window and thought how many seasons she had seen come and go in her lifetime—too many—and now they came too quickly. She had turned forty-seven years in the April just gone, twenty-six more than her mother had had. She shook herself slightly and tried to banish these strange thoughts that came into her head now.

Charlotte's father had returned to the Willows at the beginning of September, having negotiated an excellent sale of his business and properties in Norwich, the funds from which would purchase him a substantial house just outside Mere to the North. He had viewed the said property which consisted of a large house made from stone and at least 20 acres of surrounding land, after all it would be Charlotte's legacy.

All of the preparations for the wedding which would take place the first Sunday in October—four days' time—had been overseen by Elizabeth, and just as for Stewart's wedding, the decking of the church would be done by the tenants. It was to be an early morning wedding, with just friends and family, but she had insisted that the tenants would celebrate as before on the lawn at the back of the house, weather permitting. She knew that Alexander was well loved and respected by them.

Charlotte's father had brought with him many rolls of cloth, including a roll of French white silk that he had acquired from one of his merchant links, from which would be made her wedding gown. He had also purchased—at great cost—a length of Irish lace which would go over the skirt of the gown, and be sewn in ruffles on the bodice and round the neck, as well as edging the long narrow sleeves. For warmth, she would wear a white cape with hood, the outer covering being made of white satin, while the lining would be of a soft white woollen fabric, finishing with a trimming of ermine around the hood.

The men—all three—were to be clad in the deepest cherry red velvet, a full coat with silver thread embroidered along the edges and waistcoats of silver satin, embellished with the same embroidery. Their breeches and cloaks would also be of the same silver satin, but the cloaks would be lined in velvet for warmth.

James had had his tailor and several seamstresses brought to Salisbury especially for the occasion, as her father was of the opinion that he had but one daughter to marry, and she would marry in the grandest style he could pay for.

He was a cloth merchant after all—if he could not obtain the best, then who could. He was at this very moment speaking to Spike regarding flowers. Elizabeth thought that the man was a wealth of information.

She sighed deeply, the days were shorter now, and though there was a chill in the air, when the sun appeared it warmed the face, but she knew that when the wedding took place there might be little or no warmth on that day, and she prayed that it would not rain. They would all need their cloaks to keep out the cold, especially within the church.

As for hers and Margaret's dresses, Mr Masters had brought a pale gold silk for Margaret, and for herself a deep purple. The cloth far exceeded in beauty anything that they could have obtained in London. Margaret was to have a deep red velvet cloak, made with the same cloth as the men's clothes, and for herself a velvet one of a similar purple colour to that of her dress

She was pulled back from her thoughts by the door opening.

'Am I disturbing you, mother?' Stewart asked smiling.

Elizabeth looked into her son's face and smiled back.

'Heavens no my son,' she answered, watching his face for any sign of apprehension about the wedding, but there was none.

'So you think Alexander will be happy, Stewart?' her voice was soft, and she was in need of assurance. Had she not instigated this marriage herself, it would be a tragedy if she had not read the signs correctly.

'Mother, they will be fine, they suit one another perfectly, as each has their own gentleness and kind heart,' replied Stewart, coming towards her and holding her hands.

'Oh I do hope so, Stewart, all I wanted was for him to have someone to care for him, so he would not to be alone. Was I wrong to wish for this?' There was a pleading in her tone.

'Mother, I know Alexander, he is very happy. He would never have found himself a wife, his character is too introverting for that, and you know he never lets his feeling show,' he paused to grin widely. 'Now, as for myself, I have always displayed my feelings, no matter what the consequences,' he said, nodding to her as he spoke.

'Stewart, please do not remind me of that, you were a constant trial to me, even when you were very young…'

Stewart leant towards her and spoke in her ear. 'But you still loved me, no?'

Elizabeth pulled away from him and slapped her hand to his chest. 'Oh, be gone with you, you have come here to tease me and I am in no mood for teasing. I am going to the kitchens,' she said as she pushed past him and into the corridor.

'But you still love your son…' he called after her, laughing softly.

***

William Masters walked slowly to the cottage that Spike and young Kenver occupied within the walled garden. He hoped that the man would not think him disrespectful calling on him at this late hour of the evening, but to come before would be to interrupt the man at his work, and that would be totally unpardonable. Knocking on the door, he waited.

As Spike opened the door, a look of surprise came over his face.

'Oh, good evening to you, Mr Masters sir. What be bringing you to my home at this hour of the day? There be nothing amiss up at the house is there?' he questioned.

William Masters saw the look of alarm come across the man's face and thought that he had not judged this well.

'Please, Mr Spike, you have my humblest apologies.' With that he took a step back, took of his hat and bowed. 'Your servant, sir.'

Spike's eyes opened wide in astonishment—he had never in his life been address so—opening the door, he bade William Masters to come in.

'Sir, you must excuse us but we have just sat to eat...' Spike could see Kenver's spoon poised in mid-air about one inch from his open mouth. The boy looked between his master and the stairs, getting ready to make his exit.

'Young Kenver lad, can you leave us for a bit, while I speak to Mistress Charlotte's father.' Spike nodded to him to go, raising his brows.

Kenver needed no more, but putting his spoon back to his plate, he bowed his way backwards till he reached the stairs, then disappeared up them before William Masters could stop him.

'Oh, Mr Spike, I did not mean to inconvenience you in this way, pray do forgive my impertinence.'

'Please, Mr Masters sir, do not be troubling yourself on our account, young Kenver will finish his meal as soon as we are done.' Saying this he took the plate from the table and placed it on the stone hearth next to the fire to keep warm.

'Will you sit down, Mr Masters sir?' Spike waved him to the good chair while he himself took the stool.

William Masters breathed deeply. 'My daughter holds you in such high regard, Spike, and now I see why. She loves the gardens, and would spend all of her time there if her cousin would allow.'

Spike nodded and smiled. 'Thank ye kindly, sir.'

'As you know, I am a cloth merchant from Norfolk, and have been these past eighteen years or more. Norfolk is a great place for such trade between England and Europe, even the Americas,' he paused as Spike handed him a mug of ale.

'To your good health, sir.' offered Spike.

'And to yours too, Mr Spike,' returned William Masters.

'As I was saying, Norfolk not only deals with cloth but does a great trade with the Dutch in flowers. I know there will be no flowers to be had at this time of year for the wedding, but in Norfolk there are places that nurture these flowers they import, in sheds which have windows all along the Southern wall, as to catch the sun's rays. I have purchased some of these flowers for my Charlotte, they are called Carnations, and I have chosen Red and White.' He paused again to take a sup of ale.

'In fact, I have purchased several plants, as I feel that you would be able to grow these here. I want to arrange—once I have spoken to Milady Hamilton, of course—to have one such building constructed here for that sole purpose of growing them.'

Spike was astounded. He had never heard of such a thing, and to have one built here at the willows… He had no idea of how it worked, but that could wait till it was built, then maybe Mr Masters could advise him.

'Pray would you be in agreement to manage such a building, sir?'

Spike smiled widely, and then coughed.

'Mr Masters sir, it would give me the greatest of pleasure!'

William Masters stood up and presented his hand for Spike to take.

'We have a deal then, sir. Now I bid you good night, and leave you to eat your supper in peace.'

When Spike closed the door, he leaned back onto it and shook his head in disbelief. He raised his eyes upwards and spoke.

'Oh, Merryn, did you hear that? I am well blessed.'

Walking to the stairs, he called, 'Come you down now, young Kenver, afore our dinner freezes!'

***

Just before dinner, James Fairweather had come from Salisbury with his army of tailors and seamstresses to the Willows for the final fitting of all garments. It was now only three days till the wedding.

'Stewart, can we go somewhere private to speak please.'

The urgency in James' voice made Stewart look up from his son who he had perched on his knee. Handing young Charles back to his nanny, he took James by the arm and led him into the study.

'Right, James, will you now tell me what has you so disconcerted?' Stewart motioned to James for him to take a seat.

'Stewart, you remember the fair Catherine?'

Stewart eyed him warily.

'Oh, James, how could I forget…'

'Read this letter from my father, it will explain things much more succinctly than I.' He handed Stewart the folded paper and waited. He saw Stewart's face go from shock to surprise to disbelief in as many seconds.

Stewart handed James back the letter and rubbed his hand over his face.

'James,' he began. 'James,' he stopped but at the third attempt he gained his speech. 'James, her father wants a marriage between yourself and his daughter, the Lady Catherine.'

James, whose colour was usually always heightened, looked decidedly pale at this present time.

'What am I to do, Stewart, her father and my father, I have just discovered, have been friends for years, and meet at Brooks Club at least once a week for supper when they are in town,' he paused to gain control, watching Stewart's face as a completely bewildered expression came over it.

'Why would I not know this? Well, for one I do not frequent the place myself, and two I know nothing of my father's acquaintances—he has his life, as I have mine.'

'Would your father force this onto to you James?' queried Stewart, who was also becoming slightly agitated by now.

'No, Stewart, my father would never force anything on me, he is merely making me aware that such a proposal had been received. If I choose never to marry it would not matter to him. He just wants me to be happy in my life.'

'Well, I might add, that is a relief,' answered Stewart. 'So what are you going to do?' he added.

James Fairweather stood up and walked about the room.

'I have to give her father an answer by next Friday, he wants her married as soon as possible, so no other incident like the one last year can occur again.' James continued pacing.

'She is the most presumptuous, conceited, objectionable young lady I have ever set my eyes on, and now I am meant to consider a marriage with her. Dear God, Stewart, of all the people in England, her father chose me!' His voice had risen as he spoke.

'James, calm yourself, you are not thinking rationally at this present time. Let us sleep on it this tonight and we can talk again tomorrow.'

James raised his arms up and down at his sides and shook his head.

'Why me Stewart? Why me?'

'If I knew that, James, you would have your answer.'

***

As Stewart lay in Margaret's arms that night, he told her what James had confided to him. Margaret's first reaction was shock, but slowly she started to smile, and then to giggle. Stewart pulled her away from him and looked at her.

'Margaret, this is not the reaction I had expected from you. The poor man is demented with worry, and, he has to give her father an answer by next Friday.'

'Oh, Stewart, I am so very sorry, but can you not see the irony of it all?' Margaret looked up into his eyes. 'She is a very beautiful woman you said, no?'

Stewart sat up suddenly in bed. 'That has nothing to do with this situation, Maggie, Northcott wanted her for himself, now she is to be James'.'

Margaret saw that he was clearly anxious about the dilemma and slowly began to realise the implications of such an agreement.

'Northcott will believe he has been duped yet again,' she breathed.

'Exactly,' replied Stewart.

Margaret pulled herself up and sat with him. 'What will he do? Decline her father's offer?'

'I do not believe it will be as simple as that, Maggie. Her father will be in no mind to accept his refusal, as James' father's older brother, who has no children, is a Baronet. He has named James as his heir apparent.'

Margaret opened her mouth several times to speak, but decided not to. Her mind was slowly processing the implications, when she realised that James—their James—was to inherit the title of Baronet.

'Oh my, Stewart, what will he do? Can he not delay the decision for a while, till he has had time to think?'

Stewart pulled her back towards him, and drew the covers up over them.

'Let us sleep now, Maggie, maybe tomorrow on a clear head we will see a way forward.' Saying this, he slid down into bed and pulled her tightly in.

'I love you, Maggie,' he whispered in her ear, and then slowly fell asleep.

Margaret lay there listening to his heart beating, and thought that he *never* went to sleep at night without saying that to her. She kissed his chest and whispered. 'I love you too, Stewart.'

Chapter Twenty-Nine
Charlotte and Alexander's Wedding and a Father's Pain

The three men stood fully dressed in their wedding clothes looking out to the garden; as Stewart turned slightly to Alexander, he saw that his face was relaxed. Had he been truly against this arrangement, he would never have agreed to it, he knew that, which meant just one thing, that he felt a very strong affection for Charlotte, maybe love? He had never seen him so comfortable with himself—content could be the word. They would be good for one another, Stewart agreed with himself, and, he repeated to himself, if she was only half as loving as her sister, he would be one very happy man. Turning to face him, he spoke.

'So, as you once said to me, cousin, are you ready to be married?'

Alexander smiled, turned and looked at them both.

'Yes, I am,' he answered.

It was a glorious day; the sky was a clear sapphire blue with not a cloud to be seen. There was a chill to the air, but no wind as such, and Alexander silently prayed that it remained so, just till after the ceremony.

'Are you nervous, Alex?' questioned James.

Alexander shook his head. 'No, James, I am fine, but I do believe that Charlotte is.'

'Ah,' replied James, 'that is a woman's privilege, Alex.' Turning away from the window, he raised his arm.

'Come, gentlemen, we shall leave for the church and take up our positions before the rest of the party take their leave.'

As they came out into the hall, they saw that all the staff from the house was lined up there to wish Alexander good luck. Mrs Cottle came forward and placing her hands onto Alexander's face, she pulled him down and kissed his forehead.

'God bless you and your new wife Charlotte, Master Alexander. You truly deserve to be happy.'

Stewart came up behind and smiled teasingly at the cook.

'Mrs Cottle, I am envious of this show of affection for my cousin, you never showed me such thought,' he taunted.

Mrs Cottle rounded on him placing her hands on her hips.

'Master Stewart, you terrorised my kitchen—at one time it be with frogs if I do be remembering correctly—this one never did!'

Stewart bowed deeply, still grinning. 'For that I am truly sorry.'

Mrs Cottle shooed them away with her hands. 'Be off with you now, all three of you, or you will arrive after the bride.' With that she turned and went back to the kitchen.

As they rode to the church in James' coach, James turned to look at Stewart.

'You actually took frogs into the kitchen, Stewart?' James was laughing loudly before he even finished the sentence.

Stewart chuckled. 'Well, as I recall I was seven at the time, and Pip and I had just been to the river, where we had filled a small container with the said objects. I did not know then that they could jump, to a considerable height might I add.' Stewart was laughing freely now.

'When I took off the lid, they flew out—you have never heard screams like it, the kitchen girls ran in all directions, and if my memory serves me well, Mrs Cottle came at me with a rather large wooden ladle.'

By this time, they were all laughing so loudly they did not hear or feel the carriage draw up to the church, till Carter the footmen opened the door with a smile on his face.

***

William Masters helped his daughter from his carriage, smiling happily. She was not of his blood, but they had reared and nurtured her from infancy, and if that was not the equivalent of blood in the sight of God, then what was. He loved her more than life itself, and he hoped with all of his heart that he was handing her over to a man who would do likewise. He had known Alexander but a short while, but what he had seen was a very gentle loving man. He would be here though, to watch over her, and he would know in an instant of anything that troubled her. He had made sure of that. It was not that he distrusted Alexander, he did trust him, but there were other evils in this world, as well he knew.

'Your mother would have been so proud of you today, my Charlotte.' His voice was thick with emotion.

Charlotte touched the small silver locket that her father had placed around her neck that morning, which contained a small lock of her mother's hair. She brought it up to her lips and kissed it.

Seeing the sadness in her eyes, he took her arm and tucked it safely into his, then led her through the arch into the church. Margaret's maid Millie had fashioned her hair; it was pulled back softly from her face and tied gently with a satin ribbon so as it flowed in great curls down her back. As she came up to Alexander, she saw him swallow and breathe deeply, before he took her hand in his and kissed her fingers. Alexander thought he had never seen anything of such beauty in his entire life. They were married with his mother's wedding ring, a plain silver band, which Alexander had had both their initials engraved on. When the ceremony finished, he pulled her into him and kissed her deeply for the first time.

'We will be happy, Charlotte,' he breathed, as she nodded in answer and smiled.

***

They were to spend the night at Alexander's house in Mere, before setting out in her father's coach the following day for Torquay. Margaret and Elizabeth had been there just after the wedding to decorate their room with Holly and Pyracantha berries. They had arranged the carnations that her father had brought from Norwich in a small vase and placed it on the table before the window. Spike had dried some roses from the summer and Margaret sprinkled these on the floor and into the bed.

Elizabeth smiled at her daughter. Placing a hand on her arm, she turned her.

'She will be fine, Margaret, do not worry, and I do believe that Alexander does love her. One look at his face today in that church should convince you of that.'

'Oh I know, Mother, he is a kind, gentle, loving man. I was just thinking when I married Stewart...' her voice trailed away.

'Come, Margaret, we must get back to the celebrations. I am one very happy mother today,' she said as they left the room

***

Alexander stood in their room and watched his new bride. He had taken his jacket off and untied his stock, then stood there trying to find the right words... Charlotte sat on the chair in front of her mirror, carefully taking the pins from her hair, and then she slowly turned to him.

'Charlotte, I,' he begun. She was so young, he thought, and so innocent. He saw that she was afraid, though he did not think it was of him personally. He had lain with many women in his time, but none as Charlotte was, if truth were to be told, he was as nervous as she.

She stood up and looked at him.

'Alexander, let me speak first.' Alexander nodded in reply.

'I know something of the ways of a man and woman, my mother told me what was to happen... I... I will not say that I am not afraid, for I am, do you understand that?'

Alexander nodded again.

Slowly, she came towards him, putting her hands up to his shirt and unbuttoning the collar.

'I want you, Alexander, but I am afraid... of many things,' she paused to collect her thoughts together.

'Margaret told me that what I feel when we kiss, I will feel a hundred-fold when we join.'

Alexander swallowed hard. He had not had a woman in many months, and now he must be gentle with this beautiful young girl who was now his wife, who at this moment he wanted very badly.

'What... what if I do not like what we do, what if I am repulsed by it... oh, Alexander.' She looked into his eyes for help. 'I have decided that the only way I will know these things is to...' her voice trailed away as she placed her hands around his face, pulling him down and gently kissing him.

'Help me, Alexander, please,' she breathed.

Alexander pulled her to him and kissed her deeply. He felt her body yield to his instantly. Feeling for the lacings of her bodice as he kissed her, he released them.

'Charlotte, trust me, please trust me,' he whispered.

She inclined her head as her skirts fell to the floor. In truth, he could not stop himself now even if he wanted to.

***

As they lay side by side, looking to one another, Charlotte spoke.

'Oh, Alexander, my cousin was right,' she breathed, daring to stroke his bear shoulder with her fingers. She was trembling, but not from fear, only emotion.

Alexander breathed a sigh and thanked God as he pulled her into his arms and kissed her again.

He held her tight against him, foreheads touching.

'Do you smell roses?' he asked suddenly.

Charlotte giggled. 'There are rose petals in the bed... you did not notice them?'

Kissing her deeply once more, he looked at her and smiled.

'Why would I,' he replied softly, as his mouth covered hers once more.

***

Stewart sat in the winged chair opposite Charlotte's father and watched him. The man was deep in thought, he could see that as he watched the flames flicker, his thoughts were elsewhere, and Stewart would win any wager as to where they were. The women had gone to bed and James was in the study trying to compose a letter to his father to explain why a match with the fair Catherine would be impossible.

'She will be safe, sir.' Stewart's voice broke into the silence. William Masters raised his head up in surprise.

'I said she will be safe, sir,' repeated Stewart. If he were truthful, he would not want to be inside the man's mind at this present time.

'You are a very discerning man, Mr Hamilton, like your mother,' he replied as he took a gulp of his whisky. Raising the glass to the fire, he looked at the contents.

'Mighty fine stuff this, do you import it?'

252

Stewart smiled. 'No, sir, it was a gift, you might say for services rendered.'

'Ah…' came Masters' reply.

'If it were my daughter, sir, I would be feeling just as you are now—wanting to go there and choke the life from him.' Stewart said it in jest, but her father knew the intonation behind it.

'She may not be of my flesh, but she is still my daughter,' he replied softly, breathing deeply through his nose.

'I know, sir,' replied Stewart, 'and believe me when I say she got the better bargain when she was born,' he continued. Stewart swallowed all of his whisky down in one swig.

William Masters nodded. 'Yes, Mr Hamilton, your mother did explain to me what had happened. 'God, there is so much evil in this world, and all of my life I have done my upmost to keep her from it. I cannot just stop now; do you understand that?'

'Yes, sir, I do. Just because they leave their home, it does not mean to say that you stop protecting them,' Stewart answered.

'If it is of any consolation, sir, I know my cousin; he is more like a brother to me. He would never make Charlotte do anything she did not wish to do, believe me. What I mean to say, sir, is that he would never take advantage of her.'

'I know, I know,' sighed Masters resignedly. 'But it does not make it any easier to accept, and that is no disrespect to your cousin what so ever.'

Stewart smiled; he knew the man was hurting.

William Masters thought well before he posed his next question.

'Mr Hamilton, as you know, I have bought a large house here just the other side of Mere.'

'And you were wondering if they would come and live with you there?' Stewart finished.

'God, you are so like your mother,' came Masters astonished reply.

'So I have been told,' smiled Stewart. 'I think that Alexander would welcome that with open arms, that way he will know that there is always someone with her when he is at work, someone who would protect her with their life, no?'

Masters nodded. 'He could bring his cook and butler with him, I have no house staff at present, and he could close his house, or rent it as the case may be, giving them more income.'

Stewart saw the relief on the man's face; in that he had found a solution to his problems. He also realised why he had sold up his flourishing business in Norfolk, just to be close to his daughter.

Stewart stood up. 'Mr Masters, I bid you a good night, Please stay and finish your drink, have another. I myself must go and rescue my friend James from his writing as we will not rise in the morning to see them on their way.'

'I too will retire, Mr Hamilton,' replied Masters.

As they left the room, Stewart saw Lilly sitting on a chair waiting.

''Lilly, just snuff the candles, smother the fire and go to your bed. The rest can wait till tomorrow,' he whispered.

***

Stewart lowered himself gently into bed beside Margaret, pulling her into him and wrapping her tightly into his arms.

'Stewart?' her voice was soft and sleepy. 'Did you love me when we married?'

Stewart turned her to face him.

'What ever made you ask that now?' his voice was low as he looked into her eyes.

Margaret just raised her shoulders slightly, not taking her eyes from him.

'Yes, Margaret Hamilton, I did…' he replied softly, as he turned her around again pulling her tightly into him, pushing her hair back so his mouth was near her ear. 'The love I felt for you was not a great passion, where it burns with intensity, then extinguishes itself.' Margaret could feel his breath on her neck; closing her eyes she gave a silent sigh. 'My love for you was slow, as when that first spark hits the kindling, you blow on it till you see it take flame,' he blew gently into her ear now, as his leg came over her holding her tight. Margaret pushed back into him, her heart was beating just a little too fast, 'then slowly it burns till the flames lick around the wood and it bursts with heat.' Stewart's hand came up and stroked her breast, making every hair on her body rise. 'Once the flames have died, it glows with a warmth that lasts a lifetime,' he was kissing her neck now. Margaret moaned softly. 'Often in between, gusts of wind will revive the flame throughout its life,' his hand travelled down now to her stomach, 'and then, just as slowly, it begins to fade till only ashes remain.' Turning her to him once again, he kissed her intensely. 'That is the love I have for you, Maggie.'

Margaret knew exactly what he meant, but she would ask anyway.

'And when did your love burst with heat?'

'When our son was born…' he whispered, kissing her so tenderly, feeling the wetness on her cheeks.

'I love you, Margaret Hamilton, now and eternally, you should know that.'

Chapter Thirty
Letters, Men Bearing Shovels and Disclosures

Stewart watched his cousin as he sat at his desk in the office. There was a difference about him, he knew that. He could see his mind wander sometimes just by looking at his eyes. He was thinking of something, someone—he looked content and at peace with himself, more so than he had ever seen him before. He also knew who was responsible for this change—Charlotte. One could not say that he was restless before, but there was an emptiness that needed to be filled. They had been married but one month, and already he left his work at six o'clock, by his father's pocket watch that he always carried now. No more would he be sitting here working till late, now he had someone to go home to. Stewart breathed a sigh of relief; he had been alone too long.

'Shall we go over these papers tomorrow, cousin?' Stewart asked.

Brought back from his thoughts, Alexander looked at his watch.

'If it is agreeable with you, cousin, as it is past six now and my dinner will be awaiting me at seven,' Alexander replied smiling.

Stewart smiled warmly at his cousin. 'Go home to your wife, Alex.'

Alexander turned to him and half smiled.

'Did you know I never really knew how lonely I was till I married Charlotte. Now I wake each morning with a warm body pushed closely against my own whose arms are so tightly wrapped around me, and I do not wish to leave my bed.' Alexander looked out of the window to the darkened sky.

'I do not know if you can comprehend this, Stewart, but since my parents passed when I was twelve, I have never felt such closeness as this with anyone. Oh I love your mother dearly, she is as my own, but this is… different.' Slowly he rose and pulled on his coat.'

'Alex, I understand perfectly.' Stewart laughed lightly. 'I seem to remember though your saying to me after I had been married just a short while, that I was keeping aristocratic hours.'

'Touché my friend.' Alexander smiled. 'I will just dampen the fire to be safe, so as not to burn the building down.'

He pulled a small shovel from the side and started to pile ashes onto the remaining wood that still glowed when the door opened and one of the farm workers entered, taking off his hat he inclined his head.

'Begging your pardon, Master Alexander…Oh, Master Stewart sir, I did not see ye there,' he added as he bowed his head to Stewart. 'I did think that ye must have left so I just be coming to dampen the fire for ye.'

'Thank you kindly, Joshua,' came Alexander's reply.

'You be going to your home now, I will be closing up after me, ye have no need to worry, Master Alexander.'

Alexander nodded to him and they left.

As they mounted their horses to go, Stewart turned and laughed softly. 'Even the tenants are happy that you have found a wife, Alex. You are much loved amongst them,' he reached over and tapped him on the shoulder.

'I bid you good night, cousin, maybe you can come to the house for dinner tomorrow?' asked Stewart. 'That invitation is extended to her father also,' he added.

'Thank you, I think that Charlotte would like that. She misses her cousin.' Lifting his hat in farewell, he turned his horse and rode away to Mere.

***

Stewart was just finishing his breakfast when Elizabeth came into the dining room.

'Oh, Stewart, you have three letters here.' Sorting through the mail, she held his out to him. 'I also saw my physician yesterday and he asked me several questions regarding Margaret's health, to which I replied that she was well and regular in her courses…' She paused here to look at him. 'He said to tell you that she is recovered now.'

Stewart was just about to place the last piece of bread into his mouth when he stopped. 'What did he mean by that?' he enquired.

Elizabeth looked at him and shook her head. 'He just said that all will be well now. That she had made a full recovery. Is there something wrong, Stewart?' she looked at him intently as his face changed.

Stewart shook himself. 'No, Mother, I have forgotten I asked Alex, Charlotte and her father to dine with us tonight. Maybe I will ride to Mere and tell Charlotte and her father to come stay the day here, and perhaps, if they were so inclined, stay the night?'

'That is a splendid idea, Stewart, I will inform cook, I know that she will be pleased to see them all,' replied Elizabeth, as she turned on her heal and left for the kitchen.

Stewart counted on his fingers—five months? The physician said she was well. He left the table and ran out into the corridor, mounting the stairs two at a time. As he entered their room, he saw that Millie was just laying her mistress' clothes onto the bed, but on seeing Stewart she curtsied and left.

Margaret turned on her stool and eyed him with suspicion.

'What is the matter, Stewart? Are you unwell?' she queried.

'On the contrary, Margaret Hamilton, I have never felt better in my life,' he said as he locked the door and came towards her, taking his clothes off.

Margaret's eyes widened. 'What on earth are you doing, Stewart—' but before she could finish, he had her in his arms kissing her, and then pushing the shift from her shoulders, he cupped her breasts in his hands. Groaning with pleasure, he lowered himself to his knees and proceeded to lick her body slowly from navel to neck. He felt and saw the shiver go through her as she placed her hands on his head.

'Dear God, Stewart,' she whispered as he reached her ears and pulled her hard against him, crushing her. Picking her up, he laid her on the bed, and kissed her so hard their teeth ground together.

Gaining her voice, Margaret managed to push him up and away from her to speak.

'Stewart,' she gasped. 'What are we doing?' Her voice was stopped by his mouth over hers again.

'The physician says you are well,' was all he managed to say, as he pulled her onto him.

It was over so quickly that neither could breathe for many minutes afterwards. Raising his head to look into her eyes, he spoke.

'Oh God, Maggie, do you know how long I have wanted to do that? Five months and three days,' he gasped as he collapsed back onto her.

It was then he heard the loud shouts from the hall, and then his mother screamed.

Stewart leaped from the bed, scrabbling to find his clothes, dressing as though his life depended upon it. Pulling his coat on as he left the room, he ran down the stairs.

There in the hall stood four cloaked men with shovels, while his mother was laid prostrate on the floor with her head in Mrs Cottle's lap.

By this time Stewart was in a blind fury, and as he reached the first man, he took the shovel from him and raised it high, bringing it down as quickly as it was raised. The four men backed away to the door, but stood their ground.

Stewart's eyes flashed like flint. ''Sirs, you had better have good reason to intrude my home in this way, or I will run you all through!' he bellowed. Turning to Pip, he ordered. 'Get my blade!'

Pip had sent for Spike, and as Stewart raised the shovel once more to strike, Spike stepped up from behind him and took it from his hands. It was then that one of the men came forward, giving Stewart a paper. As he read it, his face went from shock to white anger. Remembering the letters that had been delivered that morning, he pulled them from his pocket and found the one in Bearcroft's handwriting. Opening it, he read the contents quickly.

Pulling himself up to his full height, he stared at the men before him and spoke calmly and precisely.

'This is a letter from my lawyer in London, who will be here by noon today. It is quite simple, you are to leave my property this instant, or you will be shot for trespassing, and you are not to return. If you do, then you will be arrested and imprisoned, gentlemen. If you do not believe me, then read for yourself.' Here he handed the letter to the man whose shovel Spike still held in his hands. The man mumbled and took the shovel back, and then turning to the other three, he signalled for them to depart in haste.

Amidst all of this mêlée, Margaret and Mrs Cottle had taken Elizabeth into the drawing room and laid her on the sofa there. Lilly was laying a cold compress to her Mistress' head while Mrs Cottle tried to get her to sip a little brandy.

Stewart sank to a chair, still holding the paper that the man had given him in one hand and Bearcroft's letter in the other.

Many things were racing through his brain; his head at the moment felt rather like a revolving sphere, nothing would come into focus, and as he looked around the room, he could see the bewildered faces looking to him for answers, only Margaret's held any understanding, his mother though was still white to the lips. Standing up, he walked towards her, handing Margaret the letters. He lifted his mother in his arms and called after the maid to send someone for their physician, Mr Hardiman, urgently. Then he took her to her room.

Stewart laid her gently on her bed then opened the windows in her room wide, letting in much needed air. It was cold but refreshing and the fire cracked heartily as the air hit it. Then he turned to her maid.

'Molly, go get Mrs Cottle to brew something, I know that she has a potion for all that ails bless her, tell her my mother is in distress.' He turned once more to his mother who seemed to be regaining her senses somewhat. Taking her hand in his, he kissed it, laying it gently on his cheek.

'Mother, this is not of my father's doing, it is Northcott who instigated this. My father at this present time is probably on his way back to Scotland, because if he so much as owes one penny to anyone, he will be either imprisoned or transported. Of that I can swear on my life to.'

Elizabeth looked at him, trying to comprehend what he had just said. 'Northcott? But how?'

'With my father's blessing, it would seem, but he is incapable of doing anything now, you must believe me.' Stewart swallowed hard. 'The man no longer rests where he was, he is at peace in a different place.' As he said the words, he lifted his mother into his arms and held her tight.

'You need not be afraid ever again,' he whispered as he stroked her hair.

There was a tap on the door and Lilly entered, bearing a salver with a glass containing a warm decoction. Curtsying, she came towards the bed.

'Master Hamilton sir, cook be saying that this is her healing brew, it be good for what ails the Mistress. She is to sip it slowly, but be finishing it all.' Bowing again, she left the room, silently closing the door behind her.

Stewart pulled his mother away from him and held the glass to her lips.

'Mother, drink this, it is from Mrs Cottle, she has made you a healing brew.' He smiled down into her eyes. 'Remember Charles' tooth and Margaret? Please drink.' Bringing it to his nose, he sniffed. 'It smells of mint and camomile, if I am not mistaken.'

Elizabeth held onto him and did as she was told.

'Stewart, what have you done?' her voice was a whisper.

'I have done nothing, Mother, except right a wrong. Be at peace now, no one will harm you, you have my word.'

Saying this, he laid her head onto the pillow and pulled a cover over her. Then going to the windows, he shut them but left the drapes open. Lilly appeared once more, bearing a basket of logs and proceeded to stoke the fire, then there was another rap on the door and Stewart turned to see the physician and Molly, her maid, enter. Stewart bowed in greeting to the man and left the room.

He found Margaret in the drawing room, sitting with her son on her knee; as he entered, he saw her eyes search his face, then she held out the letters to him.

'Does she know, Stewart?' she questioned.

Stewart took the letters from her and seated himself next to them, taking his son from her lap.

'Yes, Maggie, she does, and I tried *so* hard for her never to find out...' He turned to look at her, pleading. 'Was I wrong to do such a thing, Maggie? Was I...?' he implored.

Margaret rested her hand on his. 'No, Stewart, you were not. All that you did was try to keep her from all this evil, for that is what it is.' She entwined her fingers in his and leaned her head against his shoulder. 'Are we *never* to be free of this man?'

There was a tap on the door, then it slowly opened to reveal both Pip and Spike. Stewart handed Charles back to Margaret and went to greet them.

'Come in please, and please forgive me as my manners are somewhat remiss, as I have not thanked you both for all that you have done.' Stewart shook both their hands in turn. Spike moved from one food to the other and looked at Pip before he spoke.

'Master Stewart sir, we need no thanks for what we did. We did it from the *heart*, sir, that begs no gratitude.'

Stewart squeezed the man's shoulder, then went to pour out three whiskeys from the decanter on the side. Handing one to each, he raised his own glass.

'Well, you have my *heartfelt* thanks then,' he said with emotion before draining his glass.

Spike sipped his before asking. 'How be the Mistress, sir, if you beg my pardon for asking?'

'Spike, her physician is with her now, and I am sure that there is nothing that a few days rest will not heal,' replied Stewart, as he could see the worry in both their eyes. He looked hard at both men watching them sip their drink.

'Please, take your drink with you and sip it at your leisure. I will tell you of any news, I promise.' Stewart spoke to both but Spike knew it was directed at him.

'Thank you, Master Stewart sir,' replied Spike before they turned and left.

Maggie smiled at Stewart as he came back.

'They will not take the glasses you know; they will go to Mrs Cottle and pour their drinks into pewter mugs. They are not used to drinking at this time of day, especially whisky.'

Stewart sat once more and took his son, who was at that moment trying to get the whole of his fist into his mouth, making choking noises. Maggie, seeing this, retrieved the fist and gave him his rattle instead.

'I did not think of that, Maggie,' he sighed.

Margaret placed her hand to his face. 'They know it was kindly meant, Stewart.'

Kissing his son lightly on the top of his head, he passed him back to Margaret.

'Maggie, I shall go now to Mr Masters and invite them to lunch, and tell them they can remain the night with us. On my way there, I shall stop to Alexander at the office and tell him he is expected also.' Stewart rose up then stopped. 'When the physician leaves, Maggie, take young Charles up and sit with Mother. If anyone can bring her out of this, he will.'

Margaret smiled, took his hand, and kissed the palm. 'Go, we will all be fine here.'

***

Stewart mounted his horse and looked at the threatening sky; all that could be said of the day was that it was grey and very cold. It was a day such as this a year past when he had stood in George Wheatley's library and contemplated his own fate. He pulled his cape around him and pushed his hat down on his head, then headed for the estate office. With luck, he would see Alexander, and then ride on to Mr Masters' house to bring them back before Edward Bearcroft arrived with James Fairweather. The day had barely begun and here they were in the vindictive grips of Northcott once more. Many things were going through his mind, but first and foremost was the fact that if the Lady Catherine's father forced James' hand, then it would be his turn to bear the wroth of Northcott next.

Tethering his horse in the stable, he went and found Alexander peacefully at work in the office with two candles lit on the desk for light and a small fire in the hearth for warmth. As Stewart entered, Alexander looked up, then seeing the look on Stewart's face he placed the quill back in its stand, closed the ledger, and came round the desk to stand in front of him.

'I can tell by the look on your face that something is badly wrong, cousin.' Saying this he took a small kettle from the side of the fire and poured two cups of tea.

'I think we may require something a little stronger than that, Alex, when I inform you of what has happened this day.' He took the mug and sat himself on a stool near the fire.

Alexander listened intently to what his cousin was telling him; when he had ceased speaking, he walked to the table and picked up the bottle of whisky there, pouring a large helping into each mug.

'On a day such as this we can drink it hot, Stewart.'

Stewart raised his mug and nodded, as Alexander paced the room for several minutes before he spoke.

'We will go now and reveal all to my father-in-law. I believe that he has a right to know this. He took us all in good faith, took me in good faith when I married his daughter. He may think otherwise now.' His voice was becoming lower as he spoke.

Steward stood up and took hold of his cousin's arm. 'Alex, this has *nothing* to do with you. It concerns my part of the family.' Stewart was stopped here by Alexander.

'Stewart, we moved the man's bones together, did we not? I am as implicated in this affair as you are, cousin, whether we like this or not.' Alexander looked intently into his cousin's eyes. 'We must go now, so that they can ready themselves to be back at the Willows before Bearcroft and James arrive.' Saying this, he shovelled ashes onto the fire and snuffed the candles, leaving the office in semi darkness. Opening the door, he raised his arm.

'After you, cousin.'

***

Stewart sat for over an hour, trying to explain to Charlotte's father everything that had happened over the past year and a half. William Masters did not offer a word, but sat quietly listening. At some points in the story, he would nod or shake his head but that was the sole amount of response that he gave Stewart.

When Stewart finally lapsed into silence, William Masters rose from his seat and poured whisky into three glasses, passing them around—he then sat once more deep in thought. Alexander caught Stewart's eye and raised his brows. It was then William Masters started to speak.

'Mr Hamilton,' he began. 'May I call you, Stewart?'

Stewart inclined his head. 'By all means, sir.'

'Stewart, there have been many difficult times in my life when things were hard to bear. I have fought off many worries and what I believed to be insurmountable problems,' he paused to take a sip of whisky. 'But in comparison to your mother's life from when she married, mine has been akin to ambrosia.' At this point, he stood up and walked around.

'You state that you requested from a bank a loan of £15,000 pounds, which, if I understand correctly, was obtained with no interest. I will instruct my bankers to repay that immediately.' Seeing Stewart stand up and begin to protest, he stopped him with his hand.

'You will not interrupt while I am speaking, young man. Is that understood?' He inclined his head in affirmation.

Stewart sat back down and thought that Mr Masters reminded him very much of his mother. When she spoke, you interrupted at your peril. He had not expected this response from the man; in fact, he had anticipated the opposite. The man was wealthy, he knew that. Had he not sold his entire Worsted Cloth company just to reside here with his only daughter?

'My humblest apologies, sir, please continue.'

'As I stated, I will pay off this debt, you and my son–in–law will bear no debt to anyone, not as long as I draw breath.' He pinched the top of his nose and walked some more.

'Your friend James is a good man, a wealthy one, but no less one with a good heart and a sense of justice. I applaud him for all that he has done for you and your family. Friends of this calibre are very few in these times, and should be esteemed.'

Stewart thought to himself that without James he could have been hung, and the man would take no recompense for what he had done for him. Instead, he had wanted to give him £15,000 pounds to pay off his father's debts. Stewart closed his eyes and breathed deeply. Masters voice brought him back from his reflections.

'Your mother is a much maligned woman. If you will pardon my saying so, Stewart, she has not seen much happiness in her life since her father died, which is a grave misfortune, as she is clearly a woman of great worth. I can see this, and I have known her but a short time.'

Alexander at this point looked up at his father-in-law and gently nodded in acquiescence. He thought his aunt akin to a saint, and would have said as much, but they had been told not to interrupt.

William Masters turned to Alexander now. 'Right, my son, go get your wife, we are going to the Willows for lunch,' he paused here to look at Stewart, 'and to meet with your lawyer, Stewart. Tell her to prepare an overnight bag for me and yourselves, she knows my needs, no need to trouble your butler, Alexander.'

Alexander stood and inclined his head to him, then left the room.

Stewart stood up. 'With your permission, sir, I did not expect this response to my revelations.'

'Stewart, I class myself as an honest and tolerant man, and if I were but half the person your mother is, I would feel greatly honoured. If you will excuse me, I will go now and request the carriage to be brought round.'

***

Stewart rode ahead of the carriage, not knowing what he was to find when he returned, so he pulled his horse down to a slow trot. At this moment, all parts of his brain felt numb, as though something was preventing it from even the simplest thought. The weather had steadily worsened, and now a rain fell with droplets so fine it was comparable to a wet mist. He knew too well that everything had started from the moment he had helped George Wheatley. In retrospection, would he have done anything differently? No. It was not in his character to turn and look the other way when people were threatened. Had this not been his downfall for most of his life, but in doing so this time, he had implicated others, namely his mother, his wife, Alexander, James, and now Charlotte and her father. He had put all of their lives at risk because of this man. Stewart pulled up his horse and sat there, wiping his face with his hands. This was between himself and Northcott—no one else. Sitting there, he nodded to himself; he would go confront the man, be done with it. If he wanted satisfaction, then he would give it to him.

'No other person will be harmed in my name—enough,' he spoke quietly to himself.

Stewart was mentally planning now; firstly, he must see his own lawyer, he would write the man and request a meeting, and then when certain things were in place, he would contact Northcott. His mind resolved, he tapped his horse gently with his heels and continued his journey.

***

His mother, he was informed as he entered the hall, was sleeping—no doubt Mrs Cottles tea had something to do with that. Then before going to see Mrs Cottle, he advised Thompson that he would need the four guestrooms prepared for tonight, as they were expecting company. He then made his way to the kitchen. Removing his hat, he coughed loudly as he entered.

'Mrs Cottle, you have my humblest apologies, but there will be another five people to lunch and also dinner this evening.'

The cook looked up from the table where she was vigorously beating eggs.

'How many, Master Stewart?' she asked slightly alarmed.

'Oh please forgive me, we have…'

Stewart was interrupted by Mrs Cottle putting up her hand. She looked at her master carefully over her spectacles, placing both her fists on the table either side of the bowl.

'Right, young sir, lunch will be cold meats, bread, pickles and cheeses. The dinner… well, you are in luck that a lamb was killed but yesterday, and I be having two fine legs in my pantry. I gather the Mistress knows nothing of this?' She raised her eyebrows at Stewart and nodded.

Stewart carefully considered his words before he answered; he could see Cook was upset, and well she might be, the time was now near 11 o'clock, and he had just informed her that she would have to prepare lunch for seven people—eight, including his mother.

'Mrs Cottle, pray do forgive me, but this whole debacle results from what transpired last year, and I am afraid that I am the instigator. I tried to right a wrong, but in doing so set in motion a series of events that even I could not have foreseen. I beg your forgiveness for all that has happened.' Stewart waited for her response

The cook breathed deeply, nodded her head, and then motioned him to leave her kitchen. As Stewart turned to go, she called after him.

'Tell my Mistress that I am brewing another tea for her, and not to be taking any laudanum!'

'What was in that tea, Mrs Cottle, if you do not mind my asking?' he questioned.

'That be lemon balm and camomile, Master Stewart.'

263

Stewart smiled and then saluted her. He heard the ladle hit the floor behind him as he came out into the passage.

Entering the hall, he was greeted by Mr Masters, Alexander and Charlotte.

'Please, come into the drawing room and warm yourselves, I will go and find Margaret.' But before he could finish, Margaret opened the drawing room door. She stood there smiling and came to embrace and kiss her sister.

'Come in and I will ring for some tea,' she smiled, taking Charlotte's arm.

'Stewart, Mr Masters, Alex, maybe you would rather go into the study?' Her eyes flicked to Stewart as she said this. Stewart looked at her and thought that if he read her correctly, Bearcroft and James were already there. Margaret inclined her head slightly on seeing his face change.

Stewart leaned into Margaret, whispering into her ear, 'I think I have offended Mrs Cottle.' Margaret just looked up at him, and her eyes said everything that she would have spoken had she been able, then Stewart turned quickly and spoke.

'Shall we proceed into the study then?'

***

Edward Bearcroft was seated behind Stewart's desk and had been speaking at length for some time. He had informed Stewart that his father had signed the legal document that he, Bearcroft, had drawn up, somewhat grudgingly, he had been told, but the alternative was imprisonment or transportation. His name had been spread far and wide throughout London in all the gaming clubs, most of which, when they were made aware, would not admit him again to their establishment. A similar edict had been placed in Edinburgh. He had then turned to Stewart and warned him that this did not mean that he would not find other means, or people, to elicit information regarding his family. Stewart knew instantly who he was referring to—Northcott, who was now privy to a very dangerous secret, but there was no evidence, thank God. Even if they dug up the whole estate, they would not find the man, and by now the ground that had been dug had resumed its previous appearance, whereby no trace could be seen of any movement of soil. He also understood that his father had made his way back to Scotland, and was last heard of in Dumfries—he must have relatives there, no matter how distant.

Bearcroft then turned to James Fairweather.

Northcott had learned of the Lady Catherine's father's proposal to James' father, of marriage between his daughter and James. This had resulted in James receiving a threatening letter—which was not signed—to the effect that if he took up the proposal, he was a dead man.

Stewart looked at his friend and shook his head. His brain was working very fast now, and he knew that he had to act even faster, and think one step ahead of Northcott, cut him off so to speak, before he could fulfil his plans.

James and Alexander looked to Stewart and knew, without him voicing a word, exactly what he was thinking. Alexander paled considerably, and James became very agitated.

'Stewart, we will organise everything, you do not need to concern yourself. I have no intention of taking the Lady Catherine as my bride and have informed my father of this.' James looked down at his hands. 'He is also aware of everything that has taken place since that night in Exeter,' Looking up once more directly into Stewart's eyes he continued. 'And I have his full support on this.' He inclined his head to affirm this.

Stewart's face was unreadable, blank, showing no emotion at all till he smiled at James and nodded back.

'I thank you for that, James,' was his reply.

Alexander was decidedly disturbed by now. He knew his cousin better than anyone, and right now he was in a blind rage, which no one could see but himself.

Chapter Thirty-One
The Ride to Bath and the Dual

Stewart sat behind his desk. It had rained relentlessly since yesterday noon, and even now there was no evidence in the grey skies above that it would stop any time soon. His mother had passed a peaceful night and was now in the drawing room with Margaret, Charlotte and baby Charles. Alexander had gone to the estate office, while Bearcroft and James were preparing themselves for the journey to Bath to meet with the Lady Catharine's father. Stewart thought that he would give anything to be with James on this journey. A tap on the door brought him out of his thoughts, as Lilly entered.

'Begging your pardon, Master Stewart, the lawyer Mr Bearcroft would be liking a word, if ye would.'

Stewart looked at Lilly and smiled. 'Of course, Lilly, bring him.'

As Bearcroft entered, Stewart stood and bowed in greeting. 'Good morning to you, sir, I trust you slept well.'

'Good morning to you too, Mr Hamilton, and yes I slept very soundly. The country air seems to agree with me; in London I rise before 5 o'clock, here it was after 8 o'clock before I came down to breakfast.'

'I am very glad to hear that, sir,' Stewart replied laughing softly. 'It is very quiet in the country and seems to sooth the nerves. Maybe the air is less heavy than London?'

'Oh you could be right, Hamilton, you could be right. There, you will find a thousand chimneys from houses pouring smoke into the air that it fair chokes a person in the winter months. I fear I will have to retire though before I can find myself a country idyll.' He waved his hand in gesture at the gardens beyond.

'Pray be seated, sir, and how may I be of service to you?' offered Stewart.

Bearcroft sat himself, looking at Stewart in a pensive manner.

'Mr Hamilton, if I may be so bold. I believe that I have some idea maybe of your character, and how your mind thinks and analyses things, do you follow my drift? Bearcroft inclined his head, still looking at Stewart.

Stewart shifted his shoulders slightly and sat upright in his chair.

'I fear, sir that you have my mother's knack of seeing into my head.'

He was stopped here by Bearcroft raising his hand slightly and nodding.

'I mean no disrespect, Mr Hamilton, but the change in the expression on your face yesterday… I would defy even the slowest of people not to have noticed.'

Stewart chewed his mouth and thought well before answering, but Bearcroft was too quick—as all good lawyers are—able to anticipate their opponent's words before they have left their mouth.

'You were thinking of murder, were you not?' he offered, raising his brows and inclining his head.

Stewart's face was blank. He could see the lawyer watching him, and no matter how he tried to conceal his feelings, he knew that it was to no avail. The man could read people like an open book. Stewart breathed in deep through his nose then let it out again before he spoke.

'How else am I to be free of this man?' Stewart's voice held an air of resignation.

Bearcroft sat back in his chair with his hands clasped before him.

'It is always best to achieve one's purpose by fair means and not criminal, Mr Hamilton,' was his reply.

Stewart closed his eyes. The man was right, he always was, and what could he achieve by killing Northcott—nothing; he would be arrested charged and hung was his answer.

'I am of the opinion, Mr Hamilton, that whatever we do in this life that is done in haste—without forethought—we usually repent these actions at our leisure, for the repercussions of our actions lasts years, and sometimes returns to haunt us throughout our entire life.' Bearcroft stopped speaking and looked at Stewart circumspectly.

Stewart closed his eyes in resignation and replied.

'Sir, you are right, as always. That logical brain of yours wins through, whereas my own. Well, let us say I have usually always acted in haste, though I may have averted an injustice at the time, I have to my recollection paid for my actions.'

'Then let us say that you will not now pay a further greater price for any intentions that may be presenting themselves in your mind?' he paused. 'Would you be in a position to travel with us to Bath this day? I think that it will be beneficial for all concerned if maybe you were there when we spoke to her father?'

Stewart thought again, just how the man managed to read his thoughts so directly.

'Sir, I will go now and speak with my mother and my wife. I also consider that it will be wise if Mr Masters, Alexander and Charlotte stay here till I return.'

'Very wise, Mr Hamilton,' Bearcroft interjected as he nodded his head in agreement. 'As they say, "*Defendit numerus.*"'

Stewart inclined his head, bowed and left the room.

***

Sitting in the coach deep in thought, Stewart could hear the voices of both James and Bearcroft in quiet conversation on the seat opposite. Maggie had understood the reason he had to go to Bath, but his mother had become very agitated at the thought, until he explained that both Alexander and Mr Masters would be staying till his return. He had come for James—he needed his support at this time, as this would be a very difficult situation, one that would take much tact and diplomacy on James' part. Her father could take the affront to mean that his daughter was now unmarriageable, when in truth she was very marriageable—her looks and wealth alone would state this. The young woman had been beguiled at an age when most young women's heads were turned to love. Now she was to be punished for making one mistake. He also knew the real reason for James' opposition to the marriage: the threat to his family that would ensue from such an arrangement. His thoughts ended abruptly as the coach stopped so suddenly, throwing its occupants into disarray.

Stewart looked from the window to see three men on horseback wearing handkerchiefs about their faces, carrying pistols, which Stewart assumed were loaded and primed. He felt inside his jacket for the small blade that he always carried there, but what good would that be against a pistol shot? Looking at Bearcroft, he saw that the man had a similar pistol concealed within the folds of his cloak.

'Better to be prepared, Mr Hamilton, do you not think so?' he said in a low voice.

Stewart lifted his cloak and jacket to Bearcroft displaying the blade in its sheath. Bearcroft nodded.

'Out!' shouted one of the mounted riders.

Stewart was the first to descend from the carriage followed by Bearcroft then James.

'Who amongst you is James Fairweather?' demanded the same rider.

Stewart pushed himself in front of Bearcroft and James.

'I am, sir, and who will be asking for me?' he questioned.

He could feel that his two friends behind him were about to protest.

'I demand that you let the others continue their journey, as it is I that you seek and have found me.' Stewart shouted as he advanced towards the man's horse. It was the instinct of survival that made him take hold of the reins jerking hard causing the man to rock to one side badly; he watched seeing him lose his balance then fall from his mount. Bearcroft took the initiative and fired at the mounted rider to his right, hitting him in the arm that held the pistol.

Stewart by this time had pulled the pistol from the fallen man and pointed it to the third rider.

'I would advise you, sir to lower your weapon very slowly. I have not been known to miss my target, and at this close range it would be impossible.' Stewart spoke so calmly but with such authority that James Fairweather walked past Stewart and relieved the man of his weapon.

In an instant the rider had turned his horse and galloped off into the distance. The man with the wound to his arm in hot pursuit at his heals.

Stewart looked at the man on the floor; pulling him to his feet he relieved him of his mask. He saw at once that he had a deep scar that started at the end of his right brow, crossing his cheek and ending somewhere near his upper lip. The man had no fear, Stewart could sense this, for him it was kill or be killed, and from the lines on his face he was not a young man, it was surprising that he had survived this long. Holding him close to his face, he said the next words slowly and clearly.

'Go tell your master that if he wants satisfaction, I will meet him in the clearing just outside the western end of Bath tomorrow morning at 8 o'clock. Swords or pistols, I will bring both.' Stewart threw the man next to his horse and nodded.

The rider did no more than mount quickly. Giving one last cold look to Stewart, he spat on the ground, turned his horse and galloped away in the same direction that the other two riders had taken.

James Fairweather stood looking at his friend, white to the lips with the pistol hanging loosely in his hand by his leg.

Stewart leaned over and calmly took the pistol from his friend. 'James, give me that, for I fear that you will shoot yourself in the foot.'

'Mr Hamilton sir!' Bearcroft's voice resonated around the countryside.

'You have just invited Northcott to a duel with you, after all we discussed this morning, not to act with haste,' the man breathed deeply.

Stewart looked at the man for several seconds before he spoke.

'Would you have had me hand James over to them? James who can neither shoot well nor fence? I could not, sir.'

Bearcroft leaned back onto the coach and seated himself in the doorway.

'Mr Hamilton, I know that it is not illegal to fight duels, but if one should die from this, do you understand what you have done? The man will not stop till one or both of you are dead!' his voice had risen as he spoke.

'Sir, I only know that if I had done this after Exeter, none of the evils that have befallen my family and others would have occurred, it is the only way to be free of him, can you not see that?' Stewart spoke with conviction.

The air about them was freezing, and Stewart saw James visible shake. James Fairweather was a calm quiet clever man, a man of peace, but also a man of justice. He understood what Stewart was doing, even though he did not agree with it. James' coachman had come down at this point and was lowering the steps to the carriage. He too looked the colour of the sky above—decidedly cold and grey.

***

It was dark by the time they reached the Lady Catherine's house in Bath. They were all tired and shaken, so it was left to the lawyer Edward Bearcroft to recite what had happened on their journey. Sir Henry Portman sat in his great chair behind his desk and stared into the fire opposite. When Bearcroft had finished, he got up slowly coming round to face Stewart.

Stewart just watched him, while trying to remain impassive. The man was even taller than he was, and twice as broad. He had hazel coloured eyes, a very straight aquiline nose and full mouth which supported a huge moustache. His hair at one time had been blond, thought Stewart to himself, but was now a mixture of white and pale yellow. When he spoke, his voice was deep and sonorous.

'My young man, you are the one that rescued my daughter, are you not?'

Stewart swallowed and blinked twice. 'I am, sir.'

Sir Henry Portman then gripped Stewart's right arm while taking the hand in his and pounding it up and down in a grip so strong Stewart thought how on God's earth was he going to fight tomorrow with every bone in his right hand bruised or broken.

'I am forever in your debt, young man, you must know this.'

Stewart just nodded, speechless.

'You have the courage of a lion, young man, but I fear not its wisdom,' he paused to turn to the fire, placing his hand on the mantle before continuing.

'How well schooled is this man with a blade or pistol?' turning to face Stewart, he waited for his answer.

'In truth, sir, the man has never beaten me with swords—with pistols? I could not say, having never entered a contest with him with such weapons, sir.'

Sir Henry Portman turned once more to the fire and tugged the bell pull hard. In less time it takes to blink, a servant appeared at the door.

'Bring glasses and whisky, and any food that is edible from dinner.' As the man turned to go, Portman called out another order.

'And bring my pistols!'

The air inside the library was charged with energy. Stewart looked sideways to his friend James and read his face instantly. Stewart knew that he was thinking; he had to tell this man—who at this moment in time was acting like a general on a battlefield—that he did not want to marry his daughter. James, who had never been anything but a loyal, selfless, generous friend to him, was now in an impossible position.

Would it be so bad though to be betrothed to the Lady Catherine? God, she was beautiful, and her father owned Berkley and Portman Square in London and huge estates in Somerset. With James' father in banking, as well as owning small estates all over England—what a meeting of minds that would be. His mind was brought back by the entrance of several servants bearing salvers of food and drink, laying them out on the table at the far end of the room. Dear God, this house was vast, thought Stewart.

'Sirs, we shall eat now and then get to our beds. We will rise at 4 o'clock when you young sir will practice with my pistols. Do I make myself clear?'

Stewart bowed in acquiescence.

Both he and James ate very little; in fact, Stewart's stomach felt as though it was turning in on itself. Having bid good night to both Bearcroft and Sir Henry Portman, they made their way up to their rooms, lighted there by two servants bearing candelabras. Taking these from the servants, they were about to go to their beds when they heard a distressed crying coming from further down the landing. Stewart put his finger to his lips, and both men listened. The crying was coming from a young girl; it was only when she spoke they knew who and why.

'Oh, Mama, what am I to do. I have been so selfish and foolish, now no man will want me, I am tainted, even though I have never. Oh, Mama please do not let Papa put me to a nunnery. I beg you, please…' her voice trailed away to sobs. 'I cannot go into one of those places, please. I will be a governess, a nanny, anything, please, Mama, I beg you…' here she started sobbing once more.

Stewart looked to his friend.

'James, she is a very beautiful young woman, and you and I both know that she is untainted, you could do worse, my friend, and after tomorrow—well, you will have no fear.'

James opened his mouth to speak, but closed it again; nodding to Stewart he went into his room.

***

Stewart stood in the grounds at the back of the house, trying to focus on the target before him; the place had been lit by torches as it was still dark at this hour. Stewart's hands were wet with sweat, and although the air outside was freezing, his body felt like it had burning embers within it. He lifted the pistol once more to take aim at the target some twenty paces in front of him. Steadying his arm this time, he fired and his target, a piece of wood, splintered into fine kindling. Stewart sighed; would he have the presence of mind when confronted with a living target to steady himself, aim and fire as he had just done? He doubted that very much. The servant behind him was readying the other pistol for Stewart—he had at least another hour to prepare.

He had sat up most of the night writing letters—one for Margaret, his mother, Alexander and lastly his son Charles. He had written out a deed for the estate, bequeathing it to both his mother and wife as custodians, to be inherited by his son on his twenty-first birthday, as he had done. This would be verified by Bearcroft and witnessed by James. There was one other letter, but that would only be used if he survived.

He felt someone take the pistol from his hands, and when he turned he saw it was James.

'Stewart, you cannot do this, it is madness,' James said in anguish.

'What would you have me do, James, is it madness to want to protect the people that I love? No, James, it has to end, and it will end today.' James said nothing.

'Is there a church nearby, James? I have to make my peace before I go.'

Hearing this, Sir Henry called to Stewart.

'My wife has a small chapel that she uses here in the house. It has been here since the house was built, way over a hundred years ago, sir. You may make use of it if it so pleases you.'

'James, I will see you in the coach.' Placing his hand on James' shoulder, he walked back to the house.

***

They arrived at the clearing in Sir Henry Portman's coach a little before 8 o'clock. Looking to the other side of the clearing, they saw a coach draw up and four people alight, one of them, to Stewart's eyes, was definitely Northcott—he would know that man's figure anywhere. Stewart crossed himself and prayed that if he were to die, then please let it be quick. Looking to James—who was to be his second—he inclined his head.

As they descended from the carriage, Sir Henry came up to him and shook his hand.

'May God and his angels be with you, Hamilton.'

Stewart thought that maybe he would need the help of more than that. He had no sword with him so he had taken two of Sir Henry's—he had at least six—and, as Stewart thought, been a Major in the British Army. You did not acquire that much authority in your character unless you were used to commanding men. Stewart looked around the field; it was desolate, not a breath of wind stirred the trees, no birds could be heard calling their chorus, and as he went forward the ground was soft and slippery underfoot with fallen leaves. He thought it felt akin to velvet as he trod placing one foot in front of the other till the two men came to meet in the middle.

Stewart's head felt quite weightless; people were talking around him but his brain could not process the words, until Northcott called his name.

'Hamilton,' came his deep course voice.

Stewart looked hard at the man; he had aged way beyond his twenty-six years, and his eyes were puffy from drink, Stewart reflected.

'I choose pistols.' His mouth curled up in one corner into a sardonic smile.

Stewart watched the man; he knew and would have wagered that he would choose these as a method of fighting—Northcott had never once beaten him with a blade. He also knew nothing of his skills with a pistol, but guessed that they were akin to his own, not as good as a blade. The pistols that Sir Henry had brought with him were alien to him also, albeit that he had had but two hours of practice this morning, but then he had only hit the target the once. Stewart swallowed.

'It will be a fair fight then, Northcott. As I guess your skills with a pistol amount to the same as my own.' He inclined his head slowly.

'I would ask one question of you, why have you persecuted my family as you have? You are wealthy beyond means; I have but one estate. I fear it is jealousy that feeds your fire, and for that I am sorry for you, as there is no cure except to rid yourself of the person you are jealous of.'

Stewart extended his hand to him, but Northcott did not move to take it, instead he spoke.

'I will see you in hell, Hamilton.'

Stewart inclined his head and answered.

'In all fairness to you, I believe you will.'

Stewart took the pistol from the box the footman held, turned around and stood with his right arm raised to his shoulder, the pistol already cocked pointing skywards.

As he looked ahead, he saw his friend James cross himself, and then came the command to take ten paces forward, turn, aim and fire at will.

Many images went through his mind as Stewart walked. He saw his mother, wife and son, then Alexander who seemed to be calling something to him, what was it? He focussed hard then heard the word—wait! In that instance, he knew that if he was to survive, he must not fire in haste, but wait to aim.

Stewart reached the count, then turned. A shot rang out as clear as the sound of a single bell toll from a church. Stewart felt nothing, as he looked at the man opposite who seemed to have turned to stone. Stewart felt a burning in his left shoulder, and when he turned, there seemed to be an excessive amount of red blood which was now trickling down his arm and dripping from his fingers. His right arm was still bent upwards with the pistol facing to the sky. He heard a voice from the side, shouting, 'Shoot, man, shoot!' Turning his head, he saw Sir Henry coming towards him. Then finding his, voice he spoke.

'Get the document please, get him to sign.'

Sir Henry was pleading, 'For God's sake, man, fire, and let us tend your wound, you are bleeding to death!'

'The document!' Stewart shouted.

He watched as the two footmen approached Northcott, there seemed to be some talk, then Northcott faced him and raised his hands; turning, he took the quill and signed.

It was then that Stewart discharged the pistol into the air, sinking gracefully to his knees and into oblivion.

Chapter Thirty-Two
Oblivion and Recovery

Stewart began to rouse from his stupor, but he could not open his eyes, they seemed to be weighted by some unseen force... two pennies perhaps? His body he thought felt the same, and then a blinding pain shot through his arm, as though his shoulder was being subjected to a blacksmiths iron... and then oblivion.

As he surfaced once more, the blinding pain was there again. He knew he was screaming, but he could hear no sound; he was immobile as though something weighted was laying over his body, pushing him down—maybe he was dead, yes that could be it, he was being buried, laid to rest, maybe he was going to hell—it was then that he gave in to oblivion once more.

Surfacing yet again, his body felt as though it was being roasted over an open fire...heat was emanating from him, or was it around him, maybe he was in hell.

The next time he surfaced it was different, he still could not open his eyes, but the weight on his body had gone; the hardness underneath him seemed to have been replaced with something soft and cooling to his skin, which was still burning—maybe God had taken mercy on him and he was taking him to heaven, he lapsed back into oblivion again.

As he came back to consciousness once more, he heard mumblings, was it singing? And there was light coming through his eyelids now; try as he may though he still could not open them.

The next time he floated up from the void he managed to raise his eyelids just a fraction, his body was still heavy and numb, but what he saw were shadows moving; finding he could not focus to anything, he closed them and let the darkness take him once more.

Now he heard voices, distinct voices; he had no notion of what they were saying as it seemed to be in some foreign language. He tried his eyelids again, and this time they opened further, but to no avail, as what he saw were just blurred images. Once more he was drawn back into the abyss.

When he emerged from the fog this time it was different; he heard the voice clear... '*His fever has broken.*' Fever? What fever? Maybe that was why he felt as though they were roasting him on an open fire. If he could only focus his eyes, but nothing again. Then he felt a warm liquid being placed to his lips and being forced into his mouth, his first reaction was to swallow; it was hot but no taste. He was thirsty, yes that was it; he was thirsty so he swallowed every drop that was placed in his mouth. When they finished, he was tired, how could one get

274

tired from drinking? But he was. Could he move his fingers? Yes, the fingers of his right hand were definitely moving; he was tapping them up and down frantically now, maybe whoever was with him would notice, then they would know that he was not dead. Once again, he surrendered to the emptiness.

Someone had his hand held in theirs now, oh it felt so good to be touched; they were stroking his forehead, and the hand felt so cool on his brow, for it was a hand, he knew that. Thank God, he thought, they knew he was alive; they would not bury him.

Coming back to consciousness this time, he managed to open his eyes more. He could see distinct blurred images now moving about before him, and someone seemed to be pulling and wrapping his left shoulder. Yes! He could definitely feel it! He tried his right hand again and more success; he could lift the hand up to the wrist. There was a deep voice beside his left ear, and the words were clear to him now. *'There is still some slight infection, but he is at last starting to heal—no seepage from the wound now.'* What wound was this person speaking of? He must be hurt, but where, how? More liquid was poured into his mouth which he swallowed gratefully. He slept again.

This time his eyes opened, not fully, but they opened. He looked around him now and things began gradually to come into focus. He was in a huge bed, propped high on a mountain of pillows. Someone was sitting by the window reading; he tried to bring his vision clearer but it tended to slip back now and then to fuzziness. Stewart blinked several times to try and clear his eyes; it was then he saw her. He tried hard to call but no sound came from his mouth, so he pulled at the bedclothes hoping that the noise would bring her head up. Success! She was coming towards him, smiling and… yes she was crying; why?

Margaret took his right hand in both of hers bringing it up to her lips to kiss the palm, and then holding it tight against her cheek she spoke.

'Oh God, Stewart, my love, my heart, my soul, you have come back.' He had only time enough to blink then the sleep took him once more.

***

He had lain near death for two days, with fever and infection, till the surgeon discovered a small piece of cloth had been embedded in the wound. Once this was removed, then cauterised, there was only the fever to battle with, and battle they did. They soaked him hourly with freezing water from the well till his body shook so much they had to stop. Then one night one week into his fever, it broke; he sweated so much that they had to change the mattress twice, but after that he slept in peace, waking only to be fed some broth, bathed and have his wound dressed.

Now when he woke his eyes focussed better, his body still felt alien to him, and it was all he could do to raise his hand from the bed. Looking to the window he could see huge flakes of snow falling fast, whirling up and round hitting the window and covering it. The person he now saw by the window bent over her embroidery was his mother.

'Mother,' he breathed, but that was enough as Elizabeth was by his side in an instant. She stoked his face, her eyes searching as she pushed his hair back from his forehead.

'Oh, Stewart, do you know how many times we thought we had lost you?' her voice trembled badly. 'Margaret has just gone to eat something—she has not left your side since we came, the day after the duel…' her voice trailed away. Leaning forward she kissed his brow.

The door behind his mother opened quietly, and Stewart saw Maggie standing there. It was as though she floated towards him—she came so quickly. His mother rose, kissed him once more, then turning to Margaret she held her tightly.

'Go and rest now, Mother, I am here.'

Elizabeth turned once more then left.

Margaret sat on the bed taking his hand in hers she linked her fingers with his. His eyes searched hers, and she knew that he would not be awake for long.

'Kiss me' was all he managed to mime with his lips.

She moved herself forward and leaning into him placed her lips to his. When she sat back, he was asleep once more.

***

Lady Jemima Portman came up to her husband as he sat in his study at his desk. She was nearly as tall in stature as her husband, holding her body upright with her head held high. Her face alone told you of her aristocratic breading without hearing her voice, which was firm and authoritative like her husband's. Resting her hands on his shoulders, she leaned forward and placed a kiss on the top of his head. Sir Henry Portman reciprocated by patting his wife's hand.

'He will live, Jemima?'

'Yes, Henry, he will, but there were times when I really believed we had lost him you know.'

'I know, my dear,' he replied as he kept his hand on his wife's and squeezed it.

'Do you know what day it is tomorrow, Henry?' she asked as she looked out into the blizzard, which still seemed to be blowing.

'My dear, as always, I have no idea; please tell me.'

Jemima Portman smiled, and then brought her hand up to cup his cheek. 'It's Christmas Eve, Henry.'

Sir Henry turned sharply in his chair looking up anxiously to his wife. 'My dear, do we have anything to eat?'

Cupping her hands about his face and kissing him, she laughed. 'Henry, my dearest, there will be a feast, please do not worry yourself about anything. What I really want to know,' continued Jemima Portman, 'is how we are going to get that wonderful young man James to marry our wayward daughter.'

'Has he refused outright?' asked Sir Henry with some trepidation.

'Nooooo, but he has not said that he *will* either. I think he needs some more persuasion, and I do believe I know just the person who could maybe do that.'

'Jemima,' Sir Henry eyed her warily. 'I know about your subterfuge. I do not want this young man scared away for good, do you hear me?'

'Of course, Henry, do not worry yourself, we will have a beautiful August wedding,' she patted him on the head, kissed him once more and left the room.

Sir Henry Portman scratched his head and cursed. 'I can command a whole battalion, yet I still cannot get my wife to do as I tell her.'

Jemima Portman put her head around the door once more. 'Henry, just so as you are aware, I have threatened Catherine with the Nunnery.'

'Jemima!' yelled a very disgruntled Sir Henry, whose voice could be heard throughout the house.

'Henry,' she chided, 'keep your voice down, we have a very sick person in this house,' she added as she closed the door.

***

As they heard Sir Henry's raised, voice Alexander looked to James.

'When is your father due here?' he enquired.

James sighed. 'Sometime this evening I believe.' James shook his head. 'Oh, Alex, I thought he was dead; the blood just drained from him like a slaughtered sheep. We tried to staunch it, but it was not until they applied that hot iron did it stop.'

Alexander looked at his friend with empathy.

'It took three men to sit on him. Sir Henry lay on top of him while Lady Jemima poured whisky over the wound to stop the infection. Having no other substance, she said it was the next best thing; the screams, Alex, they will haunt me, I know that.' James paused. 'Then they had to repeat it all again, as the surgeon found a small piece of cloth embedded in the wound; it caused the infection, dear God.' James put his head in his hands.

Alexander walked to the window as the tears came; he did not want James to see him cry—he should have been there. Hearing the door open, Alexander rubbed his hands over his face trying to calm himself before he turned round. As he did, he saw his aunt coming towards him and instinctively clasped her into his arms, she was sobbing uncontrollably.

'He is finally awake, Alexander; he knew me and Margaret,' she said as she buried her head into Alexander's chest.

'Come, sit, Aunt, I will give you something to drink to calm your nerves,' he offered.

'I will be fine, Alex, her Ladyship is brewing me a tea—another Mrs Cottle, I fear.' She settled herself on a chair and wiped her face with her handkerchief.

'Did you know that she went to war with Sir Henry? She helped in the battlefield hospitals, caring for the wounded and dying; she is a very strong woman, Alex,' added Elizabeth

277

James' voice cut in. 'The daughter I fear has taken traits from both of them; she is a very stubborn lady.'

Alexander could not help but laugh. 'She is a lady with audacity, I think,' he replied, 'and, I think that life would never be dull with her, James.'

Elizabeth looked around her. 'Where is Mr Masters?'

'Be still, Aunt, he is with Charlotte, nanny Daisy and young Charles up in the nursery,' answered Alexander.

***

William Masters sat watching his daughter play with her nephew. She would make a good mother he was sure of that; she was kind, loving and patient, but she was also still young, and although he wanted a grandchild more than anything, he could bide his time. He thought back to his wife and how they had waited those first years together for the child that never came. Then he looked at Charlotte and thought what a true blessing she had been to them both. What one man had thrown away, they had loved and cherished.

'Mr Masters sir, can I get you anything?' Daisy's voice came into his thoughts.

Looking up at her he smiled. 'No, my dear, I am fine.'

He watched Daisy now and knew that she had that quality also. She would have made a wonderful mother; what makes a young lady as herself choose to care for other children and not her own.

Daisy knew what was in his mind; had not many people asked the same question of her? This was her calling she knew. At first, she had wanted to take holly orders, be a bride of Christ, but her father had said—and very wisely—that her gifts lay elsewhere. As she sat folding the small clothes, she looked up at him.

'Mr Masters sir, I understand what you are thinking.'

William stood up abruptly. 'Please, Mistress Daisy, I meant no disrespect to you, that I should openly show you my thoughts. Can you please forgive me?'

'Mr Masters sir, I am not offended. I have been asked that question many times, and each time I give the same answer. I wanted to join the sisters and take holy orders. I thought my father, being a Minister in the church, would approve. Instead, he told me that my destiny lay elsewhere, as he had watched me with the children of the parish, how I visited them, comforted them when they were ill, so, I became a nanny, and if I am honest with myself, it is just where God wanted me to be.'

William came to stand in front of her now; bowing his head he smiled. 'If I may be so bold as to say so, you are one *exceptional* young lady, Daisy.' Bowing once more, he left the room.

Charlotte looked to Daisy. 'Sometimes, Daisy, men do not understand us at all,' she smiled.

***

Robert Fairweather and Edward Bearcroft arrived around 8 o'clock that evening. Having settled themselves in their rooms they came down to the study to meet with Sir Henry.

To look at, Robert Fairweather was just an older version of James, and just as amiable. He had a welcoming smile and mild manner; it was easy to see where James acquired his qualities.

'Good evening to you, Henry, how is young Hamilton?' he enquired.

Sir Henry Portman inclined his head. 'Good evening to you too, gentlemen, our young Hamilton seems to be holding his own at last. He is very weak and sleeps most of the hours of the day, and as yet he is only taking small amounts of broth, but he spoke for the first time today, be it only a few words.'

Walking to a dresser, he held up the decanter of whisky. 'Will you join me, sirs?' Not waiting for an answer, he poured three very large measures.

'I will not disturb him now, but will take you to see him tomorrow,' he paused slightly, gathering his words. 'I do not know if you have seen him before, Robert. I know that you are somewhat acquainted with him, Edward, but he is but a shadow of his former self.' He stopped to walk the room

'Once he starts to take food again, what I want you to know is that he is quite skeletal. The lad has not taken solid food for nigh on three weeks now. Two of those weeks might I add we did not know if he would live.' Sir Henry Portman drained his glass. 'God, the lad nigh bled to death, the stupid buffoon, he would not discharge his pistol till that man signed the document, his life's blood draining from him.' He poured himself another measure and sat.

'Robert, I owe him for my daughter and you for your son's life. I gather that Edward has informed you of what happened on the road to here that day?'

Robert Fairweather nodded. 'What can we do, Henry?' he asked.

'At the moment: nothing. We have brought all of his family here, and they will remain here for Christmas and New Year; when the time comes, and he is fit to travel, he will be conveyed home in my coach—there to heal and restore to health.'

'And his wound?' queried Robert Fairweather.

'The shot went through the muscle at the top of his left arm—quite how it missed the bone there. Well, he will lose some movement in the shoulder, the surgeon informed me of that, but in time he will get most of the movement back in his arm. The surgeon had to debride the wound a little as he found a fragment of cloth from his shirt embedded, that is what caused the inflammation, fever, then he packed it with some poultice made with honey and dressed it. Dear God, he fought me so I had to lay myself upon him, while your son James sat on his legs and the physician held tight to his arm. I have seen men fight when injured in battle, but nothing like that.'

He crossed once more to the dresser and refilled his glass. Looking to the other two men he saw that they had hardly touched theirs.

The silence was split when a loud gong sounded somewhere in the hall outside.

279

'Gentlemen, let us now go in to dinner and I will introduce you to everyone.' He raised his arm for them to precede him out of the door.

As they came out into the hall, Bearcroft caught Sir Henry's arm.

'I have all the letters with me that he wrote, as well as the copy of the document signed by three parties. Do you have somewhere safe that these can be stored till such a time I may speak with young Hamilton and ask him what he would like me to do with the letters to his family? He may wish to keep them; he may wish them to be destroyed. The document is another matter. I have one copy kept in my chambers, the other is for young Hamilton to keep.'

Sir Henry nodded. 'We will talk again tomorrow, as I fear young Hamilton will be in no fair mind to choose at this present time.'

***

In the morning Sir Henry gathered everyone into the large drawing room. It was huge, Elizabeth observed, stretching along the right front of the house. The snow was still falling heavily obliterating all view from the windows, the lower ones having filled with the soft white substance. Elizabeth thought it must be at least five inches thick now—even deeper—as it had snowed relentlessly for two days. As with all snow, there comes an eerie silence, and the countryside shone with its brilliance, even though there was no sun. She was desperately worried for Margaret, who was at this moment bathing her husband—she would let no one else touch him—not even Lady Jemima. She stayed with him day and night, leaving only to take her meals and nurse Charles. Elizabeth rung her hands; how much longer could she undertake these duties without falling ill herself. His valet Pip was with them—he had insisted he come—and yesterday, for the first time, he had shaved him with Margaret's help.

She looked to Alexander now; he had told her that he must leave after the celebrations—the Estate would not run itself—there were too many things to be done, bills to pay. So after Twelfth Night, he Charlotte and Mr Masters would leave. Please God, that by then Stewart would have gained enough strength so that Alex could talk with him, for as of this moment Stewart was not aware of anything.

'Good morning to you all,' Sir Henry's voice resonated around the room as he greeted everyone.

Elizabeth smiled to herself and reflected that from the many years in the army the man did not know how to speak softly.

'My physician and surgeon have been to see young Hamilton this morning and they say that the wound is healing nicely. There is no evidence of further infection and that from this moment all he needs is peace and quiet so that his body can heal. I wish to convey to you that my home is open to any, or all members of his family that wish to stay for as long as is needed to get this young man back to health. My own family will remain here till Easter time, but if it should be that he is still not fit to travel, my home will stay open to you until such time he is.'

Elizabeth was the first to speak. 'Sir Henry, there are no words that I can express, to tell you of my profound gratitude for what you have done for my son. Without this, he would be dead, I know that.' Her voice faltered and she put her head down looking at her hands.

Alexander stood up. 'My aunt is... overcome by your kindness and generosity.'

Sir Henry stood and put up his hand to stop him. 'Alexander, please. We will all go in now to eat a VERY late breakfast, but nonetheless a needed one.' With that he waved his arm towards the door.

***

Stewart opened his eyes and looked around; he could see Margaret sitting by the window sewing. Bringing his right hand slowly up the front of his body, he stroked his clean face. This was the first time that he had woken with clear thoughts in his head, without being in a foggy daze. His eyes worked, he could see that, he no longer had to squint and strain to get things into focus. Not only that he could move his right arm up his body to his face; well, that was an improvement. He would try his voice.

'What day is this?' Stewart's voice rasped.

Margaret stood up so abruptly she scattered her work basket and all of its contents over the floor. Coming round to the bed, she took his hand and felt him squeeze hers firmly.

'It is Twelfth Night, Stewart, the day before St Stephens.' She saw him faintly smile, blink and fall asleep once more.

Margaret ran to the next room to find Pip, seeing he was not there she ran down the corridor to the nursery to find Charlotte. By the time she opened the door, she was breathless.

'Charlotte, go fetch my mother and Alexander,' she breathed, smiling broadly. 'Stewart has just spoken to me.' In a flurry of skirts, she turned and made her way back to his room.

Entering she could see that he had his right hand to his face and was blinking, coming up to him she took his hand in hers once more.

'Margaret.' His voice was so hoarse as though he had been screaming for many hours. 'I am thirsty and maybe a little hungry.' She stood turned and pulled the bell pull beside the bed several times, then with her hand to her mouth to cover her hysterical laughter she went to sit next to him once more.

'How long?' he questioned, the words came slow and rasping.

'Since the beginning of December. Please, Stewart, do not speak, save your strength.' Her tears were flowing freely now. He tried to raise his hand to her face but could not, so Margaret placed it there for him letting his fingers move softly over her cheek.

'My spirit, my love, my courage. Oh God, I love you,' she whispered.

Margaret was quietly sobbing when Elizabeth placed her hand onto her shoulder.

'He will mend now,' was all Elizabeth could say, and Margaret nodded her head still holding his hand to her face.

***

Margaret had come to sit in the library. She knew that she would not be disturbed here, and Stewart was sleeping peacefully now. Placing her hand in her pocket her fingers folded round the letter that Bearcroft had given her the night before the fever had broken, the night they thought he would die. She had not opened it, for she felt that by doing so it would seal his fate, but now he was recovering. Taking it out she turned it over, breathed deeply then eased the seal away without it breaking. Spreading the page out with her hands she began to read.

Maggie, My Heart, you are reading this now because I am no longer with you, and I have striven this past hour to find the words, how to express my love for you, but what I can say is that my life began with you so I will now try and convey what you are to me in a different way, and hope you can forgive me for what I have to do, and understand my reasons.
You are my courage my guiding light
That steers me through the raging storm
My conscience that protects me
When all my reason has left and gone
You pull me back from the brink each time
When trials threaten to engulf my soul
My constant in a world of discontent
Where all hope and sanity have flown
But if I should go or be taken
Within just the blinking of an eye
You will know that you were loved by me
With both my body and my soul
Love is unconditional, and you have given it to me as such, as I hope that I have given to you also. I will love you Maggie from the depths of my being till time stops, and my spirit will never leave you.
For you will hear me in the soughing of the trees
As you will feel my touch from the wind upon your face
You will smell me in the ripened flax within the fields
As you will taste me in the saltiness of your tears
And you will see me in the evening skies just as darkness falls
For I am around you everywhere until we meet once more
Your Loving Husband, Stewart

When Margaret could control her emotions, she folded the letter and placed it back into her pocket.

'Oh God, Stewart,' she sobbed, as she let her head fall into her hands. It was some time before she regained her thoughts, her hands and her body seemed to be shaking uncontrollably, standing she took the letter once more and held the seal over the candle melting the underside a little, and then re sealed it again. He would never know that she had read it, she would return it to Bearcroft when next he came.

***

It was three days later and Robert Fairweather sat in the study opposite his son, watching the expressions on his face as he ruminated over his thoughts while he watched the fires flicker.

'James,' he began, 'I have never, and will never, ask you to do something against your will. All I ask is that you think about this betrothal to Catherine. She would be good for you.'

'That is exactly what Stewart told me; he said life would never be dull.'

'A wise man your friend,' smiled Robert Fairweather.

'I like her well enough, Father, but she is very… strong willed.'

'And very beautiful,' finished his father.

James sat nodding to himself. 'As always, you and he are right; her mother is a force to be reckoned with though.'

'She is a Major's wife, James, what do you expect of such? Her husband runs this house like a regiment, but under this facade Sir Henry is a very kind man, I know, as he has been my friend for many years.'

James stood up and faced his father resolved. 'I will agree to the betrothal, Father, as Stewart has told me time and again I need a wife.'

Robert Fairweather stood up and took his son into an embrace smiling.

'If you need a place to run to, you can always come home, but I do not think you will once you marry, James,' he slapped his son on the back.

'Come, let us relate the good news to Sir Henry, and then I must leave here as I have urgent business to attend to in London.'

***

Robert Fairweather knocked the door lightly then opened it.

'Forgive my intrusion, Milady Hamilton, I beg just a few moments with your husband Stewart before I leave for London today.'

Margaret rose from the bed smiling. 'Please come in, sir, I will leave you to speak with him.'

Robert Fairweather raised his hand. 'No, please stay, what I have to impart concerns both of you.'

Margaret looked to Stewart then seated herself on a chair.

'Stewart, if I may call you that, I have not yet had the opportunity to thank you for saving my son's life, though *thanking you* does not convey my feelings at all.' Robert Fairweather saw that Stewart was about to speak and stopped him.

'Please hear what I have to say. You saved his life by giving your own in forfeit of his. For that alone I owe you *my* life. I wish to make you a gift of my house in Torquay. It is not a big house, but its location and views of the sea are astonishing, especially in the summer months. I have asked Edward Bearcroft to draw up the deed of transfer, and when I return to London tomorrow, I will sign it and leave your copy with him. Go there this summer; it will help you to recover in your mind as well as your body. I gift it to you with my sincere thanks for what you did, though in truth I can *never* really repay you.'

Stewart tried to find his voice but found it difficult. Margaret seeing this stood up and went to stand by him.

'Mr Fairweather, I think what my husband is trying to say is "Thank you".' She turned and smiled at Stewart.

Robert Fairweather smiled and bowed. 'My pleasure, Milady.' Then just as he came to the door, he turned.

'I do not know if you have heard, but my son has become betrothed to Lady Catherine, he said to tell you, as this would make you very happy.' Inclining his head once more he left the room.

Stewart turned to Margaret as the door closed. 'Go get the fool, please.'

***

James Fairweather stood at the bottom of Stewart's bed, smiling and shaking his head.

'Dear God, Stewart, never do that to me again.'

'I sincerely hope I will not have to, James.' Stewart swallowed hard and Margaret held his head while he drank some water.

'You are betrothed, I hear.' The smile on his face said more than words

'I am God, help me. Do you know, Stewart, we were talking in the drawing room just two minutes ago, when her father left us for a moment.' James stopped to find the right words.

'She told me she was pleased at our betrothal, then came towards me stating that we should seal our betrothal with a kiss, as she promptly placed her hands to my face pulled me down and kissed me!' James' face had coloured slightly. 'Only two seconds later her father re-entered. From the look on my face, and the position of us both, he turned to his daughter and told her to behave herself or there was always the Nunnery!'

Stewart laughed softly, then coughed and laughed some more.

'James, you will be one very happy man; *amor omnibus idem*,' whispered Stewart.

James looked from Margaret to Stewart as he realised what his friend was implying, then shook his head. 'I shall be staying for another week Stewart, and then I have to go to London to help my father. While I am here maybe we can talk some more.'

Stewart nodded. 'Is Alexander here? Can you ask him to come up?'

'I will see you later, Stewart.' James came to his friend, clasped his hand and smiled, but the words would not come, inclining his head to Margaret he left.

'Oh, Stewart, James will not know what to do with her,' she smiled.

His response was to look at her with a knowing smile and raise his eye brows.

By the time she had straightened his covers, he was asleep once more—not the dead sleep that he had been in, but the peaceful sleep of recovery.

Chapter Thirty-Three
Convalescence, a Journey and the Precious Gift of Healing

Stewart sat in the large winged chair by the window in his room. Sir Henry's estate Midcraven Hall just outside Bath was vast, he had also discovered that he also owned a house on The Crescent in Bath, and that the estate and family were affluent beyond his thinking. Sir Henry's father had been the 2nd cousin of Edward Cornwallis, the then Lieutenant General, and in hindsight had he known on the outward journey to Bath that day, exactly who the Lady Catherine had been, he would have gone straight to the magistrate. Stewart shook himself in remembrance. It was now the beginning of February and all had gone home with the exception of Margaret, his mother, nanny Daisy and Charles. Pip was still here, and as he said he would not be leaving till he, Stewart, did.

It had been two whole months now since he was wounded, the words "*tempus fugit*" came to mind, but with the reality that this time had been lost, and not spent in happiness to be remembered, as at least one month of that he had been somewhere in a deep dark void, which even he could not recall. His shoulder throbbed so at times that he wished he could revisit that void to be rid of the pain, but he had been told by the physician that this would lessen in time. The wound was still raw, even though it looked as it had healed from the out, there was still a lot of healing to take place from within.

Maggie looked ill and had lost weight, but then when he looked at himself, he thought so had he—his clothes hung on him. Sir Henry had sent for his tailor to make him two new sets of breeches, plus to alter the ones that he had to accommodate his loss. Not that this mattered, as he found it very difficult to stay upright when he walked even with Sir Henry's stick, his legs were weak. He would remedy that though, he had been walking the room whenever his strength let him.

Lady Jemima was a force to be reckoned with, and he had vague memories of her and a chamber pot which sent his heart thumping, that thought was best left to the dark void he told himself. There were other quite alarming flashes that re-appeared regarding her at times, including one lucid moment which was to do with the bathing of his body; he also chose not to let these resurface if he could help it.

He was happy for James, he had at last found himself a wife. He chuckled to himself when he thought about it. Lady Catherine was like her mother—and her father for that matter—what sort of life would he have with her? A very interesting one, no doubt. The trick for James was to curb her enthusiasm, but if her father had not managed that, what chance did James have. They would be happy, he was sure of that, even though James would get exasperated from time to time, it would do him good.

He had asked Bearcroft to keep all the letters he had written. After what had happened, one never knew when one could be taken. Life was ephemeral, to be taken away with the blink of an eye, or the firing of a pistol.

He had spoken to Alexander who had been very reluctant to leave him, but leave he must; they were like brothers, and the thought of one losing the other was beyond comprehension. They would stay at the Willows—he Charlotte and Mr Masters—till Stewart's return. He did not want the house to be left, as there was a nagging thought that festered in the back of his mind, that all was not finished. '*Praemonitus praemunitus*'—or in another phrase: forewarned is forearmed.

There was a sharp rap on the door, and when Stewart looked up, he saw Sir Henry enter.

'Good day to you, Stewart, I hope that I am not disturbing you?'

Stewart looked around him and raised his good arm. 'I am grateful for the company, sir, please excuse my not standing.'

Sir Henry flapped his hand at him. 'Be at ease. I saw my physician this morning and he asked how you were fairing. I told him that you were making steady progress, am I right?'

'Yes, sir, once I get the strength back in my legs, I will be fine. My wound can take its own time to heal.'

'Good, good. Do you need anything? As I shall be away for three days, I have to go to Wells.'

'No, sir, I have everything and more, thank you.' Stewart paused. 'I have something to ask you, sir. Northcott knew how to handle a pistol, of that I am sure now, how did he miss my chest?'

Sir Henry seated himself on the large trunk at the end of the bed.

'Do you remember my making you practice on that morning?'

Stewart nodded.

'How did you find the pistol?'

'In truth, sir I do not remember,' replied Stewart, puzzled now.

'When you fired it, did you not feel it kick up and to the right?' Sir Henry looked at him smiling.

At the same time, realisation set into Stewart brain. 'Dear God, he aimed for my heart!'

Sir Henry nodded at him. 'The man could have struck any target at that distance; he was *very* good with a pistol. I know how my pistols respond, and I hoped that if you by chance were able to detect this and aim, you would hit something significant.'

Stewart felt his stomach churn and bile rise in his throat.

'The bowl if you would not mind sir!' exclaimed Stewart.

Sir Henry just got it under his head before Stewart wretched into it. Placing the bowl in Stewart's lap, he pulled on the bell pull and within moments a servant appeared.

'Fetch water and Milady Hamilton now!' he barked, handing the bowl over and requesting another clean one.

'My sincere apologies, sir,' began Stewart.

'I have some brandy, Stewart, shall I call for some?' but before Stewart could say no, he had once again pulled the cord.

'Bring brandy and glasses, be quick!'

'I can assure you, sir I will be fine.'

'The colour of your skin would not agree with you, and neither do I,' he said as he bounded to the door throwing it open. 'How long does it take to get brandy!' he shouted.

He was pushed rather unceremoniously back into the room by his wife. 'Henry, will you keep your voice down? Margaret is trying to sleep and so is her son!' Coming across, she put her hand to Stewart's head. 'You have no fever.' Then turning to her husband, she demanded. 'What have you been giving him?'

Everyone turned as the door opened suddenly.

'Is there something wrong?' Margaret's voice held a little uneasiness in its tone, as she stood there with her son in her arms.

'My dear, I fear my husband has upset him, though quite how I have yet to fathom,' stated Lady Jemima, turning to look rather disconcertingly at him.

'We were talking of the duel,' Sir Henry said defensively, 'then suddenly he wretched into the bowl. Well I thought that there might be a return of the fever,' Sir Henry added with some trepidation. 'One cannot be too sure with wounds,' he finished, eyeing his wife, lest an onslaught from her was about to be launched once more.

'He is fine,' Margaret replied. 'You reminded him of the fear that had enveloped him on that day, and his stomach reacted—it always does.'

'If you are sure that all is well, we will leave you to your peace,' responded Lady Jemima as she took her husband by the elbow and out of the door.

Margaret's face was covered in a warm smile as she stood looking at Stewart, who raised his brows at the retreating Lady Jemima and Sir Henry.

'How would you say young James will fare with Lady Catherine?' Stewart grinned.

Margaret shook her head in reply. 'Very well, now, Stewart, would you like to see something quite amazing?' she offered as she put young Charles to the floor.

The moment his bottom hit the floor boards, the young Charles leaned forward and began crawling on all fours towards the trunk at the bottom of the bed. Margaret watched with pleasure at the changing expressions on Stewart's face, as their son reached the said trunk, then heaving himself into an upright position proceeded to walk along it with the aid of his arms which were resting on the top. Having reached the end, he once more dropped to the floor and crawled towards Stewart; grabbing Stewart's legs, he pulled himself upward again. Margaret was with them now, lifting Charles up onto his father's lap.

'Do you see how clever our son is?' she laughed gently, kneeling beside them.

'What... when did he accomplish this new ability?' he queried in amazement.

'Yesterday afternoon was the first time, then again this morning, and since then he has been doing this all around the nursery.' Margaret smiled with sheer enjoyment.

'Our son is learning new skills every day, Stewart, and nanny Daisy informs me that it will not be long till he walks!' Margaret's voice was full of delight. 'And he is but ten months old,' she added gleefully.

'Come near,' he whispered. 'I want to kiss you, but I have no free arm with which to hold you.'

She moved into him and held his face in her hands, kissing him deeply. Parting, he carefully lifted his left arm—which was held in a sling—away from his body, letting the fingers of his left hand stroke her face.

'You are my anchor, Maggie, do you know that? For without you, I would be adrift in the ocean, with no safe haven to come into... You are my life, my love, my soul,' he stopped to regain hold of his emotions. 'I love you very deeply, you should know that.'

Margaret held him tightly into her. 'And I you, Stewart.'

It was then a small fist came up between them, followed by a very disgruntled shout at being squashed between two very large human beings. Margaret was the first to laugh, as Stewart kissed his son's head.

'Charles, we have not forgotten you. I promise,' he said

Charles Hamilton was not of that agreement, as he struggled to get to the floor and explore his surroundings once more.

***

Elizabeth sat in her room after dinner. She had dismissed her maid Molly as she would sleep early this evening—there had been mail today, and one of these had been a letter for Stewart from Alexander. Alexander, reflected Elizabeth, usually wrote to her all of the news from the Willows, as did Mr Masters, but this one was addressed directly to Stewart. She was loath to give it to him this evening, lest it held some troublesome news regarding the estate. Better it is left till tomorrow, as she did not want Stewart to brood over its contents all night.

Mr Masters wrote her regularly, and she always looked forward and enjoyed these letters immensely. They were interesting letters regarding all the happenings in Mere and the houses. He was a kind man, Mr Masters, Alex was very lucky to have such a father-in-law, though she was sure that he appreciated Mr Masters as much as she did.

Stewart, she considered, had looked better than he had for days when she saw him this afternoon. He had taken more food, and was at last losing that gaunt appearance, Margaret on the other hand was looking decidedly tired. She would not allow anyone to take over the care of Stewart, even though Elizabeth had begged her. Things would be better once they were all home, she was sure of that.

Elizabeth looked now at her reflection in the mirror, smoothing her hand across her face. She had aged since the incident last December, then let us be truthful; they all had. Snuffing out the candle, she rose and got into bed, then leaning out, she extinguished the other that was on the table beside her. Tomorrow, she told herself, she would try Stewart with the stairs, if he could manage them, then they could all make plans to return to the Willows.

***

Margaret lay beside him, held tight by Stewart's good arm, feeling his heart beat steadily under her hand.

'You have a very strong heart, Stewart.' Lifting herself, she kissed the side of his chest causing the hairs there to rise and the flesh to goose bumps.

He turned his head to her and kissed her. 'Maggie... Maggie, I want you,' was all he said. They had not loved since before the shooting, Stewart had been too ill, and she had been too tired to even think of such a thing, but now she breathed in deeply, moving herself to lie on top of him.

'I need your help, Maggie,' was all he managed before her lips came down on his.

'Lay still, Stewart,' she answered as she knelt across him, removing her shift. Taking his good hand, she placed it onto her breast, while her right hand stroked his stomach, feeling the soft hair there which led up to his chest. She could discern all the bones of his ribs now—he had lost so much weight. Lifting her body, she eased herself onto him and moved slowly, never taking her eyes from his. Their love was unhurried and tender, till finally she stretched herself against his body as he kissed her deeply. Pushing her head up and smoothing the sweat from his brow, she looked down at him with such tenderness.

'Oh God, I love you,' was all she managed to say before she laid her head beside him.

'And I you,' came Stewart's soft reply; then they slept the sleep of children, untroubled and at peace.

***

The sun was warm on his face as he looked out to the gardens, but he knew that it was anything but warm outside the confines of his convivial bedroom, with the constantly burning fire. Had anyone informed him when he had set out with his friend James and Lawyer Bearcroft last December, he would find himself near death from a pistol wound; he would never have believed that either. He felt his shoulder, it was sore to the touch, and the slightest movement set off a pain that could be felt down his arm, through his neck and through his chest.

The arm had been immobile for two months, and the consequence of that was that everything had hardened to the point his joints had ceased to function. The elbow had been the hardest, as when he straightened his arm, he wanted to scream out, just to open his arm out to a point where it was nearly straight caused him excruciating pain, so he had placed his small dagger between his teeth and bit hard. He had been secretly applying this exercise, but with extreme caution as he did not want to reopen the wound. His fingers flexed now, and he could make a firm fist, though not tight. The lifting of the arm at the shoulder was impossible, just the slightest movement upwards and the world went black with bright white spots dancing in his eyes. He would persevere though, just as he had with the elbow.

Last night, he reflected, was the first time he had wanted Maggie. Until then he had considered that nothing worked, and that it would have been better to have died, but when he felt Maggie's lips at the side of his chest, oh God, it had dispelled all of his fears. She had lain with him every night this last month, but never touching him, just holding his hand. Yesterday, he had wanted to touch her, to feel her close to him, all those feelings of desire had awoken in him again. Stewart closed his eyes and ran his hand over his face.

He pushed the sleeve of his left arm up looking at his forearm, and then he carefully did the same to his good arm, biting the material with his teeth to pull it up to his elbow. The left arm was decidedly thinner, it was plain to see, the muscle in the left seemed to have shrunk and pulled in, and he knew that if he did not apply exercise to it then it would never work again.

'Stewart, am I disturbing your thoughts?'

It was his mother's voice and he turned to greet her.

'Good morning, Mother.'

She looked into his eyes and smiled. 'Stewart, you look relaxed today, the most that I have seen you since I first came here.'

Stewart smiled in remembrance as to why he was so relaxed.

'Let us hope that this is the turning point,' continued Elizabeth. 'I have brought you Alexander's letter; when you have read it. I will tell you my news that I received from Mr Masters.'

Elizabeth handed him the letter then sat in the window seat to wait. As he read, she watched his face change from a smile to a grin then a chuckle, till finally he nodded, smiling. Looking up at his mother, he knew what was going through her head, but he could not divulge anything, she would have to wait.

'Mother, all I can say is that it is good news, but… I am sworn to secrecy,' he said, raising his hand, 'so you will have to wait till we return, which I hope will be at the end—or before—of this month.' Elizabeth looked at him with wary interest.

'Very well, then I will tell you mine.'

Elizabeth seated herself more comfortably in the seat and opened the letter from Mr Masters; tapping it with her finger, she folded it once more and looked up into Stewart's eyes.

'I will not read the letter out to you, Stewart, but will explain exactly what he has done for you.'

By this time, Stewart was looking at his mother bemused.

'Mother, please just tell me what has happened.'

Elizabeth sighed and leant over to take his hand.

'Oh, Stewart, Mr Masters has acquired a passage for you all, aboard a friend's merchant ship to "Rapallo".'

Stewart's face showed a myriad of thoughts, as he tried to digest what his mother had just said.

'You will leave in April,' she continued. 'You, Margaret, Young Charles, nanny Daisy and Margaret's maid Millie. The ship—which I am given to understand is a large one—will leave Portsmouth sometime at the beginning of April, stopping first at Le Havre, then sailing south to Lisbon, then on through the Mediterranean to Malaga, then Valencia and up to Genova. From there, Rodolfo will meet you with two carriages to take you to his villa in Rapallo.' She paused to stoke his face. 'Oh, Stewart, the voyage alone will be a healing one, the seas should be kind at that time of year so, Mr Masters informs me, then you can stay for three whole months before returning, or longer if you wish.'

Stewart was astounded, then finding his voice, he spoke, 'Mother, my gratitude for what Mr Masters has done for me is beyond words, but… we cannot take Charles with us, he is too young, too open to disease, and the perils of what such a sea voyage could yield, it could kill him… I have made such a voyage before, have I not?' he swallowed and took his mother's hand in his. 'And Maggie would never go without him,' he finished reluctantly, and with such a tone of finality in his voice it made Elizabeth's heart ache.

Elizabeth searched his face, and could see the longing there, but also the futility in thinking that such a thing could happen. She tapped his hand, then stood and kissed his cheek.

'I understand, Stewart, but do not say anything to her for this moment, maybe there is another way forward.' Elizabeth rose and walked to the door, looking back at her son, seeing the longing on his face.

***

It was late in the evening, all the candles were out, and there was only the moon's glow falling through the open drapes onto the floor, casting its silvery glow. They had dined together in their room, and Margaret had observed that he had eaten very little food. Now as Margaret lay on her side next to him, she picked up his hand and kissed it.

'You are deep in thought, Stewart, what is it that troubles you? Can you tell me?'

Stewart turned to face her and smiled, his eyes searching her face.

'I am fine, Maggie, just tired, and, I want to go home,' he pushed his arm under her and pulled her to him, kissing her forehead.

She stoked the fingers of his left hand that lay on his chest and held it gently.

'I was talking to Lady Jemima today.' Stewart moved her to a more comfortable position and rested his head on hers.

'Did she have any news on when James might come?' he asked hopefully. He wanted his company right now.

'No, she was telling me about her life in the army with Sir Henry,' she paused here to collect her thoughts.

'She told me that her three sons were very young at that time—Catherine came later—and that when he was to leave, she could not bear to see him go alone, nor could she leave her children. Then she said she had sat one long night and weighed up every possibility. Her husband would go and maybe never return, and she would have missed those precious final years that she could have had with him if such a thing happened, her children would be there no matter what,' she paused once more. 'So, she followed her husband and left her children at home with her mother—she knew that they would be safe, no harm would come to them, save sickness,' she stopped once more.

Stewart's heart was racing now, and he was sure that Maggie could feel it, as it beat like a drum in his own ears.

'She told me that she never once regretted her decision, her children had a peaceful childhood—spoilt to extreme by their grandmother—and she had all those beautiful years with her husband that would have been lost if she had stayed.'

Stewart by this time thought that his heart would stop. Realising he had been holding her very tight, he loosened his grip.

Margaret raised herself up onto her elbow and looked deep into his eyes.

'What I am trying to say, Stewart,' she stoked his face lightly, her thumb finding his mouth and caressing its contours. '*We* will go to Rapallo, you and I, and our son will stay here, safe, with Mother.' She bent toward him now kissing him.

Stewart looked up at her, feeling the tears falling slowly down over his temples, but he did not care, then pulling her down to him, he kissed her back deeply. She had given him a precious gift, and he knew just how much that gift had cost her.

Chapter Thirty-Four
Home and Another Letter

In the drawing room of the Willows Stewart sat in the chair by the fire, its flicker resembling the images that surfaced at will now in his mind, forcing him to go over again and again the cycle of events that nearly killed him. It circled around in his head like a recurring dream, and at present there was no way to prevent these images from appearing—they floated before him causing him to relive every second. Hopefully when he boarded that ship, the wind and the sea would clear his mind.

It was the end of March, and they had been home for little over a week, when Alexander had told his mother and Maggie the news that Charlotte was with child, he had wished that he could have captured their faces on canvas, and thanked God that he was alive to see it.

'... *For you have drawn me up and have not let my foes rejoice over me...*' whispered Stewart.

'For that, Lord, I am eternally grateful,' he added, crossing himself.

His left arm was now free of the bandage that had held it up to his body. He could lower his arm, and bend it—though somewhat stiffly at the elbow—but he could not raise his arm above his shoulder. He was flexing his elbow when Mr Masters entered the room.

'Will you be well enough for the sea voyage, Stewart?' he questioned as he came to sit in the chair opposite.

'Well or not, sir, I will be going,' replied Stewart with determination.

William Masters smiled and inclined his head. 'I feel it would take a great deal more than that to stop you, Stewart,' he answered, nodding towards Stewart's arm.

'Margaret is overjoyed at her sister's condition, though I must say that the timing of such an event has come at a very difficult moment—you're departing for Italy next week,' Masters added.

'Mr Masters, there is never a difficult time for a child to be conceived, it is always a joy, a gift, and Margaret will be back well before the birth, do not worry yourself.'

Stewart stood up and walked towards the window. There was sun today and it reflected on all the new shoots of the trees in soft greens and yellows. A riot of daffodils ran along the front of the terrace, and he could just discern the clusters of early blooming bluebells around the trees in the distance, as though a purple blue mist hovered there. Mother Nature was re-inventing herself again.

'It will be a great comfort to know that you are here with them, especially for Alex. You have a shrewd business eye, sir, and this will be a reassurance to me that Alex will have someone whom he can trust, and make decisions with.' Stewart then turned to look at William Masters.

'I am in your debt for all you have done.'

'I will not dismiss that compliment, Stewart, but take it, and thank you for it. You have taken me into this house like family, and I hope that I have repaid that in kind.'

Stewart came towards him taking his hand in a firm shake.

'Oh, you have, sir, never doubt it.'

There was a light tap on the door and Lilly entered, curtsying.

'Begging your pardon, Master Stewart, but Mr James Fairweather has arrived.

Stewart turned to see James come bounding into the room. The two men hugged and slapped one another for some moments before James pulled away and looked soberly at his friend.

'Stewart, my eyes tell me that you have improved, but… you still have a long road to travel before you are completely recovered, my friend.'

Stewart smiled at him and reached out to squeeze his shoulder.

'I am fine, James, the sun and sea on this voyage will revive me, of that I have no doubt.' Stewart walked to pull the bell pull.

'But look at you! How long are you staying here with us? What of your betrothed? Have you set a date yet for the wedding?'

Stewart stopped as Lilly appeared once more, asking her to go fetch his wife, mother and Charlotte, then gave her his most engaging smile before he placed his next request.

'Could you maybe enquire—if it would not cause too much trouble to her—for Mrs Cottle to make some tea and maybe some food for my guest?'

Lilly curtsied. 'I am sure that cook will be pleased to be doing this for ye, sir.' Curtsying once more, she hurried out.

James turned to Stewart laughing. 'You have Mrs Cottle in the palm of your hand at this time, Stewart… I'll wager she would do anything that you asked, no?'

'She is trying to fatten me up, James, but alas my appetite is small at the moment,' he replied, offering James the seat by the fire bringing a chair for himself.

'So, how long are you staying with us, is this just a passing visit?'

James seated himself on the chair motioning Stewart to take the armchair.

'I am here till you leave next week, and I believe that Sir Henry, Lady Jemima and Catherine will call here on their way to London, to wish you well on your voyage, Stewart.'

'And the wedding?' enquired William Masters. 'Have you decided when and where?'

James looked at Stewart and William Masters in turn. 'It is to be in Wells on the first Wednesday in September.'

Stewart laughed. 'So Catherine got her way, for as I recall, after Wheatley's wedding, you vowed you would never have one like it.'

'I had no say in the matter, Stewart, Lady Jemima and Catherine had it all decided even before you left their home in Bath,' James responded dryly.

William Masters stood up at this point. 'If you will excuse me, gentlemen, I will go look for the women and bring them here.' Inclining his head, he left the room.

James looked askance at Stewart.

'The man is very perceptive, James, he realised that you wished to speak in private with me, so he went to delay the others... well, out with it.'

'The women have me going around in circles, Stewart, and neither I nor Sir Henry can do anything to stop them. As for Catherine,' he paused. 'She is a very forward woman.'

Stewart placed his hand to his forehead and laughed.

'It is not in the slightest bit amusing, Stewart, she kisses me—very passionately might I add—at every opportunity.'

'And your body does not want to obey your head, am I correct?' finished Stewart, chuckling heartily.

'Mmmm,' came James' reply.

'Oh, you are a good tonic for me, James, you have lightened my mood and you have been here but fifteen minutes.'

'Stewart, please, do not make light of this. How am I to survive five months of this?' came James' piqued reply.

Stewart was laughing loudly as Alexander came in.

'Please let me in on this merriment. What have I missed?' Alexander enquired.

Stewart calmed himself and turned to Alexander.

'James was just asking how he could dispel his betrothed's advances for the next five months.'

'You what!' exclaimed Alexander

'Come with me to Rapallo, James, that way you will be out of her clutches, and when you return, you will be married.'

'Do not put ideas into my head, I might just accept your offer, Stewart,' replied James

***

Sir Henry, Lady Jemima and Catherine arrived three days before Stewart and Margaret's departure for Rapallo. They would stay overnight before making their way to London to start the preparations for the wedding. It had been a cheerful and easy dinner, with everyone exchanging stories with the ease and comfort of old friends. The men had retired to the study while the women stayed on in the

296

drawing room to talk good-humouredly regarding their husbands and perspective ones.

'Elizabeth, you have a fine family here, one that respect'—she paused here to look at her daughter—'and love you deeply. There is warmth in this house that I have not found in any other home I have visited,' stated Lady Jemima.

Elizabeth smiled. 'I thank you kindly for the compliment, Lady Jemima.'

'Please, Elizabeth… Jemima is my name.'

'Very well, Jemima,' continued Elizabeth. 'I am afraid that it has not always been so though. There have been many times… well, all families go through trials.'

Lady Jemima stopped her. 'I am referring to now, Elizabeth, there is a great depth of affection here,' she inclined her head towards Elizabeth, lowering her voice. 'Believe me, Elizabeth, there have been times in my own house that I would gladly have walked away, leaving them all to fight out their differences.'

Elizabeth smiled. 'Are none of your sons married?'

'No, much to my consternation, I have found them many suitable young brides, but they just waved their hands at me, and well…' Lady Jemima's voice trailed away.

Margaret who had been half listening to her conversation turned to her sister, who she could see from her face, was anything but well.

'Charlotte, are you tired?' Margaret observed that she was very pale.

'Mother, I shall take Charlotte to her bed, I fear she needs her rest, so if you will excuse us.' Margaret nodded her head and took Charlotte by the hand.

'Come, Charlotte, let us go and retrieve your husband.'

Charlotte smiled and let herself be led from the room.

Once out of the room Margaret seated Charlotte on a chair.

'Now sit here while I go for Alex.' Not waiting for an answer, she proceeded down the corridor to the study. Giving the panel a sound rap, she opened the door.

'Forgive me, gentleman, I would speak with Alexander, if you please.'

Stewart's head turned and looked at Margaret and then at Alexander.

'Is she unwell, Margaret?' Stewart asked warily.

'She is fine she just…'

Alexander was up and out of the door before she could finish her sentence.

Margaret smiled. 'I bid you all good night.' Saying this she closed the door, and as she reached the stairs, she found Charlotte in Alexander's arms.

'I am taking her to bed, Margaret, she is very tired.' Alexander looked at his wife, the worry he felt was showing clearly on his face.

Margaret took her sister's hand and held it to her own face—she was so young—and then leaning in to kiss her, she whispered. 'It will pass, Charlotte, believe me I know.' She then watched them go upstairs. As she turned to go, she saw William Masters standing there, watching his daughter being carried away.

'She has been unwell for some days,' he began.

Margaret placed her hand on his arm. 'Mr Masters, she will be fine, in a few weeks all of these symptoms will pass—I know, as I too went through them.' She paused to see them disappear along the corridor above.

'I will go to cook, and if she is still awake, I will ask very kindly if she can brew her some mint tea. It was the only thing that helped me.'

Mr Masters nodded. 'I will go to my bed as well, please convey my good night to all.'

'I will, you have no need to worry, believe me.' Margaret thought the man looked ill himself. Having never been through such a thing with his own wife, this was all unfamiliar to him.

***

Stewart lay back on the bed smiling as Margaret pulled off his stockings. He was enjoying himself, watching her standing there with the light from the candles behind her, silhouetting her body through her diaphanous shift.

Margaret looked at him suspiciously. 'What are you thinking, Stewart Hamilton?'

Stewart sat himself up. 'Help me take off my shirt first.'

He had already taken out his good arm from the sleeve, so she slowly pulled it over his head and eased it down his left.

'Right, Margaret Hamilton,' he whispered. Reaching up he loosened the string to her shift letting it fall around her feet. He gently pulled her into him and kissed her stomach, and as his mouth moved upwards he licked her navel, slowly progressing up to her breasts. Margaret let out a soft moan, as he placed his hands gently on her buttocks pulling her in. Margaret's body by this time was covered in goose bumps, as every fine hair on it rose up with the sensations that surged within her body. He pulled her down to the bed and turned himself onto her. Holding himself up with his good arm, he looked down into her eyes.

'You are one very beautiful woman, Margaret Hamilton, and the more I look at you, the more beautiful you become, and the more I want you.' His voice was deep with emotion, as his mouth came down to bite her neck, making its way up to her ear and across to her mouth. Their union was not gentle, there was a fire within him and Margaret could feel this and responded in kind, wrapping her legs tightly round him, as he took her deeper into the depths of pain and ecstasy, till she cried out. It was then he covered her mouth with his, biting her lips.

Some moments later, Margaret stoked the hair back from his face and smiled.

'I am so sorry, Maggie, I did not mean to,' began Stewart.

She placed her finger to his lips. 'You never hurt me, Stewart,' she whispered.

He gently lifted her up onto the pillows and pulled the covers over them, and then wrapping his legs around her he cradled her in, stroking her back kissing her softly.

'When we arrive in Rapallo,' he began, 'there is a secret cove just a way down from Rodolfo's villa. I will take you there and teach you to swim. You will

298

feel so free, Maggie, with the sky above you, and the sea holding your weight, it is a feeling like nothing else I have felt in my life.' His voice held the excitement of a young child's, alive with the expectancy of what was to come.

Margaret moved closer, pushing her head into his chest. 'Is it cold?' she asked sleepily

'No, Maggie, it is warm.'

Margaret clung to him, tasting his salty skin, and feeling the power in his arm that held her. She would feel safe anywhere in the world, as long as he was with her.

'I love you, Maggie.'

'As I do you, Stewart,' she replied as sleep gently took them both.

***

As he descended the stairs in the morning, Stewart noticed several letters in the salver on the table that stood in the hall. Sorting through them, his eyes rested on one addressed to him whose handwriting he was familiar with—Edward Bearcroft. The remainder were addressed to either his mother or Alexander. Taking the letter into the study, he sat at his desk and opened it gently, as though it held some kind of explosive.

He read the letter through several times before he was able to digest its contents. These being that his father had been seen in London on several occasions over this past week. To the present day, Bearcroft was unable to establish the reason he had come down from Scotland, but it was noted that he had a copious amount of money on his person.

Stewart's heart gave an involuntary beat, and like a ghost passing over his grave the hairs on the back of his neck rose up. Placing the letter in the draw of the desk, he went to find Alexander.

As Stewart came out of the room, he saw Alexander about to enter the dining room.

'Alex, a word please, in the study.'

His voice held a note of urgency, which made Alexander follow without question. From the darkness of the hallway, the brightness of the room hit Alexander's face, blinding him for a second, causing him to shield his eyes with his hand. The sun fell into the study from both windows, as the back of the house faced east and always caught the early morning sunshine. In the winter months the sun, though weak, helped warm the room, while in the afternoons on hot sweltering summer days—the sun having progressed to the front—it was cool, catching the breeze, if any, that came across the lawn. The terrace, which ran along that side of the house, was a place of quiet shaded refuge on such days.

Closing the door behind them, Stewart seated himself at the desk, then retrieving the letter from the draw he handed it to Alexander.

'I received it this morning.'

As Alexander read, Stewart saw his cousin's face pale, then darken with anger and fear. Looking up, he spoke, 'Where in God's name did he get that money, Stewart? More to the point, what is he doing in London?'

Stewart shrugged his shoulders and looked to the garden. 'I do not know, Alex. I only know that it is impossible now for me to leave for Rapallo in two days' time.'

'The hell it is!' replied Alexander, coming to stand before him. 'The man cannot touch my aunt or this house if he came onto this property I have the legal right to shoot him for trespass—and I would.'

Stewart stood and looked into his cousin's eyes. 'I do not trust him, Alex, he is devious and cunning. If I am not here to protect my mother and this house...' his voice trailed away.

'We are, William Masters and I, we will be staying here the whole time.'

'My son will be in this house,' interrupted Stewart, 'if anything ever happened to him I could never live with myself.' Stewart rubbed his hands over his face and paced the room, speaking abstractedly.

'We must arm Spike with a pistol—I doubt the man even possesses such a weapon—a knife maybe, but a pistol? Also my valet Pip—I know that he can shoot, did he not give me lessons when I was old enough to hold one?' Stewart paced some more. 'Can William Masters shoot?'

Alexander nodded. 'Yes, in Norfolk he lived as a Merchant, and as such he had to protect his family, as the town was usually filled with sailors of one description or another—yes, he shoots quite well.'

Stewart's brain was thinking quickly now. 'I want all the tenants armed.' Taking Alexander by the arm, he stared hard into his face. 'Short of putting a fence around my estate, there is not much else I can do, Alex.' The frustration in his voice was evident.

Alexander looked at his cousin with empathy. 'Stewart, we must inform all the men here, including Sir Henry, but not the women.'

Stewart nodded in acceptance. 'Go get them, Alex, tell them I need to see them to set certain plans in place regarding the estate before I leave.'

Alexander nodded back and left.

As he came into the passage, he saw his aunt descending the stairs.

'Good morning, Aunt, it seems that all have risen early this day, the house is a buzz of excitement,' he said as he kissed his aunt's cheek.

'There is much to do before Stewart and Margaret leave for Italy in two days,' she hesitated looking round at the letters on the table. 'I must open those—and so must you, Alexander. There may be matters that need both yours and Stewart's attention.' Reaching past him, she gathered them up.

'These four are for you, Alexander—bills or orders perhaps. The other two are mine, one from my friend in London and one from my dressmaker.'

She smiled to herself. 'Strange how we instantly recognise the writing of another person.' Turning, she handed his letters to him.

'How is Charlotte? I have given instructions to cook to send a tray to her room, I will go see her after breakfast, as I would imagine Margaret is with her now.'

She placed her hand on Alexander's arm, seeing the tension in his face, reading this to be anxiety over his wife.

'She will be fine, Alexander, it will pass.' Saying this she turned and crossed the hall to the dining room.

Alexander breathed deeply. 'Oh, Aunt, I wish that it were just that, for if you knew, you would see that my wife's dilemma is the least of my worries this morning,' he murmured to himself.

***

No one spoke as they each in turn read the letter from Bearcroft, and the atmosphere in the room was strung as tight as a violin string. Clearing his throat, Sir Henry was the first to speak.

'Stewart, the man has money. From where he has obtained this is a conundrum, but obtain it he has—by fair means or foul. While he possesses this, he boasts no threat to your home, for he knows the consequences of such a threat—prison or deportation.' He stood up to pace the room.

'This should no way prevent you from leaving for Italy in two days.' Sir Henry saw that Stewart was about to interject and raised his hand to stop him.

'You will hear me out, Stewart, please. I leave for London today, and while there I will speak with my lawyer Sir Richard Sutton, who is also a Member of Parliament. We will talk with Edward Bearcroft so that we can devise a rationale on how to go forward, *should* the need arise. You my boy will leave for Italy to restore yourself to health, knowing that all here are safe, and well cared for. Do I make myself clear?'

There was a silence around the room as all eyes rested on Stewart who was at that moment standing looking out onto the lawn.

Alexander, who knew his cousin well, saw the slight inclination of his head as he turned to face the room, and sent up a silent prayer of thanks that his cousin had seen reason.

'So be it,' was all he said.

***

It was late in the evening as Stewart sat in silence with Alexander and James in the drawing room. All preparations had been finalised, and Stewart and Margaret's luggage now stood ready in the hall to be taken to Portsmouth the following day. It had been agreed that none of the women were to be informed regarding Andrew Duncan's re-appearance in London, as Stewart saw no good reason to alarm them at this present time.

Margaret's maid Millie and Pip were to accompany them on the voyage, as Alexander had pointed out, there were sufficient men in the house and on the estate to protect his mother.

It was James who broke the silence.

'The arrangement still does not sit easy with you, does it, Stewart?'

Stewart looked up from his whisky glass. 'No, James, it does not,' he stood up, walking to the sideboard to refill his glass, bringing the decanter back and filling the others, he stood in front of the fire chewing the inside of his mouth, as he tapped his glass with his fingers.

'There is something under my skin which I cannot shift. It is like a sore that you constantly irritate because you know it is there, and you want to be rid of it, but every time you annoy it, the sore inflames and returns once again.' He seated himself once more, looking into the fire, lest the flames could give him an insight at what was to happen.

'My father is that sore, just when I think it has gone, it returns once again, till I think maybe they have to take off my arm to be rid of it.'

James looked to Alexander for help.

'Stewart, he is bound by the law now never to step a foot here, or harm any of your family, be it by his own hand or others.'

'I know, James, but there is something here that does not sit right with my reasoning. It is as though I am missing a very important piece of the puzzle, and I fear that when I leave here that piece will sit neatly into its place.' Stewart closed his eyes and sat back.

'I am in no doubt that my father knows of my impending voyage to Italy. I believe he has been informed of everything that has taken place.' He sat up looking from James to Alexander with a knowing expression on his face.

'Yes, I do mean Northcott.'

'But he too is bound by a legal document, Stewart,' interjected Alexander. 'For God's sake you saw the man sign it as your life's blood ran from you.'

'And you think that will stop them?' Stewart's voice had risen, as he stood up and paced the room once more.

Alexander turned him round to face him.

'Stewart, nothing will happen—can you not see what the man is doing? He is manipulating you to the point where you cannot see reason. He has made his presence known for that sole reason; they are playing you like a child plays with a toy, shifting you from one hand to another.' Alexander swallowed to regain his composure.

'You are recovering from an injury that nearly took your life, you are still weak, you are vulnerable, Stewart, can you not see that?'

Stewart placed his glass on the table by the sofa and placed his hand on Alexander's shoulder.

'You are right, Alex. I am maybe seeing things that are not there. My mind has played tricks on me since the duel, and there are times I doubt my own sanity when things enter my head and will not be banished. I will go tomorrow, have no fear, as I know that you will not let a hair on her head be touched.'

Alexander embraced his cousin. 'Go in peace, Stewart, we are here.'

Chapter Thirty-Five
The Voyage, Rapallo and Healing

The ship was a large East Indiaman called "The Abigail". With three masts it stood around 120 feet from keel to the top of the main mast. In Millie's eyes, it was gargantuan. They stood on the dock awaiting the last of the cargo to be lowered into the seemingly fathomless hold, before embarking up the small gangplank that had been lowered for them which boasted a rope to one side to steady one's self. The smells and the sounds were so alien that Millie clung to her mistress' carpetbag for comfort; this would be their home for a month or more, depending on the weather, and she shivered slightly, not from cold but from trepidation of what was to come.

The Captain—a Mr Edwin Hume—had left the Port of London late the previous evening and wanted to set sail as soon as the cargo had been lowered and safely stored; it was he who greeted them as they came up the gangplank. Their cabins were all at the stern of the ship—Stewart and Margate's being next to the captains, had two small casement windows, then following around to the side there were two smaller cabins that Pip and Millie would occupy, which sported a smaller round window just to the side of the bunk. The conditions were somewhat cramped but adequate for their use, as most of the time could be spent on deck, weather permitting. They set sail just after noon to catching the next tide, and Pip and Millie watched as the sailors ran up and down rope ladders, unfurling sails and making secure anything that might move once they hit the sea. Pip commented that the sailors resembled a colony of ants; so quickly were their movements you could hardly follow what they were doing. The captain meanwhile stood by the wheel, watching with eyes as sharp as a hawk's, yelling quick commands where necessary.

All goodbyes had been said at the house, so there was no one to wave to as the ship left her moorings. Stewart looked upwards at the sky, and then watched the sails as they took the wind, billowing out, giving the ship momentum to propel them out of the harbour.

Turning to Margaret, he took her hands and smiled at her.

'Well, Margaret Hamilton, with God's grace we will be in Rapallo, in a month maybe. Let us just enjoy the journey for now.' Bending and kissing her lightly, he turned her to watch the dock slowly fade into the distance.

***

The voyage south from Portsmouth had been peaceful. They stopped just a few hours in Le Havre to take on more cargo, leaving on the evening tide. From there they progressed southwards, encountering just a day's rough sea when crossing the Bay of Biscay. Molly here had been the only one affected by the ships motion, but as soon as the ship passed making its way down to Lisbon, she seemed to regain her health once more.

Lisbon had been a delight; both Elizabeth and Molly had watched avidly as cargo was hoisted high up into the air and lowered down into the bowels of the ship. The weather was hot and sultry, and the smells around them seemed to come from an abundance of spices and dried fruits which were being sold openly not far from the ship in a market of sorts. Here also many casks of port were loaded, some to be used in barter for the silks they would purchase in Valencia. First though they would stop in Malaga, renown also for its wines, fruits and silk, and having reached the Mediterranean waters now, it was to Malaga that the ship was slowly sailing towards.

It was early evening, and Stewart stood behind Margaret by the rail on the port side, watching the far distant coastline disappear as darkness fell. The air here was different, holding none of the heaviness there had been while sailing down the Atlantic side.

'How does this compare to the ferry to the Isle of Wight?' Stewart's voice was soft and warm in Margate's ear.

Pushing back into him, she took his hands from the rail wrapping them around her.

'This is something that even in the wildest of my dreams I could never have imagined,' she breathed, closing her eyes as she savoured the feel of his arms that held her tight, and his body pressed against hers.

'Did I not tell you I would bring you here, Margaret Hamilton?' His breath was warm as his lips barely touched her neck making her shiver with pleasure.

Turning her to face him, he kissed her lightly. 'I think we will go to our cabin now.'

Margaret lifted her arms up around his neck and gave the slightest of nods.

They were awoken early the next morning to shouts and orders by the captain, the ship had reached Malaga.

***

The two lanterns swung in rhythm with the gentle movement of the ship as Pip and Millie sat at the galley table, finishing the last of their supper. Each was deep in their thoughts till Millie spoke.

'Mr Pip, how long have ye been Master Stewart's valet?'

Pip placed the last mouthful of bread in his mouth and chewed meditatively, choosing his words.

'I have been Master Stewart's valet since he be going up to Winchester, afore that, I was footman, but I always looked out for him, took him fishing and the like. What makes you be asking, Millie?'

'Oh, I just be wondering, Mr Pip, as ye seem more friends than servant and master.'

Pip chuckled and wiped his mouth with the back of his hand. There was an orange that had been quartered and set on a plate, the smell was sweet and inviting; picking up a quarter he put it to his mouth and bit into the flesh. Seeing Millie watch him, he pushed the plate towards her.

'Eat, Millie, it is sweet and juicy.'

Millie took a quarter and bit into it, making Pip smile at the surprised expression on her face as she savoured the taste, licking her lips in delight. He pushed the remaining two quarters towards her and nodded.

'Did ye never marry, Mr Pip?' came Millie's next question.

Pip swallowed the last of his ale and rested his arms on the table. The young girl opposite him wanted to talk a while, he could see that, so he would oblige her. She was maybe homesick or just a little lonely not having the other members of the household to talk to.

'Yes, Millie I did, but she died when Master Stewart was but sixteen, some twelve years back now.'

Millie nodded in reply. It was warm in the galley, and her clothes seemed to stick to her. Pulling her kerchief away from her neck, she fanned herself with it.

Pip looked at her; she was young, maybe a few years older than her mistress, but young anyway. What made a young girl like herself go into service and not marry and have children? Hunger and security were the answers to himself.

'Let us go sit on deck for a while, Millie, it be cool there.' Stepping out from the bench, he raised his arm for her to go first, and on reaching the deck, he found two barrels near the rail where the breeze from the sea cooled them. Together they sat in silence for a while with just the shush of the water as it passed by the hull, as the ship sped on through the night to its next port of call. A row of lanterns were set high on a rope above the rail, and several sailors could be seen going about their duties, aboard ship there was always someone on watch in case of pirates, but he would not mention this to Millie, it would no doubt terrify her.

'And you, Millie, what be making you go into service?' he questioned gently. Watching the expressions on her face, he could see the memories coming back to her.

'Me, Mr Pip, I be the eldest of nine children. I were put into service by my mother from the age of fourteen. It be in my mistress' father's house, and I were a maid there. Then when my mistress was to be married, I were told I would be a going with her as her maid.' Millie looked at her hands, then up into Pip's face.

'I knew nothing of being such, Mr Pip, but my mistress did not care, we were like companions to one another. She be but eighteen, and I not much older.' Her eyes looked out into the pitch darkness of the world around them.

'Her first husband he be a wicked man... he... when he called for her, I would always have a bath a ready for her when she returned. He would... he would beat her sometimes.' She turned to look at Pip.

'Oh not so you would be seeing, Mr Pip, but her body would be bruised. God, he were an evil man, and when he died, I did thank God and all his angels, may he rot in hell.' Her voice had dropped to a whisper.

Pip placed his hand on hers, not in familiarity, but in comfort. She looked at him with tears in her eyes.

'Oh, Master Stewart, he be loving her something fierce, I know that. He protects her always. If I had a husband, I would want one like hers.'

Pip placed his arm around her shoulders.

'Go to your bed, Millie, tomorrow we will reach Valencia, and I will take you off the ship to see the market, would you be liking that?'

Millie nodded, and then stood.

'Good night to ye, Mr Pip,' she replied.

Pip watched her go down to her cabin, and pondered that she could have been his daughter if he had been blessed with such, he would keep watch over her, and see that she came to no harm.

***

Having left Valencia behind, they were now on their last leg of the voyage, and the next port of call would see them in Genova, Italy. It was nearing the end of April, and they would have three whole months ahead of them before their return.

All were leaning on the starboard rail watching the vast island of Sardinia in the distance pass by.

'Is it attached to the mainland Stewart?' Margaret's question held both excitement and curiosity.

Stewart placed his arm around her as they watched. It was warm on deck, and above them the sky was a clear azure, while the sun's rays gave the sea an opalescent hue, it was magical.

'If my memory serves me right, I believe Sardinia belongs to the Spanish,' he answered.

'But Spain cannot be seen from here, is it not nearer to Italy?' she questioned.

Stewart smiled. 'Maggie, that holds no consequence, it is whoever holds control over a place that matters. Boundaries shift, wars are fought, and land is gifted or taken. At this moment in time, I believe it is the Spanish that hold sovereignty.'

Margaret sighed. 'When will we reach Genova?'

Stewart looked once more heavenwards. 'If the weather holds, the ship should dock in the early morning.' Turning her to face him, he took her hands in his.

'Are you excited, Maggie?'

As she looked up into his face, her eyes sparkled. 'Excitement is the least of the emotions I am feeling now.'

Stewart looked at her; she was wearing a pale green gown of the softest cotton, with her deep red hair loose about her shoulders and her luminous green eyes which seemed to hold the ocean's depth. Smiling to himself, Stewart considered as he watched her turn to the rail once more, that she resembled "*Amphitrite*", wife of Poseidon, goddess of the sea.

Yesterday had been a bad day for both, as it had been Charles' first birthday, but they would have celebrated in the house, though just how would have to wait, as any letter written would unfortunately arrive in Italy after they had departed. James, in all his infinite wisdom, had commissioned a rocking horse for him, but probably the horse would be twice the height of Charles and would be more greatly appreciated when he turned three.

Stewart smiled to himself; his friend was a kind and generous man, and he wondered with some trepidation how he was fairing with his betrothed Catherine. He wished he could have brought James with him—it would have removed him from the trials he was going through now, but convention dictated he should remain.

He turned now to watch Pip with Millie. Pip had taken her under his wing that was clear, had he not escorted her to the market in Valencia? In England there had not been much cause for protection, she was part of the house, and under the ever present, watchful eye of Mrs Cottle. Here it was different; she was one of only two women passengers, one being safeguarded by himself, the other… there were many sailors aboard, and sailors spent most of their lives on a ship—alone. They had swapped cabins, as Pip's had a door with a key, and unless otherwise detained by Stewart, he was with her at all times. Stewart mused to himself that he had assumed the role of father, just as Spike had done for young Kenver. It was age old, this protection of one's kind.

A single bell tolled out from the kitchen below, indicating that lunch was ready.

***

The cacophonous noise from the dock at Genova was overwhelming. Apart from not being able to understand a single word that was spoken, the sheer volume was an offence to the ears. The women had been placed into the larger of the two carriages that had arrived to escort them to Rodolfo's villa at Rapallo, while Stewart and Pip were awaiting their luggage to be off loaded from the ship and assure its safe transportation to the other smaller coach.

'Master Stewart, please go sit with the ladies, myself and the other servants from the coaches can arrange this. We have no need of you here now.' Pip was shouting to be heard, and rather than reply, Stewart nodded his head and left.

'My word, Milady, did you ever be hearing such a noise before in your life!' Millie's eyes were as big as saucers.

Margaret reached over and patted her maid's hand. 'Millie, all of this is new to me as well, you and I are novices, we are learning together.' Margaret was smiling encouragingly to Millie.

It was then that the carriage door swung open, making both occupants jump in surprise as Stewart leapt up into the coach.

308

'Ladies, you now have me as company,' he grinned broadly at both of them, seeing the startled look on their faces. 'I have been told that my services are not required, and that I am to wait in the coach.'

Margaret looked at Millie who seemed to be beside herself, not knowing whether to stand and curtsy or just nod her head.

'Be at peace, Millie, we are fine…' She reached over for the girl's hand feeling it tremble in her own, then looked towards Stewart with a guarded look on her face.

'My husband has a way of un-nerving people,' she quirked her brow at him in admonishment.

'I am reproved,' replied Stewart, straightening his face. 'You have my sincere apologies. Millie, if I have caused you the slightest embarrassment.'

Millie's eyes by now were as round as two brown pennies, her lips were moving but not one word was uttered.

Stewart coughed lightly, looking towards Margaret. 'I will go now and see if all is ready for us to commence our journey.' Saying this, he doffed his hat and jumped back down from the carriage.

Millie at this point was ringing her hands. 'Oh, Milady, I should not be in here with ye. I will go this minute and ride with Mr Pip.' Millie stood to go but a firm hand pressed her back down into the seat again.

'Millicent Penrose, you have done no wrong. I requested you to be here with me in this carriage, and here you shall stay, do I make myself clear?' Margaret looked at her maid and inclined her head, she then put her head from the window and called. 'And as for Master Stewart, he can ride with Pip in the other coach.' Stewart turned, grinned and gave her a flourishing bow. Sitting back in her seat, Margaret smiled at her maid.

'Believe me, Millie, when he is in a mood such as this, he is incorrigible, and you cannot stop his teasing. He can ride with Pip and annoy him,' she giggled.

Millie looked at her mistress; they had been together as servant and mistress for nearly five years, and in all that time she had never admonished her for anything. In those bad days, she had cried with her as she applied the salves to her body to ease the pain. Millie closed her eyes in remembrance; there had been just the two of them against a hostile household, they had clung together for comfort and support. But, there were boundaries that one did not cross, and Millie knew these, knew her place. She also knew that Master Stewart was an easy man, defying many times convention, but there were places where this had to be upheld. She counted her blessings every day that she had been placed with a lady such as Margaret.

Margaret was watching her maid all this while, seeing the changing expressions on her face, and knew what she had been thinking. Getting up, she came to sit next to her.

'Millie, you are my maid I know that, but you have also been my confidant in times of great darkness in my life, and for that I will always be eternally grateful.' Margaret took her hand and squeezed it. 'My husband knows the affection I hold for you, so you need never be afraid of him.'

As they approached the villa of Rodolfo Visconti, they could see many torches burning brightly outside the front entrance and as many candles burned from within. Rodolfo had come down from the villa and was at that moment greeting Stewart in a way that you would never do in England, by holding him by the shoulders and kissing him on both cheeks. Margaret looked at her maid in surprise.

'Do you think we will be greeted in the same manner?' she asked watching the two of them embrace.

Rodolfo was of the same height as Stewart and, in appearance, had the same slim and athletic build, but Rodolfo was roughly 50 years old. The man had a full head of thick dark hair streaked with grey, and had what could only be described as a classical face. He had a square jaw, with a straight aquiline nose, and such deep brown eyes they could have been mistaken for black. His whole appearance was distinguished, which illustrated his aristocratic roots clearly.

As they came towards the coach, Margaret looked at Millie, smoothing her gown down and pushing her hair with her hands to try and hide the wayward curls that had escaped from round her temples.

The door opened and Stewart helped her down with a warm but amusing smile on his face.

'Rodolfo, may I present to you my wife Margaret.'

Rodolfo stepped forwards with glinting eyes; taking her right hand in both of his, he bowed low over it and kissed her fingers.

'*Benvenuti a casa mia Margherita... sei bellissimo!*'

Margaret looked towards Stewart who seemed to be enjoying himself, then back to Rodolfo who still had her hand in a firm grip.

'Forgive me, Margherita, welcome to my home!' Again he bowed low over her hand. 'You have a very beautiful wife, Stewart!'

Stewart's eyes were alight with pleasure as he looked at her. 'I know, Rodolfo,' was all he offered as he pulled her hand into his arm and guided her up the path.

As they moved towards the villa, Rodolfo came up behind Stewart and nodded to him speaking lowly. '*Hai scelto bene il mio amico.*'

Stewart laughed and slapped him on the back. '*Sono d'accordo con te, Signore.*' As they came into the hall, Margaret pulled Stewart round.

'Stewart, you did not tell me that you could speak Italian, what did you both say?'

Stewart smiled teasingly. 'He told me that I had chosen my wife well, to which I replied that I could not agree more with him.'

Margaret blushed. 'Ohhhh,' was all she said

***

The hour was late when they were finally seated to dinner that evening. Three large candelabra burned a total of eighteen candles between them on the table, enabling Margaret to observe his wife for the first time. Maria Visconti was the most strikingly attractive woman Margaret had ever seen, with poise and grace as regal as any queen. She seemed to have a timeless elegance, even to the way that she used her hands, and inclined her head. Maria Visconti was nearly as old as her husband, though the smoothness of her face belied this, it resembled her husband's in many ways, with the straight nose and the full mouth, but, her face had a softness to it, and her skin was bronzed but not because of the sun. Given all of this, it was her eyes that were the window into her soul, they were a penetrating blue, neither light nor dark, but ones which seemed to change colour like luminous prisms. They were mesmerising.

Later in their room, Stewart was aware that there was something troubling Margaret. Sitting on the bed beside her, he pushed her hair back from her face.

'What disturbs you, Maggie?' he said gently.

Margaret turned to him. 'Not disturbed, Stewart, it is just… his wife is the most beautiful woman I have ever seen,' she breathed.

Stewart laughed softly and stoked her face. 'She is quite breath-taking to look at, I will agree with you there. You should see his daughters.'

The look Margaret gave him was warily questioning.

'Daughters?'

'Yes, Maggie, he has three, and before you ask, they are all married.' He leaned in and kissed her. 'They were spoken for when they were young,' he paused to find the right words to explain.

'Maggie, they do things differently here. Rodolfo comes from a very influential family—bankers. They were matched to other such families when they were but ten years old, then married by the time they were seventeen. It has all to do with lineage, Maggie,' he paused again to take her onto his lap. 'I will show you their portraits tomorrow, you will see for yourself.'

'Does he have any sons?' she queried.

'No, no sons. He took me under his wing when my mother sent me here, and treated me like one. We are not family, but my grandfather and his father were great friends, and Rodolfo stayed many times in our home while he was up at Cambridge. He knows my mother very well, and he is a very educated man, Maggie.'

Margaret leaned against him, linking her fingers with his. There were so many things she did not know about this man, her husband, but she would learn them in time, just as she had revealed her past, he would his one day.

'I love you deeply, Margaret Hamilton, that's all you ever need to know,' he whispered.

***

Breakfast in Rodolfo's villa was an elaborate affair. Mountains of hot food decked the table along with fruits from his orchard. At this moment only Rodolfo and Stewart sat to eat, as it was very early and the women were still sleeping.

'Try some coffee, *mio amico*, it is very good I assure you. I import it.'

Stewart sipped the dark brown liquid, it was slightly bitter, but not an unpleasant taste.

'You are used to tea, no?' offered Rodolfo.

Stewart smiled and nodded.

'I would assume that one gets used to this after a while,' replied Stewart, taking another sip, but this time savouring it in his mouth.

'Sì amico, you must try the fruits also, they are grown in my orchard.'

There was a peaceful silence as both men enjoyed their meal. Stewart looked around the room remembering the last time he had been here, he had been an angry young man, but Rodolfo had such a way, that you unburdened your inner most thoughts to him. He had sat here many times, and on his boat, talking for hours while Rodolfo listened. He was a kind man, but also very stringent, and he had shown him that by enraging his father, he was also hurting his mother. In hindsight,, he had been right of course.

Rodolfo sat back in his chair, wiping his mouth slowly with his napkin, choosing his words before he spoke.

'You were wounded, were you not, amico?' Rodolfo was studying Stewart intently. His soft brown eyes taking in every nuance that his face went through, keenly watching for any change in his behaviour.

Stewart sighed and nodded. 'I was, sir.'

Rodolfo nodded once more. 'When we have finished here you will show me and my physician Paolo Galvani, then we can implement a course of *esercizio* for you, no?'

'I am very grateful for that, sir.' Stewart inclined his head. 'It has caused me some discomfort on this trip, but I have continued to move my arm as the physician in England advised.'

'We will get you well again, *mio figlio*,' Rodolfo replied, and saying this he placed his hand on Stewart's arm.

'Rodolfo, you have done much for me, you healed me that last time I came, and now,' began Stewart, but he was stopped by pressure from Rodolfo's hand.

'The last time you came, you hurt here.' Rodolfo placed his hand on his heart. 'And here,' he then placed his fingers to his temple. 'Your family did much for me also, and I hold your mother in very high regard.'

Stewart looked at the man with many questions in his eyes, and Rodolfo understood and smiled.

'I will tell you some day when maybe we have a few days to spend to talk and to listen to one another, no?'

Stewart smiled once more nodding in acquiescence.

Rodolfo stood up pushing his chair back. 'We will go to my study now, as my physician will be here within the hour. The women can take their meal at their leisure.'

He then spoke something very quickly to one of the servants, who immediately collected their used dishes, while another laid out fresh for Margaret and Maria.

***

They had been in Rapallo now for over two weeks, and the regime that Stewart had been given was not arduous as such, but painful in the beginning. The physician had stated that for his shoulder to work, he had to exercise using the hydro technique, but as there was not a hot spring in or around Rapallo, the nearest being to the north near the mountains. Rodolfo and Stewart would go down to the private cove early every morning, and then again in the early evening to perform the movement functions he had been given in the sea. The water would bear the weight of his arms, allowing them to be lifted more easily.

The first exercise was to place his hands to his chest, and then slowly lift his elbows till they were level with his shoulders, repeating this many times while he was submerged to his neck in the water. The process at first caused Stewart extreme pain, but as the days passed it became easier, and once mastered without pain in the water had to be repeated on land.

The next step was to hold his arms out straight in from of him, then keeping them straight, push them to the sides till they were in a line level with his shoulders again. These processes were repeated again and again, till by the third week Stewart had regained a great deal more movement in his left shoulder. All of this was to encourage more movement in the joints, which had become stiff with lack of use, once this was established, then building on the muscle could be undertaken.

As Stewart returned one evening he took Margaret to their room.

'Maggie, undress to your shift and put on your robe.'

Margaret looked at him as thought he had lost his mind.

'Listen to me, Maggie,' he coaxed all the while he was undressing her. Taking her hand, he guided her through the house down a side exit which led them to the sea. When they reached there, he took her robe, then taking her hand in his he walked her to the seas edge.

As the water lapped at her feet, she jumped, startled by its chill, her toes sinking into the soft sand beneath them.

'How does it feel, Maggie?' he asked gently; he could see the mixed emotions in her face.

Stewart removed his breeches and lifted her in his arms as he waded out till the sea lapped at his waist.

'Trust me, Maggie,' was all he said as he lowered her into the sea.

Margaret shuddered perceptibly as the water lapped over her. She felt as though there was a great pressure on her body, and she clung to him.

'Relax, Maggie, I will not let you go.' His voice was a whisper in her ear, reassuring and safe. Slowly, she let her arms relax from his neck.

'Lay back, Maggie, I have you,' he encouraged.

As she looked up into his face, she smiled and lay back in his arms. The evening was warm and still, and the sea looked like a sheet of glass as the sky reflected into it. The sun was just beginning to set, and she could see the sky darkening in the distance, there was not a sound except for the waves lapping on the shore.

'Did you ever feel such freedom, Maggie?'

Slowly he turned in a circle, letting the water push past her shoulders, as her shift floated out around her legs. Margaret closed her eyes and breathed deeply. Then Stewart let her legs drop to the floor, holding her all the while, to steady her against the seas pull. Bringing her into his arms, he kissed her deeply.

'I think we will come again tomorrow, yes?' he said, smiling at her in acceptance.

Margaret inclined her head as she pressed her body close to his.

'Come, we will go back now and rest before dinner,' he whispered in her ear.

Margaret knew what he meant, as he picked her up and carried her to the shore.

***

The breeze blew cool through the open window, cooling their bodies as they lay entwined on the bed. Stewart was gently stroking her spine while kissing all the parts of her face.

'I told you I would take you into the sea, did I not?' Though she could not see his face, his voice held a smile within it.

'You are my soul, Maggie, the part of me that is everything good and just. Without you I am only half a man and I could not subsist if I did not have you there to guide me.'

He pulled her against him, holding her so tight she thought she could not breathe. He wanted her again, she knew that, just as she wanted him. Closing her eyes, she melted under the power and pressure of his body as he took her, not gently but with an urgency to tell her that neither was whole without the other.

Chapter Thirty-Six
Abduction

It was mid-July and William Masters was sitting on the terrace with his daughter, enjoying the coolness of the early evening, watching the sun's shadows lengthen as it slowly began to set. He sat looking at her as she embroidered some small article of clothing, and he thought that she looked both content and happy, the sickness of the early months having passed, leaving her radiant.

'Did your aunt Elizabeth say when she would be back from Mere?' asked her father.

Looking up Charlotte smiled. 'No, Papa, she went to see her friend Jacqueline, who had just received a new parcel of embroidery silks from France.'

William Masters rubbed his chin. The hour was late, even for Elizabeth; if she had not returned by the time Alexander arrived, they would go look for her.

Suddenly, raised voices could be heard from within the house, making the hairs on the back of William Masters' neck rise.

Standing up, he nodded to his daughter. 'I must go and see what is happening.' With that he was inside the house before Charlotte could reply.

The sight that awaited him froze him to the marrow. Elizabeth's footman and coachman stood in the hall in a state of dishevelment that could only mean they had been in a fight of some kind, or set on by thieves.

'Carter? What has happened? Where is your mistress?' the words came out of him like the repeated fire of a pistol.

'Oh, Mr Masters sir,' William could see that the man was close to tears.

'He has taken my mistress, he said he be having the right, the magistrate also said this, but, Mr Masters sir, he cannot take her, he cannot.'

William Masters' stomach gave an involuntary lurch, and his hands started to shake. Swallowing deeply to try and control his voice, he spoke.

'Who has taken her, Carter?'

'Why her husband, sir, Mr Duncan,' replied Carter in shocked disbelief.

It was at this moment Alexander entered. The look on his face told William Masters that Alexander knew exactly what had happened.

Looking to his father–in–law, he shook his head.

'Thomson, take Carter and Fulton into the kitchen and get Mrs Cottle to feed them, and give them something strong—brandy, if we have any.' Taking off his hat and coat, he turned to William Masters.

'You and I need to talk in the study, sir.' As they turned to go, Alexander saw Charlotte standing in the passage, her embroidery clutched tight to her. Coming towards her, he took her in his arms. She was shaking, he could feel that. Looking around he called to William to get nanny Daisy, then guiding her Alexander took her into the drawing room and sat her on the sofa.

'We will find her Charlotte, you have my word,' he said as he held her hands which were as cold as ice. Seeing a shawl draped over one of the winged chairs he took it and wrapped it around his wife's legs.

'Charlotte, everything will be well, you have to believe me, we will get her back.' It was then that Daisy entered.

'Master Charles?' queried Alexander.

'He is asleep, being watched over by Lilly, sir,' came her answer.

Alexander nodded. 'Please sit with Charlotte, as I have to speak with Mr Masters urgently.'

Daisy came across the room, and sitting next to Charlotte, she took her hand. 'We will be fine, Master Alexander, you can go about your business, I will stay right here.'

'Thank you,' was all he managed to say before he left the room.

***

William Masters was pacing the room; several times he stopped to speak but no words would come, till finally Alexander broke the silence.

'We have to get legal advice, sir, and for that I must leave with all haste for Salisbury, with the vain hope that James will be there and not in London or Bath.' Alexander paused.

'We do not even know as yet where he has taken her; all Carter and Fulton were able to inform me was that they were requested to get down from the coach, then my uncle's men took the reins, riding away with my aunt and her husband inside.' Alexander put his head in his hands.

'Dear God, why? Why?'

'Can the law do nothing to stop him?' shouted Mr Masters who had at last found his voice.

Alexander shook his head once again. 'No, sir, he has every legal right to take his wife wherever he chooses under the law, she has no rights at all, not even to divorce him. I am informed that only an act of parliament can do that,' he paused once more.

'But that is not all, they tell me that he also has the rights to beat her if he so wishes, and there is one woman who can stand testimony to that better than anyone: Margaret, my cousin's wife.' Alexander's voice held such bitterness within it.

William Masters looked at Alexander astounded. 'Dear God, man, what are you saying?'

'She was beaten, abused and used from the tender age of eighteen, and all with the blessing of her father,' came Alexander's cold reply.

316

William Masters sank down heavily into a chair. He thought of his own daughter, and the kind man who stood before him, he could never imagine allowing that to happen to Charlotte—the man would be dead.'

Alexander rubbed his fingers at the sides of his temples and over his brow. 'I must go and find James.'

As he turned to leave the room William Masters grabbed his arm.

'You can go nowhere at this time of evening. *WE* will leave at first light, and if we have to go to London, then so be it.' No sooner had his words been spoken, there was a knock on the door. Alexander looked at William with trepidation before calling, 'Come in.'

Spike opened the door gently and stood hat in hand at the entrance, looking at the astonished faces of the two men who stood before him.

Bowing to both he spoke, 'Master Alexander, Mr Masters sir, wherever you be a going, I will be going with ye.' He saw the two men begin to protest and stood his ground. 'If you do not allow me, then ye will have to dismiss me, for I will be a going with ye. Pip and myself swore an oath many years ago to be protecting our Mistress. Pip be elsewhere at this present time, but I will not be a breaking mine now, sirs.'

Alexander looked at the man before him. Seeing the determination and love for his mistress written on his face, he could not forbid this man, no more than he could William Masters. Holding out his hand to Spike, Alexander nodded.

'We will leave for Salisbury at first light to find our friend James. It could mean that we may have to travel as far as London.' Alexander stopped to look at Spike. 'We have to seek help from James' lawyer Edward Bearcroft.'

'You have no worries with me, Master Alexander. I may not be as young as I was, but I can still be riding a horse, and use a blade if need be.'

Alexander turned and went to the desk to pour three whiskies, but was stopped by Spike.

'Begging your pardon, Master Alexander, I will not be partaking, as I wish to have a clear head for our journey tomorrow.' Bowing to both, he continued. 'I will see ye both at first light on the edge of the gardens.' With that he turned and left.

***

Having reached Salisbury, they were told that James Fairweather could be found at the house of Sir Henry Portman, at The Royal Crescent in Bath. The three men acquired a room at the Sun and Lamb Coaching Inn in the town, but Spike refused to stay with them, instead he slept in the stables guarding the horses, and was fed a hearty breakfast by one of the serving maids in the morning. Spike mused to himself that he had had the better arrangement.

The ride to Bath was a long one, stopping once, only to take refreshment for themselves and rest the horses; it was late afternoon when they finally arrived. As they dismounted, Alexander looked around him at the crescent of houses that swept out facing a stretch of parkland; they were majestic in themselves alone, and the people that lived in them… well they were wealthy beyond his dreams. The last two times he had been here he had had not the time or the presence of mind to take in such beauty; now with the sun low in the sky it shone on all the windows at the front of the houses, as though they glowed from within. Shifting his jacket slightly and trying to tap some of the dust from his clothes, he mounted the stairs to the front door.

On receiving them, Sir Henry was stunned beyond credibility at what had transpired. They would not only have Bearcroft's help but that of his own lawyer Sir Richard Sutton, who was at this present time in Bath drawing up documents regarding the purchase of a house in the Crescent for his daughter Catherine and James. In fact, James was with him at this present time, but would return by dinner.

'Did you say that your gardener came with you?' queried Sir Henry.

Mr Masters smiled. 'Believe me, the man is more than just a gardener, sir. He and Milady Elizabeth have been friends since they were very young. When he knew what had befallen her, nothing would have stopped him from coming with us.'

'Where is the man now?' Sir Henry asked, looking around, thinking that he might be at the back of the room.

'He is with your servants, sir, he would not even enter by the front door,' answered William Masters.

Sir Henry nodded slowly in reply.

'My wife, thank God, is in London with her daughter, to be fitted—for the hundredth time might I add—for their wedding attire, else she would have the whole country in uproar.' He turned and walked towards the door. 'Come, we will await James in the library.'

***

It was late in the evening, and as the men sat in the library, Sir Richard explained yet again that there was not a court in the land that had jurisdiction to command Andrew Duncan to bring his wife back. She was his wife, and as such, she was his to command.

'We must wait to see what his demands are, for he will have demands, of that I am certain. Where is her son?'

Sir Henry moved uneasily in his chair and coughed softly. 'He is still in Italy, recovering from his wound. When he hears of this, dear God, he will kill the man.'

'They were my thoughts exactly,' commented Alexander, 'better he is where he is, with the chance we may be able to secure her safe return before he arrives back in England at the end of August.'

'Quite,' said Sir Richard.

***

Elizabeth sat in the corner of the carriage watching her husband. The fear that had first encircled her had subsided slightly, as she now saw that he meant her no harm—or so it seemed. Exactly where they were headed, she had no notion, but as they progressed, her instincts told her that it was north. He had not spoken a word since he took her and her coach that afternoon; by now she was sure that the whole house knew, and were maybe in pursuit of her. On thinking on a more logical basis, this could not be so, as how were they to know in which direction. Elizabeth pulled her shawl around her, it was becoming dark now, and she felt chill. One thing she was certain of, she must stay calm at all costs. Her fear would only give Andrew Duncan an edge; he would like no better than to have her at his mercy.

'Well, Lizzie, how will you like being my wife again after so many years?'

Elizabeth jumped—his voice was low and smooth, not demanding. She stiffened slightly, and pushed herself into the corner, then trying to steady her voice she spoke.

'What are you talking about, Andrew? We have been separated for over twenty-three years, your wife? How can you call me so?'

From the dimness within the carriage, she saw his mouth go up into a smile which she knew of old held no warmth within it.

'We are still married in the eyes of the law, Lizzie, or had you forgotten that I have every right to claim you, take you where I will, and do what I will.'

Elizabeth knew that had it been day, he would have seen her face pale, but she assumed that he could also sense her fear, he was not a stupid man, and her heart was beating so fast now she could hear it pounding in her ears. Her first thoughts were to calm herself; it would do her no good now to swoon; if she did, then he had won.

Her voice cracked slightly as she went to speak, coughing lightly she tried again.

'Have you not thought, Andrew, that my family will be in pursuit of us?' It was a gamble, but one she was prepared to take.

He laughed softly. 'Come now, Lizzie, we both know that could not be, for if they did, and they took you, then they would be the kidnappers in the eyes of the law.'

As Andrew Duncan leaned from the window, he called for the footman to look for an inn to rest for the night. Elizabeth froze.

'Just so you know, you will sleep with me, Lizzie, so that I can keep an eye on you, and if I decide to take my pleasure of you, I will.'

She knew—hoped—that he was just trying to terrify her—he was doing it very well if that was the case—so that she would not attempt to escape, but she also knew Andrew Duncan well; and if he were to drink, there was no telling what he might do. Though in all fairness he had never once hurt her.

The coach pulled up and as she descended, she saw a sign above the door denoting that it was "The Miller of Mansfield", a coaching house of some substantial means, within the boundaries of Oxfordshire. Dear God, had they driven that far!

They were shown to a room with a large latticed window which overlooked the road. There was a bed set into one corner of the room beside the window, and under the window was a table with an old mirror. Screened off on the other side, Elizabeth gathered, was the chamber pot. She shuddered at the thought. Three candles burned in the room, one in the sconce above the bed, the other two were placed each side of the mirror.

'I would take off your gown, Lizzie, as you will not have another till we reach our destination. The maid will bring up hot water for you to bath, and I will go and secure us some food, which we will eat here.' He had pre-empted her thoughts of eating in the tap room downstairs. 'I do not want you to be bothered with such people as frequent the dining area of this establishment.'

Elizabeth stood there, staring at him as though he was speaking in some foreign tongue.

'My man will keep watch outside, so that no one bothers you.' He smiled but not deviously, but the intonation was there: do not bother to try and run, you will not succeed.

***

Alexander sat deep in thought in the library of Sir Henry's house in Bath; it had been two days nearly since his aunt had been taken. Edward Bearcroft was now with them, having arrived late the previous evening. The man had been tracking Andrew Duncan for some time now, and as far as he was aware, they were on their way back to Dumfries, on the borders of Scotland, where he had apparently been staying with some distant relative, a minister. Tracking him as he progressed to his destination was another matter. The only information he could ascertain was where they *had* been, not where they were going. This had been a closely kept secret, lest they were forestalled on their journey, he surmised. He did not hear James Fairweather enter till he spoke.

'Alex?' his voice was low. 'You realise that there is nothing that can be done until they reach their destination.'

Alexander breathed deeply through his nose and stood up.

'I only know, James, is that if we do not find her within the month, my cousin—your friend—will kill him.'

James came to stand in front of him, taking his arm. 'We will get her back before then; I am sure of that.'

Alexander turned his head sharply to look at his friend. 'How! We do not even know what he wants in return. The Willows? It is not my aunt's to give. Does he mean to make Stewart give him the estate? Or sell it and give him the money? Dear God, James, HE WILL KILL HIM FIRST!'

James rubbed his hands over his face several times. 'I know, we must get her back at all costs.' As James said this, an authoritative voice spoke from the door.

'That is precisely what we will do.' Edward Bearcroft came in and seated himself in a chair. 'But we have to wait until they have arrived at their destination—the house in Dumfries—it will be much easier than chasing a moving target,' he paused to look at both men. 'We have to be prudent, in that he must not suspect we are pursuing him.'

'We have people pursuing him?' questioned James.

'But of course, that is how we are acquainted with the fact that they lodged overnight in Oxfordshire on the first day, further than that we will not be aware of, as it is too great a distance to report back.'

'Just how long will it take them?' questioned Alexander.

'It is my belief that they will follow on up the west side of England, through the Shires—Warwickshire, Staffordshire, Cheshire, Lancashire and Cumbria—till they cross the border to Scotland and Dumfriesshire. It will be an arduous journey, and a long one, as no doubt they will stop twice in each day—midday for lunch, rest, water and feed the horses, and then at night to eat once more and rest. In all probability, they will journey for over a week.' Bearcroft pinched the top of his nose. 'There is nothing we can do but wait. This has been a cautiously thought out scheme and as vigilantly concealed. There was no inclination that the man planned to do such a thing.'

Alexander paced the room several times before he spoke. 'Stewart will be home in maybe four weeks?' Then he turned to James. 'Your wedding is in five weeks, and if she is not returned before then, I swear if he harms one hair of her head, *I* will kill him.'

***

Elizabeth had lost track of the days, but she considered that they had been on the road for at least a week now. She had been told by Andrew Duncan that this would be their last night before they reached their destination the following day. As she bathed herself, she could feel that her flesh had shrunk, she was thinner and the bodice of her dress seemed loose no matter how hard she tightened the laces. She had kept her hair up in a tight bun at the back of her head, but when she brushed it at night, she could feel the dust from the road in it, it was hard to the touch—unclean—like she herself felt. He had not come near her apart from that first night—Elizabeth shivered slightly in remembrance. They had eaten their meal in silence, when he was requested to go downstairs as a certain party wished to speak with him. Elizabeth had undressed quickly to her shift, and then getting into bed she had pushed herself up against the wooden panelling of the wall which run down one side of the bed. Dear God, she had prayed that he would find elsewhere to sleep that night, but no, he had returned somewhat drunk. She had watched him undress, thinking that he had not lost his figure as most men of his age, but had kept the toned body of his youth, albeit softer now—the look that comes with age. As he approached the bed, she saw that he had left on his shirt—Elizabeth closed her eyes and sent up a prayer, for if he wanted to take her now—and he could—she would be powerless to stop him.

As he lay down beside her, she could smell the whisky on his breath. Elizabeth pulled the cover up to her chin; her whole body was rigid.

Turning to face her, his eyes roamed over her, and then he gently pulled the cover down to her waist.

'Lizzie.' His hand stroked her shoulder then down over her arm. 'Ye are still the soft rounded lass that I married all those years ago.' His voice had reverted to the Scottish bur he had when she met him. It always did this when he drank, as then he was unguarded, wanting to go back to his roots. He had stroked her face, and then his fingers moved over her lips.

Elizabeth had closed her eyes. No other man had ever touched her, caressed her, since he left. Her body was motionless, but it still remembered how to react to a man's touch. She swallowed hard.

He felt her reaction, no man was blind to that, had she not loved him deeply—once.

'Rest in peace, Lizzie, I will not disturb ye.' Stroking her cheek with his finger, he turned onto his back and was asleep in seconds.

Elizabeth remembered that she had shook so badly she thought she would wake him. How her body could have betrayed her so, but then it remembered when she had loved him, even though her mind could not forget what he had done.

Elizabeth stood now, holding onto the table and sobbed. She had lived her life through her son and been without love since she was twenty-four. She did not hear Andrew Duncan come in, and as he came up behind her, he turned her and held her into him, not in anger or wanting, but in sorrow.

'Dinnae cry, lass, yer ordeal is over. Tomorrow ye will go home to yer family.'

Elizabeth sat down heavily on a stool, her eyes searching his face. 'What are you saying, Andrew?' He had been drinking again.

'I have been a very angry, jealous, wicked, aye wicked man. I blamed yer father—and still do—for what happened, but I myself let it eat at me like a canker, and the more I let it, the more it grew. I didnae even recognise my own self, Lizzie,' he moved to the bed and sat, head bowed, his hands hanging limply between his knees.

'But this last week, being with ye, lying beside ye, knowing ye for what ye are, a kind loving woman, who did nay harm to anyone.' Andrew Duncan shook his head.

'I did mean to take ye back with me and live with ye as my wife. I thought I cannae have the estate, but I can at least have ye,' he stopped, got up and walked to the door.

'I will nay trouble ye again. I will sleep in the next room tonight, ye can go to yer bed in peace, Lizzie.'

Elizabeth called to him before he reached the door. 'Andrew, come back with me, see your son, your Grandson.'

'Nay, Lizzie, there are some bridges even ye cannae mend. I will see ye afore ye go.' He closed the door quietly behind him.

Elizabeth spent a sleepless night, as many things revolved in her head. She rose with the first light, washed, dressed and waited for Andrew to come. She heard sounds from the road outside, as already a coach had arrived, in these places no one ever slept.

Andrew Duncan came bearing a tray with hot rolls of some kind, honey and tea, and then they sat in silence eating, each to his own thoughts. As he wiped his mouth with his handkerchief, he looked up at Elizabeth.

'Tell your son that evil breeds evil, remind him of that, for he has my temper, but he has your heart. I will see you to your coach now, Lizzie.' He had reverted back to his English accent once more—he was sober and still wanted her to return.

Elizabeth sighed. 'What a waste of two lives, Andrew,' she placed her hand on his, and he turned his in acceptance and held hers.

'We learn our lessons too late, Lizzie—make sure your son knows that.'

'Our son, Andrew, our son. It was he who paid your debt.'

Andrew Duncan nodded. 'I know, Lizzie, else I would be in the colonies, or in prison.'

Elizabeth reached over and kissed his cheek, then stood and made her way to the stairs to go down to the coach.

As he helped her up into the coach, he handed her a letter.

'Please give your—my—son this. Tell him to read it sometime when he is alone and has some moments to spare. God go with you.' Nodding to Elizabeth, he closed the door, and called for the coachmen to go.

***

Elizabeth had reached Mere just over a week later. Andrew Duncan's coachmen had left her and her coach at Margaret's house, taking two horses to get them back to the Angel Inn in Mere, where they would leave the horses and make their way back north, on the next stage coach.

Elizabeth looked up at Margaret's house; closing her eyes she smoothed her hair back and straightened her dress before knocking on the front door.

Margaret's butler Giles was at a loss for words when he saw her. No word had been heard for over two weeks, and to say that he was astounded was the least of his emotions at this moment.

'Milady Hamilton! I... we...'

Elizabeth smiled and held his arm. 'I am safe and well, Giles, I just need to get to my home, but I have no coachmen to drive me.'

'Milady, I will get you two this minute, please come to the drawing room, may I bring you some tea? Something to eat? Oh my word, I have to tell cook.'

With that he disappeared into the back of the house.

Elizabeth made her way across the hall and into the drawing room. Looking around her once, she closed her eyes and breathed deeply. She was nearly home. Walking towards the window, she looked out onto Margaret's small garden where the apple trees were heavy with fruit.

'Oh, Andrew, if only we could turn back time.'

***

Alexander sat deep in thought on the terrace at the Willows. Charlotte and William Masters were sitting opposite in pleasant conversation, when, from inside the house, there could be heard many voices speaking at once. Alexander looked up at his father–in–law, and then both men ran to the door.

It was some moments before their eyes became accustomed to the darkness in the hallway, but then Alexander saw Elizabeth and stood stock still.

'Aunt,' he whispered.

Elizabeth nodded in reply, just before she was swept into his arms. Behind him Elizabeth could see Charlotte in tears in her father's arms. Holding out her hand, Charlotte came and joined them, meanwhile all around them voices were calling, and people laughing, it seemed that the whole household were in the hall.

Elizabeth looked around her.

'Where is my grandson?'

***

As Molly took the last of the pins from her mistress' hair, she loosened her shift and helped Elizabeth into the warm hip bath that Mrs Cottle and she had prepared.

'Lean you back, Milady, so I may pour water over your hair to wash it. Cook has sent me this new soap she made.' Holding it up to her nose, she sniffed. 'And I do believe it smells of lavender, Milady.'

Elizabeth relaxed for the first time in three weeks, letting Molly massage her head, cleansing her hair and body. When she had finished, she allowed her to dry her and dress her, as Elizabeth had not the energy to lift up her hand. As Molly placed the clean shift over her head, Elizabeth took her hand and looked up into her face.

'Bless you, Molly, and thank you,' was all she said.

Molly inclined her head and started to slowly comb out her mistress' hair.

'You will be having a visitor in the kitchen afore ye sit to dinner, Mistress,' began Molly, 'and cook has prepared a special dinner for ye, roast lamb, your favourite.' Molly smiled at her mistress as she looked at her through the glass.

'Welcome back, Milady.'

Elizabeth had taken Molly as her maid some twelve years ago now, it was when Pip's wife had died, and Molly was just twenty. She had served her faithfully since then, kept her council when needed, and listened when there had been no one else around.

Elizabeth's thoughts kept straying now to Andrew Duncan. He had meant to take her back to Scotland, and for them to live as man and wife, of that she was sure. He had also wanted no money for her return that too had become apparent as the days past, so why had he then released her. She had been terrified in the beginning, but as the days progressed, she learned not to fear him. He had been different somehow, but for the moment she could not say why.

Smoothing her gown down, she looked at her reflection in the glass. There were dark circles under her eyes, and her hair seemed to have more grey streaks than before. Her teeth were good for her age she thought, though she had lost three from the back the rest seemed fine. She always rubbed salt into her gums and over her teeth at night, rinsing well afterwards with a small amount of alcohol. Her father had taught her that—he had said it cleansed the mouth. Her hands were smooth, but then they would be, for what work had she ever done, embroidery and writing? Now cook's hands, and those of Spike, they showed the rigours of their labours. Andrew had had smooth hands, she remembered when he had stroked her face, beautiful hands with long fingers, just like Stewart's. Elizabeth shook herself; her mind was wandering as it had done many times since she had left Keswick. Wiping her hands across her face she breathed deeply, turned, and left the room.

As she descended the stairs, she knew who would be waiting for her in the kitchen, she smiled in expectancy at the thought. Opening the door, she saw Spike sitting drinking a mug of ale.

'Good evening, Spike,' was all she said.

Spike stood slowly, turning to face his mistress, his hands clasped in front of him. She could see him trying to speak as his mouth moved slowly as though chewing something. Walking towards him, she placed a hand on his arm and inclined her head.

'Thank you, Spike.'

His smile said everything he needed to say, as Spike knew that if he spoke the tears would come, and that would not be right in front of his mistress. Instead, he inclined his head, turned and went out the back door.

Mrs Cottle who had been standing watching this shook her head.

'Well I be...'

Elizabeth smiled, again; she had been doing that a lot in the last twenty-four hours she pondered.

'I will see him tomorrow, Mrs Cottle, and I thank you in advance for the aromatic dinner that my senses detect.'

Mrs Cottle folded her arms about her ample bosom. 'Welcome home, Mistress.'

Chapter Thirty-Seven
Return Home

Margaret sat peacefully under the shade of a hanging grape vine which seemed to stretch for ever into the distance. She had observed that Maria Visconti had been watching her for some moments before she spoke.

'Margherita, you are with child, no?'

Margaret looked at her friend in bewilderment. 'But...' the words died on her lips.

'It is on your face, Margherita, and besides, I know such things.' Her gaze never left Margaret as she spoke. 'It will be a boy child, but you will have a daughter, two in fact, and one more son.'

'But how do you know?' Margaret was stopped once more by Maria holding up her hand.

'I knew before I married Rodolfo that I would never bear him a son. I told him this.'

'What did he say?' interrupted Margaret.

Maria Visconti smiled that enigmatic smile Margaret had seen that first night.

'I wished to release him from his marriage bond, but he said, "*Non ha alcuna conseguenza, poiché un bambino è un dono di Dio*."' Maria smiled. 'It is of no consequence, for any child is a gift from God.'

Margaret was astounded at her response. 'If only my father had been that wise,' Margaret replied softly.

'Your father, I do not understand,' Maria said with some reservation.

'My mother had two sons and two daughters. My father saw no use for daughters. I was five when my sister was born, and within the week he had sold her to a wonderful man, a miller by trade. He made him a merchant on the other side of England—they could have no children of their own—and my sister was raised with love and kindness. I was sold for marriage to a man older than your husband when I was just eighteen. My sister, thank God, was spared that.'

There was so much bitterness and regret in Margaret's voice that Maria Visconti came and sat next to her, taking her in her arms.

'But you have a wonderful, loving husband now, you are his world, Margherita.'

Margaret, wiping the tears from her eyes, turned to Maria. 'I know, he is my world also.'

Maria Visconti pulled Margaret's head to her shoulder and rocked her gently, whispering soft comforting words in Italian as she did so.

***

Pip was packing the last of Stewart's things into the trunk when Millie entered carrying Margaret's gowns which had just been pressed.

'Oh, begging yer pardon, Mr Pip, I did not be knowing that ye were here, I will go and return later.'

Pip looked at her and beckoned with his hand. 'Come in, child, we can be doing this together.'

Pip watched her as she carefully folded the gowns laying them neatly into the other chest.

'Are you ready to be leaving tomorrow, Millie?'

Millie looked up from the chest and smiled. 'Oh yes, Master Pip, it has been a wonderful journey, one I could never have been dreaming of in my life, Mr Pip, but I miss home I do, and Mrs Cottle, Lillie and Daisy… and Master Charles…' her voice trailed away.

'I know, Millie,' answered Pip knowingly. 'You just want to be home, yes?'

Millie grinned broadly and nodded her head.

'Be finishing your packing now, then we can maybe take a walk in the gardens—would you be liking that Millie?'

'Yes, Mr Pip, I think I would.'

Their peace was shattered when Stewart burst into the room.

'Pip, have you seen Margaret?' Pip raised his eyebrows, looked to the side where Millie seemed to have been struck to stone and coughed.

Stewart stopped, turned towards Millie and nodded. 'My sincere apologies, Millie, I did not mean to startle you so, but have you seen your mistress?'

Millie still stood there with her hands over her mouth.

'Master Stewart, if I may speak, I do believe that the Mistress be in the garden with Milady Maria.' Pip nodded for Stewart to go. Stewart nodded back, turned and left.

'Why does he terrify you so, Millie? I be putting him in his place if he do become too mischievous. You need not fear him, he is a kind young man.' Pip's voice lowered a fraction, 'Albeit he be a bit impulsive at times,' he finished.

Placing the last of the clothes and closing the lid, he looked up at Millie.

'Right, young lady, do we be ready for our walk?'

***

The air was thick and sultry and it was only 10am. Margaret could hear the crickets singing loudly—the day would be very hot. She walked peacefully along the length of the grape vine, admiring the huge bulbous fruits hanging in great clusters underneath, wondering how such a small stem could hold such weight. Suddenly her world went black, as two hands came over her eyes, and lips

327

pressed themselves to the side of her neck. Turning, Maggie put her arms around her husband's neck.

'I was with Rodolfo and he asked if my wife had told me yet. I asked him what, to which he replied, "*Go ask*," so here I am.'

Maggie smiled, then giggled, then laughed out loud as she held his face in her hands, while Stewart's eyes darted across her face.

'Margaret Hamilton, are you telling me...' Stewart did not finish his sentence as Margaret nodded her head vigorously in answer.

Taking her into his arms, he kissed her deeply for some moments, only to release her and swing her around in his arms. Then pulling her close he kissed the top of her head.

'Oh God, Maggie, I thought, I thought,' he swallowed audibly.

'You thought, after what happened last time, I would not be able to have another child.' Margaret finished.

Sweeping her legs up, he carried her to the bench that Margaret had been sitting on, then cradling her to him, he took her hands, bringing them up to kiss her fingers.

'What more can a man ask of this world, to have a loving wife and be blessed with children. I have thought of young Charles every day, now he will have a sister or brother and a cousin!' he exclaimed.

***

Their last meal together was both a happy and sad occasion. The evening was hot, and both doors at either end of the room were open, allowing a warm sensuous breeze in from the gardens. Rodolfo had implied that he and Maria would journey to England the following year to stay for some months.

'I am not getting younger, my son, and if we do not come to visit soon, I fear we never will. With old age come other problems, no?' Rodolfo raised his glass to his wife. 'We will go, Maria, yes?' She in turn raised her glass and inclined her head to him.

Margaret thought that the Italians shared a hidden language of love and passion that the English did not, but she raised her glass to Stewart, their eyes meeting in understanding across the table.

Rodolfo stood and looked towards Stewart. 'Go, my young lovers, enjoy one another while you may, for no one knows what tomorrow may bring.' He raised his glass. '*La tua Salute,* my friends.'

Stewart stood and bowed to Maria, then came to Rodolfo clasping the man in a tight hug.

'I can never repay you for all you have done for me.'

Rodolfo slapped him on the back and then kissed him on both cheeks.

'*Dio ti benedica figlio, via in buona salute.*'

***

Margaret watched him undress, marvelling at the colour of his body. Over the weeks, from the daily exercise he had taken in the sea, the sun had coloured it to a burnished gold. They had both washed in the afternoon, inside a walled room within the garden, with barrels of water warmed by the hot Mediterranean sun. She had washed her hair and then her body, ladling the warm water over her, feeling her skin tingle and come alive. Where could they do such a thing in England? She had made Millie bathe as well, and remembered smiling when she had called to her, stating that she was out in the open, bare as an egg, washing, and what would her mother say. But when she had appeared, Margaret saw her small round face gleaming and blushed pink, as her hair dripped around her shoulders and over the robe Margaret had given her. Millie had liked it, she was sure.

The light in the room was dim, with just the one candle burning near the mirror. She could see his hair was soft and wavy about his shoulders, and he was clean shaven; slowly he came to the bed, his eyes never leaving hers, then he sat astride her, his hands smoothing her neck and shoulders, travelling down her arms then up again over her stomach to her breasts. Pulling her up to him, he placed her legs around him and then gently lifted her onto him, holding her there, looking deep into her eyes before his mouth came over hers. Taking her hands in his, he laid her back down again, keeping her hands under his beside her head, while he stretched full length on top of her. He moved so slow and gentle that Maggie wanted to scream as the sensations erupted within her, till at last she could contain herself no longer and cried out to him. Then he gradually lowered his head to her shoulder and she felt the shudder run through him.

They lay there, waiting for their breathing to ease before they moved, then Stewart lifted his head and brought his hand up to push the hair from her face, kissing her intensely.

'My God, Margaret Hamilton, you will stop my heart one day,' he said as he rolled onto his side pulling her against him.

'My body feels as though it is under some kind of strange charm when I take you,' he sighed.

Margaret laughed lightly into his chest, as Stewart pulled up the sheet to cover them from the breeze that came through the open window.

'We must sleep now, Maggie, we have a long ride ahead of us tomorrow.' He kissed her nose. 'I love you, Margaret Hamilton,' were the last words he said before she heard his breathing take on the usual rhythm of slumber.

Nestling close to him she breathed in the scent of his body, 'And I you,' she murmured, and then listening to his heart beating under her ear, she drifted peacefully off to asleep.

***

Pip and Millie stood on the deck of the Abigail watching the last sight of Genova fade into the distance, the sun was low in the sky, and within the half hour it would be completely dark. The sea was calm, and the air warm, with just the breeze as the ship ploughed its way out into the open sea. Stewart had taken Margaret below; she had been tired, and the sickness she had suffered before was manifesting itself again.

Pip turned to look at Millie and smiled. She had been on a voyage that another woman of her standing, or age, could only dream of. She had told him that it was as though she had dreamt it all, and soon she would wake up to the sound of Mrs Cottle shouting her orders. There had been a young man amongst the household in Rapallo that had been taken with her. He had watched him look her way, then follow her, making sure that he was at hand if she needed help with anything. Pip smiled to himself as he thought that Millie had not the slightest inclination that the young man thought her comely. Pip observed that when they left, the young man had stood at the back on the porch, looking very crestfallen. Millie did not understand just how lovely she was. As the night fell over them, Pip placed his hand on her shoulder.

'Let us be going to our beds now, Millie, we have a whole day at sea tomorrow.' Millie nodded and led the way to their cabins.

***

The weather had been fine till they reached the Bay of Biscay once more, where both Margaret and Millie had taken to their bunks. The ship had pitched and tossed alarmingly at one stage, but the Captain had been unfazed by it all, stating that he had sailed in weather more perilous than this around the Cape. Thankfully, they did not call into the port of Le Havre on the return journey, but sailed straight to Portsmouth.

Due to the bad weather they had encountered round the Bay of Biscay, they docked in the early hours of the morning, instead of the afternoon. The two coaches that were awaiting them, had been there some hours, and as the captain refused to unload his vessel in the dark, accommodation was found for them all at an inn in the town. The clientele within the inn were either sailors from the Royal Navy, or Merchants, and Stewart had voiced his unease in letting Millie occupy a room alone, for as they entered the establishment, many heads turned and watched the two women precede up the stairs to their rooms.

'I think it wise, Pip, that Millie shares a room with her mistress.' He nodded towards the tap room where many loud raucous voices could be heard, yelling unsavoury comments regarding the women.

'I agree with ye, Master Stewart. I will be sleeping in a chair at the bottom of the stairs this night, ye can go to your bed. I have my blade with me, and any man thinking to go in that room, will have to kill me first.'

Stewart looked at the man; he had been at his side for most of his life, more a friend than a servant.

'I cannot ask you to do that, Pip,' he responded, looking at Pip startled. 'You will get no sleep.'

'I am not asking ye for your permission, Master Stewart. I am a telling ye what I will be doing. Now, if ye be excusing me, sir, I be going to my post.'

Taking a chair from the room, he placed it firmly at the bottom of the stairs as Stewart disappeared into the darkness above.

Stewart mounted the stairs thinking that it was now around 3am and that neither man would be getting much sleep this night. It also occurred to him that the mayhem from the tap room must continue incessantly both day and night. Portsmouth was a town that never slept.

***

Elizabeth stood watching the road that led up to the house. They should have arrived in the early morning, but it was now late afternoon and there was still no sign. William had stated that sometimes ships are delayed because of bad weather, this could, as he explained, add days onto a journey, depending on the severity of it. Nevertheless, this did nothing to quell Elizabeth's fears; she wanted them home, they had been gone too long. There were many things she had to say to her son, but she would tell him everything when they had had time to rest, maybe in a couple of days. The letter from his father was upstairs, safely tucked away in her jewellery box. It was thick, maybe five or six pages long. She had known after the first night on the road that he had meant her no harm. He was changed, although aloof and terse at times, there was an underlying difference which she could not quite fathom. Contrary to what he had said that last night at the George in Keswick, he had ridden back with her as far as the Miller of Mansfield in Oxfordshire—the first stop on their outward journey. When she had asked him why he had taken her, he had shaken his head and told her it was of no consequence. His men would see her safely back to Mere, to Margaret's house there; they would then take the Stage Coach and meet him for the journey home. It did not strike her as strange then, but now having had time to consider what had happened. The men had been nothing but solicitous towards her; in fact, they had been that way since Andrew had first taken possession of the coach. They were not of the ilk that his past associates had been. Elizabeth's head was spinning, and the more she thought the more incongruous things became. What had he said that first night...

'*Ye are still the soft rounded lass that I married all those years ago.*'

Her hands came up to her mouth, as realisation came to her—he had meant for them to be together again.

'Oh, Andrew,' she whispered, understanding now the poignancy and futility of it all.

The noise of the wheels on the gravel brought her thoughts back, as she watched the coaches slowly draw up before the house.

When Elizabeth came out onto the porch, Stewart was just descending—he looked tanned and full of health—then he turned to help Margret down, who looked as though her face had been dusted with flour, so pale was she that Elizabeth thought she might collapse at any moment. Elizabeth held her by the waist, firmly nodding a greeting to her son.

'Margaret, my child, are you ill?'

331

Margaret smiled wanly. 'I am well, Mother, just with child, and I fear the sickness has taken me again this time as it did the first.'

Stewart just caught her as she was about to fall, lifting her in his arms he walked quickly into the house, calling to Lillie to bring a bowl and quickly, as Elizabeth followed with Millie in her wake.

'Oh, Milady, she has been that ill on the journey, we did stop five times. I must go now to the kitchen and ask Mrs Cottle to brew her some mint tea, for I do believe that helped her greatly the last time.'

Elizabeth waved her hand to Millie and headed for the drawing room. William was there with Charlotte, who was heavy with child, and looked like she might explode at any second. At this moment though she was cradling her sister's head in her lap as Lillie held the bowl under her face.

'Stewart, take Margaret to her room now, and when you have settled her, come down so that I can greet you properly.'

Bending to kiss Margaret on the cheek, she took her hand. 'I will come to see you as soon as I have organized things here.'

Smoothing her hand over Margaret's forehead, she watched as Stewart lifted her and took her from the room. Turning, she saw that Charlotte was standing, holding her side with her lips pursed in what looked like pain.

'Charlotte, sit down this minute,' she ordered as she walked to the fire to get a foot stool.

'Here, place your feet on this,' Elizabeth lifted her feet onto the stool, and then looked up at William shaking her head.

'This is not how I envisaged the homecoming at all.' There was laughter in her eyes, but also worry.

'Where is Alexander? Why is he not home now?'

William Masters took Elizabeth by the elbow and raised her to her feet.

'Alexander will be here at his usual time, you sit with Charlotte while I go in search of some tea, as the whole house appears to be in a state of flux at this present moment, so I shall dispense with the bell and go to the kitchen myself.'

Charlotte took her hand and smiled happily. 'It is wonderful news, Aunt Elizabeth, is it not?' Elizabeth breathed deeply and smiled back.

'It is, Charlotte, it is just that I have many things in my head at this present time, and this is just one new one to add.'

Charlotte laughed softly. 'They have not even seen young Charles yet, I believe that Daisy took him back upstairs out of the way.'

Elizabeth patted Charlottes hand and squeezed it. 'I know that Stewart will go directly to fetch him; in fact, I would wager he is with them now,' answered Elizabeth, laughing also.

***

Millie had taken Margaret's gown from her; laying her back onto the soft plumped pillows of the bed, she covered her with a sheet. As she went to go, Margaret took her hand to stop her.

'Millicent Penrose, you are a treasure to me, you know that? I wish you could find someone who would love you and take care of you, just as I have. You deserve that for you are a loyal kind loving young lady.'

Millie looked at her mistress and smiled. 'I could not be doing that, Mistress, for how would I be here to help ye? If I be having a husband and children, how could I be your maid? No, Milady, I be fine, now I shall go and get your tea.'

Margaret laid her head back and closed her eyes thinking, *Oh, Millicent Penrose, you are not fine, you deserve to be loved by a man.*

'I have brought a young man to see you, Margaret Hamilton.' Margaret opened her eyes as he placed young Charles on the bed beside her, then he watched her pull him in tight kissing the top of his head, crying and laughing at the same time.

'Oh, Charles, I have missed you so much!' She held him away. 'Have you missed your mother? Yes? No?' Margaret shook her head, rubbing her nose on his, listening to him giggle.

His response was to wriggle out from her arms, then take a handful of Margaret's hair in his fist; pulling her down to him, he placed a thoroughly wet kiss on her face, while speaking words which meant no sense at all to the receiver, only himself.

'Leave him with me, Stewart, Millie will be back soon. Go speak with your mother as she looked very worried and tell her I am fine, now that I am not being thrown about aboard a ship or on a coach.' She squeezed his hand as he bent to kiss her forehead.

***

As Stewart descended the stairs, he saw Alexander just handing his hat to Thompson. They greeted one another with a tight embrace for some moments.

'Oh I am so glad you are back, Stewart,' offered Alex.

'Why? Has something happened? Is there something wrong? As my mother looked very tired, and she was crying, but I believe it was not just from happiness to see us.'

Alexander smiled broadly. 'No, no, just the usual trials and tribulations of this house, and besides, I missed your company.'

Alexander put his arm around Stewart's shoulder and guided him to the drawing room.

'There is something I am missing here, Alex, and I mean to find out what it is,' he said, warily thoughtful.

'There is nothing, cousin, except that James' wedding will now take place on the 25th September. No doubt Sir Henry will inform you of the ramifications of that.' Alexander raised his eyebrows and smiled sardonically.

***

Stewart stretched, luxuriating in the ample softness of his own bed. Margaret was deeply asleep in his arms; she had not roused, even when he had got into bed beside her. She was… yes, exhausted was the word he looked for.

His mother had been very strange at dinner, choosing her words carefully so as not to say something that she ought not to. Alex had been too cheerful; there was something he was concealing—he could read him like an open book. William Masters had not spoken much, looking mostly at his daughter, but there were surreptitious glances to his mother and Alex over the course of the evening. Charlotte—well Charlotte and his mother had left the table as soon as dinner had finished. He would leave them all for a few days, then if nothing had been said, he would start asking questions—firstly from his mother, as he had a strong supposition that this secrecy stemmed from her.

Stewart shifted, placing his leg over Margaret's body, pulling her nearer, then he stroked her back as he drifted off to sleep, with the words 'I love you' dying on his lips.

Chapter Thirty-Eight
The Letters and Jane's Birth

Elizabeth stood by the open casement window in Margaret's bedroom, watching her son pace the lawn at the back of the house. It was time, she would say nothing to him until he had read his father's letter, then and only then would she explain the events that had taken place a few weeks previous. She knew that he would not understand it all, had it not taken her at least a week before she could put all the images in order in her mind? Her heart was heavy both for her husband and her son. Would Stewart understand, see the reason, she did not know. All those years, could he ever forgive him? But then had he not paid the money to save his father from prison or deportation, blood ties run very deep, she knew that. She would go now and give him the letter, and pray to God that his heart could find some compassion for his father, as hers had.

Turning, she saw Margaret looking at her with apprehension and questioning in her eyes. The young woman was no fool; she had had to live by her wits for most of her life. Coming to the bed, she sat down.

'Margaret, I have to talk to Stewart about some business, I may be gone a little while so I will find Charlotte and Millie to come sit with you. You must promise me one thing though, that you will NOT get up, or even attempt the stairs.' Elizabeth looked at Margaret daring her to defy her. 'Do I make myself clear?' she added.

Margaret leaned forward taking Elizabeth's hand. 'Mother, I wish I could be there when you tell him,' she kissed her mother's cheek. 'All will be well, I know.'

Elizabeth sat back astonished. 'But how—' her words were cut off.

'Charlotte told me. We are sisters, remember?'

Suddenly the room seemed too small for the two of them, and Elizabeth felt the walls closing in on her. Standing up, she squeezed Margaret's hand.

'I must go now.' Turning quickly, she left.

Stewart saw her coming towards him and breathed deeply. She had finally decided to tell him what had taken place in his absence, for something had, that was clear from everyone in the house.

Stewart could see as she came nearer that she held something in her hand, a letter of some kind—maybe she was not going to inform him; maybe it was just the post, but there was something in her eyes as she stood before him now that told him this was no ordinary letter.

335

Stewart felt strangely calm—there were noises all around him but he could hear nothing till his mother spoke.

'Stewart,' she paused to cup her hand round his face, 'this is for you, and I want you to go somewhere quiet and read it slowly. Then when you have finished, come find me in the drawing room.' As she placed the letter into his hand, she nodded her head for him to go. Then turning, she went back into the house and disappeared, as though she had never been there.

Stewart held the letter gently in his hands as if it might explode at any moment. He knew the handwriting, and his heart was now thumping loudly in his ears. Slowly he made his way into the gardens, sitting under the same tree that Maggie and he had sat that first night at the Willows when he had told his mother that he would marry her. After sitting there for some time, hearing the chattering of birds all around him, he gently broke the seal smoothing out the pages. Another letter fell from within and a Bankers draft for the sum of £15,000. Stewart's mouth was dry now, his head spun, and his hands shook uncontrollably. Waiting for his body to relax, he then placed the other letter, which he saw was addressed to his mother, and draft onto the bench beside him and read.

Stewart (My son, if I dare to call you this, as I have been no father to you)

I have begun this letter to you many times, and as many times have destroyed it. But after what happened with your mother, I feel that I owe you some kind of explanation, as to why I am (or was, for I am no longer the man I used to be) what I am.

It was after hearing of your brush with death, and knowing what you did for me—to save me from prison or deportation—that I changed. But, I digress...

As you are no doubt aware, I was the second born, and being such inherited none of the estate that my father owned. It was custom for the second born to go into the clergy. I was twenty years old then, and a very angry young man. It burned in my soul why only the first born should inherit everything. Why not share the land between the sons, so each could build a home there. But one's heritage and custom dictate what should be done (even though it be unfair).

I wandered for a time, I had the monies my mother left to me, which were substantial—I make no lie about that. But already the seeds of hate and anger had been sown, festering within me.

I met your mother when my elder brother took me to the Willows in 1759. He knew of your mother, and wanted to introduce me to her father as a prospective husband. I was, by then, twenty-nine years old, having lived in London many years as an Import Merchant. I had an office in The Port of London, and a small house in London itself.

I can tell you truthfully that your mother was the most beautiful young woman I had ever set eyes on—but I did not want to marry. I could tell that she liked me well enough, her eyes sparkled. You are a man and should know the feeling when a woman has an attraction for you; it shines from her like a beacon. My brother convinced me to marry, as then I would have an estate of my own, and if I loved my wife, well, that was another windfall. I can tell you now that I did love your mother—very deeply (and still do). I can hear you scoff here, but when you hear my entire story, you will know that I do not lie.

Your grandfather had taught your mother from an early age to be strong. If she were left alone, she could manage the estate, but there was no place there for me. I had no participation in the running order of things, it was administered by your mother and grandfather. So the seeds of resentment and hate built. I have a temper, Stewart, and you have inherited that, I know this from the many times we have met, face to face, neither backing down, but you have your mother's heart.

I say this to you now; never let your temper and hate eat at you, until you do not recognise the man you are—like I did.

I met with many insalubrious groups of people, and more than often I was so deep in drink... After your grandfather died and I discovered that I would never be master in my house, it would never be mine to leave to my son, but would pass automatically to you on your 25th birthday. It hurt my pride badly. I stayed away for weeks at a time, bringing people to the house who I hardly knew. Then that fateful night, the man that attacked me had come down from a ship in Portsmouth. I encountered him in Mere with the other two inebriates and brought them to the Willows to play cards. Your mother saved my life that night, and how did I repay her? By holding her to ransom for money. I am not fit to wipe her shoes, and I tell you this from the heart.

I know your wife, for I knew of her first husband. I must tell you that you have a woman of great worth, never, ever, hurt her or do anything that will break her trust in you. Her first husband was evil to the core, and he was widely known in London for his brutal ways, and I ask just one favour of you now—she will never tell you what he did to her, so never ask it of her.

I know that you have a son, Charles, treasure him, but be firm, and show him the code of manhood, in that he learns respect for his fellow man.

You were named after my father—did you know that? It was your mother's choice, putting her own father's name second. I have watched you grow into a man from afar, and I can say one thing, I am proud of the man you have become. But it was not of my doing, I owe that to two other men, who I think you will know without my saying their names. They and your mother made you the man you are today.

The man Northcott—the one who nearly killed you—I met in London at a gaming house. I was drunk—as usual—and he retrieved secrets from me that should never have been said. I also know that he has persecuted you for many years, he is another man akin to Robert Stanhope, and if I met him today, I would kill him without hesitation.

The taking of your mother was never meant to be as it was. I came back to Scotland after you repaid my debts and met a distant nephew who was a minister in Dumfries. He informed me that a lawyer there had been searching for me for some years. I had an uncle who had left me some money and a small house in Dumfries. I sat with that nephew many, many nights, pouring out my soul to him.

He listened, did not judge, but when I had finished, he told me that I was not a bad person, just one that had let myself be consumed with rage, resentment and hate. I had picked at it like one does with an open wound, not allowing it to heal, but by doing so, it grew bigger and more inflamed by the day.

He taught me to look at my life, to see where I could right the wrongs I had done, that my soul was not black, but if I did not stop, then I would be destroyed by my own self.

When I took your mother, I did not mean to frighten her; I wanted her to be with me, to see how I had changed—I still love her. When we reached Keswick, I knew that she would never accept me again. You must believe me when I say I did not harm a single hair on her head.

I am repaying the money that you transferred to save me; it is enclosed in a Bankers Draft for you. If you will not take it, then I wish you to bequeath it to your children as a gift from me.

I do not wish forgiveness for all the hurt and harm that I have brought on my family, for I know that could never be given. I just ask that you do not hate me. Stewart, if you ever travel to Scotland, I would welcome you—though I know in my heart that will never be, but I give you my address—26 Kirk Street, Dumfries. Remember, you are my flesh and blood, and I never stopped loving you.

Yours

Andrew Duncan (Father)

Stewart had sat there for some time; he knew this by the shadows the sun now cast around him. As he rubbed his hands across his face, he found it was wet with tears; looking at his hands now he could not quite make out how and when this had happened. His senses were slowly coming back to him, as he saw the other letter on the bench beside him. His mother, she had been waiting all this time for him to go to her; folding his letter quickly, he stood and picked up the one to his mother and the draft, placing them all safely into his pocket. Then swallowing hard and rubbing his face once more, he went to find her.

As he entered the room, he saw her looking out to the front of the house; hearing his footfall across the floor, she stood holding out her arms to him, letting Stewart enfold her into him. He rested his cheek on the top of her head, stroking her back as they cried together, each to their own grief and loss, till Stewart spoke first.

'Mother,' he swallowed hard trying to regain his composure. 'I must go and find him.' He felt his mother's arms tighten round him.

'After you have read his letter, I want your permission to show it to both Pip and Spike. Then I must settle things here and go... Maggie will understand, I know this but you must not show her the letter, for reasons you will understand when you read it yourself.' He felt his mother nod in agreement.

'Oh God, Mother, what a waste of a life... of all our lives, especially yours.' His voice had dropped to a whisper.

'You still love him, do you not? Always have, thinking that he would change and return to you.' He drew Elizabeth in so tightly now that she felt her face press into the buttons on his coat. Then let her quietly give vent to her feelings once more.

Stewart waited for her sobbing to lessen; gently pushing her away from him, he placed both letters into her hand, closing her fingers around them.

'Go rest now, then when you have read the letters, we can decide.'

***

He found Margaret sitting with Charlotte, Millie, Daisy and young Charles, who when he saw his father, came unsteadily across the room to hug his legs. Stewart reached down with one arm and lifted him up, letting his son nuzzle into his neck, placing wet kisses there, while his hand pulled at his hair, unfastening the ribbon that held it. Stewart looked lovingly into his son's face; placing his hand round Charles' head, he pulled him into him, kissing his forehead. He could feel the child going limp in his arms, and as he reached Daisy, young Charles' eyes were closing.

'You are tired, my son, what have all these women been doing to you?' he said as he gently laid him into Daisy's arms. Kissing him once more, he turned to Margaret, taking her hand in his.

'I will come back after lunch, Margaret Hamilton, and I will ask cook to send yours up to you.' His eyes were sparkling with mischief.

He bowed to all the ladies present then kissed his wife and left.

Daisy coughed and smiled. 'I will take Charles to the Nursery, Milady.' Curtsying, she left the room.

Margaret turned to Millie. 'Millie, you can stay with Charlotte and I, and share our lunch.'

Millie stood up abruptly, smoothing down her gown she curtsied. 'Oh no, Milady, I will be going down to Mrs Cottle.' She curtsied once more and quickly left.

'Well, Charlotte, that leaves just you and I...' Margaret stopped as she saw Charlotte wince and hold her stomach from beneath.

'Charlotte!' she exclaimed. Standing up quickly, she went to the mantle and pulled the bell pull several times. As Millie reappeared, she did not need telling why she had been summoned; Mistress Charlotte had started her birthing pains.

***

William Masters was pacing on the terrace, looking up at the windows above, praying silently. 'Dear God, let her be safely delivered.'

The light was slowly fading, as evening came upon them, and a light breeze stirred the trees sending a chill through the air. Alexander sat next to Stewart, his face the colour of custard, his hands hanging between his knees. He had been at the estate office when Carter had come for him, then they had ridden back in silence. Many things were going around in his head, had he not been through a night like this when Charles was born? But now it was *his* wife up there with the

339

midwife. Childbirth was a dangerous thing, and Charlotte was so small. He repeated over and over in his mind, 'Please let her not be taken from me.' Then he felt a hand on his shoulder.

'Alex, she will be fine, you have to believe me.' Stewart pressed his fingers in silent confirmation as he nodded.

Of all the things that could occur now, this was not one that he had envisaged happening. His mother no doubt had not had the time to read the letters; she had other trials to do battle with at this present time. Women, he mused, seem to handle many upheavals such as this without thinking, it was as though they were driven by some secret force that men were not privileged to have.

It was around 4am when Jane Elizabeth Hamilton finally made her appearance into the world on 30th August, 1788. She was small, perfectly formed with tufts of such fair hair it could be mistaken for pure white, and a pair of lungs equal in volume to her cousin.

The air in the bedroom was warm; both windows were open and a gentle breeze wafted in bringing with it the light scent of late roses, honeysuckle and jasmine. Four candles burned around the room—the majority having been extinguished to allow Charlotte to sleep for a while, after having given her daughter her first feed. Now Alexander sat by the window where one small candle still burned, marvelling at his daughter that he held in his hands. He had never imagined that he would one day be holding his own child—she was beautiful. As he gently glided his hand over the soft down of her hair; he felt Elizabeth's hand came around his shoulders as she leaned down to stroke the velvet cheek.

'Oh, Alexander, she is beautiful.' Then kneeling beside him, she pressed her head to his and they cried together, as Charlotte lay peacefully asleep now, with her father holding her hand.

'Come hold your granddaughter, William,' Elizabeth whispered kindly. 'Leave Charlotte be, she will sleep for some time, as she has had a long labour.'

William Masters was loath to leave his daughter, but the pull of the child that Alexander held was too much. Alexander stood, gently placing his daughter into her grandfather's arms.

'Here, Father, hold your granddaughter Jane Elizabeth.'

William Masters looked up in surprise. 'Jane?'

'That was her grandmother's name, no?' smiled Alexander as he wiped the tears from his face.

There was a light tap on the door, as Margaret entered quietly followed by Stewart. William motioned Margaret to the chair, and then gave her his Granddaughter—her niece—to hold.

'Meet Jane Elizabeth Hamilton,' he said quietly, kissing the small bundle on the head.

Margaret took the small child's hand in hers, stroking its fingers as she watched the child's eye lids flicker and then purse its lips in the peaceful movement of sleep. She gently pulled back the shawl and cupped a small foot in her hand.

'Oh, Stewart, she is the most beautiful baby,' she said softly, 'look at her small plump cheeks, arms and legs, does she not remind you of the child in that painting we saw at the friend of Rodolfo? All round and plump.' She turned to look at Stewart as he sat on the arm of the chair.

Stewart brushed back Margaret's hair behind her ear and smiled. 'She will be like her mother.' As he said this, he looked towards Alexander.

'Come now, Maggie, you must go back to bed, or else you will not be able to come and see Charlotte and Jane in the morning.' Saying this, he placed the baby in Daisy's arms, as she had been waiting patiently to take her into the nursery.

Daisy curtsied to Alexander. 'I will bring her back for her next feed, sir.'

Alexander gave one last kiss to his daughter's cheek; he did not want to let her go, but knew he must. 'Thank you, Daisy.'

Chapter Thirty-Nine
Elizabeth's Letter, Spike and Pip

It took some days for the house to settle again after baby Jane's arrival. She was a good baby, only crying when hungry or needing changing; at all other times she lay peacefully asleep in her crib under the watchful eyes of both parents and nanny Daisy. It had not been a difficult birth, but Charlotte had been very afraid. She had clutched onto her Aunt's hand throughout the birth, her eyes fixed staring at her aunt as if to say, 'Please do not let me die.' Elizabeth could understand her fears, as childbirth was a dangerous process, and countless mothers—and children—did not survive because of many problems that could occur—Elizabeth was testament to that. Charlotte's labour had been a long one, and as a consequence, she was exhausted. Her milk fortunately had come in abundance, and baby Jane drank avidly from her mother. Elizabeth knew only too well that some babies refused to suckle, no matter what, Charlotte had been spared this.

Elizabeth sat on the terrace now, breakfast was over, and she had left Charlotte—who was just today allowed to sit in a chair—in the careful hands of her sister Margaret, so she could sit for a while to her own thoughts. They must look for another nanny. Elizabeth knew that Daisy would take care of the baby while she was still here, but one had to be found for when they returned to their own house. She would enquire if Daisy knew of a nanny that she could recommend maybe of someone whose services were no longer required, someone trustworthy. Elizabeth recognized the fact that good nannies were hard to come by.

She closed her eyes now to the tears that seemed always just a breath away these past days, and let the peace of the morning wash over her, then feeling for her handkerchief, her fingers found the letters hidden deep in her pocket. How could she have forgotten them! She sighed deeply and went to stand when a hand pressed against her shoulder.

'Mother,' Stewart's voice broke into the silence. 'Go sit on the seat under the old oak in the gardens and read your letters. You will be at peace there; no one will bother you, and take as long as you must. All is well in the house.' Elizabeth looked up into her son's eyes and could see the anguish in them; he was hurting, and she knew that.

'Read mine first.' His arm came round her waist and lifted her to her feet. Then nodding to her, he watched her make her way across the lawn and disappear into the gardens beyond.

***

The day around her felt warm and tranquil as she walked through the gardens. Elizabeth reflected that the last time she had done this was after Stewart's wedding. She breathed deeply and pushed the wisps of hair from her eyes; no wonder Charlotte loved to walk here, the nature around calmed your spirit and made you feel at one with the world. This was the one constant, for no matter what man did to the earth, it would rejuvenate itself once more, just as the trees, shrubs and flowers did every spring. If only mankind were the same, and one could wash away one's sins, failings, hurt and pride, yes, that always, as *'pride goeth before destruction and a haughty spirit before a fall'*—a proverb well worth remembering, but always forgotten.

Elizabeth sat now, smoothing out her gown, and then taking up the two letters she placed hers by her side on the bench, opened the other, and began to read.

***

Kenver had seen his mistress enter the gardens and watched her from a distance. She was reading something that was clear, but it could not be good news as she was so distressed. Dropping his rake, he made to fetch Spike.

He was breathless as he came up to Spike, and started to say the words so quickly each one tumbled into the other till Spike had put up his hand.

'Kenver lad, will ye be taking a breath, I cannot be understanding a word you be saying to me. Now, breathe in, and begin again.'

'Mr Wood sir, it be the mistress, she be sitting on the bench, that one beneath the old oak, you knows the one. Oh, she be so distressed, sir, she be a reading something then crying. She did not see me, so I came to find ye, in case there be something bad happened.'

Spike held him by the shoulder. 'You did right, young Kenver, now you be going and getting yourself a drink of water from the flask over there, and I will go see Milady.' He nodded to him, then left.

As Spike approached where Elizabeth sat, he did not let her see him, lest it was something personal, that she did not want the house to know about. After all, did we all not have private moments where we just wanted to be left in peace with our thoughts? He would bid his time, and if she needed him, then he would go to her.

***

Elizabeth tried to calm herself; she wiped her eyes and took several deep breaths. She had another letter to open yet, but her mind was still reeling from

343

the first. Closing Stewart's letter, she sat with her hands in her lap and closed her eyes. How could she never have seen the anger and injustice that he had felt, was she that blind, she could read her own son like the pages of a book, know every emotion he went through, and yet her own husband? Taking up the letter, she broke the seal, smoothed out the pages, and began to read.

My Dearest Lizzie

For that is what you are and what you always will be for me. I call you that not as a term of derision, but in a term of endearment, as I always meant it to be.

Where to start, in truth I do not know, what I do know is that you are completely innocent of everything that has happened over these past twenty-two years. As I wrote to Stewart (my son,), my anger, my inadequacies, my own feelings of injustice (for they were mine and no one else's) and stubborn blindness made me the man I was.

I hounded you for money, Lizzie, to feed my addictions, and believed that I was right to do so, that I had a right to the estate… But I did not. I was meant to be just a custodian for the generations who would inherit it after, but I was so blinded by anger and resentment I could not see that. Even those that have vast wealth and properties never truly own them; they just hold them safe for the future. If they are worthy, they will preserve them. I can tell you now, I was not worthy.

I left that fateful night, not because I hated you, but if I had stayed, I would have brought you down to the depths I had sunk to, and I could not do that. My feelings of self-loathing—well, let us say my anger festered in me like an abscess. Each time I returned I intended to act differently, but when I stepped into the house, there was such an overwhelming sense of fear and antipathy from the occupants—and they had a right to that—for what had I done, brought pain and sorrow to everyone there. I can never ask for forgiveness, for I know that it could not be given, it is too late for that, Lizzie.

After Stewart paid my debts, I returned to Scotland and there met a young nephew who is a Minister in the Church. It was he who guided me, sat with me for hours talking. I could not tell you to this day what we said, I only know that he listened to me, did not judge me and finally told me that my soul was not black, and that I could redeem my self-respect. That young man taught me how to rethink my life, to try to right some of the wrongs that I had made, and never to ask forgiveness, because that can only be given by those I have hurt. It was for them to offer—if they could.

He also informed me of a lawyer who had been looking for me for several years. I had been left money and a house in Dumfries, by an uncle on my mother's side of the family. He had no children, my elder brother had the estate, and my younger brother had died many years past. In the letter to Stewart, I have repaid him the monies he gave to secure my release. At least there I can right one wrong.

The day that I took you, well I did not mean for it to happen as it did. I wanted to ask you to be with me, to show you how I had changed. God help me I never meant to cause you anguish or terror, but that is what I saw in your eyes, and I reverted to my old ways. That first night I wanted so much to take you in my arms and reassure you that I meant you no harm. When I lay with you that night and my fingers touched your arm, I felt you shake in fear of me. I knew then that I could not take you away from your home, your family. I had no right. For that part I beg your forgiveness, Lizzie.

It took me till Keswick to finally let you go. I had not intended to travel back with you, but I could not bear to let you leave my sight, so I travelled with you to keep you with me just that little while longer.

Lizzie, you have a fine family; you have nurtured them and shown them the common decencies and respect that one person must show to another, for respect is earned not taken. I have two men to thank for Stewart's rearing, one day I will gather enough courage before I die to write to them of my heartfelt thanks, for they did it well. I have watched him grow from afar, and know that he has my temper, but he is able to control it, as he has your heart—I have told him this also. Maybe one day he will be able to find it in his heart to come to Scotland so that we may speak, but I will not wish for that, for that must come from him, not me.

I will close this letter now, Lizzie, but want you always to know that I never stopped loving you. God Bless you, Lizzie.

Your husband, Andrew

It was some time before Elizabeth could control her feelings. She had sobbed till she thought that there were no more tears to come, only to find she was crying once more. She could not go back to the house yet, she had to compose herself first.

Spike watched her tentatively from afar. If she were ill, then he would go to her without hesitation, but, this was sorrow of a great depth, he could see that. After some time, he saw Stewart in the distance. He would go now, she would find comfort in her son's arms, he was sure of that. Turning, he left and went back to his work with a heavy heart, maybe she would talk to him later, if she felt the need.

As Stewart approached, he could hear his mother sobbing; seating himself next to her, he took her into his arms and held her close.

'When you are ready, Mother, we will walk a while, it will help.' His voice was comforting and reassuring in her ear, but she clung to him as though her life depended on it.

'I never hated your father, Stewart,' her voice stopped his words.

'In my heart, I always prayed that he would one day come back to me... want me again... need me. I have been alone for twenty-two years, known no other man save your father... and now... we can still never be together because there is too much distance between us, and I do not mean in miles, Stewart.'

***

345

'Just why are we going to see Spike Master, Stewart?' Pip asked questioningly, watching Stewart out of the corner of his eye for some inclination as to why the need for all of this secrecy. He had been told only that Stewart needed to talk with both of them, for what reason, or urgency, he had no idea. He only knew that when the two of them arrived at Spike's cottage, the man would go as white as a cauliflower, thinking that some terrible thing had happened up at the house. There was no way of warning him either; Master Stewart had a knack of doing this to people, did he not stop to think that the man was about to sit and eat his supper?

Stewart stopped and turned to look at him. 'I apologise, Pip, my mind is racing ahead of me today. I need you to read a letter from my father.'

Pip's jaw dropped. 'Your father, Master Stewart?'

'No, no, no, Pip, it is not what you think. It is related in some way, to the time when my father took my mother. Well, he did not mean to take her... but—' Stewart paused to collect his thoughts. 'You will understand better when you read the letter, I promise you.'

Pip was still not convinced; anything to do with his father was bad news as far as he was concerned, and Spike would think the same, he was sure.

As Spike opened the door, he looked from Stewart to Pip then back to Stewart once more.

'This concerns my mistress, does it not?' his voice held an edge of sadness and fear.

Stewart thought well before he spoke, if he read the man correctly, he had been awaiting his call.

'Master Stewart sir, Pip, you had best come in.' Spike offered with some trepidation.

As they entered, Kenver's legs could just be seen disappearing into the shadows above. Stewart placed the stone jar of ale he had brought with him on the table, as Spike offered Stewart the comfortable chair, while he and pip pulled up two wooden stools.

Spike coughed and shifted in his seat before he spoke. 'If I may be so bold, Master Stewart, I did see my Mistress in the gardens this morning, and if I am not mistaken, she be racked with grief,' he paused here for some reaction, but seeing none continued. 'There be no tragedy up at the house?' His voice now held a sense of foreboding.

Stewart answered quickly. 'Oh, Spike, no, there is a tragedy of sorts, but it does not concern the occupants of the house, it concerns my father.'

Pip turned quickly to Spike, raising his brows, his eyes wide.

'Is he... dead, Master Stewart?' asked Spike; his voice had an edge to it and was full of wariness.

Stewart looked at the two men seated before him; they were the only two men that he had taken guidance from throughout his life. Up until he went to Winchester, they taught him right from wrong, he would never have dreamt of being disrespectful; God, he would have had his ears boxed. His tutors had educated him, but these men had given him the education of life; good conduct, tolerance to others and, above all else, honesty. They were not his servants, and he could never identify them as such, for they were as uncles to him and had served him well. Just as Spike was like a brother to his mother—even if Spike would *never* see himself as such. His mother loved him as a brother, of that he was sure. Stewart had his mother's permission to show both the letters, but he would let them read his first.

'First, we will take a mug of ale, I know I need it, and I am sure that you do also.' As Stewart uncorked the jar, Spike stood and took three mugs down from the dresser for him to fill, and then all men hit their mugs together in a form of agreement, in that whatever was to be disclosed they were in it as one.

Taking the letters from his pocket, he laid the one from his father onto the table. Spike and Pip eyed one another then Pip opened the letter; pulling his stool next to Spike's, he took out his spectacles and they read together.

Stewart watched the two men intently, seeing all of the emotions that they went through as they read. Once or twice they looked up and eyed one another as if in some secret sign language. When they had finished, Pip folded the letter neatly, then handed it back to Stewart.

'Master Stewart,' Pip began as he took off his spectacles and placed them on the table, then rubbed his hands over his face, pushing his fingers deep into his eyes as though to sooth his brain.

'Master Stewart, we be knowing nothing of the agreement that your grandfather made when your mother married, or the contents of your grandfather's will,' he paused again.

'Your grandfather were a good man; he did what he thought were right to be protecting his only child. Any father, he would have done the same.' He stopped once more to get up and pace the room.

'From what I be reading, your father felt a grave injustice be done him afore he came here and married your mother.' Pip placed his hands on the table and let his head fall forward.

It was Spike who spoke next.

'Master Stewart, when the drink took him, he went into his own world. But I can say in all truth that he never once harmed a hair of your mother's head.' He stopped to look at Pip. 'The only wrong he be doing to you was to leave you.' Spike rubbed his face and then smoothed his hands over his bald head.

'Master Stewart sir, we know now that you saw everything that happened that night. From that moment you changed, you would be throwing tantrums, screaming and throwing things. Someone had to be taking you in hand, sir. Your mother was distraught, so Pip and myself, well we did our best. Master Stewart, you know the rest without my having to tell you, sir.'

Pip stood up straight. 'Master Stewart, your mother had no siblings, no relatives, other than your grandfather's brothers in Scotland. She be alone here, with just the servants... None from her mother's family. Dear God, sir, she be alone here.' He repeated as his voice trailed away.

Stewart sat there, his head bowed, as he dare not speak lest his emotions reveal themselves. Swallowing several times he looked up at the two men.

347

'I have *never* thought of you both as servants.' Standing up abruptly, he walked to the door. 'Please, allow me five minutes.' Before they could reply, he had opened the door and gone.

***

Stewart walked around the small garden several times. His head throbbed and his stomach was in knots. For the past three years, life had found a way to turn his world upside down. All the peace and healing there had been in Rapallo, had been taken away the moment his mother had handed him his father's letter, this had eclipsed everything. Would these two men now understand his necessity to go find his father? Stewart lifted his head up to the darkened sky and then closed his eyes. How could he justify this, would they see it as a betrayal? To his mother, to them even? Sitting on a small bench, he put his head in his hands.

Suddenly, he felt a cool hand on the back of his neck, then another took his hand in theirs, he knew the touch without raising his head as he covered her hand between his own.

'How long have you been here, Maggie?' he spoke with resigned softness.

She sank down next to him and laid her head on his shoulder.

'I am always with you, Stewart, no matter where you are, you should know that.'

Reaching up, he stroked her face.

'I have to go back in there, Maggie, and hope they understand why I have to do this.'

'Oh, I am sure they understand, Stewart, though they have never been fathers themselves, they know the pull of blood ties, be they good or bad,' she paused here to think before she said the next words.

'What would I say to my father if he came to me today? Well, I would ask him why? What difference was there between a male child and a female? That the females had to be discarded. We were all of his blood,' she paused once more as Stewart put his arm around her drawing her into him.

'Your father was not like that, he held no hate for you. What he hated was a system whereby only the eldest could inherit title, land. Why should one man claim everything and the others—'

'My mother has been speaking to you,' Stewart interjected quietly.

Maggie nodded her head against his chest.

'I must go in now and explain this to Pip and Spike and hope they understand my need to see him, talk with him. Do you think they will, Maggie?' He lifted her face to his and saw the answer in her eyes.

'Go back up to the house, Maggie,' he said as he kissed her softly. 'I will be fine now.'

***

Spike stirred his supper in the pot; pushing it slightly away from the fire, his heart felt heavy, and as he turned to face his friend, he could see that reflected in his face also. Nothing you obtained in life came without a price, he was certain of that—even happiness. For one person to find that, another must feel sadness.

It was warm in the room and the only sound was the soft crackle of the fire, as both men sat deep in thought. Spike turned and took his mug of ale from the table taking a long a drink.

'Pip,' he paused to look up at the man who had been his friend for many years.

'I know what you be about to say, Spike, and I am in complete agreement. The lad needs to go find his father, but he will not go until we... give our approval.' He was nodding to himself as he said the words.

Spike inclined his head in accord. 'Then let us go find him, and wish him well, Pip, for he needs to do this, to make peace with his father as well as with himself. It takes some men years to know the bounties they have had bestowed upon them. While others like you and I, who be leading more simple lives, can see this without causing others pain.'

Pip stood and offered his hand to Spike. 'We be in agreement then. The lad has been hurt enough, it be time for him to lick his wounds.'

As they opened the door, Stewart stood before them, hand raised, ready to knock.

Spike spoke first. 'Master Stewart sir, you need not be troubling yourself about us, because we give you our blessing—for what it is worth—so go find your father and make peace with him.'

Stewart looked hard at the two men before him.

'For what it is worth?' Stewart answered astonished. 'Your blessing means more to me than any other.'

Saying this, he took Spike by the hand, and then pulled him in to him patting his back; turning, he did the same to Pip. When he released him, he bowed his head slightly too both men and was gone.

Pip swallowed audibly, as Spike rubbed his eyes with his fingertips.

'Damn smoke from that fire, I will have to look at that chimney.'

Pip ran his fingers over his lips, swallowing once more.

'I be going back up to the house then, Spike, leave you and Kenver to your supper.'

A hand reached out to stop him as he turned to go.

'I think there be enough for three.' Turning, he saw Kenver slowly edging his way down, making sure all was clear. 'Do you not think so, young Kenver?' he asked.

Kenver was already taking three plates from the dresser and placing them on the table by the time Spike had finished speaking.

'Good lad, now get that bread. I have had a warming by the fire, and we can be sitting to our supper.'

Chapter Forty
The Journey to Dumfries and Forgiveness

Stewart was taking the same route to Scotland as his mother had done. He had meant to take the stage coach, but as he sat back in the comfort of his mother's coach, he was glad that he had not argued that. He had never been to Scotland, had no notion of what he may find there. Was it like any other part of England? Just that they spoke with a slightly different accent. Like the people of Wiltshire, with their soft musical lilt, he had grown up with that. He had met a man from Durham once, and he had to confess that he found it difficult to understand him at first, but after hearing him for some time, the words clicked into place. Maybe it would be a similar dialect in Dumfries.

When he thought about it, he had not travelled much at all, just to London and the West Country, where everything was familiar to him. Oh yes, he had been abroad, but just travelling to Rapallo and staying with friends.

Before he left, his mother had told him that his father had been educated in Edinburgh, along with his brothers. He had found out so much since the arrival of his father's letter, everything was new to him, but then he had never asked before, never wanted to know. Well for the first years of his life, his father had not been mentioned, so he had believed that he had none, or he was dead. He understood the reasoning behind this; they did not want to evoke the memories of that night—all that he had witnessed—that he had tucked neatly away in his brain as though it had never happened.

The journey was affording him too much time to think, and he did not need that at this present time. He had wanted to bring Maggie with him, but knew that it was impossible as she was too unwell. He had told her that he would wait until after the birth, but she had insisted that he must go now, as time at his father's age was precious, and no one knew what the next day would bring. He would never forgive himself if anything happened. She was right, as always.

He was on the last stage now, from Keswick to Dumfries. Stewart's eyes burned as he had not slept much the night before. The inn had been full, with only one small room available at the back, where the stables and the tap room were situated. Pip had come with him, but he had elected to ride outside with Carter the coachman; God, the man was stubborn. They were all armed, but, thank God there had been no incidents along the route.

The coach slowed suddenly, and Pip called from above that they were nearing the Scottish border, and did Master Stewart want to stretch his legs a bit.

Stewart smiled to himself, knowing what he really meant was did he want to piss. Yes, he did, as his bladder was fit to bursting, and if they had another three hours left to travel, well, he would never make it. Better to do it in daylight rather than in the dark.

The air outside was chill, with a mist that seemed to soak the clothes. As Stewart looked around, all he saw was green valleys and hills. Wiltshire was beautiful, but this held its own beauty, where the sky and the hills seem to merge as one. Stewart filled his lungs with air; it was so diverse here, and the landscape, even the earth had a distinct colour, rich and dark, pungent even.

'It be very different from Wiltshire, Master Stewart,' Pip's voice broke into the silence.

Stewart turned in surprise. 'I am sorry, Pip, what did you say? My mind is not with me at this present time.'

Pip looked at his Master. Who could blame him; for the last time he and his father had met they were fit to kill one another. It had been agreed that Stewart would go alone to his house; he did not want the meeting to be in any way confrontational. Pip had agreed, but he would stay back out of sight, this was his father's territory, unfamiliar ground.

'I know what you are thinking, Pip, but it will be fine, I assure you.'

It was Pip's turn to be surprised as Stewart placed a hand on his shoulder.

'Let us continue, I would like to be there before nightfall. We can then secure lodgings in the town, and rest before I meet him tomorrow.'

Going back to the coach, they started off once more, proceeding at a steady pace, Pip had lit the lanterns each side of the coach as the track was not one that had been ridden well, and in several places could not be seen at all.

They came into Dumfries town around 8pm. It was a small town, and Carter had stopped to ask of a coaching inn that they could rest the night, and were directed to The White Hart in Brewery Street. Having secured a room for Stewart, Pip and Carter took the Coach to the back. Un-hitching the horses, they settled them for the night with food and water, then found a room above the stable where they could both rest.

***

Next morning, Pip found his master sitting on a chair by the window deep in thought. Stewart had slept very little, and had washed and shaved himself and dressed before Pip arrived at 7am.

'Master Stewart, have you not slept at all?' came Pip's anxious voice from the door. He could see that his master was ready to leave, as he had on his boots, cloak and hat.

Stewart turned. 'Did you get the directions, Pip?

'Yes, Master Stewart, it not be far from here, and should be easy to find as the road is opposite a church called Saint Michael's.'

Stewart looked up at the name. 'St Michael's.' He smiled and turned his head slightly. 'Like the one in Mere, Pip.'

'Yes, Master Stewart, let that be a good omen.' Pip felt uncomfortable. He wanted to go with him, but there was no use in arguing, the man was as stubborn as himself.

'Omen or not,' smiled Stewart as he stood up. 'We will go down and breakfast now, then I will go find my father.'

***

The day was grey and wet. That fine mist that they had encountered on the stop just before the border was all around them again. Stewart pulled up the collar to his cloak and pushed his hat harder onto his head. The church was easy to find, and Kirk Street lay diagonally opposite. Stewart looked up at the tower at the front of the church and crossed himself.

'You can leave me here, Pip, I will be fine.' Stewart placed his hand on Pip's shoulder and pressed his fingers in reassurance. 'He is my father, Pip, I should not be afraid.'

Pip inclined his head and walked back down the hill.

The house he found was not large but it was substantial compared to others that he had passed. There were windows either side of the front door, which you approached by a series of small steps; also as Stewart looked upwards, he saw there were three floors. Stewart wrapped hard once on the door before him, then drew himself up to his full height and waited.

As the door opened, it looked as though there was no one there, till his eyes travelled down to rest on a small lady of late thirties, dressed in a deep blue gown of wool with a snow-white apron and cap. She smiled up at Stewart and inclined her head.

'Good day to ye, sir, will it be my master that ye seek?' Her voice was light and warm.

Stewart immediately took of his hat and bowed to her.

'Good day to you, Mistress, I seek a Master Andrew Duncan,' came Stewart's reply. He had not been expecting a housekeeper—well, in truth, he had not known what to expect. The house behind her looked clean and smelt, if he were not mistaken, of beeswax. Had they not had beehives on the Willows estate? Still did, as far as his memory served him.

'My master be over at yon church, sir, aye at St Michael's. Do ye ken the minister, sir, Michael Duncan, his nephew?'

Stewart cleared his throat before he spoke. 'I thank you kindly, Mistress.' Placing his hat over his chest he bowed again.

'Would ye be kin, sir?' queried the housekeeper, as she looked curiously up into Stewart's face. 'Ye have a likeness to Mr Duncan.'

Stewart looked at the woman for some moments before replying.

'Yes Mistress, I am his son.' Saying this, he bowed again quickly, turned, and made his way back across to the church, leaving the woman with her mouth and eyes open in surprise.

Stewart mounted the steps and stood at the front of the door in the tower, where he unconsciously crossed himself once more.

'Dear God, help me now,' he whispered to himself; his palms were sweaty and his stomach as usual was turning in on itself. In hindsight, the man had no warning that he was coming; perhaps he should have left word with the housekeeper that he would call that evening. No, he was here now; there could be no more waiting.

As he quietly opened the door, he heard them before he saw them. They were seated in the front pew before the pulpit, which was situated in the centre of the church just in front of the windows. There were stairs leading up to it, and the Pulpit—if he were not mistaken—seemed to be shaped in the form of a challis. It was like no other church he had been in before; there was no centre aisle, just two side aisles, with three rows of pews. There were stained glass windows to the sides and three tall ones behind the pulpit. A row of arches ran down both aisles supporting an upper gallery, which held more pews, and ran around three sides of the church. Stewart was amazed. This held the same name as the church in Mere where he had married Margaret, but that was the only similarity.

As he progressed into the church, his boots echoed on the stone floor, causing the minister to look up. Stewart could see that he was older than himself but still young, maybe his late 30s. From the height of his body as he sat, he could tell he was tall, with brown wavy hair, and a face similar in profile to his father's who was sitting next to him. Suddenly, he turned towards him.

'Good day to ye, sir, would ye be in need of some guidance, sir? Are ye lost maybe, or unwell?'

It was at this point that Andrew Duncan turned and stood. Stewart watched the colour drain from his father's face as he made his way down the side aisle.

'No, Michael, that is my son...' his words trailed away as he watched Stewart approach.

As Stewart stood in front of his father, many things were running through his mind. He could see that he was as tall as he was, maybe taller, but the face that looked back at him, with its fine bones and aquiline nose, was his own.

'Father...' Stewart managed no more as Andrew Duncan pulled him into him in a tight embrace which seemed to restrict his breathing and go on forever. Stewart responded in kind and felt the tears sting his eyes. His heart was beating so fast now it echoed in his ears, and then as Andrew Duncan leaned back, he took Stewart's face in his hands and kissed him on both cheeks.

Leaning back from one another again, Stewart could see his father's face was wet with tears, but then so was his own. Neither man could speak, so they hugged one another once more. Stewart knew that forgiveness always came at a price, but this was a price worth paying.

'Uncle, you should be going home now.' Michael Duncan's voice was soft and low as he placed his hand on his uncle's arm.

'Ye will both have much to talk through, many years to remember. God bless ye both.' Saying this, he turned and made his way to a small room at the side of the pulpit.

Andrew Duncan could see that Stewart was about to speak, so he put his hand gently on his son's shoulder to stop him.

'Let us go back to the house, have a glass or two of whisky, then eat and talk,' he nodded to Stewart as he turned him to walk back down the aisle with him.

***

Not a word was spoken as they made their way back to the house. He was shown into a small parlour to the left of the hallway; there were two comfortable winged chairs placed either side of the fireplace, which at this moment held a fire generating a heat that warmed Stewart's frozen bones. There was a table by the window which looked out onto the street, with four chairs placed neatly around it. Against one wall was a sofa, with a small table in front, and a round rug was laid in the centre of the room decorated with what looked to be a pattern of thistles.

Andrew held out his arm for his son's cloak and hat, handing these to the small lady that Stewart had met earlier.

'This is my housekeeper, cook and cleaner.' He stopped to smile affectionately at the woman. 'Stewart, this is Mrs Fitzpatrick. Mrs Fitzpatrick, this is my son Stewart from Wiltshire.'

The small lady curtsied, and Stewart bowed smiling. 'Your servant, Madam.'

Mrs Fitzpatrick looked to Andrew Duncan in surprise. 'You must forgive my son; they greet everyone this way in Wiltshire.' Placing his hand on her shoulder, he smiled down at her, telling her everything was well.

'May we have some bannocks? Butter and honey?' he asked.

'Och, Mr Duncan, ye know that I always have fresh bannocks in the oven. I will brew ye both some tea and bring the whisky, aye,' she added with a smile.

As Stewart seated himself in the armchair, he knew what the first question would be from his father without him having to voice it. He took the letter out of his coat pocket and handed it to him.

'It is from M… from Mother,' he corrected himself. 'She wanted to come with me, but I am afraid we have a new baby in the house—my wife's sister married my cousin Alexander.' Stewart saw the puzzled expression on his father's face. All will become clear when you read this, and when I have explained the life I have led these past twenty-two years.' Stewart felt embarrassed and put his head down to look at his hands.

'Stewart, there are a lot of things that you do not know about *me*—none of them good. I assure you—but I agree there are also many things I do not know of your life also, but I wager one thing, they are *all* good.' Andrew Duncan paused to look at his son—all those years lost because of jealousy and rage. He coughed slightly, placing the letter Stewart had given him carefully in his pocket and continued.

'I saw you married.' Stewart looked up sharply. 'Yes, I was there, hidden at the back, I watched you take your vowels, saw how happy you were, how at ease, how comfortable you were with your wife. How much you loved her, and she you.'

'Father, I can tell you now in all honesty that she is the best of me.'

Andrew Duncan put up his hand and smiled. 'I know that, for when you have a good woman, you should treasure her, for they are not so easy to find, believe me.'

Stewart knew he was talking of his mother, but said nothing.

There was a light tap on the door, as Mrs Fitzpatrick entered carrying a tray of hot bannocks—which to Stewart looked like hot, flat, bread rolls—butter, honey and an assortment of cold meats. Placing this on the low table before the sofa, she went to a small dresser in the alcove by the fireplace and retrieved two glasses and a bottle of whisky.

'I will just be bringing ye both your tea now.' Curtsying, she left the room.

Andrew Duncan poured two full glasses, handing one to Stewart. There were no candles lit in the room at the present time, as there was still daylight enough to see, but as his father offered the whisky the glass caught the fires flames within it turning the amber liquid into a golden glow, which reflected on Stewart's hand as he took hold of the stem. If you had asked him a few months ago would he be sitting in Scotland drinking whisky with his father, well he would have thought you mad. Yet here he was, and it still seemed so unreal to him, as though it was a dream and he would wake soon.

'I feel the same way, Stewart,' his father's voice cut into his thoughts.

***

They sat companionably for most of the day; the shy awkwardness slowly left them, as they began to relax, and get to know one another. They continued to talk till it grew dark and were interrupted by Mrs Fitzpatrick coming in and lighting the candles on the mantle and in the sconces around the room.

'Supper will be ready in half an hour, Master Duncan. I will come for ye when it is laid.'

Andrew Duncan nodded and smiled. 'Thank you, Mrs Fitzpatrick—for everything.'

Stewart crossed his legs and sat back at peace, looking into the fire's glow.

'Come back with me, Father. Before you say no, I can tell you that all of the household know about my coming here, and the reason.'

Andrew Duncan laid his head back, closed his eyes, and twisted the glass he held by its stem.

'Stewart, it is not so easy. Here I live a peaceful, simple life. I do not ask anything of anyone, nor they of me, except that I be civil, polite and kind to people. That is all anyone can ask of their fellow man. I am myself; I have no one to answer to, as no one has to answer to me. I have found reconciliation for all the wrong I have done, amity with those around me that I have never felt before in my life. You would ask that I give this up now?'

Stewart looked deeply into his father's eyes. There was no animosity there, no selfishness in this need, just an acknowledgment that he had come to the end of a torturous road, and found at last the peace he had looked for most of his life.

'Not for me, Father, for Mother.'

Stewart saw his father swallow deeply, and his eyes glistened. 'I tried, Stewart, but your mother could never accept me into her life now, it is too late for that.'

'I thought that of you and I, but here we are, together. I do not want to lose that again.' Stewart leaned forward, his elbows resting on his knees.

'My mother, when you took her, realised too late. By the time she did, well, you were gone. Father, she still loves you; she has NEVER stopped. She has never looked at another man, or wanted one. Please, Father, I have never begged for anything in my life, but please come back with me and talk with her.' Stewart's voice was pleading now. 'If you find that you cannot stay, then you can return here. I only ask that you try. For her sake.'

Andrew Duncan stood up and walked to the window. Slowly he pulled the drapes over to shut out the rain that was falling heavily now. Turning to Stewart he spoke.

'Where are you staying, Stewart?'

'At the White Hart, not far from here,' came his reply.

Andrew Duncan was looking hard at his son. 'Will you stay the night here? Then in the morning I will give you my decision,' he nodded as though to seal a pact.

Stewart stood up and walked towards him. 'Thank you,' was all he said before he embraced him.

'Come.' Andrew Duncan's voice was gruff with emotion. 'We will go and eat our dinner.'

***

Back at the inn, Pip had just returned to the stables. Jack Carter looked at him.

'He will be staying the night with his Father then.'

Pip said nothing, just inclined his head.

'Let us feed and water the horses, then eat and go to our own beds, Jack. I have a feeling that we will be returning tomorrow, with an extra passenger.'

'Do you think he will go back with Master Stewart then?' There was surprise as well as questioning in Jack's tone.

Pip looked up at him as he forked fresh hay into the manger. 'Knowing Young Master Stewart's flair for persuasion, I can be guaranteeing it.'

'Do you be thinking that his father has changed his ways?' Carter spoke with some reservation as he led one horse to the trough to drink.

Pip stopped and stood up from his raking. 'As it says in the bible, Jack, *'Let he who is without sin cast the first stone.'* Maybe we should not be throwing stones at him, afore we look at our own lives. What I mean is, it were the men that he brought into the house Jack,' he paused to compose himself. 'He never harmed anyone at the Willows; he just could not live there and be told what to do like one of the servants. I do not be saying that it is right what he did to our mistress, but in your house, they listen to you, do they not? Milady's father did what he did to protect her, but by protecting her she lost her chance of happiness.'

Everything went quite as they carried on with settling the horses, then they made their way inside to eat their own supper.

***

Stewart saw two large bags in the hallway as he descended the stairs; his heart gave an involuntary leap, causing him to stop halfway down. He could hear his father giving orders to Mrs Fitzpatrick saying that he did not know how long he would be gone, and if she needed anything, then she was to go to his nephew the minister, who would be looking in on her each day, on his way to and from the church. Then the door opened and they both came into the passage.

Mrs Fitzpatrick curtsied. 'Good morning to ye, Master Stewart. I trust ye will both have a safe journey back to… Wilshore?' She looked at his father.

'It is Wiltshire, Mrs Fitzpatrick, but it is of no matter.' Andrew Duncan smiled down at his housekeeper. 'I have told my nephew that if you are at all troubled, then he will come and stay here, instead of in the church house.'

She nodded to him. 'It will be strange for sure not having ye here, sir, but I wish ye well. May God find it in his mercy to help ye overcome all your difficulties.'

'Thank you, Mrs Fitzpatrick,' looking up at Stewart he continued, 'now let us eat our breakfast and then we can be off, as I think my son needs to be home as he has a wedding to go to.' Looking back to his housekeeper, he added, 'I will be back as soon as I can, Mrs Fitzpatrick.'

Chapter Forty-One
Reconciliation and Renewal of Love

As Stewart looked out from the coach, he now recognised the landscape that sped past them. They were in Wiltshire. The journey home had been peaceful; there were times where he and his father had talked animatedly, then others where they sat in undisturbed silence, each to his own thoughts. His mother had no notion that he was bringing his father back with him. She had been adamant that the man would not come, but she needed to know that he was happy in the place he had finally chosen to live. She had told Stewart that when Margaret was safely delivered, then she would go and find him. Stewart hoped that he had done right by bringing him back.

'You look perplexed, Stewart, is it I that disturb your thoughts?'

Stewart turned quickly to look at his father. 'No, Father, it is just... my mother has no idea that you are coming.' Stewart saw his father go to speak and stopped him. 'Please, Father, she wants to see you. When I left, she was packed and ready to travel, it was all that I could do to stop her, till I reminded her of Maggie.' At the name, Andrew Duncan smiled.

'So you too have a name that you call your wife. I always called your mother Lizzie...' his voice trailed off, as he looked at his hands.

Stewart watched him and then saw him touch his left hand. Stewart looked hard now; he had a ring there, how had he never seen this before? But it couldn't be, he would have noticed. NO he would not, as the times he met him they had usually stared one another down in blind fury.

'It surprises you that I still wear it, Stewart?'

Stewart looked up in disbelief. 'I,' he looked at his own hand. 'I... I never had one... Maggie has my grandmother's.'

'It was what your mother wanted. It is the one thing that I never pawned or gave up in payment. When I frequented the gaming houses, I took it off. I know that your mother still wears hers, I have seen it there,' he looked cautiously at Stewart now.

'I used to take it off when I came to the house, though God knows why,' he shook his head and wiped his hand over his nose and mouth, looking at Stewart enquiringly.

'Do you think it is wise what I am doing now? I mean upsetting a household, your mother?'

358

Stewart sat up straight and looked intently at his father. 'She needs to see you, to talk with you, no matter what has been said in the past, please, Father.'

Andrew Duncan inclined his head and sat back, just as the coach turned on its familiar way down to the Willows.

Stewart saw the front door open and Thompson come out followed by his mother. He watched her standing there, wearing a deep blue dress, her hair neatly pinned up, her hands clasped before her. If only he could warn her, but it was too late for that.

Stewart stepped down and took his mother in his arms.

'All is well, Mother, I promise you.' As he spoke the last words, Andrew Duncan stepped down out of the coach. Elizabeth's hands came up to her mouth as her eyes watered, and Stewart just caught her before she sank to her knees.

Lifting her in his arms, he called for his father to follow him into the drawing room. All eyes were on Andrew Duncan as he came up the stairs into the hall; even Mrs Cottle had come out from the kitchen, ladle in hand, watching the man cross the hall and disappear into the room.

Stewart lowered his mother gently onto the sofa then gathered the cushions and placed them at her back. Taking her hands, he looked deep into her eyes.

'Mother, I will leave you now,' he inclined his head. 'Take your time, and when you ring, I will bring in some tea.'

Standing up he left the room, closing the doors behind him. Looking around the hall, all eyes were staring expectantly on him.

'Please, give them some peace. I ask that no one disturb them, and when my mother rings, come and find me, as I will take tea into them.'

Those that were gathered either nodded or voiced agreement. Mrs Cottle stood with her arms crossed, still holding the ladle.

'Mrs Cottle, please let me see my wife, then I will come and talk with you.'

'Master Stewart, do you trust him, sir?' she looked at him with more than a little scepticism in her eyes, and her tone.

'I do, Mrs Cottle, believe me we have had nearly two weeks together. He is changed.' Stewart walked toward her and held her arm. 'Now I must go see my wife.'

Mrs Cottle nodded, turned and went back into the kitchen.

As Stewart looked up, he saw Margaret and Charlotte both looking down at him.

'Stay there, I am coming up,' he called as he mounted the stairs. 'Now, where are the children?'

As he spoke, he heard a door open and small feet scampering unsteadily as Charles ran towards his father, arms outstretched. Stewart lifted him up in one arm and swung him around, as his son's arms came round his neck in excitement, choking him. Pulling him away, he kissed him, then pulled him back again.

'God, I have missed you,' he said, then stroking the child's face and hair, he spoke again. 'Charles, your grandfather is downstairs with your grandmother, and when they are ready, we will go to see them, yes?'

His son grabbed him once more placing wet kisses on his cheek, while his hand pulled at his hair, removing the ribbon as he always did.

'Let us go see your cousin, see how big she has grown.' Kissing Margaret firmly on the lips, he cupped her face, then turned and made his way back to the nursery.

Margaret looked towards Charlotte and smiled. 'They are home.'

***

The air in the drawing room was warm; the sun was now at the front of the house giving sunlight at the far end as its rays shone across the bare polished floor, it came through mirroring the window and leaving the garden end now in a soft light. Andrew Duncan had pulled up a chair and now sat beside Elizabeth with his hands clasped gently in his lap, watching her. He could not tell from her face what she was thinking, how she felt; he only knew that her eyes had never left his face since he sat there. It was for her to speak first, after all it was he that was invading her home, her space, her peace. If she wanted him to leave, then so be it, but first he wanted her to know that he *had* changed. He was not the man he was all those years.

'Andrew.' Elizabeth sat up and reached for his hand.

She felt his fingers slowly close around her own, while all the time her eyes never left his.

'Where does one begin,' she asked and saw him move his shoulders slightly as he bit into his bottom lip. Putting her legs to the floor, she moved to the side, patting the space next to her.

'Please, Andrew, sit beside me.' She saw him slowly rise, place the chair back, then come and sit next to her, taking her hand again.

He looked down at her hand and saw his ring there; placing his fingers onto it, he moved the ring round her finger.

'Lizzie, whatever happens from now, I need you to know that I have changed. When Stewart paid that debt for me, in spite of everything that I have brought down on this house, well, I was so *very* ashamed. I went home to lick my wounds. I knew that I could not go back to Edinburgh, or Dundee, so I turned west and made my way down to the small town of Dumfries. I found lodgings, as the monies that our son sent, after paying the debts were enough to keep me for at least a few months, if I lived frugally. It was whilst there that my landlady, who could see that I was troubled, told me to go visit the new Minister of St Michael's. She said that he was a young man, just come to the parish these last two years from Dundee, and was a very kind, congenial and sympathetic person; he would listen to my troubles, and maybe help me.'

Elizabeth took his hand in both of hers now and laid it in her lap.

'Go on, Andrew,' she encouraged softly.

'Well, I went, and after a few days, my soul felt lighter, talking to him, without him judging me. I took to going every day, more for company than for comfort, and he asked about my family, my father, mother and brothers. As I talked, it was as though a light came into his eyes, it was then he told me that he was a distant nephew of mine, and that there was a lawyer who had been looking for me for several years. Well, you know the rest. After all the hurt and pain I had taken this family through, I could not, and will *never*, understand it.'

He had been looking at her all while he had been talking, never taking his eyes from hers.

'The man had left me thirty thousand pounds and the house I now live in. Lizzie, I did *not* deserve it. I knew what I had to do, and so I came for you, but even that I could not do right. When I saw just how afraid of me you were, I went back into my shell. Oh God, Lizzie, that first night with you, I wanted nothing more than to hold you in my arms and BEG your forgiveness.'

Elizabeth reached up and cupped his face. At first, Andrew Duncan had flinched backwards but then saw she mean him no harm—it was to comfort him. He swallowed hard and closed his eyes. He did not see her coming towards him, just felt her lips on his in a soft kiss. He was trembling now, the hand she held in hers was shaking uncontrollably. As he opened his eyes, she pulled him into her and held him tenderly.

'Andrew, I have never stopped loving you, never gave up hope that one day you would come back to me. I realised too late when you took me, just why you had done this thing. You must understand when I tell you that for the past two years we have been under such anguish and pain. I thought you meant to cause more, but you did not and I am so very, very sorry for that.'

Andrew Duncan pulled back. Looking into his wife's face, he saw the lines of pain engraved around her eyes, the grey wisps of hair around her temples. They were both many years older, but he knew that in their hearts, they were still young.

Elizabeth rested her head on his chest; she could smell him. Oh God, it had been so long since this man had held her close to him; even now she thought that she would wake up from a dream, but he was too real, too close.

'Please stay, Andrew, I want you to stay.' her words were stopped by Andrew pulling her close to him.

'Oh, Lizzie, if it were only that simple. In Dumfries I have a small house and one housekeeper. She cooks, cleans and does my washing. I knew of her through my nephew as she would go—and still does—to clean the church, polish the silver there, and arrange the flowers. She has no one. My life is uncomplicated there, Lizzie.'

'Then I will come with you. I am *not* losing you a second time; you cannot ask that of me.' Elizabeth was crying now and Andrew saw that she was becoming distressed.

'Lizzie, I will take you back with me if you wish, but then I will bring home again to your family, for that is where you are meant to be.'

Elizabeth was shaking her head. 'I will not let you go, Andrew, if you cannot be here, then I will go there. I too can live simply. I have no ties here save my family, they are young Andrew, and will still be there, we are not.'

Andrew Duncan sighed deeply; he knew what she meant—was he not ten years older than her? He knew that life could be taken in an instant, but he also knew that he could not ask her to live as he did in Scotland. He should never have come, it was a mistake, as now he had broken her heart again. Pulling her tightly into him, he rested his head on hers. He would stay a while, then he would go quietly, she would see it was for the best.

***

Margaret sat with Stewart in the study. It was nearly time for dinner, and no word had come from the drawing room since they arrived at 10am that morning. Getting up, she came up behind him and placed her arms around his neck.

'Stewart, how are we going to get your father to stay here?'

He turned to look up at her surprised.

'What do you mean, Maggie?'

'I mean, the man is out of his depth at this moment, and he is just coming to terms with his life. As we have been in turmoil, he has been in a greater one, one that could have killed him had he carried on.' She saw he was about to interrupt her, so she turned and sat on his lap, holding his face.

'Listen to me, Stewart, as one who has been through hell, and comes out the other side bruised and beaten, but whole no less. You have told me how he lives there, how he has found peace at last,' she stopped once more to push the hair back from his eyes that always escaped when he had played with his son.

'How old is his housekeeper?' she questioned.

'She is about forty, or thereabouts, but why Maggie?'

'Could she be a nanny, Stewart? Don't you see, if we can bring her with him, he will have fulfilled his obligation there, for he does have one. Charlotte needs a nanny to help her. Oh I am thinking in riddles. Stewart, your mother will never recover if your father leaves her again, do you not see that?'

Stewart rubbed his forehead; his head ached terribly, and his stomach was in no better condition.

'If they do not ring within the next ten minutes, I am going in.'

Margaret closed her eyes, she felt dizzy, but this was the least of his worries at this present time. Pulling him towards her she kissed him

'I love you, Stewart,' was all she could say as there was a light tap on the door and Thompson came in.

'Begging your pardon, Master Stewart sir, but your mother requests your presence in the drawing room.'

Stewart lifted Margaret off his lap, and then straightening his coat, he left the room.

He found his parents sitting on the window seat, hands clasped together, looking out to the garden.

'Are you staying, Father?' as Stewart spoke both his hands clenched and his head spun.

Hearing her son's voice, Elizabeth turned to look at him.

'Your father will be staying,' she paused to look at her husband, 'for a while.'

Stewart looked to his father and then relaxed slightly, turning to the side to bring Margaret close to him. Looking deep into her eyes, he spoke.

'Father, I would like you to meet my wife, Margaret,' he paused to bring her hand up to his lips and then kissed her ring. 'Without her, I would not be the man that stands before you today.'

Gently, he placed his arm round her shoulders and walked her to where his father was standing. Andrew Duncan bowed to her, taking her hand in his and kissed it.

'It is a *great* pleasure to meet you, Margaret.'

'And I you, Father,' she replied, looking directly into his face smiling.

Stewart heard the breath that his mother had taken, but no one else had. She had called him father.

Margaret continued. 'I thought you might like to come and see your grandson before dinner.' Margaret had placed her hand in Andrew Duncan's arm now and was guiding him to the door. 'I am afraid he has had a lot of excitement today, and I fear that he will not be sleeping early. I should add that he is just like his father.' She turned back to see Stewart's astounded look, just as they disappeared out of the room.

Stewart felt his mother's hand take his; turning he looked down at her in bewilderment. 'How does she do that, Mother, it is as though she has known him for years... I... she never ceases to amaze me.'

Elizabeth stood up and held his arm firmly, not just because her legs felt week, but for reassurance. 'She has this ability within her to put people totally at ease, what a wonderful quality to have,' she rested her head on his arm. 'I feel very light headed, Stewart. I do believe that I have not eaten anything since this morning. Did you say Mrs Cottle has the dinner ready?'

Stewart pulled his mother round and held her tight against his chest. 'Mother, he has many very difficult decisions to make, you realise that?'

Elizabeth nodded her head against him. 'If he has to leave me, Stewart, then I must accept that...' her voice trailed away as she quietly sobbed.

Kissing the top of her head, he swallowed many times to control his own tears. 'Oh, Mother, my heart, if I could take away your pain, I would.'

***

Dinner was quiet, but not strained. Introductions were made and greetings given, but throughout the evening his mother had not taken her eyes from her husband. Alexander had been quiet also, and pensive; he had held Charlotte's hand openly on the table many times throughout the dinner. Stewart believed that the only person who truly understood his parents' feelings was William Masters; the man had greeted his father like a friend, then spoke openly and frankly about his merchant business with his father, for had his father not had an import business himself with an office in the Port of London. When it was time to retire to the drawing room, his parents had gone into the study to be alone and talk privately. Stewart had taken Margaret up to their bedroom, as she had looked very pale and had held her back constantly at dinner.

'Are you well, Maggie?' he asked as he unpinned her hair. 'You look pale.'

She held his hand and stopped him. 'I am well, Stewart, I am with child, and as you know from before, the first few months for me are... It will pass, Stewart, but this with your mother and father will not pass. She turned to face him holding his hands. 'We must find a way for them to be together, can you understand that? They *need* to be together, and if I can help in *any* way, then I will,' she paused to take a breath. 'We are given one life, Stewart, we have to make it the best we can, and they have already lost twenty-two years of theirs. It is time they were together.' Her words were spoken so avidly that Stewart was taken unawares.

'Your mother loves that man, no matter what he has done, she loves him with all her heart. Can you stand by now and watch that heart break? If it were you, I would follow you to the ends of the earth. I would not care, Stewart.' Her voice had risen.

Holding her shoulders, he pulled her to him stroking her back. 'Maggie, Maggie, be still, I understand, I do truthfully.' She was crying now so tenderly he picked her up and laid her on the bed; then lying beside her, he held her tightly till her tears stopped. 'We will find a way, Maggie, I promise.' Lifting her face to his, he kissed her. 'I love you, Maggie.'

***

Andrew Duncan looked out into the darkness that was the garden beyond. 'Our son has a remarkable wife, Lizzie.'

Elizabeth came to stand beside him, her fingers touching his arm. There was not much light in the room, just two candles burned on the mantle, casting a soft yellow glow on everything. Elizabeth gazed up at her husband; he looked like an outline of a miniature, as his bold features caught the candles flicker against the darkness of the night outside.

'Andrew, that first night when you took me away, what you said to me as we lay together... that I was... *still the sweet young lass that you married.* Did you mean that?'

He turned to face her, holding her firmly by her shoulders, his eyes searching her face.

'What do you think, Lizzie? Of course I did.' His hand came up now tracing the features of her face, her eyes, her nose, her mouth. Elizabeth closed her eyes and swallowed. She was forty-seven years of age, how could she have feelings like the ones she was experiencing now. It was as though she was melting under his touch, and tears flowed down her face again, where she thought she had none left to come. He would not ask, so she would.

'Andrew,' she whispered. 'Will you lie with me now, please.' Her tears were flowing freely now, as she pressed her lips together to stop them from quivering.

'Oh my darling, Lizzie, after all that I have done to you, you still want me?' he breathed, as he sat on the chair pulling her into his lap, then raising her face to his, he kissed her slowly and softly, as he rocked her and stroked her back.

'Yes, Lizzie, I will lie with you, if you will have me.'

***

The curtains were open, and the sky was just beginning to lighten in the east, dawn was coming. Andrew Duncan pulled Elizabeth close to him, his hand memorising every soft curve of her body. How could he leave her, but leave he must, he would never be accepted here, there were too many old wounds to heal, too many lives torn apart. Maybe she would come with him, they could be happy there, but he had nothing to offer, save a small house and a housekeeper. No luxury like here, with soft beds and open spaces, gardens, fields. How could he expect her to come and live in a town, where it was cold and raining for most of the year? She was born to this, whereas he had thrown it away. But how could he leave her now, all those years alone, unloved, hated even. His heart was sore, heavy, and his soul weary. God had seen fit in all his mercy to give him another chance... it was how he used that chance that mattered now. Slipping silently out of bed, he came to the window.

Elizabeth roused, putting out her hands to feel the place beside her, finding nothing she sat up quickly calling.

'Andrew!'

At the sound of her voice he turned. 'I am here, Lizzie, by the window,' he whispered softly.

Elizabeth was with him instantly, her arms held tight around him.

'Never do that to me again, I thought you had gone.'

She was shaking, so Andrew stepped back and pulled a cover from the bed to wrap her in, and then he stood her in front of him wrapping his arms tightly around her.

'I came to watch the sun rise, Lizzie. Where I live you cannot see any of this. Is it not marvellous, the changing colours of everything as the sun touches them, turning them from grey to the beautiful shades of day. Whatever has happened in the night, the morning gives us a blank canvas to start afresh.'

She held tightly to his hands and leaned back into him, breathing deeply feeling his warmth against her back. For twenty-two years she had slept alone, only seen the sun rise when there was illness or birth or death. Today, her heart rejoiced in everything she was seeing. She would *never* let him go again, even if it meant she had to live with him in Scotland; as long as he was with her, nothing else mattered, she loved him, always had. People think that love is just for the young, but they are wrong, for the old love comes from the depths of their souls, the young have yet to find.

Chapter Forty-Two
Redemption of the Mind and the Taking of Catherine

Stewart and Alexander were in the study, going over the accounts and writing bills that had to be signed. The running of the estate did not stop for anything or anyone; for it to turn over smoothly and yield, it had to be maintained.

'Margaret looks a little better this morning, cousin, she has lost that pallid look and actually ate some breakfast,' offered Alexander

'Do not be fooled, Alex, until she passes these first months, her stomach fluctuates, as does her colour. This afternoon she could be all at sea again.' Stewart smiled at his cousin. 'Do you not remember Charlotte?'

'Still, I believe she looks healthier than I have seen her look for some time.'

'You could be right, cousin.' Stewart stopped to dip the quill. 'I think that my father has something to do with that.'

'And my aunt. Well, she is like a young girl of twenty. God, I have never seen her so happy, not even when you married or when Charles was born.'

Stewart put his head down, writing quickly. 'Yes, well, I believe my father has something to do with that also.'

Alexander sat back, laughing quietly to himself.

'My father-in-law likes the man; he says that he is very intelligent and easy to talk to. He also has a wealth of knowledge of the import trade. I gather he was a merchant before he married my aunt.'

Stewart looked up and nodded. 'He was, but my problem is how we can get him to stay,' he was interrupted by a light tap on the door as Andrew Duncan entered.

'Good morning, to you both.'

Alexander rose sharply, bowing. 'Your servant, sir.'

Andrew Duncan placed his hand on Alexander's arm. 'You do not bow to me, my lad. A Good morning will suffice, and without the sir. No one stands on ceremony with me.' With that he offered his hand in greeting.

Alexander stood for a moment, and then took the hand he offered, 'Good morning, Uncle.'

Stewart had been watching this with more than a little amusement. 'Good morning, Father.'

'Stewart, if it be convenient and an appropriate time, I would like to meet with both Pip and Spike. Would that be possible?'

366

Stewart smiled; he knew what his father wanted. 'Father, at this present time I dare not intrude in Spike's day, as he will be with his apprentice, clipping and pruning in the gardens, making ready for winter. But at around 6pm we can go to his cottage where I will tell Pip to meet us.'

'Not us, Stewart, me.'

Stewart looked into his father's face. He would do this on his own then, ask their forgiveness; he understood the reason behind it.

'I will tell Pip to be there, Father.'

'Thank you, Stewart, now Mr Masters is going to take me around the estate, as I know that you both have work to attend, and then to show me his house. So if you will excuse me,' saying this he smiled and left.

As Stewart watched the door close, he could see the laughter in Alexander's eyes.

'Before you speak, Alex—'

'Stewart, you are so like him!' exclaimed Alexander. 'His mannerisms are all yours.'

'Hmmm, my mother always said I was like him, even down to the temper. It is paradoxical though that your father should show my father around the estate.' Stewart was laughing softly. He knew why his father had done that, to say that he was not a threat to anyone here, but an outsider who had come to stay for a while.

'Come on, Stewart, let us finish, or we will still be here at supper, and yes I do see the logic in what he has just done.'

***

As Andrew Duncan left the house, there was a slight drizzle in the air. It was mid-September, and in one week Stewart's best friend James Fairweather would marry. He had been invited, sent a gold edged invitation to both the church and the wedding breakfast, but this was their friend. It was James' father-in-law that had saved his son's life, and he would talk to the man in good time, after the wedding. There were many thanks that he had to bestow to the many people who had helped his son. Coming into the walled garden, he shifted his jacket slightly, feeling the weight of it on his shoulders, like the burden he carried with him for what he had done.

Coming up to the door, he raised his hand to knock, only to find it opening.

'Good evening, Master Duncan sir.' Spike inclined his head and stepped to one side. 'Would you like to come in and be taking a mug of ale with us?'

Andrew Duncan breathed deeply. God, the man was giving him a peace offering, whereas it should be coming from him.

'I thank you kindly, Spike. It would give me great pleasure.' Taking off his hat, Andrew Duncan ducked under the lintel and entered. Looking around, he saw Pip seated at the table; there was a well-lit fire in the hearth with two pots hanging over it. One he knew to be water, and the other, from the aroma emitting from it, was supper.

'Your supper smells good, Spike, maybe I could share it with you if you have enough?' he raised his brows in asking, then looked around the tidy room. 'And where is your apprentice? I think that he should hear what I have to say, as it could prove a lifelong lesson for him.' Andrew Duncan had removed his coat and hung it behind the door, placing his hat over it.

Pip looked to Spike, lost for words. Spike nodded and then walked to the stairs.

'Young Kenver, come you down here and get your supper. We have two guests today, so there be no second helping for ye, but you can be going to Mrs Cottle later and be having some apple pie.'

Kenver came cautiously down the stairs and then bowed low as he saw Andrew Duncan.

'Good evening, Kenver, my name is Andrew.' Saying this, he offered his hand.

Kenver looked at Spike as though he had been struck deaf.

'Take Master Duncan's hand, Kenver lad, then you can lay the table and we can all be sitting to eat.'

They ate in companionable silence for most of the meal, what talk there had been was of the estate and the gardens. It was warm in the room; candles were lit on the table as well as the mantle, and there was a peace here, he thought, a sense of calm and wellbeing. Andrew Duncan looked at the three people seated with him, then wiped the last of the gravy from his plate with some bread.

'Spike, thank you, that was so good chicken, no? And the bread.'

'I be cooking the food, sir, but the bread be Mrs Cottle's.' In fact, cook had given him a chicken when she heard that Andrew Duncan was going to go and talk with him. *Take this*, she had said, *offer him supper, bad things are always better when taken on a full stomach*. She had been right; the atmosphere of that first moment had been broken by the smell of the food.

Andrew Duncan placed his arms on the table, looking at each one in turn.

'I want you to know that I come in peace, humbled, not to try to beg your forgiveness for that cannot be asked only given—for what I did to this house. I also owe the two of you a gratitude I can never repay for the rearing of my son, for you turned him into a fine man, albeit that he has my temper. He is kind and caring, and knows the difference from right and wrong.' He paused here to look at Kenver.

'You should listen to this, man,' he nodded to Spike, 'and to this man,' he said, turning his head to Pip. 'For they are wise beyond your years. They are good honest men who will guide you into manhood.' He stopped here to take a long drink of his ale.

'I have done many wrong things in my life, for which I have paid dearly for. It was not till a certain event happened that I understood the pain that I had brought to the people that I loved dearly. I went home to lick my wounds, and found a young minister who listened to my story and helped me see how I could repay, and try to right the wrongs.' He turned to look at Kenver now.

'No man should bow to me, young Kenver, for I am not worthy of that. I am human like you, but I chose a path of self-destruction. NEVER be tempted to that road.' He stopped once more to finish his ale.

'I sit here before you to ask that you do not hate me, and if you can find some empathy in your hearts, I would be eternally grateful.'

Kenver's hands were tying themselves in knots, and his eyes were as round as saucers. Pip turned to him and placed his hand on the boy's arm.

'Listen to the man, young Kenver, and learn by his mistakes. Never be eaten by jealousy, for this will be destroying your soul lad. Ye be a good boy, ye listen well, but always be remembering to be showing respect for your fellow man, for that way ye will also find self-respect, Lad.'

Andrew Duncan stood slowly; taking his coat down and pulling it on, he inclined his head.

'I bid you all a very good evening and thank you most humbly for your company and excellent food.' He turned to open the door, and then paused to look back.

'I owe you my soul, gentlemen. You know what that is for.' Bowing slightly, he placed his hat on his head and left.

The room was deathly quiet, the only noise came from the fire, which was slowly burning down now, ready to be banked for tomorrow. Pip stood and stretched a little, as Kenver collected the plates, ready to wash them.

Then Pip offered his hand to Spike. 'I think we be in agreement then, Spike.'

Spike stood, took Pip's hand and shook it firmly. 'Yes, we be in agreement. I have never seen my mistress as happy as she has been these past days. Let us be hoping that they can both find some peace together.'

**

Stewart sat in the study with his father; it was the only place that they would not be interrupted, as the house knew that Stewart used it as his office for work concerning the estate. Pouring out two whiskies, he handed one to his father, then went to stand by the window. It was early afternoon, lunch had finished, the women had all retired to the nursery, and Alexander and William Masters sat talking in the drawing room. The day outside was grey and windy; they had been hoping for an Indian summer as James wedding was just over a week away, on Wednesday 25th September, but if there was no change, then the most they could hope for was sun. He wondered how James was, as he had had no word from him since his return from Scotland. The man was harassed by his wife-to-be in more ways than one. Stewart smiled at the thought, poor James, she would have him entwined around her finger, and there would be no mercy. Standing there, he started to chuckle.

'May I join in the joke, Stewart?' came his father's voice from beside him.

'Oh, Father, it is my dear friend James. He is a kind, gentle, unselfish man, and I love him dearly, but his wife will have him eating out of her hand—if she has not already. When you meet him, you will understand.'

His father laughed, 'Oh, I think I understand, Stewart, do not all women enchant us, and we let them, because deep inside we love every moment of it. It flatters our egos and does wonders for our self-esteem.'

'You are right of course, Father,' he replied, taking a sip of his drink.

'This brings me to what I want to say to you.' Coming around, he seated himself opposite his father.

'James' father—for what I did for his son—gifted me a house which is in Torquay, Devon. It is situated in the bay right on the sea front and has spectacular views; you do not even have to leave the house to see it, as all rooms look directly out onto the sea. So while I and the rest of the family are at the wedding, you and mother will go there to spend two weeks together.' He raised his hand to stop his father from speaking.

'I have arranged everything. Margaret's cook and Butler will go with you, along with Carter, Fulton and Molly, my mother's maid. The house has been cleaned and will be ready for you from Friday of this week. So you will both leave tomorrow.'

Andrew Duncan had his head bowed, and was looking at his feet.

Stewart stood up. 'Is there something wrong, Father?'

Andrew Duncan shook his head and put his hand up. Then standing he placed his glass on the table and came to embrace his son.

'Thank you,' was all he said as he left the room.

Alexander came into the room looking back at Andrew Duncan's departing figure.

'Stewart, your father looks upset, is everything well?'

'Yes, everything is perfect,' he replied as he swallowed the rest of his whisky down in one gulp.

***

Margaret sat in front of her mirror brushing her hair, watching Stewart undress, till he sat slowly on the bed in just his shirt with a puzzled look on his face. Pushing his hair back out of his eyes, he sat with his hands on the side of the bed, head bowed.

Margaret continued to watch him; he was deep in thought, she could tell that, something was troubling him, and she had a notion she knew what that was. She stopped and put the hair brush back onto the table.

'What troubles you, Stewart? I think that I can guess, it is your mother, no?'

Stewart's eyes turned to her, as she kept her gaze on him through the mirror.

'Shall I tell you what you are thinking? You are wondering how your mother can take your father back to her bed.' She paused here to watch his reaction.

'Maggie, what are you saying?' he looked at her embarrassment mingled with shock showing on his face.

'I am saying, Stewart, that your mother is a very wise woman. We all know that your father does not intend to stay here, he has his own life now, and he

370

thinks—be it right or wrong—that no one will accept him here now. Am I right so far?'

Stewart kept her gaze and nodded.

'By taking him to her bed, she has made it very hard, or impossible even, for him to leave her. she has given your father a chance to see what he had before he left, and what he would not have if he chose to go now.'

Stewart had risen to come and stand behind Maggie.

'My mother has done this thing?'

Maggie turned taking his hands, pulling him onto the stool beside her.

'Stewart, you are a very wise man, but also naive.' She put her hand up to cup his face.

'They still love one another, need one another, *want* one another.' She closed her eyes and sighed.

'Stewart, do you think that love is just for the young? That when you reach a certain age in your life, you do not want that kind of love?' She pulled his head down to her and kissed him.

'I will want you till I die,' she whispered, and kissed him again with passion, then pulling back once more her eyes searched his face.

'Your mother will never lose him again, even if it means that she has to follow him to Scotland.' She smiled into his eyes. 'Now, I want *you* to lie with *me*, and *love me* like you always do.' She stood and pushed her shift over her shoulders, letting it fall to the floor.

Stewart shook his head slightly, then lifted her in his arms and laid her onto the bed. The only light in the room came from one candle, the open drapes and the fire's red glow. She could see his face in shadow as he bent and kissed her lightly, and then removing his shirt, he gently laid full stretch on top of her, his hands pushing the hair from her face as he kissed her deeply.

'You are a very perceptive woman, Margaret Hamilton, and so is my mother.' His words were lost as she pulled him back down to kiss him once more.

***

Stewart sat in his study, pensively looking out to the garden. He had said goodbye to his mother and father early yesterday morning; they had seemed happy and content in one another's company. If truth be told, it was the first time that he had seen his mother genuinely happy. That did not differ from the fact that he still found it strange when he saw them together. He had grown up with just his mother, with just vague memories of his father that came and went in his head like a dream. The times they met later in life were filled with resentment, in that other fathers loved their sons, why was he not loved. He knew now that this was his own fabrication of events; he also knew that his father had loved him.

Stewart put his head in his hands for about the tenth time that morning, pushing his fingers into his skull in an attempt to unscramble the thoughts in his mind.

371

It was then he heard the shouts coming from the hall. Leaping to his feet he ran from the room. As his eyes adjusted to the brightness of the hall, he saw Sir Henry Portman first; behind him was James and his father, then he saw the lawyer Sir Richard Sutton. Stewart stopped in his tracks as James came towards him.

'He has taken her Stewart,' was all he said, and Stewart saw the pain and desperation in his eyes.

'My mother?' he breathed, watching James fixedly.

'No Stewart,' came James' soft reply. 'Catherine.'

***

They were all seated in the drawing room, as the study in the Willows was small, and would not accommodate six people for more than a few hours, it was better here; a person could pace the room to help him with his thoughts, plus the fact that Edward Bearcroft had just joined them.

She had been taken while in Bath at a Milliner with her mother. Catherine had remained in the coach with the coachman. It was then that a man had come up beside the coachman with a concealed pistol under his cape and told the coachman to move quickly.

'We now know that they changed coaches just outside of the town, for that is where Sir Henry's coach was found abandoned. Then they had proceeded to Portsmouth.' Bearcroft was standing by the window as he relayed this information.

'My sources tell me that they boarded a ship—the *Poseidon*—bound for Le Havre.' He paused here to seat himself on the window seat.

'I sent my men on the next available ship, The *Poseidon*, it seems, was only bound for Le Havre to collect wines. I have instructed them to speak with the captain to ascertain where they went from there—that is of course if he knows.'

The silence in the room was as a crypt; each man sat looking at the floor with the exception of Bearcroft and Stewart, whose eyes were on each another.

Stewart addressed Bearcroft. 'It is Northcott, is it not, sir?'

'We believe so, Mr Hamilton, but he was not the man who took the coach.'

'When will your man return?' queried Stewart.

'Bearcroft breathed deeply. 'Not before night. We told him to come here.'

'Dear God, that is forty-eight hours!' shouted Stewart. 'They could be anywhere.'

Sir Henry, who had not spoken since he arrived, stood up.

'He is a dead man, if he defiles my daughter or not, he is DEAD.' His voice was calm but sonorous.

James's voice came out of the silence, soft but resigned.

'He will do what he set out to do over a year ago.' Looking up at his friend, he shook his head.

Stewart took James by the elbow and pulled him to his feet.

'You and I will take a walk in the gardens.' Nodding to him he led him from the room.

**

Margaret and Charlotte watched from the Nursery window as Stewart and James walked back and forth on the grass below. They had heard the disturbance in the hall, and then everyone had gone to the drawing room, where they had been ever since.

'Something very bad has happened,' Charlotte said as she stood next to her sister, holding her sleeping daughter in her arms.

'I know, Charlotte, but it does not concern Stewart's mother or father; this is something far more sinister. Your father and Alexander are at the estate office this morning, but they will be back by lunch, maybe then we will find out.'

She placed an arm around her sister's shoulders, stroking her niece's cheek with her finger.

'She is so beautiful, Charlotte, and so peaceful. Why cannot life always be this way?' Pulling her sister in, she laid her head against hers.

**

Stewart looked sideways at his friend; what could he say to him, had he not seen for himself what the man was capable of when they had burst into the room at the Coaching Inn in Exeter?

'James, Catherine is a very resourceful women, she will try and thwart him.'

Stewart was stopped as James turned around

'Stewart, the man is taller than you and bigger. Catherine is like Charlotte, but thinner. Are you trying to tell me that she can fight him off?'

'No, James, no, you misread me. What I mean is that she will try to escape. That is what I believe. Think of the family she is from, they are, or were, all in the army. You do not live in a house like that, without having some understanding of tactics and strategy.' Stewart placed his arm about James' shoulders.

'James, she escaped from her home without anyone knowing, made her way from Bath to Salisbury, and from there to Exeter. Does that not tell you something about her?'

James rubbed his hands over his face several times, then looking up he saw Alexander walking towards them, as he came near, he placed a hand on James' shoulder.

'James, Charlotte's father knows the captain of that ship; it is a small merchant vessel, only sailing from Portsmouth to Le Havre to take on wine. It does not travel on anywhere else. Unless they have secured another ship, they will be somewhere in the port or have driven into the countryside of France.'

James looked from Stewart to Alexander, resignation showing on his face. 'They have had over 24 hours start on us; by the time we knew of where they were bound, they had already reached their destination. Anything that we do or say now is pure speculation and hope.'

'Nevertheless,' continued Alexander, 'Mr Masters and I will be leaving for Portsmouth within the hour. My father knows many captains there, and if needs be, we will sail for France,' Alexander stated with determination.

'Then I am coming with you, Alex.' Stewart was stopped by Alexander before he could finish.

'You will be going nowhere, is it not enough that he nearly killed you last time, would you give him a second chance, cousin? You will stay here with Sir Henry and the lawyers. Charlotte is at this moment packing our bags to take; we will travel by horse, as it will be quicker, and hopefully change them en-route.'

As Alexander finished, he saw Margaret coming towards them.

'Do not worry, Margaret, he is *not* coming, he will be staying here with James.'

James turned to Alexander then. 'Oh no, my friend, I am coming with you, when they find her, I will be there.'

Stewart nodded to Alexander. 'Take him with you, but for God's sake keep him out of the line of fire.' Turning to James, he added, 'You are a man of learning, James, not of action. Be safe, my friends.' Stewart embraced both and watched them go back across the lawn. Placing his arm around Margaret, he saw them disappear into the house.

'And may God go with you.'

Chapter Forty-Three
Catherine and Northcott—The Chase

Catherine sat opposite Northcott, huddled in a deep red woollen cloak, the hood pulled around her face, and her arms tightly wrapped around her body underneath. She was furious, but scared. She would not show her fear to him though, lest he take advantage of her terror that was slowly building up inside her. Setting her mouth into a thin line, she stared hard into his eyes.

'How dare you kidnap me!' Her voice was slow but steady.

'Stop the carriage immediately or I will jump!'

Northcott's eyes roamed over her as she sat in the opposite corner, his mouth curling up in a sardonic smile.

'You have no bargaining powers with me, fair Charlotte, did you not agree to elope with me before? Do you think I will let happen again what happened then? Hamilton has paid dear for his mistake, believe me, even unto his life. Do I make myself clear? I will kill any man who tries to stop me now, even your father.'

It was cold in the coach, and Charlotte could see Northcott's breath swirl like a mist around his head every time he spoke. She pulled herself up straight and then stared unwaveringly into his eyes.

'They will find you, have no fear of that, sir. This time I will not stop in disclosing your name.' Catherine was shaking, but she held her hands tight around her waist lest he see just how much, clamping her mouth tight shut again to stop her teeth from chattering.

Northcott moved slightly, crossing his legs. 'I think not, as we will not be in the country, for within a few hours we will set sail.' He watched her closely now to see her reaction. It was her eyes that told him of her fear.

'My father is a major in the army; he will have them and the navy looking for you.'

Northcott put up his hand to stop her. 'My dear, he knows nothing of your abduction at this present time, and when he does, we will have left the shores of England.' He raised his brow in confirmation, nodding slightly.

As they reached the outskirts of Bath, the coach slowed. Northcott reached across the carriage and grabbed Catherine by the arm, pulling her face close to his he spoke.

'Get down now, and do not scream, or it will be your last.' Showing her a small dagger that he held in his left hand, he stepped backwards out of the carriage pulling her with him.

It was then that she saw the black carriage waiting just ahead.

'What are you doing?' she questioned, but his hand had tightened its grip on her arm, causing her to wince in pain.

'You did not think that I would drive to the port in this coach, did you, with your father's Coat of Arms emblazoned on the side for the whole countryside to see and track us?'

Pushing her into the new carriage, he slammed the door shut, then banged hard with his fist on the roof for it to move. Leaning out of the window, he issued his orders.

'You stop for nothing!' he yelled.

'But you have to, I need—' her voice was stopped as Northcott leaned down and retrieved a chamber pot from under the seat, pushing it into her face.

'If you need it, use it, and then throw its contents from the window.'

Catherine did not need to see, to know that the blood had drained from her face. Her head began to swim and small white dots seemed to come from nowhere from the corners of her eyes into her sight. She laid her head back onto the seat and prayed. She had to keep her mind steady if she was to survive, she knew that. She was not stupid, and did not get an attack of the vapours at the sight of blood. God, had she not grown up in a military house? She had a strong will, much to her father's consternation. No, she would bide her time now till she reached the port, knowing that she had the whole journey to plan what she could do when she arrived there.

***

By the time Alexander and William rode into Portsmouth, it was just before midnight. It had rained the last hour of their journey and both men's cloaks and hats were soaked through. Dismounting outside The Dolphin Inn, they led their horses to the stables behind.

'This is where Captain Houghton usually rests when he is in Port. We will go and enquire inside and find a room if one be available, for I fear we cannot do much till morning now.'

'How did you deter James from coming?' queried Alexander.

'Oh that was not I but her father; he did not intend to happen to him what happened to Stewart,' replied William.

Alexander nodded in agreement and followed his father-in-law into the inn. The place was stifling, reeking of bodies and smoke. Several sailors were asleep where they sat, others were playing cards. Someone somewhere was singing a sea shanty while others clapped, and as they came close to the counter, they could see the owner in quiet conversation with a young woman, who when she smiled, seemed to be missing her front teeth.

William coughed to get his attention. 'Begging your pardon, sir, but would you know if a Captain Houghton is in Port, he commands the *Poseidon*?'

The man looked up, and then wiped his hands on his apron before standing up to his full height. Alexander noted that he was taller than and twice as wide as himself, but then he had to be to run an establishment the likes of this one.

'And who be asking after him, may I know, sir?'

There was no humour in his tone, but William Masters was unfazed. Alexander pondered that he probably had to deal with such men in Norwich.

'I am a friend of his from Norwich, sir, our acquaintance goes back many years.'

The innkeeper narrowed his eyes and thought for a moment.

'Yes, he be in room five, ship came in on the evening tide today. I would not be disturbing the man till morning if I were you, he is somewhat... engaged at the present time.' The innkeeper looked at the women next to him and smiled lasciviously.

William Masters swallowed and looked hard at Alexander.

'I am sorry, sir, but I really must insist, as a young woman's life depends on it.'

The innkeeper hunched his shoulders and shook his head.

'Be it on your own head then, but I did warn ye. Take the stairs, and then turn to the right.' With that he turned away to the woman and continued his conversation.

As they came up to the door, William turned to Alexander. 'Please, do not say a word, let me speak.' Alexander nodded in reply as William Masters knocked on the door.

Alexander looked around the corridor and shuddered; it was darker than the night outside with one lone candle burning in a sconce at the far end. It smelt no better here than in the tavern below and there were very audible voices from the other rooms, denoting what type of establishment The Dolphin was. Well, he reprimanded himself, this was a sea port full of sailors, who had been enclosed aboard ship, some for many months, how would he feel himself if he were one of them? Then he remembered Charlotte and the feel of her warm body close to his. His thoughts were drawn back as William wrapped on the door a second time. His second knock received a response of cursing and shouting, then something crashed and footsteps could be heard coming towards the door. A voice was shouting as the door opened.

'There had better be a good excuse for this or I will slice your ears off.' As Houghton stepped into the corridor, Alexander saw that he wore just a nightshirt and supported a rather large knife in his right hand.

Houghton stood frozen in front of William Masters, his mouth open in shock.

'Good God, Masters, what in hell's name are you doing here!' he bellowed.

William looked hard into the man's eyes. 'I am on an errand of mercy, Houghton. When you hear what I have to say, you will understand.'

Houghton looked at both men discerning if it were a trick; having seen that it was not, he inclined his head. 'Normally, I would invite you in, but give me a few minutes and I will meet you both in the tavern below.'

'Thank you,' came William Masters only reply.

They made their way back to the tap room below, seating themselves on two stools that had just been vacated. William Masters turned to Alexander.

'We will get no food till morning, so I suggest that we do not imbibe, we need our heads clear, Alex.'

'I understand, Father,' was all Alexander said.

William looked around him, stoking his face with his hand. 'I thought I had seen the last of places like this when I left Norfolk. Now you understand why I kept my precious daughter hidden.'

Alexander closed his eyes as a shiver went down his spine. Opening them again, he saw Houghton coming fully clothed towards him. The inn had quietened; the singing had stopped and had been replaced by snores and the occasional fart, which only added to the reek. He thought to himself what a sheltered life he had led, both in Edinburgh and Mere, an angel must have smiled on him giving him such a bountiful life.

Pulling up another stool, Houghton spoke. 'Right Masters, what is it that is so urgent that a life depends on it?'

William entwined his fingers, placing his elbows on the table. 'You carried a young woman passenger with you to Le Havre two days past.'

Houghton frowned. 'The young nun bound for the Abbey there?' he questioned with surprise.

'A young woman yes, but no nun, believe me. She had been kidnapped from her father's coach while in the town of Bath with her mother, her father being Major Sir Henry Portman of His Majesty's Army, relative of the Earl Cornwallis.'

There was a silence where Houghton's mouth fell open, staying that way for several moments. Then finding his voice, he answered.

'But she was with her brother, Masters, bound to join the sisters of *Sainte Honorine*. Dear God, the man will have me flogged, then hung drawn and quartered.'

'I can assure you he will not,' was Masters quick reply. 'Did she occupy a cabin for the crossing?'

'I have no cabins on that ship, Masters, she stayed in mine till the ship docked, when she was escorted to a waiting Coach,' he replied, rubbing his forehead in consternation.

Alexander watched Houghton; he looked ill at this moment and knowing what he now knew who could blame him. He was sure that her father had sent word to the major of the barracks nearby, and he in turn had probably called upon the navy to assist him. Alexander felt nothing by empathy for the man.

'Did you say that she stayed in your cabin?' William Masters had been thinking hard. 'Was she alone in the cabin? Or did her... brother stay with her?'

'Oh God no, she was alone in the cabin, and I myself had locked the door and put a sentry outside, if you understand my meaning, Masters.'

William nodded, but his mind was still whirring. 'May we see your cabin? What I am saying is that she may have left a sign as to where she was to be taken when she reached Le Havre, if she knew that is.'

Houghton stood up quickly. 'We will go now.' Saying this he made for the door.

The night was cold, and as they walked to the quayside, a fine rain started to fall once more. The streets were busy, even for the early hours of the morning, but Alexander mused to himself that this was a port, and such places had another life after dark.

As they came up the gangway, Houghton turned. 'Masters, what are we looking for?'

'I have no notion, except that the young women is a very resourceful person. If she could have given us a sign, then she would have done so. We just have to look thoroughly in your cabin, there has to be something.' William looked to Alexander in hopefulness.

Houghton called to a sailor who was on watch to bring two lanterns to his cabin, and that he wanted them by yesterday. Masters raised his brows, while Alexander crossed himself.

As they entered, Alexander saw that the room was small, with a table under a small latticed window, which seemed to be overflowing with charts and maps. There was a small bunk to the left-hand side which consisted of a ticking covered mattress and a blanket. He looked around as the others searched the table; it was then he saw the ship's log lying on the chair.

'Sir, is that your log?' queried Alexander.

'What, sir? Ah yes, but who moved it from the shelf?' Houghton picked up the leather-bound book and opened it. 'I have not made the entry for the return journey yet, as it was too late in the evening, I was to write it up in the morning when my head was clearer, if you understand me.'

William nodded. 'Open it to the last entry if you please, she maybe left something within its pages.' He wiped his hand over his face for the hundredth time that day, feeling the grown of beard on his chin rasp as he touched it.

Placing the book on the table, Houghton felt for the leather marker that he always used and flipped the pages, it was blank.

'This is not the last page; someone has handled this, and it has not been me.'

As Alexander looked at the page, his eyes caught some writing down in the left corner.

'What is that, sir?' he asked.

'What? Where?' questioned Houghton. It was then he saw the handwriting, just two words: "*Dieppe England*".

'Dear God, he has taken her by coach to Dieppe!'

Alexander's head was spinning now; if Stewart were here, he would have read this situation in an instant and found the outcome.

'He is bringing her back to England again!' shouted William Masters. 'He is returning on another ship, but where will it dock, Portsmouth?!' he turned to look at the two baffled faces. 'Do you not see, by now he is already in England! We will go to the Harbour Master at first light.'

***

Catherine sat in her cabin aboard the *Achilles*; she was cold, hungry and most of all terrified. She had been made to change her gown and now wore a dark blue woollen one of a governess. The only sign she had been able to leave as to her whereabouts was the one she had left in the *Poseidon* log. Though food had been offered, she had eaten very little, and at this moment she felt more than a little light headed. She looked at the plate of bread and cheese that had been left earlier and decided that if she was to survive, then she must eat something; but with each bite she took, she felt her stomach churn. Catherine looked about her; there was a bottle of wine on the desk, but that was of no use to her, her head was spinning now, then her eyes rested on a jug of water, just how long it had been there she had no idea, but she poured a little wine into the glass and topped it with the water—if anything it would make the food go down easier. Slowly, she managed to consume two slices of the bread and a little cheese—which to her taste seemed slightly rancid—mayhap it was of some French variety.

The captain, a Mr Reynolds, had insisted that she remain in his cabin, just as Captain Houghton of the *Poseidon*. It was then that she heard a soft rap on the door as Captain Reynolds opened it slightly; not entering, he spoke from the doorway.

'Is there anything I can get you, Mistress?'

Catherine stared hard at the man; she knew that she was trembling slightly and put her hand back to steady herself on the table. It was then that she decided.

'*Help me.*' Her lips mimed but no sound came from her mouth.

The captain stood there for some seconds, his eyes never leaving hers. Then Catherine looked past him and back once more, miming the same words, '*help me*'. The captain then inclined his head and spoke.

'I will fetch you some fresh water then, Mistress.' Closing the door, he locked it once more.

As Captain Reynolds turned, he looked down at the deck below him, watching the man that had brought the young lady aboard his ship. She was a governess he had said, going back to England to a new post, and he had been sent to ensure her safe passage. He placed the key to his cabin safely into the pocket of his coat and came down to the deck to Northcott.

'Good evening to you, sir. I fear that it will not be a smooth crossing as the wind and elements tell me that we are in for a storm. I would advise you to go down to the galley, sir; it will be safer there, warmer and dry.'

Northcott looked up at the captain's cabin.

'I can assure you, sir that the young lady will be safe, as I shall remain on deck all the way to Southampton, so you need have no worry there.'

380

Northcott eyed the captain distrustfully.

'And if the ship gets in trouble?'

'She will be the first person I shall save, sir,' came Reynolds level reply.

Northcott nodded grudgingly. He had been on board a ship in a storm, a ship a lot bigger that the small vessel they were now sailing on. He knew what the seas could do, and besides the girl could go nowhere till they reach the port.

'I will leave her in your hands, Captain.'

There was insinuation and threat in his words, Reynolds read that immediately. As he watched him go below, Captain Reynolds looked up to the sky and sighed deeply.

'Please Lord, I *never* ask this of you, but let there be a squall this night, just a small one.'

***

It had been a bad night with rain and wind lashing against the windows of the inn; he and William had sat in the inglenook by the fire and dosed. Neither had really slept, then just before 6am they made their way to the Harbour Master's office. Alexander looked up at the sky which was just beginning to lighten, the wind had eased and the rain had stopped, but this did nothing to quell the noises around them—a port never slept. Alexander thought of the Willows at this time of day—quiet—not even the birds would have woken yet. William Masters' voice broke into his thoughts.

'Alexander, is that not Stewart's horse outside the office?' William's voice held trepidation in it.

'Dear God, something has happened,' answered Alexander, who had quickened his pace to a run as they approached the building. They were just about to enter when Stewart's form reared up in front of them, causing them to knock into one another as they stopped abruptly. For a brief moment no one spoke as each man eyed the other.

'What is wrong?' Alexander and William Masters spoke in unison.

Stewart placed a hand on both of them, manoeuvring them into the road away from the door.

'Nothing is wrong, except their ship has gone to Southampton.' Stewart watched the expressions change on their faces. 'It was never meant to dock here. Let us go somewhere private to talk.' Turning on his heels, he led them away from the dock.

Stewart looked about the inn and rubbed his chin, while his eyes roamed about the room. 'You chose your place well, I see.' There was an ironic tone to his voice.

'Stewart, Mr Masters knew that when Captain Houghton was in port, he always came here; besides it was midnight, and we were soaked to the skin. We had no choice in the matter.'

Stewart breathed deeply, 'My apologies, gentlemen, but Sir Henry received word that they had boarded another ship in Dieppe, the *Achilles*, bound back to

England. There was no one left to come after you. I would not let James, and Margaret will never speak to me again,' he added in a very sombre tone.

Alexander looked at his father–in–law. 'Margaret shouted at you?' came his astonished reply.

'Oh, she did more than that, Alex; she threw things at me and then began to pound me with her fists. I had to nearly squeeze the life from her to get her to listen to me.' Stewart lowered his voice a little. 'She said she will never forgive me. This was a Maggie I have never seen before.' He shook his head.

William Masters coughed. 'Stewart, that woman nursed you from the clutches of death, she never left your side for one moment, and she gave up something so precious to her just to take you to a place where you could heal. You now tell me she has no right to be angry, my young man?'

'Dear God, no, Mr Masters. I loathe myself for having had to do this to her, but I had no choice.'

William stood up. 'Right. I shall try and procure some breakfast for us. Alexander and I have not eaten since yesterday noon, and I am guessing that you are the same, Stewart, so if you will excuse me.'

Alexander watched his cousin, seeing the strain on his face. 'Go home, Stewart. Do you want the man to finish what he started last December? We can handle it from here as I am sure that Sir Henry has deployed soldiers now in Southampton.'

'Do you not understand, cousin,' Stewart interrupted, 'this is all because of *me*. It started with her… it has to end now.'

'I agree, cousin, but not with your life as forfeit. You will go home, and Charlotte's father and I will make our way to Southampton, as I think that is where everybody will be headed now.' Alexander watched his cousin closely for any sign of disagreement then nodded his head.

'Shall I tell you how you feel, Stewart?' Alexander smiled at his cousin. 'For the first time in your life you feel that you are not in control, am I right?'

Stewart smiled back and nodded.

'That is fine, Stewart, you have done all you can; you must step back now and let someone else take the lead. They will find her, I have no doubt of that. Go home, Stewart, please.' Alexander leaned forward and gripped Stewart's arm.

***

Catherine was finding it very difficult to stay on the bunk. As she looked around her, the cabin was littered with the debris of papers, bottles, maps and everything else that was not nailed or tied down; in fact, the ship seemed to have no weight at all, and was being tossed as a piece of kindle wood. She knew that if it sank now, there would be no escape for her; she would go with the rest of the crew to the bottom of the channel. Catherine shook her head, trying to push these thoughts from her mind and concentrate on keeping herself on the bunk. If she fell to the floor, there would be nothing to hold onto and she too would be tossed with the rest of the debris. The noise was intense; there was the roar of the wind, the creaking of the ship's timbers as well as an extremely high-pitched whine which she could not fathom at all. Her vision was also another problem to contend with, as her head was tossed rather unceremoniously from one end of the bunk to the other. At one point she thought she had gone blind, but discovered to her horror that her skirts were wrapped around her upper body, leaving her legs and lower body naked. Amidst the tumult, she did not hear the cabin door open, and it was not until Captain Reynolds stood before her, holding onto a beam above, that she realised he was there. Catherine gave a small scream which was muffled by Reynolds placing a hand to her mouth.

'Hush, child, please,' he called into her ear, then releasing his hand, he continued. 'Put these clothes on, tuck your hair up into this hat; your life and mine may depend on it.' Saying this, Captain Reynolds held out some breeches, a coat, shirt and a tricorn hat.

Sitting beside her, he spoke into her ear once more, giving her instructions that she would leave the ship as soon as it docked in Southampton with the rest of the sailors. Then taking her by the shoulders, he shook her.

'Please, Mistress, you have to do what I tell you, or we will both die.'

Catherine's eyes stared at him in disbelief. Her face was the colour of flour, and her hands shook uncontrollably.

'You must go to St Michael's square not far from the dock, then to the church there which bears the same name and ask for sanctuary.' Shaking her once more, he added. 'Do you understand me?'

She nodded slowly, then turned away and wretched onto the floor.

***

Catherine was amongst the first sailors that left the ship to secure its ropes to its moorings. Not looking back, she ran into the throng of people and kept running till she was as far from the dock as she could get. Stopping to get her breath, she looked around her; there were many people, both men and women, some selling food others just going about their business. Her feet were sore and bleeding as she had no shoes; the ones that the captain had left were too large, while her own were unsuitable for anything other than riding in a carriage. As she looked around her, she saw a woman selling pies—she would ask the way to St Michaels square.

Lowering her voice a tone and trying her best to mimic the Wiltshire accent, she spoke. 'Good day to you Mistress, can you be telling me where the Church of St Michael's be?'

The woman looked at her from feet to head, staring hard. 'And who be asking like?'

Charlotte swallowed. 'I be meeting my father there, having just come down from a ship.'

The woman grabbed her arm. 'Do you be running away from your captain, my lad? What ship do you be on? Methinks I will go ask him now.'

Catherine froze. 'Mr Reynolds do be giving me permission, as my father is sick.'

The woman still had her arm in a vice-like grip when a voice spoke behind her.

'I be Captain Reynolds, Mistress, and I gave this young lad permission—do not be troubling yourself, as I will take him there now.' Bowing lowly to the woman, he took Catherine firmly by the elbow and led her away.

Chapter Forty-Four
The Rescue

It was five days since Stewart left home. Now as he slowly made his way through the estate to the house, he had had many hours to reflect and collect the thoughts that had played out in his mind. What he would say to Maggie, would she even speak to him, as when he left she had screamed at him, '*Go kill yourself, Stewart,*' then had slammed the front door so hard it had echoed around the countryside. This was a Maggie he had never seen before. She had pleaded with him not to go, to think of his son if not her, but he had thought only of the hate he had for Northcott. When William and Alexander had left, his need to go with them had built to such a point where he could not stand to be shut up helpless within the walls of the house. Everything was about Northcott and himself; all others that had been hounded over the past years were a direct result of what happened at that inn in Exeter that night. How could he sit lamely by and watch him destroy everything? Seeing the estate office before him, he dismounted and walked towards it, then tethering his horse to a tree, he opened the door and went in. It was ice cold inside; there had been no fire lit for many days now, and as the day was grey outside, there was very little light within. Stewart walked to the desk; seeing mail that had been left there, he placed them in his pocket. There was also a bottle of whisky that Alexander kept there, and uncorking it he began to pour some into a mug then stopped. He shook his head; no, this was not the answer, he would not go home to Maggie drunk. Pouring the liquid back, he turned on his heel and left.

As he approached the house, he saw Spike in the gardens to the left. The man had stood up and looked at him; taking his hat off he nodded. Stewart walked towards the man, rubbing his hands over his face, and as he did so, he felt the three day growth of beard there. Stopping before him, he then looked down into Spike's eyes.

'I am pleased to see you home safely Master Stewart.' Spike's words were slow and even.

'Spike, I…' he began, 'how are things in the house, is everyone well?'

Spike nodded again. 'Go in, Master Stewart, and if I may be so bold, you should *never* have done what you did, sir.' Spike lowered his head.

Stewart closed his eyes and breathed deeply. 'Oh God, Spike, my temper got the better of me once more. I hope she will forgive me,' with that he turned on his heel and went up the steps to the door, then just as he was about to knock, it opened and Thompson bowed to Stewart.

'We are very glad to see you home, Master Stewart, Milady is in the drawing room.' His voice was as calm as always, betraying no emotion.

As he spoke, Stewart saw Daisy coming down the stairs with his son, who on seeing his father held out his arms, struggling to be free. Taking him from her he held him close.

'Thank you, Daisy,' was all he said.

Stewart saw her as he came into the drawing room, sitting on the window seat, looking out to the gardens. He knew that she had heard him enter, but she made no move to speak or look at him. Young Charles held tight to his father's neck, pulling at his hair, loosening the ribbon that tied it as he always did. It was as though he sensed something was wrong; now both father and son watched her, waiting for her to speak. As Margaret's head turned, Stewart saw the look of surprise in her eyes as she saw Charles.

'Very wise, Stewart, bringing our son with you as your defence, to make your peace offering.' Her voice was even, but had an edge to it.

Stewart walked slowly towards her, his eyes never leaving hers; he seated himself next to her, and then took her hand in his entwining his fingers in hers, while his eyes still held her gaze. Charles also stared at his mother, sucking his thumb, and then pulling it from his mouth, he called.

'Papa,' he said quietly, and then hid his face in his father's neck.

Margaret saw the look on Stewart's face change.

'Did he...?'

Margaret nodded to him. 'He has been calling for you since you left, Stewart.'

She saw him swallow several times before he spoke.

'I am so very sorry, Maggie.' Disentangling Charles from his neck, he lowered him to the floor; seeing him about to protest, he reached across and gave him a biscuit from the tray on the small table.

'Here, Charles, it is one of Mrs Cottles, you will like it.' Charles' small fingers gripped it eagerly, and then he put it to his mouth and licked happily.

Turning to face Margaret, he cupped her head at the back and pulled her into him, kissing her softly. He felt her yield to him as her hand came up to hold his own head, but as she pulled away from him her eyes bore into his.

'Never do that to me again, Stewart Hamilton.' Her voice was stopped as he drew her to him kissing her deeply.

Stewart felt a small hand grip his knee, and looking down, he saw his son was pointing to the tray for more.

'Papa... mmmmm.' His small head was nodding as he pointed to the tray of biscuits.

Stewart smiled at his son, picking him up onto his knee once more. 'No more, Charles, we will go to nanny Daisy now, so you can eat your lunch and let your father and mother eat theirs in peace.'

Charles put up his arms to his mother just as Margaret pulled him towards her.

'Come, I will take you,' she was stopped as Charles turned and grabbed for his father once more.

'Papa... Papa,' he called.

'Oh, so you want your father to take you, yes?' Charles' reply was to grab his father by the ear, climbing onto him. She watched him now, and looking at her son's face, she could see the starting of the straight nose that would come with age, and those large deep blue eyes fringed by long dark lashes. Running her hand through his silky soft black curly hair, she smiled.

'He is so like you, Stewart. Go, get your lunch,' she rubbed her nose into her son's, biting his cheek playfully. Charles giggled and then clung to his father once more.

Still holding her hand, he squeezed it tight. 'I will be back, and then we can have ours.'

As they left, Margaret relaxed; breathing deeply she closed her eyes and felt two large tears fall to her hands in her lap.

'If you ever do that to me again, I will kill you myself, Stewart Hamilton,' she whispered to the silence.

***

Margaret was already in bed when Stewart entered their room. She had been strange all day, watching him intently, as though he would disappear. He saw she had left two candles burning; one by the bed the other on the table by the mirror. Stewart undressed slowly, and then gently laying down beside her on his back, he felt for the ring on her hand, closing her hand around it with his own.

'My father told me... he told me that I had found a woman of great worth,' he paused to compose himself. 'He said... I should *never* betray her trust.' Turning to look at her now, he brought her hand up and kissed her ring. 'Oh, Maggie, I fear I have done this, can you forgive me?' Turning away he stared at the canopy above.

Maggie turned on her side, looking at his profile as it stood out dark against the glow from the candle which burnt beside him on the table.

'Stewart, many good people brought you back from the brink of death, you do not realise how close you were to...' She put up her other hand to stoke his cheek, it was smooth, clean shaven once more, then turned his face towards her. 'You have not betrayed my trust, Stewart, what you did was to put me in a position once again where I thought I had lost you.' Her voice trailed away as she closed her eyes.

Turning towards her, Stewart saw the tears glistening on her face. 'I am so very sorry, Maggie,' he whispered, pulling her to him holding her tightly in his arms. 'Oh God, I am so sorry. I love you, Maggie, never forget that please.'

Maggie's leg came over his thigh as her arms pulled him tightly to her.

'Never do that to me again, Stewart Hamilton. NEVER.' She breathed.

***

Alexander and William were tired, weary and sore as they approached the Harbour Master's office in Southampton. Alexander ran his hand over the four days growth of beard on his chin. William Masters seeing this smiled.

'Do not be worried, Alexander, no one here will even notice it.' He turned in his saddle to look at the crowds milling about the quayside; sailors, vendors, women and children all in the same state of dishevelment that they were. Alexander smiled back and nodded.

'Point taken, Father,' he replied.

Dismounting, they tethered their horses to a post and entered the Office. Sir Henry was there with several soldiers from a nearby regiment, and it was clear from his raised voice that the ship had docked sometime early that day, having been delayed on the crossing by severe winds and rain.

'Sir, perhaps you can inform me then just where is the captain of the *Achilles*? His ship is at anchor in the port, and I am unable to get any information from his ship's company. Well, nothing that would suffice as logical!' his voice was rising as he spoke.

It was at this point that Captain Reynolds voice shouted from the door.

'I be Captain Reynolds, and who might you be, sir, that you harass my crew and my ship in this fashion.'

Sir Henry turned several shades of red and his eyes bulged.

'Dear God, man, I will have you flogged, where is my daughter?' his voice had risen so much now that the glass in the windows rattled and passers-by had now stopped to look inside.

Captain Reynolds was unfazed; instead he just stood his ground and kept his eyes on Sir Henry's, daring him to try anything.

As Sir Henry's fist hit the table, he bellowed. 'I am her father!!!'

Captain Reynolds reply was just two words. 'Prove it.'

It was at this point Sir Henry had to be restrained by four soldiers from attacking Captain Reynolds. As they faced one another, their noses almost touching Captain Reynolds spoke again.

'How do I know, sir, that you are not in league with that bastard who took her? Confirm that to me, sir, or you will get no more from me.'

Sir Henry's mouth fell open; several times he went to speak, but nothing came forth, except that his complexion had now grown to a very deep shade of puce.

'Reynolds,' William Masters' voice called from the door.

Captain Reynolds turned and looked at William Masters in incredulity. 'What in hell's name are *you* doing here, Masters? I thought you had retired and gone to live in the West Country.'

William Masters walked towards him placing his hand on his arm. 'This is the Lady Catherine's father, Sir Henry Portman, nephew to the Earl Cornwallis.'

Reynolds eyes did not show any emotion; he just turned, doffed his hat and bowed to Sir Henry. 'My sincere apologies, sir, but I was not giving that young lady up to anyone.'

Sir Henry, who at this moment looked as though he was about to explode, just nodded. 'Now will you tell me where my daughter is?'

'I will do more than that, sir. I will take you to her, but you should be aware, sir, that she has been through a rough night at sea, and...'

Sir Henry now had Reynolds by the arm, dragging him from the office with the soldiers, William and Alexander in pursuit.

Captain Reynolds turned and stood his ground, staring at Sir Henry. 'If you do not unhand me, sir, then we will go nowhere. Do I make myself clear, sir?'

There was a moment where Alexander thought Sir Henry might hit Captain Reynolds, but common sense prevailed and Sir Henry removed his hand, nodding his head. 'My apologies to you, sir, after you,' he said as he waved his arm out for Captain Reynolds to pass.

It took but five minutes to reach St Michael's, and as they approached the door, Captain Reynolds bowed. 'We will leave you in peace to be reunited with your daughter, sir.'

Sir Henry turned to him. 'Your ship will be restored to seaworthiness, Captain, at my expense. I thank you.'

Sir Henry entered the church, quietly closing the door behind him. He could see the Clergyman at the front of the church talking to what seemed to be a small boy. He rubbed his eyes to get them accustomed to the dimness of the inside of the church, then walked slowly up the centre aisle. It was not until he came within four rows of them that he realised what he saw as a small boy was actually his daughter. His heart clenched and stopped in his chest as two tears ran down his cheeks.

'Catherine, my heart,' he whispered.

Catherine turned her head slowly, then jumped up and was in his arms in a second. Sir Henry lifted his daughter up and came and sat next to the Clergyman, who smiled, placed his hand on Catherine's head and offered up a prayer of thanks, then quietly stood up and left them.

***

Outside the church, Captain Reynolds looked at his friend; it was then that William Masters registered what he was thinking.

'You are about to ask how I know the Earl Cornwallis' niece twice removed. Well it is a long story, Reynolds, one I believe would be better told over a glass or two of ale, and from the look of your ship this morning, I can wager it will be going nowhere till it has had some repairs, no?' William raised his eyebrows in asking.

'You are right, Masters, there is a large crack in one of the smaller masts, and until it can be supported and strengthened, we will be in dock. I know of a small inn not far from here where we can get food also, as I have had nothing since dinner yesterday evening.' Reynolds was looking at Alexander as he was talking.

'Are you a colleague of Masters, sir?'

William looked at his son-in-law, who looked totally out of his depth at that moment.

'My apologies, Reynolds, this is my son-in-law Alexander Hamilton, now let us find a quiet place to talk.'

The inn was on the corner of a side street just off the square, and in comparison to other places they had passed that morning, it was very comfortable. After they had eaten, it took at least half an hour for William Masters to unravel everything that had happened to him over the past year. Sitting back now, he drank the rest of his ale.

'I will say one thing, Masters; you lead a very colourful life, my friend. The most excitement I have had was to nearly go down with my ship and all hands on the crossing yesterday. I had my suspicions regarding that man... Northcott you say?'

'Where is Northcott now, sir?' queried Alexander.

'In truth, I do not know, the ship limped into harbour just before dawn. I had smashed the lock on my cabin to give the impression it had been damaged by the storm, so that she could escape.' Reynolds took a long drink of ale and closed his eyes; he was tired and had not slept now for over twenty-four hours.

'When I locked her in the previous night, she had mimed two words to me, Masters: *help me*. And I could see from her expression that she was very afraid. Well, you know what they say, Masters, *we should be careful what we wish for*, and I in my foolishness asked God for a small squall to get the man off the deck. He replied with a tempest.' Here Reynolds crossed himself.

'So, whilst the storm raged, I re-entered the cabin to give her the clothes of a young sailor. I instructed her to put them on and then disembark with the ship's company of boys who would secure the boat when we docked. Well, you know the rest. As for Northcott, once he saw the damage to my ship and cabin, he left the ship. I have not laid eyes on him since.'

William Masters looked at his friend in sympathy. There would be many repairs to deal with before he slept this day. Standing up, he held out his hand in farewell.

'We will bid you good day now, Reynolds, and hope that the repairs can be done swiftly, for time is money, is it not?' All three men stood and shook hands.

'Come, Alexander, it is time that we made our way home, we have been away too long.'

***

It was just before sunrise the following morning that William and Alexander rode into Mere. William looked sideways at his son-in-law, seeing him rub the growth of beard he had acquired on his travels. Stopping his horse, he turned in the saddle.

'Alexander, we will go home first I think, shave, wash the filth from our bodies and get fresh clothes before we go up to the Willows.' He was nodding to Alexander as he spoke.

Alexander smiled. 'I agree, Father, as I smell like something that has been left on the dock to rot.' William Masters laughed and then kicked his horse to a trot.

***

Stewart opened the drapes in the study then snuffed the candles and put more logs on the fire. He had been up since before dawn, trying to work, but his mind was elsewhere and he found it hard to concentrate. Walking towards the window, he rubbed his eyes with the heels of his hands. If something happened to Alex and William Masters, he would never be able to forgive himself. There had been no word from James either; his father had had to travel back to London on urgent business, so James was left in Salisbury with Lady Jemima. Stewart rubbed his brow. *Rather you than I, James*, he thought. It was then he heard Thompson at the front door. As Stewart entered the hall, he saw Alex and William Masters just handing Thompson their cloaks and hats.

'Dear God, Alex, I thought you were never coming home.' Saying this Stewart moved quickly across the hall and embraced his cousin tightly. Then turning to William, he held his arm, taking his hand into a firm shake.

'Have they found her? Please tell me she is safe?'

William nodded. 'Be at peace, Stewart, she is safe and well and with her father.'

Alexander, who had been watching his cousin closely, saw the tension leave his face. The man had been concerned, not only for Lady Catherine but for himself and William also.

'Is my aunt back yet, Stewart?' enquired Alexander.

Stewart looked at him and smiled. 'No, Alex, they have not returned yet; it would seem that they like Torquay,' he replied, giving a wry smile.

Alexander wondered what he would feel was he in his cousin's shoes now, having a father return after twenty-two years and who was plainly with his mother once more; his first thoughts were that it must be very odd, and even harder to accept.

'Alex.' Stewart saw his cousin studying him. 'Go to your wife.'

Alexander roused himself from his thoughts and mounted the stairs.

'Come, sir, the study is warm as the fire has been lit some hours now, so you can tell me at your leisure what has happened, then we can all sit down to a late breakfast, as I fear Alex will not be down for some time.' Smiling to himself, he held out his arm to William Masters as they entered the study.

William talked for what seemed like hours, while Stewart listened watching the sun slowly creep into the room. It was now past mid-September and the weather was holding well. After the initial frost at the beginning the days had warmed and sun had replaced rain; an Indian Summer—the words of his mother's echoed in his brain.

'Stewart, Stewart, are you well?' It was William's voice that brought him back from his thoughts.

'I beg your pardon, sir, I was thinking of my mother.'

William studied Stewart's face and saw there a young man out of his depth with conflicting emotions.

'Shall I tell you how you feel, Stewart?'

Stewart turned in surprise to look at him now. 'I am sorry, sir?'

'Shall I tell you how you feel?' William repeated. 'You feel lost, cheated maybe, resentful,' he paused before he voiced the next word. 'Hurt?' Seeing that, Stewart was about to protest but he stopped him.

'Please let me finish; for years you have been the sole recipient of your mother's love and affections, am I right, lad?' Stewart nodded the man was very observant.

'You have grown up with your mother and the people around you... cocooned, shall we say, never spoilt, only the usual amount that every child deserves occasionally. Now, your father has returned into your lives; you welcome him there with open arms, as he is the one person you craved, though you would never admit this to a living soul. I am correct in my assumptions, no? Now that he is here, he has taken away that exclusivity that you shared with your mother. She still loves you, but she loves her husband with a different kind of love, and it is this that you are fighting with now. How have I done so far, lad?'

Stewart lowered his head, looking at his hands, nodded then spoke.

'Maggie told me that just because we get older, we do not lose that... desire... It is just different... deeper somehow... the need of one person for another... the love for one person for another.' He brought his head up to look at William Masters now.

'You are right, sir, it is the sharing of that person's love... that is what is hard to swallow, but swallow it I must for I love them both dearly, and they have their own life to live now, just as I have mine. She has nurtured me till I became a man with a family of my own, now I must give back that freedom to her once more, for her to move on. That is one reason I made them go away for a while. To find themselves once more.'

William leaned across and placed his hand on Stewart's arm. 'You are a good man, Stewart. I would be proud to call you my son. Let her be free now, for she will never leave you, you know that.'

The door behind them opened and young Charles came bounding into the room, scrabbling up onto his father's lap, immediately pulling the ribbon free from his hair so that he could wind his fingers through it.

'Papa... Papa... os, os?' He was now jumping up and down on his lap with excitement.

Margaret came forward and placed baby Jane into her grandfather's arms.

'Your granddaughter would like a cuddle, William.' Turning to Stewart, she smiled warmly. 'And your son wants you to ride with him on his rocking horse, Stewart.'

Stewart held his son tightly to him; closing his eyes, he kissed his head. 'Well, my son, I think that there will be time enough for one ride before breakfast.' Turning to Margaret, he smiled back. 'Do you not think so, Mama?'

Chapter Forty-Five
The Sword of Damocles

It was a week later when James and Sir Henry arrived. There was still no sign of his mother, and as the weather was still mild in the extreme for this time of year, Stewart hoped that they were enjoying the beauty of Torquay. When he thought of all that they had to discuss and learn about one another—twenty two years—it was little wonder that they chose to be alone. Now all five men sat in the drawing room, waiting for lunch.

'So there is still no sign of Northcott, Sir Henry?' queried William.

'It is like he has crawled under a stone and gone to the underworld,' came Sir Henry's agitated reply. 'As you know, both lawyers have done searches all over England and the army have been alerted and given a description. The man seems to have vanished into thin air, unless of course he returned back across the channel to France.'

'Has anyone been to his estate just outside Crediton near Exeter?' remarked Stewart.

All eyes turned to look at him. 'To me it seems the most logical place to look. The estate is large covering many hundred acres; a person could hide easily.' Stewart raised his hands. 'As I understand, only his mother and sister live there, with a large accompaniment of servants and tenants that is.'

Sir Henry had been watching Stewart closely. 'You do not believe that he would have the audacity to go home, do you? Dear God, the man would have to be very cunning or mad.'

Stewart smiled, choosing his words carefully before he spoke. 'Of that man I would believe anything. You need to look for the unexpected where Northcott is concerned. There is logic to his thinking, but not the sort that you or I would use.'

The room was quiet, with just the crackling of the fire and the ticking of the mantle clock. Stewart's eyes roamed over every man present, watching for any reaction. He had known the man since he was thirteen, and one thing he had learned was that Northcott NEVER did the obvious; his brain worked on a deeper more depraved level than the rest of humanity. You had to think like him and one step ahead, if you were to gain any headway.

'You have done exactly what he expected you to do, gentlemen, search the whole of England, but omitting the one place that your sense of logic told you he would never go to.'

William Master's looked into Stewart's eyes and smiled slowly, gently inclining his head.

'You have one very insightful brain, Stewart. I commend you for it, but I fear that now he would—as you say—be that one step ahead of us once more and moved on to a safer location?' William Masters raised his brows, and then looked around the room.

Stewart stood up and walked to the window. 'It will be I who he will come for.' Turning he looked at them. 'It is I who has been his target all along gentlemen. It is just when and where the axe will fall.'

James' face blanched as did Alexander's.

'Did you think that signatures on a legal document would stop him? The man is insane, but I want you all to swear that what I have said now stays with us in this room, never to be spoken of again, do I have that?' Stewart saw that Sir Henry was about to protest.

'I would have your word on that, sir, that my family will never hear of this. It is for me to deal with when the time comes.'

The room was silent once more till Lilly knocked and entered.

'Begging your pardons, gentlemen, lunch be served in the dining room.' Curtsying, she left.

Stewart coughed lightly. 'Right, gentlemen, we will now go to lunch, and afterwards Alexander, James and I will take a ride out to the estate office.' Nodding to all present, he led the way out.

***

Alexander had just coaxed the fire to burn, adding more kindling before placing some small pieces of log to catch. Rubbing his hands, he stood up and pulled a stool up next to James while Stewart lit several candles on the mantle with a taper.

'I think our Indian summer is over,' commented Alexander as he pulled his cloak tightly around him. 'I doubt that my aunt and uncle will stay any longer in Torquay once the cold returns.'

Stewart extinguished the taper and turned to face him. 'They have had three good weeks there, more than you had when you married. Tell me, James, how is Catherine? Did her experience with Northcott temper her exuberance?' Stewart smiled mischievously at him. 'Or has it made her more forthright in her amorous advances, my friend?'

James looked up at his friend. 'Her father has decreed that we will now marry on St Stephen's day. Catherine, may I add, was not of that agreement. She insists that we marry in November; her mother is of the same opinion.'

'And what is your opinion, James? You do have one, I presume,' teased Stewart.

James ran his fingers through his hair. 'The quicker, the better for my part. Then I can get back to some normality.'

Stewart looked at his cousin, and then both men laughed loudly.

'That bad is it, James?' said Alexander, still laughing.

'God, Alex, do you not remember what it was like with you and Charlotte?'

'James, Charlotte was *never* like your Catherine, you should feel very privileged that she wants you so... passionately. You will have one very interesting marriage, James.' Alexander shook his head, still laughing.

'Oh Lord, when she looks at me with those clear blue eyes of hers, my soul melts.'

'But other parts of your body remain firm, no?' Stewart pushed a mug of ale under James' nose. 'Drink this, James, it will make you forget. Just think in a few weeks you will be in heaven,' Stewart taunted.

James swallowed his ale then stood up and walked towards the desk, turning he looked straight into Stewart's eyes.

'Right, Stewart, we have gone through all the pleasantries, now are you going to tell us why you have brought us here? It is not to discuss my frustration I wager, so what is it?'

Taking a letter from his pocket, he held it out to James and Alexander. 'Read it, my friends. I found it here when I stopped on my way home from Portsmouth.'

James took the letter, unfolded it, and then both men read the contents.

You have duped me for the last time, Hamilton. You remember my words to you at the inn in Exeter?

My revenge for you is fathomless!

Now you will see just how much. You should have died that morning in Bath, another fair trick you played on me with the pistols. Did you think that a piece of paper would deter me? You should have died from your wound, but as they say, 'The Devil takes care of his own.' I have come to believe that you are the devil's spawn... a cat with nine lives... But you know what they say—chop the tail???

I will see you in hell, Hamilton, if that is what it takes.

Alexander had paled considerably and his hands shook, while James had leaned back to the table for support. The silence that ensued seemed to freeze the occupants, rooting them to the spot. Stewart was the first to move, as he took the letter from Alexander's hand and placed it once more into his pocket.

'No one will know of this; do I make myself clear?' he looked at his two friends closely. 'This is now between myself and Northcott.'

'Stewart, he could kill you at any time, at any distance for God's sake,' interrupted James.

'Oh no-no-no, my friend,' Stewart smiled sardonically, 'he will want to face me when it happens. Look into my eyes; he will want to SEE me die.' Stewart licked his lips which had suddenly become dry; in fact, his whole mouth was parched. Breathing deeply through his nose, he pulled his cloak around him then picked up his mug and drained it.

'I fear I do not have much appetite for work today, Alex, maybe we could ride through the estate, then return to the house?'

Alexander observed that his cousin was unnerved, and who would not be, for once again the *Sword of Damocles* was hanging above his head.

'I think we will make our way slowly home, Stewart,' replied Alexander. 'You must go be with your wife and son, as I will go to my wife and daughter.' Turning, he looked at James. 'And James will go to his father-in-law to be and convince him that November would be an excellent time for the marriage.'

The atmosphere had lightened, even though the threat was still there lurking just under the surface. Stewart turned and picked up the shovel from the hearth, then going outside, he brought back earth to smother the fire. Turning to face them, he nodded.

'Shall we go, my friends?'

They were mostly silent as they rode back to the house, with just a few ribald jokes thrown in James' direction to lighten the mood. As they neared it, Stewart saw his mother's coach just being led away to the stables.

'It would appear we have company, gentleman, and about time too.' Stewart moved his horse to a trot, while James looked to Alexander and shrugged his shoulders.

***

'Good afternoon, Mother, Father,' called Stewart from the drawing room door.

Elizabeth turned, beamed and came to her son, clasping him in a tight hug. Stewart wrapped his arms around his mother just as tightly and then kissed the top of her head.

'Welcome home.' Then turning to his father, he embraced him also.

Andrew Duncan was quite taken by surprise, as he had not imagined such a welcome. Stewart pushed his father back to look at him, then smiled. 'Welcome home, Father. I hope that you will be staying?'

Elizabeth came up beside her son, linking her arm in his and resting her head on his shoulder.

'He will be staying, Stewart, but first he must go back to Scotland to settle his responsibilities there. I will also go with him,' she added.

Stewart looked at both his parents closely, and then nodded his head. 'I understand, but must you go now? Can it not wait till after Christmas?'

Andrew Duncan placed a hand on his son's shoulder. 'It is best we go now, and then we can be back by Christmas knowing that all is settled and all debts are paid.'

Stewart knew what he was implying and smiled in acquiescence. 'Have you both eaten? I am sure that Mrs Cottle would welcome a chance to feed you both; she has missed you mother…'

'I will go and see her, Stewart, and yes we have eaten, then I would go and rest for a while, long journeys seem to tire me now.' She placed her hand to her son's face and reached up and kissed his cheek. 'I will see you at dinner.' Turning she left the room.

'How about you, Father, would you like some tea or a glass of whisky maybe?' Stewart stopped talking as his father placed a hand on his shoulder.

'I would love to take a glass of whisky with you, my son.'

Stewart relaxed; going to the dresser, he filled two glasses then came to sit by the fire.

Andrew Duncan sat there for some moments studying his son's face. 'There is something troubling you, Stewart, is there not?'

Stewart moved in his chair and took a sip of whisky. 'Father, the only thing that troubled me was your safe return. It was VERY strange here without my mother, like a ship without its captain.' He coughed lightly, trying to remove the obstruction that seemed to have placed itself in his throat. 'She has always been there.' Stewart's voice had dropped.

Andrew Duncan saw from his son's eyes that he was looking back into the past.

'She will always be with you, Stewart, until that time that happens to all of us when we pass on, but even then her soul will be with you, guiding you always.'

Stewart roused himself. 'I am sorry, Father, since the duel I get bouts of melancholy, the physicians tell me that it will pass. I get very afraid sometimes, Father, can you understand that?'

'I understand perfectly, Stewart, and if you were young, I would take you to my knee and comfort you, but since you are not, then I am sending you to your wife.' Standing up, he took the glass from Stewart's hand and pulled him to his feet. 'Go to your wife, Stewart, find your comfort.'

***

Stewart entered their room and finding it empty he made his way to the nursery. Opening the door gently so as not to wake either child that may be asleep, he saw her leaning over their son stroking his hair from his face as he lay there deep in slumber. Margaret turned and smiled, and then coming to him she took his hand and led them back to their room.

Closing the door quietly behind her, she pulled him to stand by the bed; reaching up, she gently pushed his Jacket off his shoulders, then untying his stock and loosening his shirt she pulled it from his beeches. Keeping her eyes on his, she slowly pushed him onto the bed, pulling of his boots and stockings, then his breeches.

Stewart was watching her closely now as she took out the pins from her hair dropping them to the floor, shaking out her hair so that if fell over her shoulders. Carefully, she undid the laces of her bodice and removed that also, then turned for him to untie her corset and skirts. She turned back towards him now in just her shift, pulling him to his feet so that she could remove his shirt. Stewart's eyes were still on hers as he pushed himself onto the bed, pulling Margaret onto him.

'Wait,' she breathed as she gently pushed away from him so that she was kneeling across him, then she too removed her shift.

Stewart gripped her waist and turned her onto the bed; rolling on top of her he kissed her so hard that his teeth ground onto hers, and then he took her fiercely and quickly as though his life depended on it. They lay there entwined for some moments; his fingers running over her face, committing it to memory as though she would disappear, his eyes never leaving hers.

'No matter what comes to pass, Maggie, always know that I love you completely, you are my soul, without you, I do not exist.'

Margaret reached up her hand, smiled and stoked his face.

'We are two halves of a whole, Stewart, neither would exist without the other.' Pulling his head down to her, she kissed him gently. 'I love you with all of my being, Stewart Hamilton,' she added, slowly nodding to him.

As they lay there, she felt his breathing ease as he slowly drifted off to sleep in her arms; she closed her eyes letting the tears fall, then kissed his brow and whispered.

'There is something bad troubling you, Stewart, and it is not the horrors that possess you in your dreams. I do not know what it is, but even if I did, I fear I would be unable to help you, and that is what breaks my heart.'

***

Charlotte had sat Alexander down in front of her mirror and was now loosening the ribbon that held his blond hair, taking the brush she gently drew it through.

'When I was a girl, and I was troubled, my mother would do this to me. It was so comforting and soothing that soon I forgot all of my worries.' She bent down to look over his shoulder and smiled at him through the mirror.

'You are troubled, I can see that, Alex.'

Alexander took the brush from her hand and kissed her palm, as Charlotte took the brush into the other hand and resumed her brushing, keeping her eyes on his through the mirror.

'It soothes the nerves,' she said as she picked up his hair and kissed the nape of his neck.

'If you do that again, Charlotte, there will not be much soothing here.'

Charlotte giggled. 'Hush,' she replied as she placed her finger to his lips. 'Relax, Alex, and let me finish. It may not take all your troubles away, but it will relax your mind and let you see that they are not insurmountable.' Leaning down, she kissed his neck once more, moving across to nibble the side of it.

Alexander pulled her down into his lap and kissed her deeply; taking the brush he threw it. 'To hell with the brush, I have a much better remedy, Charlotte.' She smiled as he lifted her in his arms and laid her on the bed.

***

James paced the drawing room. It seemed that everyone had gone to lie down—well they had someone to lie with, apart from his father-in-law, who had other problems on his mind. James stopped pacing and nodded; he would be damned if he was going to wait till Christmas. The wedding would be next month.

***

Andrew Duncan came into their bedroom and sat very gently on the bed beside his wife. Taking her hand, he kissed her fingers.

'Our son is very troubled, Lizzie, and I believe it stems from Northcott.' He held her hand in both of his now tight to his chest.

'He is waiting for him to come for him, Lizzie.' He watched to see if she would speak, but nothing came. 'The man is a predator, he will not desist till one or both of them are dead, and I am powerless to help,' he paused to stroke her face. 'Maybe we should delay our trip to Scotland till after Christmas.'

Elizabeth sat up; he could feel her hand shake in his own, and even from the dim light in the room he could see that she was ashen.

'If I am here, then maybe.'

He felt her arms tighten around him. This was not the homecoming he had envisaged. His voice was soft and gently as he spoke

'Lizzie, the man has committed *False imprisonment* against the Earl Cornwallis' niece. If caught, he will have his lands and title taken from him. I doubt they will hang him, but he will be imprisoned or sent somewhere. Do you not see, Lizzie, he has *nothing* to lose.

'But he signed a legal document, Andrew,' came Elizabeth's beseeching reply.

Andrew pushed her gently away from him, wiping the tears from her cheeks with his thumbs. 'To him, they are just worthless words on a piece of paper. He cares nothing for the law, has no sense of right or wrong. God, Lizzie, the man is an animal, and this hate goes way to far back for it ever to be forgotten, or forgiven. I should have been here all those years, Lizzie, for that I have failed my son. If I had been here, he would never have had the anger in him that he did. He felt cheated, Lizzie.'

Elizabeth was shaking her head now. 'No, Andrew, he has always had a temper, but he has never used it for evil, only for good, to right a wrong as you say. He could never stand idly by and watch one person demean another; you are not to blame, Andrew, it is just the way he is.'

Andrew Duncan sat and gently rocked his wife in his arms as he whispered over and over.

'I will find a way Lizzie, I will find a way.'

Chapter Forty-Six
The Ides of November

It was mid-morning, a day into November. Elizabeth sat at her bureau in the drawing room dealing with her letters; picking up one she turned it and saw a familiar seal. It was from Sir Henry; as she opened the seal there was a gold embossed card inside—a wedding invitation. Elizabeth smiled to herself as she read the date—Saturday 15th November, 1788. So Lady Jemima and Catherine had got their way, even James had wanted it in November in the end. It must have been decided very quickly though, as they only had a week to prepare. Elizabeth doubted if all those who had been sent an invitation would be able to attend; as she searched through the post, she saw the other three invitations. They were all to stay at Sir Henry's estate Midcraven Hall, outside Bath; the children and nanny Daisy would all be going, and hopefully Margaret would be well as she would be in her fifth month then. It meant that they had but one week to prepare themselves now, as it would seem that Sir Henry was taking no more chances; his daughter would marry James soon.

Elizabeth thought she would wear the gown that was made for Alexander's wedding; it was beautiful and by far the best gown she had ever owned, apart from her wedding gown. She closed her eyes and let her memory take over. It was her mother's gown, pure white, all lace and satin.

'Penny for your thoughts, Mother?'

Elizabeth turned quickly to see Stewart standing behind her.

'I must be a little deaf, Stewart. I did not hear you come in.'

'No, Mother, you were in another place entirely, a nice place, as you were smiling.' He bent to kiss her cheek. 'Ah, I see we finally have the invitation.' Stewart picked up his mother's card and smiled broadly, then chuckled to himself.

'What is so amusing, Stewart?' Elizabeth queried in a slightly bemused tone.

'Nothing, Mother, it is a private joke between James and I, so we have but one week to make ready, do you think we will manage, Mother, with two children in tow?' Stewart looked down at the post on his mother's bureau and his heart stopped.

'Mother, let me go through the mail, as I am sure that most of what you have there are either bills to be paid by us or monies to be paid to the estate.' Scooping up the letters, he separated the wedding invitations and handed them back to her.

'Here, deliver your invitations, and then go play with your grandson—he has missed his grandmother.'

As Stewart reached the door, he paused and turned. 'Is my father at home?'

Elizabeth looked at her son. 'No, Stewart, he has gone with William to see Spike.' Elizabeth's eyes were full of questions. 'They have gone to discuss the shed that William talked of last year—the one that would be built solely of windows on the south side to grow flowers.' Elizabeth stared at her son for some seconds.

'Is there something wrong, Stewart?' her voice and her expression said everything that she was feeling.

Stewart knew that his mother was watching him intently for the slightest suspicion that her assumptions were correct, that there was something VERY wrong.

'Mother, he wanted to speak with me regarding his housekeeper in Scotland. She is of around Daisy's age, has the experience of caring for children, and maybe she would suit Alex and Charlotte as a nanny.'

'I see,' she replied slowly, still watching her son fixedly.

Stewart smiled his most engaging smile, 'Do not be troubled, Mother. It can wait. Now go see your grandson, soon you will have another to shower with your affection, though I doubt that Charles will like that very much; having to share you.'

Elizabeth's eyes opened wide as she suddenly realised that her son was jealous of his father.

'Stewart, the love I have for your father will never supersede the love I have for you. They are different; they are not interchangeable. They are individual; each love has its own intensity and should be taken as such.' Elizabeth paused here to collect her words. 'I love you with all my heart, Stewart,' Elizabeth sighed. 'The love I feel for your father is akin to the love that you have for Margaret, just as the kind I feel for you is the same love you feel for Charles.'

Stewart was rooted to the spot, he had voiced his feelings without even knowing that he had done so, and his mother had recognised this so accurately.

'Mother I...'

Elizabeth came to stand before him, taking his hand in hers. 'I gave you life, Stewart, nothing can break that bond.' Reaching up, she kissed his cheek.

***

The letter from Northcott—for he was certain it was from him—now burned in his pocket as he made his way out to see Alexander in the estate office. The day was not cold, but it now held that autumnal chill, and as he looked around him, he could see that the ground was carpeted with brown, yellow and red fallen leaves, and the trees were slowly becoming bare. He was still disturbed by what his mother had said, but on recollection she had just voiced the truth. He had had his mother to himself for twenty-three years now, and it was still strange to him to see her with his father. He shook his head and hunched his shoulders, well at this moment that was not the most prevalent thought that possessed him. He looked around him once more as he rode; if Northcott had a mind to finish what he had started, what better time than now, as he was alone and an easy target. Digging his heels in, he urged his horse to a gallop.

Coming into the office, Stewart could feel the warmth.

'How long have you been here, Alex?'

Alexander raised his head from his ledger and smiled. 'Since seven, why?'

Stewart came towards him and placed the letter gently on his desk, as though it may explode any second.

Alexander's eyes looked down to the familiar writing, then up at Stewart.

'What does he say?'

Stewart walked towards the fire; seating himself on a stool, he held his hands out to warm them.

'I have not yet opened it, Alex,' came his flat toned reply. He turned to look at his cousin. 'You have an invitation to James' wedding up at the house. It will be on Saturday 15ᵗʰ November—two weeks' time.'

Alexander stood up, watching his cousin intently, and then picking up the letter he came round to sit opposite him.

'Here, will you not open it?' His words held more than just a question.

'Be my guest,' was all that Stewart replied as he gestured with his hand.

As Alexander broke the seal and smoothed out the paper, his brows knit together in perplexity. Looking up he held out the letter to Stewart.

'What in God's name does he mean, Stewart?'

As Stewart read the one line of writing, he smiled to himself.

'Beware the ides of November.'

'What he means, cousin, is that I will be dead by then.'

Alexander stood up and agitatedly started to pace the room. 'Stewart, he intends to kill you on the wedding day?'

Stewart shook his head. 'No, no, no, Alex. The ides fall on the 15ᵗʰ only in March, May, July and October. All other months fall on the 13ᵗʰ, or so they say.' He lifted his arm in a dismissing gesture. 'It has something to do with the full moon, Alex, he means to kill me before the wedding.'

'And you intend to let him, cousin!' remarked Alexander incredulously.

Stewart stood up and wiped his hand over his face, then threw the letter into the fire.

Alexander moved quickly; grabbing the poker he tried to retrieve the burning paper, but it was consumed too quickly by the fire's flames.

'Stewart, are you mad! That is evidence.' Alexander threw the poker down onto the hearth and paced nervously around the room. Turning suddenly, he grabbed Stewart by the arm, his eyes staring fixedly into his face.

'And you are going to sit back and let him?' Alexander was incensed, the man was not thinking with reason.

Stewart removed his cousin's arm and walked slowly to the door, then turning he spoke in a quiet, even tone.

'Alexander, unless I know the when, where and how, he has a good chance of completing his mission, except, of course, if I stay boarded up in my home like a hunted animal, which I do not intent to do.'

Opening the door, he nodded slightly to his cousin, then placed his hat on his head and left.

***

He rode hard on his way back to the house. He was starkly aware that Northcott knew his every move; the man was like a phantom, appearing and disappearing at will. The hair at the back of his neck at that moment had risen, just as the hackles upon a dog's back when he knows he is cornered. He had no intention of letting himself be killed, but, on reflection, thought that at this moment it was rather out of his hands and in the hands of God.

Stabling his horse, he walked to the back of the house and into the gardens. He could see Spike in the distance tying fresh twine, securing the rose trees to their posts to replace the ones that had rotted. Spike stood up slowly taking his hat from his head and bowing.

'Good day to you, Master Stewart, be there anything wrong up at the house?' Spike questioned guardedly.

'No, Spike, all is well.' Stewart paused, biting his bottom lip. 'Spike, what I am about to convey to you, I cannot speak about to anyone up at the house.' He waited to see if Spike would question him, but he just nodded. 'They would not understand. I have to do something, Spike.' Stewart took off his hat and started to pace. 'They would try to stop me, try to put things in place that would not resolve the situation, just postpone it and I cannot let that happen, do you understand me, Spike?'

Spike felt a cold shiver run down his spine, and his hands shook slightly.

'Master Stewart, if you are thinking to do what I be thinking you are, then I beg you not to.'

Stewart looked straight into Spike's eyes; the man knew exactly what he was telling him. 'I have to, Spike, else I will be forever looking for shadows; my family will never be safe. I will NEVER know peace.'

Spike swallowed several times, resting his hands on his spade. 'But what will become of your family without you, Master Stewart, have you even thought of that, sir?'

'Safe, Spike, safe.'

Spike crossed himself and wiped his brow with his handkerchief.

'Master Stewart, I think I will go back to the cottage and take a jug of ale, if that be alright with you, sir.'

Stewart took him by the arm and then laid the shovel down on the ground. Calling to Kenver, he informed him that his master was going back to his cottage to eat his lunch. Kenver just watched the two of them walk away, thinking to himself that he and his master had just eaten their lunch; maybe Mr Spike be unwell, he would finish his work then go and see.

Once inside the cottage, Stewart led Spike to sit in the comfortable chair, then he proceeded to bank the fire.

'Do you have any whisky, Spike?' queried Stewart, finding only the bottle of Ale on the stone floor by the dresser.

'No, sir, only ale.'

Stewart placed two mugs onto the table and poured ale into both. Handing Spike his, he pulled up a stool and sat opposite, reaching across to take the man's hand—it was ice cold.

'Spike, shall I call the physician?' Stewart was anxious now; it had never been his intention to alarm him so. Standing up, he retrieved a blanket from a small settle in the corner; wrapping this around Spike's legs he sat down once more.

'Spike, it would seem I have a knack for doing this to people. I have a hasty mind that does things without thinking first. I beg your forgiveness, Spike, as I have caused you much distress.'

Spike looked at his master and shook his head. 'You do that, lad, you do.' Spike took a long drink from his mug then let his head fall back onto the chair.

'Shall I go bring Pip? He can keep you company.'

Spike grabbed Stewart's hand, stopping him from standing.

'You be doing that, Master Stewart, and you will have your mother here in an instant, and we do NOT want that, do we?'

The door opened suddenly, revealing the head of Kenver as he peered round it.

'Are you poorly, Mr Spike?' seeing Stewart he quickly came into the room, removing his hat and holding it tight to his chest he bowed his head. 'Afternoon, Master Stewart sir.' Stewart nodded and smiled in reply.

'I did take to being a bit dizzy, young Kenver, but I be fine now, mind you, you will tell no one of this, do you understand?'

Kenver nodded his head quickly in response.

'Good lad, now go you back to your work, and I will be there directly.'

Bowing and slowly backing to the door, he left as quickly as he had come.

Spike drank the rest of his ale and sat up, folding the blanket and placing it on the arm of the chair.

'I be fine now, Master Stewart, you be going in for your own lunch, as I will be heading back to the gardens to finish the repairs. I will speak with Pip later.' Spike inclined his head and stood up.

Stewart stood also, then taking Spike into a quick embrace, he left the cottage. Leaving Spike staring after him speechless, as he watched the door close.

**

The hour was late and one candle still burned on the table near the window in their bedroom. Holding Margaret tightly in his arms, he stoked her back.

'Maggie,' his voice was low and full of sleep.

Margaret raised her head up and pushed away from him so she could look into his eyes.

'What is it, Stewart?' she whispered; she had been at that point when sleep was taking over, but one was still aware of their surroundings.

'Do you remember when we first lie together? You were so afraid you thought I would hurt you, but you still wanted me.'

Margaret reached up her hand stroking the hair from his face, her eyes searching his.

'What makes you think of that now?' her voice was full of uneasiness.

Taking her hand, he kissed her palm and then held it to his chest. 'Have I ever hurt you, Maggie?'

Margaret's eyes never left his. 'Never, Stewart, never,' she breathed.

Stewart pulled her into him now kissing her brow. 'I am very glad for that, we can sleep now.'

Margaret thought that at this present moment sleep was the last thing in her head. He was very troubled, but she could not fathom why. He had been strange these past days, and Margaret believed it to be just a passing despondency that he was prone to since the duel, but this was different. It was as though he were settling things in his mind, putting things in place, organising his thoughts for some future event, which could be good or bad. He had asked many questions, but above all he had sat with his son every afternoon, playing with him, taking him for walks, even eating breakfast with him in the nursery.

It was the nudge from her other child within her that brought her back from her musings. Stroking her stomach, as if to reassure him—and it was a him, she was sure; had not Maria Visconti told her so that day in the gardens of the house in Rapallo? She had also told her of two daughters and another son.

'You will be safe,' she whispered to her unborn child. It was the child that lay next to her that besieged her thoughts now. Tucking her head into his chest, she closed her eyes and waited for sleep to come.

***

Stewart sat before his glass in his dressing room while Pip shaved him in silence. Pip was usually very verbal while performing this daily routine, as he knew that Stewart could not answer him, and he had free reign with his thoughts. Watching him now through the mirror, he could see that he wanted to speak, his jaw was flexing badly. When he finally spoke, Stewart was unprepared.

'Would you be liking me to slit your throat now, Master Stewart, or would you be wanting to wait for the other fellow?' Pip looked up at him, inclining his head slightly.

'You have spoken with Spike then. Is he well?'

'Yes, he be fine now. If I may be so bold, Master Stewart…' Pip had stopped scraping Stewart's face with the razor, wiping the soap from it onto a towel. 'You should never have done what you did, sir. Spike be not a young man.'

Stewart stopped him by placing his hand onto the one that held the razor.

'Pip, if I do not do this, myself and my whole family will lay open to that man's vengeance; has he not done enough these past two years? Do I have to wait for him to harm—no maybe kill one of my own? It has to end, Pip.'

Pip stood as motionless as a statue, watching his master who he had known since birth. He would not stand by and see him give himself up as sacrifice.

'When will it be, Master Stewart?'

Stewart took his hand from Pip's. 'I have always been able to slip away from your ever-watchful gaze, Pip. I believe it is for me to choose, and for him to be there when I do.' Pip inclined his head.

'Such knowledge be a great burden to hold, Master Stewart.'

'But hold it you will, Pip.'

Pip breathed deeply, shaking his head, and then slowly finished shaving him.

***

Andrew Duncan came into the study, quietly closing the door behind him, and then seated himself in the chair beside the desk. Stewart turned and smiled.

'Good morning to you, Father, are we all prepared for the wedding?'

'Your mother says we will leave after breakfast on the 14th. It will give us time to make our way to Midcraven Hall, then settle and rest before the wedding on the following day.' He paused to see if there was any response from his son.

'She insists that we take all three carriages. I will travel with your mother, Margaret and yourself in hers. William, Alexander and Charlotte will ride in William's, and nanny Daisy, Molly, Millie and the children in Margaret's. Pip will ride outside with William and Andrews Valet.'

'Mother was always one to plan ahead. That is fine, Father, though I doubt that Charles will agree with it; he will want to be in ours.' Stewart laughed gently.

'If that is what he wishes, Stewart, then I for one have no objections.' Andrew Duncan paused before he voiced the next words.

'He has a very profound love for his father; he is always looking for you.'

Stewart leaned forward and placed his hand over his father's. 'I spoil him, Father, I know I should not.'

'But you want him to have what you did not,' finished Andrew Duncan; there was no malice in his words, just an air of regret for time lost.

As his father stood up, Stewart stood also taking his father into his arms in a tight embrace; releasing him Stewart studied his father's face, seeing his own image look back at him. 'You too can spoil him, Father.'

'Oh, I intend to, Stewart, you have my word on that.'

Chapter Forty-Seven
Baia Della Pace

Stewart looked down onto the lawn from the nursery window. It was only three in the afternoon but already the sky was darkening, as the days were becoming much shorter now. There was a keen wind blowing in from the north, dispersing all the leaves that had fallen and taking with it the ones that still remained on the trees; soon winter would be upon the earth. As he held his son in his arms, he thought that he might never see another autumn, so he would commit to memory all that lay before him now.

'Some day this will be yours, Charles, you must treat it with respect and love, but most of all, share its abundance with your siblings.'

Stewart smoothed his son's dark silken hair as he pulled his head into his shoulder. Charles responded by placing one hand behind his father's head and pulling free his ribbon, entwining his fingers into his father's hair as always, and then placing his thumb into his mouth he drifted slowly off to sleep. Stewart felt him go limp in his arms and gently laid him on his small bed; removing his shoes, he covered him.

'Sleep, my son, I will see you later.' Kissing him, Stewart turned to find Daisy watching him.

'I have never seen a father be with his son like you, sir. Others will not even look at them until they are grown.'

'Daisy, let us just say that I am different than most men, much to my mother's consternation I may add, but yes I want to be part of his life, not just to watch from afar, as though he were not part of my flesh and blood.'

Daisy nodded; in truth she did not know how to reply to such a revelation of one's feelings.

Stewart turned to the window once more. 'Did you know that my wife never left her nursery and saw only her mother on occasions, never left the house even, and was allowed only to walk the gardens for an hour a day when she grew older?' He turned to face her now.

'It is hard to imagine, is it not, Daisy?' Stewart smiled gently as he turned towards the door.

Daisy was speechless as she stared after her master, watching him walk quietly from the room.

Down in the drawing room, the fires burned brightly, throwing out their warmth; the drapes were still open, and as Lilly lit the last of the candles, she turned to look at Elizabeth.

'Would you be liking me to draw the drapes, Milady?' curtsying as she said it.

'No, Lillie, leave them for now. I am so loath to shut out what light is left of the day, we get so little of it at this time of year. We can close them after dinner.'

Lilly curtsied once more and turned to leave, finding Stewart just about to enter as she opened the door. Jumping back, she curtsied once again.

'Oh, begging your pardon, Master Stewart, I did not see you there.'

Stewart gave her one of his most engaging smiles and held the door for her. Lilly's reply was to blush scarlet, then head down she rushed from the room.

Stewart knew that his mother was watching him, so he turned the same smile on her.

'Stewart, if you embarrass my staff one more time, you know that Lilly—well, you make her uncomfortable, she just does not know what to make of you, you are incorrigible.'

Margaret and Charlotte laughed watching Stewart come over to his mother and taking her hand, kissed her fingers. Elizabeth gave her son a suspicious glance before speaking.

'What have you done, or what are you about to do?'

Stewart stiffened slightly, keeping his smile on his face lest he betray anything.

'Where are all the men of this house?' he teased.

Margaret stood up and came to take his arm. 'Your father is with William and Spike, planning the flower shed that they intend to build in the spring. Alexander is where he always is, at the estate office, where you should be, no doubt.' Margaret watched him purse his limps. 'Yes, where you should be as tomorrow we will all make ready for the trip on the following day.'

Stewart's mind by now was only half listening; he was calculating the hours, what time he would leave tomorrow, before dawn, then he would make it to the lake just as day would break, giving himself a brief moment of safety under the cover of darkness. He knew the way there, and so did his horse.

'Are you listening to me, Stewart Hamilton?' Margaret's hand slapped him on the chest.

'I am, Maggie.' Stewart needed to be alone with her, there was not much time, and what was left would be gone too soon. Taking her hand, he pulled her towards the door.

'I want to show you something, come with me.'

'But, Stewart, we are about to have tea, will it not wait?' Margaret protested as he pulled her further to the door.

Elizabeth who had been watching this play out with interest smiled. 'Margaret, go with him, we will have no peace till you do. I will save some for you.'

Charlotte lowered her head and smiled to herself thinking, *Just go, cousin, he wants to be with you, life is too transitory, so take it with both hands and enjoy it while you are able.*

Stewart closed the door to their room and pulled Margaret into his arms, kissing her deeply. 'Oh God, I want you, Maggie,' she was stopped in her reply as his lips came down on hers again. Releasing herself from his hold, she looked earnestly into his face.

'Stewart, tell me what it is that is troubling you, please? You are frightening me Stewart.'

Stewart swept her up in his arms and came to stand by the bed. 'I want to love my wife,' he whispered in her ear as he undid the laces of her bodice. 'And I would presume that she wants me also.' Biting her earlobe, his mouth moved slowly down her neck.

'Oh, Stewart, you know I do,' she breathed, 'but this is more than that, Stewart.' By now he had taken her bodice and corset as her skirt fell to her feet.

'Be quiet, Margaret Hamilton, we are wasting precious time; our son will awake soon and be banging on our door to be let in.' Stewart removed his stockings and shirt, and then pushed her shift over her shoulders. Standing back his eyes took in every part of her, as though committing her body to memory. Then holding her shoulders, he looked down into her eyes.

'God, I am well blessed; he gave me a wife of extraordinary beauty, one who loves me above all else, one who will never stop wanting me, but above all of these, one who would give me her soul if I asked it.' Saying this, he stroked the mound of her stomach, 'If it is a boy, we will name him Andrew; if a girl, Elizabeth or Isobel, after your mother.'

As his lips came down once more to hers, he lifted her onto the bed, his last words being, 'I Love you, Margaret Hamilton, never forget that.'

***

Dinner was very quiet; all gathered around the table were immersed in their own thoughts. Alexander kept watching his cousin, trying to define any signs of what was to happen the following day: 13th November. His hand kept straying to Charlotte's on the table, and he had eaten very little, just as Stewart had barely touched his food. Andrew Duncan also had been watching the cousins; he too felt a strange sense of foreboding, but he knew not what it was, or where it stemmed from. It was Elizabeth who broke the silence. Placing her fork on her plate, she looked around the table.

'Will someone kindly inform me of what is going on here? Could it be that all the men at this table have suddenly lost their appetite, and some the will to live?' This last question was directed at Stewart. 'We have a wedding to go to in two days, and from what I see, it might just as well be a funeral, would someone care to explain?'

Stewart leaned back in his chair and replied.

'Mother, as you know Northcott has tried to take Catherine twice before, so I am concerned that he will try his chances at the wedding, or any other devious plan he has in mind. It is the not knowing that causes the apprehension within us, it is the why, the where, and the how that puts fear into us. If anything happened to her, I would never forgive myself.'

Stewart saw his father relax somewhat, as did William; his mother still eyed him with suspicion, but he could see that even she was willing to let reason win. It was only Alexander's face that did not change. He did not look to Stewart, but merely nodded his head.

'It is true, Aunt, we are all worried, though I am sure that Sir Henry will post soldiers around the church, and in the grounds beyond, but it does not relieve us from our anxieties.'

Stewart's shoe nudged Alexander's beneath the table in thanks.

***

Stewart sat in the drawing room, his eyes looking into the fire's glow. He felt at peace with himself now, knowing that no matter what transpired tomorrow, the lawyer Bearcroft held all his letters, plus the documents of the estate. Everyone was provided for even unto his unborn child; his heart raced a little at the thought that he may never see it, know it, love it. Standing up, he walked slowly to the dresser.

'Can I offer you a whisky, gentleman? It is Sir Henry's finest; mellow and smooth, a wondrous nightcap.'

'Yes, I will drink with you, Stewart,' came Alexander's quiet reply.

Stewart looked to his father and William raising a glass. 'Will you join us?'

William smiled and stood. 'I thank you, Stewart, but no, I shall away to my bed. I am not as young as the two of you, sleep has a habit of creeping up on me very early now.'

'And I will retire also,' came his father's voice from the chair by the fire. 'It has been a long day with William, Spike, the carpenter, and the blacksmith, but I do believe that we have at least made a start with the shape of the building. By next summer, Stewart, your mother will have some wondrous new plants both in the gardens and in the house.'

'Good night, Father, William. It is just you and I then, Alex, and we have the fireside chairs to ourselves.'

Handing Alexander his glass, they sat once again in silence.

'Why do you have to do this, Stewart?' Alexander leaned forward in his chair, holding his glass in his cupped hand, averting his eyes from Stewart's.

Stewart did not reply immediately, but sat watching his cousin. Alexander was the opposite of himself in everything, fair to dark, slim to muscular, gentle and introvert, to brash and extrovert. Like two sides of a coin, each held their own significance. He was a quiet clever man, never looking for more than he should have. Could it have been his upbringing as a minister's son?

Stewart argued with himself now, for was he not respectful, always helping others and putting down those that would seek to intimidate others who were weaker than himself? Yes, there lay his misfortune, fighting battles for those who were not strong enough to fight their own. He could never look away, but if being such was a fault, God then so be it, for that was his character. He was quick-tempered, but only when seeing unfairness. He would lay down his own life for his family without question.

Stewart breathed deeply before he spoke.

'Alex, if I do not do this we, our family, and the extended family, will know no peace. We will continue to live under the shadow of evil that Northcott has created.'

'Stewart! You do not have to die to stop this,' interrupted Alexander.

'Oh, I sincerely hope not too, Alex, believe me.'

'But he has the advantage, Stewart,' answered Alexander in all earnest.

'Yes, but I have the strategy, he only has brute force.'

'What strategy, Stewart, what strategy?' Alexander was becoming agitated now.

Stewart swallowed to keep himself calm; he did not want to argue with his cousin, not tonight.

'I will choose the place and the time, though he will think it was him. It will be a place where I am comfortable, where I can see clearly, a place I am familiar with. Then I will wait for him to find me, and he will find me, Alex, for I believe he is watching me now, and has been for some time. The only thing I will not be able to control is when the first blow will strike.'

Alexander swallowed all of his whisky; rising slowly he placed the glass onto the small table near him. Turning to Stewart, he held out his hand. Stewart stood taking his hand in a tight grip, pulling his cousin into an embrace.

'I will follow you, Stewart. I will not let him take your life even if I have to give my own in forfeit.'

Stewart leaned back and held his cousin's shoulder in a tight squeeze, saying to himself, *You will not, Alex, for I will be gone before you even realise.*

'I bid you good night, cousin, I will see you tomorrow for dinner.' Stewart inclined his head.

***

As Stewart came up the stairs, he could hear his son's cry; making his way to the nursery he knocked gently on the door. Nanny Daisy opened it slightly, then stepped back as she saw who was standing there.

'Master Stewart sir, what brings you here at this hour?' Daisy curtsied still keeping the door half closed.

'I heard my son, Daisy, what ails him?'

Daisy opened the door letting Stewart into the room. Then walked to where young Charles lay very restless on his small bed.

'He is getting a large tooth at the back, Master Stewart. I have applied Mrs Cottle's clove oil and it seems to be helping to relieve the pain some.'

Stewart picked his son up in his arms.

'I will take him with me, Daisy, else Jane will get no peace tonight.'

Daisy went to stop him. 'Master Stewart, is that wise?'

'It will be fine, Daisy, I promise, please do not worry, go get some rest.'

Stewart turned and walked to the door, holding his son's sleeping form to his shoulder, turning back once more to nod to Daisy as he closed the door quietly behind him.

Daisy stood there astounded; what would her mistress say? What would Milady Elizabeth say? There was nothing she could do now, but there would be explanations asked for in the morning.

When Stewart entered their room, he could see that Margaret was asleep. He pulled back the covers, laying their son next to her and then undressed. Seeing Margaret turn he placed his hand on her arm.

'Be still, Maggie, our son was in pain from his tooth. I have brought him here with us as baby Jane will get no sleep, and maybe he will find comfort from his mother.'

Margaret who was at that moment still drowsy from sleep looked at Stewart puzzled, then whispered.

'What are you doing, Stewart? Daisy will be worried to distraction, thinking that she cannot look after her charge.'

'Maggie, it will be fine.' He soothed as he lay gently next to their son. Reaching over he kissed her, then entwining his fingers into hers he lay down, their linked hands laying over their sleeping son.

'Sleep now, all will be well. I love you, Maggie, good night.'

Maggie watched him close his eyes, mouthing silently to him with fear in her heart, *I love you too, Stewart.*

***

Stewart rose before dawn; kissing his sleeping son's head, he stroked his face. He could not kiss Margaret as she would wake and there would be questions—why was he leaving—but with her son lying beside her, she would feel his warmth and sleep on till morning. As he watched her now by the light from the window, he wanted nothing more than to take her into his arms once more, smell her hair, feel her warmth and the softness of her body close to his. Raising his eyes heavenwards, he whispered.

'Dear God, let me return this day.'

Going into his dressing room, he dressed in haste, then holding his boots in his hand he silently made his way down the stairs and across the hall. He would leave by the drawing room glass doors, as the huge oak front door would echo around the hallway and up the stairs when he closed it.

Reaching the stables, he told the stable lad that he needed to travel into Mere early to see the blacksmith. The young lad asked no questions, but did as he was bid. When Stewart left there, it was still dark, but he knew the way and so did the horse. It was cold as he rode, his hands felt numb as he held tight to the reins; was it from fear as well as cold, he idly contemplated, but that was of no consequence at this moment as his mind was racing ahead of him, and what he was about to undertake. Shivering slightly he urged his horse on.

As he approached the lake, his eyes scanned around the countryside for any movement. To the west side there was a small copse; he licked his lips, knowing what was buried there. There were many places for a person to secrete himself, clumps of evergreen bushes were scattered all around, Holly, some Box, Laurel and Yew—so tightly packed were the leaves and branches that birds could nest in safety.

Slowly he drew his horse to a halt, removed his jacket, then dismounting he unbuckled his sword from the saddle, tethering his horse to a tree; he took his sword from its sheath then went to stand by the lake. His heart was thumping in his ears now, blocking out all noise from the surrounding countryside. Stewart doubted that Northcott would use a pistol—maybe to finish, but not the initial blow. He would want to see his adversary's face, for that was the kind of man that Northcott was. Also, if the man did not suddenly surprise him, come at him from behind, well then his chances of defending himself were improved.

Now the dawn was breaking, streaking the sky with colour, there was a sort of half-light, the same as in the clearing on the morning of the dual. Stewart shook his head, dispelling the images which were crowding in now. If he was to survive, it was crucial that he kept his mind focused regardless of his fears.

He heard the whoosh of the blade as it cut through the air just in time, managing in an instant to turn himself swiftly round and bring his own sword up to block the blade's target—his head. Stewart was sweating now, taken off guard, but still managed to divert another blow aimed at the side of his neck. Stewart looked at his opponent and knew that all rules of fencing had been dispensed with; this fight would be fought with sheer brute force, and whoever was the stronger would succeed. Jumping backwards, he parried off another lunge, this time to his stomach. Stewart was by this time at the lake's edge, and knew if he did not bring his thoughts together, he would be dead.

Taking his sword into both hands, he ran forward, sweeping his weapon from side to side in quick far-reaching movements. Two of his strikes hit home as they tore into Northcott's shirt, which was slowly becoming red. Incensed by the onslaught, Northcott came towards him now in a blind frenzy, with several of his blows gashing deep into Stewart's chest. Hearing the water splash underneath his boots, Stewart realised that if he did not act quickly, he would not see another day. Bringing up his blade to stop another thrust to his stomach, he stepped to the side, gained his footing and came at Northcott with the same ferocity slicing into both his arm and thigh. Northcott gave a violent lunge to Stewart's stomach once more, but Stewart was ready and stepped aside taking the blow on his side.

Both men were sweating profusely now, and droplets of sweat were finding their way into Stewart's eyes, slightly obscuring his sight. Stewart made a tired lunge to Northcott's side, catching him just under the arm. It was then that Northcott screamed out and ran at Stewart, falling as he did so, causing his sword arm to be caught beneath him.

Stewart stood there, hands on knees, panting hard, holding tight to his side which was now pouring blood like water from a cataract, while he waited for Northcott to rise, but he did not stir. Falling to his knees, he crawled to Northcott's prone body on all fours; it was only when he pushed him up a little to see his face that he realised he was dead, he had fallen on his sword. The blade had cut deep into his stomach, slicing it from side to side, like one would cut bread.

Stewart lowered his head to the floor, thinking that he had won, but it was a worthless victory, for no one knew where he was, and by the time they discovered him, he too would be dead. But Northcott had died by his own hand—or had he—Stewart raised his eyes skywards. '*Vengeance is mine, I will repay, saith the Lord,*' he whispered to the air around him. His last thoughts were of Maggie and his son, then rolling onto his side, he gave in to the blackness that was pulling him down.

Chapter Forty-Eight
Deliverance from Evil and Family Lost

The banging on the front door was relentless and as Elizabeth came down the stairs rapidly tying her robe around her, she saw Thompson pulling back the large bolt that held it secure. By now all the occupants of the house were standing on the landing at the top of the stairs, when the door opened revealing the blacksmith.

'You must come this minute, Milady, your son be wounded badly, he be in my house, please make haste.' The man pleaded breathlessly.

'I be sending for his physician, Milady, as my wife knew who he be. Please you must come now.'

Elizabeth held on to the post at the foot of the stairs, turning round just in time to see her husband catch Margaret before her body hit the floor. Elizabeth recovered her senses and turned to the blacksmith.

'Come in, Master Blacksmith.' Turning then to Thompson who for once had dropped his mask of authoritative diplomacy, and was white to the lips, she issued her orders.

'Take the gentleman into the drawing room, Thompson, and give him a drink, we will dress directly, and have them bring the carriage round NOW.'

Turning she made her way up the stairs again, issuing further orders.

'Alexander, take your wife to the nursery then get dressed. William, please can you remain here, just in case.' Turning to her husband she shook her head. 'Take her into her room, Andrew, I will go to Mrs Cottle for some tea, then please ask Millie to get her dressed as soon as she is able.'

***

Margaret refused all other sustenance except the tea. It was warm, it was sweet and it seemed to be calming her senses considerably. Sitting on the edge of the bed, she looked up at Daisy, who was now standing at the door with a very sleepy Charles in her arms.

'Daisy, I want you to know that none of what happened last night is in any way your fault. I know the reason my husband brought our son to our bed, and it was not because of your inadequacies, please believe me. And if he is not already dead from his wounds, I will kill him.'

416

Millie looked up at Daisy, her eyes open wide. 'My Mistress is very distressed at this time, Daisy.'

Margaret turned to look at Millie, daring her to say another word.

'Millie, please, get me out of this gown.' Margaret was frantically pulling at the laces which were tight over her stomach. 'The corset it too tight and my unborn child is kicking so hard I do believe my stomach will burst, have I not a gown that I may wear without my corset please?' Margaret nervously pleaded, anxiety echoing in her voice.

Millie turned and went into the dressing room, reappearing a few minutes later with a gown of pale green soft wool.

'Here, Milady, this one be lacing up at the back, the gown be all one piece, and the waist at the front be very high, with a generous amount of material, you will be feeling more comfortable with this. Do you not remember, Milady, you wore it with Master Charles.'

Margaret had no time for recollection, but dressed quickly, then Millie scooped her hair up onto her head, pinning it there securely before pulling on her bonnet.

'You be putting this thick cape around you, Mistress, it be a very cold day out there,' Millie encouraged, as she could see the agitation manifesting on her mistress' face once more.

Margaret took several deep breaths, closed her eyes and swallowed hard. Looking from Millie to Daisy, she nodded.

'Thank you, both. We will see you later, please God.'

Coming out onto the landing, she saw both Andrew Duncan and Pip waiting for her, both dressed for the journey.

'Take my arm, Margaret, we will go slowly down the stairs, please?' he added as he saw her about to protest.

Margaret looked at Stewart's father and thought he appeared quite drawn, as though he had not slept for days; she reflected that she was not the only one in pain at the moment. Pip bowed to her, and she saw that he had already packed a large bag full of clothes and other such things he would require for Stewart no doubt. Closing her eyes and breathing deeply once more, she descended the stairs.

***

As the coach pulled up outside the blacksmith's house, Margaret looked at Elizabeth and saw the pain imprinted on her face. Your son has been a trial to you many times over, Margaret reflected, and many of those—such times—she had believed she would outlive him. Margaret's stomach was heaving in more ways than one, the child inside was reacting to her emotions, and at this moment Margaret felt decidedly unwell. She swallowed several times as the bile rose in her throat.

Stepping down from the coach, she looked to Elizabeth.

417

'Please excuse me, but I think that I am going to be unwell.' Walking quickly to the back of the coach, she wretched.

Elizabeth who had followed her held her head and offered her handkerchief.

'Margaret child, please rest in the coach for a moment, I will go inside and see what is to be done.'

Margaret placed her hand on Elizabeth's arm to stop her words.

'I am fine, Mother, we will go in together.'

The air was freezing, and the white mist that was appearing from everybody's mouths—including the horses that shook their heads and pawed the ground restlessly—just seemed to mingle with, and disappear into, the mist that swirled around their feet.

Elizabeth looked up at the house; it was as fine a house as Alexander's, made of stone, not the sort of house you would expect a blacksmith to own. Elizabeth shook her head testily and chided herself on her unkind thoughts; did not a blacksmith have every right to own a respectable dwelling?

As she entered the building, she heard her son and her physician talking in a very heated fashion from the room to her right.

'Mr Hardiman, just stitch my wounds, dress my wounds, and then strap up my chest, for I will not be missing my friend James' wedding the day after tomorrow.'

'Go sit in the dining room, Margaret, please. I wish to speak with my son before you unleash your wroth on him.'

Margaret inclined her head, and then allowed herself to be led by Andrew Duncan into the room on the left.

On entering the room, Elizabeth saw her son on a small bed at the far end under the window.

'Mr Hardiman,' Elizabeth said in greeting, inclining her head as he bowed to her.

'Please allow me a few moments with my son, before you start to tend his wounds.'

'Milady Hamilton, I will be just outside if you need me.' Bowing to her once more, he left closing the door very quietly behind him.

From the chill of the day outside, it was warm in the room. A fire burned in the hearth, and several candles had been lit to generate enough light for physician to perform the necessary tasks to treat Stewart's injuries.

Elizabeth did not speak as she came to him, pulling up a chair to sit beside him. Stewart's face blanched as he tried to move himself up onto the pillows; seeing this Elizabeth leaned forward, adjusted them, and then sat back down again. Stewart watched her, trying to read her thoughts.

'Is Maggie with you, Mother?'

Elizabeth inclined her head slightly. As Stewart looked at her face, he tried to decipher the emotions that she held. Oh there was anger there, and pain, fear and sorrow, but hidden under all of these there was sense of relief, that he had been the one to survive. The wound on his right side was burning like a furnace, and every breath he took seemed to heighten the feeling. He wondered if his mother was ever going to speak, then she reached over. Stewart's first instinct was to flinch as he thought she was about to hit him, but she just took his hand in hers.

'On my way here—' Elizabeth's voice was deep with emotion; closing her eyes she swallowed several times before continuing.

'On my way here... I was *so* angry, Stewart, there were many things that I wanted to say, shout, scream at you even, but now I am just so very grateful that you are alive.' Two large tears fell from her eyes as she tried hard to compose herself once more.

'You are stubborn, reckless.' She closed her eyes trying to dam the tears that were flowing freely now. Slowly bending towards him, she kissed his cheek. 'And I am so very proud that you are mine.' Her hand shook as she held his.

'I will get Margaret.' Standing quickly, she made for the door before he could speak.

Stewart lay there staring out of the window. This was not what he had anticipated; in his mind he imagined she would berate him, let lose all of her anger on him. Stewart rubbed wetness from his eyes quickly with his fingers as he heard the door open once more, then watched Maggie slowly come across the room. He could discern even from the dim light in the room that her face was very pale indeed. Keeping his eyes on hers, he raised his hand to her as she came near. Margaret took it and linked her fingers with his; kneeling next to the bed she lay her head in his lap, as his other hand came up and stroked her hair. Lifting her head, she gently stood and sat on the edge of the bed. Then, just as his mother's had, her tears fell silently down over her cheeks, dripping from her chin onto her dress. Composing herself, she stared into his eyes.

'If you do anything like this again, Stewart Hamilton, I will kill you myself.' Her words were stopped as he pulled her head down to kiss her.

'I might still die, Margaret Hamilton,' he replied with a smile in his voice.

'Good,' was all she said as she leaned towards him, kissing him once more. Leaning back, she stood up wiping her face with her hands, as Stewart handed her a piece of bandage to wipe her nose. 'I will get Mr Hardiman; he must attend your wounds.'

'They can wait, Maggie.'

'No, they cannot,' was her abrupt reply as she crossed the room, opened the door and called for him.

Mr Hardiman entered with Andrew Duncan, Alexander and Pip in tow. Elizabeth thought that a wise move, as they would have to hold him down to do what they had to do—better that Margaret did not hear that. Elizabeth took Margaret's hand and pulled her from the room.

'Come, Margaret, The wife of Mr Martin the blacksmith has laid out a breakfast for us, for none of us have eaten this morning, and you must eat.' Pushing her into the dining room, she closed the door and led her to the table. Mary Martin was stood there in her deep blue gown and snow white apron and cap; as they came up to her she curtsied to them. Before she could speak, Alexander came in requesting two glasses of brandy for the physician. Elizabeth thought that they could not be for him to drink, so they must be for other purposes—to cleanse the wounds maybe. Once he had departed, Mary Martin turned to them.

'Good morning to you, Miladies, if you like to be seated and take some food. The bread is fresh as I do bake it this morning, and the honey be from our own bees—the butter be mine also,' she added, curtseying once more.

Elizabeth came round the table and took the woman's hand.

'Mistress Martin, you will not stand on ceremony to us, we owe you a great debt, for without you my son would be dead now. Please can we not all sit and eat?' Elizabeth's eyes were beseeching.

'Mistress… Milady Hamilton, we be taking our breakfast early, my husband be at the forge before sunrise to stoke the furnace and see that his three apprentices are there.' Looking now towards Margaret she saw that she was in some distress and heavily with child.

'Mistress Hamilton, if I may be so bold, will you not come sit by the fire in the comfortable chair, and I will be bringing you a brew to quieten your nerves. It be one my mother gave me—it will not harm the child.'

Elizabeth saw Margaret's shoulders relax, so she took her hand and led her to the chair. Sitting herself into the other, she looked slowly around the room. It was a nice house with good furniture, including a brightly-coloured rug which sat under the dining table. Her eyes wandered around the walls now, seeing several paintings—of which she could only assume to be relatives, ancestors—then they rested on the portrait over the fireplace and Elizabeth's hand came up to her throat in alarm. There, staring down at her were her grandparents George MacMartin and Abigail Pembroke.

'Mother?' Margaret's voice broke in. 'Mother, what is the matter? You look as if you have seen a ghost.'

Elizabeth held her hand to her forehead which at this moment was decidedly clammy, and her head was spinning. Gaining her composure, she stood up.

'Margaret child, I must go find some water. All that has happened here this morning has caught up on me, and I feel I am in need of some air. Please, do not worry, I will be back directly.' Saying this she left the room.

***

Stewart watched as Phillip Hardiman held the curved needle with a long pair of fine pliers to the fire's flame. Once it was heated, he then dropped the needle into the glass of whisky. The sutures he would use were already soaking in the other glass.

'If I make a mess of this, Master Hamilton, or you should die because of it, please let it be said that I did warn you; it should be done by a surgeon.'

Stewart looked at the needle resting in the glass with a great deal of nervous trepidation.

'Did you not train under the best surgeon in London, Mr Hardiman, a Dr Hunter, I believe?'

Hardiman's eyes bore into Stewart's. 'I may have trained under the man, but I did not say I had his skills, sir.'

'You can sew, can you not, Mr Hardiman?' Stewart quipped apprehensively.

Hardiman rinsed his own hands with alcohol, then removed a suture and the needle from the glasses and proceeded to thread it.

'Please, gentleman, hold him steady. I am about to pour alcohol over the wound to cleanse it. Please lay flat, Mr Hamilton.'

Stewart moved himself down, as his father took both his arms above his head. Pip gripped his lower legs in a vice like hold, whilst Alexander sat on his abdomen. His father saw his son blanch considerably, as small beads of sweat appeared on his forehead and around his mouth.

'Before you start, Mr Hardiman, Father, can you move that bowl close to my head here, for I fear I will be in need of that very soon.' Stewart saw his cousin's lips twitch and thought to himself good-naturedly, *One day I will get my revenge, cousin.*

Elizabeth heard her son's scream as she made her way across the hall to the kitchen. Turning on her heel, she headed back to the dining room. She quickly poured herself a small whisky, then came to sit on the arm of Margaret's chair. Pulling Margaret's head into her, she took a sip from the glass letting the warm liquid burn its way down her throat and into her stomach, warming her body.

'It will be over soon, Margaret, I promise you.'

***

Mr Hardiman stood in the hall facing Mary Martin.

'Mistress Martin, your cleaning of the wounds was excellent. I found no fibres at all within them, so there was no need for debridement.' He nodded to her as she curtseyed, then turned to Elizabeth.

'The only wound that was in need of sutures was the one on his right side, Milady Hamilton. The others to his chest arms and thigh will heal in time—though they will leave scars. I have bandaged him, but these must be changed twice daily to prevent infection. I have also given Mr Duncan some laudanum and instructions how to use it, if it be needed.' Phillip Hardiman stroked his chin as he looked at Elizabeth.

'Your son is a very stubborn young man, Milady Hamilton, but maybe that is what keeps him alive, no?' he raised his eyebrows with the last word.

Elizabeth nodded in answer. 'Thank you, Mr Hardiman, for everything you have done.'

Phillip Hardiman bowed to all present in the hall, bidding them good day, then left.

As Margaret entered the drawing room, she saw Pip carefully placing a clean pillow beneath his head. Biting her lips madly to stop the tears, she came towards him.

'Have you had enough now, Stewart Hamilton?'

Margaret saw him nod slightly then close his eyes as two tears slid down his temples. Holding up his hand, he gripped hers, pulling her to the floor beside the bed. Margaret put his hand up to her cheek then kissed his palm, letting her own tears come.

'Maggie, I feel I have been doused with whisky, plastered with poultice of honey, ready to be placed into the oven and cooked,' he murmured. Margaret's mouth went up into a smile, and then she burst into nervous laughter as she rocked back and forth on her heels still holding his hand to her face.

Chapter Forty-Nine
Memories Resurrected

When Elizabeth entered the kitchen, she saw Mary Martin peeling vegetables while her daughter pulled feathers from a newly killed chicken. Seeing Elizabeth approach, the young girl stood up abruptly, sending feathers flying in all directions as she curtsied.

'Milady Hamilton!' shouted Mary Martin as though she had seen a ghost.

'Please go back to the dining room, I will bring you refreshments directly.' Looking to her daughter for support, she placed her knife to the table, wiped her hands on her apron and came towards Elizabeth.

'Mistress Martin, please pay me no mind. I am often found in my own kitchen at the Willows, do not let me disturb you in your work. I come here to talk with you in private, if I may?' Elizabeth looked towards her daughter who seemed to be transfixed holding the limp, half-plucked chicken up by its legs.

'Please be seated and continue. I just wish to talk and thank your mother.' Elizabeth nodded to the girl, who in turn looked at her mother for reassurance.

'Sit you down, Jennie, and after you be finished the two chickens, maybe you can make some tea for Milady Hamilton.'

Elizabeth pulled out a chair and sat, nodding for Mary Martin to do the same. Her head was so full of questions she did not know where to begin, maybe with the fight.

'Firstly I must express my eternal gratitude for what you did for my son. Where did you find him? Was it near here?'

Mary Martin turned to her daughter. 'Jennie, put the kettle to boil, child, I will be making that tea now I think, and then I can tell Milady Hamilton all that happened.' Pausing she looked once more to Elizabeth. 'I always find that a cup of tea helps with the telling.' Standing up, she took two china cups and saucers down from the dresser as well as the sugar bowl, then turned once more to her daughter.

'Jennie, make sure you be warming the pot before you brew, and bring that jug of milk in from the pantry please.' Seating herself once more, she looked to Elizabeth.

'Milady, the story goes back a couple of years now. Not far from here there be a lake—a beautiful place—well my daughter, she be liking to go there, even though she has been forbidden. She watches the birds you see and picks the wild flowers.' Mary Martin turned and looked at her daughter as she spoke. 'One summer day she be encountering your son there. Oh he be very courteous, Milady, make no mistake for that. Well, she happened there this morning and saw your son in fierce fighting with another man. She did no more than run back here to tell me.'

At this point, Jennie arrived carrying a tray with a china teapot and milk jug. Placing them on the table, she curtsied then went back to her chicken. Elizabeth looked around the room; it was spacious, clean, and homely, she mused, as she sipped her tea listening to the soft tearing as Jennie continued her plucking.

'Please continue, Mistress Martin.' Elizabeth stopped. 'What is your name, Mistress Martin?' she asked politely.

Mary Martin looked flustered but replied anyway. 'It be Mary, Milady.'

'Good,' replied Elizabeth. 'Mine is Elizabeth, shall we continue, Mary?'

Mary Martin looked at Elizabeth somewhat nervously—was she to address her by Elizabeth?

'Well, Jennie came to me and I went for my husband, then we all went out to the lake together with the cart. By this time the dawn had broke, but the mist still be swirling thickly by the water. We did not see them directly, but as we be nearing the water's edge, my husband saw the two bodies,' she paused to see the reaction from Elizabeth, but seeing none she continued, thinking to herself that this was not perhaps the first time such a thing had happened to her son.

'My husband got down, and on rolling one man over, he be looking up at me and shaking his head—he saw that he be dead. When he turned to the other, he do start shouting at me to bring the wagon. You be knowing the rest.'

'And the other man?' queried Elizabeth. 'Who was he?'

'That I do not know, after bringing your son here, my husband be going to the magistrate then on to the church, which is where the other man do lie.'

Elizabeth licked her lips several times. 'May I have another tea, Mary? And maybe I could take some to my son and his wife?'

'No worries to you, Milady, they have theirs already, and the gentlemen be eating their breakfast in the dining room at this very moment.'

Elizabeth leaned over and placed her hand over Mary Martin's. 'Thank you.'

As Elizabeth sat sipping her second tea, she thought hard how she would approach the other question of the portrait. Mayhap it was something that they had found when they purchased the house, but no, there was a likeness to her grandfather in Mr Martin's face, of that she was sure. Just as there was a likeness between the mother and daughter she saw before her now.

'Tell me, Mary, that portrait over the fireplace in the dining room, are they relations of yours? There seems to be a likeness between your husband and the man.'

Mary Martin sat back and smiled.

'The story goes that he be my husband's grandfather, though the Lord knows how. My husband be knowing the story better than myself, but let me be taking you to the dining room, Milady, then you too can eat.' Saying this, she stood up standing aside for Elizabeth to go before her.

'My husband will be home for his lunch, Milady, you can ask him then.' Smiling, she followed Elizabeth out of the kitchen.

As they entered the hall, Mary Martin turned once more to Elizabeth.

'Oh, Milady, I nearly be forgetting, I too be meeting your two sons, a year back now in Mere. The coach I be on was stopped by highwaymen just outside of town, but they were disturbed in their work by another coach, thank the Lord.' Mary Martin placed her hands together looking upwards. 'I be very distressed by the time we came to Mere, but your two sons took care of me, bringing me water and offering food, even finding my bag for me. You are truly blessed, Milady, having two such fine sons. They be a credit to you.' Saying this she turned and opened the dining room door for Elizabeth.

Alexander stood up immediately pulling out a chair for his aunt.

'Come, Aunt, sit and eat, you have had no food since last evening.' Taking her hand, he gently pushed the chair in behind her and then returned his own seat.

'Alexander, I have been told that you and Stewart know Mistress Martin? You helped her when the stage she travelled on was set by highwaymen?'

Alexander stopped from taking a bite of bread and smiled. 'Indeed we did, Aunt. The mistress was very upset, so we brought her some water—for that is what she requested—offered her food, which she declined and found her bag from the pile. In truth, we did very little, Aunt, except ease her mind till her husband came for her.'

'She thinks that you are bothers, you know.' Elizabeth smiled at him. 'But that is easy to understand, as you both have a likeness about you.'

Alexander smiled warmly back. 'So I have been told, Aunt.'

Elizabeth lifted her eyes to the portrait now. 'It is funny how a likeness can come down through the years.'

Andrew Duncan turned and smiled then took her hand firmly into his. 'Eat, Lizzie, then after lunch we will try and take him home.'

***

As expected, Stephen Martin came home for his lunch at twelve noon. The dining table had been cleared and relayed for lunch with two roast chickens, potatoes and a delicious aromatic soup made from the vegetables. There was fresh bread, cheeses and a ham. As Mary Martin and her daughter Jennie brought the last of the food in, they curtsied and turned to go. Andrew Duncan stood up; pulling out two chairs, he nodded and waved his arm for them to sit.

'We will all eat together, there is ample room for all to sit, Mistress Martin.'

Mary Martin looked to her husband who smiled and inclined his head, then taking off her apron, she smoothed her hair then her dress and sat, letting Andrew Duncan push the seat in for her. Her daughter did likewise, going red to the roots of her hair. Before sitting, Andrew Duncan looked around the table then at Stephen Martin; raising his glass he began.

'Sir, I believe that I speak for all those present at this table now in giving you my heartfelt thanks for what you and your family have done for us today. There are no words to express my gratitude for your unbridled kindness and support you have shown. For in truth, you saved my son's life.'

Alexander stood and raised his glass. 'I will second that.'

Stephen Martin stood now and raised his glass. 'I thank you kindly, sir, but let us say that it was done in kind and with the same generosity of spirit that was shown to my wife that day in Mere.'

Andrew looked questioningly at Elizabeth, who replied by placing her hand on his and smiling. 'I will tell you later, Andrew.'

***

Stewart knew that he had a slight fever as gooseflesh rose over his body intermittently, making him tremble slightly, even though he was sitting next to the fire. They had eaten their food with Pip in the drawing room, and then Pip had gone to feed and water the horses, leaving the two of them to their peace. Margaret sat at Stewart's feet now, watching the flames dance while she held his hand over her cheek. He had ordered Pip to sit him in the chair; he was not going to be fed like an invalid, but now he wished nothing more than to lie down.

'Maggie,' his voice held a deep tiredness. 'Can you help me back onto the bed? I think that I will sleep a while.'

Margaret rose, placing her hand to his forehead; it was very warm, but there was no high fever—yet. Carefully placing his arm about her shoulders, she walked him to the bed, lowering him gently. Plumping up the pillows, she lifted his legs up and brought the covers back over him.

'Sleep now, Stewart, you will gain your strength that way. Then maybe later we can get you back home.' She knelt beside him, stroking his face till she saw his breathing take on the even rhythm of sleep. Getting up, she returned to her own seat then lay her head back and let sleep take her also.

***

As the dishes were cleared away, Elizabeth went and stood in front of the portrait.

'Mr Martin, your wife tells me that this portrait is of your grandparents?'

Stephen Martin looked up in surprise.

'Why yes, Milady, that be true, it be passed down over the generations, and in truth this house belonged to my father.

Elizabeth's heart was beating a little too fast so she seated herself in one of the chairs by the fire.

'What a fascinating story, Mr Martin, you must tell me about it.' Her voice was a little high but calm and her hands shook slightly. Placing them firmly into her lap, she waited for him to speak.

'Well, Milady, I will tell you all that I be knowing. It goes back to when my grandfather—who came down from Scotland—inherited a house from an uncle here, the house being hereabouts I believe, and so he came and made his home here. His name be George MacMartin and he be hailing from Lochiel. After some time he married my grandmother Lady Jane Pembroke; they had two children, Milady, Jane Martin and George Martin.' Stephen Martin looked at Elizabeth who seemed to be riveted to her seat.

'Are you well, Milady, do I be going too fast for you? Would you be liking something to drink?'

Andrew Duncan who along with Alexander had been watching this play out came to stand by her.

'Do go on, Master Martin, I think it is that my wife is enthralled by your story.' Sitting himself on the arm of the chair, he took Elizabeth's hand.

'Well, as I be saying, four years after the birth of her son, Lady Abigail was taken by a fever and died. Then later in life, her son George went for a soldier over in a place called New Grenada, to a war they call "Jenkins Ear", though for the life of me I know not why. Well, they be told he were dead, Milady, and then the daughter married another Scotsman Charles Hamilton—and that is the last I know of that side of the family.'

Elizabeth's hand was gripping her husband's so tightly now his fingers were going numb.

'Please go on, Master Martin.' Elizabeth's voice seemed to come from somewhere outside of her.

'The son do come back though, but because of an injury to his head he knows nothing of who he is, or where he is from—just his name—and then a Major there be giving him a letter to go to a bank in London.'

'Coutts?' Elizabeth whispered.

'Yes, that be the one. There he found a substantial amount of monies left to him by his father—who had died two years previous and who believed his son to be dead—that portrait, and a letter telling him that they had all lived in Mere.'

Alexander who had been listening had gone to the dresser and poured his aunt some whisky. Coming over to her he handed her the glass.

'Drink this, Aunt, please.'

'There is not much else to tell you, Milady, but that he bought this house here, the blacksmiths came with it, and he settled down to his own peaceful life, married my mother Kathleen, and here I be.'

There followed a silence in the room, that if you could touch it, it would resonate. Everyone knew the implications of what had just been revealed, but at that moment none could find their voice. Elizabeth stood, slowly walking towards Stephen Martin.

'Sir, I do believe that we are related,' was all she said, as she slowly sank to the floor.

***

427

Elizabeth opened her eyes and saw that she was in a comfortable bed; Andrew was sitting by her side stroking her face, and Mrs Martin was looking anxiously from the door.

'Do she be feeling better, Master Duncan sir? It be the stress of today, a body can only take so much. I be down stairs if you need me.' With that she left closing the door quietly behind her.

Elizabeth took Andrew Duncan's hand in both of hers. 'Oh, Andrew. His father and my mother were brother and sister.'

'I know, Lizzie,' was all he said.

'He must come back to the house with us, and I will tell him there, show him his ancestors.'

Andrew nodded. 'Come, Lizzie, let us go down and see our son, but I think that we will maybe not tell him right now, as perhaps it will be more than he can tolerate at this time, yes?'

Elizabeth inclined her head and allowed herself to be lifted off the bed.

All eyes were on her as she came down the stairs. 'I am fine, thank you, just the worry of today and lack of sleep. I will go talk with my son, and then if he is well, we can go to our home.' Looking towards Stephen Martin, she added.

'Please come with us, Mr Martin, there is something I would like you to see.' She inclined her head towards him, and he nodded back.

'I thank you, Milady. I will go now to the forge, settle my apprentices, then when I close, I will come.'

Entering the drawing room, Elizabeth saw her son peacefully asleep on the bed and Margaret asleep in the armchair. Smiling to herself, she turned and left them to their dreams.

***

It was late in the afternoon when they at last arrived back at the Willows. The rain had started to fall; that calm sort of rain that fell from the sky in a seemingly straight line, there being no wind to move it. The earth smelled musky and ripe with the leaves that had fallen, which were now rotting into a kind of soft sponge beneath one's feet. The only sound to be heard was the rain drops hitting the coach—musical as a lullaby soothing one's senses.

Stewart was helped from the coach by his father and Alexander as Thompson held out an umbrella over their heads from behind to shield them. Stewart looked up, recollecting that this too had been one of James' gifts, and a very useful one. Thompson also informed his mistress that while they had been away, they had been delivered of another perambulator from Master James—this one for baby Jane. Elizabeth had smiled warmly, shaking her head as she looked towards her son.

'Now you know why I am going to his wedding, Mother. Even if you have to carry me to the church, I will be there.'

Coming into the hall, Stewart noticed that most of the staff had gathered there with the exception of Mrs Cottle; well maybe she was still angry with him, pondered Stewart. Charlotte was tearful and hugged her sister tightly, till she was led upstairs by Alexander. His mother was issuing orders, as that was her way of coping with situations such as this, and his father was eyeing him keenly, as he stood there holding his side. That was where the pain was generating from, and it felt as though someone was holding a burning piece of wood against his skin.

'I think that you should go lie for a while, Stewart.'

'Not until I have spoken with Mrs Cottle, Father,' interrupted Stewart as he made his way unsteadily to the kitchen. On entering, he saw her at the table kneading what looked to be dough; looking up she crossed her plump arms over her ample bosom and clicked her tongue at him.

'If I were your mother, Master Stewart, you have been a trial, Master Stewart, you are but twenty-seven and be having more scars upon your body than a man who has been to war.'

Stewart could see from her eyes that she was upset, so he said nothing.

'Sit you down now, before you fall down.'

Stewart gently lowered himself onto a wooden chair, and then leaned onto the table.

'You be wanting something for the pain and the fever, no? Well, I will send it up directly.' Her gaze had not left his, nodding her head she continued. 'I be very glad that you are not dead, Master Stewart, now be gone with you.'

Stewart stood very carefully, as he knew that if he did not his legs would not hold him. Holding onto the table once more, he smiled.

'Thank you, Mrs Cottle.'

He did not hear his father come up behind him till he spoke.

'Mrs Cottle, I will take him upstairs out of your kitchen.' Saying this, he placed his son's left arm around his shoulders and guided him out.

As they mounted the stairs, Andrew Duncan spoke again.

'Stewart, your body feels as though I am holding a fire in my hands. You cannot possibly travel tomorrow.'

Stewart stopped and looked hard at his father. 'No, Father, I am going, for if I do not, then he has won, and I will *not* let him win. He should have killed me this day, but by some divine grace, I am still alive. I will be going. Maggie can re-dress my wounds for me tonight,' he looked away from his father now. 'She nursed me the last time; she knows what is to be done.'

His father smiled, and then started up the stairs once more. 'When you are well, she will make you pay for this.' Stewart heard the laughter in his voice and murmured to himself—*I Know.*

***

It was close to six o'clock when Stephen Martin arrived at the Willows. As Thompson showed him into the drawing room, Elizabeth hardly recognised him; he was washed, clean shaven and neatly dressed, and even more like her grandfather in the portrait over the fireplace than ever.

'Good evening to you, Mr Martin, will you take a drink?' offered Elizabeth.

429

'Good evening to you too, Milady, and no, thank you kindly, I be fine,' he answered good naturedly, letting his eyes roam around the room. 'It be a beautiful home you have, Milady.'

'Thank you, Mr Martin, but please, can you call me Elizabeth?' She saw the startled expression appear on his face, 'Please, you will understand why when I explain things to you, pray do sit down.'

Stephen Martin bowed and seated himself in the winged chair opposite Elizabeth's.

'If you will allow me, I wish to show you something.' Getting up, Elizabeth went to the far end of the room and withdrew a large tome from a bookshelf. Coming back she placed it into Stephen Martin's lap.

'This is my family bible. I am afraid that it only goes back as far as my grandfather, for it was he who started it,' she paused here to swallow as her mouth seemed to be very dry.

'If you will not take a drink, then I will ring for some tea,' she added as she reached up to the bell pull by the fireplace and tugged twice. Turning to look at him once more, she tried to compose herself.

'As I said, Mr Martin, that is our family Bible, and if you will open it, on the first page within you will see my… our family tree.'

Stephen Martin was puzzled now; what could this lady be wanting, showing him their bible, but his curiosity got the better of him and he pulled back the stiff black cover.

As he read, Elizabeth saw his mouth move slowly over the names, pausing two or three times to go back over them again, till finally he looked up appearing more anxious than ever.

Elizabeth stood up and looked at the portrait. 'I too have a portrait similar to the one that you have in your home, Stephen.' She motioned to the one above her, then closed her eyes tight and breathed deep.

'Stephen, your father and my mother were brother and sister.' It came out so quickly she held onto the mantle shelf for support.

'But this cannot be. I… What are you saying, Milady?' Stephen Martin believed that had he not been sitting he would have swooned like a woman.

Elizabeth held her hand out to him. 'Stephen, please come with me, I wish to show you another portrait.'

Stephen Martin stood, and still clutching the bible to him was led to the other end of the room, where above the other fireplace was a portrait of his father. He put out his hand to steady himself on a chair; at this moment small white dots were appearing from nowhere at the corner of his eyes, and his stomach was churning uncontrollably.

'By the time your father came back from the war, your grandfather was dead, and so was my mother, your father's sister. But your grandfather had provided for him, possibly he always thought and hoped that he would one day return, as his body was never recovered—it states so in the bible.' Elizabeth paused here to sit, as her legs were shaking violently. 'I believe he left him an equal amount in money to what his small estate was worth.' She put her head in her hands now; her body felt drained and she wished so much that Andrew was with her.

Stephen Martin sat as though mesmerised, his eyes staring fixedly at the portrait, holding the bible so tight, his knuckles were white to the bone. When he spoke his voice was but a rasping whisper.

'My father lived a simple life. I knew nothing of what had happened, who he really be; he educated me with a governess, then a tutor.' Turning to Elizabeth, he smiled. 'He did but ask me when I were about twelve if I wanted to go away to school, to learn.' Stephen lifted his eyes once more to his father's portrait. 'I said I be happy where I was.' Turning once more to Elizabeth who he saw at this point was very distressed.

'Mil... Elizabeth, let me bring your husband please.'

Elizabeth waved her hand to him, but Stephen Martin pulled the bell cord anyway.

It was Lilly who answered, but Andrew Duncan's voice that spoke from behind her.

'Lilly, you can go back to Mrs Cottle, I am here.' His voice held a softness she had not heard before; looking up at him she curtsied then left the room.

Andrew looked from his wife to Stephen Martin, then back again, waiting for one of them to speak.

'Mr Duncan sir, I am afraid your wife,' he turned to look at Elizabeth. 'My cousin has been greatly distressed by the revelations of today. I will take my leave now,' he paused to look once more at the portrait of his father talking to him, 'knowing that I now be having a history.' Turning once more to Elizabeth, he smiled warmly. A family.'

Andrew Duncan by this time was at Elizabeth's side; looking to Stephen Martin he held out his hand in greeting.

'Please, do not be calling me sir; my name is Duncan, Andrew Duncan, and it is a great pleasure to meet you.'

'Mr Duncan, I will return tomorrow and bring everything with me, for I believe that I have letters that Elizabeth, my cousin—' He turned once more to look at her, as though it were all a dream, and soon he would wake to find the world as it was.

'I will bring my past—how little there be—for you to share.'

Elizabeth, who now seemed to be regaining her equanimity, spoke.

'Oh, Stephen, we are to travel to Bath tomorrow to a friend's wedding.' She looked to her husband for help.

'That be no problem, when you return, you must come to my home, where we can talk freely and be discovering our history together. I be overjoyed to know who my father was, to put pieces of a puzzle together, to have a family.'

Elizabeth stood at last, coming to take Stephen Martin's hand in hers.

'We will be back by the 16th, Stephen, but you and your family must come here, bring your past with you, for I have things to show you which have been stored in the attic for many years.' She placed her other hand over his and pressed gently.

'Nothing can stop time from revealing her secrets, be they good or bad. Ours was brought about by a tragedy of sorts, but nonetheless so very welcome.'

When Stephen Martin had left, Andrew Duncan pulled Elizabeth into his arms holding her tightly into him until all her tears were spent.

Chapter Fifty
James and Catherine

It would take three long hours for the coaches to reach Midcraven Hall. Stewart had sat on a seat to himself with his legs stretched out, comforted by a mountain of feather pillows to take the impact of the coach as it travelled over the many ruts and holes. Margaret who sat opposite him with young Charles was equally cosseted by pillows. Stewart slowly stretched his arms, pushing himself upright, lowering his feet to the floor of the coach. His son, seizing the opportunity, scrambled down from his mother and placed himself next to his father, laying his head on his chest.

'It has been a long ride for you too, Charles, we will soon be there.' He looked to Margaret. 'Will we not, Mama?' Margaret smiled back, pulling the blanket out and tucking them both into its folds against the cold.

'I can see Midcraven Hall in the distance now,' she pointed as she looked from the window. Turning back, she saw that her son had put his thumb into his mouth and was now fast asleep.

'How do you do that, Stewart?' she asked softly brushing the hair from her son's eyes.

Stewart looked up into Margaret's eyes and smiled slowly.

'He feels safe. Like someone else I know who also does this when they lay in my arms. Come, sit with us, Maggie. I want to touch you.'

Maggie felt herself blush. She knew of no logical reason for the reaction, except that it had happened. Coming across she sat next to their son, as Stewart pulled her head down to Charles', kissing her too.

***

They were greeted on the steps by Sir Henry and James, who gave one look at his friend and gasped.

'What by all that is holy has happened to you, Stewart?'

Stewart winced slightly then straightened himself. 'I met with something very disagreeable, James, but it was *not* going to stop my being at your wedding.'

James looked to Margaret, then to Sir Henry and finally to Elizabeth who sighed and kissed James' cheek.

'It is good to see you, James, I will tell you everything when we are all sitting comfortably inside, warming ourselves with a good hot cup of tea.' She patted James' arm and turned to Sir Henry.

'So the day has finally arrived, Henry. Jemima must be so thankful.'

Sir Henry nodded his head, but Elizabeth thought that he looked very harassed and wondered what trials both his wife and his daughter had taken him through.

'It has not been without its tribulations, Elizabeth.'

Sir Henry had been studying Stewart very keenly as he spoke, then watched as Andrew Duncan came and supported his son.

Stewart smiled wanly. 'Oh yes, sir, this is my father, Andrew Duncan.'

If Sir Henry had been eating, he would have choked; nevertheless he was giving a good impression of it at this moment.

'Dear God, lad, do you want to give me an apoplexy? First you, and now your father!' His eyes strayed down to Stewart's chest. 'And you are bleeding by the way, did you know?'

It was at this point that Stewart's legs gave way as he fell to his knees. The last thing he heard was Sir Henry's voice echoing around the countryside as he yelled his orders.

Stewart awoke in a soft bed with Sir Henry and his father standing over him. Sir Henry looked at him intently then grabbed the bowl from the side.

'You are not going to wretch, are you, lad?' There was concern in his voice. 'As I remember from last time, you had a tendency to do so.'

Stewart closed his eyes once more waiting for the room to stop spinning.

'Sorry, sir, but I had the misfortune to run into someone's blade, and I am afraid he has made somewhat a mess of me.' He looked now to his father for reassurance.

Sir Henry had already reached the door and was bellowing once more for someone to fetch his surgeon.

'Sir Henry, I will be fine, please do not distress yourself, it is just my dressing that needs to be changed.'

'I will be the judge of that, lad, once I have seen the wound. Here, Mr Duncan, help me remove his coat if you please.'

Together they stripped Stewart down to his breeches, and then peeled away the dressing.

'Dear God, man, was he intending carving you up for bacon?' Turning once more to the door, he yelled for his wife, who appeared like magic, armed with servants carrying boiling water bandages, whisky and thick pads soaked liberally with a honey poultice.

'Be quiet, Henry, we have a houseful of guests; they will think that we have an intruder within our home. Be gone with both of you and leave us to our work.'

Stewart looked pleadingly up at his father, as if to beg him not to leave him alone with the woman.

'Did you not hear me, Mr Duncan? I will call you when I have finished, and please tell his wife that she may come and sit with him if she wishes.'

Sir Henry nodded to Andrew Duncan, with a look to say it was futile to object, and then they left the room.

***

They had all been seated in library for some time now when Elizabeth finally finished her narration. Sir Henry sat watching the fire his face a myriad of thoughts, before he spoke.

'Elizabeth, I lead a very quiet life here, whereas you it seems have been visited by all the plagues of Egypt these past two years. There will be a trial, no?'

Elizabeth blanched. She had not even given a thought to the consequences of her son's actions.

'Where does the man rest at this moment? I recall you said that they had taken him to the church, so I assume they will have notified his mother and sister by now.' Although Sir Henry was talking to the people gathered, like any a good Major he was also making mental points of the next moves that his adversary would take.

He turned now to James' father. 'I will speak with both yours and my lawyer Robert, they are both here for the wedding. You say he died by his own hand?' he questioned, turning to Elizabeth again. Her reply was to nod slowly.

'Good, good, and this man Martin found the bodies and can testify to this, am I correct?' Elizabeth nodded once more.

'That and the whole debacle that ensued this time last Christmas in the fields outside Bath, will show the man up to be the killer that he was, I have no fear of that. We will all confer here the day after the wedding and put forth a strategy, but for now I will go see how the lad is. Alexander, James, come with me if you please.' Bowing slightly to all present, he left the room.

They found Stewart clean, propped up on fresh pillows and tucked up in bed. Seeing his friends, he tried to sit up.

'Be still, lad, do you want to open your wound again? Rest easy,' said Sir Henry.

Stewart looked sharply from Alexander to James.

'Sir Henry, your wife has just washed my body in the presence of two maids and my wife.'

Sir Henry waved his hand slightly. 'Do not concern yourself, lad, you will be fine.'

His wife, James and Alexander seemed to be having great difficulty in keeping their faces straight, while Stewart's turned a very delicate shade of pink.

'Do you feel any better?' queried Sir Henry. 'Your skin looks a much healthier colour now than when I saw you last.'

Stewart was tempted to reply that that was because it had been scrubbed, and suffered humiliation in front of four women, but Sir Henry was thinking on another level at this present time, and would probably see no wrong in it at all. Had she not performed this task time and time again when he was in the army? Stewart chided himself, thinking that he was NOT in the army, and the vague

435

memories of her when he was last here injured were rearing up in front of him again. He shook his head then looked at Alexander and James, daring them to say a word.

'I will leave you to your friends, Stewart, but if you need the surgeon, I will bring him.' Turning he left the room.

'I will go now also,' offered Margaret, 'our son will want food, and if I am away too long, he will come find me.' Kissing Stewart she stoked his face. 'I will come back later with your son.'

As the door closed, James turned to Stewart.

'She actually scrubbed your body, all of it?' he said astounded.

'Yes, James, she informed me it was to keep down the inflammation, and when she does this to you, I certainly hope that I am there to watch,' retorted Stewart, still pink to the roots of his hair.

'Oh God, she is to be my mother-in-law, remind me never to be ill, shot or wounded with a sword.'

Stewart laughed. 'Be quiet, you fool, and come and tell me about your wedding and the fair Catherine.'

James sat on the edge of the bed, looking at his feet. 'I will just be glad when everything is over with. I have been driven mad with the whole process.'

'Do you want me to tell you what Alexander and I am giving you as a gift?'

James watched them both closely; if they were going to play some sort of joke upon him, he would rather they did not.

'Relax, fool,' said Stewart, seeing his friend's face change colour. 'You and your fair Catherine will go to Italy next April and spend two whole months at my mother's friend Rodolfo's villa there. William and Alexander have paid for the ship to take you—and believe me, you will have four months—albeit two of those at sea—to yourselves.'

James' face went from a smile to a beam. 'God, Stewart, Alexander, you do not know how happy that makes me, four whole months away from here, on our own; bliss!' James placed his hands together, closed his eyes and raised his face upwards in thanks.

Stewart tried to laugh and stopped. 'Go now, both of you, and, Alex, please send my wife back to me.'

***

As Margaret entered, the maids were just leaving having banked the fire and lit the candles around the room. It was warm in there and very peaceful in comparison to the noise from the rest of the house. He held out his hand to her as she came to sit on the bed.

'How are you feeling now, Stewart?'

His eyes sparked as they searched her face. 'Mortified, but very clean; come here, I want to kiss you.' Pulling her to him, he held her head tight with his good arm, lest she run away again. 'Lay next to me, Maggie, I need to feel you near me,' he whispered.

Margaret took off her shoes and did as he asked, moving very gently lest she disturb his wound.

'Stewart, has James ever lain with a woman?'

Moving slightly, Stewart lifted her face to his. 'Maggie, whatever makes you ask that? In truth, I do not know. I would assume so as he is a very handsome young man and the ladies in London would find both him and his title very alluring, but you know, I have never thought to ask him.'

Margaret tucked her head back down onto his shoulder. 'He is a very amiable man, and his generosity knows no bounds; he is witty and very gentle, but there is something about him.'

Stewart sighed lifting his hand to take the pins from her hair.

'Maggie,' he breathed in her ear, 'I want you.'

Turning to him smiling, she replied, 'I know.' Then sliding gently off the bed she locked the doors, walking back to him removing her clothes slowly. As she knelt on the bed beside him, he grinned.

'Be gentle with me, Maggie.'

Margaret raised her brows; her smile was full of mischief as she leaned in to kiss him, biting his mouth. She heard the rumble of laughter in his chest as he let out a muffled '*aghhh*'.

***

Pip had shaved him and was just tying the ribbon on his clubbed hair, as Margaret waited holding his coat. He was wearing his wedding clothes, and the only other time he had worn them was for George Wheatley's wedding.

'You be pardoning me for saying this, Milady, but he should not be going this day; he has more bandages upon his body than clothes, for fear that he bleed.' Pip shook his head. 'You be one stubborn man, Master Stewart.'

Stewart stood gingerly, lest he pulled any stitches, allowing Margaret to gently slip his coat over his shoulders.

'I will be fine, Pip, as I told you I will sit for most of the service, and I do feel much better than I did yesterday.' He looked towards Margaret and smiled. 'You look beautiful, Maggie.'

Margaret wore the same gown that she wore to her sister's wedding, which had been very skilfully adapted by Millie to make the waist at the front higher, eliminating the need for a corset, and allowing for the large bump which was showing now.

'This is the handiwork of my maid—and best friend—Millicent Penrose.' Maggie turned full circle once to show what had been achieved.

As she spoke, the door opened and James entered, resplendent in dazzling cream and white silk embellished with gold.

'James, you look magnificent,' Stewart said teasingly. 'I cannot embrace you lest I cover you and myself in blood.'

James shook his head good naturedly. 'I came to inform you, Stewart, that both you and Alexander will stand with me at the front. Your family will sit directly behind you, and you can sit throughout the ceremony if you wish, but you will be next to me, my friend.'

Stewart eyes glistened as he smiled affectionately at his friend. 'I must warn you, James, that if my son is not next to me, there will be no peace throughout the ceremony.'

'Then so be it,' came James' quick reply. 'He can stand or sit beside you, and then you can wreak havoc together.'

Margaret came around and cupped James' face. 'You are one beautiful and very kind man, James Fairweather, and I hope that you will be as happy as Stewart and I. Bless you.' She reached up and kissed his cheek. 'My son by the way will be dressed just as his father—blue jacket and cream silk shirt, breeches and stockings. Now go to the church, James, we will see you there very soon.'

James came forward taking Stewart in a very gentle embrace, and then left the room.

Stewart swallowed several times, pressing his lips together.

'Maggie, may I borrow your handkerchief? I appear to have something in my eye.'

Margaret handed it to him, and then looked at Pip shaking her head.

'Well I be leaving you now, Master Stewart. I wish you all well, and hope that young Master James and his wife be very happy.'

***

Wells Cathedral was vast Stewart thought as he looked from the coach at the great West Front; he had seen it maybe four or five times before, but today there were as many coaches as people in its grounds. As he watched, he saw a man in a deep emerald green coat coming towards his coach, waving his arms and as he neared, he saw that it was a very frustrated Sir Henry.

'Stewart!' he had to pause to take breath. 'I will instruct the coachman to take you round to the North Porch; we can enter from there, and walk up the side aisle to the central tower, then across to the right hand side where you will sit. It will be easier for you that way, and you will not be jostled by the throng. Dear God, as I stand here, there must be half the population of London here today.'

Stewart looked at the man and thought he would not be in his shoes this moment, but for all that, he was manoeuvring the crowd with the precision that a Major would his troupes.

'You look splendid, sir.' Sir Henry gave Stewart a warning glare.

'And may I add so does James. We will have to wait to see the Lady Catherine.'

Sir Henry was sweating profusely; dabbing his forehead with his handkerchief, he got up into the carriage giving orders for it to drive round to the North Porch.

'My dear boy, thank God I only have one daughter, if I do not drop with an apoplexy by the end of this day. How do you feel, lad? Can you walk?'

'I am well, sir, and may I say that the colour suits you.'

Sir Henry frowned and looked at his clothes. 'This was all Jemima's idea, that we should be the same you see. James and Catherine are also. Oh, maybe I should not have spoken that; ah well, what does it matter now. I am sorry, my lad, but I am rambling.'

Stewart smiled. 'Sir, be at ease. I understand your frustration, believe me. Only one of us has a new gown and that be Charlotte; it is a very pale green. You will know her when you see her. Margaret is of the notion that she looks like a beautiful Lilly in a Lilly pond.' Stewart smiled in remembrance adding, 'She is of the same age as your daughter, sir.'

Sir Henry leaned across to Stewart. 'You can sit throughout the whole ceremony if you so wish, lad, no one will say a word.' The look he gave to Stewart was that if they did, they would be marched from the church.

'It is a splendid church, is it not?' offered Stewart. 'Not one of the biggest, but if I recall, the whole ambiance of the inside is quite astounding.'

'Let me tell you, Stewart, there are flowers in there that I have never seen before in my life. Just where Jemima obtained them is a complete mystery.'

As they stopped outside the North Porch, Sir Henry jumped down and called to one of the coachmen to assist him. Stewart was taken from the coach as he reflected, like some precious piece of china. Standing up in the sunny but cold air made his head spin for a second; holding onto the door, he steadied himself, then Sir Henry took his arm and led him in.

The organ was playing in muted tones—Water Music by Handel, he thought. He had heard it once in London at a private party there, as the guests seated themselves. It was vast inside—a beautiful piece of architecture renovated many times till now, but nonetheless stunning. God, he thought, that George Weatherly's wedding was immense, but this surpassed even that. He saw James and Alexander sitting on the far side, talking amiably together, oblivious of the throng of people behind them, and smiled secretly to himself. It was Alexander who saw him first; standing up he came towards him.

'How are you, cousin, your face looks as though you have been sprinkled with flour. Come, sit between James and I.'

Stewart gave his cousin a thoughtful look. 'Alexander, I will get through this, then you can carry me out and put me to bed for a week,' he replied good-humouredly.

'Good day to you, James,' offered Stewart as he sat carefully, easing himself back onto the pew. It was then he felt a hand take his shoulder. Turning slightly, he saw Margaret smiling down at him, their son in her arms.

'I will keep him for a while, but I am sure he will not stay with me,' she said amiably.

'Do not worry, Margaret, he will be fine, and probably sleep half way through the ceremony. I will lay him on the cushions next to Alexander.' Turning to James, he grinned. 'James, you look resplendent in your white and cream silk wedding suit. I understand that Catherine will be in the same colour?' he teased.

'This is another of Lady Jemima's ideas'—he smiled good-naturedly—'that we should match.' He paused for a second then turned towards Stewart. 'I owe everything to you, my friend, and well I will never be able to repay you.' He saw Stewart about to reply and put up his hand. 'Do you remember at Wheatley's wedding I said that I would never have one like it'—he waved his arm around him—'what can I say.'

James' father and brother, who had just come up and taken their seats behind them, both nodded their heads to Stewart. Then Robert Fairweather rested his hand on Stewart's left shoulder; no words were spoken, there was no need for them, the message was conveyed with silence. Stewart felt for Margaret's hand on his right shoulder, and then he saw his mother, father and Charlotte come into the pew next to her. Looking across the aisle once more, he also saw that Lady Jemima was now seated, as was the entire congregation behind. The organ had stopped and Charles Moss—the Bishop of Wells—stood looking down the nave. Raising his arms, up he called out.

'Let us stand.'

Stewart turned to James and whispered. 'I will stand when you take your vows, James.' To which James inclined his head.

A rustling, murmuring and coughing could be heard as the congregation rose, then silence. Suddenly the organ burst in with Johann Pachelbel's music "*Canon*"—indeed that is what was stated on the wedding pamphlet Stewart held—and as everyone turned, they saw Sir Henry lead his daughter down the nave. Stewart thought that the only word to describe her was breath-taking, but that was also totally inadequate. Her dress was of the purest white silk, which seemed to have iridescence to it, as the light hit the gown it glistened like Mother-of-Pearl. It had a high neckline with frill and long pointed sleeves which seemed to come over her hands. Over the skirt was a lace so fine, the like of which Stewart had never seen before; going round and down into a train which spread behind her at least five feet, over her shoulders to keep out the cold she had a short cape of the same material but lined in white fur. Her hair was natural just swept up at the sides and back from her face, held in place there with the family's diamond tiara. Lady Catherine Portman glowed from head to foot, and as she came up to James, Stewart heard him give a short gasp and thought to himself, *So you do not love her, aye, James?* Then smiled to himself, as everyone seated themselves once more, leaving the bride and groom to come to the centre before the bishop.

There were two hymns, the first being "*All Creatures of Our God and King*" then later "*Love Devine*", both sung by the choir and congregation. Stewart wondered at the sound as it resonated around the church—seemingly ethereal. It was here that his son came over beside him, crawled onto his lap and placed his hand to the ribbon in his hair—swiftly pulling it off—then putting his thumb into his mouth, he promptly fell asleep.

When the time came for the vows, Alexander took Charles laying him on the cushions on the seat beside him. Stewart stood and looked back at Margaret, placing his hand on the back of the pew, which she covered with her own, and then they watched as the two silver rings were placed on the respective fingers—they were married at last. James and Catherine returned back down the nave to the sound of the Cathedral bells ringing and Beethoven's *"Ode to Joy"*.

Stewart allowed Margaret to remove his jacket, then sat on the bed laying back on the pillows while Margaret took off his shoes and lifted up his feet. Just as she was about to sit, there was a tap on the door; it opened slowly revealing James and Catherine. Margaret stood up quickly and came to them.

'Come in, please.' Looking back at Stewart, she smiled. 'He is not asleep yet.'

Stewart looked hard at his friend. 'So, James, you are finally married. What was it you said by the lake that day, "Am I not a fine figure of a man, will no one have me?" Well, you have your answer, James.' Stewart looked at the vision in white and cream beside him who had lowered her eyes and turned a delicate shade of pink. 'Congratulations to you both. May you live a long and happy life together.'

James cleared his throat before he spoke. 'Stewart, you almost gave up your life for me—twice. That goes beyond friendship. Thank you—which is an entirely inadequate expression, but I thank you all the same from the bottom of my heart. We both do.'

'Are you spending the night here, James?'

'No,' came James' quick reply. 'We will go to our new home on the Crescent in Bath.'

'A very wise choice, James,' replied Stewart, smiling as he watched his friends face. Stewart then waved his hand. 'Go back to your guests, James; how many do you have down there by the way? It seems to be hundreds.'

'There are only 60 guests attending the wedding breakfast—including you. Sir Henry... well my father,' he corrected, 'would have no more than the direct family. For once he got his way.' Catherine smiled and looked up to her husband.

'Go, James, I will be down soon. I would not miss this for the world.' Stewart smiled mischievously at his friend once more.

James looked at him rather disconcertingly, wondering what he had in mind, then left.

When James and Catherine arrived at their house in Bath later that night, they found in their bedroom a bottle of champagne, two glasses and a card with just one word inscribed upon it:

Enjoy!

441

Chapter Fifty-One
Alison Northcott and Exoneration

They had been back just three days when the local magistrate, a one Alfred Mullings, came to call. He was not a tall man by any means. Elizabeth thought that he resembled an amiable bumble bee as his body was very rotund and sported no waist at all. His hair was so sparse as to be non-existent, and he had, as far as Elizabeth could count, at least three chins, each one below the other. She stood now as he came into the drawing room, taking off his hat and bowing to her respectfully.

'Begging you pardon, Milady Hamilton, for this intrusion. I will take but just a moment of your time.'

'Please be seated, Mr Mullings,' came her reply as she made her way to the mantle. 'You will take some refreshment?'

'No, no, thank you Milady,' came Mullings' quick reply. 'I need only to deliver a letter to your son, Milady, and then I will take my leave.'

'As you wish, Mr Mullings. I will ring for my son then. Pray, please be seated.' Saying this she offered him the chair by the fire as the man seemed frozen to the marrow, pulling the bell pull as she did so.

'You are not from these parts, are you, Mr Mullings?'

'How very observant of you, Milady. No, I hail from London, but took this post here when it became vacant. Believe me when I say, London is no place to be these days, Milady.'

Elizabeth looked up as Lilly came in.

'Lilly, could you ask Master Stewart to come to the drawing room please. Mr Mullings the magistrate would like to speak with him.'

Lilly's eyes opened. 'Very well, Milady,' she replied slowly, her eyes going from her mistress to the magistrate. Curtsying she left the room.

It was some minutes later when Stewart entered and as he came forward, he looked at his mother to get some indication as to what exactly the magistrate wanted.

'Ah, Stewart, this is Mr Mullings, the magistrate from Mere. He has a letter regarding the occurrence out by the lake.'

Mullings stood immediately bowing to Stewart. 'Your servant, sir.'

Stewart bowed back and told him to be seated, while he pulled a chair from the side and sat himself.

'How may I help you, Mrs Mullings? I did write a full account of what happened and my footman delivered it to your office the following day. Were there some discrepancies perchance?'

Mullings became flustered and shook his head. 'Oh no, no, no, sir. I am in receipt of that and several other letters regarding the incident, some from very prominent people may I add. I just needed to inform you as a matter of course, that the said gentleman's body was claimed by his family two days later, and taken back to his estate in Crediton. I am here to deliver a letter that was left for you by his sister, sir.' Saying this he retrieved the letter from inside his coat.

Stewart stiffened slightly, and then looked sideways to his mother as he took the letter that was handed to him.

Elizabeth spoke then. 'You must forgive my son, Mr Mullings; he was injured rather badly and has been suffering since then from his wounds. It will take a good few months for them to heal I fear.'

Mr Mullings stood up and bowed graciously to both. 'My duty is now dispatched, and so I will bid you both good day and trouble you no more.'

Stewart stood up and bowed back. 'I thank you, Mr Mullings, for taking the trouble of bringing it to me.'

With one more bow, Mullings left.

Stewart seated himself once more and tapped the letter in the open palm of his hand. 'Do I hold hell's fire in my hands, Mother, or a missive of peace?'

Elizabeth studied her son for some moments; he was tired and he looked in pain—though he would never admit it. She hoped with all her being that it was a letter of peace, an end to the hostilities and violence. Finding her voice, she spoke.

'If you do not open it, Stewart, how will you know? Go to the study and read it at your leisure, and in your peace,' she paused slightly before continuing. 'I will send your father to you if that will be of some help?'

Stewart breathed deeply and winced; it pained him when he did that, but he kept forgetting. Waiting for the pain to subside, he answered.

'No, Mother, I will not open it now. I am tired and will go lie for a while. I do not sleep easy these nights, as I tend to turn in my sleep onto that side.'

Elizabeth came towards him and placed her hand on his brow. 'You have a slight fever, Stewart; go to your bed and I will find Margaret.' Taking his arm, she helped him up.

***

It was two days later and still Stewart had not opened the letter. He sat now in his study looking at it as it sat quietly on the desk. He looked out the window to the cold but sunny landscape and asked for guidance. He had argued with his conscience for the past days, but if he did not open the letter, how would he know if the wrath of God were about to fall on him, or that he was free—free from all aggression and hate; free to live his life without looking over his shoulder or waiting for the next blow. As he took the letter in his hands, Thompson entered.

'If you will pardon me, Master Stewart, there is a Lady Alison Northcott in the hall wishing most fervently to speak with you. She claims to have sent you a letter, but, as yet, has received no reply. Would you like me to show her into the drawing room, sir?'

Stewart turned to face his butler with a look of complete bewilderment on his face.

'Did you say Lady Northcott?' Recovering his thoughts quickly, he stood. 'Please show her into the drawing room, Thompson. I will be there directly.'

Thompson bowed and left, leaving Stewart staring at the unopened letter on his desk. Picking it up, he went to break the seal, then threw it back on the desk and left the room. He did not want to read his sentence; he would hear it from the woman.

As he entered, Alison Northcott turned suddenly from looking out onto the lawn. Stewart bowed to her.

'Your servant, Lady Northcott.'

She nodded her head slightly, her eyes taking in his whole countenance as he stood there waiting for her to speak. She was of the same age as Margaret, but by appearance looked many years older—maybe she too had had her own battles.

'Mr Hamilton, if I may call you that, I have come in peace.' She saw Stewart's shoulders relax. 'If I may sit, as I have a story to tell you.'

Stewart motioned her to the chair by the fire, as he took the one opposite. Peace she had said; what sort of peace? What did she want of him? Of his family? Stewart's hands shook slightly so he clasped them together in front of him.

'Please continue, Lady Northcott. May I offer you refreshment, some tea perhaps?'

Alison Northcott inclined her head. 'That would be most kind, Mr Hamilton.'

Stewart stood and pulled the bell cord, then waited for Lilly to arrive.

'Could you bring us some tea, Lilly, and maybe if Mrs Cottle has some of her biscuits or cake, it would be most welcome.'

Lilly watched the woman in the chair, trying to determine if she were a threat to her Master; seeing none she curtsied and left.

As the door closed, Alison Northcott sat forward in her chair looking earnestly into Stewart's face. 'Please, Mr Hamilton, let me speak first for I have many things to tell you which I hope will solve the questions that you have and maybe ease your mind.'

Stewart said nothing but nodded in agreement, watching her gather her thoughts before she spoke.

'There were three of us, you know. I had another brother, younger than Andrew, but older than myself. His name was Rupert, and he was a kind, gentle child. Andrew was always mean and vicious. He would... he would trap birds and kill them just for fun,' she paused here to swallow, and her face had changed suddenly as she spoke of him.

'Lady Northcott, maybe you would like to wait for the tea?' Stewart saw her agitation and discomfort.

'No, no, Mr Hamilton, I must continue…' Closing her eyes to compose herself once more, she resumed. 'One day when Rupert was seven years old, Andrew told him that if he did not do as he asked, he would suffer—my brother had ways of persuasion. He was mad, you see, but of course I knew nothing of that then as I too was terrified of him.' She paused once more to take a handkerchief from her reticule and dab her forehead and top lip where small drops of perspiration had formed.

'One day, I saw my two brothers from the nursery window, arguing. They were standing by the well in the garden, and Andrew was pointing down into it. He grabbed Rupert by the arm and forced him up onto the well wall. Andrew was shaking him hard.' Alison Northcott breathed deeply, swallowing hard. 'Rupert fell into the well, it was then that Andrew looked up and saw that I had witnessed it all. My life was never the same after that day, Mr Hamilton, for he told me that if I disclosed this to anyone, then I too would suffer the same fate.'

Stewart had by this time risen and poured a small glass of sherry. Handing this to her, he seated himself once more.

Alison Northcott sipped it gently. 'It was only after my father died the real terror began. The episode of myself and Mr Wheatley, the Lady Catherine and yourself. Well, they were all orchestrated by him. You were fortunate, or should I say unfortunate, to have become embroiled in both. Much to your detriment, may I add.' She sat up right now, holding her head high. 'He was mad, Mr Hamilton, of that I have no doubt, but very evil as well.' Taking another sip of her sherry, she looked at Stewart directly.

'I am so sorry, Mr Hamilton, for all that has happened to you, and I realise that I am weak, and that you can NEVER forgive me for what I let occur to you and your family, but I hope that one day you can find it in your heart to find a little mercy for me.' She had been quietly crying as she spoke, then resting her glass on the table she stood up.

Stewart rose quickly with her. 'Lady Northcott, I thank you profoundly for your courage in coming here today. You should beg no forgiveness from me as you were controlled and manipulated by a man who had no soul, or had given it to darkness. I hope that you and your mother can at last find some peace in your lives, though I understand that it will take some time, as there are too many memories to be expunged—if they ever can be. But in time you *will* find your inner peace, trust me, it will come. Even now as you are racked with guilt, you must tell yourselves that it was not of your making.'

Alison Northcott nodded slightly. 'I will try, Mr Hamilton. I will try, but I will never forget, as the burden is too great; maybe over the years the pain will ease and I will at last begin to like myself again.'

She made her way towards the door then stopped. 'You never read the letter I sent, did you?

Stewart shook his head at her.

'You were afraid at what it might contain. Be at peace now, Mr Hamilton, as I too will try and find mine.'

Stewart walked with her out of the house and assisted her up into her carriage.

'Good bye, Mr Hamilton,' she called as the coach slowly made its way down the drive.

As he turned to come back up the steps, he saw his mother at the door.

'Stewart, what are you doing out here, you must come in now.' Her voice had a mother's urgency about it. 'Where is Margaret? You have tea and cakes waiting in the drawing room.'

Stewart took her arm and led her in. 'Margaret and Charlotte have gone to Mere to their respective houses there; they have things to take and things to bring home with them. Then on their return they will call for Alexander from the estate office. Now, come with me, Mother, and enjoy the tea that has been prepared, for I have something to tell you that will gladden your heart.'

***

They sat for what seemed to be hours talking, with Stewart telling and retelling what had happened. Elizabeth could see in her son's face the weight that had been lifted from his shoulders; he was tired, but it was not the tiredness of anxiety, just relief. They heard their laughter before they entered the room, and Stewart looked to his mother, speaking quietly.

'I will tell her, Mother, later.'

Elizabeth smiled and nodded. Turning, she saw the two women's flushed faces where the winter chill had reddened both cheeks and noses.

'I trust you enjoyed your trip to Mere, but where is my grandson?'

Alexander entered the room, his hair loose around his shoulders with Charles in his arms.

'He is here, Aunt. He fell asleep on the ride home, after playing with my quills—and much writing.' Alexander looked to Stewart. 'By the way, cousin, you owe me a new quill. I believe you have a fine goose feather one in your study, no?'

Stewart grinned as his son scrambled down from his uncle and ran into his father's arms; sitting back on the chair, he pulled him gently on his knee.

'I cannot lift you, Charles, as your Papa is wounded, but when I return to health, I will swing you around just as you like to be.'

Charles responded with a large wet kiss planted on his father's cheek, then pulled the ribbon from his hair just as he had done his uncle's. Elizabeth, who had been watching this, came up to her grandson and stoked his cheek.

'Oh, so you do not want to come with me to the kitchen then?'

Charles responded immediately by jumping down and pulling his grandmother's hand to take her from the room.

Stewart looked up at Margaret with mischief. 'Margaret, our son has deserted me for Mrs Cottle.'

Margaret smiled warmly back in response. 'I am going to change.'

'Come help me up, Maggie, and I will come with you.' His smile told her all she needed to know.

***

Margaret felt both warm and safe. As she lay there, she stroked the still raw slashes on his chest, feeling the crust of the wounds beneath her fingertips. They would scar, she knew that, but it was the scars within his mind that tormented her sleep. Today, though, he had seemed at peace; just maybe he was at last accepting what had passed, leaving him space to reclaim his life. As his fingers linked hers, she felt his hand lift her face to his, then he spoke.

'Maggie, I have something to tell you.'

***

Margaret had not interrupted nor spoken once, as he retold the events of the day. She lay there now, quiet and still. The evening sky was dark, and within their room the only light came from the fire. It was soothing in itself, as it gave one that sense of being secure—like a child feels in the womb—for is that not something which everyone longed for? Maggie smoothed the soft hair of his stomach, trying hard to make them all flow the same way, but they would not, for was not life itself just like that; no matter how hard you tried to follow a life of peace and contentment, there was always something that pulled you sideways, took you from your path, and many times to such devastating outcomes. Looking at his wounds now, she knew too well the consequences of that.

'Will you not say something, Maggie,' he asked quietly.

He felt her tears on his chest before he saw them; pulling her tightly close to him, he kissed her hair.

'Do not cry, Maggie, we are free.'

'If you were not wounded, Stewart Hamilton, I would squeeze the life from you.'

Stewart laughed slowly, and then turned her head so he could kiss her.

'You are my strength, Margaret Hamilton; it is because of you that I go on. When I think that I can take no more, that is when I think of you and you pull me back.' He smoothed her hair back and wiped her tears with his thumb.

'When I suffered that wound last Christmas, there were times that the darkness tried hard to take me down, but every lucid moment I had, I thought of you, and *you* pulled me back. I love you, Margaret Hamilton, you *are* my life.'

As Margaret looked at him, she thought of the letter he had written, and without wanting them her tears returned once more.

There was a sharp knocking on the door, and then his mother's voice called from without.

'Will you be coming down to dinner? Or shall I get cook to make a tray for you both?'

447

Stewart could hear the teasing in his mother's voice and called back, as Margaret wiped her face and then covered her mouth trying to stop her laughter.

'We will be down, Mother. We have no need of trays.'

'I am very glad to hear that, Stewart. Shall we say half an hour?'

'Yes, Mother, we shall.'

They waited till his mother was far enough away not to hear and then laughed together from the absolute relief if nothing else that they were free from fear. Suddenly, Margaret took his hand and placed it on her stomach which seemed to be moving slowly in many directions.

'That is your son or daughter, Stewart, the baby is growing fast now.'

He smiled broadly and then slapped her thigh as he pulled back the bedclothes. 'Up, Margaret Hamilton, we must get dressed for dinner, and you have to help me without letting me bleed on my shirt.'

***

Andrew Duncan sat at Elizabeth's bureau, looking at the plans for the Flower House that William had given him. So engrossed in the design, he did not hear her come up behind him, placing a kiss on his hair. Reaching back, he took her hand.

'It will be a grand thing when finished, Lizzie.' Andrew turned to look at her. 'Have you told Stewart about Stephen Martin yet?'

Elizabeth turned and sat on the chair next to him. It was chill in the room, even though two fires burned brightly at each end. Elizabeth pulled her shawl around her for comfort.

'I will speak to him tomorrow, Andrew. The news he received today was life changing—for all of us—so I will talk to him tomorrow morning, and try and explain. Yes, how to explain? Nevertheless, I must. I have asked Carter to bring down the contents of the small chest from the attic that may help.' Elizabeth looked into her husband's face and saw him smiling.

'I will be there if you want.'

'No, Andrew, it is something I must do. I also have two letters from my uncle that were sent to my mother when he was away. I wish to give those to Stephen.'

Andrew Duncan reached over and kissed her. It was at this point that Stewart entered the room; removing himself quickly, he turned to Margaret and put his finger to his lips.

'We will wait in the drawing room, Maggie. I think that we are the first down,' he called loudly from outside the door.

Maggie looked at him her eyes wide. 'What?' her voice was stopped by his fingers on her lips.

'My father and mother are in there, kissing,' he added, embarrassed.

Rattling the doorknob hard, he entered the room.

'Good evening, Father, Mother. Are Alexander and Charlotte coming down? And where is William?' he asked for want of a better thing to say.

Elizabeth stood and smoothed out her dress.

'William has gone to see Spike, Alexander and Charlotte are in the nursery, so we will await them here, and then go in to dinner together.' She came towards them, kissing her son and then embracing Margaret.

'Come, sit by the fire, Margaret, it is very cold this night. I do believe that we will have snow soon.' She seated Margaret by the fire; lifting her feet onto a stool, she placed a blanket on her legs. Going back to the bureau, she picked up a letter.

'We are all invited to Midcraven Hall for Christmas.' Turning back to look at her husband, she continued. 'Your father and I will not be going, as we are journeying up to Scotland; your father has many things to settle there, and we thought it would be good to go now.' She smiled warmly at him.

Stewart watched his parents and thought to himself, *So you and Father can have Christmas alone.* Nodding his head, he smiled.

'I think that would be wonderful for you both, especially you, Mother, as you have never been there. When will you leave?'

Elizabeth watched her son closely, there had been no sarcasm in his words; he was telling her to go.

'We will leave by the 10th December—weather permitting. It will take a week to get there as we will go slowly, stopping many times along the way.'

Stewart recalled when he had made the trip, and thought it very wise of his mother to take it slow.

'Mrs Cottle will have a peaceful Christmas here with the household,' she continued, 'and I have told her she may use the dining room for lunch on that day—which she will not—but the offer is there.'

'It will probably be warmer and much more congenial in the kitchen, Mother. Why do you think Charles is always there?' Stewart looked up to see Alexander and Charlotte enter the room.

'Ah, Alex, Mother and Father will be spending Christmas in Scotland—whereas you and I with the rest of the family will go to Midcraven Hall, to tease the life out of James. And I am going to enjoy that very much indeed,' he chuckled.

***

Elizabeth found Stewart in his study the following morning. As she came over to him, he half smiled and nodded. 'You have something you wish to tell me, do you not, Mother?'

Elizabeth smiled back and shook her head slightly as she sat beside him. 'It is strange—this thing we have between us—where we can read one another's minds so well. Yes, I have, Stewart, do you have time?'

Stewart looked at the ledger before him. 'I have been puzzling over these accounts all morning. If Alex were here, well he would have had it done within the half hour. Yes, Mother, I have time.'

At first Elizabeth was uncertain as to where to begin, but slowly as the story unfolded, she retold it with an accuracy that surprised even her. She watched her son's face all the while go through many changes, and at some points she stopped while his mind came to grips with a particular part of the story, then his head would nod for her to continue. It was a slow process, as she did not want to forget even one minor detail. Sitting back at last, she placed her hand upon his and waited for him to speak.

'Mother, do we have any right to this?' He waved his hand around him. 'Should it not be theirs by birth right?'

She squeezed his hand. 'No, Stewart, when you read the document that was lodged with the bank, it states categorically that when my mother died, everything passed to my father, in safekeeping for me. My grandfather left an equal sum in money—equal to the worth of this small estate—to his son, if he should ever come home,' she paused to grip his hand in both of hers. 'If it had not been claimed after twenty years, then it passed to me.'

Elizabeth stood up and paced the room slowly. 'Stephen Martin wants nothing from us, just for us to be his kin. He will come here tomorrow with his wife and daughter, and together we will piece together our lives and try to make them whole again. He wants nothing more than to have a past; can you understand that, Stewart?'

Stewart nodded in reply as Elizabeth came and pulled his head into her body. Releasing him, she sat once more, then wiped the tears from her face with his handkerchief.

'It was his daughter that found you.'

Stewart's head came up with a start. 'What, daughter? You said it was Stephen.'

'No, Stewart, his daughter saw you fighting and ran to get her father. She had been forbidden to go there, you see, but she did. When Stephen came, he saw two bodies lying still on the ground. The first one he went to was Northcott's—he was dead—then he came to you. Well, you know the rest of the story.'

'But how did they know who I was?'

Elizabeth sighed. 'His daughter had met you these two years past—at the lake.'

Realization registered on Stewart's face now; he stood up and came to the window, talking silently to himself before he turned to his mother.

'I remember her,' he breathed. 'It was the day that my father came here for the last time. I had just returned the previous night from Exeter.' He was animated and pacing now. 'I went to the lake before he came and she was there—a very small, young blonde-haired girl. Her name, if I am not mistaken, was Jennie. Dear God, she is my cousin. I told her she should not be there, it was not safe and to go home.' Stewart sat down and rested his head in his hands.

'Dear God, Mother, do you have any more revelations to tell me?'

Elizabeth stood and placed her hand under his hair at the back, stroking his neck.

'First your father, then Charlotte and now an uncle and cousin. We were an isolated family having no known relatives, and in the space of two years, well,

450

they do say, '*God moves in a mysterious way,*' or so the poet Cowper tells us in his hymn "*Light Shining out of Darkness*". From our darkness there most definitely shone a light, Stewart, be it holy or not, and I am very grateful it was there.'

Chapter Fifty-Two
The Dinner and Family Reunited

The table for the dinner had been set very carefully. Elizabeth wanted nothing pretentious; it was to be a small dinner party without ceremony. She wanted her relatives to feel comfortable and at ease. It was decided that Andrew, herself, Stephen and Mary would all retire to the study when they came, leaving Jennifer to go to the drawing room with the rest of the family. Elizabeth so wanted this to be a welcoming dinner and not one fraught with nerves, or their family believing themselves to be inferior. They were *her* family, and as such would be treated with respect and kindness.

She met Stewart in the hall as he was asking Lilly where the games' table was to be found.

'I do believe it to be in the dining room, sir. It do fold, you know, Master Stewart. The last time it be used was the Christmas afore last. I will go this minute to get Carter to bring it out for you, sir.' Curtsying she ran for the kitchen.

'Stewart!' his mother called to him from the bottom of the stairs. 'You are to be on your best behaviour when young cousin Jennifer arrives, and organise some games—not cards.' She darted him a look of "do not dare".

'Mother, Carter is this moment bringing in the games' table from the dining room, calm yourself; we will make her most welcome.' Seeing his mother's agitation, he placed a hand on her arm.

'Mother, they will feel very welcome here; you have done your very best to make them feel at ease. I wager that by the end of the evening, they will not want to go home.'

Elizabeth placed her hand to her mouth. 'Oh, there are no fires lit in the guest rooms.'

Stewart held her hands tight. 'Yes there are fires, Mother. I had them lit. It will be dark and cold by the time we finish eating; they will not want to drive all the way back to Mere, and then some... Now come see your grandson before he sleeps. I know that he will have my ribbon out in an instant, and Pip will have to re-tie it, but never mind.'

***

Charlotte brushed the shoulders of Alexander's coat and unbuttoned the last button at the neck.

'That is better.' Her eyes shone as she looked at him. 'Oh, you are one handsome man, Alexander Hamilton.' She pulled him down to kiss him, then patted his cheek and smiled. 'And you are all mine.'

Alexander laughed softly. 'You know my aunt is very anxious about tonight. She sees this dinner as a test—if they will accept her or not. She is so... well, she does not want them to feel inferior in any way. She does not understand that she has *never* made anyone feel that way. I am testimony to that.' He sat on the bed and pulled her down beside him. 'When I came here, I was but 12 years old, a scrawny boy from was the bounds of Edinburgh. I knew nothing of this life, as the one I knew was frugal, fraught with danger, and my father a Minister in the Kirk and helper of the poor and sick. I had no fine language then as I spoke with a Scottish burr, but she and all in this house took me to their hearts. Well, you know the rest. I have no need to repeat it.' He took her hand in his and kissed it. 'I know what will be going through their minds at this time, but by the evening's end, they will feel as much a part of this family as you and I.' He stood up, pulling Charlotte to her feet.

'Come, we will go down to greet them, but first we will go say goodnight to our daughter.'

***

Elizabeth saw their carriage draw up from the drawing room window. Turning to Andrew she nodded, then took his hand and together they went into the hall. Seeing Thompson she nodded for him to open the door. Stephen Martin stood there with a rather large box held under one arm, with his wife holding tight to the other.

Elizabeth walked quickly up to them holding out her hands.

'Stephen, Mary, welcome to my home. But where is your daughter Jennifer?'

Mary Martin looked behind and pulled her daughter forward.

'She be very shy, Mi... Elizabeth.'

Elizabeth looked at the fair young girl, with her eyes downcast, and her hands in knots. Putting her hand to her chin, she gently lifted her head.

'Good evening, Jennifer. I am very pleased to meet you.' Elizabeth felt her son come up beside her; she looked up at him daring him to be respectful, but she saw the light of mischief in his eyes and sighed deeply.

'Good evening to you, Cousin Jennifer. Please take my arm as we young people have been banished this evening to the drawing room.' He looked to his mother still smiling. 'But first, Cousin Stephen, Mary, good evening to you both. I hope that this is just the start of many such evenings *our* family will spend together. Now let me take that box from you. I will put it in the study.' Taking the box, he left the hall.

By this time, Thompson had taken their cloaks and hats and left the hall. Elizabeth tried to compose herself; her hands were shaking slightly and she felt flushed. Turning to Margaret, she swallowed hard and spoke.

'Margaret, these are my cousins Stephen, Mary and their daughter Jennifer. This is my son's wife Margaret.'

Margaret nodded and smiled. 'I am so very happy to meet you all,' she replied, stepping back for Alexander and Charlotte to come forward.

'And this is my nephew Alexander and his wife Charlotte,' Elizabeth continued. She felt a little breathless at this point; it was nerves she knew, but once the introductions were over, they could retire to the study. Turning to Andrew, she smiled as he came and stood beside her.

Alexander smiled, bowed his head slowly and replied. 'It is my pleasure, cousins Stephen, Mary and Jennifer.'

Elizabeth turned to William. 'And this is William Masters, Charlotte's father.'

William bowed. 'It is a pleasure indeed to meet you all. May I say that your family took me into their hearts, knowing nothing of me, were I a good or bad person; such is their generosity of heart and spirit. Stephen, you and I are acquainted and we have much work to do together on the flower house. You are a worthy craftsman, one of great skill and patience in your work, and I admire you greatly. I also observe that you share your cousin's warmth of spirit, for you have shown as much to me.'

Stephen bowed back. 'I thank you, William.'

Charlotte came forward now and took Jennifer's hand.

'Come, Cousin Jennifer, we will go into the drawing room; it is much warmer there. Do you like Tic Tac Toe?'

Jennifer's head came up and she smiled.

'Oh good!' exclaimed Charlotte, 'Then you can play with me.' Turning to Alexander, she added teasingly. 'No one here likes it, so you and I will play together.'

Elizabeth watched this in amazement, her eyes resting on William's in thanks for what he had just done.

It was at this moment that Stewart came back into the hall, looking around at everyone.

'Are we all ready to go into the drawing room? I have asked Carter to bring down several games—Fox and Geese, Journey through Europe—which is one of my favourites—and dominoes, which I can proudly say I have never lost at,' eyeing Alexander as he said it.

'No you have not, cousin, but I seem to recall some discrepancies in the past.'

Stewart laughed heartily, as they made their way through the doors.

Elizabeth watched her son go with some trepidation; if he did not behave himself, she would find ways to pay him back.

William Masters looked at her and smiled as if reading her mind. 'I will be in the drawing room with them, Elizabeth, if I see anything untoward, you have my word—I will be sitting in the fireside chair reading my book. They will behave themselves.'

***

The study was warm and inviting; two more armchairs had been brought in so that they could all sit in comfort. The two small trunk-like boxes sat in one corner, ready to disclose their secrets, and a small table had been placed on the far wall which held bottles of whisky, port and sherry, with several glasses. The drapes were pulled against the cold darkness of the night outside, and many candles now flickered out their yellow glow, giving a peaceful, welcoming ambiance to her guests. On the desk was a tray with cups, and a steaming pot of tea.

Elizabeth was the first to speak. 'You must both be frozen; it has been so very cold these past days that I thought we may wake up to snow each morning.' Taking the teapot in her hand she gestured. 'You will both take a cup? My cook Mrs Cottle makes a very good brew.'

Stephen Martin accepted his cup, thanking Elizabeth, then all sipped their tea while they exchanged pleasantries to ease them into the real reason for the dinner, and then looking to his wife Stephen Martin spoke.

'Please, Elizabeth, let me speak first.' Handing his cup to his wife, he withdrew four letters from his pocket. 'These are for you; they were sent to my father when he was abroad—these letters and one other article, were the only things that came back with him. They are yours now.' Handing them over to Elizabeth, he sat back and waited for her to open them.

Elizabeth looked at her mother's writing, her fingers tracing the strokes of the quill that made the words. Her hand had guided those strokes, a hand that she had never felt nor touched. She had never heard her voice, or felt the warmth of her arms around her. Placing the letters onto the desk, she lowered her head and quietly cried for everything she had lost, never had, and times remembered.

Stephen Martin got up and sat on the arm of his wife's chair, pulling her in to him. He could see that she too was as distressed as Elizabeth. Looking to her now, she nodded to him.

'Elizabeth.' His voice held the tightness of his emotions. 'Here be the other piece for you.' Taking a small blue velvet pouch out of his pocket, he handed it to her. 'My father be wearing that till the day he died, but did say that I was not to bury it with him, but to keep it so that she would be remembered. He be remembering nothing of her; but for him it be holding his past life, it be how he held onto his sanity, that and the portrait of the two of them which I have in my bedroom. He do say that he be taking it to war with him. He knew this as he was holding on tight to it when they found him. He like you had to be finding his life again.'

Elizabeth's hands shook as she took the pouch and then poured its contents into the palm of her hand. Looking to Andrew, her eyes searched his face.

'Open it, Lizzie,' he said softly.

She turned the locket over in her hands, looking at the engraving. On the front was a Scottish thistle and the back had two letters—**J & G**—within the same never-ending vine as her mother's wedding ring. With trembling fingers, she opened the clasp, and there on the left side was a small miniature of her mother, and on the right, encased in glass, a lock of her hair. There seemed to be a wind rushing through her ears now and through this she could hear her mother's voice talking to her, singing to her; suddenly the air in the room was suffocating. She felt the walls pushing in and her head began to swim, the last thing she heard was the sound of the singing. Andrew Duncan caught her before she fell forward and held her tightly close to him. Looking around him, he could see a salver on a table with whisky and a glass.

'Stephen, if you would be so kind as to pour Elizabeth a little of that whisky behind you on the table.'

Stephen Martin rose quickly and did as he was bid.

Mary Martin put her hand to her throat in concern. 'Oh, Stephen, what have we done.'

'Be at peace, Mary,' came Andrew's quiet reply. 'It has been a shock, as she never knew her mother, and now seeing this has made her so real to her.' He stopped as Elizabeth opened her eyes and breathed deeply.

The world was suddenly ceasing to spin for Elizabeth; she blinked twice trying to focus, the voice was still there calling her, but this time it was her husband's.

'Lizzie, Lizzie. Here, Lizzie, drink some of this, it will help.'

Elizabeth looked gradually around her and sipped the drink that was being held to her lips. Martin looked anxiously at his wife and then smiled with relief as Elizabeth took the glass. Andrew handed Elizabeth his handkerchief and drying her face she pulled herself up and slowly regained her composure; still holding the locket tight in her hand, she closed her eyes and breathed deeply several times more.

'Stephen, you can have no notion what you have done for me. My father always said that the likeness to my mother was astonishing. Now I know that to be true, for this miniature tells me that, and her hair is the same colour as my own.' Elizabeth looked up at Andrew and smiled. 'I think that maybe we all deserve a glass of whisky. Will you take a glass, Stephen, Mary?'

'I thank you kindly, Elizabeth,' replied Mary, 'but I do not be drinking whisky, but if you be having a sherry.' She glanced at Andrew as she spoke. 'Stephen will join you both, he be enjoying a glass every evening at home.'

Elizabeth reached across and touched Mary's hand. 'In truth, Mary, I do not drink whisky myself either, but today, I am ashamed to tell you, I needed it.'

'There be no shame in one's emotions, Elizabeth, for without these we would be but hollow shells, devoid of all feeling. You should be feeling honoured that you have such qualities.' Stephen was holding his wife's hand as she spoke.

'Stephen, I do not have anything such as you have brought me, but—' Elizabeth looked to the small trunk that sat in the corner. 'I have many things of your father's from when he was small and then again a young man. I have his school books and his reports from Winchester. He was an excellent scholar, your father.'

'My father be going to Winchester?' broke in Stephen, with the look of sheer astonishment on his face.

'Indeed he did, and was always top of his form. From there he went on to Oxford, where he studied Law, but I was told that the Army was always a passion for him—as you will see from the many toy soldiers in that trunk. He graduated with Honours and then took a commission in the Cavalry.'

Elizabeth paused as she saw Stephen had gone very pale. 'Are you quite well, Stephen?'

'Elizabeth, you be telling me that you have nothing to give me but papers and letters; what you be giving me now is worth more to me than any gold or silver. All I be knowing of my father is that he be a very kind, gentle man, who be learning his trade well, then giving others that same chance to be learning also. He worked hard all of his life to be giving us a good home, where there be love and affection. Oh my word, my father, he be going to Oxford,' he whispered, dumbfounded.

The tears that Elizabeth thought she had dammed began to flow once more. Coughing lightly, she replied, 'Stephen, Mary, you must stay here this night then we can spend the whole day tomorrow going through all of the mysteries that are hidden in both chests. We can take our time, live and relive our lives, to give one another the bounteous gifts of memories lost, or never known, and of those relived.'

It was then that she heard the laughter and cheerful voices coming from the hall. The door opened and as Stewart came into the room, he looked at his father who was at that moment holding his mother in his arms, and then the other occupants of the room, trying hard to determine what had happened, as everyone seemed to be distressed.

'Mother, this was to be a happy occasion,' he grinned widely. 'What have you said to our guests that they look so sad?'

'Stewart! You are incorrigible. Be gone with you to the dining room, and we will follow you directly.' She knew that she had snapped; her nerves were such at this time that she could not help herself, but she thought he should not have done that.

Stewart wished he could have taken back the words, but instead he smiled to everyone. 'My sincere apologies, Mother, everyone,' he offered, and then glanced across at his father who gave him a look that said leave now. Stewart bowed deeply and left the room.

Elizabeth turned to Stephen and Mary. 'I must apologise for my son; he has had the devil in him all day, and when he gets into these moods, nothing will stop his teasing.'

Mary Martin looked at her husband and smiled kindly. 'My daughter would be doing the same to me, Elizabeth. It must be running in the family, and do not be taken in by her shyness, for she be a mischievous child when she chooses.'

***

Making his way back down the passage, Stewart felt unsettled; his mother had rebuked him. He knew that he had done wrong, but there were other things as well, and he knew what they were too. It was as if his whole life had taken a step sideways; he was no longer the centre of his mother's world, and he was finding this very hard to comprehend, admit to even.

'Stewart.'

Margaret's voice pulled him out of his thoughts, as she came to him now, placing her arm into his, while her hand stroked his face.

'What has happened? Is there something wrong?'

'No, Maggie. I did something very stupid and my mother berated me for it. It was totally my fault; as usual my mouth went before me and…'

'But that is not all, is it, Stewart?' interjected Margaret. 'It is your father, is it not? He has replaced you and you find that hard to understand or accept, am I right?'

Stewart looked down at her, a quiet smile playing at the corners of his mouth. 'God, Maggie, how do you do that? Is there something inborn in women that they have the ability to see into men's minds, soul even?' Stewart stopped abruptly as he heard his mother coming up the passage behind him; turning he put out his hand out to stop her.

'Mother, I am so very sorry for my rashness just now. I should not have spoken as I did.' Elizabeth put her hand on his arm to still his words.

Margaret who had been watching them closely knew that she should leave; it was for mother and son. She touched his arm lightly to get his attention. 'I will go into the dining room now and see that everyone is seated.'

Elizabeth looked keenly at her son; it had to be said, but it was difficult for her. 'You find it hard to accept, do you not, Stewart? I mean your father and I.' She saw him about to protest and put up her hand. 'When you came in just now, you have always been the one to help me, comfort me, hold me.' Elizabeth closed her eyes; she was not going to succumb to tears again, there had been enough shed this last hour. 'Oh, Stewart, it does not mean that I love you any less because of this. I nurtured you before you were born, kept you safe, and when you were born, loved you with all my heart as a mother always loves her child. There will always be that bond between us—*nothing* can break that. It is something that only a mother and child can experience, as I gave you life, Stewart; you are my life. But as I let you go when you married Margaret, so you must let me go now. We can still hold one another, you are my son, my only child, and you will remain so till the day I die.'

Stewart looked down into his mother's eyes and slowly inclined his head, then pulling her into him he kissed the top of her head. 'I love you dearly, Mother, and there is a small part of my heart that will always be yours.'

Pushing her away he smiled. 'But do NOT tell Margret that. Now, Mother, let us go in and eat our dinner, else Mrs Cottle with also berate me.'

Chapter Fifty-Three
Scotland

December 10th had come around only too quickly. Stewart stood now on the porch outside the Willows, looking to the sky where a blanket of clouds hung over the countryside depicting prolonged rain or snow. *Nimbostratus,* he whispered to himself. Nodding, he remembered Rodolfo explaining that to him while they were on board his ship. Stewart thought it more likely the latter as the temperature had dropped considerably the last few days. He had pleaded with his mother and father to postpone their trip to Scotland till the New Year, but it was to no avail—his mother had been adamant; they would spend Christmas together in Scotland. Or more to the point, considered Stewart, alone. He watched now as Carter brought round her coach; their luggage was behind him, waiting to be strapped on top and at the back. In fact, they were taking very little; just one large portmanteau and a few smaller boxes. Elizabeth's maid would not be travelling with them, as they were going to his father's house, which was small in comparison and had just a housekeeper who would administer to her. This was his mother's wish—she intended to be alone with her husband.

As Stewart watched the luggage loaded, he felt his mother's hand take hold of his. Turning, he looked down into her eyes, and for some moments neither spoke.

'You will be gone longer than two weeks, Mother, I know this.' Elizabeth's other hand came up to stroke her son's cheek. 'I will miss you very much, Mother, but I understand the reason.' Pulling her into him, he closed his eyes and rested his cheek on the top of her head, just as his father came out of the house.

Stewart looked up and smiled. 'I was telling Mother that we will miss you both this Christmas; it will not be the same.'

Elizabeth looked at her son then as he clasped her to him in a tight embrace; releasing her, Stewart went to his father to do the same to him. They walked down the steps to the carriage together then Stewart watched them board the coach. At this point Margaret appeared at the top of the steps swathed in a thick cloak to keep out the chill; behind her were Alexander, Charlotte and William. They had all said their goodbyes in the hall.

As Stewart closed the carriage door, he nodded to his father. 'Please be careful, and do not travel if you think the roads will be impassable. There are many highwaymen, thieves and—' His father leaned out and took Stewart's hand.

'I will protect her, just as you have done; I promise, you have my word.'

Stewart gave the slightest nod then turned to Carter. 'Be careful, Carter, you have a very valuable cargo.'

Carter, who had a many layered cloak about him to keep out the cold, took his hat off and bowed his head. 'Master Stewart, I will give up my own life before theirs.' Placing his hat back, he took the reins and called for the horses to move.

It was some moments before Stewart came back into the house; he had watched the carriage till it was just a dot amidst the horizon of trees. Coming into the hall now, he saw Mrs Cottle standing there, arms folded and her mouth set, but he could see from her eyes that she was upset. She inclined her head and Stewart reciprocated, then watched her turn to make her way back to the kitchen.

Margaret came up behind him then and took his arm. 'We are all in the drawing room, come in, Stewart.'

As he entered, his son came running to towards him, hitting his legs and nearly knocking him off his feet. Carefully pulling young Charles up into his arms, he proceeded to rub noses with him, which Charles thought most amusing and giggled loudly.

'Shall we go ride on your horse?'

Young Charles started to jump excitedly in Stewart's arms that he nearly dropped him. His right side was still very painful, and the physician had said that the stitches could come out by the end of the week, but he must still be careful as any sharp movement or pressure could undo all the work of healing.

'Papa, ors... pease... pease!' Charles now had a firm grip on Stewart's hair and pulled the ribbon off, throwing it to the floor, still jumping up and down in an alarming fashion.

'Very well! We will go now, but first say goodbye to everyone.'

Charles turned and waved his small hand, then commenced once more with his jumping as they left the room.

Margaret shook her head and laughed. 'Poor Daisy does not know what to make of him. Stewart I mean,' she corrected as all eyes looked at her in surprise. 'She has never encountered such a man as Stewart.' Turning once more to look at the door, she added rather wistfully. 'But then neither have I.'

***

Margaret lay there quietly looking out to the night. Stewart's arm was around her and she could feel the warmth of him against her back, solid and comforting. She knew that he was not asleep, so she lifted up his hand and kissed the palm.

'It is alright to be worried, you know, and a little jealous.' She turn round quickly as she spoke the words and put her fingers to his lips to stop the answer he was about to voice.

'Stewart Hamilton, I get jealous of you also; how you are with our son, it is plain to see who he wants to be with most.' She laughed softly here. 'Oh, he loves us both, but with you there is adventure, dangerous things to pursue; with me... I am there when he is ill, I am his security that all will be well.' She took

460

her hand from his lips and replaced it with her mouth. Leaning back again, she stroked his brow, brushing his hair behind his ear. 'Your mother will be safe. He has never stopped loving her, you know, you can read it in his face when he looks at her. But anger, jealousy, call it what you will, got in the way. He felt second best.'

Stewart sighed and kissed her softly. 'You are a wise woman, Maggie. Now how will you sooth me so that I may sleep?'

Maggie laughed into his chest. 'I will sing you a lullaby.'

Stewart pulled her face up to his. 'No, Maggie, I have a better way.'

***

Andrew Duncan had decided to take the same route to Scotland as he had done before. He knew that way and felt safe in the knowledge that if they had to break their journey unexpectedly, for whatever reason, the inns were respectable enough to stay more than one night, as was the case when they reached Preston. It had been sleeting for some time, and the two coachmen—although they wore gloves—their fingers were frozen and they were finding it hard to hold onto the reins. They rested at the Old Blue Bell for two nights till the winds eased and the sleet had at last decided to stop. It was his intention that if they left early to reach Keswick that night, as after that it would leave just one last stage to Dumfries. By the time they arrived at Keswick, the snow had been falling for some hours; they could do no more but stay there till the weather once again changed. It snowed relentlessly for two days and nights, causing them to stay in their room or the small parlour that was next to the dining area down stairs. There was another family in The George who were suffering the same plight as they were. Elizabeth watched them now as the father occupied the two young boys with a game of Dominos. The wife was sitting in the seat opposite Elizabeth next to the fire, embroidering, but keeping a watchful eye on the three of them.

'It must be hard for you to travel with two young boys, how do you keep them amused?' Elizabeth questioned as she watched them teasing one another in high spirits but content in their game.

The woman looked up from her embroidery and smiled; she could be no more than thirty-five, Elizabeth considered, with a pleasant face of no particular beauty, but one that made you feel at ease.

'Ah, Milady, ma wee laddies are boisterous, but there be no a bad thought between them. They be twins ye ken, some say they cannae see the difference, but I know; that be wee Colum on the left and Archie on the right.'

Elizabeth looked closer now, and saw what she had missed before; they were the exact replica of one another.

'Do you only have the two?' enquired Elizabeth.

The woman threaded her needle neatly in her work and looked up to Elizabeth.

'No, Milady, I had another two bairns, a wee lassie younger than those two, and another lad two years older. I lost them both before two years now, from the septic throat ye ken.'

Elizabeth did see had it not taken at least five children from Mere a few years back. There had been nothing anyone could do for them as their throats swelled so badly, stopping their breath, and the poor mites had suffocated.

'I am very sorry for your loss,' answered Elizabeth.

'Och, dinnae worry, Milady, I still have two strong healthy laddies.' The woman looked at Elizabeth for some moments.

'Where are ye from, if ye dinnae mind my askin', Milady?'

'I am from Mere in Wiltshire, and my husband is from Dundee, but he now has a home in Dumfries. That is where we are headed to spend Christmas and New Year, and yourself?'

'We are from Dumfries also, but just now we have been visiting my sister in Preston. Have ye had bairns yourself?'

'Just the one son; he is married and at home in Mere.' A wistful look came over Elizabeth's face; she hoped that they knew why she had to leave them at this time, to come here to be alone with Andrew. They needed time away from the place that had caused them such heartache.

'Ah,' answered the woman, seeing Elizabeth's expression, not wanting to ask what had happened. She leaned forward slightly now before speaking. 'My name be Flora, and what be yours, if ye dinnae mind my askin'?'

Elizabeth smiled warmly. 'It is Elizabeth. I am very pleased to meet with you, Flora.'

As she spoke, she saw Andrew duck under the lintel and enter the small parlour. He looked happy, she thought; there was none of the strain she had seen while they were in Mere, as here they were free to be themselves—whoever they may be—for Elizabeth had no idea who she was at present. Coming towards her, he pulled up a chair and sat next to her.

'The snow has stopped, Lizzie.' He smiled. 'Maybe tomorrow, all being well, we can at last make our way to Dumfries.'

Elizabeth took his hand—which was frozen—and smiled; no doubt he had been outside with Carter watching the sky.

'Andrew, this is Mistress Flora, she also comes from Dumfries.' Looking round him, she nodded. 'And that is her husband and two sons.'

Andrew stood up and bowed respectfully. 'Good day to you, Mistress Flora. You must excuse me, but I have to take my wife from you for a short while as I wish to show her something.' He bowed once more, and then helped Elizabeth to her feet, tucking her hand in his arm.

'Maybe we will be seeing ye both in Dumfries, tis a small town, ye ken.' Smiling she went back to her sewing.

Andrew took her to the door of the inn and showed her what he had seen; the whole landscape glistened with such a white brilliance Elizabeth had to narrow her eyes and shade them with her hand. As the sun shone on the snow it blinded one in its intensity.

'Oh, Andrew, we have days such as this in Mere in the winter, but none compares to this.'

She leaned back into him, feeling his warmth as his arms came up and around her.

'The light is different in the north, Lizzie, it is more intense somehow, though in the towns and cities you will not see anything to match the beauty of this.' He rested his cheek on her head. 'Scotland is very cold in the winter months, Lizzie. We can go back to Mere whenever you wish to.' She heard the sadness in his words, as though he should not have brought her here.

Elizabeth reached up to stroke his cheek. 'I have not come here for the weather, Andrew, I came to be with you.' She had forgotten just how tall he was, as she turned her face up to his now. 'We can never bring back all of those lost years, but we can make the ones we have left memorable and precious. I intend to do just that, Andrew, and if it means I will live out the rest of my days here with you, then so be it, for I am never losing you again.' She saw his eyes watery, then buried her head in his chest as her own tears were only a breath away.

***

Mere was in the grip of a severe frost. The land was as hard as iron; nothing could break the surface, much to Mrs Cottle's chagrin. She had despatched Lilly to the vegetable garden to pull some parsnips, turnips and carrots, but the girl had returned some fifteen minutes later saying that the earth would not be giving anything up today; it was frozen solid. Mrs Cottle had folded her arms and shook her head, then took the shovel from Lilly, stating that she would see about that.

Spike had watched Lilly in her efforts from his cottage window, and when she had returned to the house, he had gone to fetch a small pick from the tool shed. As he returned now, he saw Mrs Cottle doing battle with the same piece of soil.

'Mrs Cottle,' Spike called as he came back into the walled garden. 'I think that maybe I be having something that will help you there. If you would step back a ways and tell me where to be digging, I will be getting your vegetables from the ground for you.'

Mrs Cottle pulled the shawl around her ample bosom and wiped her forehead.

'Oh the Lord bless you, Mr Spike. I have never seen the like of this in all the years I have been here, and the mistress gone to Scotland. If we be having this, what will it be like all of those hundreds of miles north? Oh, Mr Spike, it fair makes my heart stop, it does.'

Spike by this time was on his knees, loosening the compacted earth from around each vegetable. The anxiety in her voice was plain.

'Mrs Cottle, I not be sure if you be able to use any of these, they be frozen solid. Take them into the kitchen and see what happens when they thaw a bit.' Spike offered as he placed the vegetables into the basket.

'Thank you, Mr Spike.' Mrs Cottle looked at the man. 'You be as worried as I about the mistress, be you not?'

Spike pulled his coat up around him and nodded.

'Spike, you be getting young Kenver and come to the kitchen. I will be brewing some tea for us all as it be cold enough to freeze us all to our deaths out here.' With that she turned and made her way back.

As Spike entered the kitchen, he could instantly feel the warmth seep into his bones; moaning slightly he closed his eyes.

'Mr Spike?' questioned Kenver. 'Do you be feeling unwell?' The boy's look of concern made Spike smile.

'I be fine, young Kenver, just my bones do not like the cold too much now. When I be young like yourself, nothing worried me, but now...'

As Spike looked around him, he could see that Lilly had laid out the table with mugs and one china cup and saucer—for Mrs Cottle, he presumed—and there was freshly baked cake cut into thick wedges. He could feel the saliva start in his mouth as it watered in expectancy of the taste.

Mrs Cottle turned from the fire, holding a large white and green china pot emitting steam from its spout.

'Right now, sit you down, and, Lilly, go fetch the milk jug, honey and sugar bowl from the pantry, if you please.'

Spike sat and gestured to Kenver to do the same. Just as Lilly was coming back, Stewart burst into the kitchen, causing Lilly to stop in her tracks so suddenly she spilt some milk and Kenver to jump to his feet so quickly he hit his knees on the table, knocking over the mugs, which were at that moment rolling around on their sides. Spike's quick reflexes had saved the cup and saucer.

'Master Stewart!' Mrs Cottle's tone was enough to stop Stewart where he was.

'Why did you not ring the bell? When you do this, you be putting my kitchen in turmoil.' She gave a sideward glance to Lilly holding the dripping milk jug, and then to Kenver who was limping while watching the mugs revolve on the table.

'Mrs Cottle, you have my humblest apologies. I...'

Mrs Cottle held up her hand. 'Master Stewart, you would like tea and cake?' She saw Stewart looking towards the table, then at Spike with one side of his mouth up in a smile. 'For how many?' she added.

Stewart looked back at her and grinned. 'For five please, but when you have finished your own tea. We are in no hurry. I thank you, Mrs Cottle.'

When he had left, Mrs Cottle took the milk jug from Lilly, motioning her to get a cloth to mop the floor and then nodded for Kenver to sit as Spike righted the mugs.

'If I am thinking right, Mr Spike, you be as worried about our mistress as I be, no?'

Spike inclined his head and breathed deeply. 'It not be that I do not trust the man, for I do, as I saw how he had changed while he be here. It be... well, what if our mistress decided not to return? I would wager anything that Master Stewart be thinking the same thing right now.'

Mrs Cottle nodded her head several times as she poured the tea and then pushed the china cup in front of Spike. 'Drink that while it be hot, then you can have another with some cake.'

Spike did as he was told; he was grateful for the warmth as the liquid made its way down into his stomach, brewed to perfection, with just the right amount of sugar. He closed his eyes and savoured the taste.

'I think you be right, Mr Spike. It will be a very strange Christmas for us again this year, with all the family being away. It be like last Christmas when Master Stewart be shot, only the second Christmas in my life here that that be happening.' Her mind seemed to be wandering as she watched young Kenver drizzle honey onto the slice of cake that Lilly had given him.

Spike placed his hand on Mrs Cottle's. 'Carter be with them; he would not be letting any harm come to either one, you be sure of that.'

'I know,' she replied as she looked into Spike's eyes. 'But what if she not be coming back?'

The question hung in the air.

***

It was dark by the time the coach rode into Dumfries. Carter had lit the lanterns on either side of the coach, but this gave very little light to the surrounding area. The moon was weak, and only half showing, but the snow around them seemed to illuminate the road slightly with its whiteness. Carter remembered where to go from the time before when he had come with Stewart, but it had not been deep winter then. As they came slowly up the road, he could see some light emanating from the church windows—possibly from the candles, Carter thought to himself. Kirk Street lay diagonally across from there and was easy to find. They had stopped a while back at an inn of sorts to obtain some hot coals for the two pans which were used in the coach to warm the feet of both Elizabeth and Andrew. Carter's own feet, he considered, were not attached to his body right now, or if they were, they were frozen, and when he stepped down, likely to snap off. They had also sent word to Andrew Duncan's housekeeper Mrs Kirkpatrick to prepare and light the fires, as Andrew stated that she would only have the kitchen fire burning—she would not waste the precious peat with warming rooms that would not be used. As for herself, she would fill a bed pan with a little of the embers from the kitchen fire to warm her bed before retiring. He had said that Mrs Kirkpatrick was a thrifty lady, borne from the times when she had nothing.

Carter looked at Fulton—the footman that had accompanied himself on this long trip.

'Ed, we will take the mistress and Mr Duncan to the house, and then be going back to the coaching inn that we passed two streets back, where we can be stabling the horses and coach, and then find ourselves lodging in the rooms above the stable as they be comfortable enough, as I be a staying there the last time I came here with Master Stewart and Pip. Then tomorrow I will be returning to see what is to be done.'

Ed Fulton just nodded his head, as his mouth and jaws seemed to be frozen together. If truth be known, his whole body seemed to be frozen solid, and he could not recall ever having felt so cold before.

Andrew Duncan helped Elizabeth down from the coach, watching the condensation from their breaths whirl around their heads like a white mist in the dark evening air. The moon was high now, and looking to the horses he saw the same mist but to a greater extent, as the steam from their bodies mingled with the breath from their nostrils, swirling it up into the frozen night air. It was eerie; they resembled spectres that had just risen from the moors to ride the unearthly night searching for lost souls. Looking up at Carter, he spoke.

'We will take the baggage inside then I will come with you both to the inn and house the coach, water and feed the horses and return, for I believe that Mrs Kirkpatrick will have the room at the top of the house ready for you.' Carter looked to Fulton; they had not expected this. 'With a fire,' added Andrew Duncan with a smile on his lips as he nodded in confirmation. 'She will not see you boarded above the stables, that I do know.'

Carter touched his hat. 'Very good, Mr Duncan.'

As they alighted from the driver's seat, the door to the house opened and Mrs Kirkpatrick stood there with a candlestick held aloft, its soft light shining onto the face of Andrew Duncan, as he took of his hat and inclined his head.

'Good evening, Mrs Kirkpatrick. I trust all is well with you.'

Her face shone as she looked up at him. 'Och, Mr Duncan, welcome home to ye.' Looking around him she saw Elizabeth. 'And this be Mistress Duncan? The Lord be praised ye found her; come in, come in afore we all freeze to death.'

Elizabeth noticed the woman's eyes fill with tears as she guided them into the small parlour to the left.

'Oh, Mistress Duncan, I am so very glad ye have come. Here, sit ye down now by the fire and I will be bringing some hot tea and bannocks for ye.' Turning towards the door, she spoke to Andrew.

'The two coachmen, Mr Duncan, I have prepared a room for them, and a fire be lit there since midday so it should be warm. Ach, Mr Duncan, it is so good to see ye both,' she repeated. Wiping her eyes and smiling broadly, she turned once more to Elizabeth; taking a blanket from the sofa, she wrapped it around Elizabeth's legs. 'There, we dinnae want ye to catch cold now. I will go bring the tea.' Saying this she left the room.

Elizabeth looked up to Andrew—who had not stopped smiling since he entered the house—and took his hand.

'Lizzie, I will go with Carter and Fulton to the inn, see the horses safely stabled and the coach housed there. They know me. I have my own coach there as I have no stables. I will pay them for a week, and then weather permitting Carter and Fulton can drive your coach back. We can write to Stewart when we

466

feel we want to go home, Lizzie; the men that I used last time can drive us there in my coach.'

Elizabeth said nothing but studied his face. He had said *when* **we** *want to go home*—he was coming back with her if she wanted him to; her heart leaped and seemed to stop—if she *wanted* him to. She was never letting him out of her sight again. Andrew nodded to her, squeezed her hand and left.

Elizabeth felt the warmth of his hand still on hers as she clasped it to her, closing her eyes, breathing slowly, and then pulling the blanket around her shoulders she stood up and made her way to the kitchen.

Coming into the room, she felt the warmth and the smell of herbs envelop her. It was a pleasant, comfortable sensation—a sense of home, similar to the way she always felt when she entered Mrs Cottle's domain at the Willows. Closing her eyes, she let her senses take over as she savoured the rich smells of fresh baked bread, tea and honey, mingling with the succulent aroma of roast chicken and baked parsnips.

'Mistress Duncan, what do ye be doing here? Ye must go back now and rest by the fire, dinnae worry yourself, I be bringing yer tea for ye.'

Elizabeth smiled warmly, pulled out a chair and sat at the wooden table. 'Mistress Kirkpatrick, I am fine, and I am always to be found in the kitchen of my home in Mere. It is the warmest and most comfortable room in the house.'

Elizabeth looked at the small woman; she could be no more than thirty eight, and yet Andrew had told her that she had been through pain and loss, losing her whole family to illness but two years ago. How did one recover from that? How did one go on living when everything you loved and held dear to you had gone, been taken from you in an instant?

'Please sit with me, we can take our tea together.' Mrs Kirkpatrick sat down slowly. 'Andrew has told me so much about you. He has you in very high regard.' Elizabeth took the pot from the tray and poured two cups of tea, handing one to Mrs Kirkpatrick.

'My name is Elizabeth, and yours?'

The woman was watching Elizabeth intently, not knowing what to make of her. She accepted the cup that was given her and then pushed the sugar bowl and milk jug towards Elizabeth for her to use.

'My name is Aileen, Mistress Duncan.'

Elizabeth could see that the woman was uncomfortable; taking some sugar and a little milk she pushed them back towards Aileen.

'I met a young family on the way; they too were bound for Dumfries. She had twin boys and told me that she had lost two children but two years past.'

'Ach, I ken who yer mean, that be Flora MacIver. She lost her two bairns the same time as I lost my own and my husband At the time, I prayed to God to take me also, but he didnae hear me…' her voice trailed away as she sat with her hands curled around her tea cup.

Elizabeth thought well before choosing her words to reply. How did one survive something like that? Mistress MacIver still had her husband and two boys, but the woman who sat before her now had lost everything, for in losing her husband she lost her livelihood, her home and her family. Looking at the woman now as she stared into her tea, she thought she could not imagine. Leaning across, Elizabeth placed her hand on Aileen Fitzpatrick's arm.

Aileen looked up and smiled slowly. 'There were days ye ken when I felt as I couldnae go on; there be an emptiness inside of me, like I had everything scooped out of me, like I be hollow. Even now if I let myself be thinking too much, I didnae...' her voice died away just as the front door opened.

Andrew Duncan swept into the kitchen, bringing with him a blast of freezing air, his nephew Michael Duncan as well as Carter and Fulton.

'Mrs Fitzpatrick, do you think that the chickens will stretch to feed my nephew as well?' Andrew smiled broadly, coming up behind Elizabeth, placing his hands on her shoulders.

Aileen Fitzpatrick stood up, brushing down her apron as she did so.

'Aye, to be sure, Master Duncan, there be a plenty. Now you and the mistress take yourselves away into the parlour while I be getting these young men something to drink.' Looking at the two men, she smiled. 'Would you be wantin' tea or maybe a dram?'

Carter looked to Fulton and raised his eyebrows. 'A dram would be going down fine, Mistress Fitzpatrick,' he replied eagerly as they whisked off their hats and bowed their heads. Carter thought that tea would be good, but a whisky would warm his blood a lot faster.

As Andrew guided Elizabeth from the kitchen, he turned. 'We will take our dinner at the small table in the parlour, Mistress Fitzpatrick.'

Aileen knew what he meant. 'As ye wish, Mr Duncan.' She smiled. 'I will bring yer tea now.'

Chapter Fifty-Four
The Man with Scar

The severe frosts that had plagued Mere and the surrounding countryside had relented, now being replaced by heavy snow and for miles around the land was carpeted in a heavy layer of it; horses could travel, but the use of a carriage was maybe impossible. Stewart sat in his study reading Sir Henry's letter. They were expected at Midcraven Hall by the 23rd December, just four days away; just how he was going to get three coaches carrying eight adults and two children that far was something he did not want to consider at this present time. The best he could hope for was a slight thaw. As he read through the letter, he found that Sir Henry had also extended his invitation to their new-found family—that would mean eleven adults. Looking out to the blanket of whiteness that was now the garden, he pinched the top of his nose and breathed deeply.

He had received no word from his mother and father as yet—had they reached their destination safely? Who knew; his mind was in chaos at this present moment as he awaited Carter and Fulton's return. There was a gentle tap on the door rousing him from his reflections and William Masters entered. On seeing the startled look on Stewart's face, he spoke.

'Stewart, my lad, am I disturbing you at an inopportune time? I can come later; it is no trouble to me.'

'No, no, no, William,' came Stewart's quick response. 'Please come in, sit down. I welcome your company, sir.'

William came and seated himself in the chair beside Stewart's desk, glancing down at the letter from Sir Henry in Stewart's hand.

'Not bad news, I hope,' he queried.

'On the contrary, sir,' responded Stewart, 'he asks us to bring our new-found extended family with us; eleven adults and two children.' Stewart's voice dropped in tone as he spoke.

'Ah, quite… Would you like me to go see Stephen Martin? It is no trouble to me, as I have no work to do at this present time, and I do need to go to my own house to bring back clothes for the trip. I have a list here from Charlotte.' He tapped his pocket tentatively. 'I can call in on Martin on my way back, if you so wish, or better still, bring the man back with me so that you can discuss this with him here.'

Stewart looked at William and smiled. The man was the essence of diplomacy, in that he knew it would be better said here, with the rest of the family around to encourage this, rather than at his house or Forge.

'William, thank you. Sir Henry informs me that there will be no formal dinners, just family—ours, his and James'—but even so we will be there for a little over ten days, and I fear the children will take up most of the clothing.'

William looked at Stewart and mused that this was not what troubled him at this time; it was something a lot farther than Bath that held his thoughts now. Standing up he placed his hand on Stewart's shoulder. 'I will go now, so that I may be back before tea.'

Stewart looked up. 'William, if you could bring all three of them here, they can stay the night and return tomorrow; it will be better that way.'

William nodded, smiled and made his way to the door, stopping to turn back as he did so.

'They are safe, Stewart, believe me, and very happy.'

Stewart looked around and shook his head. 'Thank you once again, William.'

Both men looked at one another for some moments, and then William nodded slightly and left.

***

Michael Duncan sat looking at his uncle; he was happy, that was plain to see, but he was also at peace with himself and with life—he could see this also. The lines of pain and guilt had lifted from his face and been replaced with contentment and love. How many times had they sat here while his uncle had poured out his heart, his bitterness, his guilt? Now they sat in companionable silence, letting the church encompass them with its spiritual being.

'Uncle, I have something to ask of ye.'

Andrew Duncan turned his head and nodded. 'Go on.'

'I would like yer permission to ask for Mistress Fitzpatrick's hand in marriage.'

Andrew turned his head once more to look at his nephew. 'Go on,' he repeated.

'I have known her for over a year now, Uncle, and I respect her, admire her.' Here he turned to look at Andrew. 'And love her.'

'Does Mrs Fitzpatrick know this?' asked Andrew gently.

'Oh no, Uncle, I havnae spoken a word to her; in truth I dinnae ken her feelings at all, that is why I would be askin' ye if you would kindly speak to her on my behalf, Uncle.'

Andrew sat back in the pew and closed his eyes. The lad had never been married; he had devoted his life to his work in the parish and the church. Till now, he had probably never missed that part of life, the one that offers companionship, need, and love. Sitting up again he placed his hand on his nephew's shoulder. 'I would be very honoured to ask her on your behalf,

Michael, but you must remember that her sorrows are new; they happened just two years past, and she could still be grieving.'

'Oh, Uncle, I ken that, truly, it just be if there was any hope… well, that she may consider my proposal. I can wait, Uncle, I dinnae have a problem there,' his words were coming quickly now.

'Michael, you are a kind, loving, selfless person who helped me at a time when… well, when I did not want to be helped. If she cannot see you for the man you are—which I am sure she does—then you must bide your time.'

'I ken what you mean, Uncle, and that it be said with a good heart. Whatever her decision, I will accept it aye; it will be God's will.'

***

Making his way back to the house, he saw that the snow was gradually thawing, leaving behind a black sludge of snow mingled with the dirt of the road. He considered that the two coachmen would soon want to make their way back south to their own families for Christmas, and he prayed that Elizabeth would not want to accompany them. Oh she had said that she was staying, but that was before she had seen how simply he lived here in Dumfries. Shaking his head, he tried to dispel these thoughts. He would go back with her, he knew that, but he would like her to stay a while here, where they could be alone. Taking his key from his pocket, he let himself in.

He found the ladies sitting in the warm comfort of the kitchen; ducking slightly as he entered, he took off his hat.

'Good day to you, ladies.'

Elizabeth looked up, her eyes never moving from his, and in that moment, Andrew Duncan knew that she would stay with him.

Mrs Fitzpatrick stood up and made to push the kettle onto the fire.

'Ye be going into the parlour now and I will bring ye both some lunch. Will yer nephew be joining us, Mr Duncan?'

Andrew took his eyes away from Elizabeth's then. 'Your pardon, Mrs Fitzpatrick, no, my nephew has some parishioners to visit and assures me that they feed him in every house he calls.'

'He will be here for dinner, no? I will be making his favourite this night: rabbit pie.'

'He will,' answered Andrew softly, then offered Elizabeth his arm.

As they entered the parlour, Andrew drew her to the small sofa opposite the fire; leaning in he kissed her gently. 'You will be staying here with me then, Lizzie.' It was not a question and she knew that.

'Did you ever doubt that I would, Andrew?' Her hand came up to stoke his face.

'Lizzie, I have come to know that nothing is certain in this life; one can only hope.'

She leaned towards him now, placing her head on his chest. 'There is something else though, is there not?' she felt him laugh.

'Yes, there is,' he answered as he pulled her away from him. 'My nephew has asked me, on his behalf, to put a proposal of marriage to Mrs Kirkpatrick.'

***

Stewart sat back in his chair as he watched the people gathered around the dining table. Where there once had been just himself and his mother—and Alex on more occasions than not—he now saw the family and extended family that was assembled. Reaching out, he took Margaret's hand in his and pressed it gently and Margaret answered with a smile as always. She was heavy with child now; in two months they would have another son or daughter. Life moved on, no matter how hard we tried to contain it—it was then he heard the front door.

William was the first to enter the hall, followed by Alexander and Stewart. What they found were Carter and Fulton looking very tired and travel weary but happy nonetheless. Carter looked back at Stewart, took off his hat and inclined his head.

'Master Stewart sir, all be well in Scotland; your mother and father are safe and well.'

Stewart pushed forward to stand before Carter, placing his hand on the man's shoulder he smiled.

'Thank you, Carter, and you too, Fulton, you have done me a great service.'

Carter then produced a letter from his pocket and handed it over. 'This be from your father, Master Stewart.'

Stewart took the letter and felt the weight of it; many pages, perhaps his mother had included one also. He nodded to himself and placed the letter into his pocket, then looked to Carter once more.

'Come, both of you, we will go to Mrs Cottle whom I am sure will be very pleased to feed you.'

***

Carter leaned back in his chair and rubbed his stomach with his hand—there was nothing like coming home.

'We thank you kindly, Mrs Cottle, that be the best roast lamb I have ever tasted.' Fulton nodded in agreement.

'I had best be getting home now,' said Fulton as he rose stiffly out of his seat, stretching his back and arms as he did so. All he wanted now was to lie in his own bed and sleep till tomorrow evening. It had been a long journey.

Mrs Cottle looked up from her chair by the fire, 'Good night to you, Edwin, you be giving my best wishes to your wife Wenna.'

Fulton replied with a nod. 'I will be doing that, Mrs Cottle. I thank ye kindly for the dinner; now I be taking myself home to sleep for a week.'

Carter laughed softly and raised his hand in a wave of goodbye.

Mrs Cottle stood up and came to sit at the table; turning her gaze to Carter, she leaned her elbows on the table and spoke. 'So, Albert Carter, my mistress is

472

well and happy then? She be content where she be? Do they be looking after her well there?'

Carter sat up slowly and smiled. 'Mrs Cottle, our mistress be like a young girl of fifteen, she be that happy. She be either smiling or singing, and yes they do be treating her well, but just like here she is found in the kitchen with the housekeeper, a Mrs Kirkpatrick, a very respectable woman whose kitchen is as clean as yours be here.'

'Humph,' was the only reply Mrs Cottle made.

Carter felt in his pocket now and produced a letter, pushing it across the table to Mrs Cottle. 'She be a writing to you, as she knew you be a worrying about her.'

Mrs Cottle's eyes glistened as she gently took the letter into her hands; looking up at Carter, she stood holding the letter to her bosom. 'I be reading this in my room.' She paused to go then turned back. 'Albert Carter, you be a good man, and I thank ye.'

***

On returning, Stewart found the family in the drawing room; drinks had been poured by William and as he entered a glass of whisky was placed in his hand, just as William raised his glass and spoke.

'I would like to propose a toast, to the safe arrival of Elizabeth and Andrew in Scotland, and for our safe journey to Bath in a few days' time.'

'I will drink to that,' replied Stewart as he raised his glass to William. 'We have only to sort out now who goes in which carriage.'

'Stewart, I be having my own carriage,' replied Stephen Martin. 'We can travel in that and anyone else who be wanting to travel with us—your maids and nanny will be most welcome.'

'I thank you, Stephen,' replied Stewart good heartedly. Watching him he thought that the man had all the warmth and kindness of his mother, that gentle way of treating people. The trait seemed to have skipped him, but then he knew that he was like his father, in more ways than one. Looking around, he saw that the women had all congregated on the sofa and chairs by the window, talking and laughing quietly with such ease it made him smile again.

Stephen had been ambivalent to accept the in vitiation at first, but one look from his daughter's pleading eyes had convinced him. He had three men in his employ, all of whom could be trusted with the business, so he had no worry there. His main concern had been their status in life—who they were. They knew nothing of the upper classes and how they lived. Stewart had assured him that he was no nobleman himself, and yet their best friend James—who was one—was so unpretentious, you would never believe he came from the family he did. Sir Henry also did not look at people that way, and neither did his wife for that matter. Although he was fiercely protective of his family, as long as you were a good, honest, trustworthy person, that was all that mattered to him.

Stewart sat back in his chair now and closed his eyes. God, was this what peace felt like? If so, then it was worth its weight in gold. He was roused from his thoughts by Alexander's voice.

'Stewart, Margaret is tired.'

As Stewart looked at her, he saw what his cousin had; she was leaning back into the sofa, her hand pressed to her side.

'We will retire. Alex, please stay and enjoy the evening. I will tell Lilly—who I know is at this very moment perched on a chair outside—to go to her bed also. Please see that every candle is snuffed and the fires banked before you go to your bed.'

'Count it as done. Cousin, we will ride into Mere together in the morning, pick up the mail, so that we can deal with any matters before we leave.'

Stewart nodded and tapped his cousin's shoulder.

'Right. Margaret Hamilton,' Stewart held out his hand to her, 'we will retire as you need as much rest as possible, so you will be well for the trip to Bath in a few days' time.' Turning around he bowed lowly in jest. 'I bid you ladies and gentlemen a very good night. I will see you all tomorrow at breakfast—which will be served at eight o'clock exactly,' he added with a grin, knowing that they were all acquainted with Mrs Cottle's timing. 'Be late at your peril!'

***

Stewart lowered himself into bed behind Margaret, pulling her into him while pushing his face into her hair and breathing deeply.

'Mmmmmm. Margaret Hamilton, is this what true peace really feels like?

Margaret responded by pushing her body into his, pulling his leg over hers and stroking his thigh. Stewart knew the signs, and if he read Maggie right, she wanted him.

'Maggie, we cannot, it is too dangerous.'

'No, it is not,' she whispered as her hand travelled round to squeeze his buttocks. 'I want you,' she breathed as her head turned around to kiss him.

Stewart clasped her breasts in response. His last words being 'Oh God'.

***

They had ridden into Mere around 10 o'clock. Alexander had collected the mail, and then the cousins had sat quietly in the Angle Inn and drank a mug of ale. As Stewart came out of the inn, he saw a man coming towards him whose face he recognised only too well by the scar that ran from his eye to his upper lip. He stood there waiting, pulling himself up to his full height, eyes straight ahead to the man's unwavering, till the man stood before him. Stewart noted he was as tall as himself, and for some odd reason Stewart noticed that his eyes were grey-green in colour and that his skin was pock marked—a large scar from this sat neatly in-between his brows.

'Oh yes, you remember my face, Hamilton.'

474

Stewart baulked slightly at the sound of his voice but stared the man down unblinking, his face no more than an inch away from his own, then gave the slightest nod. An icy blast of cold air whirled around them, which did nothing to dispel the fetid smell of the man's breath which was as stale as last time, and as last time he knew no fear.

'Do you remember my brother, the one you shot? He died a very painful death from his wounds, poisoning they called it. Well, I am here to take his revenge and "*an eye for an eye*"; is that not what it says?'

Stewart felt the knife in his ribs, even through the cloak and his jacket. Yes, it was a knife most definitely; a pistol would have a much larger edge to it. There was no way that he could reach his own knife which he always had concealed within a pocket of the left-hand side of his jacket—he would have to divert the blade from its target. Bringing his left hand up, he grabbed the man's wrist, twisting it outwards.

The man gave a sardonic grin and shook his head. 'Oh no, Hamilton. I will not take my revenge now; I will bide my time, but just so as you know that it *IS* coming.' He inclined his head, sheathed the knife in his coat, turned and walked away.

Stewart stood there for some moments; all noise from around him seemed to have vanished till he heard Alexander's voice calling to him from the side as his hand pulled at his arm.

'In God's name, who was that man!?'

Stewart turned and blinked several times; Alexander had his attention now.

'You remember I told you of the men that held up the coach that day—before the dual? Well, he was one of them, and his brother died of the pistol shot to his arm.' Stewart's voice was flat as though he were reading something incongruous out loud.

Alexander stared at his cousin bemused, but then his face changed and paled slightly as he began to understand. 'He means to take his revenge, Stewart?' he asked incredulously.

'Evidently, and so the saga continues,' he replied coldly as he turned to mount his horse.

Alexander watched his cousin for some moments—this could not be happening again—then mounted his own. The thoughts in his brain bounced against one another like a ball being hit back and forth. They were due to travel to Bath the next day; did the man intend to hold up the coaches? Sweet Jesus in heaven; they would all have to be armed.

As they neared the estate office, Stewart pulled up his horse and dismounted.

'I need to think, Alex, before we get back to the house.' Saying this he opened the door and disappeared within.

Alexander sat for a moment to compose his thoughts, then dismounted and followed Stewart through the doorway. He found him sitting back onto the desk, his hands firmly gripping the edge, staring at his feet.

475

'Alex, when Northcott died, I thought I had seen the end of the vengeance against me, that I was free to live my life in relative peace with my family; it would seem that God has other plans and trials with which to test me.'

Alexander paced the room slowly. 'Stewart, we are to travel tomorrow, three—no four—coaches; we must all be armed, you have to see that. This man will not act alone, for all we know he has a network of criminals that will do his bidding in an instant.'

Stewart held his head in his hands and nodded slowly. 'We will also have my mother's cousin, wife and daughter with us.' Stewart looked up. 'The last time they attacked was on the outskirts of Bath; who is to say he will not do the same this time? But this time our families will be with us, as well as our children.'

There was a cold silence till Stewart spoke again. 'We must send the women and children now; he is not of Northcott's ilk, in that he will reap his revenge through others. No, he wants my blood, only me. What was it he quoted—'an eye for an eye'—my death in revenge for his brother's.'

Alexander walked to the door and opened it. 'We must go back to the house now and inform my father, Martin, Pip and our coachmen Carter and Fulton. Martin uses two men from Mere to drive his coach; Charlotte can travel with them. Margaret will travel with Daisy, Millie and the children in my father's coach, and then you, my father, Pip and I will follow in my aunt's coach, armed to the teeth.'

Stewart stood up and followed Alexander out, locking the door behind him. Alexander saw that all the anxiety had returned to his cousin's face—the peace of the last month was gone—but not only that, he was still wounded, the flesh still raw, and without much pressure, could be opened once again.

'Let us get home first, Alex, tell the men folk, and then we can decide.'

***

Margaret knew there was something wrong as she watched Stewart come into the hall. Looking now to Alexander, she saw the same expression on his face also.

'Stewart, what has happened? Is there something wrong?' her voice faltered slightly as she spoke.

'Nothing, Maggie, it is nothing to trouble you, just some business with the estate is Stephen still here?'

Margaret eyed him warily; this was more that trouble with the estate, she would talk to him later. 'William has taken him into the study, the rest of us are in the drawing room.'

'Thank you, Maggie,' he replied, taking her hands and kissing them. Looking back to Alexander who looked to be in a very agitated state of mind, he nodded for him to follow.

As Margaret watched them disappear, she felt as though her blood had turned to water. She had seen that look before; closing her eyes she placed her hand onto the stair post to steady herself.

476

Everyone in the study was quiet as they listened to Stewart speak.

'At this moment, gentleman, I feel as though I cannot take anymore, and no, I did not shoot his brother, Bearcroft did, but that is of no consequence to him. I had committed the act as surely as if I had pulled the trigger. You forget he was in Northcott's pay,' he paused slightly. 'Do you recall my saying that happiness could be taken within the blink of an eye? Well, that is just what has happened now. My life has been halted once more, as I am to be the target of another man's vengeance once again. My body is still reeling from the last two attempts on my life, how can I overcome a third?' Stewart's voice had been rising slowly as he spoke.

It was William who addressed the company first.

'Stewart, firstly we must ride to inform the magistrate of what has taken place. We must give him a description of the man; luckily, he will be very recognisable and, might I add, to follow. Second, we must all be armed, not with just one pistol but two, or more if we have them, and a knife. Thirdly, the women will travel today in my coach—it is bigger than yours, Stewart, and should be able to accommodate six women and two children. It will not be a comfortable ride for them, but they should reach Sir Henry's estate by early evening, and they can take the minimal of luggage, as we can bring the rest in the other two coaches.' He looked to Stewart and nodded. 'Also, that way we can inform Sir Henry of what has taken place.'

It occurred to Stewart as he listened to William speak that he favoured Sir Henry in many ways, especially his talent of bringing things together in a neat military fashion, thinking that he had probably had to do as much when transporting his cargo of worsted cloth.

'My coachmen will take them, along with Pip your valet, Stewart. I understand the man is very good with a pistol.'

Stewart nodded, for once he was totally out of his depth. Would it not be simpler for him to kill himself now and get it over with? Then thinking of Maggie, he knew it would not—he had too much to live for.

William continued. 'Right, Stewart, I want you to write down a complete description of the man for me,' he then turned to Stephen Martin. 'Stephen, you and I will take this into Mere and speak with the magistrate there. For all we know he could still be in the town.'

Stewart wiped his hand over his face and thought to himself that he doubted that very much. The man had probably been watching him for some time, just like Northcott, choosing his time well to approach him. No, the man was long gone back into his lair, he had delivered his message, now he would bid his time.

'William,' Stewart's voice was calm, 'if you will be so good as to go speak with the ladies in the drawing room, I will bring Margaret in here with me to tell her.'

William nodded in agreement, he understood. 'We will go now to the drawing room, and I will send Margaret back to you.'

'Thank you, William,' replied Stewart as the men left.

***

As Margaret came into the study, Stewart pulled her into his arms and closed the door, leaning against it, holding her tightly to him.

'This is something really bad, is it not Stewart?' her voice was a whisper against his chest.

She felt him nod. 'Yes, Maggie, it is.' Walking her towards the chair by the fire, he pulled her down into his lap, wrapping his arms about her and taking her hands in his.

'Maggie, do you remember my telling you about one of the men in the party that held us up that time, while we were on our way to Sir Henry's, the man with the scar on his face? Well the man that Bearcroft shot then was his brother, who has since died of his wounds.' Margaret stiffened in his arms.

'But it was not you who killed him, Stewart.'

'Maggie, that is of no consequence to him. I killed him just as if I had pulled the trigger myself. He holds me responsible, and now he wants revenge.' Before she could answer, he continued. 'Margaret, you will travel to Midcraven Hall today with the rest of the ladies.' He saw her about to protest and kissed her. 'You will travel there today in William's Coach. Pip will travel with you, and we will all follow tomorrow.'

Margaret was shaking her head quickly now. 'No, I will not leave you, I will go with you, we will go together,' she was pleading.

Stewart held her tight and swallowed hard. 'No, Maggie, that is impossible. You will be safe, and you can inform Sir Henry of what has happened.'

Margaret was shaking and crying as she looked up into his eyes. 'No, Stewart, I will NOT leave you, you cannot make me.' Her hands were stoking her stomach now, as her heart broke.

Stewart took a deep breath. 'You have to, Maggie, we have some things to do here, which include speaking with the magistrate. There will be five of us, and two coaches; every man will carry three pistols and a knife as well as the coachmen being armed. He will not risk attaching us now, but I need to know that you and the others are safe, so please, Maggie, listen to me, you must go now and pack a light bag, as we will be bringing the rest of the luggage with us tomorrow.'

He had been holding her tight against him all the while he had spoken. Slowly now he released her, pulling her face up to his. 'Everything will be fine, Maggie, you have my word, have I ever broken it when I truly meant it?'

Margaret shook her head and pulled the handkerchief from his pocket.

'Stewart Hamilton, I will keep you to your word. God help me.'

Standing up, he took her hand in his and walked to the door. 'You must go ready yourself, Maggie; we do not have much time if you are to reach there before nightfall.'

Margaret held onto his hand and took him with her up to their room. On entering, she shut the door quickly turning the key in the lock, pushing his coat from his shoulders her fingers undoing his waistcoat as she did so. Her hands were now frantically trying to undo the laces to her dress when Stewart grabbed her to stop her. Turning to him, she looked at him with such anger and need.

'Stewart Hamilton, this could be the last time that I will ever lie with you, are you standing there telling me that you will not—' She stopped speaking while her fingers were trying to pull his shirt from his breeches.

'Maggie, stop,' Stewart's voice was soft and low. 'I... I understand you I... Oh God, Maggie.' His hands were pulling at her clothes now as they fought to be free. Then they took one another so quickly neither had time to speak again.

As they lay on the floor inside the room, Margaret was clinging to him, crying softly, when there was a sharp rap on the door and William's voice called out.

'Stewart, is Margaret ready? We will be waiting in the hall.'

'She will be down this instant, William,' was all Stewart said as he lifted her onto the bed. He helped her dress in the travelling clothes that had been laid out for her, and then quickly dressed himself.

'I think that Millie will have packed your things for you, and they are probably on the coach as we speak.'

Margaret nodded; pulling the pins from her hair she wound it up into a bun and secured it once more. Taking her bonnet from the bed, she ran to Stewart, holding him tightly.

'Come, Maggie, you must go.' Opening the door he turned her toward him once more and kissed her. 'I love you, Margaret Hamilton, never, ever forget that,' he said as he pulled her out of the room to the stairs.

Chapter Fifty-Five
Journey to Midcraven Hall, Christmas, Scotland and a Betrothal

The women's coach reached Midcraven Hall around 8 o'clock in the evening. Margaret had been quite unwell, and they had had to stop three times throughout the journey. At this moment, she was being taken up to her room by Millie and Lady Jemima. When they had finally taken her clothes and settled her in bed, Margaret reached out for Jemima's hand.

'Lady Jemima, if you please, in my cloak pocket there is a letter for Sir Henry, please could you give it to him with all haste. Stewart is under attack again.'

Jemima looked at Margaret, a stunned expression on her face, and then recovering her presence of mind, she turned and retrieved the letter from Margaret's pocket. Tapping the letter lightly on her fingertips, she turned to Millie.

'Go get your mistress some tea and ask cook for a heated bed pan for her feet please.' Looking once more in Margaret's direction, she nodded. 'I will take this to Henry immediately. Just rest, Margaret, all will be well.'

Jemima entered the study to see Sir Henry's valet re-trying his stock. She indicated for him to leave them, and then placed the letter in front of her husband on his desk; taking the stock into her own hands, she deftly adjusted it. He looked up at his wife, a questioning frown on his face.

'Why have the women come here early and alone?'

'Henry, I believe if you read that letter, all will become clear.' She picked up the missive and placed it into his hands.

Margaret heard Sir Henry barking his orders from her bedroom—dear God, the man had a voice that would carry for miles. She closed her eyes, breathed deeply and prayed.

***

The other three coaches left the Willows around 8 o'clock the following morning. The first coach carried most of the luggage which would last them for the ten days they were to stay; in the second sat the four men, and in the last coach was Pip with remainder of the luggage. Stewart had argued with the man, as he had insisted that he would ride with them but on top; for once in his life

Stewart won the battle. The man was not young anymore, but he was as stubborn as any mule, even so Stewart told him that he would not have the man's illness on his conscious, so Pip had ceded and was now snugly seated in Stewart's mother's coach.

As they came out the other side of Mere Town, the coaches came to an abrupt stop. William looked out of the window and yelled at his driver as to why he had stopped, when his eyes caught flashes of red, yellow and white coming towards them. As they neared, he could see six cavalry men riding towards the coaches. *Dear God,* thought William to himself, *Sir Henry had sent the cavalry to guard them.*

The first officer—for they were officers—greeted William by removing his hat and bowing to him.

'Your Servant, sir, and good day to you. My name is Captain Fanshaw, and my Lieutenants and I are here to give you safe escort to Major General Sir Henry Portman's estate Midcraven Hall.' He then turned in his saddle, giving orders for two to ride at the back, two in the middle, while he and another would ride before the coaches.

William pulled his head back into the coach, lifted and secured the glass back up, and then looking to Stewart, he smiled. 'We appear to be having a military escort to Sir Henry's, Stewart.' As he looked around the coach, no one spoke a word.

***

As Stewart came into their bedroom, Millie who had been sitting by the window watching over her mistress, curtsied and left in a flurry of skirts. Maggie held out her hand to him, letting herself relax now—he was here. She was tired, her legs ached, and at that moment she was lying on her side with a cushion pushed under her unborn child to take the weight. Stewart smiled back; taking her hand he sat beside her.

'Margaret Hamilton, did you know that we had a military escort here today?'

Margaret sat up on her elbow and frowned. 'What do you mean, Stewart?'

'I mean exactly that, Maggie. Six Cavalry officers escorted us from the outskirts of Mere all the way here. You would think that we were carrying gold!'

Margaret's eyes opened wide as she put her hand to her mouth. 'Did Sir Henry do this?'

Stewart just nodded in reply, as he pushed her hair back from her forehead and leaned in to kiss her. 'How are you feeling, Maggie? Lady Jemima wants to know should she send our dinner up here this evening.' Stewart gave her one of his soft teasing smiles. 'Well, what shall I say?'

Maggie took his hand and held it to her face. 'I do not think that I could get out of this bed to go down to eat; the journey here yesterday was unspeakable, like you, they had to stop so that I could be ill—several times.' Margaret shuddered at the thought. 'My stomach hurts, my back hurts and my legs hurt from our son—who seemed to want to bounce his way here. So yes, I would very much like our dinner to be brought to us here.'

Stewart leaned in and kissed her once more. 'I will be back as soon as I have spoken to Sir Henry.' He patted her thigh gently. 'They told me to come to see you first,' he added, pinching her cheek, 'and I also want to tease James, but right now I am going to see our son,' he added softly into her ear, before he turned and left.

***

Sir Henry looked to Stewart. 'Who is this man that threatens you now, lad?'

'Sir, do you remember the men who held us up last Christmas? Culminating in that duel outside bath'

Sir Henry nodded. 'I do.'

'Well, Bearcroft shot one of the men in the arm. The man has since died of his wound, blood poisoning—or so I am told—and his brother, who was the man I sent back to Northcott, now wants recompense from me for his brother's death; "*an eye for an eye*" was the way he put it to me.' Stewart breathed deeply, holding his side as he did so. 'I am barely fit from the fight with Northcott a month ago. I am in no state to take on this man.'

Sir Henry had been nodding all the while Stewart had narrated. 'Can you describe the man? Have you been to the local magistrate?'

'Sir, I have done all of these things, but as you and I know, this man, like Northcott, lives in the underworld. He will only surface when he is ready to strike.' Stewart paused to take another breath.

'We were coming here with our wives and families. I felt I had to let you know what was happening.'

Sir Henry nodded his head for the hundredth time, 'Quite right, lad, you did well to inform me. I will bring an artist so that he may sketch his likeness from your description for me, then we can circulate it within each barracks, town and village. That way we will know of any sighting.'

'I thank you, sir, for all the help you have shown to me and my family, but yet again I fear I will never be able to repay you.'

Sir Henry turned to him. 'Just stay alive, lad, that is all I require. Now go to your wife, Jemima will send your dinner up to you; everyone has been made quite comfortable, you have no fear there.'

'I never doubted it for a second, sir, and thank you once again.' Stewart bowed to leave. 'Is James here yet?' he enquired, turning back.

'He is to be found in the drawing room; he looks happy enough, though I must say that my daughter has not lost any of her exuberance. She will have him running around in circles.'

Stewart's response was to chuckle. 'They will be fine, Sir Henry. She will keep him on his toes.'

Sir Henry looked at Stewart with a smile playing on his lips. 'She will at that, lad, she will at that.'

'With your permission, I shall now go and tease the life from him.' Stewart bowed once more to Sir Henry and left.

He found James talking to Alexander by the window. James on seeing his friend came to him and embraced him tightly.

'Well, how are you James?'

There was a playful smile surfacing on Stewart's mouth and in his eyes as he said it. Alexander looked to him and then to the women gathered. He would not dare rib him amongst their company. Stewart picked up on the intonation and leaned into James, talking quietly.

'Well, James, did you do as my card said?'

James laughed so heartily that all the women turned towards them.

Stewart bowed. 'Ladies, forgive me, it is a private joke between James and I.'

Lady Jemima raised her eyebrows and shook her head slightly, then went back to her conversation.

James looked to Stewart and nodded. 'I did, Stewart—both!'

It was Stewart's turn to laugh loudly now; looking to the turned heads once more he bowed again. 'Ladies, I beg your forgiveness, we will retire to the library so as not to disturb you any further.'

They had just reached the door when Catherine entered; seeing Stewart she came to him and kissed his cheek, doing the same to Alexander.

'Oh, I am so happy you could come.' Turning to James she pushed her arm tightly through his as she reached up and planted a kiss onto his lips, cupping her hand there as she did so.

'Catherine!' Lady Jemima's voice cut through the chatter. 'Come sit with us and leave the men to their own conversation.'

Catherine knew an order when she heard one, but she would not be outdone by her mother. She raised her head up to her husband and kissed him once more. 'I will see you at dinner,' she said softly.

***

Christmas Day was peaceful; there was no formality at the table and meals were simple. The only meal that was served was dinner, but that was done with the minimal of staff; the other meals were laid out on a side dresser for people to take as and what they required. Sir Henry and Lady Jemima wanted it to be a family affair, considering the company that was gathered.

Sir Henry had talked at length with Stephen Martin regarding his father. He had requested information from various sources and friends regarding George MacMartin who had been a commissioned lieutenant in the cavalry when he was posted to the Caribbean during the war with Spain there, gaining his captaincy through bravery. He had suffered a severe head injury whilst serving and had lain unconscious for two weeks. On waking, he knew nothing of who he was, where he was, and why he was a soldier. The physician who had attended him explained that all memory he had before the injury had been wiped out, and

483

would, as far as he could determine, never return. It was as though he had been re-born.

When he had been well enough to travel, they had sent him home on the first available ship. At the military headquarters in London, he was handed the letter from his father (who had by then died) which instructed him to go to Coutts Bank. Stephen Martin had been amazed at what Sir Henry had discovered, even to the fact that he had been awarded for his bravery. Something he had not known about.

**

It was now Twelfth Night, and everyone was in the huge drawing room either playing games or talking. Lady Jemima had cut the traditional "*Twelfth Cake*" and the bean had gone to her youngest son George (her other two sons were away) and the pea had fallen to Jennie. They were the elected King and Queen for the night, and were at that moment playing a highly amusing game of Tic-Tac-Toe together.

Margaret had been watching them for some time throughout the holidays. She wondered if Lady Jemima had seen what she herself had observed—the blossoming of a friendship. But of course she had, as she had the eyes of a hawk and would pick up on the slightest nuance from her son. Lady Jemima turned to her now.

'Yes, Margaret, I perceive what you do.'

Margaret turned sharply to Lady Jemima. 'I had thought it was just my fancy, but...'

'Mmmmm,' she replied. 'He has never shown the slightest interest in any of the young ladies that I have paraded before him, just Jennie.'

'What will you do?' Margaret queried with the slightest hint of apprehension in her tone.

'Absolutely nothing, my child.' Leaning close to Margaret she continued. 'I will talk to Henry, as I am sure he has not the slightest notion what is happening under his very nose.'

Margaret had by now become very quietly agitated. She would talk to Stewart later, at this moment though she saw Mary Martin coming towards her, flushed with happiness, Margaret noted, as she seated herself next to her.

'Oh, Margaret, you be giving us a Christmas that even in my wildest of dreams I could not be imagining.' Taking Margaret's hand, she squeezed it. Looking now to Lady Jemima, she continued. 'I can never be repaying you all for this hospitality, but I be remembering it for the rest of my days.'

**

Henry came into their bedroom clad in his nightshirt and sat heavily onto the bed. Jemima watched him out of the corner of her eye as she brushed her hair; he was tired, she could see that, but his brain was working like she had seen it work many times before. Several times he went to speak but refrained. Finally, Jemima turned on her stool and looked at him.

'Henry Portman, are you going to tell me what troubles you or do I have to tell you myself?'

Henry, who had been staring at his feet, looked up suddenly. 'What did you say, my dear?' he asked distractedly.

Jemima stood up and came to sit next to him; turning him slightly, she pressed her fingers into his shoulders as her thumbs needed his spine. Sir Henry laid a hand upon hers and sighed.

'Jemima, I am getting old,' saying this he took her hand and kissed it.

'Henry dearest, we are both getting old.'

'Mmmmm,' was all he said as he gently nodded his head.

Before Jemima could speak, he turned and looked at her. 'Jemima, I know what you are about to say; it is with regards to young George, is it not?' He nodded once more. 'I know generally I do not know what day of the week it is, but I can see what has happened. I would dare anyone to deny it.'

Jemima placed her arm about his shoulders and rested her head there.

'She comes from a good family, Jemima. I have delved into her grandfather's past and beyond. His line stems from the Earl of Fenwick'—he turned to look at her here—'a Jacobite no less, but that is neither here nor there.'

'How many young ladies of fortune have we shown him,' he continued, 'and he has not shown the slightest interest in any but Jennie. We do not always choose who we love, Jemima; sometimes it is done for us.'

Jemima stroked his hair from his face, then cupping it with her hands, she kissed him gently.

'I know, Henry, I know. Now we shall sleep on this, and tomorrow we will look at it again. Then leave them for a few months to see what comes, after all he will go back to his regiment when this holiday ends.'

Henry looked into her eyes. 'There is something else I forgot to tell you, Jemima; he is leaving the army to take up politics.'

Jemima stood up, pushed him back onto the pillows, then lifting his legs onto the bed, she covered him. 'We will talk this through in the morning.' Getting into bed beside him, she laid her head on his chest. 'Let us sleep, Henry.'

***

There was a full moon and at this moment it was shedding its light onto the floor of their bedroom, casting its white glow to wherever it touched. Stewart had Margaret scooped tightly into him; she had been quiet all evening and he assumed it was the child making her tired. But she had not slept at once as she usually did; she lay there now staring at the moon's reflection on the windowpanes.

'What troubles you, Maggie?' he whispered into the still quiet air around them. Margaret breathed in and exhaled slowly.

'Jennie,' came her soft reply.

'Ahhh.' Stewart turned her gently to look at her.

'Stewart, she is so young, innocent and vulnerable… like my sister when she came to the Willows. I do not want her to be hurt.'

'Maggie, we will leave in two days, she will go home and he will soon be forgotten.'

Maggie was staring at him now. 'If Alexander had refused William's proposal, my sister would never have forgotten him.'

Stewart pulled her in gently, tucking her head beneath his chin, holding her close.

'Young George will inherit land, estates maybe and wealth; it is not the same as Alexander and Charlotte. We must not interfere, but let life and God decide what will happen.' He stoked her back gently. 'And I will talk to Stephen in the morning.'

Margaret kissed his chest, 'Thank you,' she breathed.

***

Christmas in Dumfries had also been a peaceful one. They had gone to St Michael's for the Christmas morning service, returning to a meal of roast goose—which Andrew had managed to procure—with roast vegetables and potatoes. Aileen Fitzpatrick had made a traditional Scottish cake made from fruits and decorated with almonds, called Dundee. She proudly stated that its roots went back to Queen Mary of Scotland.

They had all eaten together in the kitchen when Andrew nodded to Elizabeth to take his nephew into the small parlour. Elizabeth knew the reason so she invited him to come and take a glass of whisky with her to celebrate.

'Will ye no be going with them, Master Duncan?' offered Aileen Fitzpatrick, as she lifted the last of the dishes from the table.

Andrew placed his hand very gently on her arm. 'Please, sit with me a moment, Mrs Fitzpatrick, there is something I need to ask of you.'

Aileen Fitzpatrick looked at her master, trying to discern what he wanted to say. 'Will it be something… bad, Mr Duncan?'

Andrew smiled broadly. 'No, Mrs Fitzpatrick, it is not. I hope that it is something that will make you happy; please sit down and I will tell you.'

Aileen Fitzpatrick sat down slowly, clasping her hands in front of her as she leaned onto the table. It was warm in the kitchen, and the air was still full of the smells of food and spices.

'Mrs Fitzpatrick, my nephew has asked me to put a proposal of marriage to you. These past years he has known you, he has grown to respect you'—Andrew paused slightly—'love you.'

Andrew watched as the woman's face change from surprise into what he hoped to be acceptance as a slow smiled came across her lips.

'He wants tae marry me?' she said slowly as her fingers came up to her lips. 'Master Duncan, I will tell ye in all truth, I still grieve for my husband and bairns, they will nay leave my heart, but young Mr Duncan, well I cannae explain tae ye what he has done for me,' she paused to swallow slowly. 'He wants tae marry me,' she repeated.

Andrew placed his hand over hers once more. 'Will you have him, Mrs Fitzpatrick?' He watched now as two tears ran down her cheeks. Taking his handkerchief from his pocket, he held it out for her.

Aileen Fitzpatrick nodded slowly. 'I will, Mr Duncan, I will.'

Andrew stood up and bowed his head. 'I will go tell him now to put him out of his misery; then I will send him to you.'

***

It was Hogmanay, the last day of 1788. The tradition in Scotland could be traced back to the days of the Norse invaders. Christmas was a quiet time, but Hogmanay was their day to celebrate. It was dead on midnight when they heard the knock on the door. Andrew had explained to Elizabeth the tradition of first footing; now he nodded to Michael to go and answer, and on opening it there stood one of his parishioners, a Hamish Paterson—a tall dark young man whose body seemed to fit the width of the door frame.

'Good health tae ye, Minister.' He bowed and handed him a small bag of salt and a bottle of whisky.

'Will ye no come in, Hamish, and tak' a dram wi' us?' asked Michael, stepping aside so the man could enter.

'I thank ye kindly, Minister, I will tak' a dram wi' ye.'

And so started the procession of visitors, each bringing a small gift; it was 3'o clock in the morning when the last of them came, and Elizabeth observed that both Andrew and Michael were slightly drunk. How did she know this: Andrew had revered to his Scottish bur as he always did.

Andrew Duncan stood up somewhat unsteadily and smiled. 'We will awa' tae our beds now, may God bless us all and gi' us a good year.' He nodded to his nephew and Aileen Fitzgibbons, who were to be wed the following Friday in St Michaels. Michael stood also, taking Aileen's hand; kissing her fingers he bowed. 'I will be seeing ye on the 'morro.'

Aileen Fitzpatrick smiled, nodded and went out first followed by Andrew and Elizabeth. 'Do ye not forget the candles, Michael, or we will all be burnt in our beds.' Andrew placed his hand on Michael's shoulder and followed Elizabeth up the stairs.

Once in their room, Elizabeth went to her table and started to unpin her hair. It was a small room, but it was warm. The fire was a mixture of peat and wood, and it was the peat that gave off most of the heat. Andrew came gradually up behind her, placing his hands over hers to still her fingers. Elizabeth closed her eyes and leaned back as he continued to take the pins himself, and as he took the last one, he turned her to him and kissed her slowly. Elizabeth melted into him and thought that he tasted of whisky and fruit cake, and that she felt like a girl of sixteen.

Chapter Fifty-Six
The Threat and the Return

Stewart burst into the drawing room where Margaret and Charlotte sat peacefully with their embroidery. The two women's heads came up in unison, each bearing the same startled expression.

'They are coming home; my father says they should be here by the second week in February!' exclaimed Stewart.

Margaret looked to her sister and smiled. 'You would think that they had given him wings.'

Charlotte giggled lightly. 'He has missed them so much, cousin. If my father ever went away, I would miss him terribly.'

Margaret looked at her sister now; she would never know the truth, not while she breathed. She cherished him, and Margaret recalled that she had never heard them say a cross word to one another. Stewart stood beside her now re-reading the letter.

'His housekeeper, Mrs Fitzpatrick, has married his cousin the minister, and he has given them the house in Dumfries as a wedding gift.' Stewart looked up in incredulity. 'You know what that means, Maggie? They are coming home for good.' As Stewart stood there, he remembered the letter that his father had handed him the day they had left. He had never opened it. In truth, he did not want to know if it contained the words *we will not be returning*'; now his heart was lifted and he would read the letter. Leaning down, he kissed Margaret on the top of her head, turned and left the room as though he had never been there.

Charlotte smiled. 'Cousin, I knew she would return,' leaning in, she placed her hand on Margaret's stomach, 'for the birth of your child.'

Margaret placed her own hands on her stomach. 'You have no idea how I have prayed for that Charlotte.'

***

Stewart sat at his desk in the study now, his hands placed firmly down on the top of it. Taking the key from his pocket, he unlocked the small side draw at the top. He breathed deeply as he retrieved the letter and then slowly broke the seal. As he had thought, there was another letter inside from his mother; laying this to one side, he smoothed the paper out seeing his father's bold hand jump out from the page and then began to read.

My Dearest son,

I hope that you will understand by now just why we had to go. It was not that we do not love you, or want to be with you. It was a need to be alone and to find ourselves once more. Can you comprehend what it is like to do what I have done to the one person that you loved above all else? I need to know if your mother has taken me back out of sympathy or loneliness or love. Please do not get angry, but place yourself where I am. By going to Scotland, I will know instinctively when we get there if she wants... me.

I have been out of my depth for the past four months, astounded you might say, by the kindness everyone has shown me. Oh, there was wariness as well—Mrs Cottle still is not sure of my intentions with your mother, and if the truth be told, neither are you. By coming here, I could prove to her that I had changed.

I wanted her to meet my saviour, my nephew Michael. He alone can bear witness to her what struggles I have endured. I was at war with my own soul, as when I took your mother that first time.

I beg you to realise I am a changed man, Stewart, and I will love and protect your mother till my dying breath. Please try and understand me; that is all I ask.

Your Loving father
Andrew

Stewart rubbed his eyes with his fingers; getting up he took a glass from the salver and poured himself a whisky. Coming back to stand before the window, he raised his glass.

'I am sorry, I doubted you, Father. I hope that *you* can forgive *me*.' Stewart took a large gulp, set the glass down then seated himself once more to read his mother's letter.

Stewart, My Heart,

Can you ever forgive me?

I know that you love your father now, but there is a small part deep inside you that is yet to be convinced of his sincerity towards me.

You will no doubt be shouting now, and, if I am not mistaken, bang the desk, but it is true and you have to admit to this.

Stewart looked up, and pressed his fingers to his head. 'Oh God, Mother, you know me so well. If I had read this letter when you gave it, that is exactly what I would have done.' Taking a deep breath, he continued to read.

I love your father as from the first day that I set eyes on him at the Willows; he had my heart then as he will always. You hold a different part of my heart, no less special or profound, but different.

Stewart stopped once more to compose himself. He took another mouthful of whisky and picked the letter up again.

By coming here, I hope to prove to you both how much I love you both. Your father in that I will be with him no matter where he chooses, as we have lost too much time, and time is precious now. It is as though I wish to capture my youth once more, can you understand that, Stewart?

You... you have been my constant for all of these years. A mother is a mother for life. You are part of me, part of my own flesh and blood, but we do not need to be in each other's presence to prove that love, but I do with your father.

Please accept and understand me, Stewart.

I love you with all my heart.

Your loving mother,

Elizabeth

He heard the door open and knew it was Maggie, and then he felt her hand upon his shoulder.

'Is everything well, Stewart?' she asked as she looked down at his mother's writing. 'Did you receive a letter from your mother also?'

Stewart held her hand and shook his head. 'No, Maggie, these are letters that my father gave me before they left. I never opened them. I did not want.'

It was then a small dark head pushed up under Stewart's hand. 'Papa, Papa, up.'

Stewart looked down and smiled at his son, swinging him up and standing him on his desk. Margaret took the whisky glass just in time before it met with their son's shoe.

'Papa, come ride my horse, peees.' Charles was jumping madly now, making all things on the desk shake in an alarming way.

'Stewart, take him down before he breaks something,' she exclaimed as she rescued the bottle of ink, just as Alexander came into the room.

Stewart had Charles in his arms now trying to contain him. 'Alex, Alex!' he shouted.

Alexander smiled broadly then put up his hands in defence. 'Oh no, my lad, you want to take my ribbon from my hair, you rascal,' he teased.

Charles chuckled heartily and then deftly removed his father's and threw it to the floor.

'I am afraid, Alex, that we must ride the horse before we can talk. I gather you have papers for me to sign?'

Alexander was still smiling and teasing his godson with his own ribbon, pulling away just as Charles to take it.

'Stewart, go ride your horse, we can talk in a while. I am going to see my daughter.'

As they left, Stewart looked back at Margaret. 'Read the letters, Maggie, my father's first.'

***

490

The hour was late, and Stewart had just signed the last of the papers that Alexander had brought with him. They were seated now in the two winged chairs by the fire, watching the flames leap and die as the wind drew them upwards into the chimney.

'It is good news, cousin, about my aunt and uncle. The weather should be slightly improved by the time they travel.'

Stewart looked up. 'It is, Alex, but you will have to look for another nanny now, as Aileen Fitzpatrick and Michael Duncan are to marry by the end of January.'

'That is fine, Stewart, nanny Daisy told me yesterday that her friend in London—who she writes to—has just left her post with a family there, as the boys were now both at boarding school. She is seeking a new post. Daisy has written to her and she will travel down to Mere next week. If she is recommended by Daisy, should that not be good?'

'Yes, Alex it is.' Stewart looked to his cousin now; there was something else on his mind and Stewart knew that it had been there all evening. 'Do you wish to tell me something, Alex?'

Alexander guarded his words carefully. 'There has been a stranger of late, riding in and out of the estate. He is a tall man, always dressed in dark colours. This would not have anything to do with the man that threatened you that time in Mere, would it?

'You know what he looks like, Alex, did you see his face?' Stewart's voice was calm, but Alexander saw his hand tremble.

'No, Stewart, he always keeps himself at a distance, and I am not the only one to have seen him—the tenants have too—but I have this cold feeling that it is the same man.'

'Then I must be very vigilant indeed, Alex. He will not come near the house; he will wait till he gets me alone, far from anyone.' Stewart paused. 'Do you get my meaning, Alex?'

Alexander nodded, but the relaxed composure of the evening had gone from his face.

'I have told all the tenants when they see him, to remain at a distance, but follow him, and not lose sight—they know that he is a danger to this estate.'

'Thank you, Alex, now let us away to our beds. I will smother the fire.' Taking the candlestick down from the mantle, he held it out. 'Here, take this candle. I will follow with the other. Good night, Alex, and thank you.'

Alexander nodded and left.

***

The wedding of Michael Duncan and Aileen Fitzpatrick was anything but small. The entire congregation from the church came to see them take their vows; it seemed that they were all so pleased that their kind Minister had found someone at last, and as for Aileen, they were thankful that she would no longer be alone, grieving for those that she had lost.

It was decided that Andrew and Elizabeth would stay two nights at the Coach and Horses Inn, leaving the newlyweds in peace. They were seated now in the warm parlour, having just eaten their dinner of chicken, baked parsnips and bannocks.

'The bannocks do no way compare to those made by Aileen,' stated Elizabeth. 'She has such a light touch; they melt in your mouth.'

Andrew took her hand in his below the table as they sat together in the nook by the fire. 'We will make our way back on Monday, Lizzie. We must leave them now to make their own life together and hope that they will be as happy as we are now.'

'Oh, I am sure they will be, Andrew. Aileen is still young, who knows maybe they will have their own children—God willing.'

They sat there peacefully for some time, taking in the ambience that surrounded them. The people she saw were content; they did not have much, but what they did, they shared. She saw that this afternoon when everyone brought with them a plate of food to the inn for the wedding breakfast.

'Lizzie.' Elizabeth turned to look up at him. 'I wish to tell you something, and I hope that you will agree with me, and that our son will not be angry.'

Elizabeth looked at him warily, not knowing what he would say.

'Lizzie, I want to give my nephew my house, part in thanks for what he has done for me and part because I want them to have a place to call home. Are you angry, Lizzie?'

Elizabeth shook her head and her smile said she was not. Reaching up, she placed her hand on his chest. 'Oh, Andrew, that is wonderful. I...' her words trailed away as the tears spilled over her lashes. She knew what he meant better than anyone.

Andrew Duncan stood up and took her arm through his. 'We will go upstairs, Lizzie, come.'

***

They had travelled back in Andrew Duncan's coach. He had hired two men from the village to take them; they would then return to Dumfries and the coach would be his nephew's. The weather had been good to them—cold, but no snow—so they had made it in five days. It was now the beginning of February and Elizabeth's thoughts strayed to Margaret; they would have another grandchild, and this time Andrew would be there at the birth. She looked at him now as he sat beside her, his profile so like their son's. Charles would mirror them also, you could tell, even from his young age, strange how a likeness gets passed down. She lifted her hand to the locket that was always at her neck now. There was the proof of what her father always said.

Andrew Duncan turned to her. 'Are you cold, Lizzie?' Elizabeth shook her head as he placed his arm about her shoulders and pulled her in to him. 'Only a few more hours and we will be in Mere.' He pulled up the blanket to cover her, 'Sleep a while, Lizzie, we will soon be home.'

His nephew had given him a book of poetry before they left. It was the works of a young poet who lived in Dumfriesshire and was being acclaimed as good. He opened the cover now, reading the first page.

'POEMS Chiefly in the Scottish Dialect by Robert Burns.'

He turned the page and started to read.

As the coach drew near the house, Elizabeth could see people running out of the door. It would seem they had a reception party awaiting them. Nodding to the window, she turned to Andrew.

'Andrew, we are to be greeted like royalty.'

As he watched her, he could see the unrestrained joy in her face—she had not stopped smiling.

***

Lunch had been a strange experience; people were talking, cross talking, changing seats at the table, and Mrs Cottle had made a rabbit pie in the time it took to drink a cup of tea. Not a crumb was left on the plate. It was a celebration Andrew thought, like the *"prodigal son's"* return. He being the said son, but unlike him, he had changed his ways forever. Looking around him now, he felt a sense of pride, one that he did not have the right to feel, as he had paid no part in their lives. Elizabeth had nurtured this family and made it what it is today; because of her strength and tenacity, they had become that family. She reached under the table now and took his hand. As he looked up, he saw Stewart smile and raise his glass to them in a toast.

'Andrew,' Elizabeth turned to look at him.

'I know what you are about to say, Lizzie, there is one man missing, am I right?'

'Yes, the man will never come to the house unless I command it. Oh he is so stubborn,'

'Go speak with him, Lizzie.'

'No, Andrew, we will go.'

Elizabeth stood up. 'You must excuse us for a while, as there is someone I wish to see.' As she came round the table, she stopped by Margaret. 'Margaret, please go rest for a while, you are very tired.' Leaning down, she kissed her cheek.

Alexander was the next to rise. 'And I must go into Mere to collect the post, as I am awaiting a letter from the bank.' Looking to Stewart he grinned. 'No, Stewart, we are not bankrupt; this is not from your bank but mine.' Saying this, he bowed to everyone and left.

***

Alexander was just leaving the post house, placing the letters into his pocket as he did so, when he saw a man approaching him whose face he knew only too well. Alexander stopped where he was feeling the ice slip down his spine. He

493

had no weapon on him bar a small knife. The man wore a pistol, a sword and a small knife tucked into his belt. As the man stopped in front of him, he stared hard at Alexander—unblinking.

'I wish you to tell Hamilton that I will be coming for him at the end of the month. This way he can put all of his affairs in order for he will die.'

Turning on his heel, the man was gone as quickly as he had appeared.

Alexander's head was swimming slightly, and beads of sweat were running down his temples. Breathing deeply, he walked straight into the Angel Inn and ordered himself a mug of ale. Just how he was to stop this man carrying out his threat, he had not the slightest notion. What he did know was that he had to get home—and fast.

As Alexander entered the hall, he saw Stewart descending the stairs.

'Alex, did you get the post?'

Alexander stared at him; he would know something was wrong just by seeing the expression on his face. 'Yes, Stewart, I did, and something else into the bargain.' Walking past Stewart, he made his way to the study.

Stewart came into the room, closing the door very quietly behind him.

'What has happened, Alex?' he asked flatly.

As Alexander turned from the fire, Stewart noticed that his face was drawn and very pale.

'I met with our friend again, who informed me that he will kill you by the end of February. He was giving you this information so that you could put your *house in order*. Dear God, Stewart, the man is madder than Northcott.'

'Yes, Alex, I know. But unlike Northcott, I cannot precipitate the time and the place. With him I knew that on that day if I went to the lake, he would follow. Here, the man will just await his chance and take it.'

Stewart sat heavily into a chair. 'I am not fit, Alex. I have not the presence of mind to take him on, but do it I must. I have no choice in the matter and he knows that, so he will play it to his advantage.'

Alexander sat in the other winged chair and laid his head back and closed his eyes. The warm, peaceful stillness of the room belied the turmoil in both men's heads.

'All of the tenants know,' spoke Alexander, 'as do Pip and Spike. I think that we should inform your father also, Stewart.'

'And how will that help, Alex? For in telling him, by instinct my mother will know.' Stewart stood up and walked to the window. 'We must keep this to ourselves and trust that God will deliver me as he has done on the other two occasions.'

'So you would leave it to the will of God, Stewart!' Alexander's voice had risen.

'No, Alex, but I will do my utmost to stay alive.'

Chapter Fifty-Seven

Death, Birth, a Father's Love and Rapprochement

Margaret sat in the chair in her room feeling very uncomfortable. The baby was very low now; she knew the signs from Charles—it would not be long. Looking out to the gardens, she hoped that it would be today as her back ached so and she could get no comfort from lying or sitting. Standing up, she paced a little. Stewart had gone to the estate office to see Alexander; he had seemed very agitated and worried as though he was expecting something. Looking down at herself, she smiled. *Yes*, she thought, *the baby, he would make his appearance on this day.*

There was a slight tap on the door then Charlotte came in.

'Can I get you anything, Margaret? May I help you downstairs?' As she came towards Margaret, she heard the splashing of water. Looking down to Margaret's feet, she saw the puddle beneath.

'Charlotte, I think that you had best get Mother and Mrs Penhale.' Margaret doubled over, holding tight beneath her stomach as the first pains came. 'Be quick, Charlotte, please.'

Charlotte entered the drawing room like an eddy, her skirts rustling as they swirled about her legs.

'Aunt, Aunt, please come quick.' Charlotte was breathless. 'The baby is coming.'

Elizabeth was on her feet at once, her book falling to the floor. 'Andrew, go get Stewart please, he is at the estate office, and tell Mrs Cottle to put water to boil, then Pip to ride for Beryan Penhale.' With the same wind that Charlotte had entered, they left the room.

Andrew met Pip in the hall, giving him his orders, and then proceeding to the kitchen he asked Mrs Cook to put water to boil, as the baby was coming.

'I have to go for my son; he is with Alexander.'

Mrs Cottle nodded and pointed Andrew to the back door. 'Be quicker, sir to be getting to your horse that way. The stables be just to the right.' He nodded to Mrs Cottle in thanks and left.

***

Stewart rode slowly to the estate office. He had his sword in its scabbard, which was buckled to his horse, and his pistol loaded and primed in his hand before him. This was the last day of February—it would be today, he knew. As he looked up, he saw a rider coming towards him with the same slow pace he rode himself. His hands were wet with sweat now, and they trembled slightly. Just as before, his hearing seemed to have stopped, cutting off all noise from around him. After what seemed like an age, the man came to a halt just in front of him.

'The time has come, Hamilton. I will take my revenge.'

Stewart heard now what he had not heard before; the man's voice was cultured, he spoke like himself, he was educated.

'Who are you?' questioned Stewart.

'That is of no consequence to you, for in a few short moments you will be dead.'

Stewart saw him raise his pistol and heard the distinct click as he pulled back the hammer. He raised his own pistol now, and to his disgrace his hand shook slightly. Then, without warning, a loud report echoed around the countryside, and Stewart felt something very warm and thick splash his face and run down his neck. He had not fired his pistol so it must be his own blood, but where was it coming from, his head? It was then he heard the thump as the other man hit the floor.

Stewart watched a hand take the pistol from his, and at that moment he felt as though he were floating on a very soft cloud, being buoyed along by the breeze. It was then he heard his father's voice.

'It is over, Stewart, you must come home now; your child is coming.'

Stewart looked down now and saw he was covered in blood; reaching up to touch his face, he felt the thick sticky mixture there.

'Am I hurt?' he questioned, as though he were asking could he speak.

'No, Stewart, the blood is his.'

'But I did not fire, Father,' came his astonished reply.

'No, Stewart, I did, now we must get you back home, but first we will go to Spike where you can wash and change your clothes, no one will notice. Pip can get you clean ones.' Andrew Duncan was thinking out loud now—he had to act fast.

His father's voice came across in such a calm manner that Stewart just nodded in acquiesce.

When they came near the house, they saw Spike coming out of the tool shed. He looked at both of them and bit his lip.

'Spike, there seems to be a mess just outside of the estate office, is it possible we can clear it up?' Spike inclined his head slowly. 'But first if you could ask Pip to bring fresh clothes so that Stewart can wash and change before he goes into the house.'

Coming to his senses, Spike nodded quickly this time. 'My door is open, Master Andrew, please go in, there be water in the pot over the fire and a bowl be hanging on the wall just inside. I will go and inform Pip now.'

Andrew Duncan could see that his son was still in shock as he huddled him into the cottage. Pulling the bowl from the wall, he emptied some hot water into it, then finding some towels and soap he ordered Stewart to strip. Helping him out of his jacket, he pulled his shirt over his head.

'Take off your breeches, Stewart, and wash quickly. I must go help, Spike, and Pip will be here at any minute.'

Stewart did as he was told like a small child, then stood there strip naked.

Andrew Duncan turned sharply towards him, pushing the bar of soap into his hands. 'Wash, Stewart, now!'

Stewart started to wash himself, watching the water turn red as he did so. Andrew watched him and saw what his son saw.

'Rinse your hair, Stewart, and your neck—quick.' Stewart did as he was bid, then taking the bowl from him, Andrew threw the contents into the garden and refilled it with fresh water.

'Now wash properly.'

As Stewart worked, his mind was slowly coming back to him. He scrubbed harder now, pushing his face and hair into the hot water. Stewart raised his head up and looked into his father's eyes, as Andrew held out a towel for him.

'I must go now, Stewart, do you understand me?'

Stewart nodded once more, but this time he did understand. As Andrew opened the door, Pip came in, but they did not speak—there was no need for words.

'Master Stewart, here, dry yourself and get dressed, you will have a new son or daughter soon.'

Stewart dressed himself quickly now and was just putting on his shoes when Alexander came in. The two cousins looked at one another for some moments before Stewart spoke.

'Is it finally over, Alex? Will this be the new beginning?' He paused slightly, buttoning his coat he closed his eyes. 'How can these two things be happening on the same day; what do they say, "*In the midst of life we are in death.*"'

'Stewart, please do not go quoting the scriptures to me at this moment, as it is more than I can bear.'

Stewart gave the merest of smiles; Alexander was unnerved he could tell, but no more than he was, but he could not show it. 'It is not scripture, Alex, it is from the Latin chant '*Media vita in morte sumus*' from the common book of prayer.'

Alexander shook his head. 'Come, Stewart, the midwife is with Margaret as we speak, we have to get you into the house.' Leaning in, he picked up the bowl and tossed its contents into the garden, then placing the bowl back on the wall, they left.

***

Stewart paced the floor in the study as Alexander watched him. He would not have been in his place today. If it had been himself, then he would have gone quietly mad by now.

'Why are we put through all of these trials, Alex?'

'Not me, Stewart, just you; perhaps you are ordained for some higher level.'

Stewart laughed softly. 'No, Alex, after some of the things that I have done in my short life, I should be cast to the devil.'

'No, Stewart, you have never undertaken them for gain or profit for yourself, you have done them for the good of others, that is why I can never understand why you have been persecuted so—'

His speech was stopped as Andrew Duncan came into the room. Both men stood and watched him.

'Stewart, you have another son.'

Before he could say anymore, Stewart was past him and up the stairs. He slowed himself as he reached their room, trying to compose his feelings, as he felt the tears come into his eyes. Wiping them quickly, he turned the door knob.

Margaret was sitting back on a mound of pillows holding the small bundle that was their new son. He thought to himself that she had never looked more radiant.

'Come, hold your new son, Stewart... Andrew, Henry.'

Stewart swallowed as he sat on the bed and took his son into his arms. 'Oh God, Margaret, he is even smaller than Charles, and he has... brown hair.'

Margaret placed her hand on his arm. 'No, Stewart, it is chestnut, a mixture of yours and mine, and yes he is smaller.'

'Oh God, Maggie,' he repeated, 'after all that has happened.' He swallowed several times trying to stem his tears, but to no avail. Turning around, he saw his father and mother standing behind him.

Standing up, he held out his son. 'Father, come hold your namesake, Andrew Duncan.'

Andrew Duncan sat down on a chair, holding his grandson as though he were a piece of precious china, while his mother just stared at her son questioningly.

'It is time that we took our true name.' He turned to Margaret as he spoke the words. 'Is that not right, Margaret Duncan?' Margaret reached out her hand to him, clasping his finger tightly.

'Oh I agree, Stewart Duncan, I agree.'

Andrew handed their grandchild to his grandmother then stood and took his son into a tight embrace. They stayed that way for some moments, each giving vent to their feelings as they cried together.

When Andrew released him, Stewart spoke. 'Thank you, Father, thank you.' His voice was low and tender.

Margaret and Elizabeth looked at one another; had something transpired between them that they had not been aware of? The balance had shifted for sure, but how?

Stewart rubbed his fingers over his face and eyes. 'Now I must go and bring Charles, he must be here to see his new brother.' Before anyone could answer he was gone.

Elizabeth placed baby Andrew back into Margaret's arms and sat down. She looked up at Andrew and tilted her head slightly in asking. Andrew sat down next to her, his arm around her shoulders. 'Everything is well, Lizzie, everything is well.'

He was stopped in his speech by Stewart's return. Coming to the bed, he placed Charles firmly into the middle.

'Now, Charles, meet your new baby brother Andrew.' Charles frowned and pursed his lips.

Stewart took his baby son from Margaret and laid him gently onto Charles' legs, while still keeping his hands under him. Then he spoke in a whisper.

'Look how small he is, Charles; he needs us to look after him, protect him because he is too small to do this for himself. Mother must spend lots of time with him, and we must help her. Do you understand me?'

Charles looked at his father and nodded. 'Andooo?'

'Yes, that is his name, just like grandfather, we must always love him, and keep him from harm, because you and I are older now, and we must *always* be there for him no matter what.' As he said the last words, he looked to his father.

'Now we must give him back to Mother as she has to feed him.' As he lifted him, Charles leaned forward placing a kiss on his brother's cheek.

'Come, we will go now to Mrs Cottle for milk and biscuits; she always has biscuits for occasions such as this.' Whisking his son in the air, he blew into his stomach, making Charles screech. Their laughter could be heard over the house as they made their way down the stairs.

***

It was a glorious end of March day, and as Elizabeth looked out from the drawing room window, she could see that the earth was waking once again from her slumber. In the distance was the carpet of bluebells that had bloomed there every spring that she could remember they seemed to hover just above the ground. The trees were in bud, some of them already unfolding into leaves and around the terrace were the heads of daffodils bobbing in the breeze. She thought that God was magnanimous in his gifts at this moment. The coaches were ready and waiting to take the family to St Michaels for baby Andrew's baptism, but she wanted to take one last look.

'Lizzie, are you ready?' came Andrew's voice from the door.

Turning, she smiled as she came towards him. 'I am coming, Andrew. I just wanted to take in the beauty of this day before we leave, as when we get back this part of the garden, will be in shade.' As she walked beside him, she looked up.

'What is it, Lizzie? There is something troubling you these days.'

'I am trying to fathom when the moment occurred, where something shifted between you and Stewart. I know it stems from the day that Andrew was born, but I cannot for the life of me determine when exactly.'

Andrew just tucked her arm into his and smiled broadly. 'There is always something magical that happens at the birth of a child, Lizzie, and Andrew has brought unity and peace for us, let us just savour that this day.'

***

The church was packed as the day when Charles was baptised. Their tenants and the people of the parish stood around the font now, watching young Andrew come in, held in the arms of his godmother Catherine, and followed by his godfather James. Behind them came Stewart, Margaret and Charles, Andrew and Elizabeth, Alexander, Charlotte and William, then finally Sir Henry and Lady Jemima.

Baby Andrew, like his brother, was completely at ease and oblivious at what was happening to him as he was passed from person to person. It was when James' turn came to hold him that he too was baptised, which sent Catherine into a fit of the giggles and James red to his roots.

The weather was too cold to have the tenants eat on the lawn, but everyone gathered there with a drink in their hands to toast to young Andrew. Then they drifted home to their own houses, armed with food from the house to celebrate.

The family were gathered now in the hall, waiting to go into the dining room to eat when Stewart took Margaret into his arms in full view of everyone and kissed her slowly. His mother was stunned, but Lady Jemima clapped, and then raised her glass.

'And here is to many more years for you, Stewart and Margaret; may your family grow and your love deepen.'

Catherine, seizing the opportunity, threw her arms around James' neck, only to be untangled by her mother.

'You can behave, young lady.'

Just then there was a loud wrap on the door.

'Who can that be?' questioned Elizabeth. 'Are we expecting anyone else?'

As Thompson threw open the door, Elizabeth's mouth fell open. There standing before her was the mirror image of her father.

The gentleman bowed respectfully. 'I have come to see Milady Elizabeth,' he said with a smile. 'Does she still live here?'

Elizabeth came forward staring at him. 'I am Elizabeth,' she answered, looking up into his face.

'Of course you are,' replied the man gently. 'I am your half-brother Brian Gailsforth, and I am so glad I have found you.'

There was a stunned silence around the hall, till Andrew Duncan stepped forward bowing to the man.

'We have all just returned from our grandson's baptism, will you not join us for the dinner?' Waving the man in with his arm, Thompson closed the door.

Stewart took his mother's arm, smiling warmly at her. Several times she went to speak but nothing came, so she just shook her head.

'Well, Mother, what other surprises will this day unfold for us. Shall we all go in to dinner now?' He raised his brows still smiling. 'It would seem that things have come "*full circle*"; what started with you, Mother, has returned.'

***

Bibliography

With grateful thanks to the following Websites and Books for their invaluable information. I have not to my knowledge quoted from any of these, but merely used them as an insight into the lives of people of the 18th century.

BOOKS

Addison, C.G. (1842) '*The History of the Knights Templars, The Temple Church and The Temple*' Ch. XIII P. 342 – Longman, Brown, Green & Longmans, Paternoster Row.

Beltham, P. (1987) '*Guide to St John's the Baptist Church, Frome Selwood*' Paperback Leaflet

Brook, J. (1964) '*Edward Bearcroft 1737–96) of Holland House Kensington*' London. Published in The History of Parliament: the House of Commons – Eds. L Namier, J. Brook, 1964.
Ref Volumes: 1754–1790. Published by Boydell and Brewer, Suffolk, England.

Burney, F. – '*Cecilia*' – first Published in 1782 – London: Printed for T Payne & Son, at Newgate, and T Cadell in The Strand

Colchester, L.S. Ed (1982) '*Wells Cathedral: A History*' Open Books Publishing Ltd. London

Cumming, B Ed. (2011) '*Common Book of Prayer*' – texts of 1549, 1559, 1662 – Oxford Worlds Classics - Kindle Version of e-book. Page 82

Ingamells, J. Et al. (2013) '*Brooks's – 1764–2014 – The Story of a Whig Club*' Paul Holberton Publishing, London

Jackson, Harvey H. III. '*Behind the Lines: Savannah During the War of Jenkin's Ear*' The Georgia Historical Quarterly - Vol. 78, No. 3 (Fall 1994), pp. 471–492

Lowndes, W. (1980) – '*The Royal Crescent in Bath: A fragment of English life*' – Redcliffe Press Ltd. London

Namier, Sir Lewis (1964) '*Sir Richard Sutton (1733–1802) of Norwood Park, Notts'*. London. Published in The History of Parliament: the House of Commons – Eds. L Namier, J. Brook, 1964.
Ref Volumes: 1754–1790. Published by Boydell and Brewer, Suffolk, England.

Neuburg, V.E. (Spring 1983) – '*Journal of the Society for Army Historical Research'*
JOURNAL ARTICLE - THE BRITISH ARMY IN THE EIGHTEENTH CENTURY, Vol. 61, No. 245, pp. 39–47

Page, W. Ed. (1908) ' *St Michael's Church, Southampton'* – *Southampton Churches and Public Buildings & Charities* – History of Hampshire – Vol. 3, pp. 524–537 – Published by Victoria County History (1908).

Presland, J Ed. (1920), Widgery, F.J. (Illus) '*Torquay: The Charm and History of its Neighbourhood'* – Ch. iv, pp. 64–66 – Chatto and Windus, London

Sangster, W. (1855) '*The Umbrellas and their History*' – Effingham Wilson, London

Shakespeare, W. (2017) '*The Tempest: FREE Hamlet Prince of Denmark,*' Canada: The Works of William Shakespeare. (26 April 1564 – 23 April 1616) – First Printed in First Folio of 1623 – This Ed. Quora Media E-book, 2017, – The Tempest Act 4, scene 1 – p128.
'*Yea, all which it inherit, shall dissolve,*
And, like this insubstantial pageant faded,
Leave not a rack behind. We are such stuff
as dreams are made on; and our little life
is rounded with a sleep'

Spoken by Prospero – The Tempest Act 4, scene 1 : *William Shakespeare*

White, M. (2009) – '*Wound care in the 18th Century'* – Georgian Britain – British Library Articles online
https://www.bl.uk/georgian-britain/articles/health-hygiene-and-the-rise-of-mother-gin-in-the-18th-century

***

WEB SITES

History of Mere – http://merewilts.org/history_heritage.html
http://merewilts.org/history_heritage.html
Wiltshire Council – Chapter 6: 6.1.4 – Evidence of the Angel Inn in Mere,
Wiltshire. The London to Exeter Stage, and the local Linen industry.
http://www.wiltshire.gov.uk/south_wiltshire_settlement_setting_assessment_2
008_chapter_6_mere.pdf
Flax information – The Victoria History of Wiltshire, Volume 4. OUO, 1959
https://history.wiltshire.gov.uk/community/getfaq.php?id=184
http://www.wildfibres.co.uk/html/harvest_flax.html
St Michael's Church, Mere –
https://history.wiltshire.gov.uk/community/getchurch.php?id=1409
http://www.britainexpress.com/counties/wiltshire/churches/mere.htm
http://www.stmichaelsmere.org.uk/?page_id=34
St Michael's Church, Dumfries – http://www.scottish-
places.info/features/featurefirst17129.html
St Michael's Church, Southampton –
https://www.british-history.ac.uk/vch/hants/vol3/pp524–537#h3-0013
Celtic Knot Wedding Rings – https://www.blarney.com/celtic-knot-jewelry/
Relating to Locheil, Scotland – http://las.denisrixson.com/2016/04/lochiel-
estate-in-1772-map/
Information on The Isle of Wight – and where Freshwater is situated –
https://www.iwight.com/azservices/documents/1595-Rowlandsons-1784-tour-
v2.pdf
https://www.google.co.uk/search?q=map+of+isle+of+wight+uk&espv=2&tbm
=isch&imgil=HN1UrRGbpKL8SM%253A%253BksnO8_QW8IhZpM%253B
http%25253A%25252F%25252Fwww.hot-map.com%25252Fisle-of-
wight&source=iu&pf=m&fir=HN1UrRGbpKL8SM%253A%252CksnO8_QW
8IhZpM%252C_&usg=__sFSiYyB1zlJJ-
jNSkOHBpbRRI1U%3D&biw=1280&bih=694&dpr=1&ved=0ahUKEwi-
2qHcu43TAhXoKMAKHcU0DIAQyjcITg&ei=G_fkWP7gAujRgAbF6bCAC
A#imgrc=HN1UrRGbpKL8SM:
Information on maps of Wiltshire –
https://www.google.co.uk/maps/place/Wiltshire/@51.1619562,-
2.4874703,9z/data=!4m5!3m4!1s0x487137c28922c829:0x648834f891bd9734!
8m2!3d51.3491996!4d-1
Salisbury in the 18th century – http://www.british-
history.ac.uk/vch/wilts/vol6/pp81–83
Evidence of the Mermaid Inn in Exeter –
http://www.exetermemories.co.uk/em/_pubs/mermaid-inn.php
Evidence of "The Sun and Lamb" in Salisbury – (92) Houses –
http://www.british-history.ac.uk/rchme/salisbury/pp66–72
The Stagecoach and its routes in the 18th century – http://www.historic-
uk.com/CultureUK/The-Stagecoach/

Evidence of the Swan with Two Necks in Cheapside –
http://www.wickedwilliam.com/principal-departure-coaching-inns-1819/
Evidence of Ellicott's, Sweetings Alley, City of London – Ellicott was a
fine clockmaker of that time, mine was a goldsmith.
The National Archives: Records of Sun Fire Life Insurers re: Edward Ellicott
and Co., 17 Sweetings Alley, watch makers - The London Metropolitan
Archives: City of London – dated 22 July 1797 – Ref: MS 11936/409/668729
History of Norwich – http://www.localhistories.org/norwich.html
http://www.meg-andrews.com/articles/norwich-woollens/1/1
https://www.humphriesweaving.co.uk/wool-trade-east-anglia/
History of St Thomas' Hospital –
http://oldoperatingtheatre.com/history/history-of-old-st-thomas-hospital
Use of Jane Austin's world for insights regarding 18th-century birthing –
https://janeaustensworld.wordpress.com
https://janeaustensworld.wordpress.com/tag/18th-century-children/
Childbirth in the 18th century – http://www.elenagreene.com/childbirth.html
The Servant Hierarchy –
https://countryhousereader.wordpress.com/2013/12/19/the-servant-hierarchy/
Insight into money management for a home in the 18th century –
http://www.homethingspast.com/family-costs-money-1700s/
Marriage in the 18th century – http://www.songsmyth.com/weddings.html
Life in the 18th century – http://www.localhistories.org/18thcent.html
Christmas in the 18th century – http://www.historic-uk.com/CultureUK/A-
Georgian-Christmas/
Food and drink in the inns of the 18th century –
http://www.historyisnowmagazine.com/blog/2014/6/7/food-and-drink-in-17th-
and-18th-century-inns-and-alehouses#.WTBhDZLytdg
English in the 18th century –
http://www.history.org/history/teaching/enewsletter/june03/english.cfm
Board games played in the 18th century –
http://www.localhistories.org/board.html
Crime and Punishment –
https://www.oldbaileyonline.org/static/Punishment.jsp
Regarding the Inner Temple – https://www.innertemple.org.uk/who-we-are/a-
brief-history-of-the-inn/
Banking in the 18th century –
http://umich.edu/~ece/student_projects/money/banking.html
Rapallo, Italy – https://en.wikipedia.org/wiki/Rapallo
Medical terms in the 18th century –
http://www.thornber.net/medicine/html/medgloss.html
East Indiamen Ships –
http://www.portcities.org.uk/london/server/show/ConGallery.69/The-Lords-of-
the-Ocean-Ships-of-the-East-India-Company.html

***

Quotations from the King James Version of the Bible and the Common Book of Prayer

Psalm 30:1 – '...*for you have drawn me up O Lord and not let my foes rejoice over me...*'
Proverbs 16:18 – '... *Pride goeth before destruction and a haughty spirit before a fall...*'
Sermon on the Mount – Matthew 6:34 – '... *sufficient unto the day is the evil thereof...*'
Exodus 21:24 – '... *eye for eye...*'
Romans 12:19 – '...*vengeance is mine, I will repay, saith the Lord.*'

Latin Chant in the Common Book of Prayer 1550 – 'Media vita in morte sumus' (*In the midst of life we are in death...*)

Quotes from Poetry

William Cowper, 1731–1800, Poet – "Light Shining out of Darkness"
Olney Hymns, 1779 '...*God moves in a mysterious way...*'

Glossary

https://glosbe.com › Dictionary Latin › Latin-English Dictionary

Defendit numerus	Safety in numbers
Praemonitus praemunitus	Forewarned is forearmed

https://en.oxforddictionaries.com/definition/in%20flagrante%20delicto

In Flagrante Delico	Caught unawares in a compromising situation
virgo intacta	Still a virgin
Benvenuta a casa mia Margheritasei bellissima	Welcome to my home Margaret – you are beautiful
Hai fatto una buona scelta, amica mia	You made a good choice, my friend
Sono completamente d'accordo con lei	I completely agree with you
amico mio	My friend
esercizio	Exercise
mio Figlio	My son
salute!	To your good health
Dio ti benedica figlio, abbi cura di te stesso	God bless you son, take care of yourself
La mia baia di pace	My harbour of peace
rifugio di pace	Haven of peace